Warning!
Violence and the Supernatural.

This book may be inappropriate for young readers.

The nature of vampires means extreme elements of violence. Undead monsters return from the grave to feed on living human beings by drinking human blood. Decapitation, impalement, the mass destruction of the vampires, as well as magic, insanity and the supernatural are all elements in this book. We suggest parental discretion.

Note that Rifts and the Rifts Vampire Kingdoms are works of fiction! NONE of the monsters, characters, magic or depictions are real. None of us at Palladium Books condone nor encourage the occult, the practice of magic, the use of drugs, or violence.

Compatible with Beyond the Supernatural™, Heroes Unlimited™, the Palladium (fantasy) RPG™, and the entire Palladium Book® Megaverse®!

Dedicated to Cheryl Corey for all of her help over the years.

Second Printing — January 1992

Copyright 1991, 1990, 1988, 1986, 1983 by Kevin Siembieda

Palladium Books®, Rifts®, and Megaverse® are registered trademarks owned and licensed by Kevin Siembieda. Other titles are trademarks owned by Kevin Siembieda.

Copyright © 1991 by Kevin Siembieda. All rights reserved under the Universal Copyright Convention. No part of this book may be reproduced in part or whole, in any form or by any means, without permission from the publisher, except for brief quotes for use in reviews. All incidents, situations, institutions, governments and people are fictional and any similarity, without satiric intent, of characters or persons living or dead, is strictly coincidental.

Rifts World Book One: VAMPIRE KINGDOMS™ is published by Palladium Books® Inc., 5926 Lonyo Ave, Detroit, MI 48210.

Palladium Books® Presents

Rifts® World Book One: Vampire Kingdom™

Vampire Kingdoms™

Written By: **Kevin Siembieda**

Additional Text and Ideas: **Steven Sheiring**
Editors: **Alex Marciniszyn**
Thomas Bartold
Cover Art: **Kevin Long**
Interior Art: **Kevin Long**

Additional Art: **Timothy Truman**
Kevin Siembieda
Michael Gustovich
Art Direction & Keylining: **Siembieda**
Typography: **Maryann Siembieda**

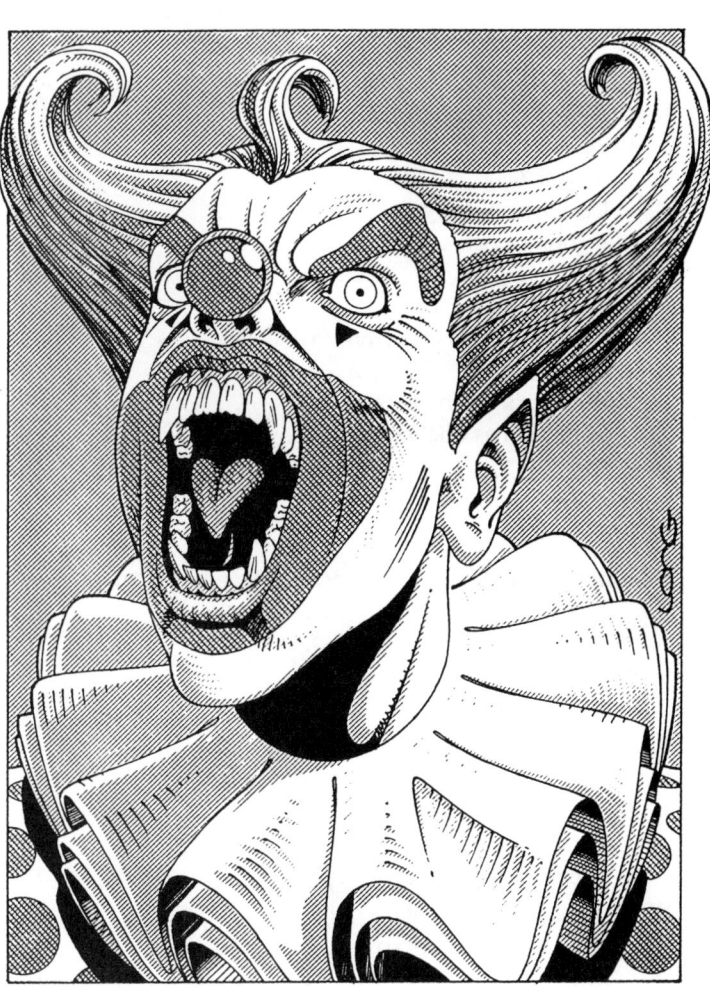

Special Thanks to Timothy and Gusto for pitching in on the art. Steve for floopers, shapers, ideas on travelling shows and other serious and silly things. Maryann and Thom for ideas on Ciudad Juarez and their enthusiasm, comments and long hours of work. Kev for his inspirational art and letting me ink some of his pencils, Julius for his encouragement, and Alex for all his efforts. Also to our fans for their insight, input, and patience.

CONTENTS

Vampires **8**
  The Vampire Intelligence 8
    Vampire Intelligence Statistical Data 10
    The Demon Familiar 11
    Destroying the Vampire Intelligence 12
  Vampire Minions 13
  Secondary Vampire 14
  Wild Vampire 15
  Vampires as Player Characters 16
    Vampire R.C.C. Experience Table 18
  Vampire Powers 18
  A lust for Blood 18
  Vampire's Bite 19
    Slow Kill: Creating Other Vampires 19
    Call & Control 20
    Mind Control: Human Enslavement 20
    Mind Control: Vampire over Vampire 22
Psionic Powers **22**
  Metamorphosis 23
  Summon Vermin 24
  Limited Invulnerability 24
  Super Regeneration 24
  Eternal Life (?) 24
  Other Natural Abilities 26
To Kill a Vampire **26**
    Weaknesses 26
    Wooden Stake 26
    Silver Bullet 27
    Garlic & Wolfbay (a.k.a. Wolfsbane) 27
    Symbol of the Cross 27
    Water 28
    Sunlight 28
    Soil of the Homeland 29
Vampire Combat Notes **29**
    Damage Table and Weapons 29
    Wood Flechette Rail Guns 30
    Conventional Squirt Guns 30
    Techno-Wizard Weapons 31
  Penalties to Strike a Vampire's Heart 32
  Vampires versus Magic 33
  Vampires versus Psionics 34
  Vampires versus Bots & Borgs 35
  Vampires versus Dragons 37
Vampires & Technology **34**
    Knock-Down Impact Table & Rules 35
    Vampire Victim Table (Insanities) 36
    Blood Loss Table 36
Vampire Kingdoms **40**
    The Northern Wastelands 40
    The Wild Vampires of Northern Mexico 41
    The Family Clan 43
Vampire Civilization **44**
    The Ideal Habitat 45
Vampire Societies **24**
    Tribal Lords 45

  Vampire Towns & Cities 47
  The Kingdom of Ixzotz 47
    The Sheriff 48
    Kryntoc Monster Protector 49
    Other Cities in the Kingdom 51
  The Mexico Empire 51
    Mexico City 51
    Tula 52
  The Muluc Kingdom 54
  The Milta Kingdom 56
Beyond the Threshold of Humankind **58**
  El Paso (Human City) 58
    The Police 59
    The Gangs 60
    King Wyatt Halloway 63
    El Paso City Highlights 64
  Ciudad Juarez 66
    The Police 67
    The Gangs 68
    Guild for the Gifted 76
  Juarez City Highlights 78
  North Side: Old North Town 78
    Slave Market 80
    Steve's Gags & Gifts 81
    Detective Agency 84
    Fighting Cock 85
    Beastiary 87
    Temple of Camazotz 88
    Feathered Serpent Tavern (Mindolar) 88
    Palace Garcia 89
    Big Gus's Apartments 91
    Mind Games Shelter 94
  West Side 94
  South Side: New Town 95
  East Side: Old Ruin Slums 95
Vampire Hunters of Mexico: Reid's Rangers **99**
    Fort Reid 101
    Doc Reid 103
    Planktal-Nakton 106
    Vyurr Kly 111
Traveling Shows **117**
  Designing Travelling Shows 118
  Mr. Drak's Travelling Circus 128
    Mr. Drak 131
    Captain Daring 137
  Night Arcade & Freak Show 139
    Mr. Esteban Morricco 140
    Mr. Lizzaro 145
    Bonecruncher the Dragon Slayer 150
The Mysterious Yucatan **153**
    Notes & Features 157
  Yucatan Overview 157
    Palenque 157
    Yaxchilan 160
    Xibalba: The Region of Phantoms 160

Tikal (Demon City) 161	Etzna 169
Uaxactun (Demon City) 164	Uxmal 169
Xultun (Demon City) 165	Merida 169
Altun Ha 167	Chichen Itza 169
Rio Bec 167	
Becan Cluster 167	**Other Monsters** **171**

Quick Find Table

New rules of Note:
- Destroying the Vampire Intelligence 35
- Knock Down & Impact Table 35
- Vampires vs Bots & Borgs 35
- Vampire Victim Insanity Table 36
- Vampire Victim Blood Loss Table 36
- Vampire Combat Notes 29
- Penalty to Strike the Heart 32
- Conventional Squirt Guns 30
- Techno-Wizard Squirt Guns 31
- Magic for combating Vampires 33
- Tarn Letters . . . . 38 & 99

Gangs (El Paso)
- K-9's 60
- Wild Cats 61
- Trogs 62
- Hammer 63

Gangs (Juarez)
- Subs 68
- Psykes 70
- Skivers 72
- Guard 72
- Night Masters (Vampires) 74
- Guild for the Gifted 76
- Priest of Camazotz 88

Monsters & New Aliens
- Agenor River Serpent 176
- Camazotz: Lord of Bats & Darkness 170
- Children of Cihuacoatl (Snake Alien) 171
- Dinosaur: Bruutasaur (Alien; Benito) 147
- Dinosaurs: Small Theropods (Speedy & Grunt) . . 147
- Dinosaur: Panoplosaurus (Nodosaur; Pokey) 148
- Dragon Slayer (D-Bee; Bonecruncher) 150
- Dr. Grey Matter (Borg) 135
- Dybbuk The Demon Ghoul 174
- Floopers (D-Bee) 132
- Incubus & Succbus 175
- Jaguar People (Werebeast) 172
- Krpt (D-Bee Monster; Oltec) 150
- Kryntoc (3 armed monster) 49
- Lyvorrk Lizard Man (Mr. Lizzaro) 145
- Mad Melody (Shifter) 148
- Mutant Cats 61
- Mii-Tar (D-Bee Ranger) 112
- Mindolar (Mind Slug) 88
- Psionic Mutant (Psi-Fi) 144
- Shapers (Animal/Monster) 133
- Spider Demon 173

- Xibalba: The Region of Phantoms 160
- Xibalba: Xibalban Demons 161
- Xibalba: Ti-Xibalbans (People of Wood) . . . 162
- Xibalba: Lord Cuchumaquiq 163
- Xibalba: Vukub-Came (The Phantom) 164
- Xibalba: Hun-Came (One Death) 165

New Optional R.C.C.s
- Cihuacoalt/Vernulian (Snake Alien) 171
- Dinosaur: Bruutasaur (Alien; see Benito) . . . 147
- Dragon Slayer (D-Bee; see Bonecruncher) . . 150
- Floopers (D-Bee) 132
- Jaguar People (Werebeast) 172
- Krpt (D-Bee Monster; Oltec) 150
- Lyvorrk Lizard Man (see Mr. Lizzaro) 145
- Mutant Cats 61
- Mii-Tar (see Reid's Rangers) 112
- Shapers (Animal/Monster) 133
- Vampire: Secondary 14
- Vampire: Wild 15
- Xibalba: Ti-Xibalbans (People of Wood) . . . 162

Reid's Rangers
- Doc Reid 103
- Planktal-Nakton 106
- Sir Raoul Lazarious 107
- Carlotta the White 108
- Pequita the Faceless One 109
- Vyurr Kly the Hunter 111
- Mii-Tar the Destroyer 112
- Meetal the Butcher 113
- Robert "Grizzly" Carter 114
- Colonel Wilding 116

Vampires
- Vampire Clowns 142
- Vampire Carnival Thieves 142
- Vampire Carnival Henchmen 143
- Vampire Intelligence 8
- Vampire Demon Familiar 11
- Vampire: Master 13
- Vampire: Secondary 14
- Vampire: Wild 15
- Vampire Powers 18
- Vampire Weaknesses 26

Maps
- Ciudad Juarez (city) . . . . 92 & 93
- Southern Mexico 50
- Mexico & Central America 158
- Yucatan Peninsula 159

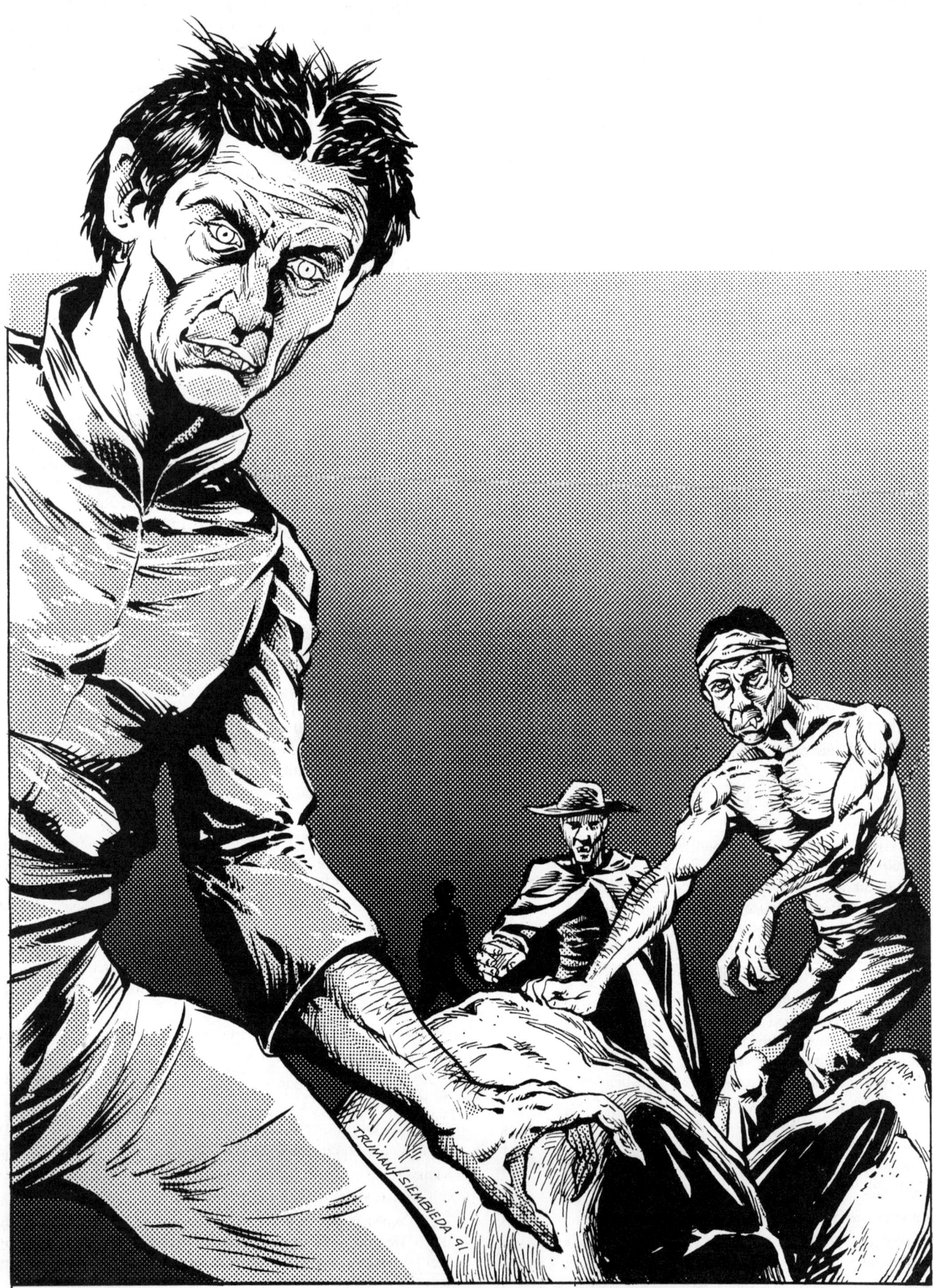

Some thoughts by the author

I've been in the publishing business long enough to know that it's stupid to think, even for a moment, that you can please all the people even half of the time. Still, it is confounding when you foolishly try to give people what they want and get criticized for it. Take the first **Rifts Sourcebook** for example, that entire books was written in response to our fan's comments. It was a mostly successful attempt to satisfy the hunger of **Rifts** players who clamored for that specific information. We had gotten request after request for more data on the Coalition and specific information about troop size, composition and deployment. More bots, weapons, equipment, and monsters were wanted too. So I wrote it up, Kev Long pounded out the illustrations, and boom, sourcebook was done. Since, the requests for that data has stopped and the sales of the book are phenomenal, I guess the first **Rifts Sourcebook** is a success. Yet in a recent (mostly positive) review, the book was criticized for to much specific detail, attention to tiny details and too much emphasis on the military and combat machines, and not enough new "world information."

It's just kinda frustrating. And, since I'm the author and the publisher, I can get stuff off my chest by publishing it in my books so I'm gonna. Hah. Seriously, I'd like to mention a couple things about the world of **Rifts**. First, there isn't much world data in the sourcebook... 'cause it's a "sourcebook," not a world book. The emphasis of the first sourcebook is *robots*, more weapons and equipment, more on the Coalition (specifically the military aspect requested by fans) and other pertinent details and data that elaborated on the information in the **Rifts** role-playing game.

Second, everybody should realize, is that **Rifts** is not a "generic" role-playing setting, but a very specific and detailed world of adventure. **Rifts** may tie into all genres and all of our role-playing games, but that does not make it generic in the least!

Often my dilemma, as the writer and designer, is how much detail and color should I put into any one book and into any one area of the world. I could write 10 adventure-sourcebooks on the Burbs around Chi-Town alone. Each part of the world is so unique and so rich in characters, possibilities, and adventures that it is hard to present just a peripheral view of the world. And in fact, I don't want to. I want to create an exciting, specific world rich in exotic wonders, memorable characters (heroes and villains), and adventures that will boggle the imagination. More importantly, we hope to create a catalyst for the creation of fabulous adventures of your own making. So you won't see any one or two books that stops with a general overview of the entire planet. Instead, you'll see one book after the other filled with interesting and hopefully unique characters, places, conflicts and ideas. I know that this detail is a bit of a departure from other role-playing games and other role-playing world settings, but I think you'll find **Rifts** far more exciting than most, with an ever expanding realm of adventure and intrigue. That's my plan. I hope I can count you in for the ride. And we'll try to make it worth the trip.

Third, "hack and slash" adventures. **Rifts** is a world torn a part by seemingly endless conflict. It is a tumultuous time where there seems to be a new would-be conqueror or supernatural danger every day. In many respects, **Rifts** is a war story with big doses of exploration, subterfuge and intrigue thrown in for good measure. The characters portrayed are the heroes that combat these threats, so there is quite a bit of combat/conflict. Hopefully, the game masters and players will create adventures that are a bit more than "hack and slash." But the idea is to have fun, and **Rifts** does offer a megaverse of adventure that the players can take in any direction they see fit.

What's with the Disclaimers?

Oddly enough, Palladium Books has received mostly positive comments from fans, retailers and distributors in the USA and Canada, regarding our warnings to the reader. However, our fellow gamers in the United Kingdom, or at least a few of the game reviewers, seem to be annoyed by them. They seem to think that a disclaimer, warning, or a reminder somehow detracts from the book. I don't see how. It is certainly not my intent to detract from four months of hard work in any way. In a review of the **Rifts Sourcebook One**, the reviewer is bothered by what he calls a "minor criticism" in that "... Kevin Siembieda insisted on reminding me every few pages that the world of *Rifts* is only fictitious." And goes on to state that, "...being constantly reminded that everything in the book is make-believe spoiled the atmosphere."

I would concur with that sentiment if it were the case, but it is not. As far as I can recall, there is only our standard, page one warning about violence and magic in the **Rifts Sourcebook** #1. There might be another comment about "reality" in regards to combat and mega-damage in the question and answer section, somewhere between pages five and ten. But I NEVER mention "make believe" or "fictitious" again, let alone constantly. I don't think once or twice in 120 pages is excessive nor should it spoil the atmosphere. This exaggeration would seem to indicate just how bothered the British are about disclaimers and warnings. That's okay. That's their opinion. And let me hasten to add that the British game publications, that particular reviewer, and most European magazines have given Palladium Books and its role-playing products far more accurate, frequent, and positive coverage than most American magazines, so I hope I have not offended anybody.

The reason for the disclaimers, warnings and/or reminders is that, we at Palladium Books are aware of the concerns of parents and young players a like. The material presented our role-playing games is "fictional" and I see nothing wrong in reminding people of that. It is a "game" of "make believe," and while one can throw himself into a night of imaginary adventure, he should also be able to realize the difference between reality and fantasy. If my occasional reminder or comments helps in that regard I am glad, because that's the idea.

Vampire Kingdoms is a book that has a couple of warnings and reminders. Why? Because, some people, especially young readers, sometimes worry about the crazy stories they hear about role-playing and the allegations that claim RPGs are linked to the occult and real demons. Of course we all think this is absurd, but I think it still bothers some people. I have found that a short statement from the author/publisher pointing out that this stuff is "make believe" puts a lot of people at ease. Maybe that sounds silly to many of you, but it happens. If a couple sentences here and there puts readers at ease then I'll continue to use them.

You won't see us pulling many punches in regard to story, action and atmosphere. Nobody, to our knowledge, has ever addressed the concept of an entire civilization of vampires. Yet if vampires did exist, unchecked, there would be thousands of the horrible fiends; tens of thousands. How would a vampire society be structured? What kind of different vampire societies might exist. How would they affect human society? Could they be stopped? Even nuclear bombardment could not destroy vampires! Yet a silver bullet or shard of wood piercing the heart will incapacitate them.

Vampires are hideous, powerful, supernatural monsters that have tantalized human imagination for centuries. Virtually every primitive culture has its legends about vampires or vampire like creatures. They are great monsters! GREAT! They are the living dead, so they're not human, not even alive as we understand life. They feed on the living and hunt only at night. A bolted door can not stop them unless draped in garlic or wolfbay. Vampires posses superhuman strength and can shape change into a demonic bat, wolf, or unnatural mist. Only the light of day sends them scurrying to their graves.

Like I said, vampires are great monsters. And I had a blast adding to their legend. Heck, I hope I made vampires more vile and frightening than ever. However, I will also be the first to remind you vampires are not real.

The Elusive Vampire Book

Many of you, who have been anxiously awaiting this book, know that **Rifts World Book One: Vampire Kingdoms** is late. That's the bad news. The good news is that it's late because its bigger than originally conceived. Initially planned at 160 pages, we first went with the smaller type, again, to squeeze in an extra 20 pages of text, the next thing we knew I was adding even more pages, monsters, and illustrations, and then Timothy Truman called and I had to have some of his artwork in here, and ...

The possibilities for **Rifts** are just so endless that the ideas just keep going on and on. I think the only disappointment for some of you, will be the lack of adventures. As the author/publisher I decided to go with vital source/world information rather than adventures. I hope to give GM's and players a better handle on the Mexican part of the world and how to develop their own, particular towns, villains and heroes by providing a general overview, but then focusing on a specific area or group. Detailed information about these people and places will hopefully crystallize what the region is like and provide Game Masters and players a template and ideas for creating their own. The city of Juarez, Mexico, Reid's Rangers and traveling shows are all examples of this. I suspect this information will be enough to spark a dozen or so adventures in and of themselves. Enjoy.

Vampires

The vampire presented in the pages of this book is not a simple monster with a page or two of basic information. Instead, we have taken the classic undead vampire of myth and examined him under a microscope. We have considered the many aspects of his nature and have speculated on how vampires might function in a society; something no other RPG has ever done. Consequently, the vampire information is presented in great detail, making him a very complex villain.

Please note that while we refer to the hideous creatures as the "true" vampires, the so-called *undead* are creatures of myth and legend. They are not real. Much of the data presented is drawn from a variety of different vampire myths from around the world, with new and original *fictional* characteristics and conclusions added (like the elemental aspect of the vampire and their societies). Other vampire like creatures are also included. As usual, some of these creatures may be loosely based on myths and legend, while others are new and original monsters. All are fictitious.

Undead Vampires

In the world of **Rifts®** there are a variety of monsters that feast on blood. Most will have specific names such as the dybbuk, succubus, and batlings; all are considered to be vampires by their nature of drinking the blood of their victims. Regardless of the abundance of blood sucking fiends, the most infamous of these legendary demons are the so-called **Undead Vampires** or *True Vampires*. The term "vampire" will generally refer to the undead/true vampire.

There are three types of Undead Vampires, the master vampire, secondary vampire, and the wild vampire (the latter two tend to be subservient to the more powerful master). The level of savagery increases from master to wild while the level of intelligence decreases. All three share the same basic powers, although the master and secondary vampires possess limited skills and abilities that the wild vampires do not.

Undead Vampires live to dominate, terrify and feed on inferior humanoid life. Humanoids are cattle to be quartered and devoured, playthings to satisfy sadistic pleasures. The hellish fiends delight in the fear, pain, and suffering of their prey, immersing themselves in dark emotions. While they require blood as nourishment, they are also psychic vampires that feed on the P.P.E. of their victims, soaking up the delectable quintessence of life tinged with the tantalizing flavor of terror and/or ecstasy that only a vampire can evoke.

Most undead vampires appear to be completely human, or in the case of the **Rifts®** world, humanoid. A true vampire is rarely alien in appearance. The vampire can be male or female, adult or child (though they tend toward adults). The physical characteristics that differentiate the undead from humans are pale (bloodless) skin color like that of a corpse, hollow and prominent cheekbones, lean and bony body (again giving them a corpse-like look; few vampires are fat), long slender fingers (often unusually long) and long finger nails. The eyes are bright and piercing (they glow red, orange or yellow when the vampire exerts his will over others, or when he is using his other powers), and, of course, they possess large canine teeth that often protrude from the upper lip. Most are said to have a "hungry look" about them, as if longing for some unnatural pleasure.

Master Vampires frequently exude an air of cold authority and confidence that is beyond the norm, like some invisible aura that makes humanoids (even non-psychics) feel strangely uncomfortable. Master vampires are the least corpse-like in appearance and tend to be attractive and a bit more meaty and healthy looking than most. Still, they are usually tall, lean, pale in color, and possess all the other physical traits of the vampire, just not as extreme. They tend to be educated, well mannered and dress fashionably, giving them an aristocratic appearance. They can easily pass themselves off as being human.

Secondary Vampires are your classic vampire, with pale, almost white flesh, thin and corpse-like bodies, canine fangs and strange eyes. They are less educated and more savage than the master and may wear fine clothes, rags, or nothing at all. Like the master vampire, they can often walk among humans unnoticed.

Wild Vampires are clearly the undead. They tend to be terribly thin, often skeletal, have long, claw-like fingernails, strange eyes, and white flesh often tinged with hues of blue, pale green or the yellow-brown of aging parchment. They frequently wear tattered rags, loin cloths, or nothing at all. Their faces are distorted by snarls and slobbering lips. Their eyes, when not aglow, have tiny pupils, no iris, reddish coloring and the crazed look of insanity. They speak in guttural tones and short sentences accompanied by grunts, growls, and howling. These creatures of the night are savage and wanton murderers who often torment their prey before they feast on their blood. They make no effort to conceal their nature. Most Vampires are noted to have foul smelling breath. Wild vampires have a particularly terrible stench for breath and a charnel smell about them.

Clear levels of superiority has created a caste system among undead vampires. The demons instantly and instinctively recognize their superior and usually bow to their better, acknowledging him or her as their lord. Only the comparatively rare *master vampires* retain a free will when dealing with other powerful vampires. But even they must answer to the **Vampire Intelligence**.

The Vampire Intelligence
Lord of the Undead

The ultimate lord of the undead is the *vampire intelligence*, a monstrous, elemental being that functions like a living virus that infects other creatures.

Vampire intelligences are malignant forces of evil dedicated to the propagation of misery. They know nothing about compassion, nor regret, and exist for the sole purpose of spreading hatred and sorrow.

They are alien beings that are beyond our understanding of physics and biology. The creatures can straddle three or four different dimensions by fragmenting their life essence and sending that life fragment to live in an alien world while other essences and its own physical body exists in another. The intelligence can divide its life-force, like an amoeba, into an army of tiny fragments. Each fragment is an extension of the multi-dimensional intelligence and is sent through a dimensional rift or allowed to be summoned by a foolhardy practitioner of magic.

Delivered into a new world, the invisible life-force must bond with a living humanoid to anchor itself to that dimension. A *willing* subject must be found within 24 hours or the essence fragment is automatically returned to its originating body. Using empathy and telepathy, the evil essence seeks out an individual who has already been corrupted by evil, hatred, greed, or dreams of power or revenge. Such a person can be easily beguiled by the promise of god-like power and eternal life.

The fool who accepts such a deal has his or her life essence torn from its living shell of flesh and blood and is then transformed into a supernatural creature of evil. The essence of the person and the fragment of the evil intelligence merge, become one, and create a new and horrible life form, the undead vampire. Humanity and a natural life are forsaken. The existence the individual once knew is lost forever and the vampire intelligence has its anchor in the physical world of that dimension. A *master vampire* has been born and the true nightmare is about to begin, for he will create other undead like himself, making the intelligence all the more powerful as he continues to spread the pestilence of vampirism among the unsuspecting people.

The intelligence can physically enter and inhabit a world if conditions are conducive to its needs. First, the monster requires 2500 or more vampires all born of its essence to serve as its anchor and lifeline to the world. Once the intelligence has established an army of vampires, it can consider inhabiting it. Once it has inhabited that world, the number of its minions can drop far below the initial 2500 required, without ill effect. The large number of vampires is needed only to enter and inhabit a new dimension and not necessary to maintaining its existence in that dimension after its arrival. But an army of vampires is just the first step to its arrival. The intelligence must have a massive and constant supply of magic energy (P.P.E.) such as that provided by a ley line nexus point. The monster also needs a regular (though comparatively minuscule) supply of humanoid blood. In earth's past, the small amount of mystic energy and the dominance of human beings made earth a barren and inhospitable environment for vampires. However, the arrival of the rifts has radically changed that. The planet Earth, itself, is so rich in mystic energy that it has become a ley line nexus point on an intergalactic level. Thus, earth has become a natural breeding ground for vampires and other creatures of magic! There are at least three or four vampire intelligences that currently inhabit Central America alone and, presumably, there are others scattered around the globe. Nobody knows how many.

An intelligence is so incredibly powerful that its presence of supernatural evil and magic can be sensed by psychic sensitives from over a hundred miles (160 km) away. To disguise its presence and to feed on the life-giving P.P.E, the creature commonly establishes a lair right on or very near a ley nexus. This location provides the horrid thing with great magic energy to draw upon to perform magic and to quench its terrible hunger, as well as providing a quick means of escape by rifting to another dimension (the creature can rift to another world that it dominates or to the dimension it originated from). The location will inevitably be a region dominated by its undead legions, thus offering it the protection of a vampire army.

The malignant creature is such a master of dimensional travel and so powerful, that once it has claimed a ley line nexus as the location of its lair, the intelligence can control the nexus. This means that no other creature can use that nexus as a dimensional gateway or draw on its usual energies (only one third the normal ley line energy can be drawn upon by beings other than the intelligence). Nothing can enter or leave through the nexus rift unless the vampire intelligence allows it. This level of control is accomplished, in part, by the intelligence's ability to syphon the magic energy into itself, feeding on it, and thereby controlling the flow of mystic energy.

Typically, the lair of a vampire intelligence is hidden deep inside a massive pyramid, gargantuan temple, or underground labyrinth. The actual inner sanctum of the lair is usually guarded by a score of vampires and a demon familiar. Deep inside is the physical embodiment of the vampire intelligence, a gigantic mound of slime-covered flesh that measures 100 to 200 feet in diameter. Six to twelve tentacles protrude from the body mound. At the end of each tentacle is a mouth equipped with terrible canine fangs. A hundred round red or yellow eyes cover the body, forming a circle around one giant central eye. All who see the intelligence recognize its maleficence and instinctively know that it must be destroyed. This, despite the intelligence's great power, makes it terribly vulnerable. Furthermore, its gargantuan size, slow speed, tremendous consumption of magic energy and need for humanoid blood and emotions to stay alive, prevents the horror from traveling except by teleporting from one location to another, or from one dimension to another. This is why the thing makes its home in a region dominated by its legion of undead. Its experiences come from the emotions it absorbs, the telepathic link with the master vampire, and from its demon familiar extension of self.

A demon familiar is created in the dimension inhabited by the intelligence. The demon is yet another fragmented part of its own life essence, only much larger than any others. The result is the physical manifestation of a humanoid extension of itself. The intelligence sees, hears, and feels everything the demon familiar experiences. The demon stands 15 to 20 foot (4.6 to 6 m) tall, with powerful arms, short, muscular legs, bat-like head, and huge bat-like wings. The demon is created so that the intelligence can experience the world around it and to help protect its entire body. However, there is no limit to the distance the familiar can travel away from the central body.

The intelligence is aware of its many fragmented extensions within each of its vampires and feels their heinous delights. The vampire intelligence also knows when one of its minions has been destroyed or placed in stasis. Fortunately, the link is not so strong that it can see, hear or know what its minions experience as they live it. Nor can it identify exactly where its many fragments are scattered or who dares to attack them. Only the few master vampires have a direct telepathic connection with the intelligence. The master can communicate with its creator up to 500 miles (800 km) away. But while the master can communicate and share his thoughts and memories with the intelligence, the creature does not see through his eyes and must conduct a lengthy and deliberate mind probe to learn all that its servant knows. However, telepathic conversations will transmit the memory of sounds and images as experienced by the master vampire. Thus, the intelligence may know the faces of his enemies although they be hundreds of miles away.

Vampire Intelligence

Alignment: Diabolic Evil
Horror Factor: 18
Size: 100 to 200 feet (30.5 to 61 m), Weight: 60 to 120 tons.
Typical Attributes: I.Q.: 20+1D6, M.E.: 20+2D6, M.A.: 16+2D6, P.S. equal to 40, P.P.: 15+1D6, P.B.: 1D6, Spd. 2D6 crawling. Can also travel through dimensions using magic.
Hit Points: 2D6×100
S.D.C.: Not applicable.
M.D.C. by Location:
  Small Eyes (100) — 5 each
  Giant Eye (1) — 300
  Tentacles (6-12) — 100 each
  *Main Body — 1D6×1000

*****Reducing the M.D.C. of the main body to zero** will temporarily hurt and impair the intelligence, but not destroy it. **Penalties:** Reduce attacks per melee to half, initiative by half, and is now vulnerable to surprise attacks. Natural regeneration ability should quickly restore both M.D.C. and hit points, unless the monster continues to suffer incredible amounts of damage.

P.P.E.: 2D6 × 100   **I.S.P.:** 1D4 × 100

Psionic Powers: Equal to a tenth level psionic.

Powers: All sensitive and healing powers, plus empathic transmission, group mind block, hypnotic suggestion, psi-shield and psi-sword (can be held in tentacles; more than one psi-sword can be created at a time).

Magic Powers: The vampire intelligence is a creature of magic. Despite its mystical and supernatural nature, it does NOT know all magic. However, all vampire intelligences know the following high level magic. **Spells:** All summoning and circle magic, close rift, dimensional portal, mystic portal, teleport: superior, time hole, restoration, calm storm, dispel magic barrier, negate magic, anti-magic cloud, and create magic scroll. In addition, the intelligence will know 1D6 spells from levels seven, five, three, and one. **Level of magic experience:** Roll 1D6 + 3 (wizard).

Natural Powers: In addition to those discussed previously, the vampire intelligence can create one additional *master vampire* for every 1000 secondary and/or wild vampires that comprise its minions. The first master vampire is considered to be the intelligence's general and right-hand vampire. A slow kill at the mouth of one of its tentacles will create a *secondary vampire*. And of course, the intelligence can create a *demon familiar* (see description that follows).

Other Natural Powers: Superior vision like that of a hawk, nightvision 4000 feet (1200 m), see the invisible, see the infrared and ultraviolet spectrum, smell blood two miles away (3.2 km), recognize the scent of human blood 90%, speaks all languages, can read Dragonese (elven), and *regeneration* of 4D6 hit points and 1D6 × 10 M.D.C. points once every melee. Regenerates entire tentacle or eye within ten minutes.

Otherwise, it possesses all the basic physical powers of the *undead vampire* legions, except that it cannot metamorph and sunlight does not destroy it. This means most forms of attack, including mega-damage weapons, fire, poison, drugs, etc., inflict no damage. Only *magic* can inflict damage to the M.D.C. of the body or otherwise affect the intelligence. Fortunately, this also means the vampire intelligence is vulnerable to the same weaknesses as the undead vampires. Wood, silver, running water and holy water inflict damage direct to hit points! Sunlight (not the magic spell, globe of daylight; it's too weak) does NOT kill the intelligence, but dramatically reduces its power. All spells, psionics, regeneration, saving throws, bonuses, physical attacks, attributes, M.D.C. etc. are reduced by 75% when the intelligence is bathed in sunlight!! Reduce by 50% if a gloomy, overcast, day.

Combat: Eight (8) hand to hand attacks per melee. Or can use magic or psionics or combine the types of attack; three by psionics or three by magic (plus two hand to hand) per melee. Each magic or psionic attack is roughly equal to two hand to hand attacks.

Mega-Damage:

Tentacle Killing Bite — 4D6 M.D.
Restrained Tentacle Strike — 6D6 S.D.C. plus P.S. bonus
Tentacle Strike — 5D6 M.D.
Tentacle Power Punch — 1D6 × 10 M.D.; counts as two attacks.

Tentacles can also be used to entangle an opponent, wrapping around a person like a python. To pull free of the tentacle a combined P.S. of 45 is necessary. An entangled foe can be crushed by the constricting tentacle at a rate of 5D6 M.D. per melee and counts as an extra melee attack. There's a 1-41% chance that both arms are pinned by the encircling tentacles. The ensnared victim is also easy prey to attacks by the other tentacles, which strike automatically if the person's arms are both pinned (can't parry).

Combat Bonuses: In addition to attribute bonuses, +10 to save vs horror factor, +6 on initiative, sneak attacks are impossible, cannot be blinded, and gets to attempt a parry on all attacks. Impervious to all forms of mind control and psionic and magic sleeps and paralysis.

Skills: The vampire intelligence knows few skills outside of magic, but it does know some. Literacy in Dragonese 98% (can read magic too), plus literate in two others, speaks and understands all languages 90%, demon and monster lore 98%. Select three additional skills from each of the following skill categories: Technical (+30% bonus), Wilderness (+30%), and ancient weapon proficiencies (W.P. Sword is usually one of them), plus two modern W.P.s (uses them in the demon familiar form). Note: The demon familiar knows everything the intelligence knows.

Notes: Other than creating vampires by the slow kill bite, the intelligence and its minions have no other means of reproduction. Vampires have been known to seduce their victims, especially those targeted for a slow kill transformation, but both male and female vampires are infertile.

Remember, an intelligence can create one master vampire for every 1000 lesser vampires. The master vampire must always be a willing victim and will always be evil. The first master vampire will have superior rank over the masters that follow later.

A vampire intelligence can only enter our world when there are 2500 or more vampires counted among its minions. But a legion of vampires is not sufficient. There must also be a huge supply of magic energy (P.P.E.) and a regular (though comparatively minuscule) supply of humanoid blood. In earth's past, the small amount of mystic energy and the dominance of human beings made it impossible for an intelligence to enter our world, although vampire intelligences essences were periodically sent to Earth and are responsible for the many vampire legends of old. Throughout Earth's history, there have been outbreaks of invading vampires (the most famous near Transylvania and throughout eastern Europe during the middle ages), but none ever led to such a massive establishing of vampire colonies as exist in the Mexico and Central America of Rifts® time. At least three vampire intelligences are known to physically inhabit Central America, possibly others. Another one is believed to exist in Africa.

Palladium RPG side note: The vampire intelligence and most other intelligences are puny *Old Ones* who were not locked in mystic slumber because their numbers were few and they are reasonably vulnerable to destruction. If these are the weak, comparatively harmless Old Ones, then what were the powerful "Great Old Ones" like? Kind of a scary thought, eh?

The Demon Familiar
An extension of the Vampire Intelligence

Alignment: Diabolic Evil
Horror Factor: 18
Size: 15 to 20 feet (4.6 to 6 m), **Weight:** 3 to 6 tons.
Typical Attributes: I.Q., M.E., and M.A., are the same as for the originating intelligence, P.S. equal to 30, P.P.: 15 + 1D6, P.B.: 1D6, Spd. 4D6 walking/crawling or 3D6 × 10 flying.
Hit Points: 1D4 × 100
S.D.C.: Not applicable.
M.D.C.: Not applicable.
P.P.E.: 3D4 × 10   **I.S.P.:** 4D4 × 10
Psionic Powers: Equal to a tenth level psionic.
Powers: All sensitive and healing powers, plus empathic transmission, group mind block, hypnotic suggestion, psi-shield and psi-sword.
Magic Powers: Same as the vampire intelligence.
Natural Powers: Same as the Vampire Intelligence; roughly equal to the undead vampire, except that the familiar cannot metamorph and sunlight does not kill it (but does dramatically weaken it). The demon's bite can turn others into secondary vampires (via slow kill).

The intelligence simultaneously sees, hears, and experiences everything its demonic extension experiences without requiring any form of telepathic communication (after all, they are one and the same).

Combat: Five (5) hand to hand attacks per melee. Or can use magic or combine the types of attack; two by psionics or two by magic (plus one hand to hand) per melee. Each magic or psionic attack is roughly equal to two hand to hand attacks.

Mega-Damage:
Killing Bite — 3D6 M.D.
Restrained strike — 4D6 S.D.C. plus P.S. bonus
Punch or Claw — 4D6 M.D.
Power Punch — 1D4×10 M.D.; counts as two attacks.

Combat Bonuses: In addition to attribute bonuses, +10 to save vs horror factor, +3 on initiative, +1 to strike, parry and dodge, +4 to dodge when in flight and can maneuver in total darkness using echo location like a real bat. Impervious to all forms of mind control and psionic and magic sleeps and paralysis.

Skills: Same as the vampire intelligence.

Death: The demon is killed when its hit points are reduced to 50 below zero. Its death also inflicts 1D4×100 hit points worth of damage to the intelligence itself and causes it terrible pain. Of course, the damage can be regenerated, but until every last hit point is restored, the intelligence is weakened and sluggish; only 6 attacks per melee.

Notes: The demon familiar is a true extension of the vampire intelligence that can be created in the dimension that the intelligence physically inhabits. The demon is another, more powerful fragment of the intelligence's life force that serves as a mobile body by which it can survey its surroundings. If you recall, the intelligence itself cannot venture far from its source of P.P.E.; the demon familiar enables the monster to venture into the world unimpeded by its vast size and energy requirements. There is no limit to the distance the demon can travel and it may be dispatched hundreds of miles away to extract revenge or to deliver mayhem. But when serving as a protector, the familiar is seldom more than minutes away, especially when trouble is brewing.

As an extension of the intelligence's life essence, the demon possesses all the memories, knowledge, and personality of the intelligence, as well as the same psionic and magic powers. Everything the demon experiences is simultaneously experienced by the intelligence and vice versa, for they are different parts of the same body/essence still linked as one. Only some of the physical characteristics such as hit points, P.P.E. and I.S.P. are different; the result of the fragmentation and different type of body. The demon always appears as a giant bat-thing with massive leather wings, powerful arms, claws, terrible maw, and vaguely humanoid shape. In many respects, the horrible creature looks like a giant bat with arms.

Destroying the Intelligence

There are only three ways to rid oneself of the influence of a vampire intelligence; destroy the master vampire(s) and all of his minions to break its ties to this dimension (this is really feasible only in the earliest invasion stage, before the master vampire has created hundreds of others), destroy the vampire intelligence, or send the intelligence to another dimension.

Stopping the Nightmare before it truly begins

When a vampire first appears it is possible to stop the evil before it is firmly entrenched. Initially, there is only the one master vampire created by the intelligence. Remember, the master vampire is the intelligence's first and only link to a particular dimension. The master instinctively knows he must feed and slowly create additional vampires (see the vampire's bite). As more and more secondary vampires are created, the intelligence's ties to that world become stronger. Each new vampire created from its essence, whether secondary or wild, helps secure the monster to the dimension it is invading. If ALL of the vampires that bear the intelligence's essence are destroyed, those ties are severed and the monster loses its hold in that world and must turn its attention to a different dimension. **Note:** Once an intelligence loses its connection to a particular dimension, it cannot enter that dimension again for ten thousand (10,000) years.

Of course, the tactic of destroying a master and his vampire legion is only feasible before there are too many vampires to combat. Typically, a master vampire will establish a base of operation and begin to create a small circle of additional vampires. For every dozen secondary vampires created, the master vampire will send 1D4 away to create their own minions at other places. This spreads and strengthens the intelligence's link to the world. If that link can be completely destroyed the intelligence is swept up in a dimensional vortex and cast into one of the other dimensions to which it is linked. Theoretically, this could be done to the vampires of South America, but as long as a single vampire lives, the intelligence can remain in that dimension to create a new master and slowly begin to rebuild its undead forces.

Destroying the Intelligence

A vampire intelligence that has thousands of minions spread across the world is firmly entrenched in that dimension. There is little hope that all its vampires can be located and eliminated. In the case of South and Central America, it is virtually impossible to destroy the thousands of vampires that have been spawned by a single intelligence. However, in such cases of extreme infestation, the vampire intelligence is likely (1-92%) to physically exist in that dimension (at least three exist in Central America). If the intelligence can be found and destroyed, ALL of his vampire legions are also destroyed, instantly turning to dust!

The task is first finding the secret lair of the vampire intelligence, then penetrating its defenses (the thing is usually surrounded by dozens, if not hundreds, of vampires and protected by its demon familiar), and killing it. Remember, the intelligence is vulnerable to weapons of wood, silver, water, and magic. The trick is to inflict such massive amounts of damage that the creature cannot regenerate quickly enough to survive. A very dangerous and difficult feat to accomplish.

Forced Abandonment

Forcing an intelligence to physically flee a particular dimension will cause a psychic shock to its system that will include its vampire extensions and will destroy 80% of its current minions. The remaining 20% of the vampires (probably several hundred) will survive, but are placed in a prolonged stasis. The forced exodus damages and drains the intelligence to such a degree that it cannot return to that world for 1D6 × 100 years. During that time, its surviving legion of vampires lay in "the sleep of Centuries" (stasis) until the intelligence returns.

A forced abandonment is caused by attacking the intelligence and inflicting so much damage that it believes its only chance for survival is to flee into another dimension. This requires tearing open a dimensional rift without the proper, lengthy, preparations to effectively sling shot it out of one dimension and into another. The slingshot rifting process only requires 1D4 + 2 minutes and most of the intelligence's P.P.E., and transports only the intelligence (even if it is covered by attacking humanoids). The action is severly damaging, though better than death, destroying the majority of its minions, including all masters. The surviving vampires will flee in panic to their place of sleep, where they will lay dormant for decades, until the intelligence returns. If all these vampires can be located and destroyed, the intelligence is permanently prevented from returning.

Vampire Minions

The Master Vampire

The master vampire is the father of the pestilence to follow. Unlike all the other vampires, the master chooses his fate. He is a human or humanoid who willingly accepts a diabolical offer in the name of revenge, power, or pure evil to become an undead. He knows full well that from that day forward he will be an inhuman abomination that feeds on the misery and life's blood of the innocent. This makes the master vampire the most evil and most like his insidious creator, the intelligence. The transformation from the living to the undead is instant, requiring only a willing soul. Once done, it cannot be undone.

The transformation into a vampire destroys all vestiges of humanity, except for some faded memories and a handful of skills. The master, as are all vampires, is reborn, or perhaps unborn. That which was once human is transformed into a completely **non-human** life form that no longer has anything in common with humankind, other than the humanoid appearance, and even that appearance is just one of several the vampire can select at will. As a result, the original human attributes and alignment are meaningless, entirely new attributes are rolled, an evil alignment selected, and a handful of skills retained (selected).

The master's new found supernatural powers are instinctively known to him. Just as he instinctively understands his place in the hierarchy of vampires and knows that he must create a legion of undead so that the vampire lord (the intelligence) may one day join them to rule the planet. Every vampire the master creates will serve to solidify the vampire intelligence's essence in this world. The more vampires, the stronger the intelligence's power, and the master's as well. When thousands of vampires exist, all born from that first evil essence of the master, the intelligence may enter that world through a dimensional rift and live among them.

Vampires are supernatural predators. Their prey, humans and humanoids. As predators, they tend to be savage hunters and run in packs. The king of all packs is the master, second only to the "ultimate creator," the vampire intelligence. Like many predators, vampires are territorial, often selecting a town, city or land area that they claim as their own. The master vampire is the king or "lord" of such communities. The lesser vampires are his subjects and the humanoids are their pitiful slaves and food supply.

The undead all see humans and humanoids as primitive animals to be corralled, controlled, fattened and eaten like livestock. The master vampire is the most arrogant and manipulative of all and frequently partakes in games and tests of cunning and power against humanoid challengers. The perceived end to such enjoyable diversions is to prove the superiority of the undead in general, and his specifically. As one might suspect, vampire masters are poor losers. Defeat and/or humiliation at the hand of a lesser being, especially true humans, is an unforgivable blow to the ego and will always require retribution. Thus, a vampire's lust for revenge is as legendary as his lust for blood. One does not begin a conflict against a vampire, especially a master or ancient secondary, unless one intends to see it all the way through to the destruction of the vampire and his legion of undead and other maleficent beings (human and inhuman) that such an evil presence attracts.

Master Vampire

Horror Factor: 14
Alignments: Any evil; radiate supernatural evil.
Size and Weight: Varies, generally human.
Attributes: The base attribute plus the number of additional six-side dice to be rolled is indicated as follows: I.Q. 14+2D6, M.E. 10+3D6, M.A. 12+3D6, P.S. 18+3D6, P.P. 10+3D6, P.E. 18+1D6, P.B. 16+2D6, Spd. 10+4D6
P.P.E.: 1D6×10
M.D.C./Hit Points: Vampires are bizarre supernatural creatures that are nearly impervious to all weapons, including *mega-damage* weapons. Fortunately, they are vulnerable to a handful of S.D.C items and magic. **Hit Point Equivalent:** 3D6×10. **M.D.C. Equivalent:** Not applicable. See *Natural Abilities and limited invulnerability*.
Natural abilities: Vampires possess a number of strange supernatural powers, including the ability to create secondary vampires, nightvision, metamorphosis, regeneration, and M.D.C. invulnerability. *See the detailed descriptions that follow.*
Psionic Powers: I.S.P.: 3D6×10, and includes mind control over other vampires which does not require the expenditure of I.S.P, and a handful of other I.S.P. based powers. *See the psionic powers description to follow.* Considered a master psionic; requires a roll of 10 or higher to save vs psionic attacks.
Combat: Six (6) hand to hand attacks per melee. Or can combine psionic attacks (as many as two per melee) with physical attacks, meaning two by psionics plus two hand to hand attacks per melee are possible. Each psionic attack is roughly equal to two hand to hand attacks. **Note:** If the master knew magic before being reborn into a vampire he retains that knowledge, but those magic abilities are frozen and can NEVER increase in experience or power. Nor can the vampire learn new magic or increase his personal level of P.P.E. points.
Combat Damage:
  Killing Bite — 3D6 M.D.
  Restrained Punch — 4D6 S.D.C. plus P.S. bonus
  Full Strength Punch — 2D6 M.D.
  Power Punch — 1D4×10 M.D.; counts as two attacks.
  Vampire versus Vampire; damage direct to hit points: All vampires, by their strange nature, inflict damage direct to hit points whenever they fight other *vampires*. This means that one vampire can kill another, although their mutual regenerative powers makes this difficult. The damage inflicted by a vampire to a vampire is as follows. P.S. attribute bonuses to inflict damage *are* applicable when vampires fight each other.
  Killing Bite — 3D6 Hit Points (H.P.)
  Restrained Punch — 1D4 H.P.
  Full Strength Punch — 3D6 H.P.
  Power Punch — 6D6 H.P.; counts as two attacks.
Combat Bonuses: In addition to attribute bonuses, +5 to save vs horror factor, +3 on initiative and impervious to all forms of mind control and psionic and magic sleeps and paralysis.
Skills: The master vampire retains the knowledge of his former life but O.C.C. skill bonuses are not applicable (forgotten), only I.Q. bonus. Skill proficiencies are frozen at the level they were at when the person became a vampire and do NOT increase. **New Skills:** Three additional skills can be selected for every 100 years of life as a vampire. All skills are at second level proficiency and do NOT increase. The available skill categories are limited to: Communication, Domestic, Piloting, Technical, Rogue, Wilderness, and Weapon Proficiencies.
Notes: Borgs cannot become vampires, but humanoids with cybernetics, including prosthetic limbs, can be transformed into vampires. The cybernetics are magically expelled from the body and new undead limbs and organs are generated.

Master Vampires are uncommon and are always evil. Thus, they are not recommended as player characters. The master vampire can be male or female, almost always human.

The Secondary Vampire
An Optional Player Character R.C.C.

The master vampire creates other vampires by a *slow kill* bite that transfers yet another fragment of the evil essence into another humanoid creature. The process, described elsewhere, transforms the master vampire's slow kill victim into a *secondary vampire*. Tragically, now that the vampire intelligence has anchored itself in the world through the master vampire, it no longer needs to find *willing* subjects. The master vampire can transform willing and unwilling victims alike into the cursed undead. With the creation of each new vampire, the alien intelligence's hold in that dimension becomes stronger.

The victims of the master are the *secondary vampires*. Despite the fact that they are usually subservient to their creator and the intelligence, and the term secondary implies a level of inferiority, they possess all the spectacular supernatural powers of the master vampire and are quite intelligent. The only two things that make them inferior to their creator/master is that the secondary vampires are a bit more savage (and therefore a bit less intelligent/clever) and they are generally subservient to their creator and most other master vampires.

Ironically, the secondary vampires can sometimes defy the vampire intelligence, perhaps because they possess a smaller portion of its essence, or because they must answer to two masters. Whether it is the smaller essence or the fact that they are a second generation extension of the intelligence, the pitiful creatures remember more about their lives as humans than any other undead. Those of evil alignment readily accept their new monstrous existence and are the least tormented by past memories. Those of a good alignment frequently loathe the monsters that they have become. Many try to fight the unnatural desires for blood and carnage, but most eventually succumb and resign themselves to an existence of evil as the dreaded creatures of the night. Yet a tiny minority do successfully win their inner battle and retain some vestige of humanity. These are the unprincipled, anarchist, and aberrant vampires who tend to operate independent of a master and away from others of their ilk. They seldom feed indiscriminately on the innocent and try to do some good with their lives. They are also the likely types to be played as player characters.

The plague of evil continues as the secondary vampires feed and/or create additional vampires by means of the slow kill. Because the secondary vampires retain more memories of their pasts than the master or wild vampires, they often target family members, friends, and loved ones as victims of a slow kill. In many cases, the feelings of love are gone, but the shadow of a memory compels them to add these people to their evil brotherhood. Unlike the master, the slow kill of the secondary vampire does not offer consistent results. Again, perhaps because these lesser vampires are not as true to the intelligence's nature or because they possess a smaller essence fragment, they do not automatically create another secondary vampire. There is trouble creating new undead. 58% of the victims of a slow kill bite will be *wild vampires*, not secondary vampires. See *The Vampire's Bite: The Slow Kill*, in the *Vampire's Powers* section.

Secondary Vampire

Horror Factor: 12
Alignments: Selfish or evil; radiates supernatural evil. Player characters who are secondary vampires, but try to fight the desire for blood and try to be good, not evil, can be unprincipled good (selfish), but their vampire instincts, cravings, and needs make a higher good alignment impossible. Anarchist and aberrant evil secondary vampires are more common than unprincipled.

Size and Weight: Varies, generally human.
Attributes: The base attribute plus the number of additional six-side dice to be rolled is indicated as follows: I.Q. 2+3D6, M.E. 6+3D6, M.A. 6+3D6, P.S. 14+3D6, P.P. 8+3D6, P.E. 16+1D6, P.B. 4+2D6, Spd. 10+3D6
P.P.E.: 1D4×10
M.D.C./Hit Points: Vampires are bizarre supernatural creatures that are nearly impervious to all weapons, including *mega-damage* weapons. Fortunately, they are vulnerable to a handful of S.D.C items and magic. **Hit Point Equivalent:** 3D4×10. **M.D.C. Equivalent:** Not applicable. See *Vampire Powers section*.
Natural abilities: Vampires possess a number of strange supernatural powers, including the ability to create additional vampires, nightvision, metamorphosis, regeneration, and M.D.C. invulnerability. See *Vampire Powers section*.
Psionic Powers: I.S.P.: 3D6×10 and includes mind control over other vampires which does not require the expenditure of I.S.P, and a handful of other I.S.P. based powers. **See the psionic powers.** Considered a major psionic; requires a roll of 12 or higher to save vs psionic attacks.
Combat: Five (5) hand to hand attacks per melee. Or can combine psionic attacks (as many as two per melee) with physical attacks, meaning two by psionics plus one hand to hand attack per melee are possible. Each psionic attack is roughly equal to two hand to hand attacks. **Note:** If the secondary vampire knew magic before being reborn into a vampire he retains about half of that knowledge (player must select the half of the spells remembered). The magic abilities remembered are frozen and can NEVER increase in experience or power. Nor can the vampire learn new magic or increase his personal level of P.P.E. points.
Combat Damage: (P.S. damage bonus is not applicable to M.D.C. attacks).
Killing Bite — 2D6 M.D.
Restrained Punch — 3D6 S.D.C. plus P.S. bonus
Full Strength Punch — 2D6 M.D.
Power Punch — 4D6 M.D.; counts as two attacks.
Vampire versus Vampire; damage direct to hit points: All vampires, by their strange nature, inflict damage direct to hit points whenever they fight other *vampires*. This means that one vampire can kill another, although their mutual regenerative powers makes this difficult. The damage inflicted by a vampire to a vampire is as follows. P.S. attribute bonuses to damage *are* applicable when vampires fight each other.
Killing Bite — 2D6 Hit Points (H.P.)
Restrained Punch — 1D4 H.P.
Full Strength Punch — 2D6 H.P.
Power Punch — 4D6 H.P.; counts as two attacks.
Combat Bonuses: In addition to attribute bonuses, +3 to save vs horror factor, +2 on initiative and impervious to all forms of psionic and magic sleeps and paralysis, and +3 to save vs magic or psionic mind control (this is in addition to possible M.E. bonus).
Skills: The average secondary vampire will retain a total of ten (10) skills. Two additional skills can be selected at levels three, six, nine, eleven, and fifteen. All skills start at first level proficiency and do not increase. The available skill categories are limited to: Communication, Domestic, Piloting, Technical, Rogue, Wilderness, and Weapon Proficiencies. See the **Vampire's Bite,** "the Slow Kill," for optional skill rules for vampire player characters.

Notes: Secondary vampires, like most Racial Character Classes, prefer to rely on their natural powers and instincts rather than the trappings of technology. As well they should, because those powers and instincts make them superhuman and the equal to any man-made power armor. Secondary vampires might know how to drive a hover vehicle and will do so when necessary, but prefer to travel, run or fly, under their own power. All vampires derive pleasure and satisfaction when they use their supernatural powers.

The majority of secondary vampires who are non-player characters (N.P.C.s) are predominantly of evil alignments, mostly miscreant and diabolic. Unprincipled, anarchist and even aberrant evil are uncommon.

Wild Vampires

An Optional Player Character R.C.C.

Wild vampires are created in one of two ways. They have either been driven insane and into their present animalistic state (often from starvation) or created by a secondary vampire. Like the master, secondary vampires can also create new vampires; however, these third generation undead are frequently flawed, one might say, mentally retarded. These misanthropes are incredibly savage and possess the meagerest of mental faculties. Most are crazed predators that are more animal than human. They are primal forces that function on instinct rather than forethought. Their lives are consumed with stalking, killing and feeding. They engage in few activities other than tormenting and hurting others. As before, the wild vampires are generally subservient to their vampire creator, master vampires, and most secondary vampires. ALL wild ones are subservient to their ultimate creator, the *vampire intelligence*.

Wild Vampires

Horror Factor: 12
Alignments: Evil or Anarchist, but most are extremely evil (diabolic and miscreant); radiates supernatural evil. The best alignment possible is anarchist, the wild ones are too savage and aggressive to fight the desire for blood or try to be good. Player characters who are wild vampires and not completely evil are still crazed and animalistic. Wild vampires of all alignments are easily provoked, attack when made angry (regardless of the consequences), fly into berserker rages and tend to be cruel. Furthermore, they love the taste of human blood and feast regularly.
Size and Weight: Varies, generally human.
Attributes: The base attribute plus the number of additional six-side dice to be rolled is indicated as follows: I.Q. 1+2D6, M.E. 4+3D6, M.A. 2+2D6, P.S. 14+3D6, P.P. 8+3D6, P.E. 16+1D6, P.B. 2+1D6, Spd. 10+5D6
P.P.E.: 6D6
M.D.C./Hit Points: Vampires are bizarre supernatural creatures that are nearly impervious to all weapons, including *mega-damage* weapons. Fortunately, they are vulnerable to a handful of S.D.C items and magic. **Hit Point Equivalent:** 2D4×10. **M.D.C. Equivalent:** Not applicable. See *Vampire Powers section*.
Natural abilities: Vampires possess a number of strange supernatural powers, which include nightvision, metamorphosis, regeneration, and M.D.C. invulnerability. As a rule, wild vampires cannot create additional vampires. See *Vampire Powers section*.
Psionic Powers: I.S.P.: 1D6×10 and includes mind control over other wild vampires which does not require the expenditure of I.S.P, and a handful of other I.S.P. based powers. See *the psionic powers description*. Considered a minor psionic; requires a roll of 12 or higher to save vs psionic attacks.
Combat: Five (5) hand to hand attacks per melee. Or can combine psionic attacks (as many as two per melee) with physical attacks, meaning two by psionics plus one hand to hand attack per melee are possible. Each psionic attack is roughly equal to two hand to hand attacks. **Note:** If the wild vampire knew magic before being reborn into a vampire it is all forgotten.
Combat Damage:
Killing Bite — 2D6 M.D.
Restrained Punch — 4D6 S.D.C. plus P.S. bonus
Full Strength Punch — 1D6 M.D.
Power Punch — 3D6 M.D.; counts as two attacks.

Vampire versus Vampire; damage direct to hit points: All vampires, by their strange nature, inflict damage direct to hit points whenever they fight other *vampires*. This means that one vampire can kill another, although their mutual regenerative powers makes this difficult. The damage inflicted by a vampire to a vampire is as follows. P.S. attribute bonuses to damage *are* applicable when vampires fight each other.
Killing Bite — 2D6 Hit Points (H.P.)
Restrained Punch — 1D4 H.P.
Full Strength Punch — 1D6 H.P.
Power Punch — 3D6 H.P.; counts as two attacks.

Combat Bonuses: In addition to attribute bonuses, +2 to save vs horror factor, +2 on initiative and impervious to all forms of psionic and magic sleeps and paralysis, and +1 to save vs magic or psionic mind control (this is in addition to possible M.E. bonus).

Skills: The wild vampire retains few of the skills or memories from his former life. Skills are limited to two ancient W.P., one modern W.P.s, one common piloting skill and three languages (not literacy). All skill proficiencies are frozen at second level; no skill bonuses apply. **New Skills for player characters:** One new secondary skill can be selected at levels two, four, six, eight, eleven, and fourteen. All skills start at first level proficiency and do not increase. The available skill categories are limited to: Communication, Domestic, Piloting, Technical, Rogue, Wilderness, and Weapon Proficiencies.

Notes: Wild vampires rarely have the patience to use technology or perform a skill, and would rather tear into an opponent with tooth and claw rather than use a weapon. The most popular weapons used by wild vampires are ancient weapons because they require close combat and spill blood. The majority of wild vampires who are non-player characters (N.P.C.s) are predominately diabolic or miscreant villains. Anarchist and aberrant evil are a rarity.

Wild Packs: Wild vampires run in packs or tribes that can range from as few as a half dozen to as many as four or five dozen. A typical pack will have about 24 members. Most packs are nomadic and will wander a vast territory that may cover thousands of square miles. The most famous vampire infested lands include the pre-rifts lands of Mexico, New Mexico, and parts of Arizona, Colorado, and Texas. The members of a pack often metamorph into wolves or bats in order to disguise their true nature and for greater speed.

Typical of larger packs, 95% of the members are wild vampires, with the remaining 5% being secondary vampires. The secondary vampires are always the dominant members of the pack. The Leader is always the strongest or smartest (frequently the oldest) and usually a secondary vampire who has been banished from society or prefers a more wild and violent life style. Smaller packs may be composed entirely of wild vampires led by the most powerful and/or aggressive wild vampire in the pack. All are subservient to the leader.

There is little structure to a wild vampire pack other than the wolf-pack like social status within the pack. Each member has a rank within the pack from leader to the lowest. The lowest members are forced to perform the most menial of tasks and are the brunt of beatings from the dominant members of the pack. To rise in stature within the pack, the wild one must challenge and fight his better. If his opponent is killed or surrenders, the vampire rises to his new position in status. Those that are too disruptive and ridiculously aggressive will be banished from the pack or killed.

Remember, wild vampires are very much like wolf packs, consumed with the hunt and feeding. They seldom establish towns or villages nor do they have much need or desire to use human technology. In fact, the wild ones are militantly anti-human and humanoids. They hate humanoid life and take great delight in destroying, molesting and mutilating it. Consequently, they tend to view the machines and trappings of humankind as repulsive.

Wild vampires rarely travel beyond their native land. In this way they don't have to concern themselves with establishing special hiding places that contain the soil of their native land. Instead, they can get away with day time dwelling places located in graveyards (mist in and out of buried coffins and crypts) or caves, or burrow into the ground (shallow graves, about three feet underground; easy to unearth).

Packs will raid the same humanoid towns over and over again. Although they may victimize the same area for weeks or months, they seldom establish a fixed lair, preferring to change locations every few nights. Likewise, they may disappear as abruptly as they arrived, moving on to other towns. Kidnapping, torturing without killing, the mutilation of livestock, howling and swearing at townspeople from the shadows or mist (fog), and other forms of terrorism, are favorite pastime activities of the wild ones.

Travelers and merchant caravans are the most vulnerable to roving packs of wild vampires and are among their favorite prey. Often the travelers are ill prepared for an assault by vampires or may not realize that they have ventured into vampire territory. If the travelers are few or can offer little resistance, the vampires will slay them all and drink their blood. They will then kill any beasts of burden, damage vehicles (will require extensive repairs to be driveable), and smash and scatter the cargo. They may steal items to wear, or weapons to use, or simply to take into the wilderness where they can do humans no good.

If the travelers are prepared for vampires (too powerful) or in great numbers and perceived as dangerous, the vampires may not attack, but may follow from a distance, shouting obscenities, threats and curses. Bands of wild vampires have been known to harass travelers in this manner, following them for miles.

Vampires as Player Characters

Game Masters <u>may</u> allow players to create a secondary or wild vampire player character or to play any of the monsters or alien races. However, this option is left entirely to the Game Master. Players should respect the GM's choice to not allow vampires or other monsters to be portrayed by players, as some GMs may find their inclusion inappropriate, awkward, or a problem that creates an imbalance in his/her campaign plans.

There are some immediate concerns in playing a vampire as a player character that players should consider before making such a selection.

A conflict of nature

First, the character may be evil, which means there is likely to be a clash between good characters in the group and evil ones. Good and evil, vampire and humanoid, is a volatile mixture. Only the most sympathetic and good vampire characters are apt to be tolerated. Good characters can not, by alignment, allow torture, cruelty, slavery, unnecessary violence, wanton acts of aggression, or the drinking of an innocent victim's blood (even if the victim is not murdered, it is still a horrible attack like rape). Confining one's hunger to brutal murderers, evil criminals, or the sucking of one's enemies may still be too extreme for many good characters. Of course, the vampire can be secretive, but the good characters must know that he is feeding on somebody and they may not be able to condone such activity even if the victims are restricted to criminals. Vampirism is a terrible act.

The vampire may be able to get around this dilemma by drinking a pint or two of blood from volunteers within his group of companions. However, this sacrifice will only be made to vampires of a selfish or aberrant alignment and who exhibit great restraint in fighting their despicable nature. Many characters may not be able to bring themselves to allow such a disgusting practice and there is always the risk that the vampire will not be able to control himself and try to suck a person dry. Under similar circumstances, the good characters may allow their undead ally to feed on the blood of the recently killed, like a scavenger, or to feed on truly evil villains already condemned to death. **Note:** Vampires cannot drink blood from other vampires.

If a satisfactory solution cannot be found, the group will find itself compelled to either reject the vampire from their group or, more likely, to kill their vampire companion (for his sake as well as the sake of innocent people).

Players who select a vampire R.C.C. should expect such an outcome and not hold it against his fellow players. This is not betrayal on their part, but a moral conviction their characters are forced to live with or suffer an alignment change toward evil.

Nocturnal Habits

The vampire character is limited to nighttime activities. While this may provide the group with a great night guard who won't fall asleep, it also means that the vampire cannot function during the day. This presents two major problems.

Problem number one. Unless the group changes its activities to mostly nocturnal adventures the vampire cannot operate as an effective member of the group. This also presents a potential problem for the game master who may find himself running the bulk of the players through daytime adventures and the vampire(s) through night adventures. This could severely damage the story's pacing and enjoyment of the game because someone or another is going to be sitting out part of the adventure. This is one of the reasons the player should get his game master to approve a vampire player character and not be upset if the GM says no. Likewise, the player who is running a vampire should make a special effort to work with both the GM and his fellow players and understand that there will be times that his character must sit out part of the game.

Problem number two is a related, but more role-playing/character oriented problem. Where does the vampire sleep during the day? How is he protected? Do his teammates transport him with them or do they rendezvous at night? If the group does not transport his body, how does the vampire travel and can he catch up to them?

The best answer to the dilemma is a combination of teamwork and resourcefulness. In the play-test, one player's character was a secondary vampire serving as a guide through vampire territory (he was of a different life essence than any of his South American cousins, or so he claimed). He was of anarchist alignment, helped his teammates, and exhibited great restraint. Consequently, the group transported his body with them when they moved during the day. The group also made an effort to engage in night activity, although they did things during part of the day as well. This co-operation worked very well. One afternoon, the group travelled across a river without advance notification and the vampire was delighted that he didn't have to worry about the trip.

Our vampire also devised a very clever travelling home. The creature of the night purchased a mega-damage van, replaced the side and back windows with solid mega-damage steel, and divided the cargo area from the driver area (with M.D. steel, of course). This gave him a self-contained, vault-like area to sleep. If necessary, one or more members of the team could drive the van while he slept, and four others could ride in the darkened crypt/cargo area with the coffin.

Inside the cargo area was his sleek black coffin (actually, it was designed not to resemble a coffin), which was also a specially commissioned mega-damage structure, locked from the inside. Breaking into the van activated a loud alarm. Tampering with the coffin caused another alarm to sound and tear gas to fill the compartment, hopefully scaring away foolish thieves. In play-test, the thieves were downright stupid and were not frightened away. Instead, they decided that something of great value must be in the black crate. They deactivated the alarm and eventually forced opened the coffin. The groggy vampire rose from his bed of soil, protected from the light of day by the walls of his van

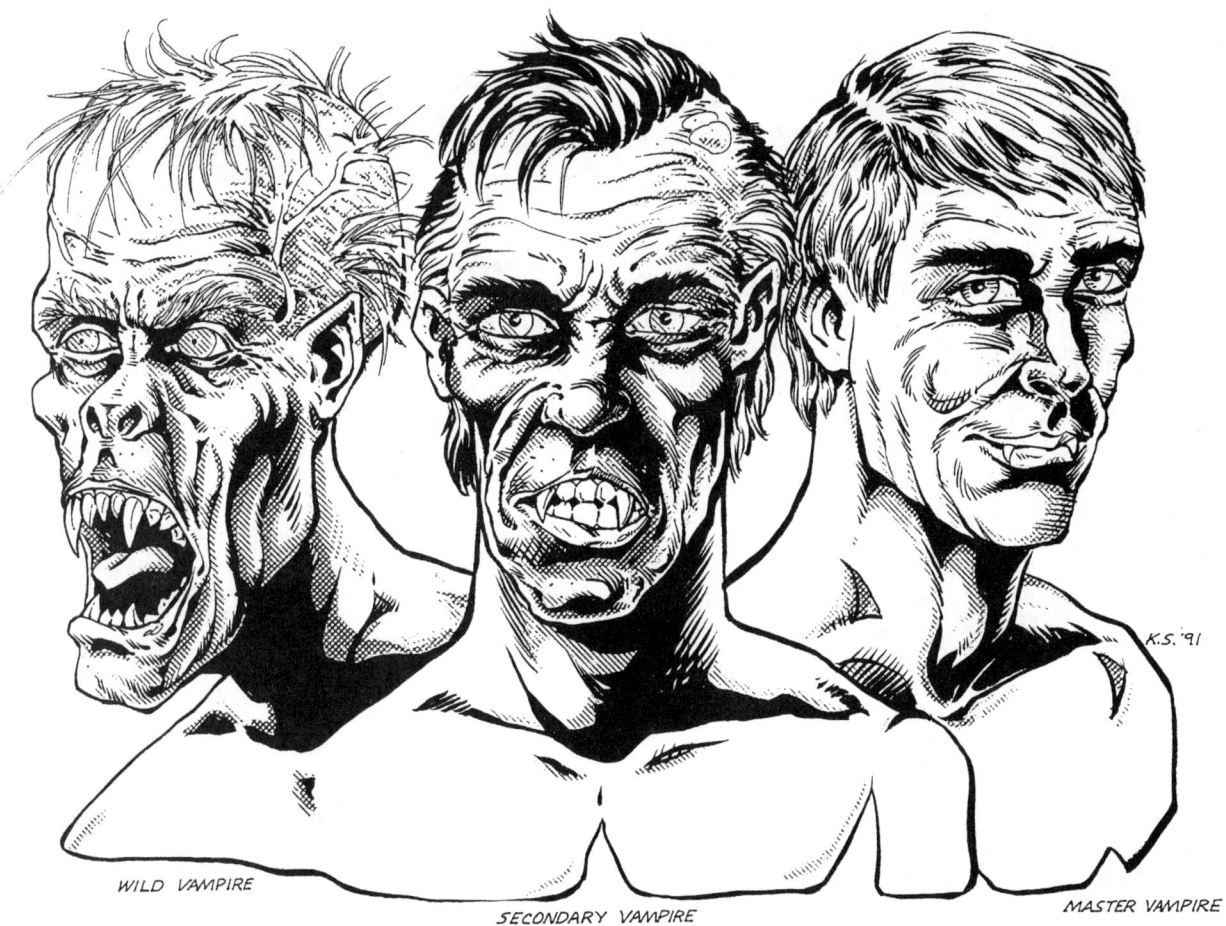

WILD VAMPIRE   SECONDARY VAMPIRE   MASTER VAMPIRE

(although a deadly stream of daylight beamed through a small exterior hole made by the thieves).

The vampire was sluggish since it was daytime and hoped to frighten the three looters away. This didn't work. Finally, the vampire used a combination of force and hypnotic suggestion to subdue them, chained them up, and went back to sleep. His humanoid companions arrived to check on the van and found the frightened crooks in chains. They left them in chains until their vampire buddy woke up, so they could get his story. That evening the vampire answered his companions' questions to their satisfaction and released his prisoners, using hypnotic suggestion to reinforce their misguided belief that he was a robot. They foolishly believed that he was the cargo; i.e., a robot being delivered to somebody. Using a vehicle as a traveling lair or mega-damage hearse is a clever one, and an idea that is probably exploited by the more intelligent secondary vampires. But there are other possibilities. The coffin could just be an oblong box of any design or construction that's carried by hand, thrown on a wagon or in the trunk of a car. If the vampire is travelling on native soil he can simply burrow a few feet under the ground to sleep during the day, or sleep in a cave or a basement, etc.

Everybody Fears a Vampire

No trust. All undead, even the rare unprincipled or trustworthy vampire, are targets for zealous vampire hunters, priests, cyber-knights, and others. Anybody might be an enemy quietly biding his time, perhaps pretending to be friendly, waiting for the right moment to strike and slay the vampire. Humanoids tend to hate and fear all vampires. The loathing and terror in the vampire dominated lands of Mexico and Central America are greatly intensified, for virtually everybody has friends or family that have fallen victim to the dreaded night stalkers.

Playing A Wild Vampire

Players who are allowed to play a vampire character may select a wild vampire rather than the more calm and cunning secondary vampire. Portrayal of such characters should depict the wild vampire as an individual with low intelligence (not likely to figure out clues nor recognize traps or lies), outspoken (mouths off at the wrong time to the wrong people), aggressive (easily provoked and likes to provoke others to fight), easily bored (tends to become tired of talk and diplomacy and would rather fight or explore; may wander off), craves action as much as blood (love to hunt all life forms, especially humanoids; would rather fight than talk) and erupts into a berserker rage when made extremely angry or on a killing spree.

Experience Table for Vampire R.C.C.s

The following experience table is to be used by players of the optional secondary or wild vampire R.C.C.s. The experience table serves as a measure of some growth and power the vampire gains with age and experience. Although some bonuses are made available, the normal advancement of skills does not occur. A vampire's skills are limited and stinted. **The typical NPC Master and Secondary Vampire** will range between levels 2-7 (roll 1D6+1). **The typical Wild Vampire NPC villain** will be much lower level, often first or second level (roll 1D4).

Experience Bonuses

1. +1 to save vs vampire mind control at levels four, eight, twelve, and fifteen.
2. +1 added to the vampire's personal horror factor at levels six, ten and fifteen.
3. +1 to initiative, strike and parry at level eight for Secondary vampires or level ten for wild.
4. +5% on all skills at levels five, ten and fifteen.
5. +2D6 Hit Points at levels two, four, eight, twelve, and fifteen.
6. Summon +1D4×10 additional rats or mice or 2D6 canines at levels four, eight and twelve.
7. Summon fog at seventh level (same as spell).
8. Secondary Vampires only! +4% to create a secondary vampire from a slow kill bite at levels six, twelve and fifteen.
9. Add one psionic experience level (4th level to 5th level) at level nine.
10. Add 2D6 I.S.P. at levels three, six, nine, twelve and fifteen.

Vampire R.C.C. Experience Table

1	0,000-5,000	8	160,001-200,000
2	5,001-10,000	9	200,001-250,000
3	10,001-20,000	10	250,001-300,000
4	20,001-40,000	11	300,001-400,000
5	40,001-80,000	12	400,001-500,000
6	80,001-120,000	13	500,001-600,000
7	120,001-160,000	14	600,001-1 Million
		15	1,000,001-2 Million

Vampire Powers

All undead Vampires, regardless of their caste level or origin, possess the same basic powers and abilities.

A Lust for Blood

As an extension of the vampire intelligence (which is always evil) vampires are compelled to engage in evil and unnatural acts. Some vampires try to fight these terrible urges and evil inclinations. Others welcome them without resistance, while others ultimately give in to the life of the undead. Remember, vampires are no longer human. They have been completely reborn as a demonic supernatural being. An alien life form that now feeds on humans. The need for humanoid (preferably human) blood is one such horrible urge that no vampire can resist for long.

Sadly, most humanoids transformed into vampires retain many memories (and skills) from their former life and may try to resist the need to feed on human blood, but the monster must feed. At some point, even the tragic *good alignment* vampire must partake of human blood. Some have tried to end their horrid existence by starvation, but this is an impossibility. A vampire's instinct to feed is so powerful that they cannot help themselves. If he is lucky, the vampire will find alternatives to actual murder, but all undead are *compelled* to drink the blood of others.

A vampire should feed on at least two pints (about one liter) of blood once every 48 hours, if not every night. The creature can try to resist the desire and fast. But, with each passing night of abstinence the hunger grows more powerful.

By the third night, the creature awakens with stomach pains and a craving to feed akin to the desires of a junky needing a drug fix. But the monster can still resist.

Feeding Frenzy

On the fourth night, the vampire looks worse than usual; more pale, with a waxy yellow hue to his skin, dark circles surround the eyes, the face and hands are covered in perspiration, and the undead is weak, suffering the following penalties: −2 on initiative, −10% on all skills. Worse, every time he smells human blood within 500 feet (153 m) of him, the vampire must roll to save versus feeding frenzy (a form of mind control/psionics), with NONE of his usual psionic bonuses to save. The slightest cut, a drop of blood, will trigger the feeding frenzy.

A failed roll means the vampire succumbs to his blood lust and runs off to feed. Only physical restraint will stop the demon from executing his dark task. The vampire must be restrained for 1D4 hours before the blood lust passes. Otherwise, the hunger will pass immediately after he has fed. Feeding will also instantly restore the creature of the night to his normal self (no penalties).

At this stage, a vampire of good or anarchist alignment has enough presence of mind to avoid attacking friends and may seek to find a victim of evil alignment to attack and drain, comforting himself in the knowledge that a good/innocent person has not suffered at his hands. Another alternative is to try to stop himself from draining so much blood that he kills an innocent victim. To do this, the vampire must again roll to save against mind control (no bonuses applicable). He can roll to save/stop after he has consumed two pints of blood. A failed roll means the undead continues to feed, unable to satisfy his hunger. A saving throw to stop can be attempted after each additional pint of blood is consumed. Obviously, several failed attempts to stop can result in the death of the victim.

For every night of abstinence beyond four, the vampire suffers a penalty of −1 to save versus feeding frenzy. At this rate it is only a matter of time before the creature must feed.

Starvation can lead to insanity

Restraining a vampire is a difficult task, but not impossible. Unfortunately, a vampire cannot die from starvation. All that a forced abstinence will do is drive the pitiful thing insane. After about three weeks of starvation, the vampire descends into an animal state. The creature cannot think or perform the simplest task. Nor can he recognize friends and companions. The tortured beast writhes in agony, the body becoming more corpse-like with each passing night. The vampire can no longer speak but only scream and howl throughout the night. His every thought is consumed with feeding. If released from his restraints, the monster will attack and completely drain (killing) the first person he encounters. During this feeding frenzy the vampire does not recognize friends, enemies or his surroundings; all he knows is that he must feed. A few minutes after feeding, the undead becomes lucid and rational, again able to think with a clear head and perform skills. His body, too, resumes its more normal appearance. The time of madness is over.

Permanent insanity

Prolonged periods of starvation, six months or more, will drive a vampire insane. Such an occurrence will turn a master or secondary vampire into a wild vampire that is more savage and deranged than usual. From that point on, the vampire functions purely on instinct, like a wolf, becoming a creature of the night that stalks and kills to slake its thirst for blood. The monster can only perform the simplest of skills, such as weapon proficiencies or pilot a simple vehicle (and not very well; at half the base proficiency). Its speech is slurred and guttural. Long sentences and involved concepts are far beyond the comprehension of the insane wild vampire. It is now a simple predator. A night hunter. An evil monster dedicated to feeding and inflicting sorrow and death. Nothing more. **Note:** Once driven insane by starvation, the vampire is permanently mad and cannot be restored to his former self or social ranking.

The Vampire's Bite

For reasons nobody can explain, not even the undead themselves, vampires are drawn to human beings. Thus, a vampire's choice for a slow kill (resulting in the creation of a new vampire) will usually be a human or a humanoid whose appearance is as close to human as possible. Likewise, the victim is likely to be attractive, especially if the vampire's intention is to create for himself an undead companion.

Victims slain for their blood or for sheer pleasure do not become vampires and can be any race, D-Bee or human. Even cattle and other animals may be slain by vampires for the purpose of mischief or mayhem, but they cannot drink the blood of animals. **Note:** Vampires rarely turn mutant animals, especially dogs, into vampires. This is due in part to the mutant's animal nature and partly because the mutant animals are perceived as natural enemies to vampires (they can sense the presence of a vampire/supernatural).

Slow Kill (creating the undead)

The Slow Kill is the ability to turn others into the undead. Vampires can turn their victims into secondary or wild vampires by performing a slow kill. To do this, the vampire must slowly drain his chosen victim a little bit at a time for three consecutive nights. On the third night, the victim is slain by having all his blood drained. Three days later, the victim rises from the grave to join his demonic creator. The new vampire will always rise as a secondary or wild vampire and will usually remain subservient to his creator, obeying his every command even if that command endangers his own life. Any intelligent humanoid can be turned into a vampire by this method.

Percentile dice are rolled whenever a new vampire is created by the slow kill of a Secondary Vampire. 01-42% means a new Secondary Vampire (subservient to its creator) has joined the legion of undead, 43-00% means a *Wild Vampire*, the insane and animal-like predator, has been created. Wild vampires are difficult to control and monitor even by their creator and are commonly banished from more civilized vampire communities to wander the land.

Wild vampires can only create other wild and deranged undead. However, they are usually too crazed, savage, or impatient to perform a slow kill. Instead, the wild ones are blood drinking predators that kill and devour their prey without forethought or plans.

A master vampire is always successful in creating a secondary vampire, via a slow kill.

If an established player character is turned into a vampire, he or she becomes a secondary vampire. The character retains some of the skill knowledge of his former life and many past memories. Skills are limited to O.C.C. skills (does not include O.C.C. related skills), but no O.C.C. bonuses are applicable (forgotten), only the I.Q. bonus remains, if any. The character also remembers half of his/her secondary skills. Skill proficiencies are frozen (minus O.C.C. and educational bonuses) at the level at which the person became a vampire and do NOT increase. The vampire relies on instinct and natural abilities rather than skills. **New Skills for player characters:** Two new secondary skills can be selected at levels three, six, nine, eleven, and fifteen. All skills start at first level proficiency and do not increase. The available skill categories are limited to: Communication, Domestic, Piloting, Technical, Rogue, Wilderness, and Weapon Proficiencies.

Humanoids with cybernetics, including prosthetic limbs, can become vampires. The cybernetic limbs and implants are magically expelled from the body and new undead limbs and organs are regenerated. Neither cybernetics nor bionics can be added to a vampire, because the vampire's regenerative system will not allow it; the skin heals too rapidly to perform surgery and the body expels foreign implants and articles in favor of regenerated undead parts.

Borgs and most supernatural or magic creatures, like **dragons**, can NOT be transformed into vampires. However, they can be killed by them.

The Passive Victim

The victim of a slow kill is immediately linked to the vampire and will offer no further resistance after the first bite. During the day, the individual is sluggish and sleepy. The character is easily frightened and will act unusually timid. Wits are dull and, when not languishing about, the individual will sit quietly by a window, staring out as if in a trance or in deep thought. Skills are at half, as are attacks per melee. The person is clearly not himself.

The suggestion of travel will meet great resistance. The victim will insist that he or she is too weary or sick or just doesn't want to travel (because he or she waits for the vampire). Force will have to be used to make the person leave the area (psionic mind control won't work; overridden by the vampire's influence). If force is used, the enchanted person will fight like a tiger with all attacks per melee suddenly back to full! Even if removed from the vicinity of the initial attack, the bond between the victim and the vampire enables the vampire to sense and find his victim's new location up to 400 miles away!

Call & Control Victim

A slow kill bite creates a mental bond that enables the vampire to telepathically "call" his victim (100 foot/30.5 m range). The victim will also obey simple verbal and/or mental commands like, "come to me" and "open the door," or "remove the crucifix." The vampire can also place the victim into a trance. While in the trance, the person is oblivious to everything around him. The entranced individual cannot react to outside stimulation, voices, or actions taken by others, nor can he take any kind of action to save himself or to help others. The person remembers nothing of the events that transpired while entranced.

Mind Control: Human Enslavement

A vampire can control a human or humanoid during a slow kill, but can also enslave a human through a series of non-lethal bites. The procedure is similar to the slow kill. For three consecutive nights the undead fiend comes to feed, drinking a small amount of blood every visit. The third attack, unlike the slow kill, does not slay the victim, but instead, the unfortunate soul is enslaved by the vampire. This is the creation of the infamous vampire slave/servant/protector. **Note:** A secondary vampire is limited to only one slave under this method. All others, servants or allies must be willing partners in evil. A master vampire can have two slaves under mind control. Wild vampires seldom have the desire to have a human slave and lack the patience to create a slave.

The enslaved person is now under the vampire's complete mind control. The slave instinctively knows to fear and obey his master. He will never attempt to run away, nor betray his master even under the pain of torture. The slave can attempt to not perform commands that are completely repugnant to him, or threaten a loved one, but he is (minus) −6 to save against the vampire's psychic power. Even if the save is successful, the person is still the vampire's obedient slave, he simply refuses to perform that one particular command. Such defiance, however, will result in a violent beating or torture. Continued defiance will incite the vampire to kill him or worse: turn him into a vampire. Only one death dealing bite is necessary because of the previous consecutive three bites and the pair's unique bond. The slave can NEVER raise his hand against his vampire master under any circumstance.

The victim of enslavement will sense when his vampire master is awake and when the master requires his services. Likewise a limited telepathic link is established in which the vampire can mentally call to his servant and his servant will hear his call. Short messages can be received this way too, such as "Come to me now, and bring the carriage (or weapons, etc.)," and the servant will automatically know the location of his master. **Range** is far greater than the Call and Control ability of a victim marked for death, an impressive one mile (1.6 km).

Breaking a Vampire's Spell

The only way to free a person from **mind control enslavement** is to slay the vampire that controls him. Once slain, the person is free of the monster's control, but will never be the same. Roll once on the random insanity table, and once on the **Vampire Victim Phobia table** (found in the *Vampire Combat Notes Section*). Also, there is a 1-70% chance that the victim's alignment will change to a better/good alignment even if he was once evil; a side effect of having been exposed to such terrible evil.

A vampire's bond between a victim of a slow kill or mind control enslavement before the process is completed (before the third bite) can be weakened and negated if the vampire is prevented from biting his intended victim. If the vampire cannot feed consecutively, the victim regains his strength and force of will. However, vampires are seldom easily dissuaded and will take to the challenge, returning to plague that individual, initiating a new three night sequence of slow kill, until the victim belongs to him or is killed. Intervention by others may force the vampire to alter his plans and first eliminate those who pose an obstacle to his inhuman desires. Of course, the only sure way to permanently break a vampire's hold over somebody is to destroy the vampire. Killing the undead assailant before the third night will save the victim from becoming a vampire or an enslaved being.

Note: All vampires can perform human enslavement and slow kill, but wild vampires seldom have the patience or need to use these powers.

Mind Control: Vampire over Vampire

When an individual is transformed into a vampire, he is reborn and recreated into a supernatural monster. The alignment is generally evil because its origin is from evil. The evil essence of the vampire intelligence merges with that of the new vampire, effectively becoming a living extension of the monstrous intelligence and thus, obedient to the creator-self. Even the few who resist the evil can feel it. Consequently, every vampire recognizes the touch of evil in his brethren, quickly identifying fellow vampires and specifically, the children of the same creator intelligence. This kinship enables the vampires to automatically sense whether or not a fellow vampire is a member of the same creator/intelligence and therefore, the same family.

Members of the same vampire family/essence instantly sense whether their brother vampire is a master, secondary or wild vampire and will treat him accordingly. Vampires that are extensions of other intelligences are also recognized, but are seen as potential rivals and enemies.

The bond that links the vampires indicates the creatures' social status within the loathsome family. The caste system establishes lords, lieutenants and servants. Each social stratum dominates those below it. The vampire intelligence is the absolute master. The vampire master (usually one for every 1000 or 2000 vampires in the family) is next in the chain of command; the first master vampire is usually the lord of all others, including other master vampires. The Secondary vampire is the typical vampire and the most common. The oldest and wisest of the secondary vampires serve as minor lords and barons, commanding or leading other secondary vampires. The wild vampires are the castaways and insane, thus, they are at the bottom of vampire society. Wild vampires serve as slaves and soldiers in larger undead communities.

Generally, a vampire will automatically acknowledge his superiors and obey them. However, some, for various reasons, may defy their superiors and attempt to act independently. When this occurs, the superior vampire will try to enforce his will through mind control.

When mind control is attempted, the attacking vampire's eyes glow bright and his words sound like thunder. The target of the mind control must roll to save versus psionic attack or fall prey to the power of the superior vampire. This degree of mind control against fellow vampires is far more powerful and complete than the similar power used to manipulate non-vampires. Mind control can be tried once every melee (with some limitations) and there is no limit to the number of vampires a dominant leader can control. A master vampire can attempt mind control on the same vampire as often as once every one minute (4 melee rounds), a secondary vampire can attempt it once every five minutes (20 melee rounds), while wild vampires are unable to mind control any vampire other than another wild vampire.

Wild Vampires: Mind Control

Wild undead are always submissive to a master vampire and usually submissive to a secondary vampire without the need for mind control. They fear and respect the *master* vampire, recognizing him or her as the revered one who began the family. They will fearfully and comparatively quietly obey the master's every command without hesitation. They will also obey the *secondary vampire*, but there will be noisy complaints, disrespect, grumbles, growls, and perhaps, arguments. Some may even attempt to exert their will in defiance, unless beaten into submission or subjected to mind control. Vampires created by a different vampire intelligence have little, if any, power over vampires of a different family, even wild ones.

Among themselves, wild vampires are quarrelsome and mean. They tend to have a pack mentality when gathered in groups, subservient to those who are stronger, smarter, or hold a higher social place within the pack. A secondary vampire will often be the pack leader.

To resist an attempt of mind control by a member of a fellow vampire family, the wild vampire must make a saving throw versus psionic mind control, but suffers penalties to do so. **A failed roll** means the wild vampire is subservient for at least 2D6 hours, after which he can attempt to defy his superior again.

Note: The power of mind control over other vampires is natural and automatic and does not require an expenditure of I.S.P.

Penalties of the Wild Vampire to resist a superior.
−10 vs Vampire intelligence (any).
−8 vs Master Vampire of the same essence.
−4 vs Master Vampire of a different essence/intelligence.
−6 vs Secondary Vampire Creator/Lord (same essence).
−4 vs Secondary Vampire (general; same essence).
−1 vs Secondary Vampire of a different essence/intelligence.
−0 vs Fellow Wild Vampire (any).

Bonuses. Vampires enjoy a high M.E. attribute which commonly provides a bonus to save versus psionic attack. This bonus applies only whenever the attack comes from a non-vampire or a vampire not of the same family/essence. It does not apply when the vampire is of the same essence.

Note: Wild Vampires are considered to be minor psionics and need a 12 or higher to save versus psionic attack.

Secondary Vampires: Mind Control

Secondary vampires regard their wild kin as mindless pawns to be used when needed and otherwise, dismissed and forgotten. Secondary vampires are impervious to mind control from wild vampires, but can fall victim to mind control by other, older, secondary vampires and master vampires. A secondary vampire will usually obey the commands of the intelligence, a master vampire, or the secondary vampire who created him, unless it goes against his own morals or desires.

To resist an attempt of mind control by a fellow vampire, the secondary vampire must make a saving throw versus psionic mind control, but suffers penalties to do so. **A failed roll** means the secondary vampire is subservient for about 1D4 hours (2D6 hours against an intelligence), after which he regains his free will and the controlling vampire must again attempt mind control.

Penalties of the Secondary Vampire to resist the orders of a superior.
−6 vs Vampire intelligence (any).
−4 vs Master Vampire of the same essence.
−2 vs Master Vampire of a different essence/intelligence.
−3 vs Secondary Vampire Creator/Lord (same essence).
−1 vs A Secondary Vampire who is 100 or more years older of the same essence.
−0 vs A Secondary Vampire who is 100 or more years older of a different essence/intelligence.
−0 vs Fellow Secondary Vampire (any).
−0 vs Wild Vampire (any).

Bonuses. Vampires enjoy a high M.E. attribute which commonly provides a bonus to save versus psionic attack. This bonus applies whenever the attack comes from a non-vampire or a vampire not of the same family/essence.

Note: Secondary Vampires are considered to be major psionics and need a 12 or higher to save versus psionic attack.

The Master Vampire: Mind Control

A master answers only to its creator, the vampire intelligence. Otherwise, the demon is free to do as it pleases, usually commanding lesser vampires. The creating intelligence rarely has specific commands or laws by which the master or even the other lesser vampires must live. The nature of vampires is anarchy. They are required to feed and propagate within the limits of what a vampire infested territory can support. Other than this, the intelligence expects its vampires to protect it and to cause suffering among the non-vampire population. How this is done is rarely a concern. Of course, the intelligence demands that its minions obey it without question or hesitation should it issue a command or require their defense.

To defy a vampire intelligence or a fellow master vampire, the master must make a saving throw versus psionic mind control, but suffers a penalty to do so. **A failed roll** means the master vampire is subservient to the intelligence for about 1D6 hours (1D6×10 minutes when under the control of fellow master), after which he regains his free will and the controlling vampire must attempt to regain his mind control.

Penalties of the Master Vampire to resist the orders of a superior.
−4 vs Vampire intelligence (any).
−2 vs Master Vampire of the same essence.
−0 vs Master Vampire of a different essence/intelligence.
−0 vs Secondary Vampire (any).
−0 vs Wild Vampire (any).

Bonuses. The master vampire enjoys a very high M.E. attribute which is likely to provide a bonus to save versus psionic attack. This bonus applies whenever the attack comes from a non-vampire or a vampire not of the same family/essence.

Note: Master Vampires are considered to be master psionics and need a 10 or higher to save versus psionic attack.

The Vampire Intelligence: Mind Control

The intelligence is the master of vampires and can enforce its will over all vampires whether they are part of its evil essence or that of another. As a rule, vampires who are part of the intelligence's essence will not consider trying to defy their creator, except under the most extreme circumstances (like being a player character).

Psionic Powers of the Vampire

In addition to the various mind control powers previously detailed, all true vampires also possess a handful of more traditional psionic powers; I.S.P. is required to use these powers. The wild has the least I.S.P.

Powers: *All are equal to a fourth level psionic.*

Death Trance	Presence Sense
Alter Aura (self)	Sense Evil
Empathy	Deaden Pain
Mind Block	Induce Sleep

Hypnotic Suggestion
Super-hypnotic suggestion (NEW, exclusive to vampires)

Super Hypnotic Suggestion (a form of mind control)
Range: Line of sight; must look victim directly in the eyes (vamp's eyes glow red or yellow when this power is used).
Duration: Five minutes per level of experience (20 minutes for the average vampire) or until the vampire is killed or willingly releases his victim.
I.S.P.: 20 per each try, whether successful or not.
Saving Throw: Standard. Does not affect characters piloting robot vehicles and seeing through the eyes of a TV monitor. However, most types of power armor and all body armor offer no protection; gaze into the vampire's eyes and you may be under his control.

This mind control power enables the vampire to place any living creature in a light trance and enforce his will over that of his victim. This power is much more than the psionic power available to mind melters. The vampire can actually control the individual as long as the command is not morally out of character or repugnant.

Vampires can be cunning and will use super hypnotic suggestion against powerful opponents such as borgs, wizards, dragons, and robots controlled by a transferred intelligence. They will also use hypnotic suggestion for the purpose of subterfuge and stealth.

Vampires are masters of hypnotic suggestion and instinctively know its limits and best application. For example: A vampire might control an opponent and tell him to, "Close your eyes and stand in a corner," or "You are very tired, go to sleep," or, "Those people need your help, go to them and help them", or, "That building's on fire, you must go and rescue anybody trapped inside"; effectively taking the character out of the battle. The closer the command is to the nature and alignment of the person, the more likely the hypnotized person is to comply without hesitation.

A command like, "Prevent your friends from entering this room," can also be effective, especially if something like, "Great danger lies beyond this room, don't let anybody enter," is added to the command. The command is an effective one because it is not abhorrent nor morally wrong. In fact, it may save lives. The hypnotized person has not been told to hurt anybody, only to try to prevent them from entering the room. The individual can use whatever methods or degree of force that would be natural for his alignment and based on his relationship with the people he's restraining. On the other hand, a command to "kill" a friend or teammate would instantly break the mind control.

The most cunning vampires will try to find out a little about the person they are about to control and work the commands to fit the individual. They love this kind of manipulation.

Telepathic Link with Minions

The *master vampire* also has a telepathic and empathic link to the legion of undead it has created (all of his/her victims who now walk the earth as lesser vampires). This link enables the master vampire to sense when one of his minions is within 10 miles (16 km), when one of his minions is in pain or killed, and enables him to summon all of his minions within a 100 mile (160 km) area. In turn, the minions will sense whether the summons is a general call to gather or whether they should come with haste because the master is in danger. The minions will also sense when the master has been slain.

Metamorphosis

A true vampire of any variety can instantly transform into a large bat, wolf, or mist. The transformation takes about seven seconds to complete, or about the equivalent of two melee attacks/actions. While in non-human form, the vampire retains its intelligence, identity and basic supernatural powers (like invulnerability), but cannot speak, perform skills, or in mist form, use its psionic powers. The types of attacks and actions are limited to the form the undead has adopted. Since each metamorphosis grants the vampire special abilities inherent to that particular animal or form (this is unlike magical metamorphosis). Thus, the bat is often used for quick escape and transportation, the wolf for spying and combat, the mist for gaining access through crevices and for escape.

One of the most bizarre abilities of the metamorphosis is that the vampire's clothing and other small *personal* articles, such as jewelry, money in pockets and light weapons (knife, light sword, handgun), all disappear, but when the humanoid shape is resumed, the clothes and personal articles all reappear. Body armor of any kind, crossbows, rifles, rail guns, missiles or explosives, large weapons, backpacks, etc., or any items that do not belong to the vampire, drop to the ground; can't be taken/metamorphed. The strange phenomenon is some innate supernatural or magic ability that is not common to any known magical metamorphosis.

Vampire Bat Abilities

Fly: Speed of 50 (35 mph/56 kmph)

Other Natural Abilities:

Sonar/echolocation: Enables the vampire to see/maneuver/fly in total darkness at full speed and see the invisible.

Ultrasonic hearing: Hears high and low frequencies; very acute. Can hear a moth's wings beating but cannot understand the spoken word (too slow).

Thermo-imaging optics: Close range, 10 feet/3 m; for sensing and seeing the heat emanations of warm blood coursing through the veins. But cannot see infrared light.

Combat: +2 to strike, +3 to parry and dodge, +8 to dodge in flight, +5% on prowl ability.

Attacks per melee: Half normal, bite inflicts 2D6 S.D.C. damage, claws 1D6 S.D.C. plus P.S. damage bonus. Can inflict vampire slow kill bite and drink blood while in bat from.

Wolf Abilities

Run: Speed of 58 (40 mph/64 km)

Other Natural Abilities: Track by scent 70% and leap 20 feet across (6 m) and about 6 feet (1.8 m) high.

Combat: +2 to strike, +1 to parry, +4 to dodge, +1 on initiative, +15% on prowl ability.

Attacks per melee: Add one to the normal humanoid number of attacks. Bite 5D6 S.D.C. damage (no P.S. bonus).

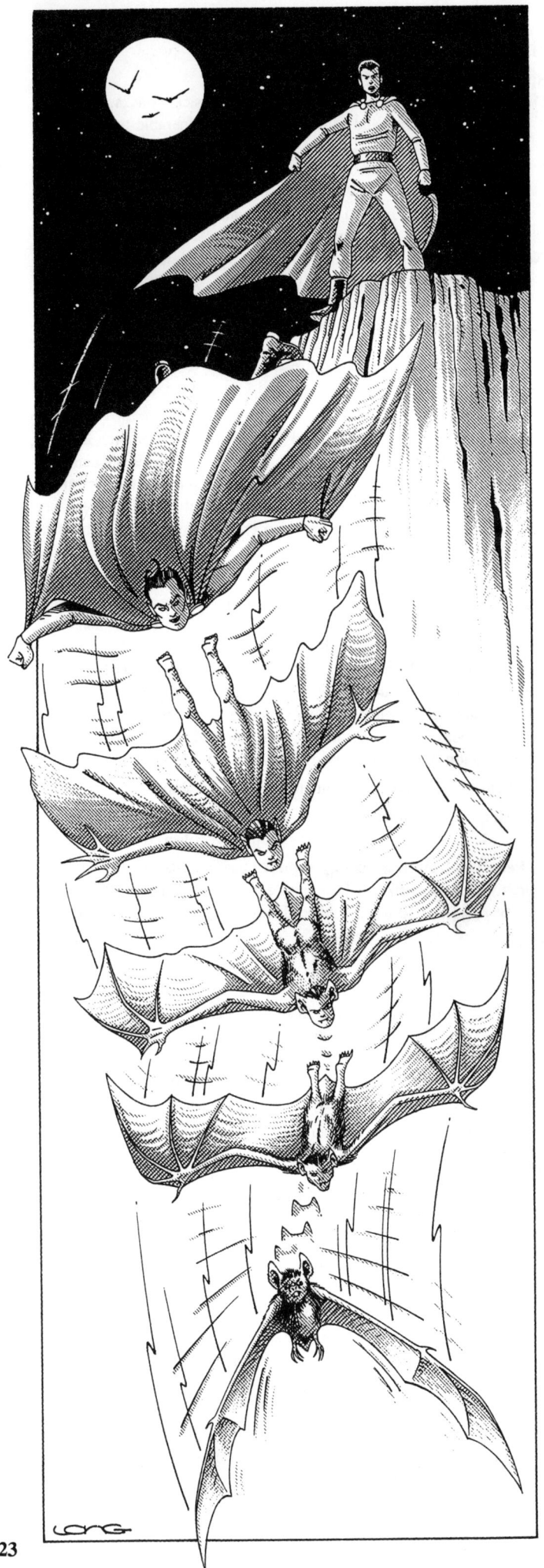

Mist Abilities

Speed: 11 (7.5 mph/12 km)

Other Natural Abilities: Impervious to all physical attacks, including wood, silver, fire, and most magic. Still vulnerable to water and elemental magic. Can slide under doors, through cracks and crevices, key holes, etc. and rematerialize on the other side.

Combat: None. Cannot attack in mist form. Can perform movement melee actions only. +10% on prowl ability (although silent, the mist is very large and obvious).

Note: Cannot use psionic powers in mist form, but can use them in animal form.

Summon Vermin

The vampire can use his earth elemental powers to summon forces of nature. In this case, vermin include rats, mice, flies, gnats and cockroaches.

The vampire can summon up to 100 rats or mice per each level of experience. The horde of rodents has a horror factor of 9 and can bite, inflicting one S.D.C./H.P. point of damage on unprotected victims as they swarm under and around people (GM Note: Roll 1D6+1 per melee for rodent damage). They also create a surprising amount of noise and are quite distracting.

Up to 500 flies, gnats, or cockroaches can be summoned per level of the vampire's experience. Flies and gnats create an annoying and icky cloud of insects (Horror Factor 6). They inflict no damage but impair normal vision and optic systems. Their buzzing also creates a massive audio disturbance, rendering enhanced hearing useless. Cockroaches (Horror Factor 9) are just disgusting, tickle when they crawl against bare flesh, crunch when stepped on, and crawl on everything and everybody in their path. Like the flies, the roaches will cause disorientation by covering optic lenses, view ports and sensors.

Duration of control: 20 minutes per level of experience

Note: The typical no-name vampire is only first or second level. The Game Master may roll 1D4 to determine the level of an NPC vampire.

Penalties from a horde of vermin: Lose one melee attack, −4 on initiative, −1 to strike, −2 to parry and dodge. Vision/optics reduced by 75% and any form of enhanced hearing is void from insects, not impaired by rodents.

Summon Canines

The vampire can summon up to six (6) wolves or dogs per each level of experience. The pack of angry looking canines has a horror factor of 8. Generally, each canine has two or three attacks per melee and inflicts 1D6 S.D.C./H.P. points of damage on unprotected victims. They can be vicious and deadly opponents and make fine watchdogs.

Duration of control: 20 minutes per level of experience

Summon Fog

Old and experienced vampires (level 7 and higher) can create a thick and unnatural fog similar to the summon fog spell. However, unlike the spell, the vampire can direct the fog to move and roll along exactly where he desires it to go. A fog is often summoned forth to cover a vampire's activities or to create fear and confusion.

The fog can cover an area of one mile (1.6 km) and is so thick that an individual cannot see clearly beyond four feet (1.2 m). Blurred shapes and shadowy figures are all that can be seen for an additional 10 feet (3 m) and beyond that, only a grey wall of mist. Within the misty curtain lurks the vampire(s), waiting to strike. Details for traveling in the fog are identical to the spell found on page 186 of **Rifts®**.

Duration: 20 minutes per level of experience (7th level means 140 minutes or two hours, 20 minutes).

Limited Invulnerability

Normal weapons of steel and energy inflict no damage to these demonic abominations. Not the blast of a rail gun nor the energy bolt from a particle beam will hurt a "true" vampire. This means that energy blasts, electricity, explosives, bullets, blades of steel, acid, radiation, disease, etc., do absolutely NO damage!! Nor does alcohol, drugs, anesthetics, poisons, toxic gases, fumes, or smoke have any effect. Fire and cold are also meaningless to the undead while they walk the earth.

The impact of a rail gun, explosion, or the power punch of a robot will knock the undead creature off its feet (loses one melee attack). But an energy blast or the bite of a sword will damage only its clothing, while its undead flesh is untouched. **Note:** See *To kill a vampire* for ways to destroy the monsters.

The vampire's invulnerability coupled with the super regenerative powers means that the creatures are not affected by poison or disease that may be in a person's blood, including cancer and AIDS; not even for a moment. Likewise, alcohol has no effect, good or bad, on vampires. Nor can vampires pass along diseases.

Super Regeneration

A vampire can survive, even keep functioning as normal, with a wooden spear through the head or a severed limb, but the undead does experience pain and can be temporarily immobilized from accumulative hit point damage. When a vampire has been reduced to near zero hit points, he knows he is in jeopardy, not from immediate death, but from lapsing into a recuperative coma that will make him vulnerable to further attack. **A vampire can fight up to 20 points below zero!**

At minus 21 the creature drops to the ground and appears to be dead. Chopping off its head will further enhance the illusion of death, but in reality, merely prolongs the time needed to regenerate. The death-like appearance is a regenerative stasis state. Unless proper measures are taken to truly kill the vampire, it will live anew, possibly regaining consciousness in a matter of minutes and fully restored in hours. A vampire must be destroyed in very specific ways or the monster will rise again, such is the vampire's power to regenerate.

A vampire can regenerate physical damage at a pace that no other known creature can equal. Entire limbs, eyes, hair, skin, grow back in a matter of minutes. The entire body can re-form overnight (8 hrs), an arm 45 minutes, a leg 60 minutes, lower body 4 hrs, upper body 6 hrs, head 4 hrs. A decapitated head left laying nearby can merge back with the body by slowly dissolving into a mist and re-forming with the body, about 20 minutes. **Hit Points are automatically regenerated at a rate of 2D6 per melee.**

Eternal Life

Vampires are said to be immortal. This is true only in a conditional sense, as there are actually numerous ways to permanently destroy the undead. But destroyed they must be, or the ghastly abominations will rise again.

Vampires may seem immortal because they are impervious to fire, cold, poison, energy weapons, and many other things that hurt or kill humans. The creature's regenerative powers and superhuman attributes also seem to grant immortality. And they never age.

Theoretically, an undead vampire can exist for millions of years. The creatures of the night are linked to their ultimate creator, the vampire intelligence. As long as the vampire intelligence lives, so does the humanoid, undead vampire. If the intelligence is destroyed, then all of its fragmented essences die with it, be it 10 or 10 million scattered across three dimensions, all suddenly crumble into dust and cease to exist. However, the destruction of an intelligence is a rare occurrence. It is far easier to deal with undead vampires one at a time, for an individual vampire can be destroyed without killing the alien intelligence.

Abilities Natural to Vampires

- **Supernatural aura.** Vampires have a very unique and distinctive aura. Any psychic who has seen a vampire's aura will recognize other vampires by their aura. The aura also prevents the vampire from having a reflection in mirrors or other reflective surfaces. The aura even makes the clothing and other items held by the vampire invisible in a mirror. This also means that still cameras that utilize mirrors in the photographic process cannot photograph a vampire, but video cameras can.
- **Nightvision.** Can see in total darkness up to 1600 feet away (488 m).
- **Smell Blood.** Can smell blood like a shark, up to a mile away (1.6 km), and has a 50% + 5% per level chance of recognizing whether it's human blood.
- **Prowl 50%.** The prowl ability stated here applies to the vampire in humanoid form. The various forms of metamorphosis add a bonus to the prowl percentage when in that form.
- **Echolocation.** This ability can only be used when metamorphosized into a bat. Enables the vampire to maneuver in total darkness and see the invisible.
- **Does not breathe.** Vampires do not breathe and can survive in a vacuum or in a toxic gas cloud with no detriment to their other senses or powers.
- **Vampires do not bleed,** except when impaled through the heart.
- **Vampires do not radiate heat.** They are cool to the touch and invisible (cannot be detected) to infrared. Thermo-imaging systems are more effective in identifying vampires as a null spot in an otherwise warm environment (especially in Central and South America) but it is not as effective as usual (−20% to read sensory equipment/thermo-imager).
- **Impervious to knockout/stun attacks.** The special knockout and stun attacks provided by some forms of hand to hand combat do not affect vampires. Martial arts throws, flips and holds (locks) are still effective in knocking the monster off balance or holding him in place, but cause no pain/damage.
- **Impervious to normal fires.** Vampires are not harmed by fire, although their clothes will burn and personal articles may be damaged or destroyed. Only when the vampire is staked and his head severed from the body, can he be burnt and permanently destroyed.
- **Not affected by heat or cold.** Neither heat nor cold impair or damage vampires. However vampires prefer hot and *dry* areas. Cold regions are often wet and humid; the undead try to avoid land where it could suddenly begin to rain.
- **Not affected by artificial light.** Artificial light does not harm nor blind vampires. They can see in artificially lighted areas the same as a human.
- **Can eat food for a taste sensation or to trick humans, but do not need to eat.** Nor do vampires have the desire to eat. Likewise, a vampire can consume an unlimited amount of alcohol without the slightest degree of intoxication. Poisoned and spoiled food will have no effect either. Accidental consumption of garlic or wolfbay causes immediate vomiting and 1D6 damage direct to the vampire's hit points.
- **Recognize other vampires** and whether they are of the same family when they are seen, but cannot *sense* the presence of another vampire.
- **Eyes glow when angry and when they use their powers.**
- **Fly 70 miles or more to feed.** Vampires frequently fly 70 to 140 miles away to hunt their prey. This is especially true of solitary hunters and small groups or when prey in one area becomes less available. The larger societies and kingdoms usually have their own human livestock and stay within a more defined area.

The trip is easy in bat form or even running in wolf form. A vampire can fly 70 to 100 miles in two hours, allowing ample time for the creature to arrive, hunt, kill, and return home with hours to spare before dawn. Since the vampire's lair could be anywhere within a hundred to hundred fifty mile (perhaps more) circle, there are actually hundreds of square miles to be searched, a difficult task.

- **Note:** The average vampire is usually quite low level, often only first or second level. The Game Master may roll 1D4 to determine the level of an average, unimportant NPC vampire, or arbitrarily assign an experience level. Wild vampires seldom achieve a level greater than fourth.

To Kill a Vampire

A vampire can withstand the fiery impact of a dozen plasma missiles, or the sizzling assault of a particle beam, making the monster appear indestructible and therefore, immortal. Yet despite the undead vampire's mind boggling regenerative powers and limited invulnerability, they share common weaknesses that can destroy them.

A vampire can be immobilized, perhaps seem dead, but unless properly eliminated, the creature can be restored to continue its evil. This is where the legends of immortality arise. And indeed the vampire can live for hundreds or thousands of years until slain.

Weaknesses

Wood	Water
Silver	Day light
Herbs	Soil
The Cross	Fire

Ironically, while a vampire can survive a nuclear blast, the terrible creatures are surprisingly vulnerable to some very common objects, including wood, water and silver. Thus, a wooden stake, arrow, spear, or silver bullet plunged into its heart will *incapacitate* a vampire, if not truly kill it. Garlic, wolfbay (often referred to as wolfsbane in pre-rifts earth), the symbol and shadow of the crucifix, and a circle of holy water will hold them at bay. Rain, running water, and the light of day will completely destroy the monsters. Holy water burns like acid. Magic can also hurt, incapacitate and contain a vampire.

The Wooden Stake

Many misguided souls believe a wooden stake thrust through the heart of a vampire kills the demon. They are wrong!!

A stake through the heart is a painful means of inflicting a state of *suspended animation*. An arrow, crossbow bolt, spear, or other shaft will all do the job. Some insist that the wood must be made of hawthorn, maple or aspen, but any wood will suffice. The moment the stake hits its mark the demon screams in pain and falls to the ground in a crumpled heap. Moments later, the ghastly fiend seems to stop breathing, blood may gush from the wound, and the body may shrivel to look like an ancient corpse or skeleton.

Dead? No.

Remove the wooden stake and, in mere seconds, the cursed demon is restored to its full strength and physical mass. The transformation is taxing and sends the monster into a feeding frenzy that forces it to hunt and kill immediately to slake its inhuman thirst for blood.

The state of suspended animation can last for eons with no ill effect. As long as the originating vampire intelligence still lives, the undead vampire can be revived by removing the stake of wood. Furthermore, because the vampire is merely locked in forced slumber and not dead, the vampire intelligence retains its link to the world.

Undead vampires are elemental in nature. The impalement of a wooden stake or shaft through the heart grounds the monster to the earth and renders it completely powerless and unconscious. Once grounded, the vampire is locked in forced stasis. In this state he is vulnerable to normal weapons and fire, but it remains dangerous. If the stake is accidentally removed or destroyed, the vampire is instantly revived. Even if the demon's body has been mutilated or blasted to bits, it will regenerate. If the head has been removed and discarded, the head will grow a new body overnight (the staked body crumbles into dust when the new body is complete). Or if the head has been severed and the stake removed from the body, the two parts will magically reunite and the creature regenerates.

The only way to destroy an undead vampire using wood is to drive a wooden stake (or silver) into its heart, rendering it helpless, lop off the head, burn the head and body in separate funeral piers, and scatter the ashes! The vampire can burn when made vulnerable by impalement by wood.

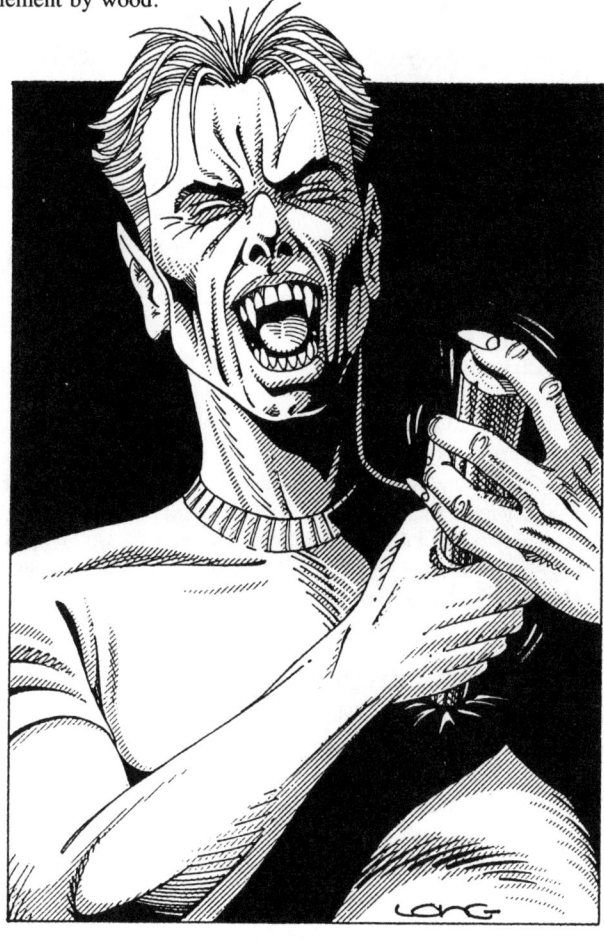

Wood in the form of spears, javelins, arrows, crossbow bolts, shafts, sharpened wood knives and swords, and clubs and staves will hurt the vampire, inflicting damage direct to Hit Points. But the accursed monsters regenerate so quickly that the damage, no matter how great, is never life threatening unless the wooden weapon is thrust into the heart.

Impalement by wood is extremely painful, especially if lodged near the heart. Impalement within three inches of the heart will cause the vampire incredible pain. The fiend loses all remaining attacks that melee as it writhes around and tries to dislodge the wooden shaft. The creature can usually remove an exposed wooden shaft/stake near its heart within one melee. If the wood cannot be grasped by hand the vampire must turn into mist to allow the wood to drop away. Or it can cut or claw away chunks of its own flesh to remove the offending object (roll for horror factor). Impalement of other extremities, including the head, can be painful, but has no ill effect. In fact, vampires are notorious for actions like getting shot with an arrow through the neck, leaving the arrow in the neck, laugh, and continue its assault, as if defying his attacker to try again. The sight is extremely eerie and requires characters to roll again to save versus horror factor. **Note** that a direct strike to the heart instantly renders the vampire helpless, preventing him from turning into mist or using any of his other powers.

The use of wood weapons can be helpful in combating a vampire. Wooden swords, knives, and clubs will cause the demon pain, but a wounded or angry vampire is a terrible opponent. If the warrior cannot finish the vampire with his weapons, the night stalker will see the attack as torture and incite the fiend to seek to inflict similar torture to his tormentor. A vampire's revenge can be a horrible thing. **Note:** The wood weapon must be made entirely of wood. An arrow or spear with a flint or steel head will bounce painlessly off the monster's hide. However, silver tipped weapons are as effective as wood. **Note:** Weapons made of wood inflict double their normal damage against vampires.

The Silver Bullet

Weapons of silver, whether they be blade or bullet, are as effective as wood against the undead. The silver must be as pure as possible to be effective. Silver diluted by impurities is ineffective. Any grade of silver that has less than 85% silver content is useless.

Silver is another element that grounds the vampire to the earth and makes him vulnerable to destruction, but like wood, the weapon can not kill the creature itself. Silver plated stakes and weapons function identical to wood. In the case of the silver bullet, the bullet must pierce the heart and remain lodged in the heart to incapacitate a vampire. If the bullet shoots into the heart and continues through and out of the body, the pain is excruciating, but the vampire is not immobilized and recovers in seconds (loses two melee attacks).

Note: A vampire can remove any foreign particles, such as silver bullets or shards of wood, by turning into mist.

Protection by Herbs

There are two herbs, again linked to the element of *earth*, that can be used to ward away the undead. They are garlic and wolfbay. Hanging either on a door, on or around window, and above a fireplace will prevent a vampire from entering one's home. Wearing the herbs around the neck will protect one from a vampire's bite. Waving the herb in the face of the undead will cause them to recoil. Nor can a vampire enter a circle made of either herb. Eating large portions of the herbs will cause the monster to retch and vomit blood.

Protection by the Symbol of the Cross

The symbol and even the shadow of the crucifix (T shaped cross) will cause the vampire to recoil in apparent fear and pain. The exact nature of this powerful symbol is not known, but its influence is world renowned. A cross held firmly in hand can be used to force a vampire away. Wearing it around the neck protects one from the vampire's bite.

The shadow or the physical touch of a cross will inflict such pain that the demon must roll versus horror factor 18. A failed roll means the fiend is temporarily racked with pain and is immobilized (cannot move/attack) for one full melee! During that melee, the monster will actually appear to smolder and burn. The touch of a crucifix or a small shadow cast by the symbol inflicts 2D6 points of damage direct to hit points. A large shadow that covers half or more of the body will inflict 1D4 × 10 hit points of damage per melee. Unfortunately, the vampire's regenerative powers prevent any permanent damage.

Death by Water

Running water can destroy a vampire. Being immersed in a river, stream or other source of running water will destroy the monster. The moment the creature is immersed in water he loses his other powers and must flee or be destroyed. Running water is like acid. Holding a vampire in or under running water for 1D4 minutes will see the body quickly burn and melt into slime, then disappear without a trace. Even rainfall can kill a vampire exposed to its cleansing waters.

Being immersed in still water, like a swimming pool or horse trough, causes great pain and 3D6 hit point damage per melee, but will not kill. However, a child's toy *water pistol* or *squirt gun* takes on a lethal meaning to vampires. The water is in motion and therefore, considered to be "running" water. Each blast from a typical squirt gun inflicts 2D6 points of damage direct to the vampire's hit points. But water damage is not as quickly healed as all other forms of damage (the vampire can regenerate 6D6 points of water damage once every four melees/one minute). Consequently, a vampire can be squirted to death by a toy water pistol. When hit points are −21 below zero, the water-logged monster melts into oblivion.

Water offers other barriers for the vampire. The undead cannot willingly cross over running water unless there is a bridge to cross, and even then the pitiful creatures must roll to save versus horror factor 16. A failed roll means the vampire cannot bring himself to cross the bridge. The monster can try to overcome his fear to cross a bridge (roll vs horror factor again) as often as four times an hour.

Another way of traversing across running water is to be transported by somebody else, sealed in a container (coffin) and taken over by boat, aircraft or other means, without the vampire's knowledge.

Holy water is water blessed by a priest whose god(s) is of a scrupulous or principled good alignment, or a god of light. Holy water splashed on a vampire burns like molten lead (3D6 hit points per vial/six ounces). A vampire cannot enter a circle drawn with holy water.

Death by Sunlight

The light of day will turn a vampire into ashes! The undead cannot survive the light or warmth of sunlight, yet another weakness tied to the four elements. A true vampire will endure 1D6 × 10 points of damage direct to hit points for every melee (15 seconds) of exposure to sun/daylight. While exposed to the light of day, the creatures of the night are powerless. They cannot use their powers and can barely move (reduce the number of melee attacks/actions and speed to one third). In a matter of minutes, they are reduced to ashes; permanently destroyed.

The magic spell, **Globe of Daylight**, does create true daylight, but it is NOT powerful enough to destroy a vampire. However, the magic globe of light is powerful enough to ward off most vampires, holding them at bay just beyond the edge of the light and preventing them from entering the lighted area.

Do not underestimate the value of this spell. In play-test, the heroes had invaded the lair of a tribe of secondary vampires to save a child who had been kidnapped by one of the vampires. The child had already been bitten two nights in a row ("slow kill") and a third bite meant being turned into a vampire. The group of heroes were faring extremely well until fate made a twist. Suddenly, they were separated into three smaller groups; ironically, the largest group (4 members, one of which a young dragon) was getting the stuffing knocked out of them. The mutant dog, a companion to the psi-stalker, laid in a pool of his own blood, apparently beaten to death at the hands of four vampires. The psi-stalker was unconscious and about to become dinner. The player bot had the child in his arms but was facing down two other vampires. The dragon, the last to enter the scene, peered through the opening of the tunnel they had just crawled through. The situation looked bad. And I mean BAD!

As luck would have it, everybody was clustered together in a 30 foot area. The player of the dragon shouts, "The dragon throws a globe of daylight in the middle of group!" The vampires shriek, cover their eyes and run out of the light, leaving their victims and opponents free from attack. They stand screaming and cursing just beyond the light, but dare not enter the lit area. That timely and smart play enabled the player characters to gather their wounded and make their escape. Further smart playing allowed them to get away. Even the dog-boy would live to fight another day thanks to immediate hospitalization.

Vulnerability (sleeping) During the Day

Vampires must sleep during the day! They cannot seek refuge in a subterranean abode, shielded from sunlight, and remain active. They are not like humans who can function during day or night. The vampire's sleep is a deep, stasis-like sleep from which they are not easily roused. However, a vampire can be woken and can function for a limited time during the day, as long as he or she is shielded from the sun.

A vampire trying to function during daylight hours is groggy and befuddled. The condition is similar to the state that a human is in for the minute after he first wakes up, only the vampire remains in the sluggish state the entire period. During this period, attacks, speed, bonuses, and skills are all reduced by half. And the entire time the vampire wants to get back to sleep. A vampire whose sleep has been disturbed is also an angry and/or threatened vampire who will react to intruders with deadly force. **Note:** A vampire may be able to force himself to stay awake for as long as one hour before collapsing into a coma-like sleep. The need to sleep the deep stasis sleep and the vampire's impaired abilities make them extremely vulnerable during daylight hours. Consequently, most vampire hunters will seek to find the vampire's lair and attack him in his lair during the day. Most vampires will move their lair the instant they find it has been discovered.

The Soil of the Homeland

The elemental nature of vampires links them to the earth, specifically, the soil from the land in which the vampire was originally turned into the undead (usually one's homeland) Thus, vampires must sleep on a bed of soil from their homeland (the place the creature became an undead). The soil of the homeland is any soil from the vampire's native continent. If bitten in North America, the undead can sleep on any soil from North America. This makes travel within the continent easy and hazard free because there is native soil everywhere. However, if traveling to a different land, the vampire must bring the soil of his homeland with him. All that's required is enough soil to create a layer of dirt on the floor of the vampire's sleeping container.

The potential danger to vampires operating outside their native land is that the soil can be stolen, destroyed, or defiled. A vampire hunter can enter the creature's lair at night, while the undead is on the prowl, and steal the soil or defile it by covering it in garlic or wolf bay, or placing a crucifix(es) on it. Covering the soil with holy water will effectively destroy the soil by contamination. Or the soil, an S.D.C. structure, can be atomized by any number of mega-damage weapons.

Without the bed of soil, the vampire cannot sleep. If he cannot sleep he will be racked in agony throughout the day and become an insane berserker beginning with the new night. That night, the mad undead will slaughter livestock and attack (not necessarily kill) 2D6 humanoids. With the dawn of the new day, the vampire is destroyed; it has no place to hide and is compelled to remain on the surface during the next day. The day's first light destroys him.

A smart vampire always brings enough soil for at least two or three alternative lairs, just in case one is destroyed.

Fire

As discussed previously, fire and heat have no effect on living vampires. But, a vampire that has been weakened by a stake through the heart is vulnerable to fire and will burn. However, unless the vampire's head has been decapitated, the demon's body may survive being burnt (50% chance) and regenerate over the next night and kill again.

Vampire Combat Notes

Damage Table
Wood, Silver, Water & Others

Not only does wood, silver and water inflict damage direct to hit points, but the damage to a vampire is far greater than to a normal humanoid. All damage is direct to hit points.

- **Wood or silver weapons; knife, sword, spear, arrow, club, bullet, etc:** Double normal damage direct to the vampire's hit points. Note that while these weapons can cause grievous pain and injury to a vampire and place the undead into a coma, the weapons cannot kill them. Plunging such a weapon into the undead's heart will cause instant and painful suspended animation (see wooden stake and silver bullet in the heart). A vampire that has received damage below zero cannot use his hypnotic or metamorphosis powers, and speed and attacks per melee are reduced to half. −21 or greater places the vampire in a coma, however, the monster's regeneration continues and the horrid fiend is likely to be back on its feet within a melee round or two. **Note:** Character's P.S. damage bonus is not applicable to thrown missle weapons like arrows.
- **The touch of a crucifix:** 2D6 damage to hit points and leaves a momentary burn mark (mark disappears when all damage is regenerated). The touch is so repulsive and painful that the undead must roll to save versus horror factor 18. A failed roll means the fiend is racked with pain and is immobilized (cannot move/attack) for one full melee! During that melee, the monster will actually appear to smolder and burn.

    When held before a vampire, the cross will cause the undead to cringe and keep away, preventing an attack.
- **Shadow of a crucifix:** A small shadow cast by the symbol of a cross inflicts 2D6 points of damage direct to hit points. A large shadow that covers half or more of the body will inflict 1D4×10 hit points of damage per melee. The creature must also roll to save versus horror factor 18. A failed roll means the fiend is immobilized for one full melee. During that melee, the monster will actually appear to smolder and burn.
- **Water gun blast:** 2D6 damage direct to hit points from a typical water pistol or rifle type toy/weapon.
- **Vial of Holy Water (6 ounces):** 3D6 damage direct to hit points. Holy water can also be spilled to form a circle that a vampire cannot enter.
- **Silver bullets:** Normal damage but direct to hit points, because the rounds are so small. A bullet lodged in the heart will inflict the same state of suspended animation as a wooden stake. Silver bullets are soft and heavy, reducing the normal effective range by half.
- **Daylight/Sunlight:** 1D6×10 points of damage direct to hit points for every melee (15 seconds) exposed to sun/daylight. While exposed to the light of day, the creatures of the night are powerless. They cannot use their powers and can barely move (reduce the number of melee attacks/actions and speed by half). In a matter of minutes they are reduced to ashes.
- **Globe of Daylight Spell:** The magic spell is not powerful enough to kill or seriously damage a vampire. However, its light can ward off most vampires, holding them at bay just beyond the edge of the light and preventing them from entering the lighted area.

Wood and Silver Weapons

Any style of knife, sword, or axe can be made of wood to use against vampires. Wood weapons inflict double their normal damage to the undead, but half damage to normal humans and animals. Note that wood weapons are less durable than metal and vulnerable to fire. Cost is about the same as similar metal weapons.

Unusual Wood Weapons:
Boomerang (high quality): 100 credits each
Wood Throwing Knife: 100 credits each
Throwing Sticks: 75 credits each
Tiger Pits: Six to 10 foot deep pits dug in the ground big enough for a man to fall into. Wooden stakes pointed up to impale, line the bottom of the pit and sometimes the sides as well. Inflicts 2D4×10 H.P./S.D.C. to normal people/animals double to vampires, no damage to M.D.C. armor.

Any weapon can be plated in silver. Silver-plated weapons inflict double their normal amount of damage direct to the hit points of vampires and normal damage to S.D.C. structures. Silver is more durable than wood, but is a softish metal and will scrape, dent, and melt more easily. Plating cost is about three times the cost of the original weapon.

Unusual Silver Weapons:
Silver-plated Spikes (knuckle or foot, 1D6 S.D.C.): 150 credits.
Plated Throwing Irons (2D6 S.D.C): 150 credits.
Plated Tiger Claws (2D4 S.D.C.): 100 credits.

Costs of Bow Weapons

All prices are typical prices for good quality weapons. Exceptional quality weapons will cost double or triple.
Short bow: 250 credits
Long bow: 700 credits
Modern Compound Bow: 700 credits
Traditional Crossbow: 500 credits
Modern Crossbow (full size): 800 credits
Crossbow Pistol (half range): 300 credits

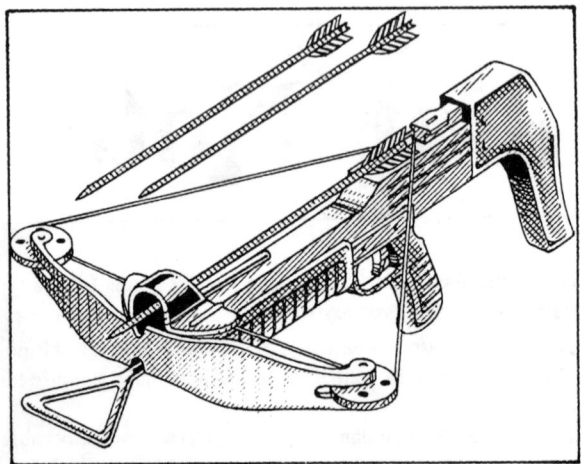

Anti-Vampire Rail Guns Modified Rounds for Combating Vampires

Vampire rounds for the SAMAS C-40R and NG-202 rail guns

Doc Reid and others have perfected special anti-vampire ammunition for rail guns; shards of wood with tiny bits of metal imbedded in the base of the wood projectiles. The blast of wood (or silver) flechettes from the powerful C-40R and NG-202 inflict reduced mega-damage because of the softer, less damaging, rounds being fired (only 1D4 M.D. per burst of 30 or 40 rounds), but 3D6×10 S.D.C/Hit Point (H.P.) damage to vampires. A called shot is still needed to strike a vampire in the heart to immobilize him. These two rail guns can inflict severe damage to vampires and blow off a head, arm or leg. 50% of the flechettes shoot right through the body. The lighter and softer wood or silver, with less iron content, has a reduced range than the typical, unmodified round; reduce by half. The great thing about these anti-vampire weapons is that no modification of the weapon itself is necessary. The change is made in the rounds fired. Thus, vampire rounds and conventional M.D. rounds can be quickly changed from one to the other. The rail guns and unmodified rounds are found in the **Rifts RPG**, page 226.

Modified Mega-Damage Rounds: A burst is 30 rounds: **Wood** inflicts 1D4 M.D. or 3D6×10 H.P. to vampires. **Silver** rounds inflict 1D4×5 M.D. or 2D6×10 H.P. to vampires.
Modified Range: 2000 ft (610 m).

Vampire rounds for the NG-101 rail gun

The blast of wood flechettes from this light rail gun inflicts only one or two M.D. per burst (30 rounds; roll 1D4: a roll of one or two equals one M.D. of damage, while a roll of 3 or 4 inflicts two M.D.), but is still quite devastating to vampires, inflicting 2D4×10 S.D.C/H.P. damage. A called shot is still needed to strike a vampire in the heart to immobilize him. 40% of the flechettes shoot right through the vampire's body. Range is half (2000 ft/609 m).

Modified Mega-Damage Rounds: A burst is 30 rounds: **Wood** inflicts 1 or 2 M.D. or 2D4×10 H.P. to vampires. **Silver** rounds inflict 4D6 M.D. or 1D6×10 H.P. to vampires.
Modified Range: 2000 ft (610 m).

Cross Spotlight

This is really a very simple device:, a conventional floodlight that has the shape of a cross painted or taped across it. The shadow of a crucifix is painful and frightening to vampires. Cost and Damage:
Flashlight: 2D6 H.P., costs 15 credits.
Large Vehicle size Spotlight: 4D6 H.P., costs 75 credits.
Huge Aircraft Signal Spotlight: 1D4×10 H.P. and vampire must roll to save vs horror factor 18; costs 2000 credits.

Conventional Water Weapons — Squirt Guns

Plastic Water Pistol: Range: 30 feet (9 m), Weight: 3 ounces (85 grams), Damage to Vampires: 2D6 hit points, Payload: 12 blasts. Cost: 5 credits.

Metal or Ceramic Water Pistol: Range: 100 feet (30 m), motorized. Weight: 2 lbs (0.9 kg), Damage to Vampires: 2D6 hit points, Payload: 12 blasts. Cost: 50 credits. Greater durability and range.

Plastic Water Pump-style sawed-off Shotgun: Range: 50 feet (15 m), Weight: 6 ounces (170 grams) for plastic or 5 lbs (2.3 kg) for metal, Damage to Vampires: 4D6 hit points; wider, concentrated blast (more water), Payload: 10 blasts. Cost: 10 credits. Greater damage and range.

Metal or Ceramic Water Pump-style sawed-off Shotgun: Range: 75 feet (22.9 m), motorized. Weight: 5 lbs (2.3 kg). Damage to Vampires: 4D6 hit points; wider, concentrated blast (more water) Payload: 10 blasts. Cost: 80 credits. Greater range.

Full size Metal or Ceramic Water Shotgun: Range: 100 feet (30.5 m), motorized. Weight: 7 lbs (3.2 kg). Damage to Vampires: 5D6 hit points, Payload: 10 blasts Cost: 95 credits. Greater range.

Full size Metal or Ceramic Water Rifle: Range: 150 feet (75.7 m), motorized. Weight: 6 lbs (2.7 kg). Damage to Vampires: 3D6 hit points. Payload: 12 blasts. Cost: 135 credits. Greater range.

Water Rifle and Water Grenade Launcher: Range: rifle is 150 feet (75.7 m), grenade launcher 75 feet (22.9 m), motorized. Weight: 10 lbs (4.5 kg), metal or ceramic. Damage to Vampires: Rifle blast 3D6 hit points; the grenade is effectively a water balloon that erupts on impact, covering its target in water (approx. 8 ounces of water to a 3 ft/0.9 m area), inflicting 6D6 hit point damage. Payload: 12 rifle shots and one grenade, must reload. Comes with 10 additional grenades and can be carried in a cloth carrying case with shoulder strap. Cost: 150 credits. Additional grenades cost 15 credits per 10; can attach water balloon, but reduces range to 50 feet and −4 to strike. The grenades can also be fired by crossbows (half range). Limited Rate of Fire: Can fire grenade only two times per melee and it takes one melee action to reload. Not available in hand-thrown grenades.

Homemade Water Grenades/Water Balloons: An ordinary child's balloon can become a lethal weapon to vampires; however, water balloons are not made for throwing and break easily, sometimes in your hand. Extremely difficult to carry more than a half dozen, even in a container, without breaking. Effective Throwing Range: 10 feet (3 m); any distance beyond 10 feet and the thrower is −6 to strike! Maximum throwing range is 50 feet (15 m). Weight: 6 or 8 ounces (170 grams). Damage to Vampires: 6D6 hit points. Cost: 5 credits for a package of 100 balloons.

Portable Water Cannon: This weapon looks like a two-handed flame thrower with hose and small, one gallon hip tank (7 lbs/3.2 kg) or five gallon backpack tank (35 lbs/15.8 kg). Range: 100 feet (30.5 m), Weight: 11 lbs (5 kg) plus water tanks, Damage to Vampires: 6D6 hit points; fires a high-pressure stream of water. Cost: 300 credits. Payload: One gallon tank: 10 blasts, five gallon tank: 52 blasts.

Vehicle Mounted Water Cannon: This is big, rail gun-style water cannon with a fifty gallon drum of water. Must be mounted on cars, bots, or buildings, or carried by borgs and characters with a P.S. of 24 or higher. Range: 400 feet (122 m), Weight: Cannon 40 lbs (18 kg) metal and ceramic, 50 gallon drum (350 lbs). Damage to Vampires: 1D6×10 hit points; fires a high-pressure stream of water. Cost: 1000 credits. Limited Rate of Fire: Can shoot only six times per melee. Payload: 40 blasts. Payload can be increased dramatically by connecting a hose to a much larger tank of water or to a city's water/sewer system, the latter is effectively unlimited. Fort Reid has several water cannon-mounted turrets along its protective walls.

Additional Water Tanks: These are simple hip tanks or backpacks that can be connected to most water weapons to increase the number of shots. Half gallon hip tank (3.5 lbs) adds 40 shots to most weapons, 20 shots to heavy water weapons. Gallon hip tank (7 lbs/3.2 kg) adds 80 or 40 shots, or five gallon backpack tank (35 lbs/15.8 kg) adds 400 or 200 shots. Costs are 10, 20, and 50 credits respectively.

Techno-Wizard Anti-Vampire Weapons!

The Vampire Cross

A special, cross-shaped, magic amulet with a power crystal (techno-wizardry) that will turn blood red whenever a vampire is within 12 feet (3.6 m) of the cross, and, as any cross will, hold vampires at bay. The crosses come in a variety of sizes and are attractive enough to be worn as jewelry. Minimal cost is 10,000 credits, more ornate pieces (jewelry, perhaps gem studded) can cost three to six times more. No mystic energy is needed to activate, always activated; radiates magic.

Techno-Wizard (TW) Water Blasters

These weapons are typical looking squirt guns or real looking automatic weapons (can not fire bullets) that appear to be empty. However, when 10 P.P.E. or 20 I.S.P. are pumped into the blaster, it will fire a high-powered jet of water. **Payload and Rate of Fire:** The typical weapon can fire 40 bursts before requiring a recharge of 10 P.P.E. or 20 I.S.P. The rate of fire is identical to automatic and energy weapons, generally meaning as often as one can pull the trigger. However, the conditions for *aimed, bursts, and wild shooting* also apply (as do automatic weapon W.P. bonuses and skills). Thus, rapid-fire is less aimed and less likely to strike than a careful, aimed shot.

The great thing about techno-wizard water blasters is that they do not require a reservoir of water, the water just magically appears, which makes them more durable, lightweight (no water weight!) and easy to use. The range is also significantly greater than conventional, toy-like water guns.

TW Plastic Water Pistol: Range: 150 feet (46 m). Weight: 6 ounces (170 grams). Damage to Vampires: 2D6 hit points. Payload: 40 blasts. Cost: 6000 credits.

TW Metal Water Pistol: Range: 200 feet (60 m). Weight: 2 lbs (0.9 kg). Damage to Vampires: 2D6 hit points. Payload: 40 blasts. Cost: 10000 credits. Greater durability. Any existing automatic pistol can be converted.

TW Pump-style Water Pistol or Sawed-off Shotgun: Range: 200 feet (60 m). Weight: 1 lb (.45 kg) for plastic or 5 lbs (2.3 kg) for metal. Damage to Vampires: 4D6 hit points; wider, concentrated blast (more water). Payload: 40 blasts. Cost: 20,000 credits. Greater damage.

TW Full-size Water Shotgun: Range: 300 feet (91 m). Weight: 3 lbs (1.35 kg) for plastic or 7 lbs (3.2 kg) for metal. Damage to Vampires: 5D6 hit points. Payload: 40 blasts. Cost: 25,000 credits. Greater damage.

TW Full-size Water Rifle: Range: 600 feet (182 m). Weight: 1 lb (.45 kg) for plastic or 6 lbs (2.7 kg) for metal. Damage to Vampires: 4D6 hit points. Payload: 40 blasts. Cost: 40,000 credits. Greater range. Any existing rifle can be converted into a water rifle.

TW Rifle and Water Grenade Launcher: Range: 600 feet (182 m). Weight: 5 lbs (2.3 kg) for plastic or 11 lbs (5 kg) for metal. Damage to Vampires: Rifle blast 4D6 hit points; the grenade is a concentrated ball of water that erupts on impact, covering its target in water (approx. 15 gallons of water to a 10 ft/3 m area), inflicting 1D4×10 hit point damage. Payload: 20 blasts. Cost: 60,000 credits. Limited Rate of Fire: Can fire grenade only twice times per melee and each grenade counts as two rifle blasts. Not available in hand thrown grenades.

TW Water Cannon Bazooka: Range: 600 feet (182 m), Weight: 5 lbs (2.3 kg) for plastic or 11 lbs (5 kg) for metal, Damage to Vampires: 2D4×10 hit points; fires a concentrated ball of water that erupts on impact covering its target in water (approx. 30 gallons of water to a 10 ft/3 m area). Payload: 20 blasts. Cost: 70,000 credits. Limited Rate of Fire: Can shoot only three times per melee.

TW Water Cannon: This weapon looks like a two handed flame thrower with hose and small, one gallon hip or back tank. Range: 300 feet (91 m), Weight: 5 lbs (2.3 kg) for plastic or 11 lbs (5 kg) for metal, Damage to Vampires: 3D6×10 hit points; fires a high-pressure stream of water the full 200 foot length, covering its target in water (approx. 50 gallons of water to a 10 ft/3 m impact area). Payload: 20 blasts. Cost: 150,000 credits. Limited Rate of Fire: Can shoot only six times per melee.

TW Storm Flares

A magic flare that is fired into the air by a flare gun or lit and launched like a rocket. Blows up 2000 feet in the air and causes a sudden rainstorm. The storm covers a 100 foot circle and lasts 1D6 minutes. Storm damage inflicts 4D6×10 hit point damage for every HALF melee round (7.5 seconds) a vampire is exposed to the cleansing waters. Cost: 10,000 credits per flare. Note: Shooting the storm flare into the vampire does NO damage and doesn't create a storm.

TW Globe of Daylight Flares

Another magic flare that is fired into the air by a flare gun or lit and launched like a rocket. Explodes 200 feet (61 m) in the air to release a magic globe of daylight that slowly drifts down until it stops and hovers, stationary, about 20 above the ground. The flare forces vampires to the edge of its light, holding them at bay and preventing them from entering the lighted area (same as spell). Typical Duration: 3D4 minutes. The globe is stationary and can't be moved. Cost: 2,000 credits per flare. Note: Shooting the magic flare into a vampire does NO damage; bounces off and away, but will still burst into a globe of light. Also excellent as a signal flare, scaring animals and lighting an area.

TW Animal Repellent Flares

This flare is a hand-held flare that ignites when a cord is pulled. It doesn't fire anything but releases a minty scent and a magic aura that will repel as many as six large animals, like wolves, and 20 small animals, like rats, mice, and bats. Typical Duration: 1D4 minutes. The magic aura covers an tiny area of about five feet (1.5 m) although scattering several around and area will increase the area of effect. Moving the flares will cause them to dissipate twice as quickly. The mint smell is only for effect. When the flare stops burning, its magic is ended. Cost: 6,000 credits per flare.

TW Modified Wood Firing Rail Gun

This is very rare and expensive weapon, said to have been developed by a techno-wizard at Lazlo with the help of a wizard from another dimension (Palladium). Any rail gun can be magically converted, but the lighter models are preferred because they can be used by more people. Like the TW water weapons, no external ammunition drum is required, only the rail gun itself; the rapid-fired wood shards magically appear. Normal rail gun rounds can not be fired from these weapons.

Damage from Rounds: A burst inflicts 1D4 M.D. or 3D6×10 H.P. to vampires.
Range: 4000 ft (1200 m).
Payload: 40 bursts per every 20 P.P.E. or 40 I.S.P.
Cost: 500,000; very rare, but becoming more common as other techno-wizards learn the magic.

TW Vampire Water Field

The TW water field is a silly, but amazingly popular device with people in the vampire plagued west. The basic device is a compact backpack that weighs five pounds. When activated by 10 P.P.E. or 20 I.S.P., an umbrella-like tube framework (no protective membrane) sprouts up and sprays water all around the individual wearing the pack (some of the water hits the wearer too, especially if moving or on a windy day). Despite the ridiculousness of the "portable shower,/73 as it is frequently called, the device does keep vampires away. A vampire will suffer 3D6 H.P. damage every time he steps into the shower of water. Duration: Five minutes. Range: 2 feet around the wearer. Cost: 50,000 credits.

Other Techno-Wizard Devices

TW Underwater Ley Line Flyer

These are underwater versions of wing boards and are of a very similar design, with directional water flaps instead of air flaps. The board rides under the waves, along ley lines, at a speed of up to 45 mph (72 km). Costs 1 P.P.E. or 2 I.S.P. to activate. Duration: until the pilot stops or the ley line ends. Initial creation cost in P.P.E.: 50, need swim as fish spell. Market Value: 5000 credits.

TW Underwater Scooter

Looks like the conventional underwater scooters except for the strange crystals and doohickey toward the engine. Costs 20 P.P.E. or 40 I.S.P. to activate. Duration: Six hours. Speed 60 mph (96 km). Initial creation cost in P.P.E.: 250, need swim as fish, wind rush, and energy field spells. Market Value: 50,000 credits for a one-man scooter, 75,000 for a two-man scooter. Optional Features: Add 25,000 for a conventional back-up motor. Add 500,000 to add a protective 100 M.D.C. energy field (costs an additional 10 P.P.E. or 20 I.S.P. to activate, duration one hour or until M.D.C. is depleted). Add another 100,000 for a breathe without air bubble (duration one hour, costs 10 P.P.E. or 20 I.S.P. per hour).

TW Water Sled

Looks like the conventional jet sleds used by water skiers to skim across the water, but is TW powered and has great stability. Costs 20 P.P.E. or 40 I.S.P. to activate. Duration: Five hours. Speed is 100 mph (160 km). Initial creation cost in P.P.E.: 270, need swim as fish, telekinesis, and energy field spells. Market Value: 50,000 credits for a one-man sled, 75,000 for a two-man sled.

TW Sailboat

A sailboat with an oversized fan in the rear, facing the sail. When the TW fan is activated it creates its own wind to drive the sail. Costs 10 P.P.E. or 20 I.S.P. to activate. Duration: Three hours. Can maintain a speed of about 30 mph (48 km). Initial creation cost in P.P.E.: 210, wind rush and energy field spells. Market Value: 30,000 credits for a small six-man yacht, 50,000 for larger fishing boat (holds 20 people), plus cost of boat.

TW Hover Yacht

A techno-wizard designed hover watercraft. Costs 20 P.P.E. or 40 I.S.P. to activate. Duration: two hours. Can maintain a speed of about 150 mph (240 km). Initial creation cost in P.P.E.: 350, requires the spells, levitation, float in air, wind rush and energy field. Market Value: 100,000 credits for a small six man yacht, 250,000 for larger fishing boat (holds 20 people), plus cost of boat.

TW S.C.U.B.A — wetsuit and diving gear

A special, breathe without air respirator, with a small air tank attached, is worn instead of the normal air tanks and hose. Costs 5 P.P.E. to activate. Duration is 20 minutes, but can be instantly refilled/reactivated by an additional 5 P.P.E. or 10 I.S.P. Also effective against toxic fumes or in an airless environment. Initial creation cost in P.P.E.: 200; breathe without air spell. Market Value: 10,000 credits.

Super Swimmer Diver's Suit: This is a simple air mask and skin diver's wetsuit with a crazy looking contraption built into the belt. The TW gizmo instills the magic powers of swim as a fish and breathe without air. Costs 11 P.P.E. or 22 I.S.P. to activate. Duration: 15 minutes. Initial creation cost in P.P.E.: 600. Market Value: 50,000 credits.

TW Night Goggles

The magic goggles that enable a person to see in the dark and see the invisible. Range of vision is 120 feet (36.5 m). Costs 25 P.P.E. or 50 I.S.P. to activate. Duration 15 minutes. Initial creation cost in P.P.E.: 140, modified Eyes of the Wolf spell. Market Value: 50,000 credits.

TW Thieves Gloves

The gloves appear to be normal leather, with a metal plate on the top, knuckle part, with wires running along the seams of the fingers, and with crystal studs on the knuckles. Gives the wearer the power of magic concealment (palming) and escape. Requires 16 P.P.E. or 32 I.S.P. to activate. Duration is 15 minutes. Initial creation cost in P.P.E.: 200, concealment and escape spells. Market Value: 250,000 credits (the gloves sale is prohibited in many towns).

Penalties to strike a Vampire's Heart

Long Range Attacks

It is difficult to strike the heart when shooting with any type of long range weapon, whether it be a crossbow or a gun. **Long range** is considered to be 20 feet (6 m) or more. Attackers must make an aimed, *called shot* to strike and must roll a 19, 20, or higher to strike. **Bonuses to strike** are applicable! Vampires cannot parry an attack from a gun or bow. Thrown weapons like a spear or knife can be parried or dodged.

Close Range Attacks

A close range attack is the usual hand to hand combat or sword play. It encompasses a range up to 20 feet away; a distance that can be closed within one melee action (a few seconds) and close enough to have a good view of a target. From this range the character's normal attacks and bonuses apply. The only condition is that the combatant must state that he is "trying to pierce the heart" before he strikes. The player must announce a *called shot* for gun play or bow weapons. The vampire opponent gets his usual option to parry or dodge the close range attack.

Attacks on an Incapacitated Foe

The old method of "stake 'em while they sleep" is a sure fire way of hitting one's mark. The attacker can easily aim and hit the heart of a sleeping or otherwise immobilized vampire. Such an attack would be an automatic hit except for the vampire's horror factor aura and the nervousness the attacker is likely to feel. Thus, there is a slim chance that the *point blank* attack may miss. Roll to strike as normal; a roll of 1-4 misses the heart (a last minute twitch, deflected by a rib, etc.). The wooden stake (or whatever) has pierced the vampire's chest, but just missed the heart by a fraction, but still does damage. The vampire is now awake, in agony, and angry. A roll of 5-20 is a definite strike, rendering the fiend immobile.

Note: This rule applies only to sleeping or incapacitated foes and not close combat.

A Natural 20

The roll of a natural 20 (unmodified by bonuses) always strikes the heart unless the vampire's parry or dodge roll is a natural twenty.

Vampires versus Magic

Harmless and Weak Magic

Vampires are impervious to virtually all forms of **magic mind control,** including sleep, charismatic aura, befuddle, fear, heavy breathing, trance, domination, compulsion, wisps of confusion, words of truth, and all curses. The **id barrier** is the only mental/emotional afflicting magic that has full effect on vampires. **Turn dead** and **animate and control dead** have no influence on the *undead*.

Similarly, magic that withers or impairs the physical body has no or little effect on vampires. Agony, paralysis (any), sickness, life drain, wards, heal wounds, negate toxins, impervious (all), restoration, metamorphosis (any), and transformation have no effect on vampires. **Blind** and **mute** will affect a vampire, but the duration is half. **Petrification** has no effect! **Speed of the snail** and **fly as an eagle** has full effect!! **Swim as a fish** will impart the ability to swim, but does not protect the vampire from the water (water kills). **Wind rush** has no effect.

Magic especially useful against vampires

Mega-damage magic energy, such as fire ball, call lightning, wall of flame, etc., inflicts half damage direct to hit points (the listed M.D.C. damage is considered hit point damage, but divide by half). S.D.C. spell magic does not hurt the undead. But while magic can hurt and incapacitate a vampire, it cannot kill him.

Circles of protection will keep all vampires, except the master, outside their borders. Likewise, the undead cannot enter a place that has been protected by a **sanctum** incantation nor can they pass through or over an **impenetrable wall of force**.

Constrain being and **banishment** will also protect/force away all but the master vampire from an area. **Summon and control entity** and **exorcism** do not apply to vampires; no effect. **Summon lesser beings** can be used to summon wild vampires and recently created secondary vampires; the master is impervious to the summons.

Blinding flash will temporarily blind a vampire, just as a **cloud of smoke** or **sandstorm** will impair the monster's vision and senses. **See aura** or **sense evil** will help identify a vampire (vampires do not register as magic). **Invisibility:** Vampires cannot see the invisible except when in bat form. **Telekinesis** can hurl wooden weapons toward the heart at a distance and often with greater accuracy than thrown weapons, and from behind too. **Carpet of adhesion** and **magic net** are both excellent means to temporarily stop a vampire, but the undead can easily escape by turning to mist.

Vampires are fooled by **illusionary magic**, thus, **multiple image, mask of deceit,** and others are useful spells. **Apparition, horrific illusion** and **hallucination** are effective only if the image is something frightening to a vampire, like running water, a crucifix, dragon, etc.

Summon and control storms can be extremely deadly to any vampire caught in a sudden downpour!

Magic weapons inflict hit point damage rather than mega-damage when used against vampires.

Note: Although magic can be tremendously useful in combating the undead, the vampires must still be destroyed in the time-honored fashion of being staked and burnt, or exposed to sunlight, or submerged in water, to be permanently destroyed.

Vampires Versus Psionics

Impervious to some forms of psionics

Vampires are susceptible to psionic attacks, although they are impervious to mind control, including **empathic transmission, exorcism, hypnotic suggestion, mind wipe** and **mind bond**. Likewise, **pyrokinesis, electrokinesis, bio-manipulation, induce sleep** and **healing touch** will not work on vampires.

Psionics that affect Vampires

Normal **empathy** (to sense the vampire's emotions), **telepathy, presence sense** and **most other psionic powers** are effective against vampires and function as they would against a human foe. **The danger of using telepathy** on a vampire is that the monster can use his own hypnotic suggestion or super hypnotic suggestion on the telepathic person without gazing into his eyes. Normal save vs psionics. **Sense evil** (most vamps radiate supernatural evil) and **see aura** are useful in identifying a vampire. Sense magic will not indicate a vampire; they are not considered creatures of magic.

The **psi-sword** inflicts hit point damage to vampires rather than mega-damage, but cannot permanently destroy a vampire. The **mind bolt** also inflicts hit point damage (rather than S.D.C.) but at half damage. **Hydrokinesis** is an especially lethal psionic power when fighting vampires. A water spout inflicts 4D6 hit points of damage to a vampire per each gallon of water hurled. One gallon of water can be hurled/manipulated per level of the psionic.

Telekinesis is perhaps the most lethal of all the psionic powers because the psychic can telekinetically strike from behind or hurl a barrage of light wood weapons at the vampire.

Vampires Avoid Technology

Don't need it!

The vampire, despite his or her earthly origin, is driven by the instincts of a predator. Those instincts include the desire and enjoyment of hunting/stalking prey, killing, aggression, domination, and a feeling of superiority over non-vampires and lesser vampires. This latter feeling of superiority tends to make the monsters arrogant, condescending and cruel. Fortunately, they also tend to become overconfident and sometimes careless when dealing with other life forms. This is true even of the barbaric wild vampire. Many a vampire, especially among the older, more experienced master and secondary vampires, believe themselves to be immortal or even demi-gods and the lords of humankind.

The feeling of superiority and godhood is in part derived from their supernatural powers. They are invulnerable, with the exception of a handful of peculiar weaknesses and possess the ability to shape change as well as numerous other inhuman powers. They instinctively know how to use their every power and, with time, can learn strategies and tactics that make them all the more powerful. The use of these powers are extremely pleasurable and reaffirms their non-human and superior nature. Most vampires soon revel in the fact that they are not human, even though they may have seen themselves as cursed or as a monster for the first few weeks of their new existence.

As a result, the undead tend to shy away from human technology, vehicles, robots and equipment. In most cases, human constructs are too restricting or simply inappropriate to a vampire's needs. Even mega-damage body armor and robot power armor are distasteful. For one thing, they impair the natural senses and one cannot enjoy the smell, taste or touch of a kill. More importantly, such body shells prevent metamorphosis and create a feeling of claustrophobia. Why wear the human trappings when one is nearly as powerful without them? Why acknowledge humanoid accomplishments by cherishing their things? No, a vampire needs none of the trappings of humankind.

Vampires and Weapons

The one article of technology that vampires do utilize is weapons. Vampires are known to carry an ancient type weapon (especially knives, swords, and morning star/spiked maces), as well as a light wood or silver weapon or two (to use against rival vampires), and about a third (33%) carry an energy pistol or rifle. The energy weapon is a useful tool against M.D.C. armor and multiple opponents. It is much faster to blast away an opponent's armor than to tear it apart by hand. Still, the typical vampire on the prowl will be unarmed, or armed with only an ancient style weapon. Energy weapons and other limited technological devices are most typically encountered near and in vampire lairs or when a vampire is knowingly about to engage a mega-damage opponent(s) in combat.

Note: Vampires are fond of magic weapons, especially those that are elemental in nature.

Vampires and Body Armor

Although vampires enjoy limited invulnerability, they are vulnerable to some simple and common things such as wood, silver and running water. These weaknesses are a negligible danger when combating a foe who is not prepared for a vampire. However, an opponent who is knowledgeable about vampires and armed for combating the undead, can be a deadly encounter. Consequently, master and some secondary vampires occasionally wear mega-damage body armor. Obviously, mega-damage body armor will prevent an S.D.C. object, such as a wooden stake or spear, from penetrating the heart and no damage is done to the armor. This means the armor must be destroyed first, before the deadly S.D.C. weapons can be used. But vampires and armor don't mix.

The vampire's elemental nature prevents the creature from being sealed away from nature. This is the reason for the bed of soil and other conditions and weaknesses. Thus, a vampire feels terribly claustrophobic and panic stricken when incased in body armor or power armor. They need to feel the wind on their skin and the dirt under their feet.

Most importantly, body armor *prevents* the vampire from using metamorphosis; can not even change to mist. The metamorphosis ability is second nature to vampires, and to have that ability stripped away is intolerable. The vampire must be able to shape change at will, in an instant, without having to worry about shedding his armor. Again, this is part of the fiend's supernatural and elemental essence. To take away their ability of metamorphosis is akin to dressing a hawk in body armor that prevents the predator from flying, its most natural ability. The hawk is comfortable, slow, and no longer as formidable without flight, although it still has claws.

What all this means is that vampires will rarely wear any sort of body armor, relying on their natural invulnerability and regenerative powers. The few that do wear armor will only wear ancient Roman or Greek style chest and arm plates similar to dog-boy armor. Such armor can be quickly removed (in less than one melee; 15 seconds or less). This type of armor has a mega-damage range of 20 to 40 M.D.C. and once the armor's M.D.C. is destroyed, the vampire is vulnerable to traditional vampire slaying weapons. Of course, body armor doesn't negate the affect of the cross, garlic, wolfbay or sunlight, nor does it give them a reflection in a mirror.

Hit and Run Tactic

Vampires are cunning and instinctive supernatural monsters of amazing power, versatility, and adaptability. They rely on their powers and react to combat on an instinctive level. This lends them a certain savage and treacherous edge as evident in the "hit and run" tactic. When a vampire falls to around 12 hit points, it instinctively knows that it is in jeopardy. Rather than continue the fight, the vampire will momentarily flee and hide. After a minute or two the horrid thing attacks again. The few minutes of avoiding combat enables the creature to regenerate its hit points to a much more formidable level, if not entirely back to full strength. The regenerative powers of the vampires give them a massive edge and the fiends realize this and use it to their maximum advantage.

Lasers

Inevitably, people wonder, if lasers are amplified light, do they inflict any damage on a vampire? The answer is no. Lasers are not sunlight, but artificial light. Artificial light has no damaging effect on the undead, thus, a laser blast is harmless.

Vampire versus Robot

Robots are not living creatures and therefore, are not vulnerable to the undead's blood lust, slow kill, mind control, or hypnosis. The gaze of a vampire has no influence on a robot. Only robots with *transferred intelligence* are susceptible to mind control/hypnotic suggestion, because the bot's mind is that of a living, intelligent creature (this happened in play-test, to everybody's dismay). Obviously, a bot has no fear of being bitten and transformed into a vampire. However, a vampire's *killing bite* does inflict mega-damage!

Characters inside robot vehicles are only vulnerable to vampire mind control if they stare directly into his glowing eyes from a view port or outside of the robot. Viewing a vampire on a video monitor/camera eliminates the creature's hypnotic influence (vamps can't control people via television). Characters in *power armor* are vulnerable because they use normal vision and optical enhancements for normal vision, not a view screen.

Vampires cannot turn into mist and enter a robot. Nor can a vampire turn into mist and enter a giant robot vehicle, unless the hull has been breached. Environmental armored units, such as robot vehicles, power armor, many military armored vehicles, and even environmental body armor, are either airtight environmental units or designed with gas filtration systems and/or have independent oxygen supplies. If these vehicles can travel underwater or in radioactive or other lethal environments without ill effect, no vampire is going to be able to gain entry as a mist.

Vampire versus Borg

Partial reconstruction and **full conversion borgs** are NOT vulnerable to a slow kill bite; i.e., cannot be turned into a vampire because they are as much, or more, machine than human. If you recall, bionics often has a disruptive affect on creatures of magic. However, borgs, though bound to a mechanical body, are also creatures of flesh controlled by a living brain, thus, they are vulnerable to mind control and hypnosis (even though their eyes may be mechanical).

Borg characters seem to get cocky when combating vampires because they typically have a high mega-damage body armor and are constructed of mega-damage artificial limbs. While their armor and invulnerability to a slow kill affords a borg greater protection than the average human, they are far from invulnerable. During one play test session, a borg was literally torn limb from limb by a trio of vampires, but survived to be repaired. A fellow adventurer, a Simvan warrior clad in heavy Coalition mega-damage body armor, was slain when a pair of vampires literally tore his armor to shreds during a prolonged melee. The death blow happened when the last of the M.D.C. armor was depleted and the vampire attacker punched from behind, inflicting 4 M.D. (equal to 400 hit points/S.D.C.) to the character's fragile humanoid body (punched right through him). The character had actually beaten one of the vampires into apparent death/coma twice, with a wooden staff, but the fiend kept regenerating to consciousness within a melee or two. But such are the dangers of invading the lair of a vampire gang.

Note: Characters who have limited bionics, but the amount of bionic augmentation is less than a partial reconstruction (all four limbs plus implants are bionic), ARE vulnerable to a slow kill and can be turned into a vampire. In such cases, the limited bionic or cybernetic limb(s) and implants are magically expelled from the body and new undead limbs and organs are generated. Neither cybernetics nor bionics can be added to a vampire.

Knock-down

The punch from a robot, robot vehicle, power armor, or from a borg, does no physical damage to the vampire, but the force of the blow is likely to knock the fiend off his feet. Being knocked down or off one's feet means losing one melee attack/action that round. Mega-damage explosions from missiles and grenades may knock the vampire down too. **Note:** Energy beams, automatic weapons, shotguns, and revolvers do NOT knock a vampire down because they deliver minimum force.

Optional Combat Rule for Non-Vampires.

This same rule for knock-down from impact or the force of a blow can also be applied to all characters in body armor. Not applicable to power armor or robots. Game master's option.

Knock-Down Impact Table

The following is the likelihood of knocking a vampire off his feet (losing one melee attack) by the amount of damage inflicted.
1-4 M.D.: No chance. Withstands the blow.
5-12 M.D.: 01-30% chance of being knocked off feet.
13-20 M.D.: 01-50% chance of being knocked off feet.
21-30 M.D.: 01-70% chance of being knocked off feet.
31-40 M.D.: 01-90% chance of being knocked off feet.
41-60 M.D.: 100%! Knocked off feet.
61 or more M.D.: 100%! Knocked off feet and stunned! Loses all attacks/actions that melee round (15 seconds).

Grappling

While the robot, power armor or borg may not be able to hurt the demonic thing without wood, silver, water, etc., a constant attack (e.g. an unrelenting battery of punches, kicks, grappling), can keep the vampire too busy and off balance to attack them or anybody else. Superstrong characters protected by mega-damage power armor, bionics, or body armor can also grapple, pin, entangle, or crush/squeeze (bear hug) a vampire. As long as the character hangs on or keeps the fiend unbalanced, the vampire is incapacitated and cannot attack others. Remember, with the possible exception of giant robots, the vampire can inflict a mega-damage bite even when entangled/pinned. Likewise, a vampire can perform a metamorphosis into mist to escape the strongest hold. But this too is good, because the vampire will lose time and attacks changing from one form to another, especially mist.

Vampire Mist

No, a vampire in mist form cannot be sucked into a vacuum cleaner or similar suction device! Nor can it be blown away (wind rush). The mist is an unnatural substance guided by an intelligence. Remember, the vampire is virtually invulnerable to all attacks, including wood and silver. Water sprays and holy water will not significantly hurt the mist but will hold it at bay or force it back. Likewise, a line or circle made of, or a door covered in, garlic or wolfbay will also keep the mist at bay. *Day/sunlight* is the only force that can destroy a vampire in mist form.

A vampire cannot attack nor use psionics/mind control while a mist. Only movement and observation (sees and hears) are possible.

Vampire Victim Tables

Being a victim of a vampire's slow kill and/or mind control is a traumatic experience that leaves a lasting mark. Roll on the following table when a character has nearly been transformed into a vampire by slow kill, or was nearly a victim of mental enslavement (or was enslaved), died/coma at the hands of a vampire, or other very traumatic events inflicted by vampires (GM's discretion). A phobia is a deep, overriding fear stemming from a traumatic event. Exposure to the object of the phobia may cause the individual to run away, hide, avoid it, cry, or become hysterical or frozen in fear.

01-10 Total Darkness
11-20 The Full Moon; seen as bad luck, prefers to stay indoors, not travel nor go outdoors during a full moon.
21-30 Graveyards
31-40 Bats and bat-like creatures, especially vampire bats.
41-50 Tall, thin, pale strangers, especially if corpse-like.
51-60 Wolves, especially wolf packs; uncomfortable around mutant dogs too.
61-70 Sudden fog and strange mists.
71-80 Coffins, tombs, and funerals.
81-90 Rats (12 or more) or bugs (swarm of 100 or more).
91-00 Underground tunnels, especially tombs/catacombs.

Blood Loss Table for Victims of Vampire Bites

The average person only has about 8 pints of blood. Losing three or more pints is life threatening. Note that a vampire's draining bite is not like a knife wound that damages the body; the real damage is the loss of the blood. A transfusion or magic healing can restore a person to near normal within an hour.

- **Losing one pint of blood** causes no ill effect, damage or impairment. The body replaces the lost pint of blood in about three weeks. A person can safely donate/lose one pint of blood a month. Losing two pints will make the person feel tired, run-down, a bit anemic and more susceptible to disease (see next description).

- **Losing two or three pints of blood** is the reasonable limit before a person experiences seriously negative effects. It takes about six to eight weeks for the human body to replace the blood naturally. There's a 1-20% chance that a victim of a bite that drains him of two pints of blood will pass out for 4D6 minutes. Afterward, the person will feel a bit sluggish and tires more easily. This run-down sensation lasts for about a week; with the following penalties. **Penalties:** −2 on initiative, −1 to strike and loses one melee attack for 1D6 days. **Note:** Receiving a transfusion of one pint of blood or a healing touch/spell that restores 15 hit points will bring the person up to snuff (no penalties) in an hour.

- **Losing four pints of blood** is getting into the danger zone. There is a 1-80% chance of passing out for 1D6 hours. The victim is extremely weak, can barely move, needs to drink fluids to avoid dehydration and sleeps 12 to 18 hours a day. **Penalties:** Speed is reduced to 10%, attacks/actions per melee are reduced to one, skills are −50%, no bonuses to strike, parry or dodge apply. Can move around for a period of minutes equal to the character's P.E. before collapsing exhausted or even passing out (1-60% chance of passing out for 1D4 hours). **For example:** A character with a P.E. 12 can exert himself (with the previously described penalties in place) for 12 minutes of activity before collapsing and must rest or sleep for at least an hour before he is able to exert himself for another 12 minutes. The weakened condition and penalties last 2D4+3 days with rest or 1D4+1 weeks if the person refuses bed rest and continues to exert himself. Such a foolish person is subject to numerous collapses, fever and much sleep (at least 14+1D6 hours a day). Will have to be carried/transported by others to travel.

A blood transfusion adding a minimum of two pints of blood will reduce the recuperation period to 8D6 hours (back on their feet in a day or two and pretty much back to normal, no penalties).

Magic or psionic healing can also restore the victim of blood loss. The equivalent of 30 hit points of healing will restore two pints of blood and the person will be up and around without penalty within 1D6 minutes, although the person will feel nauseous and tired for the rest of the day. The equivalent of 15 hit points being healed will restore one pint of blood and the person will be able to function, but remains weak; speed and attacks are half, −20% on skills, −2 on initiative.

- **Losing Five or Six pints of blood puts the character in great jeopardy!** The person falls into a light coma. Medical or magic treatment is required! Without medical treatment, the person never regains consciousness and will die within 4D6 hours.

Receiving medical treatment and three pints of blood will restore the person to life; roll save vs coma/death with a bonus of +10%. The person can be back to normal after 1D4 days of rest. Feels a bit under the weather for an additional week; tired, sluggish.

Magic or psionic healing will restore the person much more quickly and will offers a +5% to save versus coma for every 10 hit points pumped the a individual.

- **Losing Seven pints of blood is near death!** Almost all the blood has been drained. Unless a transfusion to add blood is started within 20 minutes, the person will die.

Receiving medical treatment and four pints of blood is likely to restore the person to life; roll save vs coma/death (no special bonus). The person can be back to normal after 1D6+2 days' rest. Feels a bit under the weather for an additional week; tired, sluggish; −2 on initiative. **Possible brain damage!** Roll percentile dice: A roll of 1-33% means permanent brain damage; reduce I.Q. by one (1) point.

Magic or psionic healing will restore the person much more quickly and offers a +5 to save versus coma for every 20 hit points pumped into that individual, but there is still a chance of brain damage. **Remember**, the equivalent of 15 hit points from magic or psionic healing restores one pint of blood.

- **Losing Eight or more pints of blood means death.** Only extensive and immediate (within five minutes) medical treatment has any chance for survival. But even this is a remote possibility; −40% to save versus coma/death.

Immediate magic or psionic healing is another slim possibility to save the victim of near total blood loss. Again, the person must be treated within five minutes. A restoration spell will bring the person back to normal without side effect. Numerous healing touches (the equivalent of 60 hit points) may also save the individual; roll save vs coma as normal, but with side effects. **Side effects are likely.** Role percentile dice. 1-40%: Permanent brain damage; reduce I.Q. by 2 points. 41-65%: Roll on random insanity table. 66-80%: Permanent physical damage; reduce P.E. and hit points by 1D4 points. 81-00%: Lucked out, no damage. A restoration spell can be performed later to eliminate the side effects other than insanity.

Note: Vampire societies or vampire lords with humanoid slaves sometimes drain a person of 5 or 6 pints and then command a healer or mage to heal them with magic or psionics. This can be done, but is very emotionally and mentally taxing. After the fourth time, especially over a short period of a week or two, the victim will develop insanities. Roll once on the **Vampire Victim Phobia Table** and once on the **Random Insanity Table (Rifts,** page 19).

Dragons

Dragons are supernatural beings and creatures of magic, consequently, they can inflict damage to vampires through magic or from a punch.

A dragon's punch/claw inflicts 2D6 points of damage direct to hit points.

A dragon's kick inflicts 3D6 damage direct to hit points, a leap kick does 5D6 H.P. to vampires, but counts as 2 attacks.

A dragons's bite inflicts 2D4 damage direct to hit points.

A dragon's magic breath (any) inflicts 3D6 damage direct to hit points.

Note: P.S. attribute damage bonus is added to the damage inflicted to vampires.

Although a dragon can severely damage, even rend a vampire limb from limb, such physical attacks cannot kill it. The usual method of staking, decapitation and burning is required.

Dragons cannot be turned into vampires by any means.

Vampire attacks on Dragons

Combat is a two-way street. And while the dragon can injure a vampire, a vampire can injure a dragon. The normal mega-damage is applicable from punches and the likes but **a vampire's killing bite** inflicts 1D6×10 M.D. to dragons (although dragons cannot be turned into vampires).

Note: Other creatures of magic are generally considered to be natural enemies of the vampire. But not all supernatural monsters/demons are creatures magic.

Psi-Stalkers & Mutant Dogs

Psi-stalkers were born to hunt supernatural vermin such as vampires. Stalkers automatically sense and recognize the supernatural presence of a vampire from 600+ foot radius (*Sense psychic and magic energy*), and can track them to their lairs like a bloodhound (*Sense supernatural beings*). Their resistance to psionic attack (+4) makes them difficult to mind control and their empathic relationship with animals enables them to identify vampires in wolf or bat disguise.

Most of all, vampires have a high P.P.E. which doubles when slain; the psychic food of the psi-stalker. However, the P.P.E. of the undead is not available until the creature is permanently destroyed. Driving a wooden stake into the heart does not kill the undead and releases no potential psychic energy. Only death by sunlight, water, or the process of staking, followed by decapitation and burning truly kills a vampire. It is only then that the vampire dies and the P.P.E. is available to consume. But this too is helpful, because the psi-stalker cannot be fooled into thinking an undead opponent is slain. If there is no release of P.P.E. then the monster still lives.

Intelligent mutant dogs are equally suited for the task of hunting and slaying vampires. Their awareness of the supernatural (sensing abilities similar to the psi-stalker's) alerts them instantly to the supernatural presence. Dogs instinctively feel supernatural creatures to be a threat and will act against the potential supernatural threat with deadly force. Plus the ability to track by scent, keen hearing and hunting instincts make intelligent mutant dogs a dangerous foe.

Exploring Central America

Letters from Erin Tarn

The Journey Under Way

Erin Tarn, February, 101 PA

It has been 20 years since I last considered exploring the vast, empty lands to the south of Lone Star. To this day I have nightmares about my one, near fatal encounter with a vampire in the Lone Star territory, near the Rio Grande River. Yet I feel compelled to return and find the truth. Is it my infernal curiosity that nags at me, or is it the conscience of an old woman who feels she has left a job undone? I do not know myself. Perhaps it is a little of both.

Many people look to me for guidance. More people than I'd like give my every word meaning, sometimes far more meaning than I ever intended when I penned it. Even my letters, such as this one, inevitably see print and take on some special significance or serve to exhibit some special insight. If that be my fate, so be it. I cannot change what I am. This being the case, I guess I do feel that I have an obligation to find the truth about the southern lands said to be the kingdom of the vampire. If the stories I continue to hear have any measure of truth, I must find out. For if they are true, it is time that we civilized people rose up to liberate our southern brothers from what must be a hellish existence.

Thanks to the unauthorized publication of **Traversing Our Modern World**, I am again a hunted enemy of the Coalition States. Many, I dare not say whom, have offered me sanctuary, but I have no wish to bring ill to these generous and kind people. Instead, I have decided to take this opportunity to travel west and south. Here, the Coalition has few eyes to follow me and there are many lands which I have yet to explore thoroughly. I suspect this will be an old woman's last great adventure. Wish me luck and remember me in your prayers, I fear I will need them.

The Rio Grande River

Erin Tarn April 10th, 101 P.A.

The history books before the time of the rifts indicate that the Rio Grande River was little more than a long, winding mud puddle. Of course, this is an exaggeration, but the point is that the pre-rifts river was not the river we know today. The Rio Grande River of our time is truly a river of great measure. It snakes its way along the border of Lone Star territory (the old American state of Texas), from the Gulf of Mexico to the San Juan Mountains in Southern Colorado. It is approximately 2000 miles long, about 100 miles longer than the days of old, and measures between 100 feet (30.5 m) to 1200 feet (365 m) wide, depending on the location. The depth of the river, or so I am told, is as shallow as 10 feet (3 m) in some spots (we are looking for one such place now, so that we may cross), to about 80 feet (24 m) deep.

We are currently encamped near New El Paso, where we understand the river is shallow and the current is weak, so that our horses can swim across (our robot vehicles could cross at any number of places without difficulty). If we can not find such a location, we may have to arrange passage on a ferry boat at **New El Paso**. We hope to avoid this, as New El Paso is a dangerous city, renowned for its decadence and cruelty. The cattle baron who rules the small kingdom is a man by the name of *Wyatt Halloway*. King Halloway is a strange and wild-eyed individual with cold, clammy hands and a sinister smile. I had the displeasure of meeting him when I was a much younger woman and he had just risen to power after the sudden, accidental (?) death of his father and his two oldest brothers. If ever there was a snake in human form it is Wyatt Halloway (I mean no disservice to snakes by this comparison).

Perhaps it is my imagination, but having travelled along the Rio Grande for several days now, I cannot rid myself of the feeling of foreboding and desolation. We have passed scores of burnt or otherwise demolished bridges and the broken remnants of riverboats. Signs too, posted by local inhabitants and erstwhile adventurers, warn of the vampires across the river. One plaque nailed to the burnt and crumbled skeleton of a bridge read, "Cover not these waters lest you give passage to the demons barred by these sacred waters." This is the typical sentiment of the inhabitants. The swollen river is seen as a godsend by many local inhabitants as it seems that the worst variety of *vampires* can not cross over water. Myth? We shall see.

Vampires and Water

Erin Tarn April 30th, 101 P.A.

We have been encamped here, near New El Paso, for nearly two weeks. My guides have thought it best to wait until a local skirmish passes before we move onward. The fear is that we may be mistaken for cattle rustlers if we do not. It also appears that we may have to solicit passage from King Halloway to insure our safety. I wonder what that will cost us.

At any rate, this pause in our journey has given me the time to write you of my, so far, distant encounters with vampires and the tales we have heard.

Running water, and some say, any large body of water, will kill a vampire if the demon is immersed in it. Furthermore, what most would call true vampires, the undead, cannot pass over running water. I would not believe this had I not witnessed the phenomenon firsthand. On several occasions we had seen what we believed were vampires. Glowing red or yellow eyes and shadowy figures watching us from across the river, yet never did they cross.

One might think, surely they cannot cross the river by swimming through the cleansing waters, but certainly the fiends could metamorph into a bat and fly over, high in the sky. But this is not true. One moonlit night, a small pack of vampires were calling to us from across the river. They jeered and swore, hooted and snarled, but none dared to cross the river. Suddenly, they transformed into giant bats before our astonished eyes and flew into the night, away from the river.

The creatures cannot pass over the water under their own power, even from a high altitude. However, I am told that a vampire can be transported across water by a willing humanoid by means of boat or aircraft, but that the vampire must be contained in a sealed box, or blindfolded and restrained in a vehicle, and cannot know he is being taken over water, otherwise he will panic, fight to break away, and flee away from the water. This seems to imply, to me, that water represents some sort of deep rooted *phobia* rather than a physical obstacle. Likewise, vampires can cross over water on a bridge (if they can control their fear) because the bridge is an extension of the earth and is, itself, rooted to the earth on either side of the river. The talk of earth, water, air and the elements, makes me wonder if vampires are not elemental beings.

Holy Water, that is, water blessed by a priest or shaman, is said to be like acid to a vampire. If splashed on the flesh, the flesh will burn. If poured on the ground the vampire cannot step over it. However, I am also told that the person using the blessed water must believe in the god and sanctity of the water/blessing.

Believe it or not, we are all armed with **squirt guns!** Yes, children's toys. The toys/weapons fire a blast of water. The water is in motion and therefore, *running water,* and is said to inflict painful damage to the living dead. The people we have spoken to are so convinced of its success that we have decided to try it. In one village, a travelling techno-wizard had created and sold a ridiculous contraption that was little more than a portable water sprinkler that showered water all around its wearer. The contention was that the shower of harmless water acted a force field against vampires, preventing them from touching the wearer. I imagine there is some logic to the silly thing.

If water is a key to a vampire's vulnerability, then it does make sense that tribes of vampires may live in the American States of Arizona, New Mexico, Texas and Central America. The climate is hot and dry. The land mostly devoid of tall trees, instead covered in shrubs and tall grass. It is a land where one can survey his surroundings for miles around. Little rain graces the land meaning the vampires need not worry about the threat of destruction from a sudden cloudburst.

Vampire Legends

There appears to be at least a handful of different types of vampires. Even among the true vampires, there are three, possibly more, types of demons. The most powerful are the vampire lords or masters. These are supernatural beings who have entered our world through a rift. They appear mostly human but are intelligent and powerful monsters. It is they who command entire legions of undead. Rumor has it that they can even learn magic and may use human weapons and technology.

The victims of the master vampires sometimes rise from the dead to join their masters. These so-called "undead" are humanoids transformed into vampires. They possess most of the supernatural powers as their master, but are less intelligent and much more savage. It is unclear to me, at this time, why some victims of vampires rise from the dead and others do not.

Then there are other blood-drinking demons and creatures from the rifts that are not the traditional or "true" vampire, but possess similar supernatural powers or the hunger for human blood. Virtually any monster that drinks humanoid blood is a vampire of some kind.

The following enumerated facts (?) are about true vampires and are universally agreed upon by the residents along the Rio Grande.

1. Vampires stalk at night and sleep by day.
2. The light of day will turn a vampire to dust.
3. Water will hold at bay, hurt and even destroy a vampire.
4. A wooden or silver stake, driven through the heart, will kill a vampire. A wooden arrow or silver bullet will hurt or kill them.
5. Vampires are impervious to all other types of weapons, including particle beam weapons, rail guns, and explosives (I find this difficult to believe).
6. Vampires can metamorph into the shape of a bat, wolf, or mist.
7. Vampires posses superhuman strength.
8. Vampires can regenerate entire limbs overnight.
9. Vampires feed on humanoid blood. Animal blood cannot be substituted.
10. The victim of a vampire is cursed to walk the earth as an undead until slain.
11. Vampires are always evil and savage monsters.
12. The purest heart is not safe from a vampire.

Despite this frightening journey into a land supposedly dominated by these demons, I am confident that humankind has persevered, and with luck, the stories of vampires and even vampire kingdoms are exaggerated myths.

Juarez, Mexico

Erin Tarn, May 3rd, 101 P.A.

We are on the vampire side of the Rio Grande River. Our first few days were spent in the squalid city of **Ciudad Juarez**, which is built on the bones of the original, pre-rifts city of Ciudad Juarez. Never have I seen such filth and decadence. Even New El Paso is a safe and happy haven compared to Juarez. Everything and anything is for sale. And I do mean everything, from illicit human services to magic and more exotic pleasures. Several public and private arenas offer a variety of blood sports. Strange herbs, shrunken heads, animal feet, livestock and unidentifiable animal(?) organs are sold on every street corner. The poor are everywhere. Human life has little meaning, and the squalor is beyond words. Days away, I can still taste the bile of the city in my mouth. It is a wonder that our visit went without incident.

We spoke briefly to some of the inhabitants of Juarez who seemed to confirm the rumors about nomadic vampire tribes and of a vampire kingdom deep in the south. The official word is that Juarez is free of vampires. However, the peasants tell us otherwise, relating countless stories of people slain or stolen away in the night. Of course, in this terrible place the fate of the missing could be in the hands of a hundred different fiends, none of them vampires.

All confirm that the safest route of travel is along the ocean coastline and the few rivers and tributaries. Our route is a more direct and perhaps more dangerous one across land. Our ultimate goal is to reach the site of old Mexico city, now said to be a city of vampires. Depending on what we encounter there, we may move on into the rain forests of the Yucatan and perhaps into the Land of a Thousand Islands (South America).

Erin Tarn has not been heard of since this last letter.

The Vampire Kingdoms

The pre-rifts Mexican Empire and Central America (Guatemala, Honduras, Nicaragua, Panama, etc.) is the domain of the undead. Wild tribes of vampires roam the northern plains, like packs of wolves, from Monterrey to the Rio Grande River. Generations of people have spoken in whispers about the great and powerful vampire kingdoms that exist to the south, but no man from the north has ever seen fit to investigate. Actually, that is not entirely true. Numerous rogue scholars and scientists have gone to investigate, but few have ever returned. The survivors tell an alarming tale of the wild vampires that roam the Mexican highlands, and of the terror that fills the simple farmers and sheepherders on whom the undead prey. They also tell of human towns built in and on the water, for vampires fear water. But of these few explorers, even fewer have ever ventured near the ruins of old Mexico City or beyond, which is the reputed land of the vampire kingdoms.

The Coalition

In recent years, the stories of vampires have reached the ears of the paranoid Coalition States, inciting them to conduct their own investigation. Thus far they have only been able to confirm the existence of an alarming number of northern, wild vampire tribes. Two CS expeditions reported "sane and organized" vampire villages near the pre-rifts cities of Tampico and Veracruz before contact was lost. The Coalition, secretly working out of **Lone Star, El Paso,** and **Juarez** as northern bases of operation, continue to send in teams of investigators. A half dozen CS spies have infiltrated **Reid's Rangers** and work among the rangers as insignificant people at the fort. Yet the CS cannot bring itself to believe that the undead, though their numbers be frighteningly high, are intelligent or organized enough to function as anything more than a tribe of savages, despite data to the contrary gathered at Fort Reid.

The reason for the erroneous judgement is that the Coalition's own research shows that the millions of square miles of northern Mexico is inhabited by the animalistic, wild vampires. By their estimation, the number of intelligent vampires is minuscule, as few as one in thirty. A mistake that could spell the Coalition's doom if they ever waged a military campaign in Mexico, which is exactly what the vampires want. Fortunately, except for a few coastal sites and reserves of fossil fuels, Mexico offers few resources that appeal to the Coalition. It is the existence of a supernatural menace that prompts the CS to continue halfhearted investigations.

The Northern Wastelands

The Vampire's Great Deception

Far to the south, on the bones of pre-rifts Mexico City and the ruins of the Maya before them, are the vampire kingdoms. Towns and cities of submissive humans and D-Bees are ruled by the undead. It is here that the source, or more correctly, "sources" of the undead are found. Several different vampire intelligences are responsible for the creation of these hell-spawned kingdoms and fight among each other to assert themselves as the true master of the land. They are monstrous beings of pure evil. Supernatural forces of incredible power that seek to dominate each other, as they dominate the puny people of this forgotten land. The result is armies of undead warring against the other as each different vampire intelligence tries to make its kingdom the dominant master of the land. Unholy allegiances are made and horrid "things" from other dimensions are recruited to help win the conflict. Creatures and god-beings that harken back to the Maya gods of legend are called upon and walk the Earth again, but not always to the vampires' benefit.

Regardless of the wars and many supernatural skirmishes, the different vampire factions have united in one brilliant scheme, the creation of the wild vampire filled northern wastelands. The Coalition States' perception of the Mexican wilderness is exactly what the vampires want. Most of the vampire intelligences have banished their **wild vampires** to the northern plains. Wild vampires have no place in the comparatively serene vampire societies. They are too unmanageable and animalistic. Some undead societies actually destroy their wild kin, or place them in suspended animation (staked through the heart), where they lay quietly sleeping until needed as an army to defend the kingdoms. At such a time, they are awakened by the removal of the stake and set loose to feed on their attackers. But most are discarded, forced to wander the northern plains or be destroyed. However, this is not such a terrible fate, for the wild ones dislike the constraints of formal society and prefer to run free and unrestrained in the wild. The north country means freedom. No laws, no rulers, no restraints. They can act and do as they please without interference by their dominant brothers.

The creation of the northern wastelands plagued by wild ones serves two purposes. One, it removes the potentially disruptive and antisocial wild vampires from society. Two, it creates a perimeter defense of naturally aggressive, bellicose, and savage warriors to defend the thousand mile stretch of territory between the vampire kingdoms and the domain of man. Equally important, the territory of wild vampires creates some important and intentional illusions. First, it makes humans afraid to enter the territory. Second, it keeps the daring, and adventurous from travelling far to the south. Third, even humans that travel a thousand miles into the Mexican interior find an inhospitable land of vast, open plains, sweltering heat, simple communities of farms and animal herding humans, and more wild vampires. Fourth, this paints a picture of a primitive, undeveloped, and hostile environment not worth the effort to extract from the wandering vampire tribes. The sameness of the land accompanied by the emptiness of apparent resources (not even pre-rifts ruins are plentiful) and the ever present danger of the wild vampires, discourages most explorers from travelling any farther. It is simply too dangerous and unrewarding.

Last, and perhaps most importantly, the presence of the wild vampires creates the illusion that the undead are savage, barely intelligent brutes that traverse the land in roving packs like animals. The false impression leads most observers to surmise that the Mexican vampires represent little threat to beings of superior technology and intellect. The rumors about vampire societies and kingdoms are dismissed, because the wild undead, so often observed, are incapable of establishing any such kingdoms (which is true). Thus, the powers to the north remain ignorant of the secondary and master vampires and underestimate the true power and potential danger the undead pose to the world.

Confirmation of the existence of intelligent, organized, and socialized vampires would certainly urge splintered human and non-human factions to unite in the common cause of destroying the undead, as had happened in Earth's past and on many other worlds. But if the perception that vampires are mindless savages that operate like a supernatural wolf pack can be maintained, then humans and their kin will ignore them. Oh, of course, even savage vampires are seen as disgusting, horrible creatures that should be destroyed, but they cannot be compared to the perceived threat that an intelligent monster evokes. Instead, they are seen as inferior creatures that fall to the superior intellect and technology of man. Just as the intelligent vampires hoped, their deception has succeeded and they are ignored. Relegated to the category of some potential problem to be worried about in the distant future. After all, the savage vampires keep to the wastelands of the south where few humans or D-Bees alike are known to exist (another false perception) and thus offer little danger to the Coalition or the other growing kingdoms that are cradled in the cool, wet climes of Middle America and the old Canadian Empire. So the belief continues that the vampires are stupid, mindless predators quarantined in a hot and presently, undesirable land. A belief that allows the intelligent vampires to quietly prosper, expand and plan for the future.

The Wild Vampires of Northern Mexico

Northern Mexico is a vast savanna of flat grasslands and scrub broken by rolling hills and mountains to the west. The native people are predominately low tech farmers and animal herders. The primary crops are maize (corn), wheat and cotton. Livestock includes goats, sheep and some cattle. The inhabitants of Mexico learn vampire lore at an early age. Most wear crosses, amulets, or garlic to protect themselves. Wooden knives, swords, spears, and crossbows or short bows are the commonest anti-vampire weaponry. The youngest child knows the threat that vampires represent and also knows how to defend against them and the methods to destroy them. Still, it is these people who are the main targets of the marauding, wild vampires, for their numbers are too many and their power too great to stave off indefinitely.

Wild vampires lack organization and self control. Although not entirely accurate, it is best if one thinks of *wild vampires* as wolves or similar animals that tend to hunt in packs. Wild vampires do have a greater intelligence than the smartest animal, but they are animal like in the sense of their vague society, methods of hunting and reliance on instinct rather than logical thought. However, unlike animals, they are far more cunning, resourceful, utilize simple and effective tactics, are incredibly savage, and kill for pleasure.

The lone hunter and small groups

Many wild vampires do not associate with the larger packs. These lone-wolves wander the land as a solitary hunter, or in pairs, or tiny groups of three to six. These hunters tend to be less aggressive, preying on lone individuals who have strayed too far from their village or travelling companions. The lone hunter will also prowl around villages, stalking children, women and the sick or elderly; all easy prey. Like a hungry tiger the wild vampire strikes, killing or subduing his prey to feed on the life-giving blood. Once filled, the creature of the night leaves the carcass to find other amusement.

A lone predator or a small group of undead will attack small groups of people, but will usually flee if their quarry proves to be too powerful. But even the lone hunter can be a formidable foe and may fight to the death, taking many with him.

Wild vampires are always on the move. Although they may hunt within a particular range, covering an area of 50 to 200 miles (80 to 321 km), they are constantly on the prowl and have no specific lair. Every morning or every few mornings, the vampire has a different resting place. The lone hunter will typically burrow three to six feet (0.9 to 1.8 m) into the earth or cover himself with stones and earth to hide from the killing light of day. Actually any place devoid of sunlight can be a sanctuary. Vampires have been found sleeping in the caskets of others, in mausoleums, ruins, caves, abandoned huts, the trunks of vehicles, fruit cellars, dry wells, barns, under haystacks, inside barrels, etc. Remember that most wild vampires are natives of Mexico/Central America and need no special earth or container. The soil of Mexico/Central America is the creature's native soil. Thus, they can safely travel mile after mile, to the jungles of the Yucatan or to the bank of the great river in the north (the Rio Grande). Some are completely nomadic and may travel everywhere, from the mountains to forested lowlands. Others will settle on one specific hunting ground. Few wild vampires will establish a residence inside a town or consider the people/prey of his hunting ground to be exclusively his.

Note: Most solitary wild vampires or small groups will back down to a larger group of vampires and vampires of a higher class (secondary or master). Nor do lone hunters care about vampire clans; i.e., associating with vampires whose creation can be traced to the same intelligence.

Wild vampire large groups

Large groups or packs of wild vampires are the real danger to humans. Again, the wolf pack analogy is the logical comparison. The solitary predators join other hunters to create a group. As a group, the pack has dramatically increased its power by way of greater numbers and flexibility of options and tactics. The capture of prey is easier and the availability of prey is more plentiful because the larger group can attack larger and more powerful groups of humanoids that might otherwise be too powerful for one or two vampires. No more skulking in shadows waiting for the lone individual to wander away from his group. No. The larger vampire pack can attack a band of travelers with little fear. Their pack members, fueled by successful attacks and the excitement of their fellow hunters, motivate the night hunters to become all the more confident and aggressive. Even a medium size pack of 20 to 40 will consider laying siege to a travelling caravan or village. Like wolves, perhaps even in the shape of wolves, the vampires will run down their prey, exhausting it until it drops and they can feed, or scaring members of the herd/community to act foolishly, divide their forces or run scared. A small group of prey is an easy target for a pack of vampires.

It is among the larger groups of wild vampires that the aspect of human-like intelligence and cunning becomes evident. The vampire pack often uses simple, but effective tactics that would normally be impossible for a simple-minded animal. They may use stealth and surprise, appearing without warning. It is not uncommon for a pack of vampires to invade a town quietly, attacking the most remote homes and working their way into the village until they have drunken their fill. In these cases, the rest of the village or town's residents are not aware that they have been attacked until dawn when the gruesome discovery of slain villagers occurs.

Other tactics include the creation of distractions to lure smaller numbers of their opponents out to them. This can be done by kidnapping a child, woman, or important villager, or destroying property or threatening crops and livestock. The tactic of divide and conquer is one of their favorites. If distraction doesn't work, the undead might attack one portion of the town and force defenders to rush to protect that location. When they do so, the vampires strike at the weakened position.

Another advantage any vampire group has over earth-bound humans and D-Bees is their supernatural powers. By turning into a bat the undead have instant flight, greater mobility and aerial reconnaissance capabilities. As a wolf they have greater speed and enhanced senses. Mist provides complete silence and ease of entry. The vampires instinctively and tactically use all of their powers to their advantage. The most brutal and destructive vampires take advantage of their supernatural invulnerability by setting a home or an entire village or grassland on fire. The vampires are impervious to the blaze but their prey is not. Fire creates distraction, poor visibility, mass panic, destruction and divides the enemy; everything an attacker could hope for. People trapped in a burning structure not only have to worry about attacking vampires but the additional worry of surviving the heat, flames, falling debris,

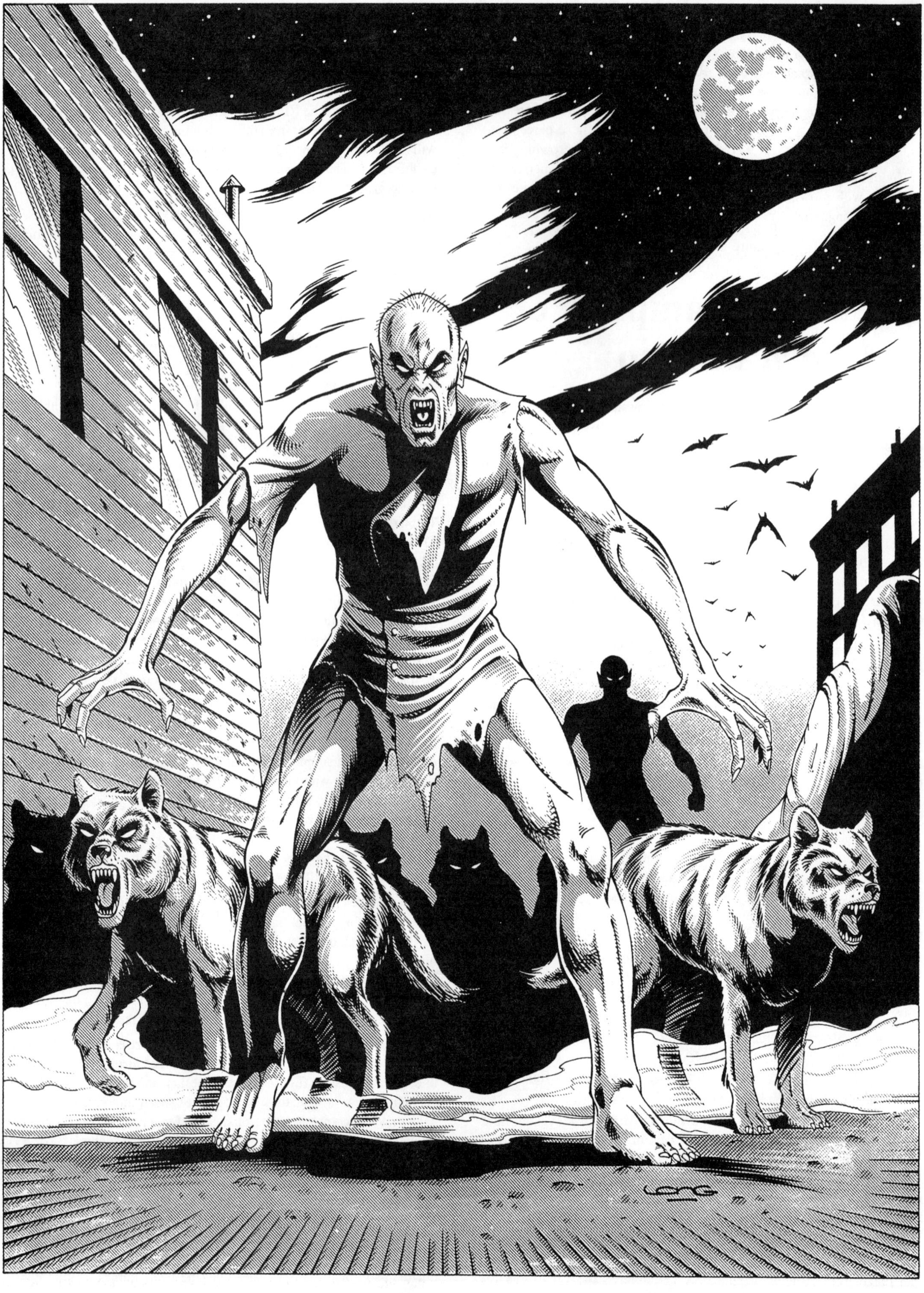

and perhaps rescuing others. The vampires can walk, unharmed, through the fire, and are impervious to most falling debris (impalement by collapsing wood is a remote concern). Surrounded by the blaze, they can continue to attack and even feed on a person who is on fire or otherwise injured.

Many wild packs become so cocky or conniving that they will try to blackmail an entire community. Frequently the tactic is successful. What happens is the vampires let the community know they are present by spooking them. Animals are slaughtered in the field, frightening strangers with glowing eyes appear and disappear into the night like specters, strange mists, packs of wolves that show no fear of fire or of man, and frightening shrieks and howls in the night are all part of the process. Once the proper atmosphere of terror is achieved, the vampires announce their presence and deliver their ultimatum: "Give us what we need and we will soon depart. If you do not fight us, most of your people will remain among the living." This usually means welcoming the wild vampire pack into the town without resistance, tolerating their degrading words and punishing actions, and allowing them to feed on many of the townsfolk. Few vampire packs will promise no deaths, but the odds are that they will kill few (1D4). Instead they will drain dozens to the point of unconsciousness or weakness (drinking about 4 to 6 pints of blood from each) and leave. A few will inevitably die from over zealous feeding, or because they insulted their attacker, or tried to resist. Children are usually spared such a nightmare, because adults have more blood. Large, overweight individuals are the human cattle of choice because their plump bodies contain more of the precious fluid (generally 2 to 4 pints of more blood than the average person). After the pack has feasted, they leave. However, they are likely to return every two to four weeks if they live in the area, or every few months if nomadic wanderers, to feed again and again. Such towns and villages are considered grazing locations. Places where the vampires can come to feed without fear of conflict. A sad, but all too common fate of rural communities that cannot fight back.

Wild vampire packs that consider a particular area their domain will chase away and/or kill other individual vampires and wild packs that try to feed on their property (the people) and invade their domain (the land). The territorial nature of the vampires can lead to some incredible conflicts between warring, rival packs, with the humans and their blood the prize for the winner. A vampire pack may mark its territory by displaying humanoid corpses, skeletons, skulls, bones or warning signs (rock carvings on boulders or stone monoliths) at key locations. Wild vampires who ignore the warnings are frequently killed or chased away. Only a powerful secondary vampire, group of secondary vampires, or a master vampire, will not be molested. Remember, wild vampires are typically submissive to any secondary or master vampire.

Villages that rebuke a wild pack and successfully hold them at bay, may cause that pack to flee, never to return. Or they may create a demonic enemy that will plague them for years. The pack regroups or flees only if their intended prey proves to be too deadly. Even wild vampires believe themselves to be vastly superior to human beings and all similar intelligent life forms. This sentiment reinforces their aggression and also causes them to be wild and reckless. An angry or humiliated vampire will act out of vengeance and attempt to hurt his humiliator in at least some token way. This might result in the attack/murder of a key person in the town or the butchering of a child or female (they don't quite understand why, but the undead know that this sort of thing distresses human beings). Or they may destroy property, set fires, and cause other problems before they disappear. The pack may return from time to time to test their strength against this old foe or to extract more revenge.

A small pack is about a dozen members strong; typically all are wild vampires. **A medium size pack** will have 20 to 40 members and is likely to be composed entirely of wild vampires. However, a secondary vampire or other powerful being may be the pack leader. **Large packs** can range from 50 to 120 members. The leader of large packs must always be a smart, feared and powerful leader, or leaders. Typically, this means one or two secondary vampires serve as the leader (a master vampire rarely wastes his time on wild ones). However, other powerful (frequently supernatural) creatures that are not vampires can become the leader, or one of the dominant members of a vampire pack. Powerful and evil necromancers (any powerful practitioners of magic), dragons, witchlings and demons are all potential candidates for leader or elite members of the pack. Whether a secondary vampire or powerful non-vampire, a forceful leader is necessary to command and control a group of more than 40 wild vampires. Lesser demons and monsters sometimes join the medium and large packs as lowly, subservient pack members and also function as daytime protectors. However, a vampire pack seldom has more than 15% non-vampire members.

The family clan

Large groups of wild vampires are more clan oriented than any other. The main power within a wild vampire pack is likely to be vampires that are linked to the same intelligence, meaning leadership is often a matter of sheer numbers and brute strength. Vampires created by other intelligences are usually welcome, but they must remain subservient to the dominant clan that leads the pack. Those of different vampire families will never rise to the same level of authority as those of the ruling clan.

The hierarchy of wild vampires is fairly loose and much like a wolf pack. The dominant members are acknowledged as being superior and are given a wide berth by the submissive, lower pack members. There is no formal label of power other than leader and clan kin. Nor is there a distinction by wealth based on the ownership of possessions. Wild vampires have little need for material goods. They are animalistic predators that live off the land and constantly travel, thus hauling around possessions can become a liability. Instead, the hierarchy of the pack provides social benefits.

The leader and dominant clansmen get first blood and first choice of potential victims. They also direct and control the activity of the pack. It is the pack leader and his clansmen who decide what are the strategies and tactics of the pack, acts of vengeance, the form the vengeance will take, who lives, who dies, what direction the pack travels, where they stop, how long they stay, etc. Lower pack members are expected to obey and to serve the leader(s) and the dominating clan members. To defy the pack by ignoring or disobeying orders is to challenge the authority of the leader and his kin. Offenders know they must leave the pack forever, or to expect punishment (beaten or killed) and to be relegated to being the lowest man in the pack. The alternative is to challenge the current leader for his rule (usually a fight to the death). Note that any member of the pack is free to leave at any time, but may not be allowed back into the group and will have to begin at the bottom of the pack if he is allowed to return.

Activities other than feeding

Wild vampire packs, like most predators, spend a great portion of their time hunting and wandering. Being instinctive, elemental creatures, they enjoy the outdoors and the primordial pleasures of simply hunting, running, flying, and traipsing through the wilderness. Like a wolf pack, they have few needs or desires for civilization or socialization on a human level. They are happiest when running free across the prairies and stalking prey. Unlike wolves, wild vampires are supernatural demons that do not limit their killing to providing food. They are malignant fiends who crave blood and the destruction of all that is good, pretty, or human. As a result, wild vampires will exert a certain amount of energy for causing mischief, pain, death and destruction for the fun of it.

Malicious mischief can be as harmless as pranks and name calling. Wild vampires are notorious for cat-calls and insults from the darkness. They will follow caravans and spend hours cursing and making threats, like an annoying cat wailing at the stars. Wild vampires love to terrorize people by making threats and implying danger. To that effect, they will voice threats, make scary suggestions, growl, howl, fly by overhead, throw sticks (as well as stones, bones, animal organs, rotting carcasses, etc.), stare from the darkness with glowing eyes, leap forward in a mock attack, and so on. The more frightened the targets of these psychological attacks the happier the vampire tormentors.

Wild vampires are also known for killing wild animals, house pets and the slaughter of livestock. Frequently the animals will be desecrated by having their entrails strewn all over, or placed on doorsteps, porches and vehicles. Frightful images may be drawn in blood (vampires cannot drink animal blood) on the sides of buildings, vehicles, or on the ground. Carcasses or entrails may be hung, like ornaments, from lamp posts and tree limbs. Sometimes the wild ones slaughter animals just for the fun of killing, not to frighten or torment, but simply to kill. Finding a dozen bison, wild horses or dinosaurs gutted and mauled in the middle of nowhere is a common sight for wilderness scouts. Finding such a grisly sight can be useful, because a fresh slaughter of that nature is the calling card indicating that a vampire pack is operating in the vicinity and enables one to prepare for nocturnal visitors.

Wild vampires also engage in vandalism, smashing windows, breaking, stealing or hiding equipment, overturning vehicles, starting fires, freeing livestock, etc. Other fun and games at the expense of non-vampires can include torture, beatings, rape, and games of chase and beat. The chase game usually involves a captive who is allowed to escape. The vampires chase him down, like hounds tracking down a fox, beat him and allow the person to escape again, only to be hunted and caught and beaten again. Oddly, the victim of such torment is seldom slain. Perhaps his reward for an evening of sadistic pleasure, or to serve as a living symbol of vampire superiority and that it is they who dispense life and death.

Vampire Civilization

Most people think of vampires as slobbering, savage monsters that defy the laws of nature and man. The picture of the snarling brute is the common image of the vampire because we think of the creatures that attack by tooth and claw; a very animalistic picture. But that is a picture that applies only to wild vampires, and the solitary hunter or small groups of undead (wild and secondary) that stalk from village to village. The nomad and the wild vampire do not represent vampire society.

The socialization or civilizing of vampires is something the people of earth have never witnessed. In Earth's past, the mystic energy of the ley lines were not powerful enough to attract many vampire intelligences, and though vampires have walked the earth since the advent of man, the undead were never able to establish a foothold on this planet.

There have only been a few times in Earth's past that vampires have come close to establishing a domain for the undead. One such time occurred during the pre-rifts Middle Ages of Europe. A period when hundreds of thousands of people perished from "the pestilence." Pre-rifts historians incorrectly attributed this period of death exclusively to the "Black Plague," also known as the "Bubonic Plague," "the Pestilence," and the "Wasting Disease." Death swept Europe. In many instances, entire villages and towns were obliterated. The Bubonic Plague was real, but it is interesting to note that during this exact same period *vampire hysteria* reached unprecedented heights. At no other time in human history (pre-rifts) was the belief in vampires more prevalent. The majority of peasants, particularly those of Eastern Europe (Hungary, Poland, Romania, Transylvania, Bulgaria, Russia, etc.), steadfastly believed that "the pestilence" was spread by the undead. Indeed, the vampire's power to summon and control rats and mice (rats and poor sanitation are considered the major causes in the spreading of the Bubonic Plague) may have contributed to the perpetuation of the plague.

It is also interesting to note that the symptoms of the plague and the symptoms of the "wasting disease" are very similar. The Wasting disease has the symptoms one exhibits when subjected night after night to a vampire's "slow kill" bite, which transforms that person into a vampire himself. The victim becomes thin, pale, weak (from blood loss), feverous, loses his appetite, stares out windows as if waiting for somebody, is languid and sullen. The bodies of those who fell victim to the plague and the wasting disease, as well as those said to have been killed by a vampire and those who were suspected of being a vampire, were burnt, usually after being staked through the heart and decapitated. Scores of plague infested (vampire infested) towns were burnt to the ground.

The belief in vampires was so wide spread during this period that it reached the shores of France and England. While modern, pre-rifts scholars may have attributed this hysteria to superstition and mass trauma, the scholars and highest authorities of that day were called upon to rid the land of the pestilence. Town magistrates, mayors, dukes, barons, princes, bishops, priests, and military commanders all led the search for vampires. They also conducted or supervised the ritual of staking, decapitation and cremation of the suspected monsters. There were countless stories regarding the official exhumation of graves that revealed the slumbering demons. Many cases were documented and existed until the time of the rifts.

Apparently, humankind was triumphant in stopping the vampires' invasion of Europe, although the cost in human life was greater than any of the World Wars. How many other vampire invasions were thwarted is lost in time, no tangible records remain. Some scholars, like Erin Tarn, have speculated that Central America may have been the site of one such invasion, citing the blood sacrifices of the Maya and, particularly, the Aztecs of Mexico. Their legacy of human sacrifices and bloodletting makes one wonder. But here too, the vampire invasion seems to have been crushed, perhaps by the arrival of the Europeans to the new world. We can only guess.

The eruption of the ley lines and dimensional rifts has transformed the Earth into a haven for vampire intelligences and their minions. In the past the flow of P.P.E. energy was too weak to support the massive P.P.E. feeding monsters. Only a handful of places like the Yucatan, England, China and a few other ley line power centers offered comparatively large amounts of the life sustaining energy, but not quite enough. Furthermore, these places were dominated by swarms of humans, which made infiltration by vampire minions difficult. The Earth belonged to man. But that was then.

The priests and wizards of the ancient Olmec, Maya, Aztec, and others, knew of the magic energies that flowed through their lands and had utilized them for eons. It is at the location of ley lines and nexus points that great stone pyramids, temples and cities were erected. The infamous human sacrifices of the Aztec and Maya were magic rituals that used the blood of captured enemy warriors (or more to the point, P.P.E.) to summon rains during periods of drought, to see the future, cure disease, defeat an enemy and to speak to the gods. Twentieth Century scholars saw these ceremonies as entirely religious, superstitious and symbolic; however, men of magic in Rifts-Earth can appreciate the genius of these ancient people and correctly recognize the mystic ceremonies to draw on P.P.E., create magic and open rifts. The entire Maya culture was linked to the movement of the stars. The priests (sorcerers) were so skilled that they could accurately calculate lunar and solar eclipses (a feat that amazed 20th Century scientists), the solstice, equinox, planetary alignments, the seasons, positions of the moon and stars, the rising and setting of the sun, and even the calendar year was an accurate 365 days! All of this information is critical in determining the precise moment when the P.P.E. of the ley lines surges to their maximum power. It is this same abundance of potential psychic energy (P.P.E.) that has drawn vampire intelligences to this part of the world.

The Ideal Vampire Habitat

Rifts Mexico and Central America, Circa 102 P.A.

Never during any time in Earth's history have the undead established a stronger hold on Earth than they have since the Time of the Rifts. Unknown to humans and D-Bees anywhere in the world, the vampires have conquered the Mexican heartland and parts of the Yucatan and South America.

Mexico and the American west is an ideal habitat for the following reasons.

1. **It is hot and dry.** Annual rainfall is less than 12 inches (300 mm). A dry habitat, with minimal water is important to creatures that can be destroyed by running water or a sudden rainstorm. The extreme heat to cold desert nights means nothing to creatures who are impervious to heat and cold. Besides, as creatures of the night, it is the chill of the night breeze that the vampires experience, not the blazing heat of the daytime sun.

    Northern Mexico and the American west offers a terrain of grass and scrub, mostly devoid of trees, providing the vampires' humanoid prey and enemies few places to hide. A settlement of humans or a travelling caravan can be seen miles away, especially from the sky. The common dependence of humans and most humanoids on water, food and shelter means the legions of undead know the locations where humans are most likely to congregate; again, making them easy targets.

2. **The weather changes of the seasons is minimal** compared to the wet winters and springs experienced elsewhere. **The winters** are dry and snowless, except in some of the higher mountain elevations to the north. The average winter temperatures are 50 to 70 degrees Fahrenheit and a scorching 90 to 120 in the spring and summer. Less than 12 inches (300 millimeters) of rain falls in an entire year.

3. **The periods of daylight hours and nighttime darkness** are more evenly divided throughout the year. The closer one is to the equator, the more equal the hours of day and night, with little or no distinction, in terms of daylight, between summer and winter. At the equator day and night hours are approximately 12 hours each throughout the entire year. Unfortunately for vampires, the equator falls along the tropical jungles of Venezuela, Columbia, and the upper portion of the Amazon. As one might guess, the undead avoid this wet and rainy land except during the dry season or during desperate times.

4. **Lightly populated and inhospitable to humans.** The uncomfortable temperatures and the vastness of the deserts, arid steppes, and savanna (grassland and scrub) makes the land undesirable to humans when there are far more pleasant regions to the east and north to conquer. The American west and Mexico is of little interest to most people.

5. **Old Mexico City — Vampire Central.** Mexico City falls at the border where grasslands turn into forest. Although it receives twice as much rainfall (about 600 mm/24 inches), the amount of rain is still comparatively light and the winters are *dry* (and the winter nights a few hours longer). This territory is also ideal because the land is much more conducive to human and D-Bee habitation, providing the vampires with their most important requirement for survival: human cattle on which to feed. The territory around Old Mexico City is also abundant with magic energy, which serves the vampires needs as well.

6. **The Yucatan: A safe haven for the vampire intelligences.** The wet tropical rain forests of the Yucatan and Central America are less appealing and more dangerous to vampires, but are an important resource they can plunder. It is a place where the undead can raise human livestock, and grow the food for their livestock, and hunt wild humans (free communities). **Most importantly,** the Yucatan abounds with the vast mystic energies necessary for the vampire intelligences to survive in this world.

The Yucatan is the center of ley line energy in Central America. Hundreds of ley lines and dozens of nexuses dot the countryside. The ancient pyramids and temples of the Maya and other ancient cultures still mark the exact locations of many of the most powerful nexus junctions. Some of these ancient structures have been rebuilt by the vampires or other users of magic, and new edifices have been erected to warn travelers of danger. Only Atlantis, China, and the British Isles have a greater abundance of mystic energy.

These epicenters of magic energy are the lairs of the vampire intelligences. The close proximity of the vampire intelligences power/food source and their close location to their vampire minions is a superior feature of the Southern Mexican and Central American environment. The dense tropical forest helps hide the intelligences' presence, makes them difficult to get at, and the ley line energy not only provides an abundance of energy-food, but with additional energy and power for their magic and protection. Add to this the remoteness and seclusion of the area, the small number of humanoid enemies, and the predominately low tech level of the natives, and the environment is absolutely perfect as a breeding ground for vampires! And remember, unlike their undead creations, the intelligences are not vulnerable to water or sunlight.

Note: Vampires with a background in magic and the vampires daytime protectors with mystic powers, can also use the ley line energy to increase their power and defend their undead lords. Frequently, vampires capture and hold nexus points to prevent enemies from using the ley line energy against them.

Vampire Societies

Like human societies, there are a large variety of different types of vampire kingdoms and communities. The descriptions that follow are the most typical types of communities, but there can be a vast number of slight to extreme variations. Note that the vampires discussed in this section are predominately secondary vampires led by one or two master vampires and the vampire intelligence. Ninety percent of the wild vampires are relegated to the northern highlands, deserts of Mexico and the American southwest. Note that vampire intelligences are seldom found to inhabit the cities occupied by their minions.

Tribal Lords

Vampire tribal lords are usually one to as many as a dozen vampires who have become the rulers of a tribe or village of humans or other non-vampire life forms. Generally, one or two vampires (typically seen as husband and wife, brother and sister, or parent and child) have become the tribal chief(s) or village ruler. Any other vampires in the community are subservient to the ruler and are seen as the chief's family members or his chosen people, and therefore, lesser lords of the community. As the lords of the tribe, the vampires are its most honored and esteemed members. Only the chief and his or her second in command have a higher status.

In many cases, the people revere the vampire chieftain as a god. Any other vampires belonging to the tribe are seen as demi-gods in their god's pantheon, or as his children, family or chosen people.

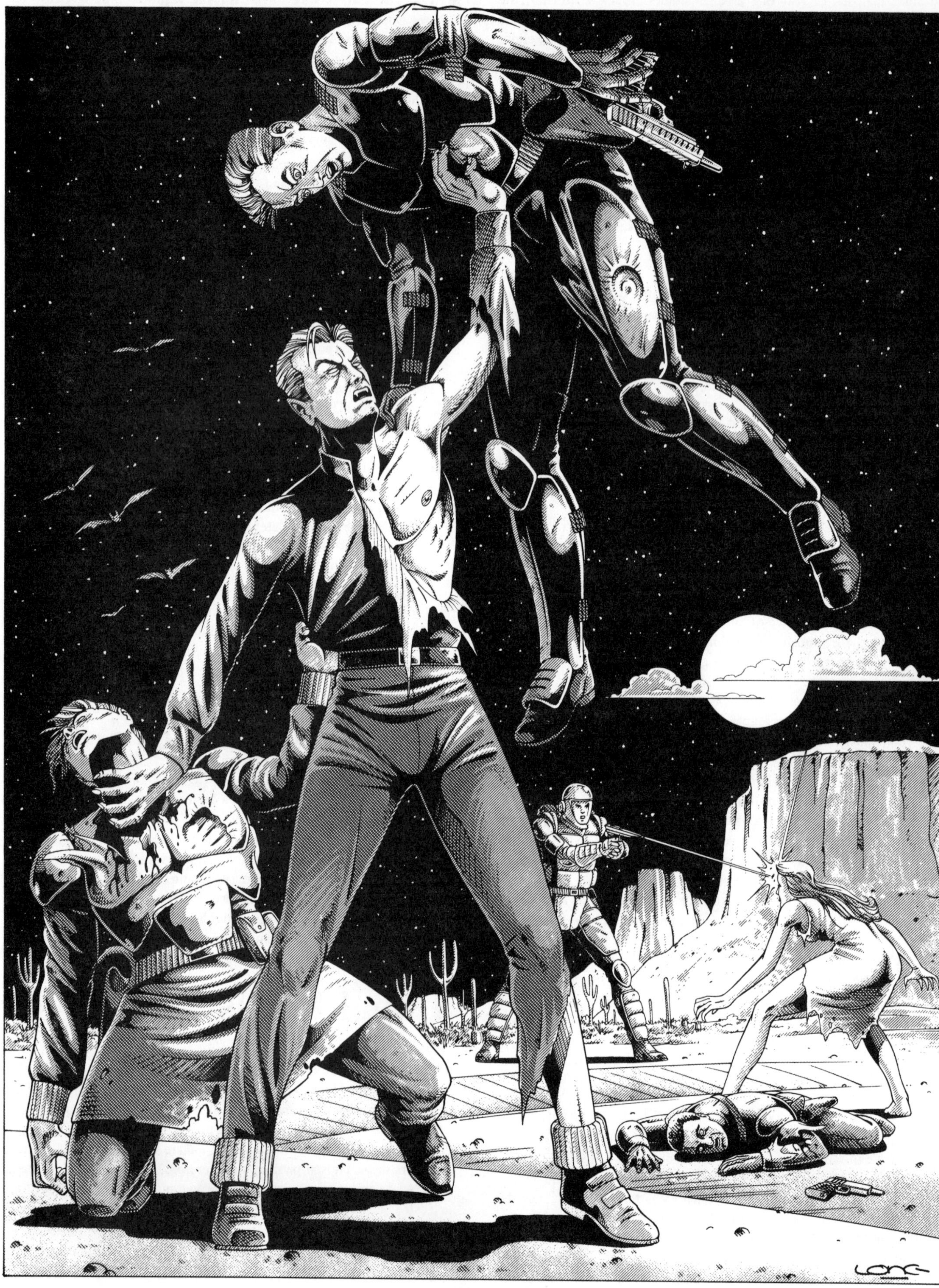

Typically, these loyal subjects are honored to be chosen by a god and offer their blood and allegiance to their god(s). Depending on the disposition of the vampire chieftain, he and his chosen may be feared or loved. In either case, the vampires do not kill their subjects, but drink only enough blood to slake their thirst. If loved by the people, the blood will be offered cheerfully and the acceptance of one's life fluids is seen as a great honor. Some may even boast of how many times the god-chief has selected him/her to satisfy his thirst. If feared, the people may dread this ritual, but comply out of terror. After all, how does a simple man fight a god?

As unbelievable as it may sound, many of these tribal communities love and revere their god-chief and his chosen people. They honor them with dance and song, feasts in their honor, acts of heroics, protection, and treat them with the respect one would give a king and his court. Perhaps most difficult for northerners to believe is that the vampires act and function as lords and protectors of their people. This is not a game. These people are the vampires subjects/property and, as such, the vampire lords protect and nurture what is theirs. Some may even love their subjects, as much as a god-being or demon can love any of his pets. Despite appearances to the contrary, the vampires' motives are always self-serving. They do not slay the people because they are cattle providing them with blood/food. Furthermore, their loyal and happy (or submissive and terrified) subjects protect them while they sleep. The symbiotic relationship keeps both vampire and non-vampire alive and prosperous in a dangerous land. In many regards, the relationship is a simple matter of trading goods and services. Hundreds of these vampire ruled tribes and villages are scattered throughout Southern Mexico, the Yucatan and Central America. **The typical community** includes 4D6×10 human subjects and one to 2D6 ruling secondary vampires.

Vampire Towns and Cities

The roots of domination

Before we explore some of the specific types of vampire societies and kingdoms, it is important to understand how it is that the undead minority dominate the non-vampire majority. And why people allow it to happen.

While it is true that even in the vampire infested lands of Mexico, non-vampire humanoids outnumber the average vampire by at least ten to one, the supernatural nature and powers of the undead dramatically alters the odds. Any one vampire is more than a match for any two or three humans, possibly twice as many, depending on the circumstances. One must consider that the majority of the southern communities are simple farming villages with little or no high technology, meaning no mega-damage body armor, weapons or magic to help them in their rebellion against their demonic masters. There is also the problem of the vampires daytime protectors, undoubtedly several townspeople loyal to their demonic masters for whatever reason. There is also likely to be a handful of extraordinary daytime defenders, whether they be demons, skilled and physically augmented warriors (bionics, bots, power armor, etc.) or powerful sorcerers. The protectors will have to be eliminated first (and quickly). A mass rebellion must be carefully orchestrated, for if one vampire survives he will return with others to extract their terrible revenge (and about half of the vampires will have secret lairs). A failed rebellion will mean the torture and death of dozens of the rebellion's leaders and torment for all.

Furthermore, there are thousands of vampires roaming the countryside, looking for human prey. Thus, even if a rebellion was successful and all the current vampires were killed, how long would it be before new vampires conquered them, masters who may be worse than their predecessors. There are also other monsters and demons as bad or worse than the vampires. Vampire rulers/owners will protect the village against other menaces, both humanoid and supernatural. Sadly, many people are stuck between a rock and a hard place. Often the only alternative to vampire domination is death. Those who chose life must think of their families and often find themselves trapped in a life of slavery, quietly waiting and dreaming of the day they may be free.

There are two major types of vampire dominated communities, the ones that are predominately human occupied and those that are predominately inhabited by the undead.

The most common are the communities composed mostly of humans. Only 25% to 35% of the population is vampire, the rest are normal humans and/or D-Bees. Typically, the undead and their humanoid subjects live and work in the same community, mingling freely with one another. In such communities it is often difficult to distinguish vampire from humanoid slave.

The less common vampire community is one that has a central city occupied almost entirely by the undead, with a dozen smaller communities of humanoids all around it. These tend to be the more savage and less sophisticated vampire cities, typified by **Ixzotz.**

The Vampire Kingdom of Ixzotz

Population Breakdown:

Ixzotz City: 1500 secondary vampires, one master vampire, one intelligence; approximately 500 humans.

Surrounding 30 mile area: 20 humanoid communities of farmers and raisers of livestock surround Ixzotz. Each town has roughly 4D6×100 people and 4D6 secondary vampire overseers; approximately 45,000 total people (30% D-Bee).

Entire Ixzotz Kingdom: Approximately 4700 active vampires. 72,000 humanoids. Remember this is the oldest and therefore largest of the vampire kingdoms in regard to the number of vampires.

Ixzotz (Eesh-zotz) is the oldest vampire kingdom in Mexico. The central city of Ixzotz is located on the bones of the pre-rifts city of **Aguascalientes,** along a ley line that connects to the Aztec pyramid at Tula (a nexus) and an indian ruin 44 miles (70 km) northwest of the city. **Ixzotz** is the central city of the vampire kingdom and populated primarily by vampires (68%). Ixzotz is a cruel dictatorship and the humans it controls are its abused slaves.

The few hundred humans that occupy the city are servants to the vampire elite. They wear collars and chains and are anemic. All of the city's humans are completely submissive to their demon masters, never raise a hand against them, and are petrified of strangers. Like most of the non-vampire population, these people have been the slaves of vampires for generations and know no other way of life. They are uneducated, unskilled (not even as skilled as a first level vagabond O.C.C.), and physically and psychologically abused/conditioned.

The humanoids that live around the vampire city are slave labor and cattle on which the vampires feed. The people are uneducated farmers and raisers of animal livestock. They live quiet, hard days of labor, either working for the vampires by constructing buildings, making furniture, and other things desired by their masters, or working the fields or tending their animals so that they can feed themselves. Approximately every 30 days, the community is besieged by a thousand vampires who come to feed on their blood. The doors to houses are expected to be open and the people to willingly bare their necks. Children under the age of 12 are typically exempt from the feeding. When the vampires are done, they leave, it as simple as that.

The vampires inhabit the old city of Aguascalientes, much of which had been rebuilt before the vampires seized control. Half of the city has electricity and indoor plumbing. The overall level of technology of the city is about equal to the Americas of the 1950's. During the day a visitor is struck by how deserted the town is. There are apartment buildings, houses, saloons (social gathering places), theaters, dance halls, gambling casinos, a hospital, an arena, and sheriffs office, but few people. One can't help but to notice that 50% of the windows in all the buildings have been bricked-up, boarded, or covered by heavy drapes and shutters. The streets are empty except for packs of 2D6 dogs that bay noisily at the visitors, and an occasional, pale skinned person dressed in rags and chains scurrying to hide in the shadows. If one these pale inhabitants is physically stopped and questioned, the individual will be panic-stricken and plead to be released (20%, male and female, will faint). He or she will refuse to answer most questions, but will be quick to deny that he is afraid of anything other than the strangers questioning him. If asked about vampires, the character will insist that "there are no vampires here. Absolutely none!/73 If released the person will run into the nearest building and hide, but then run to get the sheriff. If the person is not released immediately, he will begin to scream for help.

Help will arrive in the form of the sheriff, a huge, muscular, Brodkil demon who is a partial conversion borg, bristling with bionic weaponry and slinging a borg rail gun. He will be accompanied by four deputies; another brodkil demon and what appears to be two ogres, all clad in crusader armor and carrying pulse rifles. The fourth is a human in robes (5th level shifter). All are of evil alignments, but surprisingly polite, in a gruff and threatening sort of way. They will demand the immediate release of any citizens. Failure to comply will incite a battle. Four other similarly armed deputies are moving up behind the strangers to support the sheriff; gunfire will send them attacking within one melee.

Obeying the sheriff's requests will meet with courteous treatment from him and his men. He will try to answer any questions the best he can. He will name the city. Explain that the person(s) they were speaking to are stupid slaves who don't know anything. Explain that the majority of the people are away for a religious ceremony, or cattle roundup, or harvesting crops, or similar special event, but that they'll be back tonight. Depending on the situation and on the visitors, he will either try to encourage them to be on their way, or will invite them to stay, booking them rooms, at reasonable prices, at the hotel near his office.

Ixzotz City Highlights

The Sheriff

The sheriff and his deputies will be encountered sooner or later because one of the vampires slaves or protectors would catch wind of visitors in town and radio or run to get the sheriff. The sheriff and his men are the vampires daytime protectors. They will usually lull visitors into a false sense of security and then waylay them. Intruders may be captured to be questioned, tortured, and then enslaved or eaten/drained of blood by the vampires. If they seem too dangerous, or an immediate threat, they are killed immediately.

The sheriff is a brodkil demon, Miscreant, I.Q. 11, M.E. 20, P.S. 30 (both real & bionic), P.P. 17, Spd. (bionic) 220 (150 mph/241), all others average. Body M.D.C. 250, plus body armor 100 M.D.C. Name: Prevv, a 5th level warrior with partial bionic conversion; bionic legs, one bionic arm, weapons, implants and body reinforcement. Bionics include: Laser finger blaster (1D4 M.D.), silver-plated retractable knuckle claws (3D4 S.D.C.), particle beam forearm blaster (6D6+6 M.D.), energy chip arm port, concealed ion rod (4D6 M.D.) in right leg, secret compartment in left leg (contains vibro-knife and two plasma grenades: 5D6 M.D.). Also has a multi-optic eye (right), amplified hearing and headjack, and oxygen storage cell. Weapons: In addition to bionics, he is armed with an NG-202 rail gun (1D4×10 M.D.), and a pair of vibro-swords (used as daggers, 2D6 M.D. each). Also has access to a dozen plasma grenades, six fragmentation grenades, another rail gun, a giant size crossbow (bolts inflict 3D6 S.D.C.), and vampire killing weapons (for use against rival vampire kingdoms).

Deputies include: Ten 4th level Brodkil demons (only one is a partial borg), all are diabolic, can turn invisible at will and have 250 M.D.C. bodies, and are armed with pulse rifles and rail guns (see **Rifts Sourcebook** for further data about the Brodkil). Plus, four ogres and six D-Bee headhunters, all third level and armed with pulse rifles and clad in crusader body armor. **The one human** is a psychotic shifter (5th level, miscreant) who likes vampires and has agreed to help protect them if they allow him to experiment with rifts and summonings. His secret companion, hidden at his feet, is a minor earth elemental. All of the deputies have access to hover cycles and jet packs. These are all the day time protectors, other than the vampire intelligence itself and its demon familiar, that they think they need.

Note that in the event of a daytime city assault, the 500 slaves will try to fight with clubs and the occasional energy weapon (3% will have M.D. weapons) and the 20 or so willing servants will fight too (includes two heavy Titan combat bots and two Multi-Bots). The sheriff or one of his men can also activate a legion of 50 NG-W9 light labor bots (100 M.D.C.) and 30 NG-W10 heavy labor bots (150 M.D.C.) if necessary. Don't forget that packs of dogs roam the streets, alerting the inhabitants of intruders. And can also be controlled to fight for the city.

The Hotel

The hotel is a front to help make the town look authentic and peaceful. The ogre and six D-Bees (all are 3rd level headhunters) that run the hotel are in on the deception and work with the sheriff, booking visitors into lavish rooms that are under surveillance (hidden cameras and bugs). Then when the visitors are relaxing, like taking a shower, the sheriff and his men attack and capture them. Captives are taken to the M.D.C. constructed jail house.

The Jail

The jail is across the street from the, comparatively small, sheriff's office. It is one of the original pre-rifts buildings and may have been the police headquarters. It covers a quarter of a city block and is four stories high, with nearly 100 offices (none are used). 1D6+1 of the deputies and 2D6 of the human slaves are usually hanging out in the main lobby and prison portion of the building.

The prison area has 40 good, solid S.D.C. prison cells and 30 mega-damage cells (200 M.D.C. each; installed in recent years). Each cell can hold as many as four prisoners without overcrowding. Half also have M.D.C. wall manacles and chains (10 M.D.C. each).

The large 30×60 foot open office area is devoid of furnishings except for three medical surgery tables and some M.D.C. chains and manacles built into parts of the wall and floor. Blood stains the area around these items; sometimes used as a torture and feeding area.

Note: 30 vampires live and sleep in the remote areas of this building.

The Arena

A large, domed stadium is the Ixzotz arena. The most popular, formal place of night entertainment in the city. Vampires enjoy engaging in and observing contests between vampires and humans and other creatures. Captive adventurers often find themselves in the arena, pitted against a vampire(s), monster or demon. Some of the contests are genuine competitions and gladiatorial style battles, many are sadistic games and torture. A dozen vampires live in the offices at the arena.

The Hospital

The hospital is another large building that is empty except for one small wing that services the human slaves and mercenaries. There is also a blood storage reserve that contains approximately 4000 gallons of human blood.

In the basement morgue area of the hospital are modified storage rooms that contain slab after slab of staked vampires. There are 300 wild vampires and a 100 secondary vampires who have submitted themselves to suspended animation by being staked. They lay here as reserve warriors in case of battle. If they are needed, four NG-W9 bots have been programmed to run down the aisle removing the stakes to bring the undead back to life, hungry and in a killing frenzy.

Note: 50 active vampires live and sleep in the remote areas of the hospital.

The Old Convention Center

The convention center is a crumbling ruin near the center of town and directly on the ley line that cuts through the city. The building is obviously abandoned, but continues to serves a sinister purpose, for this is the lair of the Ixzotz vampire intelligence. Unlike many intelligences, Ixzotz has elected to live among his minions in the middle of his capital city. His specific lair is on the first floor main convention, exhibit hall. He is old, cunning, and over-confident. He believes that no one would suspect his presence in the city, so that is where he lives. His demon familiar is always near and 100 secondary vampires live in the convention center to protect and serve their creator.

A treasure-trove of gold, silver, and gems worth about 100 million credits, in addition to a couple dozen magic items (scrolls, TW devices, etc.), CS Enforcer (half M.D.C. is gone), 100 Northern Gun weapons, 12 one ounce vials of Chichen Itza healing water, and the skull of a dragon.

The Casino Royale

The casino is a popular gathering place for the undead and is the abode of the Cranston Octolan, the head master vampire. The entire penthouse is his lavish apartment. Ten beautiful slave women wait on him, hand and foot. Six male slaves complete his entourage of servants. Although Master Octolan has a huge master bed room, his sleeping compartment is a hidden, mega-damage, closet-like chamber (200 M.D.C.). It would require 3D4 hours of thorough searching to find the concealed compartment. Tampering with the exterior of the compartment, even touching it (covered with heat and motion sensors), will cause a shower of acid to come spraying on anybody within four feet of the chamber; inflicts 2D6×10 S.D.C. damage per melee; stops when the sensors detect no more activity or until the acid is depleted, 2 minutes/8 melees. Further tampering will cause an additional acid shower, as well as trigger a silent alarm to the master's personal protector and the sheriff's office. Octolan can evacuate his coffin chamber by turning into mist and traveling through a narrow, concealed tube to a reserve M.D.C. coffin in the basement (this one is hidden behind a brick wall near one of the old air-conditioning units).

Master Octolan, Prince of Ixzotz: Second in command after the vampire intelligence. Diabolic, I.Q. 23, M.E. 20, M.A. 24, P.S. 30, P.P. 20, P.E. 21, P.B. 22, Spd. 23; 30 P.P.E., 120 hit points. Mean, vindictive, and supremely arrogant. 10th level, 287 years old as a vampire, looks 30.

Master Octolan's protector is a horrific thing from some hell-spawned dimension, called a Kryntoc. The brute stands 13 feet tall, has three powerful clawed arms, bulging eyes, slime covered mouth (no teeth) and mega-damage skin.

Kryntoc: Horror Factor 14, **Alignment:** Diabolic

M.D.C.: 210 M.D.C, Natural Body Armor (4D6×10)

Weight: 2 tons, **Height:** 13 ft **Age:** unknown

P.P.E.: 6D6, **I.S.P.:** None

Attributes: I.Q.: 11, P.S.: 30, P.P.: 19, P.E.: 22, Spd. 19, all others average.

Disposition: Tough and mean. Likes to fight and kill, often competes in the arena. Totally loyal to Master Octolan.

Experience Level: Equal to an 8th level headhunter.

Natural Abilities: Teleport up to 60 feet (18 m), flawless, but must see or know where it is porting to; there is no limit to the number of times the monster teleports a day. Is impervious to energy weapons (vulnerable to kinetic weapons, explosives, magic and psionics), keen vision, sees the infrared spectrum and has a thermo-heat sensor to guide its attacks. Climb 70/60%, prowl 45%, track by sight and smell 60%, leap up to 40 feet (12 m) high and lengthwise, and can roll with a fall from over 500 feet and not even be stunned.

Combat Skills: Supernatural.

Attacks Per Melee: Six (6) attacks per melee. Critical strike from behind/surprise attack.

Bonuses: +6 to strike, +9 to parry, +6 to dodge, +4 on initiative, +6 to roll with punch or impact, +4 to save vs magic, poison, and psionics, +6 to save vs horror factor.

Damage: Claw or Kick: 3D6 M.D., Power Punch/Claw: 1D6×10 (counts as two attacks), Leap Kick: 6D6 M.D., inflicts double damage from behind/surprise attack.

Note: 50 vampire elite and 50 slaves live and sleep in the private rooms on floors 4,5, and the basement (top floor is Master Octolan's abode, 1, 2, & 3 are gambling and gathering places for the undead) remote areas of the hospital. Forty million credits' worth of gold and gems are also hidden in three massive safes in the casino.

Houses and buildings

The rest of the vampire population is scattered among the thousands of houses and buildings throughout the crumbling city. All are secondary vampires of 1D4+4 levels of experience. They amuse themselves by tormenting their slave population and flying into the western hills and

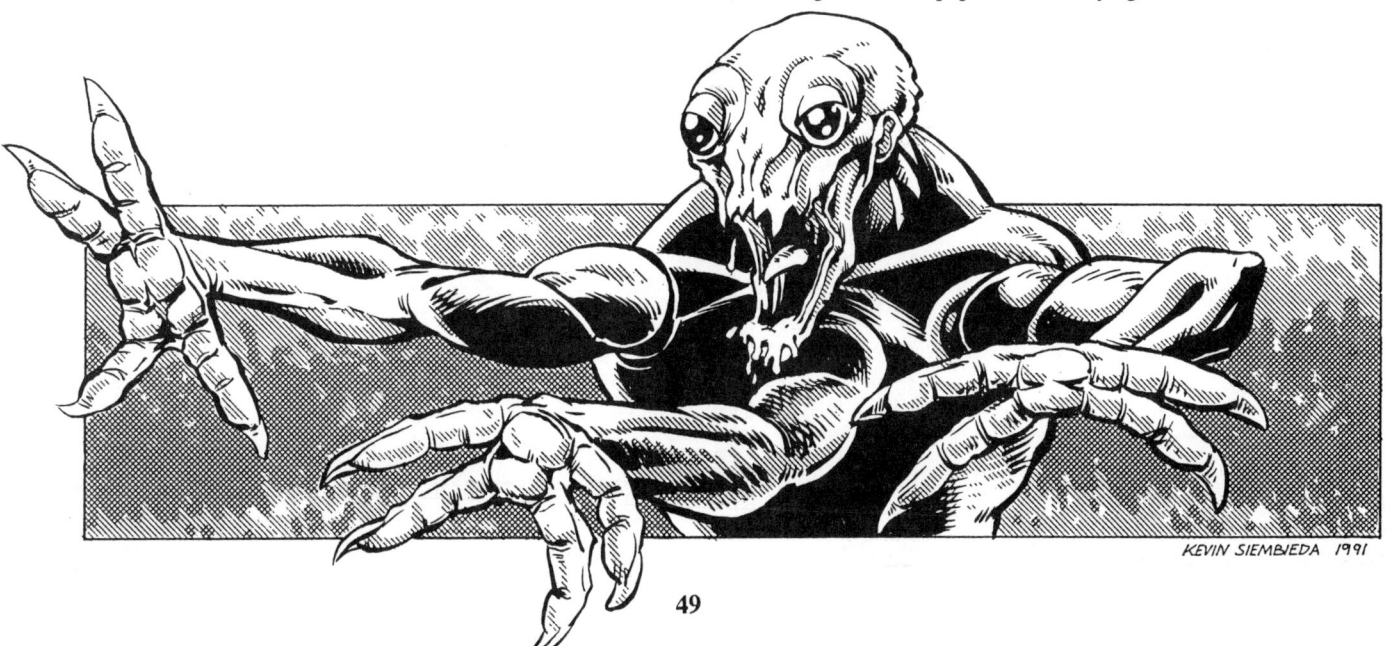

KEVIN SIEMBIEDA 1991

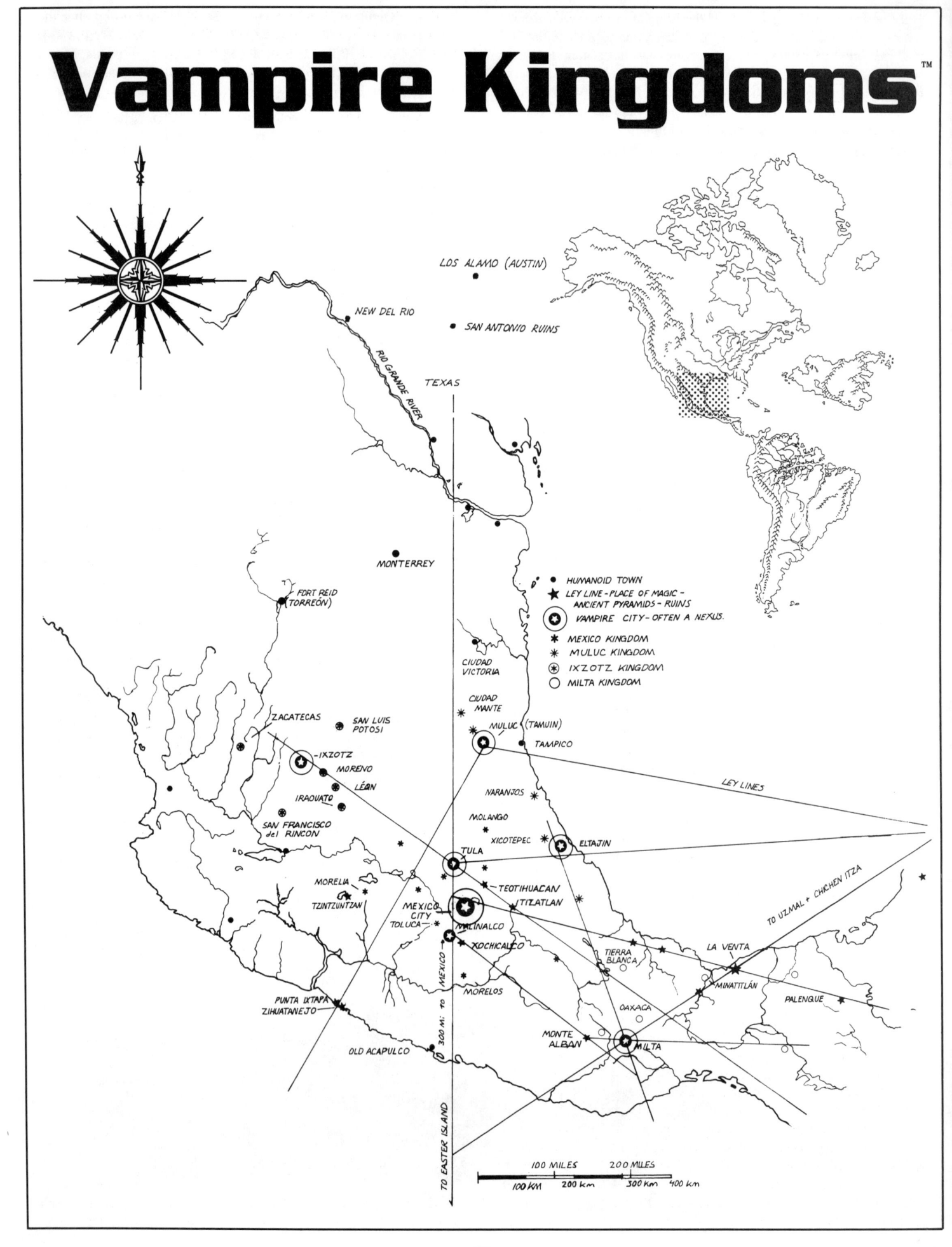

Vampire Kingdoms

- • HUMANOID TOWN
- ★ LEY LINE - PLACE OF MAGIC - ANCIENT PYRAMIDS - RUINS
- ⊛ VAMPIRE CITY - OFTEN A NEXUS
- ✳ MEXICO KINGDOM
- ∗ MULUC KINGDOM
- ⊛ IXZOTZ KINGDOM
- ○ MILTA KINGDOM

Locations shown:

- Los Alamo (Austin)
- New Del Rio
- San Antonio Ruins
- Rio Grande River
- Texas
- Monterrey
- Fort Reid (Torreón)
- Ciudad Victoria
- Ciudad Mante
- Zacatecas
- San Luis Potosí
- Ixzotz
- Moreno
- León
- Irapuato
- San Francisco del Rincon
- Muluc (Tamuin)
- Tampico
- Naranjos
- Molango
- Xicotepec
- Eltajin
- Tula
- Morelia
- Tzintzuntzan
- Teotihuacan
- Itzlatlan
- Mexico City
- Toluca
- Malinalco
- Xochicalco
- Morelos
- Punta Ixtapa Zihuatanejo
- Old Acapulco
- Tierra Blanca
- La Venta
- Minatitlán
- Palenque
- Oaxaca
- Monte Alban
- Milta
- Ley Lines
- To Uxmal + Chichen Itza
- To Easter Island
- 0 300 Mi. to Mexico

Scale: 100 Miles / 200 Miles / 100 Km / 200 Km / 300 Km / 400 Km

50

northern plains in search of new humanoids to play with and destroy. They also engage in minor skirmishes with the rival vampire kingdoms of Mexico and Muluc.

Other Cities of the Kingdom

Six satellite cities are found at the pre-rift cities of **Zacatecas, San Luis Potosi, Monero, Leon, San Francisco del Rincon,** and **Irapuato.**

Zacatecas is the northern most city, located in the mountains 110 miles (177 km) from Ixzotz. Zacatecas is a town of 433 secondary vampires. All around the town are dozens of tiny villages (40% D-Bee) composed of 5D6×10 villagers. Most are sheep- and goat-herders, but farmers are present as well.

San Luis Potosi is about 80 miles (128 km) east of the central city. Here resides a second master vampire and 790 secondary vampires, among a populace of 1500 humans. This area is the agricultural center of the Ixzotz kingdom (for its human population, of course). Farms fill the countryside, broken only by little villages and some cattle ranches. Another 4000 or so humans labor in the fields. Actually, these are the lucky ones, for their lives are fairly normal, although under the yoke of demonic oppression. They are visited only three or four times a year to be feasted upon by their masters, for they must be strong to continue their work in the fields.

Monero is a nightmare town. It is effectively a cattle town where livestock is bred and groomed for slaughter. Only in this case, the livestock is not animals, but human beings. The town is located about 30 miles (48 km) south from Ixzotz and 20 miles (32 km) north of Leon. 220 vampires live at or near Monero (half live and sleep in the pre-rifts ruins about two miles north of the vampires' Monero). It is a filthy town of weather-beaten, wood buildings and a few M.D.C. bunkers, occupied by a small troop of mercenary demons, like the brodkil, and inhuman D-Bees; about 200 in all (1st to 4th level scouts, vagabonds, headhunters, and monsters). They protect and manage Monero. All humans, including fellow slaves, are kept miles away from the horrible town. Runaways from the Monero food pens are hunted down and killed on the spot, no exceptions. The vampires don't want word of the food pens spreading to the work slaves for fear that it would cause a panic.

The food pens are huge, fenced in pavilions that resemble giant aircraft hangars (in fact Monero could be mistaken for an airfield from the sky). Each so-called pen is a giant barracks that houses approximately 200 adult humans (no D-Bees) and has a large courtyard/field contained by an electrified fence, for the people to exercise. The people are pale, weak and apathetic. The entire scene is frighteningly reminiscent to the Nazi concentration camps of pre-rifts times. The human cattle are given the best foods to eat and toys to play with. They are not required to work or do anything but eat and reproduce. Every two weeks their vampire masters come and feed. Those who die are given to the inhuman mercenaries to eat or are taken to the processing plant where they are butchered for meat and their bones ground to dust for fertilizer. **Note:** There are eight food pens (approx. 1600 adult human cattle and twice as many children) and one processing plant. Average life expectancy at the food pens is 30 years old.

Leon is a town built among the ruins of the old, pre-rifts city of the same name, populated by approximately 5000 humanoids (20% are D-Bees). In many ways it is the best community for the human slaves of Ixzotz. The housing is good, the tech-level is about equal to the turn of the 20th century, 60% of the buildings have indoor plumbing, and the people are allowed to lead fairly normal lives. Most are farmers and sheep- or pig-herders, but many are also craftsmen (carpenters, smiths, builders, artisans, etc.). They are the vampires' work force and secondary food producers for the humanoid population. They are also called upon as soldiers to defend the kingdom if threatened by invaders. Half the male population is equipped with energy weapons and light M.D.C. body armor provided by the vampires. Best of all, the vampires come to feed only once or twice a year. **Note:** A meager 50 secondary vampires govern and supervise the city of Leon.

San Francisco del Rincon is the newest addition of the Ixzotz kingdom. It was a humanoid town that grew too big, too close to vampire territory and caught the eye of the Ixzotz vampires. The population of approximately 3800 humanoids (50% D-Bee) has not yet accepted the vampires as their lords and masters, thus there is continual insurrection. Residents are constantly trying to escape into the hills, attacking their would-be masters with sharpened pieces of wood, and general disobedience, even after the vampires slew 1100 fellow townspeople just last summer, after a futile rebellion. **Note:** The minions of Xibalba have secretly fueled the flames of rebellion by supplying weapons, equipment, and encouragement, and have helped stage a few escapes. Why? Why just to stir up the pot and see what comes of it; hopefully, some delectable chaos. 600 secondary vampires are trying to whip the town into shape.

Irapuato is also one of the newer Ixzotz towns and begins to encroach on the territory of their rival, the Mexico Kingdom. It was specifically established to test the tolerance of the rival kingdom. It is occupied by 1000 secondary vampires and a legion of nearly 4500 sub-human D-Bees; mostly orcs, goblins, and similar stupid, strong, and blood thirsty types (one third are armed with energy weapons and M.D.C. body armor, the rest are equipped with traditional vampire killing weapons). In addition, a score of demon sorcerers (average 4th to 6th level) and a hundred demon warriors are part of their ranks. The army has sat at Irapuato, doing little for the last five years. However, they do dispatch the occasional raiding part to destroy border villages and stake vampires, slay vampire travelers, steal supplies, and cause malicious mischief. A war between the two kingdoms, at Irapuato if nowhere else, is inevitable. Over the five years over 3000 humanoid pawns have died and over 200 vampires on both sides.

The remaining vampires are scattered throughout the kingdom, involved in their own affairs. Some travel to neighboring regions, looking for trouble from both humanoids and rival vampire kingdoms.

Doc Reid has learned of the Ixzotz, Mexico City and Muluc vampire kingdoms. His subsequent discovery of rumors about the food pens at Moreno from a talkative mercenary that once worked at the food pens (killed after torture by the Doc), Ixzotz has become the first target in his holy crusade against the undead. He has already established a few tiny outposts along the mountain rivers and has spies as far south as San Luis Potosi and Ciudad Victoria.

The Mexico Empire

Population Breakdown:
<u>Mexico City</u>: 1700 secondary vampires, one master vampire, approximately 65,000 humans. The vampire intelligence is at Tula, 70 miles (112 km) north of Mexico City. The original master vampire is the ruler of Mexico City and answerable only to the intelligence.
<u>Surrounding 30 mile area</u>: 12 humanoid villages, mostly farmers and raisers of livestock. 4D6 secondary vampires oversee their smooth operations at each and represent the authority of the Empire; approximately 14,000 total people (40% D-Bee).
<u>Entire Mexico Empire Population</u>: Approximately 2900 active vampires (none staked). 185,000 humanoids (30% D-Bees).

Mexico City
Capitol of the Mexico Empire

Without a doubt, the Mexico Empire is the most advanced and civilized of all the vampire kingdoms, and Mexico City is its crowning jewel. Pre-rifts Mexico City was obliterated by earthquakes, storms and ley line eruptions during the great cataclysm (90% of the population over 13 million were killed in Mexico city alone), but much of the city has been rebuilt under the management of the vampires. Although the humans are effectively slaves and food for the undead, they are treated with dignity and kindness. Their unusual relationship is one of mutual co-operation and unity, even though the vampires are the ruling power and can be a bit cruel and demanding at times. The tech-level is close to that of the pre-rifts cataclysm. Streets are paved and kept spotlessly clean (by the humanoids). All buildings have indoor plumbing and electricity, there is low volume manufacturing, advanced farming, and an education system for the humans; 60% of the population is literate in Spanish. There is free time for humanoids, recreation centers, theaters, saloons, restaurants, dance halls, stores, and everything else one would expect from a major metropolis. The city is about the size of Ciudad Juarez in the north, only newer, nicer, cleaner, has no gang problems, minimal crime, and is growing.

The humanoids and vampires maintain their astoundingly civil and friendly relationship because these vampire rulers have made an effort to create a certain degree of freedom and mutual prosperity. The vampires do remind the humans that they are a conquered people and that vampires are their superiors. But they also acknowledge the humanoid's ingenuity and abilities, and give them freedom to live their own lives. The Mexico Empire vampires are no worse than any human dictatorial regime, and better than most in the present day world of **Rifts**. The vampires make the laws, administer punishment, and rule the people in a mostly, fair and equitable way. The humans and D-Bees who abide by the law can live long, happy lives.

The friendly environment between the humans and vampires of the Mexico Empire exists for three major reasons. **1.** The vampires have made an open effort to create a human-like society where the people would enjoy an appreciable degree of personal freedom and control over their world. The humans in any even have a right to assembly, vote on city issues, and have representatives (elected by the humans) to express their views, concerns and needs in how they are governed to the vampire city council. **2.** The vampires of the Mexico Empire have deliberately kept their numbers low and do not make a spectacle of their supernatural nature. The lower number of vampires means less demands, especially for blood, on the human slave population. However, low numbers is potentially dangerous by conventional vampire wisdom. It means the vampires can become grossly outnumbered by both humanoids and rival vampire kingdoms. But this plan may work for the Mexico Empire, if their human subjects will stand with them, not against them, in times of conflict. **3.** The vampires do not personally come and suck a person's blood. Instead the citizens are required to donate a pint of blood every three weeks. The blood donations are rotated in such a manner that there is always an ample supply of blood without taxing the community or straining the individual. Every big business has an employee blood donation clinic in the office and there are numerous public clinics for the rest of the population. The giving of blood has become so commonplace, quick (about 30 minutes), and painless that most people don't even think about it. There is even an incentive program for those who donate blood, within the limits of human safety, earning bonus points and receiving prizes, cash rewards and vacations! The gentle, clinical collection of blood has done a great deal to remove the monstrous aspect of the vampire. There are even laws and punishment for vampires who "go wild" and attack a citizen to feed.

As a result, the majority of the humanoid population is loyal and fairly trusting and supportive of their supernatural rulers. However, not everybody is content. There are humans and D-Bees who fear and hate their vampire masters. They may have a comparatively good and normal life, but a bird in a gilded cage is still a prisoner in a cage, and they resent their captivity. Vampires, in general, are predominately evil and the majority make a point of showing their superiority, freedom and power. They are frequently condescending, arrogant, and slap and degrade their human slaves. Non-vampires of the Mexico Empire are second class citizens and they are reminded of this often.

Conversely, there are vampires who see the laws and rules of the Empire as forcing them to coddle and dote on their human inferiors. They have difficulty understanding why humanoids should have any rights. They see things very black and white: humans are the slaves, vampires are the masters. To these misanthropes, humans are their playthings and food, nothing more. These vampires (about 25% of the population) are outspoken and belligerent. They are typically the cruel master or boss, and mistreat humanoids in general. They are also the ones most likely to go on "wild" feeding sprees, attacking citizens on the city streets or fly off to the wilderness on hunting trips so that they may feed as vampires are meant to feed, on living prey.

Regent Augustus Obregon, Ruler of Mexico City, Second in command of the Empire after the vampire intelligence; I.Q. 25, M.E. 26, M.A. 27, P.S. 28, P.P. 18, P.E. 19, P.B. 24, Spd. 30; P.P.E. 40, 160 hit points. Aberrant evil, honorable, loyal, insightful, confident, and fair, but also a stern disciplinarian, decisive and merciless. 7th level, 137 years old as a vampire, looks 25.

Tula

The site of the Aztec ruins at Tula, about 70 miles (112km) north of Mexico City, has been transformed. It is not so much a city as a fortified encampment. About a hundred buildings fill the Tula. A third are military style, mega-damage bunkers that house troops and robots. But it is the impressive pyramid of Tula that is the all imposing structure of the town. This is not an ancient ruin but a modern construction to house the vampire intelligence of the Mexico Empire. The impressive structure covers two city blocks at its base and looms 400 feet (122 m) into the clouds. One might think the prominence of the pyramid makes it any easy target, but the edifice has both technological and magic protection. The average wall area is 20 feet thick with an M.D.C. of 2000 per 10 foot area. In addition, the Tula pyramid stands directly on a powerful ley line nexus connecting it to the nexuses, at **Uxmal** and **Easter Island** among others.

The pyramid is specifically designed to completely harness the mystic energies that flow within it in ways unlike many others in the world. One of the dimensional features of the pyramid is that the intelligence can make the entire structure temporarily disappear into the limbo dimension without, and can manipulate the passage of time. Time can be suspended so that for those within the pyramid, hours may pass, but outside, only a few minutes have gone by. Or time can be accelerated so that for those inside the pyramid only a few minutes have passed, but outside it has been hours. Or time may pass normally. The maximum amount of time that can be warped is 24 hours and time must always advance, even if it is very slowly; it can never be completely stopped nor can one travel backwards in time. To teleport such a massive structure rooted to a particular dimension by ley lines is difficult and taxing, consequently the maneuver can be performed once (gone and back) every 72 hours. If the intelligence is slain while in the limbo dimension the pyramid will instantly return to the Tula, Mexico location and begin to deteriorate (see the death of the intelligence that follows).

Inside the pyramid are several active dimensional portals. Stepping in the portal will instantly transport the person to a new location on Earth or to a completely different world. Earthly locations include the pyramid at Uxmal, the Milta Vampire Kingdom (at Milta), Punta Ixtapa, Acapulco, Easter Island, Calgary (Canada), St. Louis Archway rift, Old Detroit, Atlantis and Stonehenge and an obscure location in China. **Portals to other dimensions** include the Palladium World (RPG), Xibalba (the real dimension, not the Yucatan microcosm), a strange pre-historic Earth-like world (dinosaurs, lizard people and dragons) and one of its other vampire ridden worlds. Others may be opened at any particular time.

Inside are approximately 50 secondary vampires, 1D6x10 humanoid assistants/slaves, and a variety of entities and other dimensional beings. A common visitor to the pyramid is a regular dimension travel companion who is a Neuron Beast (1-72% likelihood of being present). A dimension travelling Sowki is also a regular guest (1-50%) and both are friends who will fight to the death to protect their friend (and controlled dimensional gateway to other worlds).

Killing the Tula Intelligence

Killing the vampire intelligence at Tula will have the usual effect on his minions, but will also adversely affect the great pyramid. The intelligence is the single element that controls the ley line energy and all the magical and dimensional aspects of the pyramid. If slain, there is nothing to contain the energy within and the pyramid erupts like a volcano. Within 1D6 minutes after his death, the pyramid begins to rumble and shake as if being struck by an earthquake. 1D6 minute later, the M.D. walls begin to crumble. Explosions can be heard and waves of blue-white magic energy can be seen erupting from various rooms. 1D6 minutes after that, the controlled dimensional portals rift open, unleashing 3D6 monsters from a variety of different dimensions, none of them are friendly. 1D6 minutes after that, the entire building continues to fall apart. Anybody inside will suffer 4D6 M.D. every melee (15 seconds) and 2D6 M.D. to people outside, within 100 feet (30.5 m) of the collapsing structure. Huge chunks of M.D.C. concrete and steel are hurled 1D4×1000 yards/meters into the air, showering the surrounding ten mile (16 km) area with debris (2D6×10 if hit by a chunk of the debris; dodge is possible). 1D6 minutes after debris is shot into the sky, the pyramid explodes! Anybody inside the building has a 1-50% chance of being hurled into the limbo dimension (see the *Yucatan for a description about this dimension*) all others suffer 1D6×1000 mega-damage. Fortunately, it is a contained blast and inflicts little damage beyond its walls; 2D6×10 M.D. to a 300 foot (91.5 m) radius and every psychic, psi-stalker, and practitioner of magic within a thousand miles will feel the impact and be stunned for one melee (15 seconds). Psychics and men of magic within a hundred miles will suffer a terrible headache for 1D4 days as a result of the P.P.E. backlash. The Nexuses at Uxmal, Milta and off the Pacific Coast will suddenly surge and there is a 1-33% chance that a rift will open at each location (lasts 3D4 minutes then closes).

The Mexico Empire's Defenses

The Tula Pyramid is an important means of defense because it can be used to summon a variety of supernatural creatures; demons, elementals, humanoid warriors, etc. But the Empire must also rely on its citizens and conventional war machines.

The militia: On the high-tech end, the vampires have turned some of their humanoid slaves into a defensive militia. Approximately 4000 troops are found at Tula, with another 2000 patrolling the lands controlled by the Mexico Empire. In addition, each major city has a militia of about 1200 active troops. All are the equivalent of second and third level Coalition grunts and technical officers. 20% have undergone partial bionic reconstruction. Special equipment, like robot vehicles and heavy weapons, are primarily items that have been captured, stolen, or secretly purchased. In case of an invasion, the average citizen is also expected to fight, and they will, especially against other vampire kingdoms.

High-tech manufacturing and equipment: Tula and Mexico City have the ability to recharge energy clips and repair most weapons, M.D.C. armor, vehicles, borgs and bots. Mexico City has limited cybernetic and bionic manufacturing and installation capabilities. Mexico city also manufactures urban warrior and crusader body armor, motorcycles, hovercycles, common types of vehicles, and vampire slaying weapons like silver-plated and wood weapons, water guns (no TW items) and bow weapons. The Empire controls two small silver mines, providing them with ample amounts of silver and silver weapons. The most common energy weapons include the L-20 pulse rifle, the Wilk's laser pistol and most Northern Gun items. **Note:** Live horses and horse-drawn wagons are a common means of transportation, especially among the humanoid populace in farm areas and the smaller communities.

Robots and power armor: The most precious and limited items are the extremely expensive mega-damage robot vehicles and power armor suits. Current resources include: 6 SAMAS, 2 CS Enforcers, 2 Behemoth Explorers, 8 Titan Reconnaissance Robots, 10 Titan TR-001 Combat Robots, 3 Titan TR-002 Explorer Robots, 6 NG-V7 Hunter Mobile Guns, 12 NG-V10 Super Labor Robots, 2 NG-M56 Multi-Bots, 1 Glitter Boy, 2 Triax X-10 Predator Power Armor, 12 Triax T-21 Hopper Power Armor, 12 Titan Power Armor, and 20 NG Samson Power Armor. **Note:** Half of the pilots in the armored division are under vampire enslavement/mind control, the others are Mexico Empire citizens. The presence of such a large percentage of mind controlled humans is to prevent the free-willed humans from considering rebellion by seizing control of the robot defenses. However, the large majority of the free-will humanoids in the militia are loyal to the Empire, if not entirely loyal to the vampires themselves. The armed forces will fight to the death to protect their fellow citizens and their cities.

Magic: In addition to the supernatural allies and monsters that can be summoned at ley line nexuses, the Mexico Empire also has a couple dozen elite men of magic, mostly 1D4+4 level ley line walkers and shifters.

Medical: Each major city has a large and excellent hospital and a half dozen smaller, modern, top-notch clinics (all are experts in blood transfusions and storage). Most have laboratories and facilities equipped with the most up to date equipment and a well trained staff of body fixers, cyber-docs, holistic doctors, psychic healers, and nurses. Key personnel are typically mind controlled and the facility itself is run by the vampires. The standard field equipment for the militia is a bit limited, but sufficient to give patrols a portable bio-scan, robot medical kits (both), and first-aid kits.

Tula population: Approximately 9,000 humanoid city residents (10% D-Bee), in addition to the 4000 to 7000 troops and visitors. Tiny farms and livestock villages dot the countryside around Tula.

Other Cities of Note within the Mexico Empire

The Mexico Empire vampires own and control Teotihaucan, Itizatlan, Malinalco, and Xochicalco, all ley line focal points/ruins. A small nexus is found in northeast Mexico City, Teotihaucan and at Malinalco.

Teotihaucan is a small, modern looking city about 30 miles (48 km) northeast of Mexico city. Its most significant feature is its two ancient pyramids (builders unknown, predates the Aztec; perhaps Toltec). Once a historical park, the pyramids are now part of a fenced-in military installation that houses half the city's militia and six resident men of magic (two are shifters). Both of the pyramids are considered ley line nexus points and offer great mystic power.

Around the military installation is the city, complete with an arena for bullfighting, a popular sport at Teotihaucan. Population: Approximately 19,000 humanoid city residents (30% D-Bee), plus another 1200 in the surrounding 50 mile (80 km) area.

Itizatlan is a comparatively small, agricultural town. Its two most distinguishing features are that it is a central storage area for crops and sits on a ley line. **Note:** The land all around Mexico City and throughout the Mexico Empire is dominated by intensive agriculture. The principal crop is corn/maize, with some wheat, coffee, tobacco, and cotton. Cattle, pigs and sheep are also raised. Population: Approximately 7,000 humanoid city residents (30% D-Bee), plus another 1200 in the surrounding 50 mile (80 km) area. Tiny farms and livestock villages dot the countryside around the larger cities.

Malinalco is the agricultural center of the Mexico Empire. The city is the second largest in the Empire (only Mexico City is bigger) and rich in farm and pastoral lands. In many respects it is simply a smaller version of the capital city, with a de-emphasis on manufacturing and a focus on agriculture. A score of food processing, storage and distribution facilities are at the heart of the city's activity. But the most important aspect of the city is the ley line nexus that is controlled by the "weather wizards." The nexus is used by a cadre of magic users (ley line walkers, warlocks/elemental masters, and shifters/summoners) under the employ, control and supervision of the vampires, who control the weather of the 50 mile (80 km) area around Malinalco and for the Mexico Empire in general. The wizards summon and dispel rains and elemental forces that promote optimum farming conditions and perform feats of magic that produce exceptional results. A full militia of 1200 troops are posted near the nexus and another 1200 patrol the city and neighboring farmlands. Population: Approximately 37,000 humanoid city residents (20% D-Bee), plus another 3200 in the surrounding 50 mile (80 km) area. Tiny farms and livestock villages dot the country side around the city.

Toluca is another important community, with an emphasis on raising cattle, mostly cows and pigs. It is a sprawling, modern looking city about 30 miles (48 km) southwest of Mexico City. Population: Approximately 5600 humanoid city residents (20% D-Bee), plus another 1000 in the surrounding 50 mile (80 km) area.

Morelia is one of the farthest border towns and is in jeopardy from attack by the Ixzotz Kingdom. The tech level of the city is about 25% less than the other central cities, with a mixed focus on raising livestock (pigs, sheep and cattle), agriculture, and mining (oil, silver, lead, zinc and iron). The town and surrounding area is patrolled and monitored for Ixzotz aggression. About 20 miles west is a minor place of magic, a half mile long ley line. At the center of the ley line is the Tzintzuntzan ruin. Population: Approximately 6600 humanoid city residents (40% D-Bee), plus another 500 in the surrounding 50 mile (80 km) area.

Xochicalco is the site of an ancient ruin about six miles from the Malinalco nexus and in the northern point of a ley line power triangle. Consequently, Xochicalco is about twice as powerful as a normal ley line (though less than a true nexus). The ruins are occasionally used by the weather wizards of Malinalco and other sorcerers sanctioned by the Mexico Empire. The site is owned and controlled by the Empire. A small town surrounds the ruin. Population: Approximately 680 humanoid city residents (30% D-Bee), plus another 1000 in the surrounding 50 mile (80 km) area.

Morelos (not to be confused with Morelia) is the most southern of the Mexico Empire's major towns and cities, although the Empire lays claim to all of the southern land from Punta Ixtapa to Old Acapulco (now a citrus fruit plantation) and Ometepec. The principal produce of Morelos is pigs, maize and tea. It is a quiet but growing community of about 13,000.

The Muluc Kingdom

Population Breakdown:
Muluc City: 1800 secondary vampires, one master vampire, approximately 29,000 humans. The vampire intelligence is located somewhere in the Yucatan. The original master vampire is the ruler of Muluc City and answerable only to the intelligence. Muluc City is located about 200 miles (320 km) north of Mexico City. A second master vampire is found in the city of Eltajin and responsible for many of the raids into the Mexico Empire. Eltajin is about 110 miles (176 km) northeast of both Mexico City and Tula.
Surrounding 30 mile area: Dozens of tiny humanoid villages, mostly farmers and raisers of livestock. A typical village will contain 2D6×100 humanoids and 1D4×10 secondary vampires to dominate them.
Entire Muluc Kingdom Population: Approximately 4000 active vampires, plus another 1000 in suspended animation (staked). 70,000 humanoids (30% are D-Bees).

The Muluc Kingdom is of middle to low technology, about equal to the pre-rifts 1950's America. Much of the population is scattered among scores of tiny villages and towns of farmers, fishermen and raisers of livestock. Only the cities of Muluc (the largest city) and Ciudad Mante are comparatively modern towns. But the entire kingdom operates on the more traditional means of vampire dominance and oppression.

Human enslavement and mind control are the principal means of maintaining control over their humanoid population. For every secondary vampire there is a mind controlled human slave/servant. The human slaves serve several different purposes. In addition to being food and manpower, the victims of mind control function as the protectors of their master and his undead kin. They also serve as spies, keeping an eye open for rebellious attitudes and actions by their fellow townspeople. Their unholy allegiance to the vampire lords and their place within every aspect of the human community means that it is incredibly difficult to keep secrets from, or to act against, the vampires without their discovery.

In some cases, it is difficult to know, with certainty, whether a person is a vampire's mind slave or not. This is compounded by the fact that the Muluc Kingdom continues to create new undead on a regular basis. This means a new, not previously known, mind controlled slave is introduced within the community fairly frequently. The secrecy is maintained by feeding on a part of the body that is not as obvious as the throat. The blood of a victim does not have to be drawn from the neck, so the more careful and deceptive vampires create their slaves by biting less obvious areas, thick with veins, like the forearm, wrist, and leg.

The presence of the mind controlled slaves also reduces rebellion because they are (or were) the friends, family and loved ones of the remaining free-will population. Striking at the vampires will mean killing many of their mind controlled slaves who aldo happen to be the father, mother, sister, brother, cousin, friend, wife or husband, parent or child of somebody within the community. Killing a loved one who is not of his right mind is not a prospect which many people are willing to take. They are still the loving people they once were, only forced to do evil by the more powerful will of their demonic, vampire master. Like puppets of flesh and blood, they have no choice but to do as their vampire puppet-master directs.

As one might expect, the atmosphere at these villages and cities is one of apathy, despair, paranoia, and secrecy. The people look pale and drawn. Their eyes are dark and empty; no sparkle of life, no joy. They all lack emotion and even the children go about their daily chores in a quiet, zombie-like manner. The people have been emotionally beaten into being submissive drones.

Dealing with Strangers

The people live, but are less alive than their undead masters. They show little emotion to the arrival of strangers; not fear, not joy, not apprehension. They simply continue on with their drone-like activities. They will answer questions quickly and briefly. The tiny handful who might wish to warn a stranger, especially near dusk, will first look around to see if one of the many mind slaves are watching (for to give warning means death or worse). Children will just stare at strangers forlornly and scamper away if approached.

The most animated and friendly people will be the vampire mind slaves. They will engage travelers in friendly conversation, answer questions, and offer goods and services. Generally, their orders, in regards to strangers, are to ascertain their purpose for travelling in this territory and their military/physical strength. Then they are to make them feel at ease and keep them in town until the vampires rise with the setting of the sun. Then the visitors will be attacked and either destroyed or captured. Captives are usually added to the *blood pool*, a fate worst than death, or become mind controlled slaves of new vampires and join the work force.

The Muluc Blood Pool

The blood pool is a technological horror used to supply the vampires with their precious blood. A blood pool facility is found at Muluc City, Mante, Naranjos and Eltajin (the second largest city in the Kingdom). Thousands of humans are hooked up to life support and blood draining machines. They are emaciated, more than half are permanently crippled or retarded, all are weak and suffer from muscle atrophy. The blood suppliers are never allowed to get up from their beds, so most, with the passage of time, suffer from muscle atrophy (the muscles wither and become useless from lack of use/exercise). A third of the people are comatose. All are thin, pale and weak.

The people are kept alive by means of medical life support systems, nutrient fluids/intravenous feeding, and magic. The blood is drained on a daily basis. The amount of blood taken is always dangerously close to life threatening. However, state of the art medicine combined with magic and psychic healing keeps the people alive and producing blood. Many of the healers involved in this horrid operation are mind slaves, other supernatural monsters and creatures of evil. Horribly, the average life expectancy of these blood supplying human cattle is five to eight years.

The Problem with Muluc

The humanoid cattle of Muluc are well controlled by fear and despair. The problem of the Muluc Kingdom is mismanagement. Too many Vampires are continuing to be created. Soon it will be impossible to provide sufficient food/blood. The situation is already straining the blood pools to the maximum. A number of vampires find that they must supplement the blood pool rations by occasionally feeding on the slave population or by traveling into other territories to hunt for prey.

Overpopulation of Muluc vampires will force them into military conflict. The Kingdom will find it necessary to conquer other human communities and vampire kingdoms to supplement their dwindling food supply. However, war could cripple or destroy the Muluc Kingdom. Unfortunately, the vampire intelligence that dominates the Kingdom is quite savage and this is the way it wants things done. Furthermore, the intelligence's savage and aggressive nature makes the prospect of war seem logical and appropriate. It sees the other vampire kingdoms as rivals to its power that will have to be destroyed sooner or later anyway. It might as well be sooner.

The Muluc Kingdom relies far too heavily on its legion of vampires and their supernatural powers as its principal resource. This places too much strain on its human stock and on the vampires themselves. A significant loss of manpower would cause mass starvation of the vampires, and a significant loss in the number of undead will make the kingdom vulnerable to attack by neighboring vampire kingdoms, as well as humans. But such events seem inevitable. The Mexico Empire, with its 180,000+ humanoids, is a very alluring target. Border skirmishes and mass kidnappings of humans in the Mexico Empire are becoming increasingly frequent.

The City of Eltajin

Eltajin is the second largest city in the Kingdom, with approximately 1100 vampires and 16,000 humanoids (35% are D-Bees). The importance of the city is that it controls a major ley line nexus that is part of a triad that connects with the powerful Milta and Uzmal nexuses to the south and east. A second master vampire by the name of Anna Dominguez, rules the city. She was a sixth level ley line walker who still possesses a frightening amount of mystic knowledge, and is the friend of a witch (major pact) who is her constant companion and protector. Her palace is located on top of a rebuilt pyramid at the nexus. Anna and her vampire minions are responsible for the majority of raids on the Mexico Empire.

The city possesses little pockets of high technology, like the blood pool facility and an occasional food processing plant, but is primarily a low tech, agricultural town. Crops include citrus fruit, sugarcane, cotton and some maize. The humanoids are fearful and obedient. A small band of about 500 mind controlled humans serve as the vampires' protectors and secondary military force. An additional 2000 free-willed humans (closely monitored by the mind slaves) comprise the remainder of the Eltajin non-vampire forces. Among the mind controlled armored defenders are 24 CS SAMAS power armor units, 4 CS Enforcer bots, one CS Abolisher and 9 NG-Samson power armor. Another 600 mind slaves are scattered throughout the city to monitor the populace. **Note:** Eltajin is located about 150 miles (257 km) south of Muluc City and 110 miles (176 km) northeast of both Mexico City and Tula.

The Milta Kingdom

Population Breakdown:

Milta, Capital City: 1000 secondary vampires, one master vampire, approximately 19,000 humans. The vampire intelligence is located somewhere in the Yucatan. The original master vampire is the ruler of the capital city and answerable only to the intelligence. A second master vampire rules the city of Minatitlan.

Surrounding 30 mile area: Dozens of small, humanoid villages, mostly farmers and raisers of livestock. A typical village will contain 3D4 × 100 humanoids and 1D6 × 10 secondary vampires to dominate them.

Entire Milta Kingdom Population: Approximately 2800 active vampires, plus another 500 in suspended animation (staked). 60,000 humanoids (40% are D-Bees).

The Kingdom of Milta is the youngest of the vampire kingdoms. In structure and function it is a combination of Muluc and the Mexico Empire. Like the Muluc Kingdom, it presently dominates and degrades its humans, using fear and mind controlled slaves to control the humanoid population. Also like the Muluc Kingdom, technology is low and the kingdom's primary resource is its legion of undead. Like the Mexico Empire, Milta is experimenting with giving its human population more freedom and has established a modern blood donation hospital and contribution system (like Mexico) at its two largest cities, Minatitlan and Milta. Likewise, the powers behind the Milta Kingdom are striving to make technological advancements, with plans to make modern cities. To this end, the Milta Kingdom has entered into a tentative (and unheard of) peace treaty with the Mexico Empire. The treaty is a mutual non-aggression pact with a provision for trade relations. Milta controls the largest oil refinery in Mexico. The Mexico Empire has need of oil and petroleum products and the Milta Kingdom has need of their technology and political expertise if they are going to reorganize their present governmental structure. With threats from the Ixzotz and Muluc Kingdoms from the north, west and east, the non-aggression pact with Milta allows the Mexico Empire to concentrate on military action against those two kingdoms without having to worry about potential assault from the south as well. Note that the non-aggression pact simply means that the two kingdoms agree not to attack each other, but neither is obligated to help or protect the other from third party attackers.

The city of Milta is located in the southern hills of Mexico, about 300 miles (482 km) southeast of Mexico City. Its most important feature is the Milta ruins that mark the ley line nexus. The ruling master vampire has his lair near the ruins. The city is spacious but dirty and comparatively primitive. The Kingdom's humans are mostly farmers, growing rich crops of citrus fruit, coffee and maize, as well as raising cattle and pigs.

Minatitlan is the second largest city in the Milta Kingdom and, by far, the most technologically advanced. Over 15,000 people reside in the industrial city, with 80% working in the oil drilling stations and refineries. Heavy manufacturing of oil equipment, pipes, and conventional work vehicles are also capabilities of the town. A second master vampire and about 800 secondary vampires oversee the smooth operation of Minatitlan. The city has become a bit of an experiment in the Milta Kingdom's consideration to allow its humanoid population greater freedom. The vampires here are less brutal, allow the humanoids more personal time and expression, and they do not physically assault them to feed. Instead, the humanoids report to a hospital on a regular schedule to donate a safe amount of blood through sanitary hospital methods of transfusion. The morale among humanoids at Minatitlan is generally high and talk of progress and democracy is common. **Note:** The La Venta nexus is about 30 miles (48 km) to the east. The nexus is not part of the Milta Kingdom and is reputed to be the lair of Death Weaver demon spiders. An unknown nexus exists about 60 miles northeast of Teirra Blanca on the unofficial border where the kingdoms of Milta, Muluc and Mexico Empire meet. Two ancient ruins mark the ley line that runs parallel to the Gulf coast.

The Strongholds of Man

Tampico Military Protectorate

Tampico is not a kingdom nor a thriving city, but it must be given mention because of its strategic and commercial importance. The ruins of old Tampico lay smashed and battered from the tidal waves and hurricanes that battered the coast during the Coming of Rifts. But a tiny, new town has sprouted up admidst the ruins. Tampico is more of a fortified encampment of humans and D-Bees than a town. You see, a band of mercenaries came into the possession of a map the showed the location of a substantial oil field in the Gulf of Mexico. The merc's travelled along the Gulf coast to Tampico and found the oil. They have since established a small, but powerful military fort/encampment around the oil drilling operation and sell crude oil to the notable kingdoms of Northern Mexico and the southern states of the old American Empire. They have maintained the oil drilling and exporting operations for nearly seven years, despite the fact that the area is located in the vampire ridden Kingdom of Muluc.

In all honesty, the mercenaries have no idea that Muluc is a *vampire kingdom* or that other vampire kingdoms exist. They have heard some rumors, but choose to ignore them. As for the abundance of vampires (they have lost hundreds to vampire attacks), everybody knows Mexico is crawling with the damn demons, but a vampire kingdom? Impossible. This misconception is perpetuated by the fact that the soldiers have not explored the surrounding territory. The mercenaries have one goal: to get rich from the Tampico oil fields. This is their complete, selfish and narrow focus. They don't care about vampires or anything else. To this end they have seized control of a tiny, but valuable piece of land, and have devoted all of their energies to the development and defense of that tiny area.

To that end, they have established a small army of elite mercenary veterans to hold and protect the area and a small town of laborers to work the oil fields. Neither the workers or the mercenaries venture more than 10 or 12 miles beyond the Tampico city limits. Although they know not the extent of the vampires' dominance over the land, they do acknowledge that vampires and monsters plague the land. Thus, they avoid travelling through what they perceive as the desolate and demon filled hills of the Mexican gulf. The oil is transported by boat or bot along the coast or through the Gulf of Mexico, further avoiding vampire intervention. The encampment's close proximity to the waters, off the Gulf coast, also unwittingly serves to keep vampires at a healthy distance. The Tampico operation is surprisingly small, but efficient, well organized and growing.

The Tampico defenses are designed to counter both man and vampire. The most sophisticated vampire defenses and weapons are deployed as well as giant robots, borgs and power armor. Those who aren't borgs, juicers, or men of magic, pilot bots or power armor. Eight Glitter Boys, 14 Triax Ulti-Max, 12 Triax Dyna-bots and a captured CS Spider-Skull Walker are part of the Tampico defenses.

The Muluc vampires find these humans wedging themselves into even a tiny fragment of their domain, an insult. Just knowing that they are present drives the Muluc vampires crazy with frustration. However, despite several attempts to roust the humanoids, they have failed at great cost in the way of lives of both humanoid slaves and undead alike. For the moment, the Tampico elite combat veterans are too well fortified and powerful (outgun them in technology), plus their close proximity to water and their use of water makes them all the more difficult to eliminate. The Muluc vampires have decided that the Tampico operation is just an annoyance and an embarrassment, but as long as the humans dare not extend their territories or numbers, they offer little, if any, danger. However, on the other hand, the Muluc vampires have also considered an all-out siege to destroy the humanoid encampment. **Note:** The Mexico Empire fears that Tampico will attract the Coalition or other humans to their land. But they too have no current plans to eliminate Tampico. Milta and Ixzotz have no idea that Tampico is a humanoid stronghold.

Tampico Population Breakdown:
Fort Tampico: 800 laborers (1D4 levels of experience), 1150 mercenaries (1D4 level headhunters, crazies, juicers, borgs, ex-soldiers, wilderness scouts, practitioners of magic, psychics, and adventurers; 45% are D-Bees). Organized and run like a military operation. All the men receive a quarterly percentage of the profit based on rank, seniority and quotas.
Surrounding 20 mile area: About a dozen vampire-free fishing villages, with perhaps as many as 3000 people, are found on the coast. An additional half dozen fishing villages are under the control of the vampires. A dozen farm villages dot the surrounding inland area, 90% are slaves of, or allied to, the Muluc Vampire Kingdom. Contact with these communities is infrequent and very rare. Travel beyond the ruins of old Tampico is uncommon.
Area Notes: The city of Muluc, the Muluc Vampire Kingdom's capital city, is less than 80 miles (128 km) to the west. Other Muluc Kingdom communities surround Tampico. If not for the Gulf of Mexico, Tampico would be lost to humanoids.
Tampico Allies/Customers of Note: Monterrey, Ciudad Juarez, El Paso, The Pecos Empire, New Del Rio, Los Alamo (old Austin, Texas), and occasionally, Kingsdale (Missouri). The Coalition States has only recently become aware of Tampico's operations and has yet to make any conclusions about it. The CS is leaning toward considering Tampico a hostile force because it trades with enemies of the States, like the Pecos Empire and Kingsdale.

Monterrey

Far to the north, some 150 miles (276 km) south of the Rio Grande River, is the town of Monterrey. The town is a small, filthy place with dirt streets, ramshackle houses, and lawlessness. It is effectively a southern outpost used by the Pecos Empire as a rest spot, watering hole, and sanctuary by the Pecos barbarians. Thus, it is a haven for vagabonds and bandits. The only businesses of note are a blacksmith, carpenter, a hidden mechanic's garage with a secret fuel depot (can repair most common vehicles and M.D.C. body armor, recharge E-clips, etc.), and a half dozen saloons and boarding houses.

The regular town population is a meager 900 people, 50% are D-Bees, 30% are bandits who are hovercycle gang thugs and members of, or associated with, the Pecos Empire. The rest are farmers and raisers of livestock. Typically an additional 1D6×100 vagabonds, bandits, adventurers or other transients can be found in the town and in the surrounding ruins of the pre-rifts city of Monterrey. However, the town, though dilapidated, is five times bigger than its average population. These buildings are used only when the Pecos Empire comes to town. The typical bands of Pecos brigands will roll into town once a month. The average group will range around 3D4×10 members in need of water, rest and repairs. Small bands of scouts and nomadic biker gangs will contain as few as 4D6 members, and the largest groups will range around 1D6×1000. The large armed forces are an uncommon sight, and arrive about once every 12 to 18 months, rarely more often.

Monterrey is often plagued by gangs of wild vampires and solitary secondary vampire hunters. However, there is no known vampire or mind controlled slave living in the town. Whenever a vampire is discovered, the bandits or mercenaries hunt him down and destroy him. Ninety-nine percent of the people wear crosses and carry some form of vampire-killing weaponry. Crosses, wood weapons and bow weapons are the most common. Only the Pecos thugs and travelers have the more sophisticated anti-vampire weapons.

New Del Rio

New Del Rio is located on the banks of the Rio Grande near the ruins of the pre-rifts city. It is located in the middle of nowhere in the old American state of Texas. About 400 miles (643 km) to the northeast is the powerful, human kingdom of Los Alamo. New Del Rio is a poverty stricken and vampire-ridden kingdom of about 50,000 humanoids (50% are D-Bees) ruled by a tyrannical and decadent family. In recent years it has become a haven for outlaws and has established strong trade with the Pecos Empire. The kingdom is avoided by most travelers, and the city itself is filthier and more dangerous than Juarez. Gangs and thugs control the streets. Except for the very few elite rich and powerful, the level of technology is poor, equal to about the turn of the 20th century. Only 30% of the buildings have electricity and 60% have working indoor plumbing. 90% of the people are illiterate farmers or laborers on cattle ranches owned by the ruling family. There are few merchants or hotels, and those that do exist are rat-traps with poor quality merchandise.

Wild vampires terrorize and feed on the inhabitants in the outskirts of town or farmers away from the city, but they are so bold that roving gangs sometimes run through the streets. There are also approximately a hundred secondary vampires that have lairs within the city itself.

Los Alamo

Is a modern, high-tech kingdom that keeps to itself. It is completely self-sufficient, vampire free, and considered an oasis in the middle of the parched Texas plains. However, the kingdom's policy of isolationism means that it rarely opens its gates to travelers and avoids contact with the outside world, including the CS and the Pecos Empire.

Ciudad Victoria

The city of Victoria harbors nearly 14,000 inhabitants, 60% of which are human. The city is sprawled along the banks of the Rio Bravo River and in the river itself. Many are the houseboats and floating platforms of the city dwellers, much like the junks of Hong Kong. Over 30% of the overall population lives on the water. Fishing, farming and raising livestock are the primary means of self-support. The technology level is low, about equal to the turn of the 20th century, although the occasional hover vehicle and giant robot is evident. There is an open market (most foods and basic goods), five carpenters, boat builders, saloons, two dance halls, a city square and a handful of other merchants that sell goods and services for the common, daily needs of the city's inhabitants. Travelers are a rarity.

The use of water has kept the trouble with vampires to a minimum. Irrigation ditches, canals, and sprinkler systems are integrated throughout the city complex. Those who live farthest inland are in the greatest danger, but a night militia patrols the streets and outer areas. Among the militia are 50 young men trained by Reid's Rangers, and Grizzly Carter, himself, has visited the city in just the last year. No vampires are known to inhabit the city, but vampires are known to find shelter among the neighboring ruins of the pre-rifts city of Ciudad Victoria.

Travelling beyond the threshold of Humankind

One must realize that beyond the tentative borders of the Coalition and the Midwestern strip of human civilization, the remainders of the old American and Canadian Empires are wilderness. Within that wilderness are thousands of tiny villages, towns, cities and kingdoms, each with its own ruler, laws, and prejudices. The laws of the land are the laws enforced by the landholder(s). The laws may be fair and just, or cruel and inhuman, or virtually nonexistent.

As one travels farther away from the borders of human jurisdiction, the tolerance, and presence, for non-humans/D-Bees, non-Coalition outlooks toward life, and the proliferation of magic increases dramatically. Between one town and another there are often hundreds of miles of hostile wilderness. And civilization may be little more than a public well, a dirt road, church and a dozen farm families. The typical village will range from two to a hundred families, a town 50 to 500 families, and a city may have a population of 5000 to 50,000. However, west of the Mississippi River, the size of the rural communities is typically half, and their numbers few and far between, except for clusters of communities at locations like El Paso and Ciudad Juarez.

In some of the wilderness communities, it is humans who are the monsters to be feared and loathed, especially in remote areas of the far west and Canadian north country. In others, humans and D-Bees live side by side as brothers (true decadence in the eyes of the Coalition). Strangers are often viewed with suspicion and fear. And the people give them a wide berth. This is especially true if south of the old American border where white people, humans, bots, borgs, and travelers of any kind are a rarity in the vampire and demon-ridden lands. Here, in the old Mexican Empire, supernatural and monstrous creatures dominate the land and humans are either slaves, playthings, or food.

El Paso

Estimated Population: 29,000
Racial Breakdown: 45% Humans (5% psionic, 10% augmented)
  26% D-Bees
  24% Mutant animals (65% are dogs)
  5% Others (borgs, bots, dragons, etc)
Average Transient Population: 6000 additional people.
Tech Level: High/Modern and Magic
Surrounding Communities (100 mile radius): 8,000 (50% human, mostly farmers or sheep and cattle herders, low tech level).

El Paso is generally considered the last vestige of civilization in the American southwest. To the north are the badlands of New Mexico and Colorado, followed by the northern forest wilderness that starts in Wyoming and extends deep into Canada. This is hostile territory, with few people of any origin. The Calgary, Alberta area thrives with D-Bees, monsters and insane wizards. West of El Paso are the prairies and deserts of Arizona, Utah, and Nevada, and the wastelands and wildernesses of California. South of the Rio Grande technology has been lost. The old Mexican Empire is reduced to wide open steppes, populated by tiny communities of peasant farmers, sheepherders, vampires and supernatural terrors. The new Juarez City is about 70 miles (112 km) directly south of El Paso, across the Rio Grande. It is easily twice the size of El Paso, but it is not considered a place for civilized people.

El Paso is a fairly large city compared to what's found around it. Other than Ciudad Juarez and Lone Star Coalition outposts, there are no cities for 500 miles around, and only a handful of small villages and the occasional one-horse town. Visitors from the Coalition megalopolises of the east may find El Paso to be comparatively tiny, primitive and dirty, similar to some of the better Burbs, but compared to Ciudad Juarez, and most other wilderness communities, it is a sparkling clean paradise.

The streets are wide to accommodate giant robot vehicles, trucks and all-terrain vehicles. Half of the streets are paved, a quarter are covered with gravel and only the smallest or newest streets are still dirt roads. The city is constantly alive, with travellers arriving and departing daily. *Merchant Avenue* is the commercial center of town and full of stores, shops, restaurants and entertainment. People, both travellers and residents alike line the streets. Street bazaars and festivals are frequent events.

As the last great trade center in the west, El Paso is on the list of places to go for most western travellers. It is a place to replenish supplies, buy new clothes, repair robots and vehicles, sell artifacts, furs, and other goods, get medical attention, catchup on the latest rumors and news, and just plain relax. El Paso is surprisingly well policed, truly free of vampires (well, 95% of the time; remember, people are coming and going all of the time), and an overall safe haven for humans and D-Bees alike. All the CS has is a tiny diplomatic embassy on the outskirts of the city, the Coalition has no influence over the city. The occasional CS military personnel seen on the streets are there, like all visitors, to relax or replenish supplies (and to do a little spying). The CS troops and diplomatic ambassadors do not enjoy special treatment of any kind, and are often the butt of practical jokes, name calling and cheerful ridicule.

The Police

The El Paso police are an efficient, well trained, and mostly honest group of peace keepers, half of whom are composed of equal parts ex-headhunters, ex-wilderness scouts, ex-Coalition soldiers, and borgs. The mix of humans to D-Bees is about 60/40; all get along well. The average cop is the equivalent of a 1D4+2 level soldier or headhunter, but wise to the ways of the streets (special bonus of +15% to streetwise skill; all have streetwise) and experienced vampire hunters. They are surprisingly tolerant of roughhousing by rough and tumble wilderness folk and non-human visitors. Most of the police will work to break up and stop a brawl or rowdiness without drawing blood or imprisoning the offenders. They understand the trials of wilderness life and the need to let out a little steam, so they are willing to cut the noisiest and most belligerent drunk a bit of slack. However, only the foolish take this act of kindness as an indication that the El Paso police are weak-kneed sissies. The cops are tough, canny, alert and experienced in all types of combat. Furthermore, while they are willing to dismiss disorderly conduct, drunks and roughnecks they are diligent in crushing crime and vampirism. They show no sympathy to thieves, con-artists, molesters, bullies, or murderers, and are twice as tough if the victims of these criminals are city residents or the residents of some of the surrounding villages. **Note: The police force also serves as the militia/defenders of the city.**

Police Statistical Data:

Average level of experience: Fourth.

Standard Body Armor: Street Patrols are in bright white Bushman body armor, 60 M.D.C., while perimeter patrols wear tan Bushman armor; both have the word "Police" and an I.D. number emblazoned on the armor and uniforms. Undercover police may wear street clothes and disguises. Short-range radio built into the armor and in cars.

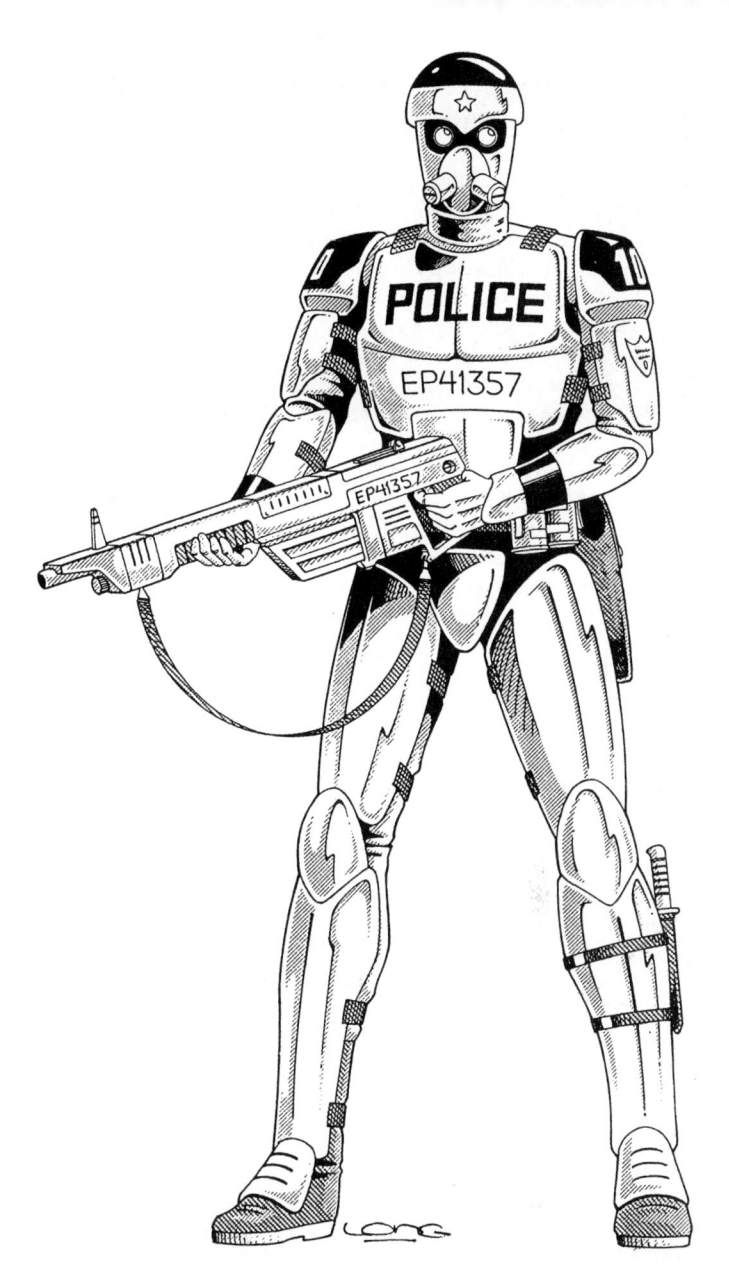

Standard Weapons: All police are issued a neural-mace, vibro-knife, 9 mm automatic pistol (13 shot clip, 2D6 S.D.C. damage, normal bullets, and clips of silver bullets are provided), a silver cross, pocket mirror, Wilk's 320 laser pistol, and a TX-30 Triax ion pulse rifle. A dozen wooden stakes, mallet, extra clips of silver bullets, water pistol and water cannon are also standard issue, but usually kept in the trunk of their hovercar.

Unit Breakdown:

1. **800 police patrol** the city streets on foot and in squad cars (hover and land rovers).
2. **200 hovercycle & motorcycle police.** Fast moving one man units, often operate in pairs. The motorcycles and hovercycles are armed with a forward laser and mini-missile launchers.
3. **50 "Skyjockey's," police** that monitor the city from the air in Flying Titan power armor. This squad also has a dozen Sky King hovercraft.
4. **50 Desert Dogs:** 38 mutant animals and 12 borgs (dispatched in pairs) patrol the villages and 100 miles of land around El Paso.
5. **Mechanized Division** (98 plus 49 labor bots): 20 full conversion borgs, 30 partial reconstruction borgs (use jet packs or police hovercycles), 10 Flying Titans, 8 NG Samsons, 4 Triax X-10 Predator power armor, 2 Triax X-1000 Ulti-Max power armor, 2 Glitter Boys, 2 Titan Reconnaissance bots, 4 TR-001 Titan combat bots, 6 TR-002 light combat bots, 6 NG-7 Hunter Mobile Gun bots, and 4 NG-M56 Multi-Bots. The city also has at its disposal 20 NG-W9

light labor bots, 20 NG-W10 heavy labor bots and 9 NG-V10 robot labor vehicles (see **Rifts Sourcebook #1** for new bots).

6. **Psi-Division:** All are 4th level unless otherwise noted. 20 detectives with major psionics (otherwise city rat O.C.C.), 12 mutant dogs (four are 6th level), four psi-stalkers, six operators (all 6th level), three bursters, two mystics (both third level), five mind melters, one cyber-knight (Sir Henry Curry, Psi-Division's second in command, 6th level), and Ramone Portillo, an 8th level Mind Melter, is the head of the division. Often work undercover.

7. **Magic Squad (16):** An elite squad of police that investigate and protect against supernatural and magic problems. Luis Santeogo, an 11th level ley line walker, heads the squad. Other members include, second in command, Anton Gruber, a sixth level shifter, a pair of seventh level mystics, a pair of 5th level techno-wizards and a pair of fourth level ley line walkers, along with eight seventh level police officers (ex-soldiers, half have minor psionics) versed in lore and experienced in handling vampires and other supernatural menaces. Often work undercover; half are D-Bees.

El Paso Gang Problems

El Paso does have one perennial problem that the police and city administrators have not been able to solve, gangs! There are four major gangs operating in El Paso; the K-9s, the Wild Cats, the Trogs, and the Hammer. With the exception of the militant, human supremacists that compose the Hammer, the majority of the gangs consist of uneducated and unskilled mutant animals and D-Bees. El Paso's close proximity to the Coalition State of Lone Star and openness to all life forms means the city finds itself the home of runaway dog boy soldiers and mutant animal refugees fleeing Lone Star. Not only do intelligent, mutant dogs find their way to the city, but felines and other, apparently experimental, mutant animals, including bears, horses, cattle, apes, and rodents. Fortunately, the CS's creation of mutant animals is less prodigious than its bots and borgs.

The K-9s

The K-9s, as one might expect from the name, are renegade, mutant dogs that have fled the Coalition's Dog Boy troops or from Lone Star's laboratories. The gang is predominately mutant dogs, but any mutant animal, except felines and birds, are permitted to join the gang. However, non-canines can never attain the highest positions within the gang.

The K-9s

Breakdown: 390 total members: 60% dog, 20% rodent, 10% cattle, 10% other (including five bears, four badgers, and a pronghorn antelope).

Common Gang Member Alignments: Anarchist, Unprincipled, Aberrant and Miscreant.

Colors: Dark blue leather jackets, clothing and armor decorated with leather straps and metal studs. The gang insignia is a howling wolf's head. It is usually worn as a large patch on the back of jackets and armor or a smaller patch worn on the front of T-shirts and jackets over the left breast.

Standard Vampire Weapons: These items vary widely among the members of the K-9s gang ranging from a handful of wooden stakes and silver cross, to crossbow, water weapons and silver bullets (revolvers and automatic weapons are common).

Mega-damage Weapons: Can be anything, but the K-9s' favor vibro-blades, vibro-claws, and pulse rifles.

Body Armor: The Gladiator, Crusader, Juicer and Coalition Dead Boy armor are the most common among the K-9s, but are usually accessorized with leather straps and metal studs.

Bionics and Cybernetics: Only 10% of the K-9s have 1D6 cybernetic implants.

The Gang Leaders: "The " leader of the K-9s is a mean, old German Shepherd and CS veteran (9th level Dog Pack R.C.C.) by the name of Zeus. A long battle scar is etched deep across one side of his face and over a blind eye. Zeus hates the CS for treating Dog Soldiers like worthless cannon fodder and caused him to desert six years ago. He is bitter, cranky, intolerant and tough as nails. He sees himself as a father figure to other mutant canines and tries to help the misguided and homeless by giving them a home in his gang. Unfortunately, Zeus does not live by any law other than his own (aberrant evil alignment; has his own code, but too bitter, violent and spiteful to do anything but evil). Body armor is a suit of heavy CS Dead Boy armor. Weapons include a C-18 laser pistol, C-14 Fire Breather rifle, a C-27 heavy plasma rifle, vibro-claws, sub-machinegun with silver bullets, water pistol, wood cross, and stakes. Illiterate, but excellent warrior and strategist.

Second in command is a young, strong, wolf named Eric. He is a 5th level Dog Pack O.C.C. soldier too. Zeus and he are like father and son. Alignment: Aberrant.

Sigmund, a lakeland terrier, is a gang member of high standing and close to the two leaders. His old master, a CS scientist, educated him in ways deemed as inappropriate by the Coalition. His master was killed while resisting arrest for treason (because he educated a dog in human knowledge) and Sigmund escaped. He is not a fighter but more of a City Rat O.C.C. (6th level). Skills include: Literacy in American, speaks American 98%, Techno-can, Spanish and Gobblely, computer operation, program computer, computer hacking, photography, pilot hovercraft, cook, dance, play the piano, pick locks, pick pockets, streetwise, and prowl. NO combat training; two attacks per melee. Alignment: Unprincipled.

There are also dozens of leaders of smaller segments of the K-9s that are all sorts of breeds, from fox and coyote to terriers and bulldogs.

Gang & Criminal Activity: Spend most of their time hanging out and bullying mutant felines, birds, supernatural creatures and rival gang members. Known for drunkenness, brawls, and petty crimes like vandalism, theft, breaking and entry, and assault. Occasionally sell their services as mercenaries, scouts and thugs for merchants, travellers and fellow criminals. Seldom molest humans (a result of the dogs bond with humans). The bloodiest confrontations are with mutant cats, alien looking D-Bees, the Coalition, vampires and monsters. One of the K-9s' favorite pastimes is hunting down "vamps" and "decap 'em," meaning finding vampires and destroying them. Their next favorite pastime is rumbles with the Wild Cats and gangs from Ciudad Juarez.

Note: Unless you're a feline, the K-9s will always protect humans and D-Bees alike from the Coalition and vampires. For this reason they are the least pestered by the police.

The Wild Cats

The Wild Cats gang is another gang of mutant animals that has popped up four years ago. For the last five years, the scientists at Lone Star have been trying to develop a mutant soldier that is a silent, stealthy hunter. To this end, a variety of felines have been used as test subjects. Unfortunately, the feline predator is instinctively a solitary hunter and does not function well within a large group nor exhibit the loyalty of the dog soldiers. This has made the felines unpredictable and dangerous.

Several such mutant felines have made their home in El Paso. They have created the gang of mutants and D-Bees known as the Wild Cats. Unlike the K-9s, whose members are predominantly of canine origin, only the leaders and lieutenants of the Wild Cat gang are actually mutant cats. The other gang members are humans and D-Bees.

The Wild Cats

Breakdown: 260 total members: 5% feline, 30% human, 35% D-Bee, 10% mutant rodents, 10% mutant cattle, 10% other mutants (including psychics).

Common Gang Member Alignments: Diabolic, Miscreant and Anarchist.

Colors: Tan leather jackets, jump suits, clothing, and armor. The gang insignia is a snarling cougar's head. It is usually worn as a large patch on the back of jackets and armor or a smaller patch worn on the front of T-shirts and jackets.

Standard Vampire Weapons: These items typically include wooden stakes and mallet, silver cross, crossbow, water weapons and silver bullets (revolvers and automatic weapons are common).

Mega-damage Weapons: Can be anything, but the Wild Cats' favorites are vibro-claws and vibro-swords, crossbows, spears, and precision laser pistols and rifles.

Body Armor: The Urban Warrior, Explorer, and Huntsman armor are the most common among the Wild Cats.

Bionics and Cybernetics: 20% of the Wild Cats members have 1D6 cybernetic implants or 1D4+1 bionic implants, weapons or limbs.

The Gang Leaders: The ultimate leader of the Wild Cats is Donna the Dark Kitten (a sort of pun name that has stuck with her), a mutant black panther. She is very intelligent (I.Q. 22), beautiful (P.B. 23), savage and ruthless (miscreant alignment). She is quickly developing a strong criminal organization that has already developed relations with the Black Market. Most of her lieutenants are fellow mutant felines and include a female lynx, four cougars/mountain lions (both females), three tigers (one female), one African lion, and five domestic cats (two are female). One D-Bee and two humans have risen to the rank of lieutenant and are considered to be quite fortunate.

Note: All of the Dark Kitten's chief henchmen are clever and capable. They are typically mutant Dog Pack type R.C.C.s trained in military combat or espionage, or are effectively the City Rat O.C.C. with an emphasis on rogue skills and stealing.

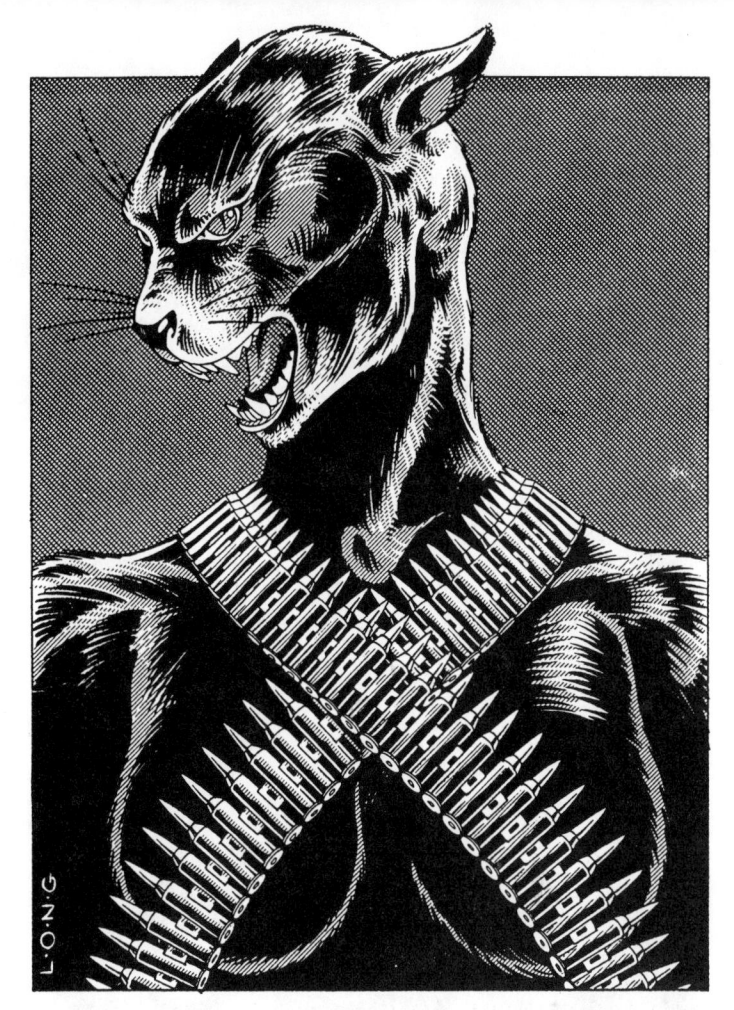

Gang & Criminal Activity: The Wild Cats are more organized and involved in serious criminal activities than any of the other gangs. They are known for violent brawls, gang wars, robbery, theft, breaking and entry, extortion, assault, assassination and murder. They are very territorial (especially the mutant cats) and dominate one specific section of town, which is consider Wild Cat territory. Of course they conduct their criminal activities throughout the city, but that one portion is considered their home/sanctum/lair. The Wild Cats have no loyalty to anybody except to their gang, and have sold their services to the Coalition, the Black Market, unscrupulous merchants, and other criminals. The bloodiest confrontations are with the K-9s, the Hammer and gangs from Ciudad Juarez.

Note: Nobody is safe from the Wild Cats. They are aggressive, arrogant and cruel. The police suspect the gang of many crimes but have insufficient evidence to prove it. Even when a perpetrator is known to be a member of the Wild Cats, it is virtually impossible to find him if he is given protection in Wild Cat territory. The citizens of El Paso dislike and fear this gang more than any other

Typical Mutant Cats

Domestic Cats, Lynx & Bobcat: Roll 3D6 for each as usual, but add +2 M.E. and +3 P.P.; special bonus of +1 on initiative. Skill bonuses: +5% to climb, +5% to swim, +10% land navigation, +10% prowl.

Cougar/Mountain Lion: Roll 3D6 for each as usual, but add +3 P.P. and +2 to spd; special bonus of +1 on initiative. Skill bonuses: +10% to climb, +10% to swim, +5% to prowl, +10% land navigation, +10% to all track skills.

Tiger: Roll 3D6 for each as usual, but add +4 P.S., +6 P.P., +2 P.E.; special bonus of +3 on initiative. Skill bonuses: +20% to swim, +10% to prowl, and +5% to tracking skills.

African Lion, Leopard & Jaguar: Roll 3D6 for each as usual, but add +4 P.S., +6 P.P., and +2 to the P.E.; special bonus of +2 on initiative. Skill bonuses: +10% to climb, +10% to swim, +10% to all track skills.

Note: All skill bonuses are in addition to R.C.C. skill bonuses.
Natural Abilities: Base swim ability is 50%, climbing 40% and track animals 20%; all three abilities can be selected as skills instead and improve as the characters increase in experience. Keen hearing, good sense of smell, sharp vision, and nightvision (120 feet/36.5 m).
Coalition Training: Either Soldier, in which case skills and weapons are the same as the Dog Pack R.C.C., or as an espionage agent.
CS Espionage Training for Mutant Cats: R.C.C. skills tend to focus on hunting and assassination. Intelligence, detect ambush, pick locks, pick pockets, sniper, tracking, and wilderness survival (all get a +10% bonus), plus land navigation (+10%), track animals (+10%), prowl (+10%), radio: basic (+10%), speak American (+15%), pilot hovercraft (+5%), hand to hand: assassin, and select three physical and four W.P. skills. Two additional skills can be selected at levels one, four, eight, eleven and fourteen. Available skill categories are limited to communications, domestic, electronic: basic, espionage (+5%), medical: first aid or holistic, physical, pilot (conventional type vehicles, not bots), rogue (excluding computer hacking), technical, W.P. and wilderness (+10%)

Ogre and Orc members of the El Paso Trog Gang.

The Trogs

The Trog gang recruits non-humans, mostly poor and uneducated D-Bees and mutants, but also has a small number of humans. The humans are completely normal, although usually big, muscular, not too bright and uneducated. The rest of the gang consists of the deformed, scarred, retarded, psionic, and alien in appearance or ability (super powers from **Heroes Unlimited,** etc.). The Trogs are the oldest gang in the city, but the mortality rate is high from frequent gang wars, and some of the other gangs have more enticing recruitment. This is really a gang for macho punks looking to prove how tough they are with their fists and a gun. Its members are mostly thugs, bullies, petty crooks and the downtrodden. Most are bitter and resentful of those who are handsomer, more popular, smarter and wealthier than they, and it is these people who are the targets of most of the Trogs' crimes.

The Trogs
Breakdown: 272 total members: 50% D-Bees, 20% mutants, 10% psychics, 20% humans (often deformed or retarded, and always uneducated).
Common Gang Member Alignments: Anarchist and Miscreant.
Colors: Black leather jackets, clothing and armor decorated with chains and large metal spikes. The gang insignia is a spiked ball and chain. It is usually worn as a large patch on the back of jackets and armor. The majority of the gang members also have the insignia tattooed on their biceps, and many wear a ball and chain attached along their shoulders or waists, with the spiked ball dangling down.
Standard Vampire Weapons: These items vary among the members of the Trogs gang but typically include a giant, silver or wood spiked clubs or, silver-plated ball and chain, silver-plated throwing spikes (1D4 normal S.D.C damage, 2D4 to vampires), wooden stakes, wood crucifix, spears and crossbow (the Trogs prefer hand to hand combat). **Note:** All members of the Trogs must learn W.P. Chain, W.P. Blunt, and W.P. Targeting (for throwing spikes, throwing knives, spears and crossbows).
Mega-damage Weapons: Can be anything, but the Trogs' favorites are the neural mace, vibro-knife, grenade launchers, plasma and pulse rifles.
Body Armor: The Gladiator, Coalition and Juicer body armor, usually accessorized with chains and metal spikes.
Bionics and Cybernetics: Only 15% of the Trogs have 1D4+1 cybernetic or bionic implants, weapons or limbs.
The Gang Leaders: The "Octopus" is the leader of the Trogs. He is a four-armed giant, 13 ft tall, usually clad in Gladiator body armor (120 M.D., giant size). The giant is of a race known as Rahu-men, from the world of Palladium (fantasy RPG). He is surprisingly intelligent considering the rest of his gang (I.Q. 17), a phenomenal fighter (eight attacks per melee, expert hand to hand, 23 P.P., knows all ancient type W.P.s at 8th level proficiency) and a major psionic (resist fatigue, resist hunger, resist thirst, mind block, object read, presence sense, sense magic, see aura, and sixth sense).

The second in command is a human mutant known as Mister Green (6th level City Rat O.C.C., I.Q. 11, P.P. 20). He is a 6 foot, 9 inches tall body builder and street boxer known for his muscle, green skin and unnatural super powers. Powers modified from Heroes Unlimited: 1. Bend light enables him to deflect/parry laser beams (same as normal parry), to see the infrared and ultraviolet spectrum of light (100 ft/30.5 range), and to fire a harmless beam of colored light (any color) 100 feet (30.5 m). 2. Energy expulsion (light): Fires a laser beam from his fingertips. 1D6×10 S.D.C. damage or 1D4 M.D. damage. Can also radiate light like a human light bulb (equal to 300 watt bulb, will not harm vampires). 3. Impervious to fire and heat, including magic fires. 4. Turn self invisible at will, unlimited duration, no limit to the number of times he can turn invisible. Can still be detected by heat and motion sensors. Also provides a natural M.D. of 3 (better than nothing).

There are also dozens of secondary group leaders. All are typically city rats, wilderness scouts, vagabonds or psychics. The typical gang member is usually a vagabond or city rat.
Gang & Criminal Activity: Spend most of their time hanging out and bullying handsome, wealthy people and rival gang members. They are known for rowdy drunkenness, violent brawls, vandalism, vehicle theft, muggings, kidnapping, assault, and murder. Occasionally, they sell their services as mercenaries, scouts and thugs to merchants,

travellers and fellow criminals. The bloodiest confrontations are with the Hammer gang, the Coalition and vampires (they see fighting vampires as macho). Mostly they like to fight.

The Hammer (humans)

The Hammer is a gang of fascist human supremacists and a constant source of turmoil in the city. They continually wage attacks against the other gangs, assault and plunder non-human citizens and are involved in a variety of criminal pursuits.

Rumors suggest that the Hammer is secretly supported by the Coalition States (Lone Star and/or Chi-Town). The gang is unusually well equipped and seems to have vast resources, even though they are not as self-sufficient as their rivals. It is unlikely that their meager energies in crime could support them, as the members of the Hammer expend most of their energy harassing and terrorizing non-humans. But there is no proof that they are supported by the CS.

The Hammer
Breakdown: 200 total members: 80% humans, 10% human psychics, 10% bionically augmented humans (borgs).
Common Gang Member Alignments: Anarchist, Miscreant, and Diabolic.
Colors: Khaki/tan color leather jackets, clothing and armor. Many wear buckskin style, soft leather outfits. The gang insignia is a hammer. It is usually worn as a patch on the back of jackets and armor and/or on the shoulder of jackets and clothing.
Standard Vampire Weapons: These items vary among the members of the gang, but typically include 9 mm sub-machineguns with silver bullets, water cannons and pistols, wooden stakes, wood crucifix, and crossbow. **Note: All members of the Hammer learn W.P. Sub-machinegun and Energy Rifle.**
Mega-damage Weapons: Can be anything, but the Hammer's favorites are the ion pistol, particle and pulse rifles. 10% (the elite squad) own and operate power armor, including three SAMAS. Well-equipped with energy weapons (40% CS) and ammunition.
Body Armor: The Coalition, Bushman and Explorer armor.
Bionics and Cybernetics: Only 30% of the Hammer have 1D4+2 cybernetic implants or 1D4+1 bionic implants, weapons or limbs.
The Gang Leaders: The leader, Captain Mark Riddley, is a mercenary who served eight years in the CS armed forces as a Military Specialist (8th level). He allegedly quit the army to become a mercenary and finally settled down in El Paso. The captain and his elite squad often disappear, presumably on secret missions or mercenary work. Many believe he and his closest men are Coalition spies.

The 20 elite members of the Hammer include 10 ex-Coalition soldiers all of whom once served under Riddley, four full conversion borgs, two psi-stalkers and three SAMAS pilots and a burster; all are 6th level.

There are also dozens of secondary group leaders. All are typically city rats, wilderness scouts, vagabonds or psychics. The typical gang member is usually a vagabond or city rat.
Gang & Criminal Activity: Actively harass, beat up, molest, torture, vandalize D-Bees and mutants. They are known for violent brawls and anti-D-Bee demonstrations, vandalism, robbery, muggings, kidnaping, assault, terrorism, assassination and murder all directed at non-humans, mutants and D-Bee sympathizers. They frequently sell their services as mercenaries, scouts, spies and thugs to merchants, travelers, the Coalition, and fellow criminals. The bloodiest confrontations are with the D-Bees, the Trog gang and the Juarez gangs the Subs and Psykes.

King Wyatt Halloway

King Halloway is an adventurous cattleman who struck it rich in El Paso. He owns over a million acres of land and two silver mines. His ranch-estate is located about 80 miles northwest of El Paso (which he also effectively owns). El Paso is built on his land, constructed with his money and labor, and the big arena and most of the saloons, gambling halls, larger merchant establishments and hotels are owned by him (61% of the city is King Halloway's).

Wyatt Halloway is a shallow, insensitive person who thinks only of becoming more powerful and wealthier; the motivation for everything he does is the attainment of one or the other. In the midwestern cities, Halloway was nothing but an ornery, two-bit punk, but out in the wild west he has become a king. He is infamous for doing everything in a big way, with a lot of pomp and fanfare. He is celebrated for bringing civilization to the wilderness and renowned for his generosity (when he decides to be generous). King Halloway is also infamous for his mean temper, spiteful and cruel nature and terrible acts of revenge. The saying in El Paso is, "You're better off taking your chances with the vampires than with Wyatt Halloway if he's looking to get you," and many have done just that. One becomes an enemy of King Wyatt Halloway by humiliating him (privately or publicly), accusing him of wrong doing, insulting him or attacking him in any way (business, reputation, property, etc.).

Halloway has surrounded himself with rough and tumble mercenaries, headhunters, and low-life scum as employees on his ranch. They serve as ranch hands, cowboys/wranglers, and members of Halloway's private army. They are all surprisingly loyal and subservient to their boss, because they are paid big money, enjoy their work, and see Halloway as a growing power in the west. It is these scoundrels who are sent out to extract revenge on those who have offended King Halloway. They will rustle cattle, destroy property, beat, murder or do anything else Halloway asks of them. **Halloway's troops** consist of approximately 800 headhunters (25% have been given Triax X-10 Predator power armor, all 1D4 level), 300 wilderness scouts (1D4+1 levels), 250 mutant canines (average 2nd level) 200 borgs (40% are full conversions; 1D4+2 levels), 120 juicers (average 3rd level), 75 crazies (average 3rd level), and a dozen practitioners of magic. In addition to the armored division which consists of six Glitter Boys, 24 Titan TR-001, 24 Titan

TR-002, 12 TR-003, 6 NG-V7 Hunter Mobile Guns, and 4 X-500 Forager Battlebots. A dozen Triax Dyna-Bots also patrol his estate.

Halloway sees himself as the supreme being in this part of the country. He resents the Coalition's presence and sees them as a threat to his domain. His dealings with them are always on his terms and in his favor, like selling the CS cattle and silver at inflated prices (the CS is his biggest buyer). Furthermore, he is diplomatically coy and uncooperative, but in a friendly and careful way. He may allow the CS a diplomatic embassy in El Paso, but it is in the worst location in town. Likewise, the people and his own men treat the CS soldiers and dignitaries poorly, except when it involves matters that might benefit Halloway or his town. He sees the Coalition as a potentially useful but undesirable ally, so he always holds his cards close to his chest when dealing with them.

King Wyatt Halloway

Alignment: Miscreant
Hit Points: 39, **S.D.C.:** 30,
M.D.C.: Body Armor
Weight: 165 lbs, **Height:** 5 ft, 11 inches,
Age: 41, **P.P.E.:** 9, **I.S.P.:** None.
Attributes: I.Q.: 12, M.A.: 11, M.E.: 25, P.S.: 17, P.P.: 14, P.E.: 15 , P.B.: 12, Spd: 11
Disposition: Supremely arrogant, condescending, callous, selfish, easily angered. Has great personal drive, almost an obsession to become rich and powerful. Yet, insecure and sees even innocent remarks and incidents as inflammatory or deliberately demeaning. Those who embarrass him, or are demeaning or against him are "dealt with, " themselves embarrassed, beaten, molested or hurt in some way; Halloway is extremely petty and vindictive.
Experience Level: 8th level vagabond who turned to business.
Magic Knowledge: None
Psionic Powers: None
Combat Skills: Hand to hand: basic.
Attacks Per Melee: Three (3)
Bonuses: +1 to strike, +2 to parry, +2 to dodge, +2 to roll with impact, +2 to pull punch, +5 to save vs psionics.
Weapon Proficiencies: W.P. Rifle, W.P. Energy Weapon, W.P. Energy Rifle, W.P. Blunt.
Weapons: Favorite weapon is the NG-P7 particle beam rifle, NG-Super pistol and bolt action rifle for hunting.
Body Armor: Bushman or Titan power armor.
Bionics & Cybernetics: Gyro-compass.
Money: Has over 250 million universal credits, liquid and at his disposal. The silver mines are estimated to be worth 200 million annually and the cattle are worth another 100 million annually. Non-liquid properties, business assets and holdings are estimated at close to a billion dollars.
Skills of Note: Streetwise, palming, computer operation, literate in American, speaks American and Spanish, math: basic, horsemanship, land navigation, hunting, skin animal hides, radio: basic.
Note: Wyatt Halloway's family also lives on the ranch. They include his two teenage sons, one 13 year old daughter (wife was killed by vampires five years ago), his worthless, alcoholic brother Bryannt (5th level city rat), Byrannt's equally worthless sons (4; 16, 17, 19 and 20 years old, first level cowboys, snotty, arrogant, miscreants), Uncle Willy (a sweet guy, 6th level body fixer), Aunt Ester (Willy's sweeter wife), and cousins Thelma and Candice (both are babes and smart too).

El Paso City Highlights

Note: El Paso has two prosperous silver mines and a huge cattle industry, consequently, the prices of beef, cattle, silver and silver products (jewelry, anti-vampire items, etc.) are about 40% less than the standard costs elsewhere.

The El Paso Magic Shop

The shop is large and filled with shelves of books, jars, vials and boxes. The aisles are wide and clean and smell of incense. Zalfeel, the owner, is a gnarled, little D-Bee who stands 3 and a half feet tall. He looks to be 80 years old but nobody knows. Zalfeel claims, with a wink and a nod, to be 20. He is disarmingly cheerful and pleasant, and extremely observant (in a Sherlock Holmes kind of way). He dresses like a cowboy and is in love with the pre-rifts American Old West. In fact, he has nearly 100 different pre-rifts western novels and history books about the west for sale in his store (2000 credits each). **Zalfeel:** An alchemist (NPC) with a magic skill equal to a 10th level techno-wizard. Anarchist alignment, 67 hit points, 20 S.D.C., I.Q. 22, M.A. 21, M.E. 15, P.P. 17, P.B. 8, all others average. Has a coyote as his animal familiar.

Zalfeel is assisted by two 4th level techno-wizards, a 4th level ley line walker, three floopers and 12 clerks, all of whom are literate in American and know basic math (taught by Zalfeel). All are polite and helpful. The floopers are usually sent to deal with people who look to be more like curious travelers than paying customers.

The store sells a variety of items, including pre-rifts artifacts (Pepsi cans, books, video discs, and knicknacks), some indian artifacts (statues, arrowheads, pottery), fine condition and authentic old west six-shooters, as well as modern replicas, and new books, including all of Erin Tarn's. There are city maps of El Paso, Ciudad Juazez, and Lone Star City. Video and music discs, herbs, holistic medicine herbs and poisons, silver bullets for most common weapon calibers, and silver-plated knives, swords and arrowheads. Every techno-wizard (TW) type of vampire weapon is also available along with TW converted weapons, TW flaming sword, TW lightning rod, TK-Flyers, etc.

Magic items include amulets of protection against the supernatural, protection against sickness, protection against insanity, see the invisible (costs 150,000 credits) and turn the undead (most cost around 60,000 credits each). **Scrolls** are usually limited to first, second, and third level, at a cost of 1000 credits per spell level and another 1000 credits per level of strength. Typical spell strength and duration is equal to a fifth level wizard. Spells fourth level and higher cost two or three times more and many spells are not available (**Note:** Zalfeel's and/or the GM's discretion).

Magic services include the placement of wards on an item (8000 to 15,000 credits per ward), casting immediate spells on a person or items, such as breathe without air, float in air, fly, fly as an eagle, heal wounds, etc., (2000 credits per level of the spell being cast, plus as much as 100% may be charged as a difficulty fee; not all spells are available; remember, that's a 10th level spell if cast by Zalfeel) and the removal of curses (50,000 to 100,000 credits depending on the curse, no guarantees of success).

Information is also available. But nothing is overtly dangerous, secret or valuable. The floopers and salesclerks are full of miscellaneous information about El Paso, Juarez, the gangs, and rumors around town. There is no need to pay for the information, just ask and be friendly. Everybody is pretty outspoken about the Coalition (don't like 'em much) but are careful not to say to much and nothing derogatory about Wyatt Halloway or his family.

The Traveler's Inn House

A large, popular hotel with 500 rooms. The rooms are austere, but provide ample space, closet, desk, comfortable bed, and a private bathroom. Average cost is 75 credits a night. Fancier rooms cost 150. Security is fair; the rooms clean. The owners are a husband and wife and their large family of sisters, brothers, uncles and cousins run every aspect of the hotel. The first floor also offers a meeting lounge, saloon (seats about 60 patrons, 5 credits a drink), barbershop (15 credits a haircut, no fancy styles), tobacco shop and a small kitchen that can provide soups, sandwiches, salads, and breakfast at about 15 credits per meal.

Note: There are numerous other hotels, motels, boarding houses and flophouses in El Paso. The filthiest and cheapest cost 20 to 40 credits a night and are in gang territories or bad neighborhoods. The best cost 200 to 400 credits a night and are in the nicest neighborhoods (owned by the Halloway family).

The Open Market

A huge city square, or fairgrounds, where over 200 merchants, farmers and vendors of all kinds, come to sell their wares. Merchants include sellers of spices, herbs, tobacco, corn and vegetables, flour and grains, fruit, fresh meats, smoked and salted meats, jerked beef, poultry, fish, candy, flowers, hats, ponchos, baggy cotton shirts and pants, sandals, rope, sacks, wooden stakes, crossbows, bolts and arrows, and livestock, including horses, mules, cows, pigs, sheep, goats, chickens, geese, ducks, and dogs. There are also a dozen different artisans, blacksmiths, carpenters, tailors, silversmiths, silver jewelry makers, men for hire (both laborers and mercenaries), pawn booths, fortune-tellers and healers. Prices are generally average to 20% below standard market value, but quality varies dramatically, from poor to excellent.

Note: Silver bullets cost 45 credits per box of 96 rounds; most calibers available.

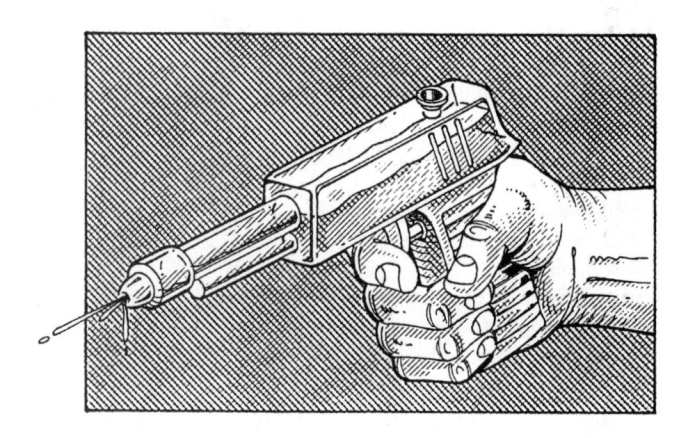

The Halloway Armory & Outfitter

A gigantic six-story building that covers half a city block. It is an extremely well equipped store for all of one's adventuring needs. Services include weapon repair, energy clip recharging, body armor restoration, power armor repairs, and general mechanics. Prices on everything are standard to 5% less.

Equipment: Tents, sleeping bags, backpacks, cloth and leather sacks of all sizes, saddlebags, riding tack, plastic, clay and glass jars and containers, canteens, wineskins, portable stoves, lanterns, flashlights, lighters, flares, cutlery, string, rope, wire, spikes, grappling hooks, insect repellents, pocket sewing kit, pocket tool kit, gasoline, kerosene, knee boots, leather and cloth gloves, hiking boots, fishing nets, fishing poles, fishing line and hooks, SCUBA gear, paddles, life preservers and similar outdoors items.

The weapon section includes vibro-knives and short swords, pocket knives, hunting/skinning knives, throwing knives, wood knives, swords, silver-plated weapons, crossbows and bolts, bow and arrows, spears, quarterstaves, walking sticks, wood stakes, mallets, wooden crosses, and a full selection of vampire weapons including techno-wizard weapons and flares.

Guns include 9 mm pistols (normal and silver bullets; a box of 96 normal bullets is 30 credits, silver bullets cost 70 credits), sub-machine-guns, and rifles, the entire line of Northern Gun energy weapons and most of Wilk's laser products, and rail guns. Silver bullets cost 60 credits per box of 96 rounds, all standard calibers are available; special orders are possible at double the cost and a 200 credit set-up fee.

Power Armor: NG Samson power armor and Titan power armor, and the occasional Triax Terrain Hopper.

Body Armor: Urban Warrior, Plastic Man, Bushman, Huntsman, Explorer, Juicer, Dog Pack and Crusader.

Vehicles are limited to wastelander and highway-man motorcycles, hovercycles, Big Boss ATV, horse drawn wagons, canoes, sailboats, rowboats, motorboats (seat 4), underwater sleds, sails for sailboats, and similar items. Will be glad to help find and select a suitable vehicle or horse for a 2% commission.

Robots: Usually has 1D4 bot vehicles from the Titan series, one EX-5 Behemoth Explorer is parked in the back lot, and is also likely to have a couple of NG-V10 Super Bot-Vehicles (labor), and an NG-V7 Hunter Mobile Gun. The big item in robots is **the basic bot horse** (Simple intelligence is all that is available, minimal I.Q., loyal, obedient, basic program: trained in animal-like functions; 150 M.D.C., 5 year nuclear power source). Costs: Pony 3 million credits, Medium size horse: 4.3 million, Large horse: 5 million. **Extra Features:** Additional 100 M.D.C. 100,000 credits, additional 200 M.D.C. one million credits. Speech and Skill Programs: Domestic 55,000 credits, technical (speaks 5 languages, knows lore, and operates computer) 220,000 credits, wilderness (select 5 appropriate wilderness skills) 175,000 credits, espionage (intelligence, detection) 95,000 credits, espionage spy (tracking, escape, photography, pick locks) 260,000 credits. **Note:** Programs same as found in **Rifts Sourcebook #1,** prices 5% to 10% higher. Real animal appearance: Looks like a real horse, with fake fur, eyes, and other cosmetic features. Cost: Horse 200,000 credits. **Note:** Weapons and other features as found in the **Rifts Sourcebook #1** are all available at a cost of about 10% more.

Official Wilk's Laser Store

Sells exclusively Wilk's laser products at 10% less than standard market prices. Also repairs lasers of all kinds and recharges E-clips (Wilk's E-Clips are recharged at a 25% discount). In addition to weapons and tools, the store also sells a variety of other Wilk's products, including cybernetic finger lasers (tools and weapons), telescopic, laser targeting, gun sight (3000 credits; 2000 ft/609 m), pocket laser distancer (1500 credits; 5000 feet/1524 m), infrared distancing binoculars (1500 credits; 2 mile/3 km range), high-powered laser flashlight (400 credits; 1000 foot beam), laser spotlights (1500 credits; 1000 foot beam/305 m, illuminates an eight foot/2.4 m circular area; for mounting on vehicles), and conventional flashlights and lanterns.

River Side Taxi & Guide Service

The garage and dispatch station for the biggest taxi service in El Paso; a fleet of yellow hover-sedans and all-terrain vehicles. Costs 1 credit a minute or two credits a mile, whichever is applicable. Also offers the services of wilderness guides (3rd or 4th level) as a guide the area. Will travel up to 500 miles away (cash advance required), but will not cross the Rio Grande River. Costs a flat fee of 200 credits a day, vehicles and supplies not included (but can be arranged).

Daylight Ferry Service

Located on the banks of the Rio Grande is one of the two legitimate ferry services for a hundred miles. The service has small ferry boats for passengers traveling on foot and by animal, and large barge types for transporting vehicles, robots, wagons, and shipping crates. The service opens at sunrise and stops an hour before sunset. It is ILLEGAL to travel the river at night, punishable by steep fines and the termination of the business, so there is absolutely no way the Daylight Ferry Service will transport anybody across the river at night (no matter how high the bribe). Fees: 10 credits per person and two suitcase size pieces of luggage. Additional luggage costs 10 credits per 100 lbs, unless it goes freight, which costs a minimum of 250 credits per 500 pounds. Big shipments and livestock get a special rate of 500 credits per ton, but are low priority.

Speedway Boating

Located on the other end of town is a small ferry that transports only people, at a cost of 8 credits a head. A bribe of 50 credits or more might allow a passenger to squeeze on board up to 200 lbs of luggage. The Rivera family runs the business, and like the other ferry service, stops all service at night. However, Old Man Rivera, a retired, 72 year old wilderness scout (8th level, anarchist) and wino, has been known to sneak people across in his rickety, old rowboat (sits three plus Rivera) for 50 credits per person.

Old Man Rivera will also sell his services as a guide to the streets of Ciudad Juarez. The cost is a mere flagon of wine (about 5 credits) and 50 credits for six hours of his time; no limit to the number of travelers he's conducting the guided tour for (although he will strongly suggest that people keep him plied with wine or beer). One of the travelers must provide transportation or they walk the 70 miles to Juarez and costs an extra 50 credits. Unfortunately, there is a 1-75% chance that before the end of the tour, Rivera will pass-out, drunk as a skunk, and will remain unconscious for 2D4 hours. Furthermore, the old man disappears at the first sign of serious trouble, leaving travelers stranded in a dangerous city. There is nobody to complain to about the old man because he doesn't work for or represent anybody (although he will imply that he works for Speedway Boating). The old man disappears for days, sometimes weeks, on his little excursions. Skilled in avoiding and warding off vampires.

The Mystic Travel Service

This is a small, one-story, wood frame building with ornate decorations and impeccable exterior and interior designs. The service is extremely limited, costly, but takes less than a minute. An old ley line walker (9th level) and his grandson (3rd level line walker) will teleport as many as six individuals and two tons of luggage to a handful of predesignated areas for 25,000 credits one way. Locations are limited to Ciudad Juarez (just out front of the Merchant Pony Express office), Amarillo, Wichita Falls, Lone Star City, or anywhere up and down or across the river, up to 900 miles away.

The Wild Bronco Arena

The Wild Bronco is "the " arena to see the best fights, races, and events (of course, owned and operated by Halloway). It is as big as a football stadium for outdoor spectacles like horse racing, visiting circuses and carnivals, monster wrestling, major gladiatorial fights and other big events. As if this were not enough, inside the structure is an auditorium for theater and concerts, two dance halls, four taverns, snack bars, concession stands, and two indoor arenas for local fighting competitions, and cock, dog and other animal fights. All gambling is operated by the Halloway Management and security is handled by Halloway's mercenaries. The taverns offer strong booze at reasonable prices, two to five credits a drink.

El Paso Psychic Healer Society

Psychic healing is performed at reasonable fees. Psychic diagnosis 70 credits, negate toxins (booze, drugs, poisons) 200 credits (psychic purification), heal minor wounds, cuts and bruises from a barroom brawl costs 75 credits, stab wounds and/or blood loss (healing touch) 100 credits, internal injury or grievous wounds requiring several healing touches and enhanced healing 3D4×100 credits, depending on the severity of the wound. Curing of minor diseases costs 500 credits (healing touch and increased healing), psychic surgery (4000 to 32,000 credits, depending on the severity, sometimes more), exorcism 10,000 credits per entity. They will also heal pet and work animals for comparable fees.

The clinic is spacious and sparkling clean. It employs 15 fifth level psychics with healing powers, three seventh level mystics, a simvan healing woman banished from her tribe (9th level) and 12 assistants. A fifth level mind melter runs the clinic. Halloway permits the clinic to exist on the condition that their fees are competitive or higher than the hospital's and that they pay him 15% of their profit.

The Halloway General Hospital

A 12-story hospital that covers a city block and is equipped with the best modern medical facilities money can buy. Its spacious emergency rooms and 24 hour clinics are typically visited by gang members, bar brawlers, and roughneck adventurers and wilderness folk. Psychic healers are especially useful in the ER for quick stabilization of the most serious injuries. Suturing cuts, fixing bruises, and bandaging wounds will cost 4D6×10 credits, depending on the degree of difficulty and time, transfusions cost 150 credits a pint, setting broken bones costs 2D4×100, surgery and implants can cost 6,000 to 40,000 credits, depending on the severity and complexity of the surgery, and a typical stay at a hospital costs approximately 350 credits a day. **Note: Citizens of El Paso enjoy a 50% discount for all medical treatment and medicine, compliments of Wyatt Halloway.**

Ciudad Juarez

Into the Mexican Frontier

Estimated Population: 77,000
Racial Breakdown:
   39% Humans (5% psionic, 10% augmented)
   35% D-Bees
   19% Mutant animals (65% are dogs)
   5% Others (borgs, bots, dragons, etc)
   2% Vampires
Average Transient Population: 16,000 additional people.
Tech Level: High/Modern and Magic
Surrounding Communities (100 mile radius): 6,000 (50% human, mostly farmers or sheep and cattle herders, very low tech level).

Seventy miles (112.6 km) south of El Paso, just beyond the Rio Grande River, is Juarez City (note: "Ciudad" means city). Built on the ruins of the pre-rifts city of the same name, Ciudad Juarez is the only known city in the vampire ridden lands of the Old Mexican Empire. Except for rumors of vampire kingdoms deep in the interior, only tiny villages and small towns are believed to dot the vast plains and southern rain forest.

The city looks like the cantina scene out of the pre-rifts movie, *Star Wars*, only it looks like that everywhere in the city. Its streets are narrow, dusty, dark, overcrowded and alive with throngs of mutant and alien life forms (and downright monsters). Headhunters and adventurers of a hundred races stroll through the streets in full armor, with mega-damage weapons strapped to their sides. Gunfights in the saloons and in the dirt streets are a daily occurrence, as is the finding of a half dozen dead bodies every morning.

Juarez is the watering hole for every rogue within a thousand miles. It is a haven for scoundrels and renegades of all kinds. Other than El Paso (often accused of being "sissified" because a man must check his weapons and armor at the city gates), Ciudad Juarez is the only other place to purchase supplies, repair vehicles, buy and sell goods and equipment, relax and spend money. As a pleasure resort for the decadent and illegal, Juarez has no peers (except, perhaps, Atlantis). It is said that anything can be bought in Ciudad Juarez and especially if it is bannded in more civilized places. Gambling, drugs, sex, slaves, murder, magic, the exotic and the forbidden are all commodities at Juarez. A saloon, gambling hall or arena can be found on nearly every block. Body-Chop-Shops (and cyber-snatchers) offer an array of mechanical augmentation at discount prices.

The Police

The Ciudad Juarez police force is a haphazard militia that is as corrupt and brutal as the criminals and gangs they allegedly protect the citizens from. Many are street punks and city rats who grew up and joined the gang known as the "Juarez Police Force." They joined the police to bash heads, grab some glory and/or respect, or to make good money (even become rich through bribes, pay offs, extortion, and the sale of information and services). The majority (60%) includes city rat, vagabond, and wilderness scout O.C.C.s of 1D4 level experience; most are illiterate.

Only about 20% are truly an efficient and well trained fighting force. These are men and women who have been on the police force for years and have developed excellent urban combat skills. Half are literate. Average level of experience is 1D4+4 levels, equal to the CS grunt, CS RPA or wilderness scout.

The remaining 20% are headhunters, wilderness scouts, Coalition soldiers, crazies, juicers, borgs and other warrior types who have enlisted with the Ciudad Juarez police. While all are not evil or corrupt, many are self-serving and most view life and their job pragmatically and often dispassionately. Thus these men and women are callous, tough, and often, savage law enforcers. Average level of experience is 1D4+1.

The mix of humans to D-Bees on the force is about 55/45; all get along fairly well. **Note:** The police force also serves as the militia/defenders of the city.

Good Cops ... Where?

Out of the entire police force the honest police officer not on the receiving end of some sort of criminal alliance and payment is definitely in the minority, a mere 15%!!

These ragged champions of justice tend to get the lousiest assignments and are slow to get promotions. **Typical Alignment:** Most are scrupulous and unprincipled and a few are principled and anarchist. **Typical Experience Level:** The average good cop is the equivalent of a 1D4+2 level CS grunt, headhunter, but wise to the ways of the streets (automatically gets the streetwise skill at +20%), and are experienced vampire hunters. This means they know the modus operandi of the gangs, Black Market, corrupt police and vampires extremely well. They know all the trouble areas and the troublemakers of note.

The good lawmen are tolerant of vandalism, roughhousing and petty crimes, like stealing a car for a joy ride and petty theft, committed by the youths of the slums, especially "basically good" kids. The police will break up a brawl or rowdiness with force, but will send the offenders home with a warning and a crack on the head or behind. A joyrider, petty thief or vandal will be on the receiving end of long lecture, a couple smacks in the mouth or on the behind, a stern warning, and may be publicly humiliated, or forced to perform some public service for the community. These same police are intolerant of gangs (some even of the vigilante Guards), drug dealers, body-chop-shops, murderers, rapists, professional criminals, and vampires. They fight these evil forces mercilessly and to the full extent of the law.

For the most part, the neighborhood people and members of the Guard gang respect and often love these valiant men and women. To show their appreciation the people will frequently give the police officers treats of food, drinks, candy, pastries, and other goodies. Some of the businesses will offer them discounts on the goods or services they sell. When these street soldiers are in trouble the citizens and members of the Guard rush to their aid.

Police Statistical Data

Average level of experience: second to fourth.

Standard Body Armor: Street Patrols are in dark brown Bushman body armor, 60 M.D.C., or beige Urban Warrior body armor, 50 M.D.C., both have the word "Fed" and an I.D. number emblazoned on the armor and uniforms. Undercover police may wear street clothes, disguises, and any type of body armor. Short-range radios are built into the armor and in squad cars.

Standard Weapons: All police are issued an NG-57 heavy ion blaster, NG-L5 laser rifle, Wilk's laser wand (tool), 9 mm automatic pistol (20 shot clip, 2D6 S.D.C. damage, normal bullets and clips of silver bullets are provided), a wood crucifix, and billy club (1D6 S.D.C.). However, any weapons of their own selection and purchase can also be used. Triax pump weapons and pulse rifles are popular additions. A dozen wooden stakes, mallet, extra clips of silver bullets, water pistol and water cannon are also standard issue, but usually kept in the trunk of their hovercar or dune buggy style squad car.

Unit Breakdown:
1. **4000 police patrol** the city streets on foot (pairs) and in squad cars (hover and land rovers).
2. **600 hover cycle & motorcycle police.** Fast-moving one-man units operating in pairs and four-man units. The motorcycles and hover cycles are armed with a forward laser and mini-missile launchers; typically ATV Speedster and highway-man motorcycles.
3. **200 "Sky Jockeys".** Police that monitor the city from the air in NG-Samson power armor (120 suits in stock) and Sky King hovercraft with full weapon systems (150 vehicles).
4. **Mechanized Division** (168 plus 80 labor bots): 30 full conversion borgs, 40 partial reconstruction borgs (use jet packs or police hover

cycles), 10 Flying Titans, 24 NG Samsons, 12 Triax X-10 Predator power armor, 4 Glitter Boys, 6 Titan Reconnaissance bots, 12 TR-001 Titan combat bots, 12 TR-002 Titan light combat bots, 12 NG-V7 Hunter Mobile Gun bots, and 6 NG-M56 Multi-Bots. The city also has at its disposal 48 NG-W9 light labor bots, 20 NG-W10 heavy labor bots and 12 NG-V10 robot labor vehicles (see **Rifts Sourcebook #1** for new bots).

5. **Psi-Division:** All are 3rd level unless otherwise noted. 48 detectives with major psionics (otherwise city rat O.C.C.), 48 mutant dogs (half are 4th level), 12 psi-stalkers (half are 6th level), 12 operators (half are 7th level), nine bursters (half are 5th level), five mystics (one is 6th level), and 12 mind melters (four are 5th level, two are 8th level).

Juan Sanchez, a 10th level nega-psychic (master psionic from **Beyond the Supernatural**), is the head of the division. His abilities include: All psionic saving throws are automatic and is even closed to psi-communication (roll to save versus psionic attack, even from things like see aura, object read, empathy, telepathy, healing, etc.). Disrupts group magic/rituals by disrupting/negating eight magic P.P.E. points for every one of his personal P.P.E. (has 24 P.P.E.; 12 in BTS but doubled in Rifts world; 24 × 8 = 192 points of magic energy that can be negated). Anti-Psychic Bonuses: +9 to save vs psionic attack (includes M.E. attribute bonus too, M.E. 21), +5 to save vs magic, +5 save vs possession, +4 to save vs horror factor and impervious to magic curses, illness, sickness, words of truth, trance, domination, and voodoo (including voodoo style circles).

6. **Magic Platoon (32):** A group of special police that investigate and protect against supernatural and magic problems. **Lavana**, a 7th level ice dragon (female), heads the squad. Magic Knowledge: 60 P.P.E., all level one spells plus befuddle, chameleon, repel animals, escape, telekinesis, carpet of adhesion, magic net, fire bolt, call lightning, tongues, magic pigeon, eyes of Thoth, turn dead, banishment, exorcism, dispel magic barrier, negate magic, protection circle: simple. Psionic Powers: Healing touch, increased healing, psychic diagnosis, mind block, object read, sense magic, total recall, and alter aura. And the usual ice dragon abilities (**Rifts,** page 101).

Other members include, second in command, Mario Antonio, a sixth level ley line walker, a pair of seventh level techno-wizards, a pair of 5th level mystics, a pair of fifth level shifters, another four third level shifters, six third level line walkers, along with four fifth level psi-stalkers, ten fifth level police officers (ex-soldiers, half have minor psionics) versed in lore and experienced in handling vampires and other supernatural menaces. Often work undercover; one third are D-Bees.

The Government of Ciudad Juarez

The city government is more corrupt than the police. They show little interest in justice or the people. They crave power and seek only to preserve that power. The government calls itself a democratic republic. It has a president, vice president, treasurer, secretary, police commissioner, city council, district representatives, and other city administrators. There are even public elections every eight years. However, the political machine is oriented to the perpetuation of the bureaucracy, the division of the poor and the wealthy, and to maintain the current power structure. Those in office have held their positions for over 20 years.

Juarez Gangs

Like El Paso, Juarez has its share of gang problems, including rivalry and rumbles from visiting El Paso gang members. About 20 different gangs (city rat and vagabond O.C.C.s) have claimed some part of the city as their own, but most are small and insignificant (10 to 40 members) when compared to the rest of the criminals and decadence of the city. The Black Market, for example, has many strong holdings in Juarez, operating half the body-chop-shops, private (illegal) gladiatorial arenas, and many of the taverns, pawn shops and gambling places. There are also guilds and political organizations that are corrupt and powerful influences on the city.

Of the gangs, there are only five of any significance, the *Subs, Psykes, Skivers, Guard,* and *Night Masters*. These gangs are fairly large in membership and are the cause of daily trouble and criminal activity.

The Subs

The Subs gang has been around for over 40 years, making them the oldest gang in Ciudad Juarez. They are a "D-Bees and mutant animals only" group, usually allowing only the ugliest and most inhuman looking to join, hence the name "subs," as in "sub-humans." They are your typical tough punk gang of bullies and thugs who use their physical might to get what they want. They see themselves as the kings of the hill who get their way by force. They are quick to accept any challenge, especially against a human or vampire opponent. The Subs hate humans, vampires and the more handsome D-Bees. They are obnoxious, mean-spirited and bellicose, especially when dealing with humans and formal authority. They even give the Black Market trouble from time to time.

The Subs' typical criminal activities include robbery of all kinds, brawling (bar and street fights), arranging gladiatorial fights (often kidnapping people off the street to be new gladiatorial combatants), fighting in the arena themselves, beating up and/or killing humans (they hate humans), and selling their brawn as a service to the unscrupulous. Services for sale include theft, vandalism, acting as a bodyguard, beating people up, breaking limbs, torture, and murder. The more violent the better. They will inflict injury on any creature, human or D-Bee, but will *never* knowingly work for a human or a vampire.

The Subs are archenemies of El Paso's predominantly human and arrogant *Hammer* gang. There have been many a bloody rumble between these two gangs on both sides of the Rio Grande. The *Trogs*, also from El Paso, have bumped heads with the Subs on numerous occasions. The Trogs and the Subs see each other as a sort of brother gang, since both are composed of inhuman D-Bees. Unfortunately, this makes them rivals, each feeling the need to prove that they are better than the other. This has led to frequent brawls, shouting contests, loud chest thumping and challenges of skill, brawn and courage (the latter usually involves outrageously foolish and deadly risks), but seldom are these encounters the bloody skirmishes waged against other gangs.

The Subs

Breakdown: 420 total members: 60% D-Bees, 20% mutant animals, 10% non-human psychic R.C.C.s, 7% other (horribly deformed humans, borgs, shapers, goblins, black faeries, creatures of magic, etc.), and 3% are full conversion borgs.

Common Gang Member Alignments: Anarchist, Miscreant, and Diabolic.

Typical Gang Member O.C.C.: 1D4+2 level city rat, vagabond, scout, or headhunter.

Colors: Red leather clothing and armor, and a red headband. The gang insignia is an inhuman skull with large brow ridges above the eyes and large canine teeth (bigger than a vampire's). It is usually worn as a large patch on the back of jackets and armor or on the front of T-shirts and robes.

spears, and automatic weapons, particularly machineguns and sub-machineguns that fire silver rounds. Several of the strongest also use rail guns that can fire both conventional rounds and slivers of wood.

- **Mega-damage Weapons:** Can be anything, but the Subs favor larger, more destructive weapons such as the Triax pump weapons, rail guns, ion blasters, plasma and particle beam weapons. Many also utilize magic weaponry; flaming swords and daggers being the current rage.
- **Body Armor:** The Gladiator, Crusader, and Coalition armor are the only types worn by the Subs, and are usually bristling with leather straps and metal studs.
- **Bionics and Cybernetics:** 50% of the Subs will have 1D4+1 cybernetic implants, 20% will have 1D4 bionic items, either bionic weapons or artificial limb(s) of great strength (P.S. of 20+1D6). 3% are full conversion borgs.
- **Gang & Criminal Activity:** Actively harass, beat up, molest, torture, and rob humans and handsome D-Bees. They are known for violent brawls, vandalism, robbery, muggings, kidnapping, assault, terrorism, and murder, all directed at humans, pretty D-Bees, and the wealthy. They occasionally sell their services as mercenaries, scouts, and thugs to merchants, travelers, the Guild for the Gifted, and fellow criminals. The bloodiest confrontations are with the Ciudad Juarez police, vampires, and the El Paso Hammer gang and the Coalition.
- **The Gang Leaders:** The Leader of the Subs is the famous city gladiatorial champion of six years ago, **Vlad the Invincible**, a Dragon Slayer! He loathes humans almost as much as vampires. Likes to belittle, harass and hurt humans.

Horror Factor: 12, **Alignment:** Miscreant
Hit Points: Not applicable, **M.D.C.:** 500 M.D.C.
Weight: 3900 lbs., **Height:** 19 feet tall (5.9 m),
Age: 121 **P.P.E.:** 90 P.P.E., **I.S.P.:** None
Attributes: I.Q.: 12, M.E.: 17, M.A.: 11, P.S.: 38, P.P.: 24, P.E.: 23, P.B. 4, Spd. 14.
Experience Level: 9th level Dragon Slayer! hand to hand: martial arts and boxing; six (6) attacks per melee. Good, forceful leader.
Magic Powers: Knowledge is limited to lore, but the giant possesses some innate magic powers. Invisibility (equal to superior, but can only turn self invisible), see the invisible, energy bolt (S.D.C. damage energy bolts can be fired from fingertips), and negate magic (same as spell). Also impervious to magic fire, impervious to normal fire, cold, and S.D.C. weapons, has a great resistance to magic, inflicts M.D.C. damage from punches (4D6 M.D.), bites (6D6 M.D.), kicks (5D6 M.D.) and other attacks. Special bio-regeneration instantly restores 1D6x10 M.D.C. three times per day.

Bonuses: In addition to attribute and combat bonuses, +3 to save vs magic, +3 to save vs psionic attack, +5 to save vs horror factor, +1 to parry, +2 to dodge, and +3 on initiative, one additional attack or action per melee.

Energy Aura (special): An invisible aura of energy adds 100 M.D.C. (subtract damage from this energy aura first) and covers everything the giant is wearing or holding. Depleted M.D.C. from the aura is restored within 24 hours. The additional effect of the mega-damage aura is that the energy field turns ordinary, hand-held S.D.C. weapons/items into M.D.C. extensions of the giant! Thus, a strike from an S.D.C. giant sword, club, dagger, or uprooted tree inflicts the 4D6 M.D. of a full strength punch from the giant. See Bonecrusher in the **Night Arcade and Freak Show** for a full description of the Dragon Slayer's powers.

- **Skills of Note:** W.P. Targeting, W.P. Sword, W.P. Blunt, W.P. Chain, W.P. Energy Rifle, W.P. Heavy Energy, languages include Spanish, American and Gobblely.
- **Favorite Weapons:** Giant size pole arms and chain weapons and a TX-500 Rail Gun (strong and big enough to use one-handed). Range:

Standard Vampire Weapons: The mix of these items varies widely among the members of the Subs gang, ranging from a handful of wooden stakes and silver crosses, to crossbows, wooden swords,

4000 feet, mega-damage: 6D6 M.D. per burst, 13 bursts per 390 round belt. Has conventional and vampire rounds.

Body Armor: Dragon skin armor (shirt and pants), looks like very fine scale mail, 224 M.D.C. (has seen some wear). Weight: 1000 lbs. Penalty: −30% to prowl and reduce speed by 20%. Market value in Juarez is 200,000 credits (resale is 500,000 credits).

Second in Command is a D-Bee brute named "Gabby," a facetious name because he is a quiet, sullen and burly, 300 lb mound of muscle and flab. He is an 8th level thief with assassin hand to hand skills and background. Also has a knack for torture. Hates humans and psychics. A good leader and excellent planner; clever, daring and resourceful. Doesn't take part in many physical activities himself, but orchestrates many of the gang's crimes. 55 years old.

Third head honcho is a psychotic human who calls himself "Deader Dead Boy." He is often behind the more wild, flamboyant and brutal fights and crimes. Deader, as he's usually called, is a 7th level crazy! Really crazy. He is an ex-mercenary who takes particular delight in torturing and/or killing Coalition Soldiers. His living quarters is filled with trophies from scores of kills, most notably, dead boy body armor, helmets, a dozen dog pack skulls and CS military paraphernalia. Most of his personal weapons and equipment are captured Coalition items. His favorites include SAMAS Power Armor (has 2 full suits, which he can pilot expertly), CS heavy Dead Boy armor, every vibro-weapon made (his most favored is the vibro-claws), C-12 laser rifle, C-27 plasma cannon and CR-1 rocket launcher. Also likes the Triax pump rifle and pistol. He's also handy with a sling and short bow (W.P. Targeting). **Insanities:** Multiple personalities: The dominant personality is the miscreant "Deader Dead Boy," the second personality is "Blood Thirsty Bob" (also Miscreant), and the third personality is "Norman the Psychopath" (Diabolic). See **Rifts,** page 61, for personality descriptions. Also obsessed with killing Coalition Soldiers and government officials. Age 27.

The Psykes

A band of criminals who call themselves the *Psykes* (pronounced "sikes") dominate the streets of the west side. They tend to be much more intelligent, organized and subversive than most gangs. The gang consists of a mixture of humans and D-Bees whose only requirement is to possess at least minor psionic powers. The greater one's psionic abilities and cunning, the higher their position within the gang. Although all true members of the Psykes gang must have psionics, the gang also employs a network of non-psychic runners, spies, and snitches in its organization.

A nicer section of the North Town slums, on the west side, is controlled by the Psykes. It is the only part of town that is truly vampire free. It is also Black Market free; the Psykes operate ALL the illegal businesses on their turf. The gang's network of spies and lookouts (not to mention psychic premonitions) warn them of any Black Market or government sponsored assaults. They also deploy what they call "soldiers," usually psi-stalkers, dog packs and bursters, to eliminate trouble before it happens. It is the soldiers that are the most obvious force on the streets, but it is the quieter, less obvious leaders and elite, master psionics who are the most feared, for they possess the deadliest psychic powers.

The Psykes

Breakdown: 245 total psychic members: 40% psychic humans, 25% psychic D-Bees, 10% psi-stalkers, 15% mutant animals (90% are dogs), 5% other mutants, 5% other. 98% all have some degree of psionics, 50% are of psychic R.C.C.s and 30% have major psionics, the remaining 20% have minor psionic powers. Plus another estimated 300 non-psionics compose their network of street spies, snitches, lookouts, runners, and petty crooks (typically 1D4 level city rats and vagabonds).

Common Gang Member Alignments: Anarchist and Miscreant.

Typical Gang Member O.C.C.: 1D4+3 level mind melter, burster, dog pack/stalker, or city rat with minor or major psionics.

Colors: The majority wear bright, multicolored ponchos. Their insignia is an eye (as in the psychic third eye) which many members have tattooed in the middle of their forehead (30%) or over their heart (40%).

Standard Vampire Weapons: Most carry a wood cross, silver dagger, and water pistol. Full vampire combat gear as used by Psykes "soldiers" on an extermination patrol include wooden stakes, garlic, wood cross, crossbow or wooden spear or javelin, two silver daggers, a revolver with silver bullets, and a shotgun filled with silver pellets or a water cannon. Magic may also be used.

Mega-damage Weapons: High-tech, lightweight, rapid-fire and long range weapons are preferred; Wilk's laser weapons and pulse rifles are a favorite. Techno-wizard weapons and devices and other forms of magic are also popular.

Body Armor: The Urban Warrior, Plastic Man, Bushman and Coalition style Dog Pack armor are the most common, but others can be used (usually concealed under the poncho). A handful of members use Titan power armor and the Triax Terrain Hopper.

Bionics and Cybernetics: 15% of the Psykes have 1D6 cybernetic implants. None have bionics.

Gang & Criminal Activity: The psykes are busy establishing a strong, organized crime network with gambling houses, fences, body-chop-shops, prostitution, drugs, and manipulation. Known for daring robberies (especially of Black Market establishments), mind control, extortion/blackmail, protection racketeering, confidence games and murder (frequent clashes with members or employees of the Black Market, the Guard and Juarez police). Hated and feared by the people.

Note: There is growing rivalry between the Psykes and the Black Market and the Guild for the Gifted. If the gang continues to grow and prosper they will inevitably come into conflict with these two powerful forces. Fortunately, such a conflict is years away. The Psykes leadership is careful to be secretive, discreet, and tries not to antagonize the Gifted. The Psykes are engaged in the same types of criminal activities as the Black Market, which means they are affecting the B.M.'s profit. This has led to minor skirmishes and a few bloody clashes between the two, however, the Black Market underestimates the Psykes' strength and potential.

The gang is seen as an independent, elite and exploitive criminal organization that does not fraternize much with those outside its organization. Consequently, they are not liked by the average freelance crooks and thugs, other gangs, or the citizens of Juarez; although the Psykes also have their own network of paid informants and loyal street punks.

Gang Leaders: The top gun of the Psykes is a 13th level mind melter, known as "The Eye" (her real name is a secret, looks Mexican). She is a strong, ruthless leader with an aptitude for leadership and organization. Any male who treats her with disrespect is punished (usually psionic torture). Anybody who tries to usurp her power is killed in a terrible way. Attributes & Skills of Note: I.Q. 17, M.A. 20, M.E. 22, P.B. 12, all others average. Age: 33. Alignment: Miscreant. Can speak American, Spanish, Gobblely and Dragonese 98%, literate in American 83%, basic math 98%, dance 83%, horsemanship 88%, pilot hovercraft 98%, hand to hand: basic, W.P. sub-machinegun, W.P. energy rifle, pick pockets 88%, and streetwise 73%. Psionic Powers: 230 I.S.P., presence sense, object read, see the invisible, see aura, sense magic, sixth sense, mind block, telepathy, clairvoyance, alter aura (self), nightvision, impervious to fire, impervious to cold, impervious to poison, resist fatigue, summon inner strength, bio-regenerate (self), exorcism, detect psionics, psychic diagnosis, psychic surgery, increased healing, healing touch, and psychic purification. Super Psionics: Electrokinesis, hydrokinesis, super telekinesis, telekinetic force field, mind block auto-defense, group mind block, mind bolt, psi-sword, psi-shield, mentally possess others, mind wipe, mind bond and telemechanics.

Second in Command is Steven Trenton, a 9th level mind melter; age 27. He is tough, self-reliant, a good leader and deadly (Miscreant alignment). Psionic Powers: 208 I.S.P., Bio-regenerate (self), deaden pain, detect psionics, induce sleep, alter aura (self), death trance, ectoplasm, levitation, impervious to fire, impervious to cold, resist thirst, resist fatigue, nightvision, see aura, see the invisible, sense magic, sixth sense, mind block, astral projection, empathy, total recall. Super Psionics: Bio-regeneration: super, bio-manipulation, empathic transmission, hypnotic suggestion, mind wipe, P.P.E. shield, psi-shield, psi-sword, pyrokinesis and hydrokinesis.

The Skivers

One of the most violent criminal gangs is the Skivers (pronounced "skeevers"). They are thugs and city rats who make a living as cyber-snatchers. Cyber-snatchers are considered the lowest of the low, even in Juarez, because they attack, maim or kill people in order to steal their cybernetic or bionic body parts for resale to Body-Chop-Shops. Cyber-snatching is so prevalent that the unscrupulous cyber-docs pay a mere 5% of the retail value in credits or 8% in trade for cyber components or services.

Cybernetic retail prices are about 25% to 35% less than standard prices in other cities. Body-Chop-Shops are pretty blatant and many advertise with colorful neon signs and/or have hawkers on the street corners trying to lure potential customers into their establishments. Several have recently offered the promotional deal of, "Bring in the artificial part, and we'll implant/attach it at half price, or install two for the price of one." Frequently, 1D4 Skivers or other cyber-snatchers hang around the alleys and darkened entrance ways near chop-shops and hotels looking for victims for their bloody trade. A likely candidate will be followed and attacked later that night or perhaps days later, depending on the perceived strength of the intended victim and the strength of the cyber-thieves. Typically, the Skivers will outnumber their opponent three to one and they always try to catch their victims off guard. They have also been known to plunder corpses, the wounded and helpless, attack ambulances, and raid insufficiently protected clinics. They generally live high on the hog, fight dirty, fight hard, and die young. The Skivers tend to avoid antagonizing other gangs, but are hated by most. The Guard will shoot Skivers on sight!

The Skivers

Breakdown: 198 total members: 40% humans, 40% D-Bees, 15% mutant animals, 5% others.

Common Gang Member Alignments: Anarchist, Miscreant, and Diabolic.

Typical Gang Member O.C.C.: 1D4+2 level city rat, vagabond, or headhunter.

Colors: Black leather jackets, dark leather clothing and armor decorated with leather straps and metal studs. The gang's insignia is a chain saw dripping blood. It is usually worn as a large patch on the back of jackets and armor or as a smaller patch worn on the front of shirts and jackets.

Standard Vampire Weapons: These items vary widely among the members of the Skivers gang but typically include a half dozen wooden stakes, a crucifix, water pistol or water cannon, and silver bullets (revolvers and automatic weapons).

Mega-damage Weapons: Can be anything, but vibro-knives, vibro-sabres, vibro-swords, M.D. chain saws (inflict 1D6+2 M.D., but requires a P.S. 20 or higher to use), and cybernetic and bionic weapons are their favorites. Heavy damage energy pistols and grenades are also popular. Jet packs and the highway-man motorcycle are the usual means of fast street transportation; 60% are equipped with weapons.

Body Armor: The Plastic Man, Urban Warrior, and Coalition Dead Boy armor are the most common, but are usually accessorized with leather straps and metal studs.

Bionics and Cybernetics: 80% of the Skivers are augmented with 1D4+2 cybernetic implants plus three Black Market Cyber-Specialty items (see **Rifts,** pages 235 & 236). 30% also have one bionic limb and two additional bionic features (weapons, etc.). 5% (10 gang members) are partial reconstruction borgs with bionic arms, legs, feet, hands, four other bionic features (weapons, extra limbs, etc.), LI-B2 light infantry body armor (270 M.D.C.) and three cybernetic features.

Gang & Criminal Activity: Spend most of their time hanging out, getting drunk or high, getting into brawls, robbery, muggings, and stealing mechanical augmentation. Notorious for maiming, killing and brutalizing the victims of their cyber-snatching, as well as for vandalism, theft, armed robbery, breaking and entry, assault, and murder. Occasionally, sell their services as mercenaries, thieves and thugs to merchants, travelers and fellow criminals. The bloodiest confrontations are with the Guard. Ignore vampires and other monsters. Treat the police with disdain but try to avoid combat with them.

The Gang Leaders: The leader is a D-Bee junkie named **Wily Willie**, an intelligent, 7th level city-rat, hacker and thief. He has a good head for numbers, strategies and tactics, and is a charismatic leader (M.A. 22), but has a weakness for drugs, booze and babes. He is shiftless and lazy, and always has an eye open for the quick buck. Even when drugged-out he can be cunning and resourceful. In fact, if he spent more time being "straight" and actually spent time with his gang members (who idolize him), the Skivers could be an efficient criminal organization.

Second in command is a human, 9th level Mystic named Francisco Cruz. He's like the tough staff sergeant in the trenches holding the troops together. He's not a genius (I.Q. 9), but has a lot of enthusiasm, guts, and common sense. Psionic powers are: clairvoyance, exorcism, sixth sense, healing touch, bio-regenerate (self), see the invisible, see aura, telepathy, and bio-manipulation. Magic Spells of note include: Globe of daylight, sense magic, sense evil, befuddle, energy bolt, chameleon, climb, concealment, fear, levitation, turn dead, float in air, invisibility: simple, fool's gold, swim as a fish, tongues, and magic pigeon. 105 P.P.E., 66 I.S.P.

The Guard

The Guard is more of a militant vigilante group, organized as an unofficial people's militia, than a gang in the traditional sense. They wander the streets, protecting the citizens of Juarez from criminals, vampires, and evildoers. The main targets of the Guard are vampires, supernatural monsters, D-Bees and humans who prey on innocent people, particularly the citizens of Juarez. Consequently, while the Guard might intervene in an obvious attack on a traveler/visitor to Juarez, they will not get deeply involved with strangers. However, the victimization of a Juarez citizen, theft, rape, assault, murder, especially at the hands of an outsider or monster race, will send the Guard on a vendetta. The Guard will track down the perpetrator and deliver onto him/them their own violent justice.

The justice of the Guard is brutal. Bullying, demeaning and insulting behavior and minor assault against a Juarez citizen, D-Bee or human, will earn those responsible (including those who may have been a peripheral party to it) a vicious beating and lecture on respect toward others and a warning to get out of Juarez and/or to keep their nose clean while visiting "their" city. Thieves will receive a similar beating and all of the thieves' valuables will be taken and given to their victim(s). Murderers, rapists, and molesters are killed; sometimes beaten and tortured first. Vampires and supernatural monsters responsible for any crimes against a citizen are killed without hesitation.

The Guard is the only gang that is allowed passage in or through other gangland territories, as long as they do not interfere with gang business and let the gangs take care of their own. Most gang leaders respect or fear the Guard and will listen to anything a Guard leader has to say. They have even been known to kill one of their own gang members when the Guard can prove that the accused is guilty of some atrocity beyond redemption. This gives the Guard a great deal of influence on the streets. The Guard has not fought another gang in over eleven years.

The Juarez government has come to recognize the influence the Guard has over the people, who see them as heroes, and over other gangs, who stay out of their way or cooperate with them. This makes the government very nervous, fearing the Guard is an inevitable political adversary that could one day threaten its corrupt and uneven rule. As

The Guard

Breakdown: 2700 total members: 50% humans (10% are men of magic), 30% D-Bees, 10% mutant animals (mostly dogs), 10% other (including psychics, borgs and bots). Plus there are thousands of families in the slums the Guard tries to protect, who will offer the gang members sanctuary in their homes, report rumors and suspicious people and incidents, and act as spies and informers.

Common Gang Member Alignments: Unprincipled, Anarchist, Aberrant.

Typical Gang Member O.C.C.: 1D4+3 level city rat, wilderness scout, headhunter, or rogue scholar.

Colors: Dress entirely in black or dark grey clothes, and body armor with brown or red boots and gloves; often wear a black hood, ski mask, or stocking to cover the face. A white or silver cross is evident as a patch on the shoulder, chest or back. Many members also have a silver cross laying across a wooden stake tattooed on their arm. All wear a silver cross around their neck.

Standard Vampire Weapons: Minimum gear: Pocket mirror, silver cross, wooden or silver-plated machete (1D6 normal S.D.C damage, 2D6 M.D. to vampires), vial of holy water and six wooden stakes. Maximum vampire gear: Mirror, wood or silver cross, wooden knife or silver-plated machete, crossbow (or short bow and arrows), water pistol or water cannon, automatic pistols with silver bullets and six wooden stakes and mallet.

Mega-damage Weapons: Vibro-blades, magic weapons, and energy handguns of all kinds, because they are easy to conceal and long-range weapons are clumsy in close-quarter city battles. Wilk's and Triax pistols are favorites. But virtually any kind of energy weapon can be used.

Body Armor: Explorer, Urban Warrior, Bushman and Huntsman body armor are the most common to the Guard; frequently (but not always) concealed under bulky clothing or robes.

Bionics and cybernetics: Cybernetic implants (a la City Rat O.C.C.) are far more common than bionics. 40% have 1D4+1 cybernetic augmentations, while 5% have 1D4+2 bionic implants, limbs or weapons.

Gang & Criminal Activity: Spend most of their time patrolling the streets as well-meaning vigilantes. They will question suspicious characters and will detain, beat up and even kill criminals caught preying on the citizens of Juarez or innocent travelers. They are especially ruthless against cyber-snatchers and vampires, attacking without hesitation and with murderous intent. Known for inciting unrest among the people, brawls, destroying public property, vigilantism (taking the law into their own hands), as well as vandalism, theft, breaking and entry, assault, and murder (though usually against criminals and evil beings). Occasionally, the Guard will aid or join forces with other well-meaning people to combat oppressors of the people, vampires and evil in all its guises. The bloodiest confrontations have been with the Skivers, vampires and monsters. They are constantly on the lookout for the undead and eliminate them. They generally avoid trouble with the other gangs and are respected by the people and most other gangs.

Note: Because of the massive support of the people and the respect from other gangs, the police try to ignore the Guard whenever possible; some of the honest policemen even work with the Guard to help clean up the city. However, most of the Juarez police are corrupt and evil, thus they will kill (when there are no witnesses), frame or otherwise discredit members of the Guard whenever they can.

Gang Leaders: The leadership is divided between three different individuals. **Octavio Diaz** is an elderly 9th level rogue scholar (63 years old) and the spiritual heart and soul behind the Guard. He is literate in American, Spanish and Techno-can, and knowledgeable in computers, math, biology, medicine and lore. **Clive Winston,** a 7th level cyber-knight and director of strategies and tactics (32 years

a result, they persecute and punish the Guard worse than any of the others, never realizing that this makes them all the more respected and revered, especially by the gangs.

old). And 27 year old, **Lupe Estaves**, an 8th level city rat who is intelligent (I.Q. 20), super resourceful, a charismatic leader (M.A. 21) and driven by deep compassion. All are concerned with the plight of the people, both D-Bee and humans, who live in poverty and who are the constant victims of vampires, gangs, brigands, corruption and evil. If the police will do nothing for their people, then they will take the law into their own hands. Although extremists, often acting as police, judge, jury and executioner, these are desperate times in a place devoid of true justice.

The gang is broken down into divisions and squads. Each division has its regional leader, each squad a captain. Each division is responsible for protecting and assisting the people of a specific neighborhood. The squads function as a civilian militia or police force, patrolling the streets in groups of six to ten armed members. They try to dispense justice by protecting the innocent, stopping crime, chasing away brigands and killing vampires. The divisional leaders and the less violent or physically capable members of the Guard assist in community affairs, organize public protests, repair homes, and find food, clothing and shelter for the poor, etc.

The Night Masters

The official hype from the police and the city government is that Ciudad Juarez is vampire free! Unfortunately, that is the farthest thing from the truth. Hundreds of vampires enter the city, lost in the sea of transients that come and go from the city on a constant basis. Hundreds of the undead live in the city, feeding on transients and peasants. Many of the vampires are lone individuals or members of small clans or families of 3 to 10 members. However, there is a vampire gang that roams the streets of Ciudad Juarez. They are the Night Masters.

The Night Masters are a known force, yet despite the valiant and almost obsessive efforts of the Guard and the feeble efforts of the police, none have been able to find the vampires central lair or rout them from the city. The vampire gang members present themselves as a group of superior beings and engage in blatant, often advertised crimes and attacks to prove their superiority. They are extremely well organized and directed by good tacticians. The citizens fear the Night Masters more than any of the other gangs.

The old cemetery is the location of the main lair. About 40% of the gang members live in the natural labyrinth of caves and tunnels underneath the cemetery. 10% live scattered throughout the cemetery in buried coffins and the occasional mausoleum. Another 20% of the Night Masters use a two level basement of a pre-rifts building (40 feet underground and unknown to the city people) near the cemetery. The others live in secret locations within the city, often in the homes and businesses of humanoid, mind controlled servants. The master vampire's secret lair is the villa of an influential city official who is his mind controlled slave.

The Night Masters
Breakdown: 212 total members: 75% human in appearance, 20% human-like D-Bees in appearance, 5% other (mutant animals, ugly D-Bees, etc.). All are secondary vampires.
Common Gang Member Alignments: Diabolic, Miscreant, and Anarchist; no good alignments.
Typical Gang Member O.C.C.: 1D4 level secondary vampires.
Colors: None, but tend to wear dark clothing. The gang insignia is a broken femur bone, which they often leave at the scene of a crime or battle as their calling card. A handful (less than 10%) wear the insignia on their clothes, but most prefer to be inconspicuous. Obviously their fangs are another trait that identifies vampires.
Standard Vampire Weapons: Many of the undead do carry weapons that will hurt other vampires, most notably, wooden stakes, wood and silver weapons, crossbows, and silver bullets (revolvers and automatic weapons).

Mega-damage Weapons: Can be anything, but these undead seem to favor vibro-blades, vibro-claws, and laser weapons.

Body Armor: Typically none, though some will wear dog pack or juicer style armor (about 30 M.D.C.) that can be easily taken off to allow for quick metamorphosis. Frequently decorated with bones and skulls of previous victims.

Bionics and Cybernetics: None

Gang & Criminal Activity: Spend most of their time humiliating, bullying and hurting humans and non-vampire life forms. Known for vandalism, arson, deadly brawls, theft, black mail, terrorism, assault, torture, murder, mass murder, and vampirism. Occasionally, they will sell their services as mercenaries, spies and murderers to other evil, supernatural creatures. Humans and human-like D-Bees are the primary targets of their attacks. The bloodiest confrontations are with humans, the police, the Guard, the Psykes, the Subs, and the El Paso K-9s; especially the K-9s.

The Gang Leaders: As one would expect, the leader of the Night Masters is a master vampire called the **Master Night**, real name Pedro Ortega. He is an ingenious fiend (I.Q. 23 and M.E. 20; diabolic alignment, 9th level vampire, 60 years old, looks 30) with an aptitude for subterfuge and espionage. He uses guerilla, hit and run, tactics of assault, robbery and terrorism. His supreme arrogance and disdain for the living encourages him to frequently alert the police or news media (radio/TV) of his intentions and often, the specific location/person/target of his crimes. To his thinking, this proves him and the undead to be superior beings when they succeed in their task despite the humanoids' advanced warning and precautions. About half of his vampire legion are spawn of his creation and therefore, completely loyal to him. The other half are vampires and vampire clans created by and linked to other vampire intelligences, but who have joined the Night Masters for their own safety and to better molest and destroy humans. Most of these are fairly loyal and subservient to Master Night.

Second in command, Ray Flint, is the first secondary vampire created by Master Night. He is a sixth level vamp, smart (I.Q. 18), charismatic (M.A. 24) and a resourceful leader. Ray is often the man who leads daring assaults against humans and other gangs. Miscreant alignment. Looks 40, is nearly 60 years old.

A vampire of note is the handsome and youthful looking (P.B. 16, looks 20 but is 142 years old), 9th level, secondary vampire, Emanuel Rodriguez. His master and most of his clan were destroyed over 70 years ago. He joined the Night Masters because of their cocky and vindictive attitude toward non-vampires. Emanuel is highly regarded by his fellow vampires and by Master Night, but will never attain a high place in the gang because he is not linked to the same vampire intelligence as the gang's leader. He often secretly acts on his own agenda, but will never betray the group (Anarchist alignment).

Julia the Night Mother is a Witchling (see **Rifts Sourcebook #1** for full description), a demonic sorceress of supernatural origin. She hates most other intelligent life forms and delights in being the Night Masters' daytime guardian and protector. Julia admires Master Night for his treachery, deceptions, and skill at inflicting misery. The creature is 100 percent loyal to him and his gang. Sometimes the witchling accompanies the undead on raids, stepping in to add a little magic, or to help an escape, or to enjoy a little murder and mayhem herself. **Statistical Data on the Night Mother:** Horror Factor: 14, Diabolic, 7th level witchling, 121 P.P.E., I.S.P.: None. M.D.C.: 200. Combat: Three physical attacks (1D6 M.D. per punch or by weapon) or three magic attacks. Bonuses: +2 to strike, +4 parry and dodge, +2 initiative, +3 to save vs psionics, +5 to save vs magic. Abilities: I.Q. 14, M.E. 21, P.S. 10, P.B. 4, Spd 27 flying/hover, all others average; impervious to poisons & drugs, impervious to fire and cold, prowl 70%, turn invisible at will, bio-regenerate 4D6 M.D.C. per hour. Magic: 121 P.P.E., spells of note: Cloud of smoke, befuddle, energy bolt (S.D.C.), fire bolt (M.D.), circle of flame, call lightning, wind rush, carpet of adhesion, sleep, minor curse, sickness, spoil, trance, death trance, turn dead, mask of deceit, mystic alarms, concealment, detect concealment, sense magic, see aura, see the invisible, reduce self to six inches, magic pigeon, ley line transmission, tongues, calling, and heal wounds.

Note: Other protectors include a score of mind controlled human servants and packs of dogs. Furthermore, some of the other vampires who live in Ciudad Juarez, but who are NOT gang members, will still warn the Night Masters of impending attacks and of rumors and information on the streets. Many of the undead consider the Night Masters to be the champions of their kind and will offer them reasonable aid whenever appropriate (including helping gang members hide/escape, removing stakes when nobody's looking, creating distractions and attacking assailants engaged in combat with the Night Masters, etc.).

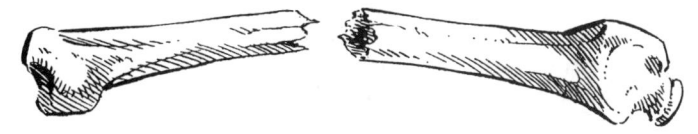

No Vampires in Ciudad Juarez?

The "official" position of the Ciudad Juarez city government is that Juarez is an absolutely vampire free community! The Bureau of Vampire Affairs is resolute about their claims that the police and militia have destroyed all vampires and keep the city streets free of the undead. Billboards with slogans like, "Say NO to vampires", "Ciudad Juarez, death to the Undead," "Vampire Free Juarez, the haven of the Rio Grande," and "Walk the streets knowing that your police keep them free of vampires," are everywhere. The government controlled radio and TV stations chime every few hours about being vampire free. Of course, this is all hype and bull feathers. The government has never been able to eliminate vampires from its city and hundreds of vampires prowl the streets and alleys every night.

The government does admit that the vampires of the Mexican wilderness are attracted to the city, like sharks to blood, but that the police are on the job and eliminate them or chase them from the city quickly and efficiently. Indeed, the police are fairly quick to act on calls regarding vampire attacks in progress (less than 10 minutes, which is far better than their usual 30 minutes to an hour for most crimes) and act with great bluster; a good performance to keep the people happy. The majority of vampire victims are beggars, street people and travelers, so the deaths of these nameless victims go mostly unnoticed and are easy to conceal. The undead learned long ago that keeping a low profile by feeding on the homeless, D-Bees and non-residents will cause few serious repercussions.

The presense of the **Night Masters** vampire gang is an embarrassment to the ruling body, so they pretend they don't exist. It is the contention of the police that the Night Masters is a tiny gang, or cult, of depraved humans involved in vandalism, terrorism, murder, cannibalism, and necrophilia. And that these crazed individuals only pretend to be vampires to strike fear into the citizens and to discredit the police. To prove their point, the Juarez police have (literally) produced evidence to support their claims. They have many signed confessions from alleged, imprisoned (or executed), Night Master gang members, which admit that they are human terrorists dedicated to anarchy and terror. A recent televised daytime execution of a human Night Master depicted a supposed gang lord, complete with filed, fang-like teeth, and cybernetically altered ears (pointed), odd eyes, and psychotic behavior. Critics of the police claim it was all a theatrical sham (which it was), but the police insist otherwise. Generally, the crimes of the Night Masters are attributed to other gangs, criminals, and monsters, or covered up, or ignored.

The Guild for the Gifted

The Guild for the Gifted, also known simply as "The Gifted," is not a gang, but it is yet another influential organization of self-serving people who operate within Ciudad Juarez. The Guild is a combination trade union and exclusive club for powerful men of magic and the occasional psychic and super-powered being (excluding vampires). The majority of the members are practitioners of magic (75%), nearly a quarter are master psionics (20%; many are Mind Melters) and the remainder (5%) are rogue scientists, rogue scholars, and supernatural beings who hold arcane knowledge, power, and/or artifacts (i.e., some pre-rifts or alien machine, weapon, magic item or knowledge).

The Guild for the Gifted keeps a low public profile and avoids police entanglements. Of course, this does not mean that they are not involved in illegal activities, quite the contrary, it's just that they are very quiet and discreet about it. The Guild has its hand in everything it can. The goals of its members are the acquisition of wealth, power and revenge by means of magic, blood sacrifices and manipulation.

The citizens of Ciudad Juarez avoid all members of the Guild for fear of becoming victims of human sacrifice, plagued by bad luck, besieged by demons, or becoming the target of the Guild's many supernatural and mortal enemies. They know the Guild as a source of evil and insanity. Rumors tell of nightly magic rituals, blood sacrifices, visitations by demons and god-beings, summonings of monsters, wizard feuds and depravities of all kinds. In this particular case, the rumors are very accurate. Next to the police, city government and the black market, the Guild for the Gifted is the most powerful and wealthy force in Ciudad Juarez.

The Sanctum is a huge five-story mansion (with a basement and a secret sub-basement) that serves as the Guild's headquarters and home for about half the members. The other half own their own mansions and/or are off causing trouble in some other part of the world. The Sanctum is off bounds to the public and not even the police are allowed beyond the reception area and lounge (most are terrified to go any farther). The place is protected by magic, wizard familiars and supernatural servants. Every room is enchanted with the "sanctum" spell, and wards, mystic alarms, and magic circles are everywhere. Thus, it is a truly safe haven for its members and those it chooses to protect from both man and the supernatural.

The Library is a famous collection of modern, pre-rift, and otherworldly books and video discs about magic and the supernatural. It includes books on history, lore, gods, demons, monsters, vampires, other dimensions, dimensional travel, and learning magic. Also includes books and scrolls with usable circles, rituals, and magic spells. The members of the Gifted and special guests are allowed supervised access to the library. The library and its contents are protected by wards, other magic and *guardians*, as well as the wizards and psychics in the Sanctum at the time. A quartet of stone golems (all 7 ft tall) guard the entrance, with two outside the entrance door and two inside the library. A pair of zombies clad in Coalition equipment (plus another pair of zombies that accompany Fineous, the Librarian) are among the more obvious safeguards.

The Circles of Stone is a place of summoning used by the Gifted just outside the city limits. It is a small ley line nexus point where three ley lines (each about 5 miles long) intersect. The location is denoted by a small, Stonehenge-like circle of 15 foot stone pillars and archways. This is where the Guild of the Gifted performs all their most important and powerful summonings, dimensional travel and the opening of rifts. The place is shunned by the locals and authorities alike, and most wizards who are not Guild members honor the Guild by <u>not</u> using the place themselves.

The Guild of the Gifted (Magic)

Breakdown: 113 total members; very exclusive, very elite, very powerful. 50% humans, 30% D-Bees, 20% other (dragons, demons, witchlings, faerie folk, monsters, godlings, aliens). Employ about 200 non-magic "associates," including low level practitioners of magic (level 6 and lower), assassins, spies, informers, and mercenaries on a regular basis to do the more mundane chores. In addition, they have several corrupt city officials and police on their payroll.

Common Member Alignments: Anarchist, Miscreant, and Diabolic, a few are Aberrant, none are of good alignments.

Average level of the 113 Members: 11th level (roll 1D6+9)

Colors: None per se; tend to dress in rich silk robes and the most expensive clothing. Usually ladened with expensive gold and gem encrusted jewelry and magic amulets and talismans.

Standard Vampire Weapons: Pocket mirror, gold cross or magic amulet, and magic.

Mega-damage Weapons: Magic spells, scrolls, magic weapons, vibro-blades and energy weapons of all kinds; often include hard to find and expensive items such as Triax weapons and techno-wizard items.

Body Armor: Typically worn only when a battle is anticipated, and then usually Explorer or Bushman and, more commonly, magic armor (techno-wizard or other magic).

Bionics and cybernetics: Only a few have some bio-system type cybernetic implants to replace damaged limbs, eyes, or internal organs. No augmentation for the sake of augmentation.

Gang & Criminal Activity: Robbery, assault, kidnapping, extortion, murder, assassination, and human sacrifice. Most of their criminal and murderous ways are for the purpose of gathering more wealth, power, magic, and the extraction of revenge. They often sell their mystic services and favors to government officials, the police, wealthy merchants and any who can afford their price (often a debt that will see payment in the way of favors and information collected time and time again). The Guild of the Gifted is often called upon by the government and the police to assist them in dealing with supernatural menaces and delicate matters such as assassination and clandestine operations.

Note: The power and reputation of the Guild is such that the thousands of rogues and brigands that fill the streets will "give" (the more foolish will try to sell) information to win the favor of a guild member (and perhaps be able to get a discount on magic items, or receive aid or advice from the Guild member at a later time). Furthermore, the Guild owns (have paid off) several key people within the government and police, as well as hundreds of informers and musclemen within the police department who will warn them of trouble, keep them apprised of developing situations, lose evidence, give them illegal access to prisoners, provide access to police files, and who will ignore crimes committed by the Guild and/or frame innocent people. Consequently, the members of the Guild of the Gifted seldom encounter problems with the police or the government.

Members of Note within the Guild of the Gifted:
Fineous Clydesworth — The Librarian

Alignment: Diabolic
Species: Human, **Age:** 78,
Height: 5 ft 7 inches, **Weight:** 134 lbs.
Attributes: I.Q.: 24, M.A.: 9, M.E.: 14, P.S.: 8, P.P.: 11, P.E.: 10, P.B.: 8, Spd. 9, **P.P.E.:** 12, **I.S.P.:** None, not psionic.
Hit Points: 62
Level of Experience: 12th level Rogue Scientist.
Areas of expertise: Archaeology, anthropology, biology, both chemistry skills, both math, computer operation, computer programming, radio: basic, demon & monster lore, literacy: Dragonese, American, Spanish, Techno-can, Euro, also speaks those languages plus

Japanese, Faerie Speak, and Gobblely, all at 98%. Special abilities (tied to lore and literacy knowledge): Recognize and identify magic wards, circles, runes, and symbols (including Dragonese/elf/Palladium RPG magic). Identify magic enchantment and potions (82% chance) and magic items (75% chance). Can actually perform magic rituals if given explicit written instructions and can read/use magic scrolls (needs to draw P.P.E. from a blood sacrifice, willing participants, or ley line to use a scroll).

Magic and Weapons: NG-57 ion blaster and a vibro-dagger. Wears an amulet of Turn the Undead and a magic charm (+1 to save vs magic & psionic attack). A large gold- and diamond-studded Egyptian style necklace (worth over 150,000 credits as jewelry alone) is a magic talisman that contains the spell teleport (superior). Scrolls include: 8 heal wounds, 3 restoration, 2 blind, 2 chameleon, 2 invisiblity: simple, 4 globe of daylight, 4 befuddle, 4 magic net, 4 call lightning, 4 see the invisible, 6 Eyes of Thoth, 2 superhuman speed, 2 constrain being, 2 banishment, 2 exorcism, 1 anti-magic cloud, 1 id barrier, 1 impenetrable wall of force, 1 transformation. All are at 11th level.

Note: Fineous is a malicious fellow who takes great delight in misleading adventurers (especially those of good alignments) into trouble with other Guild members, the police, evil forces and the supernatural. He seldom leaves the Sanctum, and is often the host to visitors and oversees the library. Two zombies, clad in heavy Dead Boy body armor and armed with CS vibro-claws, C-18 laser pistols, and C-12 assault laser rifles, have been created to protect and assist the old man. They obey the librarian's every command. Fineous has several scary stories about the zombies and will always make a chuckling comment about the fates of those who dare to oppose the Gifted.

Devon Drilfraun — The Lord of the Sanctum

Alignment: Diabolic
Species: D-Bee (elf), **Age:** 148, looks 30,
Height: 6 ft 7 inches, **Weight:** 194 lbs. Tall and slender.
Hit Points: 68
Attributes: I.Q.: 20, M.A.: 14, M.E.: 14, P.S.: 16, P.P.: 15, P.E.: 15, P.B.: 24, Spd. 12, **P.P.E.:** 197, **I.S.P.:** None, not psionic.
Level of Experience: 13th level ley line walker (wizard).
Areas of expertise: Magic, administration, analysis, strategy and tactics. Cool under the worst conditions. Literacy: Dragonese, American, Spanish, also speaks those languages plus Faerie Speak, and Gobblely, all at 98%. Demon & monster lore, faerie lore, both math, computer operation, radio: basic, pilot hovercraft, horsemanship, W.P. energy pistol and W.P. energy rifle.
Magic and Weapons: JA-9 Juicer variable laser rifle, TX-11 sniper rifle (3D6 M.D., 1600 ft range, 20 shot clip, +1 to strike, aimed or wild shots only), TX-16 pump rifle (4D6 M.D., 1600 ft range, 16 rounds), silver short sword, flaming sword (4D6 M.D.), mantle of invulnerability (3× daily, 10th level, lasts 10 melees or 2.5 minutes, see **Rifts,** page 178), techno-wizard thief gloves (look like metal or gauntlets, have concealment, 6 P.P.E., and escape, 8 P.P.E., spells/abilities, 8th level), and an amulet of Turn the Undead. Also scrolls of metamorphosis: insect, time hole, and memory bank.
Spell Knowledge: All first, second and third level spells, plus fire bolt, call lightning, life drain, sickness, spoil, speed of the snail, locate, calling, transferal, wards, create zombie, summon rain, sanctum, repel animals, stone to flesh, water to wine, remove curse, cure minor disorders, words of truth, negate magic, dispel magic barrier, dimensional teleport, and close rift.
Note: Lord Drilfraun is the master of the Sanctum. It is his duty to oversee the management of the Guild House (also his home) and the day to day routine of the Guilds functions and activities. He is generally regarded as being second or third in command of the Guild.

Rasputin the Grey — Guild High Lord

Real Name: Rasputin Tanrovich
Alignment: Miscreant
Species: Human, **Age:** 48
Height: 6 ft, **Weight:** 180 lbs.
Hit Points: 59
Attributes: I.Q.: 20, M.A.: 24, M.E.: 21, P.S.: 17, P.P.: 15, P.E.: 18, P.B.: 19, Spd. 14, **P.P.E.:** 219, **I.S.P.:** 61, minor psionic.
Level of Experience: 14th level Shifter (summoner).
Areas of expertise: Magic, summoning, diplomacy, deceit and manipulation. Maniacal with delusions of grandeur. Literacy: Dragonese, American, Euro (the Old Russian Empire is his native land), also speaks those languages plus Spanish and Gobblely, all at 98%. Demon & monster lore, both math, computer operation, radio: basic, pilot hovercraft, hand to hand: expert, W.P. energy pistol and W.P. energy rifle.
Magic and Weapons: JA-9 Juicer variable laser rifle, TX-11 sniper rifle (3D6 M.D., 1600 ft range, 20 shot clip, +1 to strike, aimed or wild shots only), TX-16 pump rifle (4D6 M.D., 1600 ft range, 16 rounds), silver short sword, flaming sword (4D6 M.D.), mantle of invulnerability (3× daily, 10th level, lasts 10 melees or 2.5 minutes, see **Rifts,** page 178), techno-wizard thief gloves (look like metal gauntlets, have concealment, 6 P.P.E., and escape 8 P.P.E., spells/abilities, 8th level), and an amulet of Turn the Undead. Also scrolls of metamorphosis: insect, time hole, and memory bank.
Spell Knowledge: All first, and second level spells, all protection and summoning magic (summon shadow beast is one of his favorites), plus call lightning, fire ball, circle of flame, fuel flame, blind, mute, globe of silence, animate/control dead, turn dead, exorcism, banishment, shadow meld, invisibility: superior, mask of deceit, multiple images, transferal, negate magic, dispel magic barrier, anti-magic

cloud, create magic scroll, id barrier, sanctum, eyes of Thoth, eyes of the wolf, words of truth, oracle, teleport: lesser & superior dimensional portal, and close rift.

Psionics: Minor psionic, 61 I.S.P., presence sense and object read.

Note: High Lord Rasputin the Grey is linked to a supernatural intelligence known as the Grey One, Lord of the Shadows; origin and powers unknown to all but Rasputin. Rasputin usurped the leadership of the Guild seven years ago when he murdered the original founder.

He is perceived as a great and cunning leader and has won the respect and fear of his fellow guildsmen. With Rasputin's guile and ingenuity, the guild has grown to be the secret power it is today. Half of the Guild is fiercely loyal to him, a third is complacent and the minority envious.

He is reputed to associate with demons and a shadow beast or two is always at his side to protect him.

Ciudad Juarez Highlights —— Old North Town (The Guard, The Gifted, Vampires, others)

Note: Only the highlights have been detailed. There are other saloons, residences of notable people and places like gas stations, power stations, water plants, etc., but they have not all been indicated because the player characters are not likely to ever visit them. Ciudad Juarez is fairly detailed to provide players with an idea of how cities might work.

The North Town is and older, an densely populated part of town that is filled with homes and merchants. It is a popular place for travelers, with many hotels and places of entertainment. Although considered to be The Guard's territory, all the gangs frequent Old North Town, especially the Merchant Districts.

The small area farthest north, near *The Sanctum of the Guild for the Gifted*, has been rebuilt and renovated over the last decade and is considered one of the nicer neighborhoods in Ciudad Juarez. It is also home to many of the members of the Guild for the Gifted. The Guard are seldom seen in this part of Old North Town, which is often referred to as "New North Town," because of the many renovations. New North Town stretches from descriptions number one to number thirty-eight.

The Guard operates across the street from The Sanctum in the old, crowded and crumbling neighborhoods of Old North Town (#39+).

1. Maliki's Curio Shop. The shop is small and overcrowded with shelves of books, boxes and boxes. The aisles are narrow and a musty smell permeates the place. Yet the establishment is surprisingly clean, and though crowded, it is not cluttered.

The owner is Maliki, a tall, elderly fellow with a pale complexion, thick white hair, beginning to peak at the temples, dark eyes and pointed ears. He is quite striking for a man obviously in his late 60's (really a 349 year old elf). His air is that of authority and nobility. He is always dressed in the finest, brightly colored green, yellow, and blue silk robes, and speaks with a thick Dragonese accent. He is usually fairly polite, especially toward the educated gentry, scholars and those who treat him and his staff with courtesy. Loudmouths, pushy bullies, roughnecks and the idiotic are not tolerated and are likely to find themselves magically expelled from the shop (and/or treated poorly and greatly overcharged).

Maliki is a long time member of the *Guild for the Gifted*. He is an 11th level air Warlock (a la Palladium RPG) and an amateur scholar (Anarchist alignment, 67 hit points, 20 S.D.C., I.Q. 17, M.A. 19, M.E. 15, P.P. 15, P.B. 22, others all average). Consequently, the focus of his magic is air related spells, such as globe of daylight, invisibility, fingers of the wind, thunderclap, summon & calm storms, call lightning, wind rush, and similar. **His three clerks** are all attractive young women (Maliki has a weakness for young women), who also happen to be novice warlocks, studying under his tutelage (one is a first level warlock the other two are unable to cast spells, but can see, speak with, and command air elementals).

A quartet of invisible, lesser air elementals protect the curio shop, as well as assist in its cleaning and stacking of goods. Many times Maliki or one of his shop clerks will bark out a command in an alien tongue (air elemental) and suddenly boxes will begin to move or come flying down an aisle, seemingly by themselves (really one of the air elementals).

The store sells a variety of items, including pre-rifts artifacts (Pepsi cans, books, video discs, and knickknacks), Aztec artifacts (statues, arrowheads, pottery), new books, including all of Erin Tarn's, detailed maps of Juarez, video and music discs, herbs, holistic medicine herbs and poisons, silver bullets for most common weapon calibers, and oddities of all kinds (shrunken heads, the skulls of strange creatures, weapons/items/artifacts of alien construction or origin, supposedly real vampire teeth, but are really the fangs of animals, etc.).

Magic items include amulets: protection against sickness, protection against insanity, and turn the undead; the occasional techno-wizard item is available from time to time and scrolls too. **Scrolls** are usually limited to level one to third level, at a cost of 500 credits per spell level and another 200 credits per level of spell strength. Typical spell strength and duration is equal to a fifth level wizard. Spells fourth level and higher cost two or three times more, and many spells are not available. (**Note:** Maliki and the Guild will not sell scrolls that might hurt them or their corrupt government buddies, consequently, the sale of powerful scrolls may be forbidden and many spells are not available.)

Magic services include the placement of wards on an item (8000 to 15,000 credits per ward, performed by associates at the Guild), casting immediate spells on a person or items such as breathe without air, float in air, fly, fly as an eagle, purification, heal wounds, metamorphosis into mist, etc. (1000 credits per level of the spell being cast, plus as much as 50% may be charged as a difficulty fee; all spells must be air oriented), and the removal of curses (30,000 to 120,000 credits depending on the curse; usually done with a scroll or through one of the other Guild members).

Information is also for sale. Only Maliki handles the sale of information. While his clerks might offer info, little of it is of great value; the kind of data one can get on the streets. Maliki, on the other hand, sells secret and dangerous information. The price can range from as little as 1000 to 4000 credits for tips like where one might find a particular person or item, important rumors, government plans/activity, transport of prisoners, locations of prisoners, plans for prisoners, hangouts of gang leaders and key people in the city, etc. Top secret or lifesaving information can cost tens of thousands, sometimes hundreds of thousands. Of course, not even Maliki or his fellow guildsmen know everything, so there may be times when information is not available or inaccurate. Likewise, the information is never data that could hurt the Guild for the Gifted or the Juarez city government. In fact, the information that is often provided at the most reasonable prices is data that will ultimately help the Guild, such as the location of enemy forces and competitors. Maliki and the Guild often set-up adventurers by giving or selling information that will in turn give them additional information or an advantage. **For example:** Maliki knows that the group is looking for revenge against so and so. He sells them the location and other data they need, but also feels them out as to what they might have in mind and when they plan to take action (sometimes his information will already tell him a lot, like, "The one you seek can be found at the Peacock Club at mid-night."). He knows full well that the group is going to attack this person. He may or may not care about the outcome, but does know that they will cause a major incident. An incident that may serve as a cover or as a distraction for the Guild's own illicit activities. If it is a Guild enemy, somebody in the shadows may see to it that the group is successful in killing their foe (secret assassinations are among the Guild's specialties).

2. **Juanita's Boarding House.** A medium-size boarding house that caters to the better off visitors who are planning to stay a while in Ciudad Juarez. The four-story, brick and wood frame building offers 18 sparkling clean, bright, cheerful and roomy suites. Each suite has a large bedroom, equally large sitting room, kitchenette, private bath, and television, all for 300 credits a night. Security is good; vacancies few. The owner and her large family of sisters, brothers and cousins run every aspect of the boarding house. The first floor also offers a meeting lounge with bar (seats about 60 patrons) and a small kitchen that can provide soups, sandwiches, salads, and breakfast at about 12 credits per meal.

3. **The Golden Pheasant Restaurant and Catering.** This three-story brick building is one of the most popular places to dine on the north side of town. The first floor is a formal restaurant, dimly lit, and richly decorated. The highest quality live musical entertainment adds to the atmosphere. Private dining rooms and soundproof booths are also available for 50 to 100 credits (plus meals). A typical meal costs 40 to 150 credits, but is the finest food in the city.

    The second floor is a dining hall for gatherings such as parties, weddings, anniversaries, and celebrations of all kinds. The walls are adjustable and can be setup to divide the floor into four separate areas of medium size to one huge room. The third floor can be used for dining in an emergency, but is actually a hardwood ballroom.

4. **Santiago's Clothing.** Santiago's is a small tailor shop of the finest quality. Hand fitted clothing made to order. Prices are about 10 times the cost of rack clothes; a suit, cloak or coat will run 1D6x1000 credits and a ballroom dress double.

5. **General Store.** Sells household goods, including detailed maps of Juarez and El Paso, vague maps of Mexico (shows all of southern Mexico as wilderness), basic clothing, bolts of fabric, sewing machines and equipment, soaps and shampoos, beauty products, aspirin, band-aids, towels, cutlery, kitchen utensils, toys, candy, fruit juices, soda, beer, dried fruits and nuts, snack foods, and a wilderness outfitters section with basic items, including tents, knapsacks, sleeping bags, backpacks, sacks, bags, carrying cases, canteens, straps, rope, tool kits, flashlights, lamps, and Urban Warrior, Plastic Man, and Crusader body armor. Prices are standard and quality is good.

6. **Winston's Cyber-Shop.** A small body-chop-shop with connections to the Guild for the Gifted. It is a clean, efficient and surprisingly reputable cybernetics and bionic repair and implant clinic. Prices are about standard, which means they are much higher than the numerous, less reputable, cyber-body-chop-shops found throughout the city. The shop is completely safe and protected by the Gifted.

7. **Good Cheers Saloon.** A neighborhood bar. It is dark, loud, air-conditioned, and offers a variety of good quality booze, from beer and wine to tequila and whiskey. Prices are good, at about 4 credits a drink. Known to be one of the less dangerous watering holes and popular with the city gentry. Information in the way of rumors and common knowledge can be collected from the bartenders; nothing juicier.

8. **The Duke's Card Parlor & Saloon.** This two-story establishment is a popular saloon and gambling hall. The most popular card games are poker and blackjack, although other card games are played, along with shooting craps. The drinks are strong and cheap (about 3 credits a drink) and the money plentiful. At any given time there are at least 20 games in progress and the place never closes. The

down stairs is the open, general gaming and saloon, the second story is the site of private, high stake games.

An eighth level simvan warrior is the head bouncer (Aberrant evil, 30 hit points, 90 S.D.C., I.Q. 10, P.S. 20, P.P. 23, P.E. 27, Spd. 26, wears a suit of dragon skin armor, 190 M.D.C., completely loyal to Duke). He is assisted by a full conversion borg, three fifth level crazies, two juicers, and four zombies (all, except the zombies, are 4th level). The owner, Duke, is a fifth level Chinese Demon Dancer wizard (aberrant evil alignment, summoner/shifter type magic, I.Q. 17, M.E. 21, P.P. 20; an excellent gambler) who is waiting acceptance into the Guild for the Gifted. Consequently, he is quick to offer the Guild information and perform favors.

Surprisingly, the gambling is pretty on the up and up, with a minimum of cheating in favor of the house.

9. **The Serpent Claw Bar.** A popular tavern frequented by practitioners of magic and psychics. A sanctuary spell prevents violence inside, while two fourth level practitioners of magic (one is a mystic, the other a ley line walker, both are D-Bees) manage the place and keep their customers serene with fine drinks and finer female entertainment (dancing, singing and illicit). The alcohol is of superior quality, costs 8 to 10 credits a drink. The owner is reputed to be a great horned dragon, almost always out of town on business.

10. **The Juarez National Bank.** Change/sell gems, gold and silver into credits, apply for loans and credit cards, store your valuables in top security (and magically warded) private vaults, get precious ores and gems appraised. The bank services the local merchants and the Guild for the Gifted. Secretly operated by the Guild.

11. **North Town Slave Market.** Life has little value in Ciudad Juarez, thus it is bought and sold like everything else in this city. The North Town Slave Market is clean and pleasant compared to the other slavers in town. It is a towering ten story building that houses over 300 slaves (60% are D-Bees). Most of the slaves are uneducated criminals (typically 3rd level city rats and vagabonds/thugs) sold by the city government to keep the prisons from getting overcrowded. Others are D-Bees captured in the wilderness and sold as slaves. About 10% of the Ciudad Juarez's population are slaves.

The cost of a slave varies with the subject's training, discipline, age and physical attributes. Prices range from as little as 1000 credits to 60,000 credits. Most average out at about 30,000 credits ($1D6 \times 10,000$).

The North Town Slave Market also offers an **employment service for mercenaries**. Juicers, crazies, borgs, headhunters, wilderness scouts, wizards and D-Bees can be hired through the market. Most are mercenaries down on their luck and forced to sell their services through the Slave Market. Services include personal bodyguard, security guard (home or business), armed delivery, armed scout/wilderness guide, detective, surveillance, assassination (very discreet), and brutality (beating somebody up, breaking a leg, blowing up a car, etc.). Average rates are 300 credits a day plus expenses (ammunition, vehicle repairs, room and board, etc.) for levels two through four, 600 a day for experience levels five and six, 2000 to 6000 a day for experts seventh level and higher. The need for special equipment like power armor, robots, and magic will cost extra and can easily double or quadruple the daily rate. The Slave market manages all moneys taking 60% for themselves (acceptable to most in their employ). As one might guess, the North Town Slave Market does NOT officially condone nor encourage illegal activity on the part of its mercenaries, but does in fact allow them to pursue all avenues of conduct. The market's only concern is discretion and they may not protect or defend "wanted" criminals.

The slave market is run by a triumvirate of owners, all ex-military; one is a ninth level CS military specialist, one is a 10th level partial reconstructed borg, and the third is a 10th level CS RPA robot pilot (still owns his SAMAS as well as a fine collection of power armor suits, including a Triax Ulti-Max). Under their employ are the following notables: a mated pair of Simvan monster riders and their rhino-buffalo mounts, a Shemarrian warrior and her A-002 Monst-

Rex, and six Brodkil demons (see **Rifts Sourcebook** for details on these non-human warriors).

12. **North Town Motel.** An eight-story motel with 160 rooms. Clean and fairly secure. Includes television and private bath; costs 120 credits a night.

13. **The Power House Armory (Robots & Armor).** A large, six-story, modern building of reinforced steel and concrete (50 M.D.C. per 10 foot area) houses the premiere dealer in brand new, perfect condition, mega-damage armor, robots and weapons. The Power House Armory sells the following at 10% above market. **Power Armor:** Triax T-21 Terrain Hopper power armor, X-10 Predator power armor, and Titan power armor. **Robots:** Triax X-500 Forager Battlebot, DV-12 Dyna-Bot, the entire Titan Robot series, and the NG-V10 Super Bot-Vehicle (labor). **Body Armor:** Bushman, Explorer, Juicer, and Gladiator. **Weapons:** All Triax weapons available to the Americas, all Wilk's laser products, both Juicer assassin energy rifles, NG-P7 particle beam rifle, and rail guns.

    The five, small, two-story buildings next door are: 1. Weapon repair and energy clip recharging. 2. Body armor restoration. 3. Electronics shop. 4. Power Armor repair. 5. General mechanics shop. Robot repair is done inside the big building.

14. **Opie & Bea's Fix-it Shop.** A young boy (6th level operator, scrupulous alignment) and his Aunt Beatrice (an 8th level operator, principled alignment) run this all-purpose repair shop. They clean and repair weapons, recharge weapons, fix computers, appliances, and vehicles of all kinds. Cousin Joeber and two D-Bee assistants help with the work. They are all 4th level vagabonds who know basic electronics, computer repair, automotive mechanics, and carpentry (all are of unprincipled alignments). Prices are reasonable and the workmanship is very good to excellent depending on who did the work.

15. **Floyd's Hair Salon.** An ex-juicer, known only as Floyd, is a masterful barber and hair stylist (unprincipled alignment, I.Q. 8, P.S. 17, P.P. 23, all others average; looks 60, is really 40). The wilder the cut, the better. He is incredibly fast and nimble, seldom taking longer than a half-hour for the most complex hairdo, and his hair styling is the most popular in town. Prices are fair, at 20 to 50 credits a do.

    His assistant is Eduardo Ramirez, a full conversion borg with special bionic scissor attachments for his hands and two additional bionic limbs. One limb is equipped with a laser scalpel finger, utility laser finger and chemical spray (filled with hair spray, mousse, and hair conditioners). The other hand has four retractable finger blades. The borg also has a retractable vibro-blade, knuckle spikes, garrote wrist wire, forearm laser blaster (2D6 M.D.) and a concealed ion rod (4D6 M.D.) in his leg, along with multi-optic eyes, bionic lung and speech translator. A 3rd level borg, anarchist alignment. Likes Floyd but thinks he is a better hair stylist.

16. **Lebeau's French Cuisine.** A small restaurant and pastry take-out bakery. About a dozen tables are available inside and another dozen outside; cafe-style. Classic pre-rifts French music is piped in through loudspeakers. A typical meal is 15 credits. Pastries run about 1 or 2 credits each.

17. **Hogies-Heroes.** A take-out shop specializing in submarine sandwiches called "U-Boats"; delectable, quickly made sandwiches, hot and cold. Take-out only. Sandwiches cost 4 to 10 credits. Also sells a variety of popcorn; one credit per 16 ounce bag.

18. **Lovie's Jewels.** A quaint, little jewelry shop that specializes in gem stones, jade, and silver. Her best selling items are an array of diamond-studded silver crosses and knives. Will buy and sell gem stones at fair prices.

19. **Benito McGoo's Optics Center.** Sells optical systems for adventurers, including gun sights, binoculars, telescopes, nightsight goggles, infrared and multi-optic systems, cameras, video recording equipment, and even a small selection of cybernetic eyes (no bio-systems). Standard prices.

20. **Sergeant Carter's Gun Shop.** This is a prosperous, little gun shop that specializes in automatic weapons, pistols and revolvers. Sells every caliber and type of ammunition, including silver bullets. Also repairs guns and sells a small selection of crossbows and silver-tipped bolts. Prices are 10% below average.

21. **Senor Jayney's Resale Shop.** A scuzzy, little pawnshop that pays 30% of the average market value on anything from guns and computers to cybernetics and magic items. Promises to hold pawned items for 60 days before selling them, but hot-selling items tend to get misplaced (sold). Sells most items for 30% below average market value, but there is a 1-50% chance that the item will be flawed. Roll percentile dice: 1-25% the item is broken and needs minor repairs (costs 2D6 × 10 credits to fix), 26-50% the item is filthy and requires 1D4 hours of careful cleaning to get it into working condition (1-25% chance that the cleaned item is worth 50% more than what it was sold for).

    The owner is Senor Jayney (pronounced Ay-nee), a swarthy, 5 foot, 3 inch, 220 pound, beady-eyed con artist who has a sales pitch and a special deal for everything in the store. Jayney is a 5th level city rat oriented to being a thief (miscreant alignment, I.Q. 9, M.E. 15, P.P. 18, all others average).

22. **Steve's Gags & Gifts.** A strange, little souvenir shop that sells a ton of silly and ridiculous trinkets, including cheap sombreros (fall apart in a matter of days), ponchos, beaded necklaces and bracelets, wooden crosses (large and small), puppets, papier-mache masks, baskets, whistles, pinatas, fire crackers, sparklers, itching powder, dribble mugs, mugs with false bottoms (holds four ounces more than it appears), plastic vomit, whoopie cushions, joy buzzers, fake vampire teeth, rubber stakes and mallets, fake blood, trick vampire mirror (a 3-D hologram of a growling vampire appears in the mirror when viewed at just the right angle; yes, Steve knows vamps have no reflection, but loves the gag anyway), vampire postcards (vamp rising from coffin, graveyard, severed head, etc.), vampire hunter photographs (3 different life-size action poses of figures fighting the undead; person inserts his own head/face and the picture is taken), the Vampire Almanac (see #108 for description), rubber bats on strings, rubber tarantula spiders, real tarantula spiders, shrunken heads (fake and real), pet lizards, cactus juice ("great thirst quencher," but tastes terrible), detailed map of Juarez, a large variety of water pistols, and "authentic" Mayan luck stones.

    The luck stones are about the size of an old silver dollar and can be carried in a pocket or worn on a string of leather or chain around the neck. Mystic Mayan symbols are carved into ordinary polished stone or jade circles about a half inch thick. Believe it or not, these are real magic amulets. **Magic bonuses:** +1 to save vs magic sickness and minor curses, and holds vampires at bay like a crucifix. Where Steve learned to make the luck stones or from whom he might have purchased them is a mystery. Luck stones sell for 300 credits each (no accumulative effect by wearing more than one).

    The owner, Steve, is a large, happy fellow who is a master of bad puns and terrible jokes. Every object he sells has a gag line or funny story behind it. Get him going and he can be as bad as a flooper or shaper. Of course, a sincere appreciation of his humor may net the person a complimentary glass of cactus juice and a 10% discount. Steve is a retired adventurer who enjoys relaxing and being with people. He love juicy rumors as much as a bad pun. If one can tolerate his humor, Steve can be an excellent source of free information (or inexpensive; buying stuff from his store makes him a bit giddy and loosens his lips). His favorite topics are city politics, the Guild for the Gifted, and sports; Steve knows every arena and the sporting events going on in town.

    Steve is a 5th level scholar; scrupulous alignment, stands 6 feet 2 inches tall, weighs 280 lbs, I.Q. 15, M.A. 13, M.E. 8, P.S. 24, all others average. Cybernetic implants include a universal headjack and ear implant for amplified hearing (great for hearing customers whisper and picking up rumors) and sound filtration, as well as one bio-system infra/ultra eye.

23. **Tomas' Rare Antiquities.** A high-class pawnshop and store that deals only in the rarest, most dangerous, and illegal (at least in the Coalition States) artifacts. The artifacts can be Mayan, Aztec, pre-rifts, alien or magic. Prices are about 50% higher than market, but the items are 100% authentic and in superb condition. The wealthy and men of magic are among his most loyal patrons.

   Tomas (pronounced Toe-moss) is not interested in mundane or mangled artifacts (will not purchase), but will pay 50% to 100% of typical market for truly strange, rare and well-preserved items. Books, video discs, art, and magic (can read scrolls and use some techno-wizard devices) are his favorite collectibles.

   Tomas is a 9th level scholar with a background in archaeology, astronomy, advanced mathematics, and computers (knows all computer skills). He is fluent in American, Spanish, Euro, Dragonese, and Techno-can and literate in each. He can also speak Gobblely 75%. Unprincipled alignment, I.Q. 25, M.E. 19, P.S. 14, all others average. Minor psionic: 45 I.S.P., object read and mind block.

24. **Bakery.** Sells fresh bread, buns, rolls, taco chips, corn tortillas, meat pies, donuts and honey. Everything is under two credits.

25. **The Sanctum of the Guild for the Gifted.** This is the five-story mansion owned and operated by powerful men of magic who have great influence on the city. The mansion is surrounded by a 15 foot stone wall marked with mystic symbols. Between the wall and the mansion is a garden area with a sprinkler system (also useful against vampires). To the north and east of the Sanctum is a tree filled park that is always green and healthy, even in times of drought. A well and fountain in the form of a wizard is always flowing with pure, delicious water.

   City folk stay away from the Sanctum, both day and night, for the wizards are known to be incredibly dangerous and consort with zombies, demons, monsters and dragons. **Note:** See the gang section for the complete description on the Guild of the Gifted.

26. **North Town Police Station & Jail; Precinct #1.** One of the few police stations manned by a police force that actually protects the citizens is Precinct Number One. Of course, it is their charge to take care of the affluent citizens of the "New North Town" area and the merchants in that area (numbers 1-38). The police turn a blind eye to the activities of the Guild for the Gifted and always take their side in any dispute. The Guild has such influence over this police station that they are allowed to examine evidence, given access to police files and schedules, and secretly interrogate prisoners.

27. **The Villa of Fineous, The Guild Librarian.** A large villa owned by the wizened librarian at the Sanctum. It is also the site of some wild parties.

28. **The Estate of Carlos Garcia.** Senor Garcia is a wealthy nobleman with ties to the Black Market (specifically smuggling, gambling and drugs). He owns Palace Garcia, a rough and tumble gambling casino. He is also a renowned vampire slayer and a reputed assassin (7th level city rat assassin, diabolic alignment, I.Q. 14, M.E. 18, M.A. 16, P.S. 19, P.P. 21, P.E. 18, P.B. 12, Spd. 22; millionaire worth over 50 million credits and another 10 million in gold and gems). Another place known for its parties.

29. **The Estate of Rasputin The Grey.** This palatial, five-story mansion is the home of the High Lord of the Guild of the Gifted, Rasputin the Grey. Like the Sanctum, the estate is avoided by local folk and is said to be haunted. Indeed, a half dozen shadow beasts roam the estate, ever vigilant for intruders, and a black faerie is a permanent guest in one of the more remote bedrooms. The basement is a temple for the Grey One. The mansion is protected by magic and conventional means and is frequently the visiting place of supernatural beings. See the section on the *Guild for the Gifted* for full data on Rasputin the Grey.

30. **The Gentlemen's Club.** An exclusive club for the wealthy. Members are predominately rich humans and human-like D-Bees. Visitors must be approved and accompanied by a member and pay a nominal entrance fee of 100 credits. The four-story club offers a quiet sitting room, large lounge and bar stocked with imported libations, a second, small lounge and bar, card room (reserved for quiet evenings of card gambling), a small library with about 1000 contemporary and pre-rifts books, second floor ballroom, weight and workout room, showers, jacuzzi, sauna, and 10 private rooms (all with bed, couch, easy chair and table and six chairs) that can be reserved by members for private meetings. Seldom visited by the members of the Guild for the Gifted, but a place frequented by non-Guild practitioners of magic, government officials and the snob rich.

31. **North Side Music.** A small shop that sells musical instruments and music recordings (one inch discs). Also offers voice and music lessons for singing and the guitar. Good quality, good prices.

32. **The Starlight Theater (and Brothel).** This is a small theater that caters to the illicit rather than the dramatic. 14 different half-hour performances are exhibited from 8:00 p.m. till four in the morning. Shows include scantily clad dancing girls, strip-tease artists, and live sex shows. Watered down whisky, rum, and tequila cost two credits a drink, while shots of a 150 proof rum cost four credits. Entrance fee is 25 credits, allowing the person to stay as long as he wants. Six burly mutant dogs serve as bouncers (each is a 4th level Dog Pack and has a minimum P.S. and P.P. of 20, anarchist alignment).

   Upstairs are a dozen, simple, clean, small rooms with a bed and sink with running water. These are used by the theater's prostitutes. Prostitution is not illegal in North Town, so there is no fear about police, but thugs, jealous boy friends, and wives can be the cause behind violence and trouble. The girls typically charge 60 to 160 credits per hour of their time. A popular place for the middle class and wealthier visitors.

33. **Lydia's.** Lydia's is a two-story wood frame building that caters to the gentler needs of rich men. The first floor has a manicurist (30 credits per pair of digits), hair salon (50 credits for a hair cut), tobacco shop (also sells snuff, hallucinogenic drugs, cocaine, and marijuana), and Lydia's business office. The office is a large, comfortable lounge. The furnishings are lavish and comfortable, with a couch, two love seats, two comfy armchairs, a sitting table and desk. Her private chambers are behind her office.

   The second floor has eight comfortable rooms with air-conditioning, bed, sink and shower. Each is the quarters of a beautiful young lady of the night. Each woman has a P.B. of 19 or higher, are all healthy, disease free, and very discreet. One is a mutant cat who sometimes acts as a spy for the El Paso Wild Cat gang.

   Lydia is a master psionic with a talent for healing and prophecy, offering a variety of discreet services to her gentlemen callers. She will gladly heal the wounds/scars from a barroom brawl or the claws of another woman (costs 1D6x100 credits depending on the severity of the wound), cure venereal diseases (500 credits; healing touch and increased healing), psychic diagnosis (75 credits), instant sobriety from booze, drugs, or poison (400 credits, psychic purification), psychic surgery (5000 to 50,000 credits depending on the severity) and other healing services. Lydia is also clairvoyant and empathic, enabling her to foretell the future (usually by reading tarot cards). **Lydia:** Anarchist alignment, 7th level mind melter, 223 I.S.P., knows all healing and sensitive psi-powers as well as bio-manipulation, empathic transmission, hypnotic suggestion, mind bond, mind wipe, and telekinetic force field. I.Q. 12, M.E. 23, M.A. 19, P.B. 15, all others average. Age 32, human, 5 ft 6 inches tall.

34. **Punta's Magic Shop.** A young female sorceress (Maria, 3rd level ley line walker) and her father, a retired member of the Guild for the Gifted (Punta, a 12th level ley line walker), own this magic shop. The front of the establishment is covered with windows and

has a skylight, so sunlight fills the store. It is a bright, cheerful place, although there is the occasional demonic looking statue and monster's skull. Two goblins and an orc (considered D-Bees) work the back, stockroom, section of the store, while either Maria or Julio (4th level techno-wizard) and a sales clerk named Anna, deal with the customers. Only occasionally does Punta make a personal appearance at the store (he and his daughter live up-stairs on the second floor). Of course, the building is protected by wards and magic circles.

Magic items include talismans, amulets, scrolls, techno-wizard devices and a large variety of other magic items such as gryphon claws, flying carpets, etc. (**Note:** Many of the magic items listed in the Palladium RPG & Adventures on the High Seas are available in this shop. The **Rifts Conversion Book** will contain exact conversion info and new magic items.) Some of the store's hottest selling items to travelers are vampire crosses, TW-water blasters and flares. Also sells a variety of crystals and gem stones ideal for techno-wizardry.

35. **Riverview Movie Theater 1 & 2.** A popular movie theater that specializes in the showing of pre-rifts films (and occasionally, new, usually bad, contemporary films). The pre-rift films are the most popular and are rerun regularly. A "hot" film will show for four to six weeks, while a fair to good film will show for two weeks. There are two theaters that show two different films. Cost of admission is 30 credits per person.

36. **The North Star Hotel.** A 15-story complex that can accommodate 600 patrons. Rooms are clean, 80% have private baths, and security is good. Nice view of the park on the west side. Rooms cost 100 to 150 credits a night.

    South of the hotel is the guarded parking garage (the four squares on the map).

37. **The Pyramid Hotel.** An older and 20-story hotel that offers 200 bargain rooms on floors 16, 17, 18, and 19, (50 credits a night; no private bathroom, communal bathroom and shower on every floor), 200 quality rooms on floors 6-15 (80 credits a night; larger and have private bathroom), and 120 luxury rooms on floors 2-5 (120 credits a night, large, private bath, TV). The first floor contains the hotel's offices, lounge, bar, and two huge restaurants (food is fair to good, average cost is 20 credits a meal). The top, 20th, floor is divided into six massive penthouse suites. One is the residence of the hotel owner, Emanuel Juarez III, and at least two are available at any given moment (cost 1200 credits a night). Security is fair, upkeep reasonably good, service is good. Half of the hotel's staff are D-Bees.

38. **North Town Mechanics & Gas Station.** A competent mechanics shop able to repair vehicles and minor robot problems. Reasonable prices.

39. **The North Juarez Apartments.** An eight-story apartment building for the middle-class residents of New North Town. Security is excellent, the apartments are nice, service is good. Costs about 3000 a month to rent; few vacancies. Note: generally down wind of the stables next door.

40. **Wilbur's Stables.** Sells, buys, and rents horses, pack mules, donkeys, and has a team of four camels. Also offers veterinary services for horses, shoeing, and grooming. Renting a good riding horse with riding equipment costs 30 credits an hour or 150 for a 10 hour day or 800 credits for a full five days. A work horse (plow, pull wagon, pack mule) costs 20 credits an hour or 120 for a 12 hour day, or 600 credits for a full five days. All rentals require a 500 credit deposit to cover loss of equipment, in addition to agreeing to pay all expenses incurred from theft, injury or death of the animal. A typical work horse costs about 4000 to 10,000 credits, pack mule or donkey 3000 to 6000 credits, a good, trained, riding horse costs 10,000 to 40,000 credits, superior riding or race horse can cost as much as 10 times more. The camels are not for sale.

Wilbur and his family are psi-stalkers, which makes them superior animal handlers. Wilbur is a 7th level wilderness scout who love horses and is seen talking to them all the time. He is a slick and savvy businessman with a keen eye for quality horses and a passion for racing them. His sons are all 3rd and 4th level wilderness scouts, his daughters are considered wild psi-stalkers. Average alignment is anarchist, but there is strong family loyalty.

The six smaller buildings behind the main building are the blacksmith and additional stables. Operated by the large family of psi-stalkers: pa (Wilbur), ma, six sons, four daughters, Uncle Buck, Aunt Louisa, and their four boys and two girls. They also employ six pig-face D-Bees (orcs) and four small, pointy-eared D-Bee midgets (kobolds, who make excellent blacksmiths and prefer to work nights).

41. **Wainwright and Carpenter.** A quality manufacturer of wagons, wheels, barrels, tables, large and small ornamental crucifixes, furniture. Unfinished products, items not yet stained, varnished or painted, are half price.

42. **The North Town Lumberyard and Mill.** Produces and sells wood material for carpentry, such as two by fours, wood planks, beams, doors (wood and some metal/M.D.C. doors), molding, windows, paneling, wood roofing tiles/shingles, barrels of wooden stakes (12 for 2 credits, made from scraps), wood arrows and crossbow bolts (12 for 8 credits), mallets, rope, wood pegs, nails, screws, bolts, spikes, hammers, saws, paint, paint brushes, glues, resin, varnish, lacquer, sandpaper, tar paper, tar, and lime. Employs 100 full-time workers (50% are powerfully built D-Bees, a dozen are giants).

43. **Gomez the Coffin Maker.** Simple, cheap, unfinished wood coffins cost a paltry 400 credits. Fancy coffins range from 2000 to 6000 credits. A mega-damage coffin costs 50,000 credits per 100 M.D.C., with a maximum of 300. He will also build to special specifications, including airtight seal, secret vents or openings, locks, alarms and M.D.C. armor and more. Gomez is a self-serving pig who makes coffins of any specification without asking questions. To his way of thinking, he can argue that he has never "knowingly" built a special coffin for a vampire, but who else would require the unusual features he often includes (he claims the rich and eccentric).

Gomez the Coffin Maker is also called Mr. Ghoul-mez by the local kids and gang members. He is a 5th level operator with carpentry knowledge. Diabolic alignment, I.Q. 12, M.E. 18, P.S. 18, P.P. 15, all others average. Tall, 6 ft, 5 inches, thin, pale, yellow teeth, dull eyes, and looks to be about 40. Greedy, petty, and selfish, he will work for anybody who will pay the price. Hoards 200,000 credits worth of gold and gems in a secret compartment (100 M.D.C., with complex electronic lock and two tumblers) in his bedroom on the third floor of his building. The Night Master gang and other vampires frequent his establishment (stays open till midnight) and also protect him and his business from unfriendly forces. Nobody has ever proved that Mr.G works for the undead, but many suspect the truth. He employs one fellow fourth level operator, two 7th level D-Bee carpenters, four 5th level human carpenters and four laborers/assistants (all orcs).

44. **Morley's Mortuary.** This three-story building, next door to the coffin maker, is a funeral home. It is a nice, serene place with helpful morticians, and a variety of parlors, from simple, with two couches and wood folding chairs, to fancy, with numerous couches, armchairs and padded folding chairs. Coffins (40% purchased from Morley) generally cost 3000 to 8000 credits (simple wood costs 1000 credits), mortician services (prepare, preserve, present the body) cost 500 credits, parlor rental is 100 credits for the simple, and 1000 for a fancy parlor. Cremation is 100 credits, interment in a cemetery costs 1200.

Mr. J.P. Morley is a 6th level medical doctor turned mortician. He sometimes performs autopsies for the city government and individual clients (costs 500 to 1000 credits depending on the difficulty) and secretly sells human organs and cybernetic parts to the body-chop-shop across the road (#46). Miscreant alignment, I.Q. 11, P.P. 14, all others average. Has squirrelled away over six million credits, nearly half of which came from his sale of body parts. Secretly employs a quintet of grave ghouls to dispose of bodies (instead of cremating the bodies as he was paid to do) by eating them and to dig graves.

45. **North Town Florist.** A pretty shop that specializes in bridal bouquets and funeral arrangements. Prices are fairly reasonable.

46. **The Better Body (chop-shop).** This is your classic hole in the wall body-chop-shop. It is filthy, poorly lighted, and smells of blood and disinfectants. But prices are "slashed to the bone," about 40% less than the normal cost for organ transplants and cybernetic implants. Bionic parts are a rarity, but even they are 20% to 30% less than standard market value and bionic repairs are possible. The shop will also perform minor surgery, like removing bullets, suture knife wounds, etc., for a mere 1D6×100 credits, without reporting the incident to the authorities. This doctor is frequently used by the Skivers gang and underworld scum of all sorts.

    Doctor Vincent Lee is the owner and chief surgeon. He is a 9th level cyber-doc of great skill when he's not too drunk or on drugs. Miscreant alignment, I.Q. 15, M.A. 15, P.P. 20, P.B. 14, all others average. Age 55; usually depressed and sullen, doesn't give a shit about anybody. Spends most of his money on alcohol and cocaine.

47. **Chapel; Weddings Cheap** is all the pink and white neon sign says. This is a quickie marriage chapel. No blood test is needed. The marriage license is prepared on the spot. A quickie, no-fuss wedding costs 20 credits and takes five minutes. A longer, more formal wedding costs 50 credits, takes 15 minutes and has canned music and flowers. Formal wedding ceremonies and catered receptions are also available for about 1D6×1000 credits. The second floor is the wedding hall for large affairs.

48. **The Remmington Detective Agency.** This is a semi-respectable detective agency that seems to be continually embroiled in controversy and trouble. They are well liked by the neighborhood and seen as a positive force. The agency's detectives have an excellent rapport with the Guard Gang and the Guild for the Gifted, but are hated by the Juarez Police, Psykes and Night Masters.

    The head of the agency is **Josh Remmington**, a one-time member of Reid's Rangers (one reason for the agency's popularity), and pretty good amateur painter of Western themes. 7th level military specialist (ex-Coalition/Free Quebec military) and power armor pilot (CS SAMAS & Triax X-10 Predator). Skills of note include disguise, escape artist, pick locks, forgery, intelligence, tracking, wilderness survival, computer operation, literate in American, hand to hand: expert, W.P. targeting, W.P. energy weapons, robot combat: basic, pilot robot and power armor. I.Q. 14, M.E. 11, M.A. 17, P.S. 18, P.P. 18, P.B. 20, all others average; human, age 35, 6 feet tall, unprincipled alignment. Minor psionic: 56 I.S.P., object read and sixth sense.

    Victorio Truman is Remmington's erstwhile partner, a 5th level city rat and major psionic. Skills of note include radio: basic and scrambler, surveillance, computer operation, computer programming, computer hacking, pick locks, pick pockets, prowl, streetwise, literate in American, speaks American, Spanish, and Gobblely. I.Q. 17, M.E. 15, M.A. 10, P.S. 20, P.P. 17, P.B. 15, all others average; human, age 27, 5 feet, 8 inches tall, anarchist alignment. Major psionic: 60 I.S.P., mind block, presence sense, object read, see aura, see the invisible, telepathy, total recall, and sixth sense.

    The agency also employs two secretaries, two fourth level psi-stalkers, four fourth level dog pack mutants, four third level city rats skilled in surveillance, two 5th level headhunters, and a second level ley line walker (knows a total of 12 spells; magic is mostly 1-3 level spells suitable for espionage, like climb, chameleon, detect concealment, breathe without air, fingers of wind, blinding flash). All are of anarchist or unprincipled alignments.

    Services include locating missing persons, locating stolen goods, surveillance, photography of subject, wire tappings, breaking and entry, stealing (for a good cause; i.e., stealing a stolen item from the thief who stole it in the first place), personal body guard, security guard, etc. **Fees** vary from client to client. They would like to charge at least 75 credits an hour, or 600 credits per 10 hour day, plus expenses (ammunition, film, gasoline, bribe money, repairs of equipment, etc.); sometimes get more (hazardous assignments might command double or triple), other times less. Their tendency to champion the underdog often means getting paid less and exposure to dangerous situations.

49. **Seeligson & Jordan Attorneys and Counselors.** A pair of good-hearted rogue scholars, originally from New Lazlo, who work as attorneys. Both men know their way around the bureaucracy of the city government and the corrupt police force. They will never knowingly become involved in criminal activity and avoid defending gang members, the Guild for the Gifted, or the Black Market. Legal consultation may be given free or at greatly reduced rates to the needy, but average rates are 300 credits an hour.

    Jordan's main legal interests involve helping travelers who have been fleeced by criminal organizations or persecuted by the city government. He can arrange bails, pay fines, and defend clients in court. He boasts an impressive 70% winning record for court cases against the city and police force and is dreaded in court. Many city attorneys will plead out or drop a case the moment they find out that Jordan is willing to take the case to court. He is extremely literate (reads and writes American, Spanish and Euro 98%), fluent in Gobblely and Dragonese 88%, and is an avid collector of old books and art. 8th level rogue scholar and attorney at law. Scrupulous alignment, I.Q. 17, M.A. 24, M.E. 20, all others average. Age 40; human. Loyal friend to Seeligson, who he greatly respects and trusts.

    Seeligson is the crafty senior partner. His specialty is insurance fraud, medical claims, and business law. He is also a fairly competent computer hacker (76%) and a master at negotiation and bluffing. 11th level rogue scholar and attorney at law. Scrupulous alignment, I.Q. 19, M.A. 20, M.E. 18, all others average. Age 54; human. Loyal friend to Jordan, who he greatly respects and trusts.

50. **N.T. Money Exchange.** Will turn gold, silver, gems and jewelry (not artifacts, vehicles, weapons, mortgages, or magic) into instant credit. No questions asked. No proof of ownership required. Pays 55% of market value for Juarez credit, or 40% for universal credit. This is a Black Market operation. Quiet, efficient, and protected. Employs borgs, crazies and juicers for security (1D6 level).

51. **Old-World Style Beef & Leather.** A small, smelly butcher shop that sells beef in its many forms: steaks, roasts, stew beef, ground (hamburger), sausage, slices, livers, kidneys, brains, tongues, feet, eyes and snout. Also sells some poultry. Plus a section of the store sells leather goods: belts, straps (studded and plain), strips, watch bands, hats, tanned leather (cowhides), etc. Good prices.

52. **Felix's Fruit Market.** A medium size market that sells plums, guava, avocado and other fresh fruits, dried fruits, jams, fruit juices, ciders, honey, some vegetables, spices, dairy products, and eggs. Reasonable prices for good quality food.

53. **Town and Country Vehicles — Used Car Lot.** Sells used and rebuilt automobiles, motorcycles, hover cycles, common hovercraft, and the occasional jet pack, mountaineer ATV, sky king and wing board. Conventional engines are the norm (few techno-wizard engines). Prices are 30% to 50% below new vehicle prices (vehicle M.D.C. is typically 10% less). Fair to good quality. Will pay 30% market value for used vehicles in good condition, 10% in poor shape. Has own mechanics.

54. **Open Market.** Scores of different vendors and farmers sell their goods at this large market. Merchants include sellers of spices,

herbs, tobacco, corn and other vegetables, flour and grains, fruit, fresh meats, smoked and salted meats, jerked beef, poultry, fish, candy, flowers, hats, ponchos, baggy cotton shirts and pants, sandals, rope, sacks, wooden stakes, cross bows, bolts and arrows, and some livestock such as chickens, geese, ducks, pigs, sheep and goats. Prices are generally 20% below standard market value, but quality varies from fair to excellent.

55. Tinker's Shop. Makes, fixes and sells simple items made of metal such as belt buckles, clasps, pins, pots, pans, knives, kitchen utensils, fishing hooks, animal traps, manacles, chain, horseshoes, nails, hammers, bells, and wind chimes. Smith in back of building. Standard prices.

56. Sherman's Potter Place. A maker of a vast variety of pottery, dishes, platters, bowls, clay jars, mugs, and wind chimes. From simple clay to fine ceramics. The local saloons are major purchasers of the simpler mugs. Fair prices, good to excellent quality.

57. The Fighting Cock. A favorite indoor arena, gambling place and saloon. Every night different animals are pitted against each other; rats, cocks, dogs (include coyote and wolf), wild cats or dogs versus wild boar or other fierce animal, bull and boar wrestling (humanoid vs bull or boar, bare-handed), boxing or wrestling (humanoid vs humanoid). Prize money of 200 to 1200 credits or equivalent in gold is given to the winner of the contest, as well as earnings from side bets with fellow patrons or the house.

The saloon offers strong and cheap drinks, two credits each, but is limited to corn liquor moonshine (powerful stuff), tequila, and beer.

The owner is Pedro Delgado, a 6th level scholar (I.Q. 12 all others average, miscreant alignment) who lives vicariously through the fights and excitement at the Fighting Cock. He is a simpering, mean, back-stabbing wimp who has no combat skills. The only time he fights or exerts himself is when he has Night Hawk and/or several of his strongmen to protect him and to subdue his foe for him. Pedro pays the police for favors and to overlook trouble, in return he gives them information and has his men do an occasional special job for the police. Consequently, The Fighting Cock is a hangout for some of the corrupt members of the Juarez police force (1D6+1 are present 80% of the time).

His manager of the fights is a burly, 7th level crazy known as The Night Hawk. I.Q. 11, M.E. 14, P.S. 27, P.P. 20, P.E. 21, Spd. 36, all others average; hit points 82, S.D.C. 124. P.P.E. 25, I.S.P. 52, psionic powers: impervious to fire, levitation, telekinesis, plus the crazy's powers of enhanced healing, bio-regeneration and special bonuses. Insanities: Phobia: snakes, Obsession: gambling (loves it, gambles all the time), Affective Disorder: disgusted by anything sticky, Crazy Hero: nighttime complex in which he believes his M.O.M. powers and abilities occur only at night (fights like an average man during the day), thus he is active all night and sleeps most of the day. Hates vampires, likes to kill them.

The indoor gambling arena also employs Ferdinand, a 4th level juicer and sometimes, wrestler/fighter in the arena (P.S. 30, P.P. 24, anarchist), two 3rd headhunters in NG-Samson power armor, four bouncers, all of whom are 3rd level Ogre fighters and four second level Orc fighters; all possess a strength of 24 and are anarchist and miscreant alignments. Pedro also employs two goblin thieves (4th level, miscreant) to pick pockets and keep an eye out for troublemakers. Off-duty policemen may step in to give a hand in getting rid of brigands or to shakedown gullible visitors (bribes and pay-offs are split 50/50).

58. The House of Healing. Psychic healing is performed at reasonable fees. Psychic diagnosis 50 credits, negate toxins (booze, drugs, poison) 250 credits (psychic purification), healing minor wounds, cuts and bruises from a barroom brawl costs 50 credits, deep stab wounds and/or blood loss (healing touch) 100 credits, internal injury or grievous wounds requiring several healing touches and enhanced healing 3D4 × 100 credits depending on the severity of the wound, cure of minor diseases 500 credits (healing touch and increased healing), psychic surgery (4000 to 24,000 credits depending on the severity, sometimes more), exorcism 10,000 credits per entity. They will also heal pets and work animals for similar fees.

The House of Healing is run by three elderly sisters (each is a 12th level psi-healer, anarchist alignment, 64, 65 and 67 years old). They also employ ten, fourth level psychics with healing powers and a fifth level mystic. All are women.

59. **In God's Image.** A quaint artisans' shop where craftsmen make statues of old Aztec and Mayan deities, carved out of wood, stone and jade. 75% are copies based on real Aztec and Mayan statues and carvings. The figures are popular souvenirs for the wealthy and art minded persons. Prices are 1D6 × 100 credits, except jade carvings which cost 4D6 × 100 credits, depending on the size and complexity of the statue.

60. **Temple of Coatlicue and the Aztec Gods of Light & Dark.** A pyramid shaped temple dedicated to Aztec gods of earth, air, moon, sun, death and war.

61. **Good Food Snack Shop.** Sells cold drinks: water (1 credit), soda, fruit juice, cactus juice, beer, wine, ice cream cones (hand dipped; 6 flavors), chocolate, sugar candy, honey, syrup, bread, corn chips, hot chip dip, flaky cinnamon and sugar chips, popcorn, and cheese sticks. Everything is quite tasty and ranges in price from 1-6 credits a serving.

62. **Robot Horses & Canines.** A small robotics shop that specializes in the sale of robot horses and dogs. Also repairs and reprograms robot horses and dogs. **The basic bot horse** (Simple intelligence is all that is available, minimal I.Q., loyal, obedient, basic program: trained animal like functions; 150 M.D.C., 5 year nuclear power source) costs: Pony: 3 million credits, Medium size horse: 4 million, Large horse: 4.3 million. **Basic bot dog:** Small 1.2 million credits, Medium: 2.1 million, Large: 3.7 million. **Extra Features:** Additional 100 M.D.C. 100,000 credits, additional 200 M.D.C. one million credits. Speech and Skill Programs: Domestic 55,000 credits, technical (speaks 5 languages, knows lore, and operates computer) 220,000 credits, wilderness (select 5 appropriate wilderness skills) 175,000 credits, espionage (intelligence, detection) 95,000 credits, espionage spy (tracking, escape, photography, pick locks) 260,000 credits. **Note:** Programs same as found in **Rifts Sourcebook #1**, prices 5% to 10% higher. Real animal appearance: Looks like a real dog or horse with fake fur, eyes, and other cosmetic features. Cost: Horse 200,000 credits, dog 120,000 credits. **Note:** Weapons and other features as found in the **Rifts Sourcebook #1** are all available at a cost of about 10% more.

63. **Official Wilk's Laser Store.** Sells only Wilk's laser products at 25% less than standard market prices. Also repairs lasers of all kinds and recharges e-clips (Wilk's E-Clips are recharged at a 25% discount). In addition to weapons and tools, the store also sells a variety of other Wilk's products, including cybernetic finger lasers (tools and weapons), telescopic, laser targeting, gun sight (3000 credits; 2000 ft/609 m), pocket laser distancer (1500 credits; 5000 feet/1524 m), infrared distancing binoculars (1500 credits; 2 mile/3 km range), high-powered laser flashlight (400 credits; 1000 foot beam), laser spotlights (1500 credits; 1000 foot beam/305 m, illuminates an eight foot/2.4 m circular area; for mounting on vehicles), and conventional flashlights and lanterns.

64. **North Town Taxi Service.** The garage and dispatch station for North Town taxicabs, a fleet of blue hover-sedans. Costs 1 credit a minute or two credits a mile, whichever is applicable.

65. **Mexicalli Rose Restaurant.** Mexican cuisine, good food, excellent wine. Typical meal costs 10 to 18 credits.

66. **The Third Eye — Fortune Teller.** This is a pleasant little shop that offers palm reading, tarot cards and playful fortune-telling, nothing too extreme or serious. Four attractive young women perform the showman-like (fake) card and palm readings. The cost is 10 credits and the fortunes are always good and the advice helpful. Only the attractive, middle-aged woman who owns the shop possesses any real psionics.

Madame Dolores is a 9th level vagabond who has learned to use her major psi-abilities for profit. Powers include clairvoyance, empathy, see aura, sense magic, deaden pain, and psychic diagnosis (I.Q. 12, M.E. 19, all others average; 76 I.S.P, anarchist alignment). Madame Dolores is a secret member of the Psykes gang. Psychic readings are impressions from viewing the aura and empathy, combined with expert theatrics, and cost 50 credits. Psychic diagnosis costs 100 credits (this may be used to answer concerns about problems and anxieties, as well as health questions). Clairvoyant readings cost 200 to 600 credits. Deadening pain costs 20 credits.

67. **Laser Villa (video CDs).** This establishment boasts of having over 10,000 one and three inch video discs and over 20,000 music discs. Videos include contemporary dramas, comedy, and instructional vids (very important in a society where 80% of the people are illiterate). All are bilingual (American & Spanish); simply program your vid player for the desired sound track. A typical contemporary vid-disc sells for 75 credits. Music discs sell for 25 credits. Also sells pre-rift music discs for 2D6 × 1000 each; has 4D6 × 10 in stock at all times. And sells the occasional pre-rifts video disc for 4D6 × 10,000; has 2D6 in stock most of the time (kept in a safe). Also sells CD players and blank, recordable discs.

68. **North Side Massage Parlor.** "Get rid of those kinks and stiff joints from sleeping under the stars or a hard day's work!" Over 30 male and female, certified, expert masseurs. 20 minute quickie is 40 credits, a regular hour session is 90 credits. Massage and chiropractic bone manipulation is 150 credits. Use of the sauna and showers is an additional 20 credits.

69. **A-Plus Energy Weapons.** A weapon smith that specializes in energy and high-tech weaponry. Selection includes all vibro-blades, neural mace, all Wilk's laser weapons and tools, L-20 pulse rifle, and all common Northern Gun weapons, including the rail guns, and energy clips. Also sells parts for the NG Samson power armor (can not do repairs), gun sights/optics, smoke grenades, flares and recharges energy-clips. Prices are 10% less than list.

70. **North Town Computers & Electronics.** A well equipped store that sells computers of all types and sizes, language translators, laser distancers, electro-adhesive pads, sensory equipment, medical systems (including robot medical kits), video and/or audio disc players, cameras, watches, surveillance equipment, and tool kits. No cybernetics. Prices are standard.

The salespeople will always refer their customers to the **Wilderness Outfitter** for other goods and products or just as a store to visit. The other store is owned by their cousins.

71. **Complete Wilderness Outfitter.** A well equipped store for all one's wilderness needs. Prices on everything are standard to 5% less. It sells tents, sleeping bags, backpacks, cloth and leather sacks of all sizes, saddlebags, riding tack, plastic and glass jars and containers, canteens, wine skins, portable stoves, lanterns, flashlights, lighters, gasoline, kerosene, flares, rope, spikes, grappling hooks, insect repellents, pocket sewing kit, pocket tool kit, fishing poles, fishing line and hooks, knee boots, leather and cloth gloves, hiking boots, SCUBA gear, sails for sail boats, and similar outdoors items.

The weapon section includes vibro-knives and short swords, pocket knives, hunting/skinning knives, throwing knives, wood knives, swords, silver-plated weapons, crossbows and bolts, bow and arrows, spears, quarterstaves, walking sticks, wood stakes, mallets, wooden crosses, and a full selection of vampire weapons, including TW-weapons and flares. Guns include 9 mm pistols (normal and silver bullets; a box of 96 normal bullets is 30 credits, silver bullets cost 70 credits), sub-machineguns, and rifles, and the entire line of Northern Gun energy weapons. **Body armor** is limited to Crusader, Plastic Man, Huntsman and Explorer.

Vehicles are limited to the wastelander and highway-man motorcycles, canoes, and underwater sleds. Will be glad to help find and select a suitable vehicle or horse for a 2% commission.

72. **North Town General Hospital.** A 10-story hospital with fairly modern medical facilities and psychic healers (a few wizards too). Its emergency room is typically full (psychic healers are especially useful in the ER for quick stabilization of the seriously injured). Suturing cuts, fixing bruises, and bandaging wounds will cost 4D6×10 credits depending on the degree of difficulty and time, transfusions cost 100 credits a pint, setting broken bones costs 1D4x100, surgery and implants can cost 6,000 to 40,000 credits depending on the severity and complexity of the surgery, and a typical stay at a hospital costs approximately 250 credits a day.

73. **North Town General Professional Building.** This is a six-story annex to the hospital that includes a massive pharmacy, scores of laboratories (blood, chemical, toxicology, forensics, etc.), radiology and nuclear medicine, ultra-sound facility, morgue, and administrative offices.

74. **The Merchant's Pony Express Office (Merchants on Wheels).** A branch of the famous travelling merchant company and mail delivery service. These cheerful lunatics will try to deliver a package anywhere in Northern Mexico, North America and most of Canada. Fees vary depending on the size, weight and number of packages, the distance of travel and the potential dangers involved. They are best at delivering small packages that can be carried by one or two delivery men. A delivery from Juarez to El Paso only costs 40 credits, same day. From Juarez to anywhere in Lone Star, or to Fort Reid, costs 150 credits, 1D4 day delivery (some of these bandits are hard to find). From Juarez to Chi-Town, 1000 credits and also 1D4 day delivery. To Free Quebec, 2D4 days, at a cost of 1600 credits.

All the delivery men and employees of the Merchant's Pony Express are cheerful, courteous, trustworthy and reliable. A Flooper is the Juarez office manager.

75. **Phil's Used Cybernetics.** Phil is an arthritic, 11th level headhunter (with two bionic arms and weapons, miscreant alignment) who has retired to run a used cybernetics shop. All the usual cybernetics and many bionic (50%) items are available at 50% the standard cost. Of course, all need cleaning, recharging, and many are slightly damaged (reduce M.D.C. by 25%). Phil is lewd, rude, loud and he has the manners of a rhino-buffalo. He will pay 10% of market value for cybernetics in good condition and 20% for bionics. Also buys the occasional robot part, but only at 5% of market. No questions asked. A dealer for the Skivers gang.

76. **Herbs & Medicine Shop.** A grungy looking holistic medicine pharmaceutical shop that sells all kinds of herbs used in folk medicine, including arsenic, cocaine, narcotic roots and flowers, hallucinogenic mushrooms and peyote, garlic, wolfbay, salt, spices, and prepared salves and lotions for burns, insect bites and rashes. Also sells love, charm and healing potions (same as Palladium RPG).

77. **Horsefitter, Smith & Riding Shop.** Shoes horses, sells riding equipment, food bags, blinders, saddlebags, spurs, picture books on horse care and riding, rope, and basic riding clothes like hats, ponchos, boots, and leather goods. The big selling item is lightweight, M.D.C. barding (horse body armor) made from the same substance as the plastic man human armor. Cost: 32,000 credits, 90 M.D.C., weight: 40 pounds (18 kg).

78. **The Beastiary.** A huge, concrete, M.D.C., two-story building with 20 foot ceilings, that sells horses and exotic animals. Sells good quality riding and work horses, mules, and occasionally, cattle, elephants, rhino-buffalos, and dinosaurs. Prices are a bit higher than usual. Main income is from the sale of exotic animals and monsters. Few of the monsters and wild animals are tame or trained, although they may appear so when handled by the simvan, psi-stalker or mutant dog handlers. No refunds.

Monsters and animals can include anything from a rift found within a 500 mile area of Juarez. Most wilderness scouts and adventurers know of the Beastiary's desire to purchase (and sell) strange creatures, so they bring in a constant supply of strange monsters. Sometimes the monsters are one of kind oddities, some are creatures of magic, like the unicorn, pegasus, and shaper, while others are aliens, mutants and the demonic. The cost for such a beast can be as little as a 1000 credits or as much as a million. Most of the larger exotic animals, like housebroken dinosaurs, gryphons and tuskers, drop in around the 10,000 to 40,000 credits range. Trained pegasus or manticore and top quality horses will garner 80,000 to 150,000 credits. Two recent imports are magical wing tips (6000 credits a pair) and fire worms (8,000 credits each).

One of the shop's best selling beasts of burden (great for pulling carts, wagons, lumber, etc.) is the nodosaur family of dinosaurs. The nodosaurs include the panoplosaurus, silvisaurus, and nodosaurus, all of which travel in small herds of 1D6×10 near the Rio Grande and other rivers of northern Mexico, New Mexico and Kansas. They are surprisingly smart (for an animal) and gentle, heavily armor plated, and herbivores that feed on the grass and plants that grow in and around rivers and lakes. Nodosaurs are very sturdy, powerful (average P.S. 30 to 60), slow-moving (average speed 22 to 33) beasts that are about the size of a rhinoceros. One nodosaur is equal to a team of four horses in raw pulling power. Average cost is a low 2000 to 6000 credits (mainly because it can be difficult and expensive to feed the three ton animals). **Note:** See Mr. Lizzaro in the *Night Arcade and Freak Show* for a description of a panoplosaurus.

Normal animals for sale include a variety of birds (mostly parrots and songbirds, 20 to 120 gold each), lizards, turtles, foxes, dogs, the occasional jaguar and ocelot, weasels and ferrets. Most critters sell for under a hundred credits, jaguars and ocelots cost 500 credits.

79. **Sunshine Vampire Exterminator Agency.** This is a group of 13 well-meaning and fairly competent, professional vampire exterminators. The group is composed of 3rd and 4th level city rats, wilderness ,scouts and headhunters turned vampire hunters. The only psychics in the group is a 5th level mutant dog, named Waldo, who is the owner's best friend and a 3rd level mystic; both arm themselves with TW water shotguns, storm flares and globe of daylight flares. The owner is a 4th level wilderness scout and a member of the Guard (scrupulous, I.Q. 9, M.A. 19, M.E. 17, P.S. 19, all others average).

The exterminators are of good or selfish alignments and are generally cheerful, swashbuckling wiseguys who know everything there is to know about vampires and are literally dressed to kill! Half are members of The Guard. Standard anti-vamp equipment includes Bushman body armor, passive nightvision optics, a silver crucifix around the neck, a large wooden cross tucked in the belt, 9 mm pistol (20 shot) with silver bullets (and six extra clips), NG-Super pistol (M.D. weapon), water pistol or rifle, a dozen stakes and a mallet, silver plated knife, and a Wilk's laser flashlight with a cross taped to the lens. Exterminators are sent out in pairs to handle one or two vampires (cost 150 to 400 credits) or a team of four to six men is sent to confront three to eight vampires (800 to 1500 credits). One member of the team will be a partial cyborg or in power armor and equipped with a wood flechette firing rail gun, while another will have a water cannon, particle beam rifle and a globe of daylight scroll.

They also sell the Vampire Almanac (see #108 for description), vampire protection kits (25 credits gets you a 10 inch wood cross, a small cross on a cheap chain, a ring of garlic, pocket mirror, four wood stakes and a mallet), a dozen stakes for six credits, rings of garlic for six credits, and an instructional video (made themselves) called How to Protect Yourself from the Undead (45 minutes, 30 credits).

80. Temple of Camazotz (Mayan Deity — Ruler of Bats). The temple is a church of darkness whose priests deal with vampires, mysticism and dark forces. The god Camazotz is said to be a powerful alien intelligence who can control wild bats, darkness, death, and even exert his will over the undead. It is further said that he lives in the jungles of the Yucatan — the land that is and is not. The building is a dilapidated looking, two-story, wood frame edifice lit only by candles and filled with pungent incense. A 20 foot tall totem pole-type statue, carved from a tree stands in front of the temple. The statue depicts four bats with grotesque faces. The temple's doors are always open and one of the five priests, Mayan H-men (shaman/holistic doctor/exorcist/healer), is always available for consultation and healing.

All the H-men are humans of about 5th level experience and anarchist or miscreant alignments, except the high priest who is 8th level and miscreant. The vampires are somewhat fearful and respectful of the priests and will never attack them. Thus, the Camazotz H-men often act as liaisons between the undead and the living, arranging deals between vampires and humanoids, and sometimes use the undead as their minions. The Camazotz H-men also preform blood rituals to exorcise evil spirits and demons, predict the weather, cure sickness, and foretell the future. They can also metamorphosize into a bat or tarantula (same as spell). Despite the aura of evil surrounding the temple, the peasants of Juarez frequently turn to the Camazotz H-men for advice, to rid them of vampires and evil spirits, and for healing. The price? Typically a couple gold pieces, food or livestock and a pint of blood!

The temple is also a refuge for vampires, but the undead, like the peasants, are subservient to the priests. While the priest may give advice, protection, and food (the blood he has collected), in exchange, the vampire must perform him a service or favor. The favor may be helpful to the priest or the peasants, like killing or chasing away a demon or brigand, or performing manual labor, or the favor may be of evil intent, like robbery, brutality, terrorism, or murder. Such is the way of the Camazotz priests.

81. The Feathered Serpent Tavern. A tavern frequented by the homeless, beggars, punks, D-Bees and the worst criminal low-life; the locals often refer to it as the "assassins' den." The owner is Slymac the giant (troll), a long-time resident and retired warrior (9th level assassin). It is rumored that his son, Trool, dabbles in demonic summonings (2nd level shifter). In the last year the tavern has gotten worse than ever as a haven for the evil. Drinks are strong and cheap, a mere ONE credit per mug.

The Feathered Serpent serves as a recruitment and employment center for evildoers, with murder and assassination the house specialties. The murderous patrons are often employed by the Psykes, Black Market and other criminals and malefactors. Slymac cuts the deal, arranges payment and assigns somebody to the task. He keeps a reasonable 30% as an agent's fee. However, there is more than what meets the eye.

The true power behind the tavern's den of murderers is a supernatural creature known as a Mindolar or "Mind Slug." The horrid, larva-like intelligence was foolishly summoned by Slymac's son, but his inexperience has proven to be the family's undoing. The young shifter failed to control this greater being and became its mind slave. Father, mother, sister, and the workers at the tavern were all to become its victims. The few that managed to fight the monster's power were killed. The mindolar's bite places its victim under its complete control (identical to the domination spell, only the duration and range is infinite). A single mindolar can control as many as 200 mind slaves, but at this point the mind slug at the tavern is content with 73 (including a police captain, three police sergeants, a couple local merchants, Slymac and his family, the tavern's staff, and numerous thugs). **Note:** Its existence is known by the priests of Camazotz (#80), but they have an arrangement with the monstrosity. **Itazal The Mind Slug:** H.F. 16, diabolic, 7ft long, 200 P.P.E., Hit Points 9000 (equal to 90 M.D.C., can regenerate 4D6×100 H.P. every hour), vulnerable to all attacks, except mind control and illusions. Psionics: 800 I.S.P., all psi-sensitive powers, exorcism, sleep, healing touch, and increased healing, +10 to save vs psionics, +10 vs H.F., +3 vs magic. The slug lives to control humanoids and to inflict pain and sorrow.

82. Moonlight Taxi. A small, independent taxi service with a fleet of 32 automobiles. Costs 2 credits a minute or two credits a mile, whichever is applicable. Also rents bicycles at a cost of 50 credits for a 24 hour day.

83. Silversmith. Sells pure silver bars (300 credits a pound/0.45 kg) and silver-plated weapons. Silver bullets cost 90 credits for a box of 96 (superior silver content), silver-tipped arrows and crossbow bolts at 30 credits a dozen, silver-plated daggers and pocket knives for 2D6×10 credits, as well as silver crosses, chains, jewelry, goblets, silverware, and other silver items, at good but highish prices.

84. Automatic Mechanic & Gas Station. A dirty but competent service station for wheeled and hover vehicles. Reasonable prices.

85. The Tlaloc Shop. Tlaloc was an Aztec god of rain. This shop sells every variety of techno-wizard water weapons, TW SCUBA equipment, TW underwater flyers, conventional water weapons, vials of holy water (6 ounces, 20 credits), good wine (magically converted water to wine), and the purest, freshest water in town (25 credits per half gallon/1.9 liters), as well as dozens of water containers and medallions of the god Tlaloc. The owners are a husband (6th level techno-wizard) and wife (5th level ley line walker). They employ three third level techno-wizards and four shop clerks (ordinary people). Prices are standard.

86. Alfredo's Leather & Whips. This is a leather shop that caters to the gangs. Leather goods include jackets, pants, capes, and boots, spiked and studded gloves, wristbands, straps, belts, caps, face masks, etc. Also sells bull-whips, cat-o-nine-tails, leather strips, unfinished rawhide strips, handcuffs, lengths of chains, ball and chain type weapons, and accessories. Prices are on the low side.

87. Quality Used Weapons & Armor. Well, the quality isn't there, but the items are cheap. Nothing new, all used, no refunds. **Mega-Damage body armor** with half its original M.D.C. for 60% off the list price! Most of the armor is pretty battered and scarred, but a good substitute for warriors low on cash and in need of some protection. **Weapons** include crude wood stakes (12 for 4 credits), a variety of ragged looking crossbows, bolts and arrows, revolvers, automatic pistols, and many of the Wilk's and Northern Gun weapons. These guns may not look fancy, but work fine (although they don't come with charged E-clips). Cost is 25% less than the standard, list prices. A sweet talker and/or quantity purchaser (eight or more energy weapons) can increase that discount to 35%. **Vehicles:** Occasionally has a used motorcycle, hover cycle or Big Boss ATV for sale, half off.

The shop is owned by an ex-mercenary D-Bee by the name of Sploss (6th level wilderness scout, ogre) and run by his D-Bee employees, mostly orcs and goblins.

88. The Vasquez Tattoo Parlor. Another popular place for gang members and young toughs. A small tattoo, about the size of a silver dollar costs 30 credits, medium (6-8 inches) 75 credits, large (12-15 inches) 150 credits. Special or intricate designs will cost 50 to 100 credits more. The six tattoo artists are very skilled.

89. The Sentinel Parking Garage. A six-level parking structure that is patrolled by armed guards. Comparatively safe. 10 credits and hour; only a 4% chance of a vehicle being stolen. Owned and operated by the Black Market.

90. The Desert Inn (a gang hangout). A filthy, smelly, dark, and dangerous saloon and flophouse. Rooms cost 20 credits a night (no private bathroom; community privy is down the hall). Drinks are cheap, poor quality liquor, costing two credits a drink. Nobody asks for names, identification, or questions anybody about anything. Questions at this place can get a person killed. Likewise, the police seldom arrive, even to investigate shootings, until 2D6 minutes after a gunfight is over.

The Desert Inn is a favorite hangout of the **Skivers gang** and occasionally, the Subs and Psykes. The Skivers and other hoodlums use the Inn as a convenient location to observe the patrons coming and going to the Palace Garcia. Muggings, cyber-snatching, beatings, murder, and car theft are common nightly occurrences in this neighborhood.

91. The Palace Garcia. A rough and tumble gambling casino owned by the wealthy noble, Senor Carlos Garcia (see #28 for Garcia estate). The building is a large eight-story structure with three towers and the appearance of a castle or palace. It is the largest and one of the most popular gambling casinos in the city. **Floors 8, 7, and 6** contain 80 luxury hotel rooms leased or given to special clients, wealthy visiting gamblers and business associates. **Floor five** is used as a brothel and drug den where guests can enjoy carnal pleasures and/or a variety of drugs. **Floor four** contains storage rooms, a huge bar and ballroom. **Floor three** contains the private offices of the casino, surveillance (all public rooms including floors 1-5 and the basement, are monitored, except the casino's private offices), auxiliary lighting and electrical system, security, living quarters for 50 employees, Garcia's private office and a few storage rooms. **Floors one and two** are the casino areas. Over 200 gaming tables offering every game of chance one can imagine, two dozen different card games, craps, roulette, coin tossing, knife and dart throwing, slot machines, and others. Most of the games are fixed so that the house wins 72% of the time. Profit is split between Senor Garcia (30%) and the Black Market (70%), who is the sponsor of the casino. Garcia has an excellent rapport with the Black Market and they trust him completely (he would never betray or cheat the B.M.).

The basement has an indoor arena that seats 200 and is used for special events (about three fights/competitions a month). Big matches cost 1000 credits a head and admittance is by invitation only. The basement also contains the heating, cooling and electrical systems for the building (monitored and locked away behind M.D.C. walls and metal doors; guarded by magic, men and technology). The vault is also in the basement and heavily protected by men, magic and technology. 1D4×One million credits' worth of gold and valuables are in the safe at all times, plus important documents, I.D. cards, and 96 bearer universal credit cards with 50,000 credits each (can be used by anybody). However, to steal from the casino is to steal from the vengeful Black Market. Thieves will be hunted down and terminated (after recovering as much of the stolen goods as possible).

The Palace Garcia is also an excellent source for gathering information (especially with the complex audio-visual surveillance system). Happy gamers and drunks have a habit of talking too much, bragging, and flashing valuables.

The security force includes 12 headhunters, 12 juicers, 6 full conversion borgs, 6 power armor pilots, 6 psi-stalkers, 6 dog pack, 4 Brodkil demons (all have some bionics), 2 bursters, 2 ley line walkers, 2 mind melters, 2 assassins with major psionics, and a thunder lizard dragon, ALL of whom are 5th level experience. An additional 48 low-level security people (1st and 2nd level city rats, vagabonds, scouts, and grunts; men and women) patrol the floors of the casino, watching for trouble, breaking up fights, catching pickpockets and escorting/bouncing drunks, punks and troublemakers out of the casino. Plus half the game dealers are criminal city rats and thieves of 1D6 levels of experience.

92. Palace-Side Escort Service. An armed escort service that will provide 2, 4, or 6 heavily armed security guards and an M.D.C. armored vehicle to transport wealthy visitors and big winners at the Palace Garcia to the bank or their homes/hotels. All fees are based on an hourly rate per pair of escorts. Armed and armored headhunter/merc escorts cost 300 credits an hour, juicers and/or crazies 800 credits, borg and/or bot escorts cost 1000 credits, ley line walker/wizard and juicer or borg 1200 credits, mind melter and dog boy or psi-stalker 1200 credits, or the deluxe dragon (fire, ice or thunder lizard) escort 2000 credits. All are 4th to 6th level and trustworthy (they get half the fee and are serious warriors, dedicated to their job).

The escort service is bonded and registered with the police and recommended by the casino. Although presented as an independent business, Palace-Side Escort Service is owned and operated by Senor Garcia. 30% of its profits goes into the pockets of the Black Market.

93. The Supernatural Protection Agency. This is an independent escort service and detective agency owned and operated by supernatural creatures. The agency is open to all sorts of protection and escort assignments, as well as vampire extermination, and supernatural pest control (chase away evil spirits, faerie folk, demons, etc.), and cares little about ethics or morality, thus they will protect known hoodlums, suspected criminals, and evil characters, as well as good and honest people foolish enough to hire them. All the monsters at the agency are surprisingly trustworthy and rarely attack or abandon their employers. They are just mean, ugly, and villainous.

An armed escort will consist of a pair of heavily armed and psionic or magic security guards and an M.D.C. armored vehicle. Protection and extermination/pest control fees are based on an hourly rate per pair of escorts/exterminators. Armed psi-stalkers, or psi-stalker and mutant dog, cost 400 credits, necromancer and a pair of zombies or skeletons 500 credits, werebeasts 700 credits, mind melter and psi-stalker 900 credits, dragon slayers 1000 credits, ley line walker and mystic 1000 credits, ley line walker and warlock (earth, air, fire or water) 1500 credits, succubus or incubus 1200 credits, sowki demon and mutant animal or psi-stalker 1500 credits, thornhead demon and brodkil demon 1800. Most are 3rd to 5th level (when applicable).

A husband (8th level) and wife (10th level) team of shifters own and control the Supernatural Protection Agency. Both are intelligent, literate, and miscreant evil. Sometimes hired by the Palace Garcia, members of the Guild for the Gifted, and the wealthy.

94. The Electronic Man (Body-Chop-Shop). A well stocked cybernetics and bionic chop-shop. Fairly clean, very competent cyber-docs. Prices are typically 40% below market for cybernetics and 20% less for bionics. A purchaser of body parts and artificial parts from the Skivers gang.

95. The Blazing Saddle Dance Hall & Saloon. A large, clean, and lively place with a first and second floor ballroom and bar. The third floor is divided into four medium-size, private dance halls that can be rented for private parties. Drinks are good quality and fairly priced, at 3 to 6 credits a drink. A popular night spot.

96. Windsong Carriage Service. A small stable of a dozen horse-drawn carriages that will take visitors, lovers, and shoppers on a romantic or luxurious ride down the market district and the North Town Park (near the Sanctum) for 40 credits. Will also serve as a taxi service at the rate of 40 credits an hour. The carriage drivers are a good source for collecting gossip and having the parts of town identified ("Don't go there, Psykes hangout," or "Worse chop-shop in town," etc.).

97. The Queen Bee. A fancy dress and jewelry shop. Someplace for the casino's winners to spend their winnings. Prices are average, quality is good.

98. The Ace Pawnshop. A friendly, brightly lit pawnshop that buys and sells valuables. Pays 30% to 50% of real, Juarez, market value, but will sell the item in 10 days. To buy back the pawned item, the individual must pay a 10% premium based on the money received. As one might suspect, this is a Black Market operation.

99. Millie's Loan Agency. An independent loan shark that pays the Black Market 20% of earnings as protection money to let her operate. Borrowers must have collateral such as a vehicle, robot, weapons, bionics or cybernetics (has the Electric Body chop-shop remove parts), etc., to get a loan, or a known resident. Interest is 10%, compounded daily! Failure to pay a debt may result in getting beaten up, legs broken, fingers chopped off, and murder. Millie is not a nice person (Diabolic alignment, city rat, I.Q. 15, M.A. 18, P.P. 13, P.B. 15, all others average).

She has a network of thugs, snitches, spies and city rats to do her dirty work for her. She sometimes employs members of the Subs and Skivers. Really a two-bit operation.

100. The Peacock Club. A four-story nightclub with expensive drinks, live entertainment, and lots of atmosphere. A popular place among wealthy travelers, high-ranking police officers, and men of magic. The third floor offers quiet, high stakes card games. The fourth floor is the owner's residence and storage.

101. West Side Hotel. A nice, clean, comfortable 16-story hotel with 600 rooms. Average room costs 90 credits a night, a suite (double the size) 175 credits. All rooms are small, but have a double bed and private bath.

102. Jail house. A grungy, three-story jail house/prison facility that has 100 separate cells, and 12 high-security solitary cells (air tight). On a wild night the entire jail will be filled with drunks, vandals, and brigands.

103. Police Station Precinct #7. This crumbling, five-story, stone building is the main police station for this part of town. They usually have their hands full dealing with petty crooks, gangs and trouble around the casino and street crime. 30% are on the Black Market's payroll, 10% are on the Psykes' payroll, another 40% are just plain corrupt and will take bribes from anybody. These cops are tough, streetwise, and often brutal.

104. Fire Station #9. The neighborhood fire department. The Casino has top priority.

105. The Jaguar's Den (Secret Psykes Hangout). A dangerous saloon for the rough and tumble. It is frequented by criminals, corrupt police officers, arena gladiators, prostitutes, wilderness adventurers and mercenaries. It offers both strong liquor and hard drugs to its patrons at low prices (2 credits a drink). A card game or two is usually in progress, brawls are frequent, two-bit crooks panhandle their ill-gotten goods, beggars pander for a handout (inside and on the streets) and ladies of night look for a man's favor. Despite all of this, or perhaps because of it, the two-story tavern is always packed. Seats are premium items, forcing the majority to stand or mill about.

The Jaguar's Den is secretly owned by the Psykes and is used as a safe-house for its members (secret rooms in the basement) and as a means of gathering information.

106. The Mid-North Arena. This is the second most popular arena in town, hosting sporting events and gladiatorial combat. Something is happening nearly every night. Monster wrestling is the most popular.

107. Xilonen Restaurant. Xilonen is the name of an Aztec maize goddess, and of crops/fertility in general. The restaurant offers traditional Mexican cuisine. An average meal costs 15 credits. Beer and wine are also served, 2 credits a glass.

108. Dagger Inn & Souvenir Shop. An establishment that panders to the people who attend the arena. Beer and non-alcoholic beverages are sold for one credit per glass, meat tacos, and tortillas, corn chips, and spicy sauces round out the snack foods.

Souvenirs include photographs and posters of gladiatorial champions and monsters, banners, flags, toy guns, toy wood swords and daggers, rubber vampire stakes, toy wood shields, slingshots, wood crosses, maps of Ciudad Juarez, mugs with gladiators or monsters painted on them, souvenir kites, rubber balls, and other odds and ends. Most everything costs between three and ten credits.

Also sells a variety of nice pocketknives, throwing knives, machetes and silver-plated knives and silver 9 mm bullets. A favorite item among tourists and travelers headed into Mexico is the **Vampire Almanac**. Every year there is a new edition, with lots of pictures (for the illiterate and semi-literate) and important data. Information includes: 1) The exact times of sunrises and sunsets for the Juarez/Northern Mexico area. 2) Location of major waterways, with a map of Mexico (becomes less accurate 400 miles beyond Ciudad Juarez and inaccurate regarding the Yucatan & Central America). 3) Rainy season. 4) How to identify vampires & known vampire powers (80% accurate). 5) Items that ward away vampires, like crosses, magic amulets, garlic, etc. 6) How to kill a vampire (clearly illustrated). 7) Things that hurt a vampire. 8) Famous vampires, personalities, myths, & legends (includes Reid's Rangers). 9) Travel tips and other miscellaneous information.

109. **Auto Parts R Us.** A three-story building crammed with tons of engine and vehicle parts for the do-it-yourself mechanics. Has parts for most common wilderness vehicles, including most makes of motorcycles, hover-cycles, dune buggies, jeeps, Big Boss ATV, Mountaineer ATV, motorboats, and outboard motors. Reasonable prices. Owned by the Mendez family (Uncle Bob and kin).

110. **Mendez's Mechanical Wizards.** As the name suggests, this is a mechanics shop that employs skilled operators, mechanical engineers and techno-wizards. Prices are high, but the turn around time is amazing (half normal) and the workmanship is impeccable. Can repair all types of vehicles, including cars, trucks, hovercraft, jet packs, aircraft, boats, and robots, as well as generators.

111. **Techno-Wizard Conversion House.** Also owned by the Mendez family, this small shop will convert conventional engines into techno-wizard machines or power sources. Mainly converts weapons, engines, small generators and appliances. Can also recharge P.P.E. devices. Fees are reasonable but on the high side.

112. **The B.B.B.P. (Betty's Blackmarket Body Parts).** Yes, another body-chop-shop that specializes in the selling of cybernetic items of all kinds at 20% off, and bionic parts at standard list prices (an occasional 10% discount is offered on select items), all allegedly brand new. Installation is also offered at 10% less than standard. This is a fairly clean and competent facility, sanctioned by the Black Market (Betty pays 40% of the profit). She purchases most of her stock through the Black Market (consignment basis), but also buys 20% of her stock from cyber-snatchers, like the Skivers. Betty is a diabolic, 6th level cyber-doc with a taste for gems, rich men, and action. She prefers to leave the medical work to her staff while she enjoys life at the Palace Garcia, nightclubs, and arenas. From time to time Betty will perform undercover investigations for the Black Market and is suspected (no evidence) in the murders of three public officials who opposed the BM. Cybernetics include a left sensor hand and bionic arm with fingerjack, finger camera, finger gun (silver bullet), wrist needle and drug dispenser. Other items include a lung oxygen cell, toxic filter, and bio-system infra/ultra eye (left eye).

113. **Civic Meeting Hall.** A dilapidated, three-story, city building that is made available to the citizens of Juarez for neighborhood meetings, dances and civic events.

114. **The Glib Goblin.** A three-story tavern and meeting hall. It is one of the Guards' frequent meeting places. Prices are cheap, at one and two credits a drink. The owner and the bar manager are members of the Guard.

115. **Boat Builder.** Makes and sells wood canoes, rafts, row- and sailboats, small yachts, and barges; mostly special orders. Main work facility is near the river. Also repairs boats.

116. **Fire Station #10.** The neighborhood fire department. The lumberyard and brewery have top priority.

117. **North Town Tax Collector.** City assessing department for Old North Town. This building is easy to find because it is covered in foul graffiti all the way up to the second floor windows.

118. **Dog Catcher.** Tries to catch and terminate stray dogs, cats and vermin; a losing battle.

119. **Police Station Precinct #8.** One of the recently refurbished stations. Its main priorities are to keep the Subs gang from raiding the Brewery and to keep riffraff on this side of the wall (the wealthy neighborhood of New Town is just beyond the wall). Police officers on hover cycles and on foot, patrol the length of the wall constantly.

120. **The South Wind Brothel.** Humans, D-Bees, and women of two dozen other races (70 women in all) sell their bodies for a pittance, 2D4 × 10 credits. This is not a safe place and is visited by gang members (spontaneous rumbles erupt weekly on the doorstep), thieves, and hoodlums of all kinds.

121. **The South Wall Theater & Freak Show.** A big, three-story, concrete building with a 40 foot high ceiling on the main floor (seats 2200) and 20 feet high ceilings on the other two floors. The entertainment includes comedy shows, minstrel shows, rock concerts, dancing girls, stage magic, and the occasional visiting attraction. **The freak show** is located on the second floor. It presents a menagerie of strange, alien animals, a caged and chained gryphon (an improperly healed broken wing prevents it from flying, chronic pain makes it vicious), a pair of juggling shapers, lobotomized Cihuacoath snakeman (mostly drools, but scary to see), a three-headed goblin, and other oddities. Some of the more intelligent freaks perform in the shows or put on special shows.

122. **The North Town Brewery.** This facility is big, fifteen stories tall, and provides half of the city with its alcohol, namely corn liquor, tequila, rum and beer. It also manufactures rubbing alcohol and preserving chemicals for the mortuaries.

123. **The Family Clinic.** An appalling body-chop-shop and doctors' clinic that caters to the poor. Treatment and services, including surgery and cybernetics, are half of what they'd cost at the hospital (#72), but the doctors are terrible and their work quick and shoddy. Suturing wounds will always leave scars, bones may not be set correctly (1-30% chance), diagnoses are often incorrect (1-35%; administer general antibiotics and painkillers for everything), and sells narcotics to patients long after they have healed, and will sell drugs at a 100% markup to anybody (effectively a drug dealer). Save vs coma/death is an appalling 1-32% (horrendous life support facilities and treatment). The Family Clinic is owned and protected by the Psykes.

124. **East Wall Pool Hall.** Another gang and hoodlum hangout. If you're looking for a fence, thief or con-artist, this is the place.

125. **Big Gus's Apartments.** A clean, well kept, five-story, brick, apartment building that contains a tattoo parlor, dentist, barbershop, candy store, and meeting/dance hall. It is a known haven for the

OLD NORTH TOWN — GUARD TURF

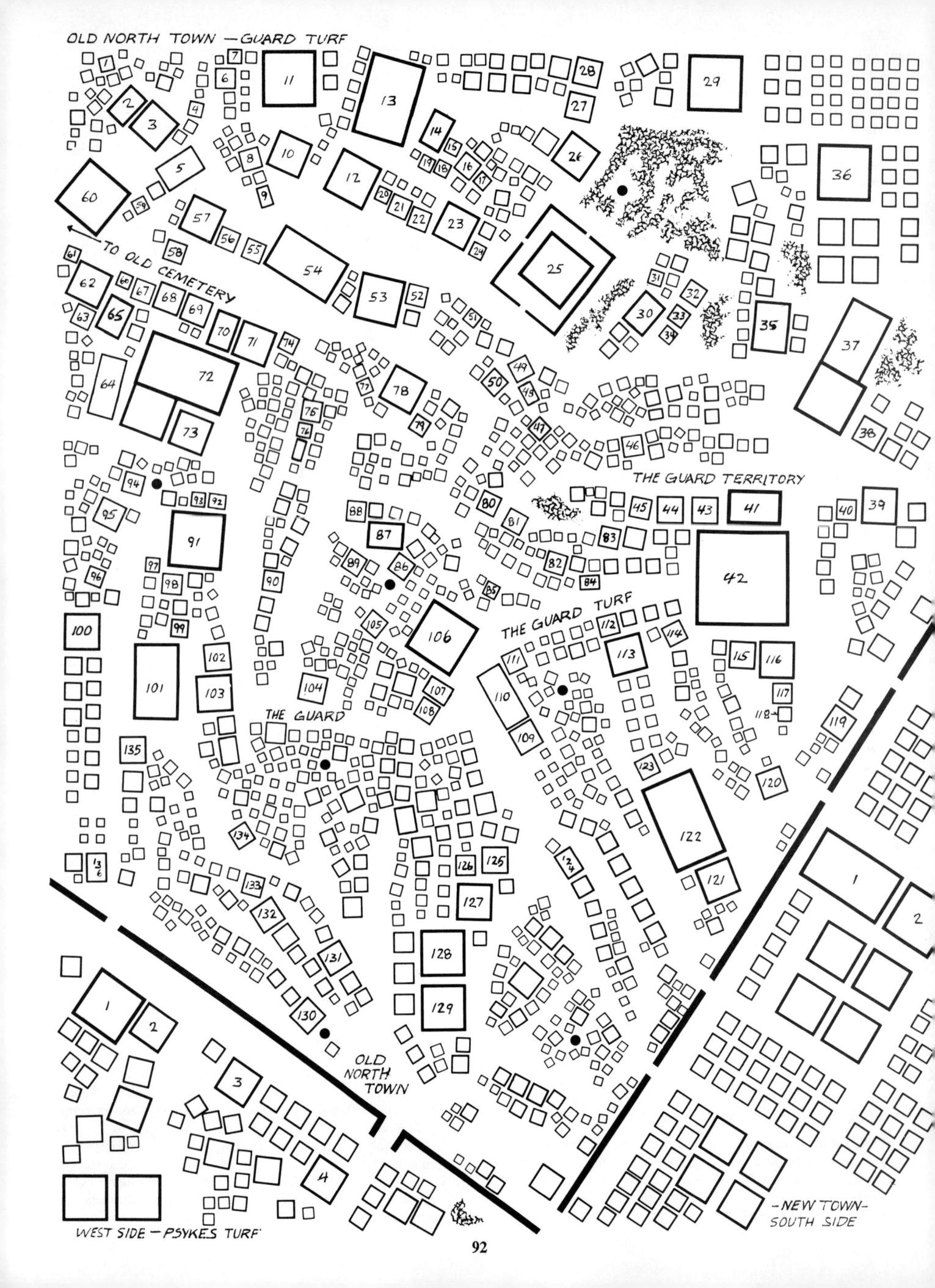

TO OLD CEMETERY

THE GUARD TERRITORY

THE GUARD TURF

THE GUARD

OLD NORTH TOWN

WEST SIDE — PSYKES TURF

— NEW TOWN — SOUTH SIDE

EAST SIDE — THE RUIN SLUMS — SUBS TURF

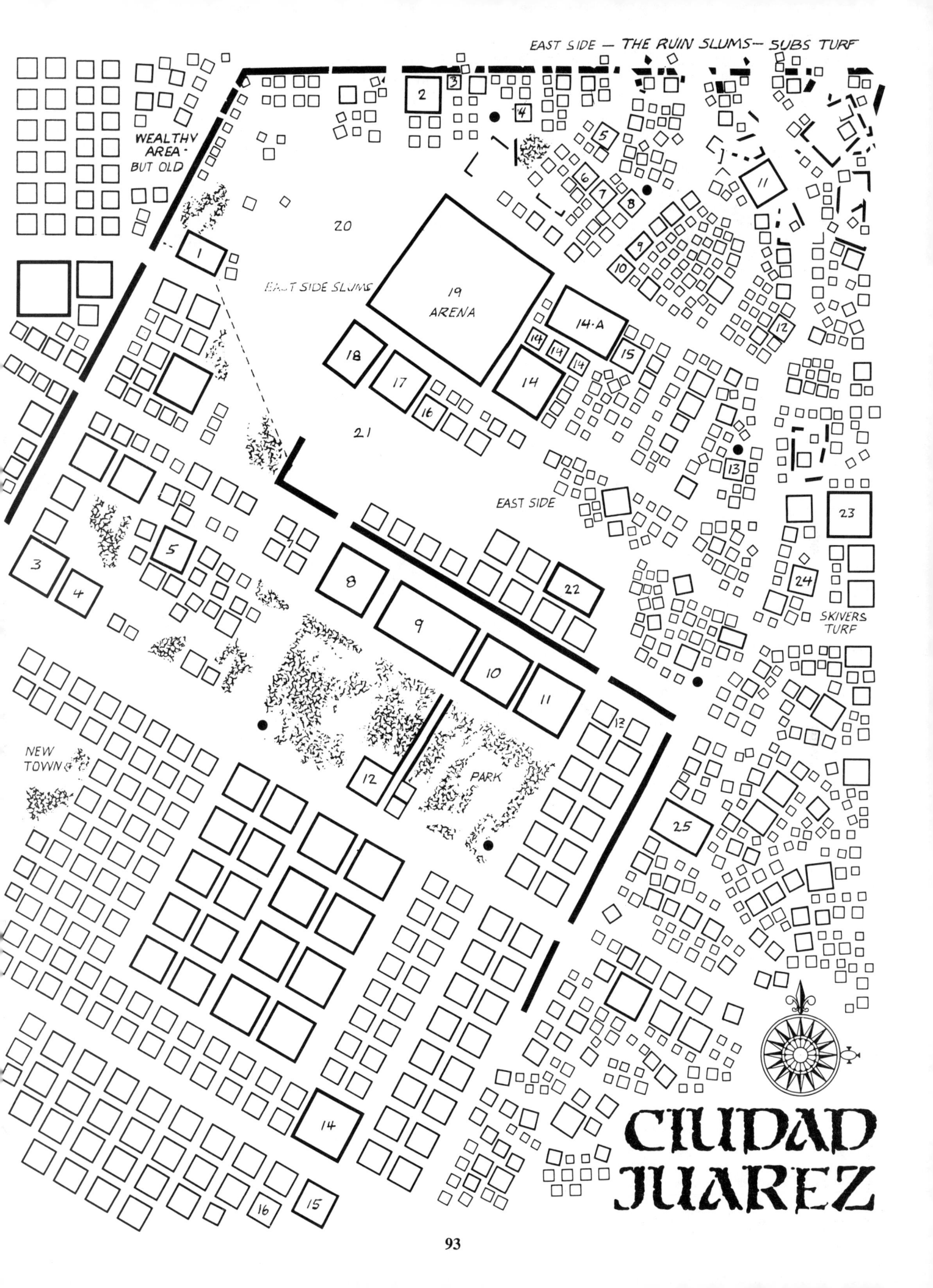

WEALTHY AREA - BUT OLD

EAST SIDE SLUMS

19 ARENA

EAST SIDE

SKIVERS TURF

NEW TOWN

PARK

CIUDAD JUAREZ

neighborhood; free of drugs, vampires, and vice. It is also a suspected center for the Guard (half of its 80 apartments are leased by families and members of the Guard).

Gus is a bronze-skinned, 20 foot (6.1 m) giant (Jotan from Palladium RPG), with long, flowing hair and impressive muscles. He is a warrior of renown, having defended the city against vampires and demons alike. Principled alignment, hit points 900 (equal to 9 M.D.C.), I.Q. 9, P.S. 30, P.P. 26, P.E. 28, all others average. Possesses a fabled magic battle-axe from another world that spits M.D.C. lightning bolts (4D6 M.D.), returns on command when thrown and is seemingly indestructible. Gus also has a suit of specially constructed armor (210 M.D.C.). He is gentle with maidens, children and animals; intolerant of vampires, demons, and evildoers.

126. Outdoor playground. A hangout for local children, with slides, swings and monkey-bars. Big Gus and the Guard keep a vigilant eye on the shabby, little park.

127. North Town Recreation Center. A dilapidated and overcrowded city building that provides two swimming pools, a boxing ring, dance hall, cafeteria, full-size gymnasium, game rooms (ping-pong, darts, checkers, etc.), a dozen classrooms (painting, crafts, basket weaving, cooking, dance, sewing, first aid, woodworking, etc.), and meeting rooms.

128. West Star Hotel. An inexpensive and shabby hotel for those who can't afford one of the better hotels. Rooms cost 35 to 60 credits a night; only half have private bathrooms (the 60 credits ones). Security is poor, prostitutes, junkies, and crooks are common guests.

129. The Carmen Movie-Plex. 12 small movie theaters offer a variety of contemporary films, mostly comedies and adventures. Costs 5 credits.

130. Northwest Bank and Exchange. City operated bank and money exchange. The Psykes use this bank for their laundered money.

131. West Side Men's Club. A seven-story den of iniquity that has the appearance of being a legitimate men's club. Facilities include a massage parlor, hair stylists, small library, lounge, bar, a dozen private game rooms (gambling) and meeting rooms (where prostitutes and drugs are available at reasonable prices). The women are clean and attractive (about 30 of them; 50 to 100 credits an hour) and the drugs are of good quality. **Owned and operated by the Psykes. Thirty Psykes gang members have lavish living quarters on the upper floors, as well as private offices.**

132. Mind Games Shelter. A large, three-story place of psionic entertainment. The surroundings are richly decorated in expensive materials and furnishings. There are a few large meeting rooms for group involvement and twenty smaller rooms for individuals and groups of four or five. Services include hallucinogenic drugs (300 credits for 1D4 hours of hallucinations), psionic tests of combat (200 to 1200 credits), hypnotic suggestion (200 credits per suggestion), empathic transmission (300 credits), sensory deprivation via bio-manipulation and telekinesis (temporarily blind/deaf/paralyzed while being suspended in air, made to fly, spin, etc.; 1000 credits), bio-manipulated masochism (300 credits), mind bond (10,000 credits), mind wipe (erasure of painful memories, dangerous information, etc.; 3000 to 12,000 credits), psionic healing (100 to 1000 credits, no psychic surgery), and magically induced illusions and metamorphosis (5000 to 10,000 credits). Certainly a place for those with exotic and decadent tastes.

The owner is a sadistic, 10th level mind melter by the name of Cyril Lombardi. He loves to subject people to pain, terror and strange experiences. He has delusions of grandeur and toys with the idea of attempting to usurp the leadership of the Psykes. However, for the moment, he has decided that he has more freedom as a lesser gang member, and freedom to do what he wishes is all-important to this madman. Diabolic, I.Q. 18, M.A. 17, M.E. 24, P.B. 15, all others average. Psionics of note: 245 I.S.P., empathy, sixth sense, summon inner strength, nightvision, alter aura, bio-manipulation, empathic transmission, hypnotic suggestion, mentally possess others, mind wipe, mind bond, P.P.E. shield, telekinetic force field, telekinesis (super), and hydrokinesis.

Anna Le Broch, a miscreant, ninth level, ley line walker who was declined membership to the Guild for the Gifted, is Cyril's partner and companion. Her specialty is illusionary magic, sickness, curses, and metamorphosis (knows all). She has a vendetta against the Guild for the Gifted and she and Cyril often embarrass and antagonize its members. Anna is easily as cruel and arrogant as Cyril and enjoys taking (and pulling off) high risks. I.Q. 15, M.A. 20, M.E. 14, P.B. 18, all others average. Minor psionic: 65 I.S.P., presence sense and astral projection.

Both Cyril and Anna are valued members of the Psykes, although a bit uncontrollable at times.

Mind Games employs two sixth level mind melters, four third level mind melters, and two fifth level mystics; all are of miscreant alignment and enjoy their high paying jobs. Half are members of the Psykes. They also employ six prostitutes, six female helpers and 10 male assistants.

133. The Golden Arm — Body-Chop-Shop. A fairly clean, well managed chop-shop. Offers brand new cybernetic implants at a 30% discount and basic bionic augmentation (partial conversion) at a 20% discount. Certain special (basic/common) cybernetic items are reduced to 50% due to the shop's war with the body-chop-shop across the street. Owned by the Psykes.

134. The Ultra-Man — Body-Chop-Shop. A good quality facility, nearly identical to #133 except that it is owned by and operated by the Black Market.

135. Mama's Boarding House. An old, four-story school turned into a boarding house. No private bathrooms, two communal wash-and-rest-rooms on each floor, no showers or bathtubs. Rooms are large and clean. Only 45 credits a night. A total of 36 rooms, plus shabby lounge and dining hall (serves soups, stews, bread and salads at 8 credits a diner). Security is poor.

136. The Lonely Rider Bathhouse. A two-story building that provides bathing facilities for travelers; used primarily by wilderness scouts and the homeless. A 20 foot swimming pool is a giant communal bathtub (water is scuzzy, only 5 credits), six large communal showers (segregated male and female areas, 8 credits), and 40 private bathrooms with tub and shower (20 credits per half-hour).

West Side (Psykes Territory)

The west side, located in the southwest portion of Ciudad Juarez, is separated from the older, poorer Old North Town by an inner city, mega-damage wall (30 feet/9 m tall). The west side is mostly residential, with the occasional neighborhood store, tavern, and a large shopping mall. The middle class live in this section of town, although most work in North Town or the East Side Ruins. The Psykes are among the commuters who live in the nicer neighborhoods, but perform most of their criminal work in the larger, poorer areas of the city. However, they do operate a few places on the west side and violence does follow them to their west side homes.

1. The Western Sky Hotel. A popular, luxury hotel. 240 rooms, all have private baths; top security. Typical room costs 150 credits a night. Bigger, nicer rooms cost 250 credits. Several spies for the Psykes work at the hotel.

2. Security Garage. Hotel parking garage with valet parking and armed guards (less than 2% chance of robbery).

3. The Three-Armed Casino. A small, but nice, quiet casino controlled (not owned) by the Psykes. All the usual card and parlor games common to gambling casinos. Good security.

4. **The Portillo Estate.** The estate of a wealthy businessman and one of the four partners that own the Three-Armed Casino. Rafael Portillo is a prominent member of the Psykes and his estate is a safe-house for the gang. Armed guards patrol the grounds.

South Side: New Town

New Town has the largest and prettiest houses. This is the abode of the wealthy and the city government's officials. It is protected by the best the police have to offer, private guards, and high-tech security systems. The area is mostly residential.

1. **The Five Star Hotel.** The biggest and most luxurious hotel in the city. All rooms have a private bathroom, and bar. 400 rooms are available in this 16 story, mega-damage edifice. Average room is 400 credits a night, luxury suite 2000 credits, penthouse suite 3000 credits. The hotel also has a five star restaurant (average meal is 75 credits), hair salon, book and video store, lounge and bar. Security is the best!
2. **New Town Health Spa.** A luxurious health spa with an olympic size swimming pool, extra large gymnasium, 8 workout rooms, four saunas, four massage parlors, jacuzzi, private showers, private lounges, etc.
3. **Police Headquarters.** The newly built administrative offices and police headquarters; a super mega-damage structure (100 M.D.C. per 10 foot area). Houses some of the police elite. Patrol the dividing wall and wealthy New Town neighborhood.
4. **Police Armory and Garage.** Police weapon and vehicle storage and mechanics' garage. Heavily guarded, same M.D.C. structure as the police headquarters.
5. **City Morgue.** Numerous high-tech laboratories, forensics, pathology, chemical analysis, cyber-docs, psionic healers, psychic sensitives, etc. A busy place.
6. **City Jail/Prison.** High security. 300 jail cells and 50 solitary confinement cells.
7. **City Services Buildings.** Sewage, garbage disposal, maintenance, restoration, vampire affairs, etc.
8. **Criminal Court.**
9. **City Government Building — Ruling Body.**
10. **Civil Court.**
11. **Tax, Gambling, Merchant Administration and Licensing Bureau.**
12. **Immigration.** Tries to register D-Bees, psychics, practitioners of magic and foreigners coming into the city, but only 40% are accounted for. Surrounded by the city park. The black dots on the map indicate public fountains.
13. **City Administration Buildings.** Includes private government library (books, videos, and artifacts), public records, health department, housing department, recreation department, water department, etc.
14. **City Governor's Estate.** Top security, heavily guarded.
15. **New Town Library & Museum.** A beautiful library (new and old books, contemporary and pre-rifts video and music discs) and museum (pre-rifts, post-rifts, and Aztec artifacts) exclusively for the wealthy inhabitants of New Town; all others restricted.
16. **Police Station Precinct #20.** A brand new police station charged with protecting the library-museum (#15), which has recently been subjected to vandalism by the Subs and others, and the protection of the wealthy neighborhood of New Town. Police officers on hover cycles, jet packs and on foot, patrol the area. Most of these police officers are green recruits (1st & 2nd level), but well armed and tend to shot first and ask questions later.

East Side: The Old Ruin Slums (Subs & Skivers Turf)

The "Old Ruin Slums" is the oldest, ramshackle and most dangerous part of town. It gets its name from the old thirty foot wall that once served as part of the city's fortifications, but over the decades the wall has been subjected to mega-damage battles, gang wars, vandalism and deterioration. Huge, gaping holes are everywhere. Half of the buildings should be condemned and rebuilt, many have been abandoned by their owners years ago and have become a refuge for the homeless and squatters. The city government doesn't care about this section of the city because it is the habitat of the poor, beggars, homeless and the inhuman. 80% of the population in the overcrowded streets are D-Bees; 50% of which are orcs, goblins, hob-goblins and other ugly humanoids.

Thousands live on the streets in the open, gathering as groups or gangs of beggars, hobos, or joining the Subs (official gang). Needless to say, these people resent (many loathe) the wealthy and prettier humanoids, humans in particular. The old ruin slums, with its thousands of homeless, is also the most victimized by vampires.

1. **The East Side Medical Clinic.** A run-down four-story, brick building that is forced to handle ten times more patients than they can possibly handle. Most of the staff are well-meaning and dedicated men and women of medicine, but are so overworked and pressured that they can not give the people their complete or proper attention. Thus, mistakes are made and many are lost due to improper treatment or inadequate facilities.

    Suturing wounds will often leave scars (1-40%), bones may not be set correctly (1-20% chance), diagnoses are too often incorrect (1-30%; administer general antibiotics and painkillers for many different ailments). The save vs coma/death ratio is an impressive 1-56%, considering the terrible conditions. The head of staff is an 8th level body-fixer with psionic healing abilities (Principled alignment, I.Q. 14, M.E. 19, P.P. 17, all others average; major psionic: 72 I.S.P., has all healing psi-powers, except resist fatigue, exorcism and detect psionics). Prices are a quarter of what the hospital would normally charge and many pay only what they can afford, which isn't much.

2. **The Lopez Flophouse.** A ramshackle six-story building that was once a boarding house. Five credits gets you a blanket and a place on the floor for the night. Ten credits gets you a cot. 15 credits, a cot in a semi-private room shared by only 1D4 other people. No private rooms are available. An additional five credits will give one access to the showers (cold water only). Three credits will buy a plate of beans, stale bread, and glass of water. A public rest-room is found on every floor; all are filthy, graffiti covered and smell like ... well, stink horribly.

    The place is always crowded with 2D6x1000 people. The top floor is the home of the family that owns and operates the building, including several uncles, aunts and cousins. It is off limits to the patrons of the flophouse and is protected by a quartet of 4th level D-Bee headhunters, and at night, it's rumored that demons protect them.

    Papa Lopez is a 5th level vagabond with a knack for business. He is also the mind controlled servant of a third level secondary vampire (once his friend) by the name of Miguel Sanchez.

    Mama Lopez is said to be a witch. Indeed, she is a second level mystic. Psi-powers: 48 I.S.P., clairvoyance, exorcism, sixth sense, bio-regeneration, detect psionics, object read, see aura and astral

The Slums of Ciudad Juarez.

projection. Magic is limited to see the invisible, cloud of smoke, befuddle, chameleon, fear, energy bolt, impervious to fire, levitation, turn dead, and armor of Ithan; 52 P.P.E. points. I.Q. 9, M.E. 12, M.A. 11, all others average; miscreant, willingly works with the vampires, whom she sees as business partners (they help keep the peace and her business prospers).

The vampire Miguel (3rd level, diabolic) and nine fellow secondary vampires, live and feed at the flophouse. Four, including Miguel, live on the sixth floor with the Lopez family and are believed to be the night watchmen and assistants. Five live in hidden in the basement. All, other than Miguel, are first level vampires and miscreant evil. They predominately feed on the sick and dying and on vagabond transients not from these parts. Nobody suspects that any vampires live or work at the flophouse.

3. **The Hole in the Wall Pool Hall.** A Subs gang and hoodlum hangout. Drinks are big, strong and cheap; 1-4 credits each (Subs pay half price). There are always 4D6 members of the Subs gang present at any time. They hate humans and pretty humanoids. All are bullies looking for trouble and a quick buck. Generally 1D4 level experience, anarchist and miscreant alignments, extremely loyal to the Subs gang; arrogant and mean.

4. **Katie's.** A house of prostitution populated by D-Bees and another popular hangout among the Subs. A lady's time costs 20 to 50 credits an hour. Gunfights, stabbings, and brawls are common.

5. **Power Man's Cybernetics — Body-Chop-Shop.** A dark and grisly looking place of business that specializes in Black Market cybernetic weapons, disguises, and bionic arms and weapons. Cybernetics are 40% less than standard market value and bionics are 25% less. Also performs basic medical services for punks and brigands at half of what the hospital charges and with no questions. However, there is a 40% chance of minor scarring from all types of surgery and a 35% chance of getting an infection from cybernetic surgery. The owners of this rat nest are quick, sloppy, and compassionless. They purchase 50% of their product line from Skivers and other bodysnatchers and crooks. Pay the police to ignore them.

6. **General Store.** A small but fairly well stocked general store. Average prices.

7. **Butcher Shop.** A popular store that sells beef, pork and poultry. Low prices.

8. **The Stake & Mallet Tavern.** A popular saloon and gambling hall. A headless skeleton with a stake in its ribs swings from a rope over the bar. Drinks are one and two credits, the gambling is serious, the patrons are loud and tough. Knife throwing, arm wrestling, and card games are played in the main, smoke filled tavern area. The high stake games of cards and craps are on the second floor. Ladies of the night rent the eight rooms on the third floor (30 credits gets one an hour of the lady's time, a wash basin and cot; human and D-Bee females). The Stake & Mallet is the site of nightly brawls and trouble. The owner is an ogre warrior (6th level, anarchist, I.Q. 11, P.S. 25, P.P. 20, P.E. 18, all others average) and his place is popular among ogres, orcs, goblins and the Subs and El Paso Trogs gangs.

9. **East Leather Goods & Accessories.** A store that caters to the gangs. Sells whips, ropes, manacles, handcuffs, nightsticks, nunchaku, knives, vibro-blades, M.D.C. chain saws, hair dye, and a huge variety of leather clothing, belts, straps, bands, caps and boots; studded, spiked, and plain. Prices are average on the low side.

10. **The Colorful Peacock Tattoo Parlor & Hair Stylist.** The tattoo parlor is the official place to get "colorized," offering a mind boggling number of tattoo designs. Another popular place for gang members and young toughs. A small tattoo, about the size of a silver dollar costs 20 credits, medium (6-8 inches) 50 credits, large (12-15 inches) 100 credits. Special or intricate designs will cost 50 to 100 credits more. The eight tattoo artists are master tatoo artists. The oldest is also skilled in holistic medicine (5th level) and offers his medical expertise to those he likes (costs a third of what the hospital charges; no surgery).

The second floor is **Adam's Chunk-Out Hair Salon,** specializing in punk style hairdos, dyes and make-up. A typical haircut will cost 10 credits, a creative "Chunk-a-Do" costs 30 to 50 credits.

11. **Rickety Wall Dance Hall.** A crumbling, four-story edifice that serves as a dance hall, meeting hall and indoor arena. Every night, except Fridays, there is dancing on two of the floors. The only alcohol is moonshine, for a credit a mug.

Friday nights are fight night! 1D4+3 fights will be exhibited. Admission is 5 credits a person. Ample side betting with the house and fellow attendees is plentiful.

12. **The Wizard's Hut.** A place run by a crazy, old wizard who sells healing potions, amulets, the occasional scroll or TW item, and magical services. Magic Services: Healing touch (150 credits per touch), cure minor disorders and illness (100 to 400 credits), remove curse (10,000 credits), place curses on people (1000 to 6000 credits; very discreet), summon demons or monsters for people (usually to perform acts of vengeance, brutality and murder; costs 10,000 to 60,000 credits. Will summon something or send one of his mummies, animated dead, shadow beast, or vampire or demon helpers/associates). **Old William the Wizard,** looks to be over 100, diabolic, 10th level Shifter, 249 P.P.E., spells of note: all summoning, all protection, all control and domination spells, create mummies, animate and control dead, apparition, mask of deceit, calling, locate, call lightning, blind, speed of the snail, carpet of adhesion, circle of flame, and armor of Ithan. **Note:** Has four mummies, a Brodkil demon and three goblins (two are 4th level thieves) as helpers. Also associates with a couple dozen different vampires, including the leader of the Night Masters. He will sell his goods and services to anybody, human, D-Bee, vampire, or supernatural menace. Often requests payment in gold, gems, and blood rather than credits.

13. **O'loc's Armory.** New and rebuilt weapons of good quality. Lowish prices, no refunds. **Mega-Damage body armor** with half its original M.D.C. for 50% off the list price. Most of the armor is pretty battered and scarred, but a good substitute for warriors low on cash and in need of some protection. Selection is limited to Gladiator, Crusader, Urban Warrior, and Dog Pack armor. Also sells new gladiator armor at a 10% discount. **Weapons** include crude wood stake (12 for 5 credits), a variety of crossbows and bolts, bows and arrows, revolvers, automatic pistols, the L-20 pulse rifle and many of the Wilk's and Northern Gun weapons. New weapons cost the standard price, but rebuilts are 25% less than the standard price. Has the occasional rail gun and TW weapon at full price.

14. **The Romerez Stables.** Sells, buys, and stables horses and pack mules. Also offers veterinary services for horses, shoeing, and grooming. Occasionally sells cattle too. Stabling a horse or mule costs 50 credits a day and includes basic grooming, water and hay. Better quality food will cost an additional 20 credits a day. A typical work horse costs about 3000 to 10,000 credits, pack mule 3000 to 6000 credits, a good, trained, riding horse costs 15,000 to 40,000 credits, superior riding or race horse can cost as much as 10 times more.

Romerez and his family service the stables, along with 20 work hands. Paco Romerez is a 6th level wilderness scout who love horses and selling.

The main showroom and stable for horses available for sale is #14-A, behind it are three smaller, additional stables. Behind them is the livery stable and veterinary facility, along its east wall are four additional livery stables.

15. **The Romerez Blacksmith.** The large blacksmith that is part of the Romerez livery complex. In addition to showing horses, the blacksmith makes nails, chains, manacles, and maces. Prices are all average, high quality. Romerez employs a Jotan giant as an ironworker and four kobolds.

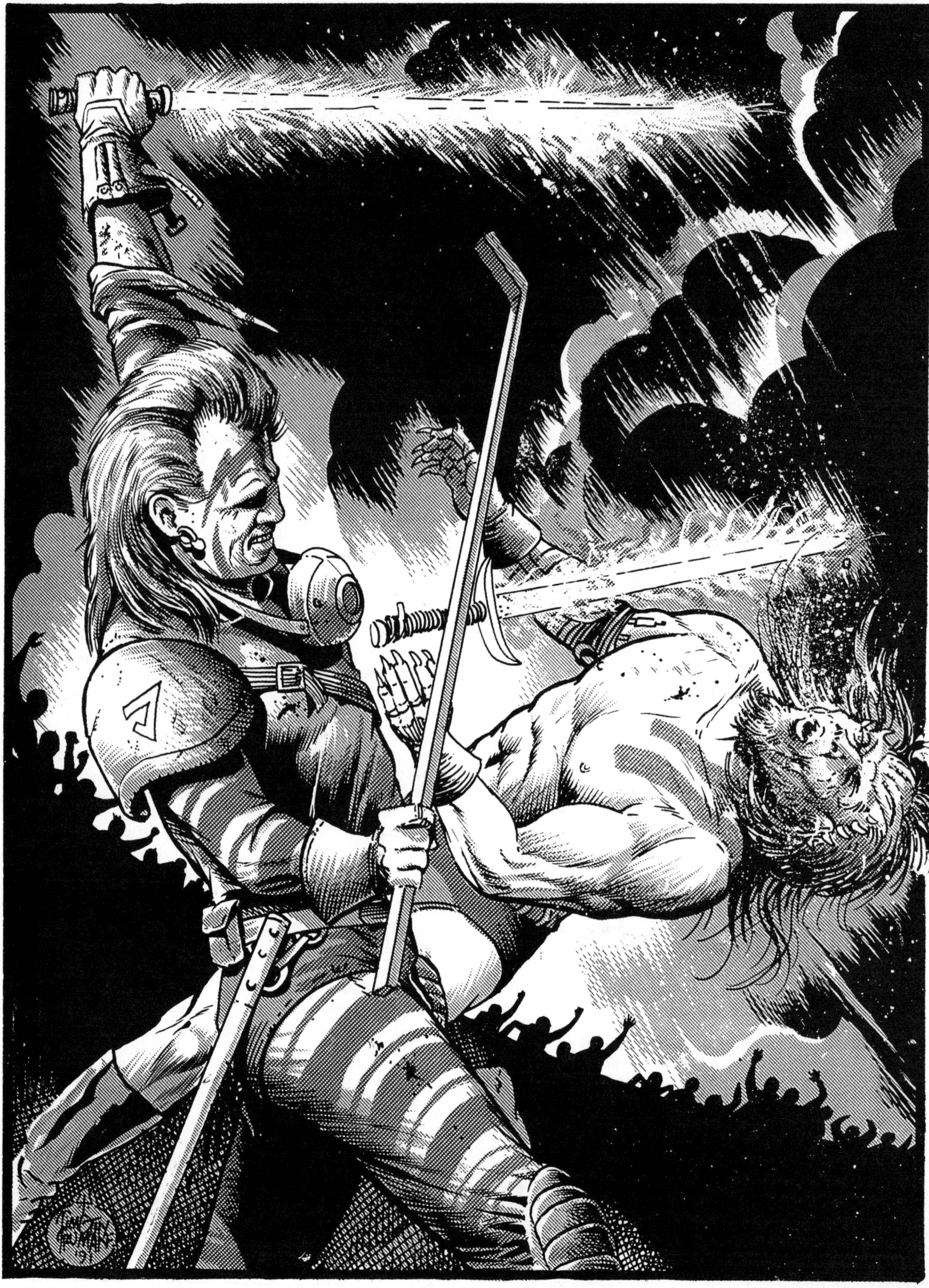

6. **Arena Mechanics & Gas Station.** A competent mechanics' shop, able to repair most vehicles and perform minor repairs on robots and power armor. Reasonable prices.
7. **The Mayfair Nightclub.** One of the nicest places to eat and relax. Entertainment includes dancing girls, tasteful strip-tease, minstrels and singers. The food is excellent (costs 15 to 30 credits) and offers a selection of liquor, beer and wine (average drink is 3 credits). A hot spot in town for visitors, city workers, and the better off residents. Always packed on days the Juarez Arena has major attractions.
8. **Guarded Parking Structure.** A pre-rifts style parking structure with an armed patrol. Can accommodate 1000 cars, costs two credits an hour, valet parking; only a 7% chance of one's vehicle being stolen, stripped or vandalized.
9. **The Juarez Arena!** This is a place that attracts the rich and poor from all over Ciudad Juarez. **Monday** night shows include practice horse races, practice gladiatorial fights and performing clowns, jugglers and tumblers. Regular admission is 5 credits for the cheap seats, 25 credits for the good seats, and 100 credits for front row seating. Monday is family night, so the cost of admission is only 2 credits.

   Tuesday through Friday are the horse, dog, and dinosaur races. City run gambling is available near the arena entrance, but the wandering Black Market and Pyskes gang bookies offer better odds and potentially bigger pay-offs. **Saturday and Sunday** are fight nights with 10 to 20 different fights, including bullfights, monster fights (humanoid vs monster), monster wrestling, monster vs monster, and gladiatorial contests. The regular events are sometimes interrupted by public executions and parades (both are crowd pleasers and it only costs one credit for up-close bleacher seats).
10. **Open area (parking & homeless).** A large open area that was once a residential section that burned to the ground. It is used as a parking lot during events at the arena, as a gathering place for residents, and, at night, as a place where the homeless can set up camp and sleep under the stars. A very dangerous place during the night; filled with desperate people, criminals, and stalked by hungry vampires.
11. **Open area (parking and homeless).** Identical to #20. Nearby are the homes of middle-class merchants and city government workers.
12. **Police Station — Precinct #1.** This was the old police headquarters before they moved to nicer quarters. The building is still one of the major police stations and is a mega-damage structure (50 M.D.C. per 10 foot area). Some of the meanest, toughest, most corrupt policemen in Juarez are stationed here. Many of the troublemakers are sent to this location as punishment. Their main concern is controlling the gangs and keeping crooks, gangs, and beggars out of neighboring New Town, home of the rich and elite.
13. **East General Hospital.** Basically the same as #72 in North Town, only a third its size. The two neighboring buildings are the professional building and the administrative offices.
24. **Wainwright & Carpenter.** A builder of poor quality wagons, wheels, barrels, tables, crucifixes, furniture, and coffins. Unfinished products, items not yet stained, varnished or painted, are half price.
25. **The Rio Apartments.** A ten-story apartment building for the poor working-class residents of the east side slums. Security is poor, the apartments cramped and dirty, service is poor. Costs about 800 a month to rent; few vacancies. **Note:** Many small, local shops are just east of the building, including a taxi service, general store, fruit market, butcher and dairy market, poultry market, bakery, fabric shop, hardware store, small CD shop, potter, clothing store (work clothes, shoes, boots and hats), and saloons.

The Vampire Hunters of Mexico

Doc Reid and his Vampire Hunters

An excerpt from the writings of Erin Tarn; Circa 101 P.A.

From Wichita Falls, all along the Rio Grande, and far beyond New Ciudad Juarez, people tell the tales of **Reid's Rangers**. Virtually every peasant in every village we have encountered since Wichita has an array of tall tales about the great **Doctor Kenneth Reid** and his fearless vampire hunters. Many of the stories sound like fantastic faerie tales, perhaps with some nuance of truth at their roots, but tales that have been so embellished that it is impossible to tell what is true and what is fantasy. Even those who insist that they have personally witnessed the good doctor or one of his vampire hunters in action, spin tales too fantastic to be believed.

Never before have I witnessed such fervor about a folk hero as I have seen in these people. "Doc Reid and his Rangers," as the doctor and his troop of warriors are called by most frontier folk, are loved by all. The man has been elevated to the status of a saint in the hearts and minds of these simple and too often tormented people. All speak of the doctor and his rangers with the highest regard and reverence. A farmer, exhausted from his 14 hours of labor in the fields, will suddenly become aglow when somebody asks about "Doc Reid." With renewed energy, the man will relate his favorite yarns and inevitably end the dissertation with a sign of the cross and a, "God bless Doc Reid," or a prayer to the "savior of the land," as the doctor is alternately called.

If the stories can be believed, the doctor and his rangers are responsible for destroying thousands of vampires and routing entire tribes of the demons, forcing them back into Mexico. A few years ago, Doc Reid and the rangers headed into Mexico, taking his crusade to the "heart of the evil." I must have heard the following statement a thousand times, "You think we have vampire troubles now? Oh, you should have seen the vampires before Doc Reid. This is much better. Bless his soul."

I now give you a list and brief description of Doc Reid and the most notorious of his Rangers as the people describe them. As you will see, the people see them as the symbol of courage and strength.

Doc Reid. Depending on the perspective of the storyteller, the good doctor is described as tall and handsome to short and common in appearance, young to late 50's, powerfully built to deceptively slender and average. All agree that he comes from a city in the northeast, although, again, that place of origin appears to be in dispute, as Chi-Town, Whykin, Manistique and Iron Heart have all been credited as his place of origin with equal regularity and certainty.

Planktal-Nakton is a wizard-philosopher of great power and Doc Reid's right-hand man. He is a solemn, compassionate, and courageous champion of good who consorts with the gods of light.

Raoul Lazarious is the captain of the Rangers and said to be one of the greatest cyber-knights to ever walk the Earth. He was trained by the hand of the legendary Lord Coake, is said to be just as noble, and has been sent by Lord Coake to combat the denizens of evil that plague this land.

Carlotta the White is a sorceress, so pure of heart that she is impervious to the powers of the undead. She is the lover of Captain Lazarious.

Mii-Tar the Destroyer is an inhuman D-Bee both massive and monstrous in appearance, but has the heart of a warrior and the soul of a child.

Robert "Grizzly" Carter is an ancient wilderness scout said to have accidentally drunken from a spring of eternal youth. Locals insist that Grizzly Carter has roamed these lands for over 200 years and is a master of the long bow.

Vyurr Kly the Hunter is a famous psi-stalker scout renowned for the battle of Eagle Peak where he is credited for single handedly slaying 110 vampires during a three night siege. He was one of three survivors of this famous battle against the undead. Vyurr Kly is also known for his flamboyant use of twin flaming swords.

Meetal the Butcher is a frequent companion of Vyurr Kly and is one of the other survivors of Eagle Peak. She is a psi-stalker of great prowess and equally great savagery as a hunter. She is called the "Butcher" because she severs the heads from all those she slays.

Pequita "The Faceless One" is said to be a dragon, or demon, or demi-god with the power to shape change. She possesses great magic power and never wears the same face twice.

The preceding descriptions provide a fair indication of the larger than life portrayals of Doc Reid and his Rangers by the local people. The stories are so consistent that one must wonder whether they are fictional heroes of myth or real people who have been deified by a superstitious and downtrodden people. I have done some of my own investigations and this is what I have learned. My spies in *Lone Star* confirm that a group of bandits calling themselves Reid's Rangers do exist. Their leader is a man called Doc Reid. It would seem that the great liberator of the people has had his share of conflicts with the Coalition, which in and of itself would make him a hero in the eyes of many. There are a half dozen official incidents between CS troops and Reid's Rangers and I am told there are as many as three dozen other conflicts secreted away in CS confidential files, including an impressive raid on Fort El Dorado.

According to my Lone Star sources, **Doctor Kenneth Reid** was a small time criminal who operated a successful body-chop-shop in the Coalition city of *Free Quebec*. He is middle-aged, 6 feet tall, slender in build and well educated. After a rather devastating encounter with Coalition authorities, Doctor Reid disappeared for four years, resurfacing in the west. After a short while, stories of "Doc Reid," the vampire hunter, and his band of warriors began to surface. When or how Doctor Reid met and gathered his present associates is not known. According to Coalition propaganda, it was the CS who forced Reid and his "bandits" to flee to Mexico to avoid capture and punishment by the Coalition. But my sources disagree, citing the fact that the CS troops sent against Reid's Rangers suffered defeat after defeat and were never able to find the Rangers' base of operation.

Planktal-Nakton is a name that is immediately known to me. If this is the same man (and the descriptions I have heard would seem to confirm that he is), this "hero" is the notorious necromancer and one-time commander of the dreaded **Federation of Magic.** He is responsible for much carnage and death in the East as the leader of the devastating three year campaign of terrorism known as the **Revenge of Blood**. Thousands of innocent people, living in CS territory along Chi-Town's eastern borders, were slaughtered in the name of revenge. The necromancer is also known for human sacrifices and countless other crimes against the Coalition and humanity. Like Doctor Reid, he disappeared and, for the past decade, has been believed dead. His mystic powers are legendary. I find it difficult to believe that this maleficent murderer could now be on the side of the angels.

If I recall correctly, **Raoul Lazarious** is another rogue with a passion for murder. He is a cyber-knight and did study under the legendary Lord Coake, but was banished from *Coake's Cyber-Knight Legion* for conduct unbefitting a knight. Sir Lazarious' misconduct included extreme and unnecessary violence, torture and brutality in combat. Again, if my memory serves me correctly, Lazarious was a fanatic who saw himself as the hand of god and acted as judge, jury and executioner.

A psi-stalker named **Vyurr Kly** was one of the valiant heroes of Eagle Peak. He and 1300 other warriors made a last stand against a horde of 600 vampires that had been sweeping the land and destroying all they encountered like demonic locust's. 459 vampires were destroyed, the rest fled in retreat, and thousands of lives were saved. Only three of the 1300 lived to tell the tale, Vyurr Kly was one of the three and is credited for slaying over a hundred vampires. But it is also true that Vyurr Kly is a tempestuous wilderness scout given to drunkenness, brawling, cattle rustling and roguish mischief.

As for **Grizzly Carter**, tales of this lone wanderer and champion of the weak have existed for well over a hundred years. He has been a favorite subject of folk tales for generations. I suspect his inclusion among the new folk heroes is a simple matter of the old merging with the new. The other notables within the Rangers are local figures of prominence who, like Vyurr Kly, have earned reputations as being both heroes and rogues.

Reliable records place the first appearance of Doctor Reid at April 90 P.A., 11 years ago. I can attest that there was no "Doc Reid" or "Reid's Rangers" when I visited the area 20 years earlier. And I did not begin to hear the stories of the Rangers until four or five years ago. Evidently, Reid's Rangers became a formal and active group around August that same year (90 P.A.). I find it unlikely that a real group of warriors could establish such a monumental reputation in such a short period of time. But then these "Reid's Rangers" seem to have collected quite an impressive crew.

Our current plans for travel will place us near the reported location of Doctor Reid's Mexican fortress. If our information is correct, we may pay a visit to the illustrious Doctor Reid on our travels into the Mexican interior.

Reid's Rangers

Any characters travelling south of the Rio Grande will hear tale after tale of the living legends, "Doc Reid" and "Reid's Rangers". **Doc Reid** is the greatest hero of Mexico, New Mexico and Texas, and is known throughout the west. He is followed in renown by Robert "Grizzly"

Carter, Raoul Lazarious, Carlotta the White, Vyurr Kly and Mii-Tar the Destroyer; pretty much in that order. The stories tell of feats of great courage and incredible power triumphantly pitted against vampires and other forces of evil (especially supernatural menaces). Any native from the area (including player characters) will regard Doc Reid and the most notorious of his Rangers as demi-god like champions of goodness and purity. To actually meet any member of the Reid's Rangers is an honor. To meet one of the more famous Rangers like Sir Lazarious or Vyurr Kly, or the Doc himself, is an honor to be remembered and cherished for a life time. To fight at their side is an honor beyond measure.

Like most legends, there is truth to the tall tales. Much more truth than most give credit. The men and women who compose the famous members of Reid's Rangers are bold, powerful warriors committed to the destruction of the undead and their supernatural kith and kin. They have ridden hundreds of communities of vampire vermin saving tens of thousands of lives. The exact number of undead who have perished at their hands is unknown but must range into the thousands. The Rangers have won the love and respect of the people and the hatred of the undead.

The Place of Dreams
Fort Reid, The Home of Doc Reid and his Rangers

Estimated Population: Fort population, approximately 7300.
- 25% are Humans under the age of 21; mostly peasant warriors.
- 20% are Humans over the age of 20; many are mercenaries.
- 30% Non-human; mostly poorly trained D-Bee warriors.
- 25% are workers and families who are permanent residents of the fort town.
- Average level of a typical Reid's Ranger is one to third level (roll 1D4) wilderness scout or headhunter. Seasoned veterans are in the minority (about 20%) and range from 4th to 8th level (roll 2D4).
- Another 1000 Rangers wander Mexico and Central America destroying vampires and evil wherever they are found. Fort Reid serves as their central base of operations.
- At any given time, an additional 2000 or so Rangers are scattered on missions throughout the territories of Mexico, New Mexico, Texas and Arizona. A handful may roam as far north as Canada and as far east as Missouri.
- Another 2500 peasants, mostly families, live in tiny villages scattered around the fort.

At first glance, the fort and the Rangers are everything the stories attribute them to them. The fort is an impressive structure with a great stone wall enclosing the interior of a small town. There are various training areas inside and outside the walls of the Fort. Giant robots stroll down the wide avenues as do an endless variety of humanoid life forms. Just as the hype states, people of all kinds are welcome if they come to fight evil. The buildings are patchwork structures made of stone, wood, clay, steel or mega-damage materials and often a combination of them all.

It is a bustling community, full of vim and vigor. A hundred or more new recruits gather in every diner and fill the streets. Their words are filled with dreams of crushing evil, becoming famous, and the virtues of being one of Reid's Rangers. A visitor or new recruit might imagine that this must be a modern day *Camelot* and these are the knights errant who will travel the land righting injustice. The illustrious members of Reid's original Rangers are found inside these hallowed walls too. When not off leading a campaign to right some wrong, the likes of Raoul Lazarious, Grizzly Carter, Carlotta the White, Mii-Tar the Destroyer, Vyurr Kly the Hunter, Meetal the Butcher, and the others, teach the recruits the art of combat and beguile them with tales of adventure. They are the elite, the Knights of the Round Table at this new Camelot. They are the measure for those who aspire to be like them. It is a heady feeling just to be at the fortress. To brush shoulders with legendary heroes is ecstasy.

If this be the new Camelot, then Doc Reid is King Arthur; reborn to lead his warriors on a noble journey into the pages of history. Indeed, the fame and glory seem assured. At least 60% of those who join the Rangers come just to become one of Doc Reid's knights, to become one of Reid's Rangers. The would-be-heroes trek across miles of open prairies and desert. They come by the hundreds from all walks of life. Their dream, to live and perhaps die as one of Reid's Rangers. It is with this desire to become a Ranger and their fanatical faith in Doc Reid and all that he, and they, hold dear, that the seeds of destruction are sown.

The majority of volunteers who come to the fortress are farmers and sheepherders. Many are mere children, boys in their early teens, others are young men and women with high ideals and soaring spirits. Few know anything about making war or slaying vampires. They are given two to four weeks of the most rudimentary combat training, taught the basics of vampire lore, given suitable weapons for the task, dubbed Rangers, and sent on missions that the best trained soldier would be hard pressed to win. When they die, and they die by the truck full, a story of bravery and sacrifice is sung in their name. In death they have become titanic heroes, martyrs for a great and noble cause. For their families, their lives and deaths seem to have been given meaning. In their home villages are they remembered as the valiant who fought bravely to free their families from the tyranny of the vampires. Their graves are covered with flowers and gratitude. It was enough that they were members of Reid's Rangers, there are no questions regarding how or why they died; they died as heroes, because they were Reid's Rangers. For Doc Reid, their deaths serve to inflame more youths to come running to join the ranks of the Rangers so that their brethren can be avenged and to make freedom a reality. Perhaps a noble sentiment and a righteous death if not also the fuel for madness.

The cycle of death perpetuates Doc Reid's mad delusions of godhood, fuels his crusade against the undead, and drives his quest for his own immortality. Seldom does the Doctor consider the consequences of his actions which have condemned so many to their graves. He believes the stories of his own divinity and omnipotence. It is his destiny to be the savior of the land. And a god can do no wrong. Blood must be spilled so that the dream can continue. Sacrifices must be made. He accepts this, as do the thousands who so willingly place their lives in his hands. Doc Reid ignores critics, for how can others, outsiders, question his motives? How can they speak of injustice and cruelty when they do not understand, or lack the courage themselves, to make the dream of freedom from the vampires a reality? It is a good dream; a bold dream that Doctor Reid holds dear. But his methods and the motives of some of his lieutenants may turn the dream into a nightmare. The dream-quest is already an obsession.

Equipment & Forces at Fort Reid

Standard Issue Weapons:
- L-20 laser pulse rifle
- NG-57 ion blaster
- Choice of 9 mm pistol with silver bullets, or crossbow with 24 wood bolts, 6 med. explosive (2D6 M.D.), 6 smoke.
- Silver cross medallion and 10 inch wood cross.
- 24 wooden stakes and mallet.
- Conventional water pistols (psionics are given TW water pistol and rifle)

Note: Additional E-clips, silver bullets, wood stakes, arrows, crossbow bolts, specialty arrowheads and other ammunition are all plentiful.

Standard Issue Equipment:
- Urban Warrior body armor for new recruits (level 1-3), choice of Bushman, Dead Boy, Crusader, Gladiator, for veterans (levels 4+).
- Portable language translator.

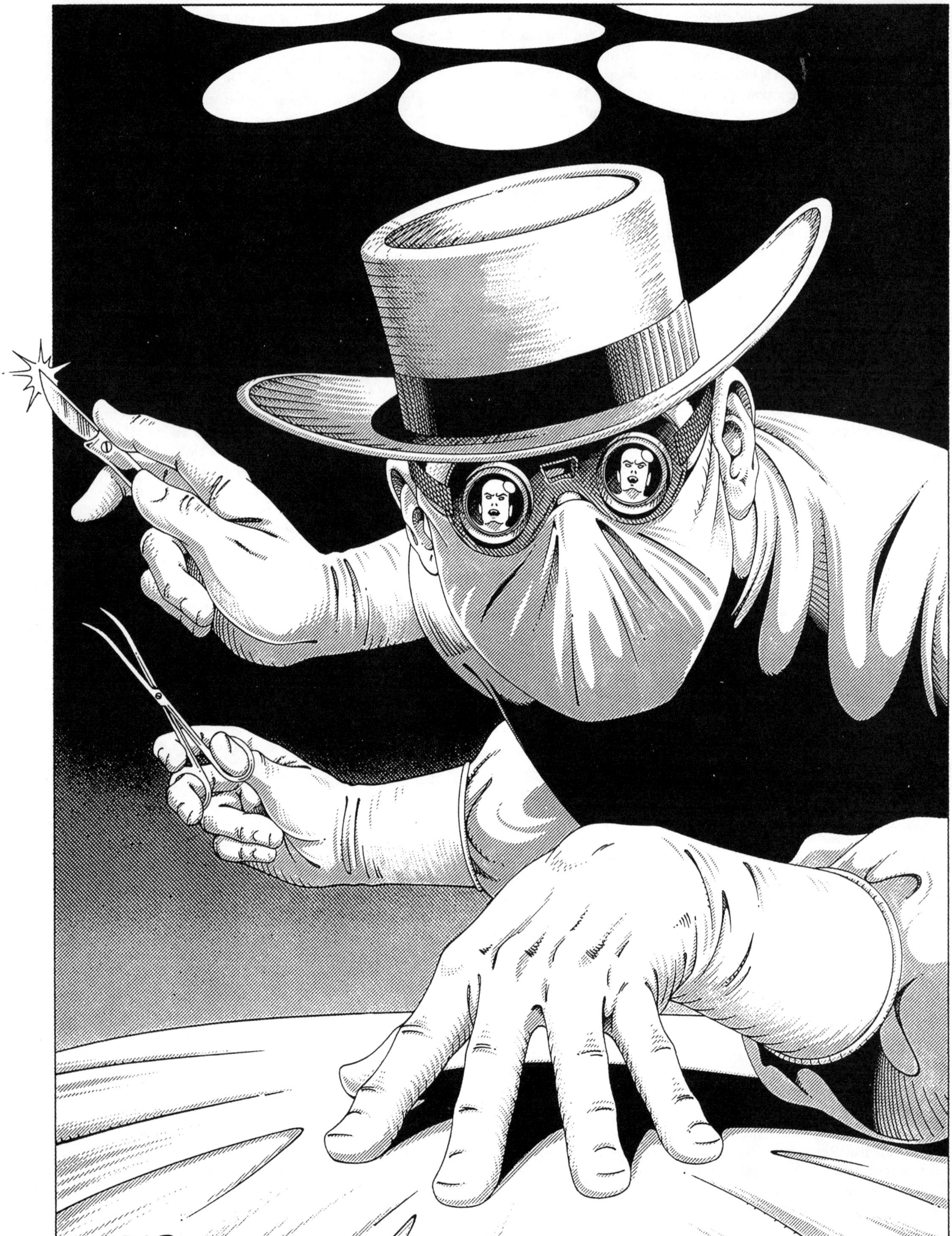

- Choice of horse, motorcycle or hover cycle.
- General equipment: Flashlight, compass, utility belts, backpack, sleeping bag, canteen, food rations, short-range radio, handcuffs, pocket mirror, boots and clothing. A place to sleep (barracks), food and medical care are supplied to all rangers.

Equipment Available on assignment:

Vehicles: Virtually any basic vehicle is available, including hover vehicles, robot horses, real-live horses, Big Boss ATV, Mountaineer ATV, Sky King, jet packs, five CS Mark-V APCs and 21 CS Sky-Cycles, but their numbers are limited, so issued only on an assignment basis.

Weapons: Most of the weapons listed in the **Rifts RPG** are available, especially Northern Gun weapons. Wilk's and Coalition weapons are a bit less common, but a great deal of the weapons and equipment have been stolen from the Coalition. Conventional water weapons, bows and arrows, crossbows and bolts, wood weapons, and silver-coated weapons are plentiful. Techno-wizard (TW) water weapons and vampire round (wood flechette) rail guns have a limited availability. Triax and other weapons are scarce, but a few are available.

Robots and power armor: The most precious and limited items are the extremely expensive mega-damage robot vehicles and power armor suits. Current Fort Reid resources include:
17 SAMAS (50% have a reduced M.D.C. of 185)
3 CS UAR-1 Enforcer Robots
1 CS Spider-Skull Walker
4 Behemoth Explorer Robots
11 Titan Reconnaissance Robots
7 Titan TR-001 Combat Robots
5 Titan TR-002 Explorer Robots
2 NG-V7 Hunter Mobile Guns
2 NG-V10 Super Labor Robots
1 NG-M56 Multi-Bot
4 Triax X-10 Predator Power Armor
72 Triax T-21 Hopper Power Armor (20% have an M.D.C. of 120)
48 Titan Power Armor (All in perfect condition)
60 NG Samson Power Armor (25% have an M.D.C. of 200)

Equipment Note: Other robots, vehicles, weapons and equipment may be owned by the individual Rangers, either brought in with them when they joined (typical of ex-mercenaries) or purchased with their own money.

Medical Facilities:

Medical facilities are excellent, with a fully equipped, up to date hospital, a staff of body fixers, cyber-docs, holistic doctors, psychic healers, and nurses. The standard field equipment is a bit limited but sufficient to give patrols a portable bio-scan, robot medical kits (both), and first-aid kits.

The People Behind the Legend

Being a Ranger is a badge of glory in and of itself. To achieve the notoriety that the *original* Rangers have attained is to become a demi-god, with all the power and respect that comes with godhood. The peasants lavish them with love and humble generosity. The Rangers get the best food, best accommodations and the most ardent attempts to satisfy their every desire (sometimes including carnal and decadent pleasures). Even acts of cruelty and mischief are explained away and dismissed by the people; the famous heroes of the Reid's Rangers need make no excuses for their actions. They have absolute freedom. Every door is opened for them. Every favor given at the slightest hint. Every man and woman adores them and every child aspires to be like them. They ride where they want and do what they please. Even the Coalition and the Vampire Kingdoms fear them.

Sadly, like most legends, the inspiring tales of shining heroes, pure of heart, are not entirely true. The original Rangers include fanatics, despots, rogues, murderers and glory hounds. They each have their own motives for joining Reid's Rangers, but it is the heady nectar of fame and glory that serves as the drug that keeps them intoxicated and loyal to the Rangers.

The Original Reid's Rangers

Kenneth "Doc" Reid, famous leader and megalomaniac.
Planktal-Nakton, necromantic ley-line walker of great power.
Raoul Lazarious, General of the Rangers and a cyber-knight.
Carlotta the White, military lieutenant; companion of Lazarious.
Mii-Tar the Destroyer, military lieutenant; D-Bee monster.
Vyurr Kly, famous hero of Eagle Peak; psi-stalker.
Meetal the Butcher, hero of Eagle Peak; psi-stalker.
Robert "Grizzly" Carter, legendary hero, said to be immortal; elf.
Pequita the Faceless One, mysterious shape-changing mage; changeling.
Note: The original Rangers rarely gather as a combat unit. Instead, two or three will lead a band of newer Rangers on heroic missions. The following is the preferred selection of allies commonly selected by the famous Rangers.

Sir Raoul Lazarious and Carlotta the White are always together. The two will occasionally elect to work with Vyurr Kly, Mii-Tar, Pequita, and Planktal-Nakton (or any combination thereof).

Grizzly Carter and Meetal the Butcher frequently work together. They have been known to enlist the company of Vyurr Kly, Mii-Tar, and to a lesser degree, Raoul Lazarious and Carlotta.

Of course, there are times when these characters must work with someone they don't care for whether they want to or not.

Doc Reid and Planktal-Nakton seldom participate in combat missions as they are far too busy maintaining operations at Fort Reid. The two are often seen together.

Doc Reid
Founder & Leader of Reid's Rangers

Real Name: Doctor Kenneth Reid
Alignment: Miscreant
Hit Points: 67, **S.D.C.:** 30, **M.D.C.:** Bionics & Body Armor
Weight: 188 lbs, **Height:** 6 ft, **Age:** 45, **Species:** Human
P.P.E.: 7, **I.S.P.:** None
Attributes: I.Q.: 22, M.A.: 29, M.E.: 11, P.S.: 24 (main bionic arms and P.S. 20 on the additional pair of bionic arms), P.P.: 21 (bionic), P.E.: 13, P.B.: 12, Spd: 176 (bionic; 120 mph/192 km)
Note: Having submitted to partial bionic reconstruction, Doc Reid cannot be transformed into a vampire.
Disposition: Friendly, warm, cheerful, attentive, enthusiastic, and charismatic. Very kind and compassionate to the poor and downtrodden (his people). But also considers himself to be a god and is above the law. Thus, he quickly becomes disenchanted, intolerant and mean to those who do not treat him like a god or who dare to question his motives and decisions. He can be capable of great callousness, cruelty, and murder. The ends (his ends) always justify the means (his means). Tends to talk quickly and in an excited and raspy whisper; a bit hyper.

Doc Reid loathes vampires and is committed to their genocide. He continues to perform countless atrocities on the creatures which he sees only as horrible monsters and not fellow intelligent life forms. As such, vampires are far less than animals and receive no mercy, no compassion, nor humane treatment of any kind. He instills these sentiments in his Rangers and any who will listen to him (which are many).

Insanity: Obsessed with attaining fame, glory and immortality (at least in the annals of history). Craves the adoration of millions which is the driving force behind to his altruistic and compassionate deeds. Believes himself to be a god destined to save the mortals enslaved and tormented by the undead. His delusion of godhood is making him less in touch with his own human frailty and he may, one day, become convinced that he is indestructible, immortal, and superhuman, but that day is still a long way off.

Experience Level: 11th level cyber-doc; third level borg.
Magic Knowledge: Only myth and lore.
Psionic Powers: None.
Combat Skills: Hand to Hand: Basic
Attacks Per Melee: Five (5). Critical strike on a natural roll of 19 or 20, kick attack (1D6 S.D.C.), and Judo flip (1D6 S.D.C.).
Bonuses: +3 strike, +3 parry, +3 dodge, +12 S.D.C. damage, +4 roll with punch or impact, and +4 to pull punch. 96% likelihood of instilling trust or intimidation (M.A.), +8% skill bonus (I.Q.).
Weapon Proficiencies: W.P. Knife and W.P. Energy Rifle are both at 11th level. W.P. Sword, W.P. Energy Pistol and Archery are at third level.
Weapons: Blade weapons are among the doctor's favorites, including a set of 12 silver plated scalpels (1D6 S.D.C. damage each), a pair of wooden throwing knives (1D6 S.D.C. damage), and a matched set of a silver handled vibro-knife and vibro-sword, both of which have a four inch silver spike at the end of the handle so they can be used against vampires (1D4 normal S.D.C., double vs vampires).
Additional vampire hunting weapons include: A compound bow and three dozen arrows (3rd level proficiency), large silver cross medallion, motorized water pistol with a half gallon capacity, four vials of holy water and a dozen stakes (hammers them in with bionic hand).

Other weapons of choice are his bionic arsenal and the NG-E4 plasma ejector (rifle), Wilk's laser weapons and Wilk's laser scalpel.
Body Armor: LE-B1 light espionage bionic body armor, 135 M.D.C., is worn when involved in covert operations. LI-B2 light infantry armor, 270 M.D.C., is worn when faced with combat situations. Both have a large silver cross painted on the chest.
Bionics & Cybernetics:
  The Legs
  Concealed laser rod in right leg: 3D6 M.D., 3000 ft/914 m range. A secret compartment in the left leg contains a small wood crucifix, two vials of holy water and six wooden stakes. A secret compartment in the right leg contains an RMK and an IRMSS robot medical kit along with a first-aid medical kit and a Wilk's laser scalpel.
  The Arms
  Wrist needle and drug dispenser in the right arm. Holds four doses of 1) antibiotics, 2) tranquilizer/sleep drugs 3) truth serum, 4) paralysis drugs, 5) poison (6D6 S.D.C./H.P. damage). A computer & calculator are also built into the right arm.
  A retractable vibro-blade (2D6 M.D.) is built into the left arm along with a laser finger blaster (1D4 M.D.), and shooting knuckle spikes that fire four silver spikes (can fire one at a time or simultaneously; range 100 ft/30.5 m).
  Additional pair of arms with a P.S. and P.P. of 20, M.D.C. of each hand is 5, each arm 25. Extremely useful in performing operations.
  Others
  All head and throat features including bionic lung, loudspeaker, headjack, speech/language translator, molecular analyzer and modulating voice synthesizer (see **Rifts,** page 242). Clock calendar and radiation detector. Note that the eyes are normal human eyes.
Money: Doc Reid is not interested in personal wealth, although he has a tidy sum of about 40 million in gold, artifacts and credits socked away. Fort Reid is a prosperous military community with well over a billion credits worth of equipment, weapons, robots, bionics, and medical facilities.

Skills of Note (includes I.Q. bonus): Medical doctor (general) 98/98%, M.D. of Cybernetics 98/98%, pathology 98%, forensics 98%, biology 98%, chemistry 98%, chemistry: analytical 93%, computer operation 98%, computer programming 98%, math (all) +98%, literacy American and Spanish 98%, language American and Spanish 98% (bionic speech translator: all nine major languages at 98% but drops to 78% when 3 or more people are speaking), pilot automobile 98%, horse 88%, hovercraft 73%, lore: demons & monsters 83%, and streetwise 68%.

Description: Doctor Kenneth Reid is a brilliant and talented doctor of cybernetics. However, there has always been a sort of dark, yet altruistic side to the doctor which has driven him to live on the edge of danger. In the Coalition State of Free Quebec, he abandoned his regular practice to establish an illegal body-chop-shop and quickly made a name for himself as the "safe doctor." Doctor Reid's intention was to service the poor who needed cybernetic prosthetics and organs but could not get authorization through proper channels.

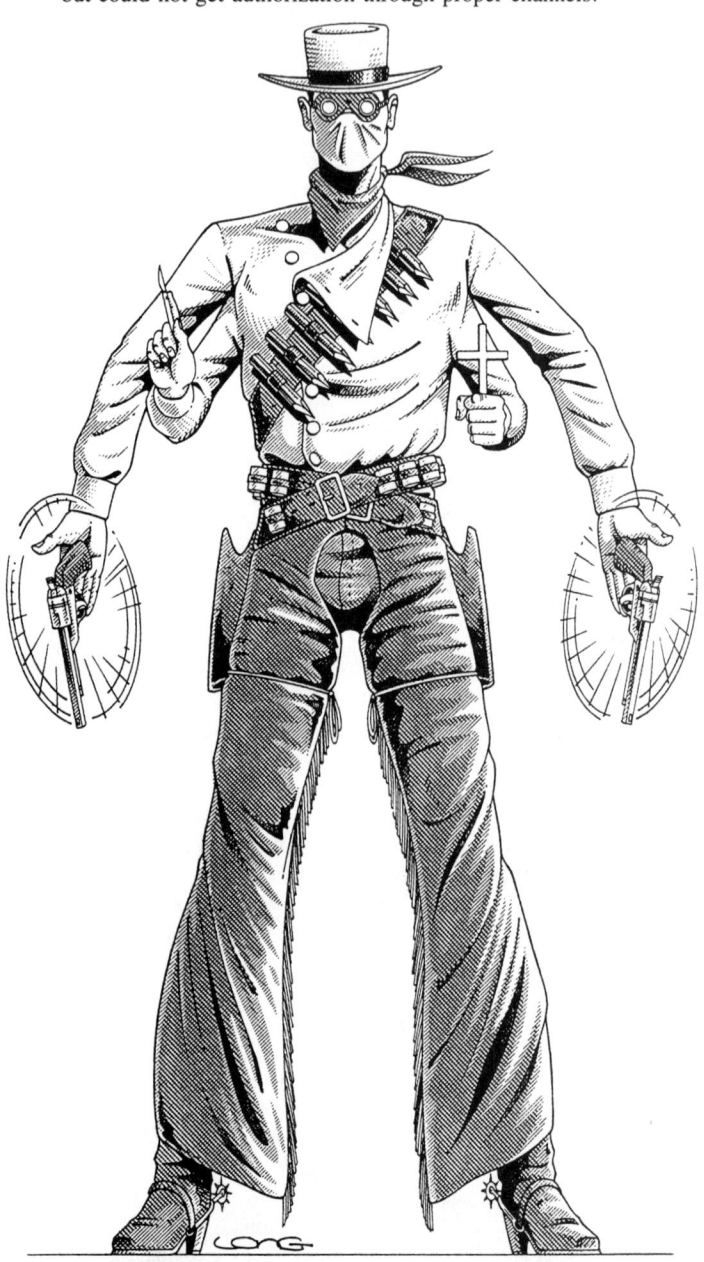

A big fan of heroes depicted on illegal, pre-rifts video discs, the doctor pictured himself as a swashbuckling champion of the downtrodden like those portrayed by Errol Flynn, Clint Eastwood, Charles Bronson, and Mel Gibson. Unfortunately, in addition to being egocentric, the doc had a taste for the good life, money, and power. This led to his involvement with the Black Market transforming his quiet little body-chop-shop into a haven for elite members of the Black Market and other criminal organizations. The body-chop-shop prospered and grew. Doctor Reid's ego also grew, causing him to be careless. He had the wealth now he wanted the recognition. Yet even then, the Coalition authorities turned a blind eye and a well paid hand away from Doctor Reid's activities.

Success and power allowed Doctor Reid to expand into the area of *bionic augmentation*. He became enthralled with the potential of bionics, added bionics to his own cybernetics, and eventually subjected himself to partial bionic reconstruction. Shortly after his bionic reconstruction, the authorities raided his chop-shop. His blatant criminal activities could no longer be ignored; bionic augmentation was too dangerous and Doctor Reid was too arrogant. Thus, the CS decided to make an example of him. To the consternation of authorities at Free Quebec, Doctor Reid escaped, avoiding Coalition troops, assassins, and bounty hunters. The man simply disappeared.

Kenneth Reid stayed in hiding for four years, selling his unique service to various outlaw gangs. It was during these years that he befriended the sorcerer, **Planktal-Nakton**. The necromancer had grown disillusioned with the **Federation of Magic** and had fallen into a deep melancholy. He viewed the Federation as being "like frightened children given to flinging stones at their parents." He craved adventure, glory, and power. The two men became instant friends.

Fate drew the pair to the **Pecos Empire** for a short period. The vampire problem of the southwestern territories struck a cord with Doctor Reid and an interesting scheme was hatched. Planktal-Nakton liked it. They gathered a few compatriots from the Empire, such as the inhuman juggernaut **Mii-Tar the Destroyer, Vyurr Kly the Hunter** and **Meetal the Butcher**, and traveled to New Mexico. A dramatic battle that liberated a village from a powerful tribe of vampires drew the attention of the cyber-knight **Sir Raoul Lazarious** and his companion, the beautiful, **Carlotta the White**. Raoul needed purpose and direction in his life and Doctor Reid gave it to him. None could dispute the nobility and valor of a campaign against the undead. Nor could one be accused of brutality in a battle against hell spawned monsters. Raoul and Carlotta loved the idea of banding together with other champions in savage combat against vampires. The pair joined the group and would eventually become its military leaders.

One morning, the legendary **Grizzly Carter** stood in their camp. He had apparently snuck past the sentry, made coffee and, with a fresh pot of brew in hand, began to suggest strategy for "their" next vampire assault. He never asked to join the group, he just did. Everybody recognized him. No body protested. He's been with them ever since. **Pequita the Faceless One** simply joined them during a pitched battle and has been with them ever since.

Doc Reid of Today

Kenneth Reid's search for wealth, power and glory seems to have been satisfied with the creation of his famous vampire hunters. Doc Reid and Reid's Rangers are renowned throughout Mexico, Texas, and New Mexico, and their tales have even spread into Arizona, Utah, and Colorado. Reid's Rangers are the heroes of the age. Other than the vampires, Doc Reid and his Rangers represent the power in Northern Mexico, from the Rio Grande to the border of the Vampire Kingdoms near Mexico City. Unfortunately, Doc Reid is quite mad.

In addition to the good doctor's obsession with destroying vampires and supernatural forces of evil, he is also convinced of his own divinity and destiny as "the Savior of the Land." His close friendship with the necromancer Planktal-Nakton has also introduced him to new ideas and a fascination with the undead and death. Doc Reid has decided to uncover everything there is to know about the undead and has spent the last two years conducting horrific experiments on vampires. While these experiments have indeed made the Doctor the foremost authority on vampires (vampire lore 98%), they have also revealed a dark and demented side that even unnerves Sir Lazarious and Grizzly Carter, the two most seasoned and hardened warriors among the Rangers.

As stated previously, Doc Reid perceives vampires as inhuman monsters that do not warrant the same humane treatment one would give an animal. Thus, his experiments are akin to those performed by the Nazis on prisoners in concentration camps during the pre-rifts period of World War II. Typical "experiments" include torture to determine how much pain a vampire can endure before he is driven insane, amputating limbs to observe or demonstrate the vampire's regenerative powers, inflicting damage by sunlight, water, etc. in order to study their effects, forced starvation of vampire subjects (a process that also results in madness), dissection on living vampire subjects as callously as one might dissect a frog, and the list goes on. The Doctor delights in the torture of the undead defending his actions with the quip, "Nothing I might do to these monsters is comparable to the suffering and horror they have inflicted upon humankind since the dawn of time."

As for Doc Reid's duties as the spiritual leader of the Rangers, he is unequalled. For all intents and purposes, he is a living god. The Rangers and uneducated wilderness folk hang on his every word. There is no man, woman or child who would not sacrifice his own life to save Doc Reid's. His words and spirit radiate hope, confidence, grandeur, wisdom, glory and power. He can seduce, entice or incite an audience faster and better than Emperor or Joseph Prosek. He is the heart and soul of the vampire hunters who flock to him.

As an administrator and commander of men, Doc Reid is terrible. While he can breathe life into words and ideas, he feels little true compassion toward the men and women who die for him or for his words. Nor does he feel deeply for the people he claims to liberate. They are all just parts of the puzzle. All are elements of this illusive thing called immortality. He can mold the people like a sculptor molds clay, but like the artist, it is his vision that shapes the clay which is all important. The people, like the clay, are only the medium used to shape the artist's vision. Worthless mud dug from the ground until the sculptor blesses it with his vision and spirit. Such is the distorted perception of Doc Reid. Consequently, he has little time for matters in administering law, judgement, or justice. Nor for the simple matters of organization, assignments, combat targets, the conduct of his troops, etc. These are left in the hands of his lieutenants; other madmen such as Planktal-Nakton and Raoul Lazarious.

Doc Reid seldom leaves the fortress, being too consumed in his horrible research, speech making (keeps morale high), and the duties of a deity. This arrangement is encouraged by his Rangers who would rather have their leader safe at home than risking his life on the field of battle. Still, the mad Doctor enjoys going on the occasional reconnaissance mission or to investigate, firsthand, unusual activity and situations that require the full attention of the living god. His friend and advisor Planktal-Nakton always stays near (in the fortress or accompanies him on travels) and personally selected the Doctor's ever present bodyguards, a pair of 6th level psi-stalkers, a 5th level borg and a 7th level mystic.

If confronted with accusations that one or several of the rangers are guilty of a crime, atrocity, injustice, negligence, or cruelty, Doc Reid will lend a patient and concerned ear. Then, after having listened to the complaint/charges, he will frown and make a fatherly and wise statement like, "Why must some men tarnish what is good by succumbing to corruption? I thank you for your honesty and strength of courage to tell me of this matter. It will be taken care of." Unfortunately, the matter is turned over to one of the doctor's trusted commanders who forget about the incident entirely. Such matters are generally under the jurisdiction of *Planktal-Nakton, Sir Raoul Lazarious, Carlotta the White,* or *Colonel William Wilding*, all of whom are among the Ranger's most evil and corrupt leaders. Doc Reid will always look to his original Rangers for their opinions, guidance, or rectification of the matter. He will never believe anything terrible about the original Rangers. NEVER! And will always trust their word over anybody else's.

Planktal-Nakton the Necromancer
Advisor, Judge, and Administrator

Real Name: Unknown
Alignment: Diabolic
Hit Points: 86, **S.D.C.:** 30, **M.D.C.:** Body armor or magic
Weight: 210 lbs, **Height:** 6 ft, 5 inches,
Age: 41, **Species:** Human
P.P.E.: 183, **I.S.P.:** 57, minor psionic
Attributes: I.Q.: 18, M.A.: 10, M.E.: 17, P.S.: 18, P.P.: 14, P.E.: 21, P.B.: 12, Spd: 11
Disposition: Strong, quiet, confident, secretive, and cunning. Always cool and intelligent under fire; a fast thinker. Seems sinister and dangerous even to the casual observer under the most pleasant conditions.

Completely loyal to Doc Reid for two reasons. First, the Doctor is his means to power. Under Doc Reid, Planktal has attained complete freedom to wreak havoc (upon the vampires) and at the same time to build an empire of people who praise his actions and brilliance. It is everything he could hope for. Second, Doc Reid is the only person who has ever been a true friend to him. He cares deeply for the man.

Often conspires with Lazarious and Carlotta whom he can often manipulate. Colonel William Wilding is his right-hand man (it was Planktal who arranged for the Colonel to become head of Fort security). Doesn't trust Grizzly Carter or Pequita the Faceless One. He greatly underestimates the other famous rangers, thinking of Vyurr Kly and the others as bumbling fools when compared to him.

Insanity: Sadistic, loves to inflict pain and death. Obsessed with death and the dispensing death.
Experience Level: 9th level ley line walker and necromancer (magic that focuses on blood sacrifices and death)
Magic Knowledge: P.P.E.: 183. Spell strength 14 (victims need 14 or higher to save). In addition to the usual line walker abilities (see **Rifts,** pages 83-84), Planktal knows the following spells and rituals.

Necromancy Type Spells: Banishment, control/enslave entity, constrain being, summon lesser being, exorcism, turn dead, animate/control dead, life drain, sickness, spoil, create mummy, create zombie, and death trance.

Offensive Spells: Globe of daylight, speed of the snail, fear, blind, call lightning, fire bolt, magic net, energy disruption, horrific illusion, negate magic, invulnerability, superhuman strength, superhuman speed, trance, and domination.

Other Spells: Chameleon, shadow meld, armor of Ithan, energy field, impervious to fire, protection circles simple and superior, see the invisible, swim as a fish, fly, eyes of Thoth, tongues, words of truth, heal wounds, sanctum, talisman, close rift, and Id barrier.

Magic Scrolls: Summon and control rain (2), time hole (1), transferal (1), teleport: superior (1), metamorphosis: animal (2), remove curse (1) and summon shadow beast (1).

Psionic Powers: I.S.P.: 57, minor psionic. Only two powers, alter aura and mind block.
Combat Skills: Hand to Hand: Basic.
Attacks Per Melee: Four (4), Critical strike on a natural roll of 19 or 20, kick attack (1D6 S.D.C.), and Judo flip (1D6 S.D.C.).
Bonuses: +1 to strike, +2 to parry, +2 dodge, +2 to roll with impact, +5 to S.D.C. damage, +4 vs horror factor, +2 save vs psionics, +6 save vs magic (O.C.C. & P.E. bonuses), +3 save vs poison, +4% on all skills (I.Q. bonus).
Weapon Proficiencies: W.P. Knife, W.P. Sword, W.P. Revolver, W.P. Energy Rifle.
Weapons: Magic: A pair of Gryphon Claws, magic gloves that inflict damage like claws; can be mentally regulated to inflict 2D6 S.D.C. or 1D6 M.D.C. damage. Lightning Rod (see **Rifts,** page 96).

Conventional weapons: Silver plated Falchion sword (1D8 S.D.C.; handle is gold plated and gem studded, worth about 12,000 credits), .357 Magnum (4D6 S.D.C. normal damage) loaded with silver bullets (holster contains 32 additional silver bullets and has a quick loader device), JA-11 Juicer variable energy rifle, and a gem studded silver cross is worn around the neck (worth 10,000 credits). Additional vampire slaying equipment may be taken on vampire combat missions, including stakes, water pistol, holy water and extra crucifix.

Favorite Weapons: Always wears gryphon claws, lightning rod, and .357 Magnum (and holster). Always takes JA-11 variable laser rifle on field missions.
Body Armor: May wear light Urban Warrior armor under robes or into combat (uses magic for main protection).
Bionics & Cybernetics: None
Money: The evil necromancer has a fortune in gold, gems, and pre-rifts artifacts (namely a huge library of books and video and audio discs) worth 20 million credits. In addition, the mage has a 15 million credit line with the black market, 8 million in universal credit, and connections with the Federation of Magic that could bring him additional revenue if he ever decided to use them.
Skills of Note: Demon lore 79%, basic math 98%, streetwise 56%, prowl 69%, land navigation 56%, wilderness survival 79%, skin & prepare animal hides 74%, intelligence 83%, radio: basic 89%, computer operation 84%, horsemanship 78%, pilot hovercraft 98%, literacy: American 79%, and languages: American, Spanish, and Dragonese 98%.
Description: Planktal-Nakton is a powerfully built, black, human male with dark, ominous looking eyes. He radiates an aura of authority, strength, cunning, and power. In many areas, it is Planktal who is the power behind Reid's Rangers and the loose knit kingdom the Rangers have inadvertently created. He exhibits absolute loyalty to Doc Reid. He is always subservient to the Doctor, for the sake of appearance if nothing else, knowing full well that Sir Lazarious and others might challenge his authority as leader if the good doctor was gone. He also realizes that, while he *may* be a significant force behind the Rangers, that it is Doc Reid who symbolizes the Ranger's spiritual center. Without the charismatic Doctor, the people might question his methods and goals. With the Doctor to cover and approve of his activities, Planktal can do as he pleases. It is of little consequence to him that he sits in the shadow of the great Savior of the People, Doc Reid, as long as it is he, Planktal-Nakton, who holds the reigns of power.

Under the mastery of Doc Reid and the might of the Rangers, the necromancer has attained complete freedom to wreak havoc (upon the vampires) and at the same time establish an empire. He can slaughter hundreds of vampires in the most vile of ways and be praised a hero (and he so loves to kill). Likewise, he can send thousands to their doom or kill hundreds of innocent by standers all in the name of freedom and still be heralded as the hero. It is every thing he could hope for.

Above and beyond his own delusions of power, Planktal-Nakton does respect and care for the one person to ever call him friend and mean it with every fiber of his being, Doctor Kenneth Reid. The Doc is the only person to have ever won the heart and friendship of the sociopathic wizard. It is a friendship cherished by the necromancer and has given cause for both men to risk their lives to save the other.

Planktal-Nakton's magic education was in the ways of the ley line walker, but at an early age, took a twist toward necromancy. Whenever possible, the mage will perform a blood sacrifice whether the sacrifice is necessary or not. Presently, he tries to limit the victims of his blood sacrifices to incapacitated (staked) vampires, but in the past he frequently used humans and D-Bees, as well as animals. The mage is fascinated with death, dying, and murder as it relates to magic and power (P.P.E. doubles at the moment of death). Vampires are especially interesting to him as they defy one's conventional understanding of life and death. He is drawn to them because they are harbingers of death and undeath and its almost as if he can control death if he can control vampires. Vampires also offer a large amount of P.P.E. when slain, making them ideal for blood sacrifices.

The necromancer is not one to be trifled with. The enemies of Planktal-Nakton have a nasty habit of mysteriously dying. The necromancer is an excellent strategist, but takes no chances, eliminating potential opposition and trouble makers immediately. He is the administrator, judiciary and law at Fort Reid.

The mystic minions of Planktal-Nakton

13 mummies clad in crusader body armor. Weapons are limited to a silver plated falchion sword (1D8 normal S.D.C. damage or 2D8 H.P. damage to vampires) and a vibro-sword (2D6 M.D.).

8 zombies clad in heavy Coalition dead boy armor. Weapons include a motorized water pistol, 6 wooden stakes, a crucifix (worn around the neck), vibro-sword (2D6 M.D.) and a Coalition C-27 plasma cannon (see **Rifts**, page 203). An additional **two zombies** always guard the necromancer's sanctuary.

Note: For complete information about mummies see **Rifts**, page 185 and for zombies see page 187.

Sir Raoul Lazarious
General and Commander of Reid's Rangers

Real Name: Same
Alignment: Aberrant evil
Hit Points: 54, **S.D.C.:** 97, **M.D.C.:** 240, Samson Power Armor
Weight: 220 lbs (all muscle), **Height:** 6 ft, 7 inches
Age: 25 **Species:** Human Cyber-Knight
P.P.E.: 25, **I.S.P.:** 69; considered a major psionic.
Attributes: I.Q.: 13, M.A.: 15, M.E.: 24, P.S.: 25, P.P.: 23, P.E.: 19, P.B.: 19, Spd: 22 (15 mph/24 km)
Disposition: Arrogant, bold, confident, tricky, deceitful and cold. Thinks his way is the best and only way of doing things. Tends to be extremely demanding, pushy, and impatient. Beats and belittles those who don't understand or obey him immediately. Treats most people in a condescending manner; a bully in knight's clothing.

He is merciless in combat, loves to fight and to win, which means he fights dirty/cheats. Will often seek revenge if he loses. Enforces his own feeling of superiority by humiliating or torturing defeated opponents. Has his own very twisted code of ethics and is completely loyal to Doc Reid and the ideals behind the Rangers (like I said, he's twisted).

Lazarious has his suspicions about Planktal-Nakton, but likes his style and considers the necromancer to be his equal and an ally. He loves Carlotta the White, whom he thinks is the most beautiful and mystical creature he has ever known. Colonel Wilding, in charge of security at Fort Reid, is also a friend and ally; they rode together for years. Of all the others, Vyurr Kly is the most respected for his fabulous combat abilities, but frowned upon for acting the fool. Grizzly Carter is despised as being too soft, a coward and a weakling, as is Meetal the Butcher. Mii-Tar the Destroyer and Pequita the Faceless One are considered capable warriors and loyal companions, but too weak and emotional to be truly great warriors or true allies.

Insanity: Borders on sadism, obsessed with winning and needs to test himself constantly on the field of battle.
Experience Level: 8th level Cyber-Knight
Magic Knowledge: Only Lore.
Psionic Powers: I.S.P. 69; major psionic. Powers are limited to see the invisible, sixth sense, summon inner strength, and, of course, the cyber-knight psi-sword (3D6 M.D.).
Combat Skills: Hand to Hand Martial Arts: Automatic kick attack (2D4 S.D.C.), Karate kick (1D8 S.D.C. plus damage bonus), jump kick (critical strike), paired weapons, critical strike on a natural roll of 18-20, pin on roll of 18, 19, 20; entangle, crush squeeze (1D4 S.D.C. damage), climb rope 89%, sense of balance 90%, and back flip 98%.
Attacks Per Melee: Five (5)
Bonuses: +6 strike, +9 parry, +7 dodge, +7 roll with punch/impact, +3 to pull punch, +10 S.D.C. damage, +5 save vs psionic attack, +2 save vs magic, +2 save vs poison, 45% chance to impress/charm.
Weapon Proficiencies: Archery, W.P. Sword, W.P. Spear/Polearm, W.P. Energy Pistol, W.P. Energy Rifle.
Weapons: Psi-sword (3D6 M.D.), NG-202 rail gun (with wood flechettes; see description under body armor, used only with power armor), Triax TX-30 ion pulse rifle, long bow, sabre halberd pole arm (3D6 S.D.C. damage, 6D6 damage to vampires, silver plated), broadsword (1D8 S.D.C), vibro-sword (2D6 M.D.) and 4 plasma grenades (5D6 M.D.) and two #3 fusion blocks (4D6×10 M.D., 10 ft blast radius). Wears a talisman given to him by Planktal-Nakton: Invulnerability (3).
Body Armor: NG Samson Power Armor (see **Rifts**, page 212) for reconnaissance into known enemy/vampire territory and for heavy combat, otherwise wears Gladiator body armor (casual wear and light reconnaissance). Both suits of armor are gold and silver in color (except for reconnaissance suits which are brown). Note: Special vampire ammunition for the NG-202 Super rail gun ammunition fires shards of wood with tiny bits of metal imbedded in the base of the wood projectile. The wood flechettes inflict only 1D4 M.D. per burst (60 rounds) to normal targets, a fraction of the rail gun's usual damage, but 3D6×10 S.D.C/H.P. damage to vampires. A called shot is still needed to strike a vampire in the heart and immobilize him (but is +1 to strike). This weapon can inflict severe damage to vampires and take off a head, arm or leg. 50% of the flechettes shoot right through the body. The lighter and softer wood (or silver) has less magnetic material which reduces the gun's range by half, to 2000 ft (609 m).
Bionics & Cybernetics: Cyber-armor (A.R. 16, 50 M.D.C.), underwater eye (bio-system), oxygen storage cell (30 minute supply), toxic filter, and gyro-compass.
Money: Carries 3D6×1000 in gold and/or gems on him at all times, as well as 150,000 in credit. Another 900,000 worth of gold, gems and artifacts, along with a cool million worth of credits is hoarded away back at his quarters at Fort Reid.
Skills of Note: Body building, boxing, wrestling, climbing 98/92%, gymnastics (see combat skills; prowl 30%), general athletics, swimming 98%, preserve food 69%, track animals 60%, tracking (humanoids; espionage skill) 65%, detect ambush 70%, escape artist 70%, intelligence 65%, wilderness survival 70%, radio: basic 80%, horsemanship 83%, pilot robots & power armor 77%, robot combat: elite: NG Samson Power Armor, paramedic 85%, demon lore 80%, literacy: American 85%, anthropology 70%, and languages: American, Spanish, Euro, Gobblely, Dragonese all at 98%.
Description: Sir Raoul Lazarious is a big man with bulging muscles and a long mane of golden hair. His voice is deep and authoritative,

his demeanor regal and haughty. Everything a classic hero should be. Only Sir Lazarious is a maleficent force disguised as good. In his own way he tries to help people, but his motives are to achieve personal reward in the way of glory and power. He believes himself to be superior to the common man and is probably the greatest warrior to ever live. He expects others to hang on his every word and obey his every command. His advice is the best. His opinion the only opinion. People can either do things the right way (his way) or the wrong way (not as he prescribed). Those who question his ability and authority are considered fools who deserve whatever fate befalls them, since they are not wise enough to listen to his words or to enlist his aid (without question). Those who openly question or defy him are seen as challenging his superiority. They are either treated with disdain, mocked, put in their place by humiliation, or beaten and/or destroyed in any number of ways.

A typical example of Sir Lazarious' petty ego is an incident at a village near El Paso. The village was threatened by a band of wild vampires who swore to destroy them. As luck would have it, a platoon of Reid's Rangers, led by the famous Sir Lazarious, heard of their plight and arrived that very morning. Unfortunately, the village elders questioned Sir Lazarious' battle plans and refused to allow the Rangers to have their way with the village women as a reward (payment). The great hero snorted and rose ever so slowly, saying, "My dear man, you question my strategies and my motive, yet it is you who called for our aid. Then, you refuse the hand of friendship from the great Sir Raoul Lazarious, General Supreme of Reid's Rangers? You dishonor my name, the Rangers, and the name of the men whom you've asked to offer up their own lives to protect yours. Sir, I am appalled. Still, I will accept your apology if you recant your previous words. I beg you reconsider your position, for without us, you are lost." The village chief tried to explain that the "price" of the women was too high and that they merely questioned the "wisdom" of the proposed plan, asking only for reassurances and clarification. Sir Lazarious smiled sarcastically, showing his displeasure, shrugged and said, "How can a general of a hundred battles make a ... a farmer understand military tactics? As to your other criticism, can there be a fair price placed on one's life? Sir, I will be in my tent, should you change your opinion." With this, the noble knight departed for his tent.

Sir Lazarious and his army stayed the day, enjoying the hospitality of the villagers food, drink and company, but the village elders would not agree to Lazarious' conditions. Shortly before dusk, Sir Lazarious and his men rode out of town. From a hilltop they watched the vampires come and lay waste to the village; 958 people died. After the carnage, a tear rolled down the cheek of Sir Lazarious. He turned to his captain and said, "We have witnessed an atrocity this night. And by all that is holy, these simple farmers shall be avenged!!" The atrocity, you see, was not his, but the massacre by the marauding vampires. The next night he found the vampire band responsible and destroyed every last one, suffering only four casualties. Of course, he was heralded as a great hero. In his own twisted mind he had punished the villains, destroyed the evil, and avenged the innocent. Such are the ways of Sir Raoul Lazarious and the men who serve under him.

"Silver," The Robot Horse

Sir Lazarious' favorite vehicle is a large, grey, steel robot horse named Silver. **Speed:** 293 (200 mph/321 kmph). **Robot Armor:** 450 M.D.C., 1600 lbs. **Intelligence:** Simple, equal to an I.Q. of about 7. **Alignment:** Aberrant evil; completely loyal to Lazarious. **Skill Program:** General Military. **Power Source:** Techno-wizard/five year. **Optics:** Advanced robot system. **Sensors:** Bio-Scan medical survey unit and micro-radar. **Weapons:** Eye laser (1D6 M.D.) and hooves (kick, stomp). **Combat:** Four attacks per melee, front kick/stomp 2D6 M.D., rear leg kick 3D6 M.D., leap kick 4D6 M.D. and a 50% chance of knocking opponent down (loses one attack), counts as two attacks. **Bonuses:** +2 to strike, +2 parry, +4 to dodge, +3 on initiative. Robots are found in the **Rifts Sourcebook One**.

The Rangers of the Lazarious Platoon

General Lazarious can command thousands of troops, but this is a rarity. The Rangers usually operate in small groups of four to eight and seldom larger than a full platoon of 32. The Lazarious Platoon, named after its famous leader, is one of the most elite forces in the Rangers. The troops that comprise the fighting force are all experienced soldiers and loyal to their commander.
Platoon Leader: Sir Raoul Lazarious
Second in Command: Carlotta the White
The 30 Soldiers: Alignments are aberrant evil (30%), miscreant evil (30%), and anarchist (40%). Average level of experience 5th.
One burster, 5th level, D-Bee, miscreant.
One psychic healer, 5th level, D-Bee, aberrant.
One mystic, 7th level, human, anarchist.
One techno-wizard, 5th level, human, aberrant.
One ley line walker, 6th level, anarchist.
One dog boy, 4th level, mutant bloodhound, anarchist.
Two full conversion borgs, 3rd and 4th level.
One partial reconstructed borg, 5th level.
Two crazies, both 7th level.
Three juicers, all 4th level.
One chief scout, 8th level, Simvan warrior, aberrant.
Four wilderness scouts, 5th level.
Five headhunters/rangers, 4th level.
Armored squad (6): One SAMAS (5th level), two NG Samson (3rd level), two Triax X-10 Predator (5th level), one T-21 Terrain Hopper, (5th level).

Carlotta the White
A Captain of the Rangers and Consort to Sir Lazarious

Real Name: K'rl-Ota
Alignment: Anarchist
Hit Points: see M.D.C., **S.D.C.:** N/A, **M.D.C.:** 400 Natural Body Armor
Weight: 125 lbs as a woman, 8 tons as a dragon.
Height: 6 ft, 4 inches as a woman, 15 ft as a dragon (30 feet long),
Age: 99
Species: Palladium Ice Dragon.
P.P.E.: 70, **I.S.P.:** 30
Attributes: I.Q.: 19, M.A.: 18, M.E.: 21, P.S.: 29, P.P.: 16, P.E.: 22, P.B.: 27, Spd: 26 (18 mph/29 km running) or fly 50 mph (80 km).
Note: Really a dragon who is usually metamorphosized into the shape of a beautiful woman; few know the truth.
Disposition: Tends to keep to herself (associating with Sir Lazarious), quiet, but cocky, arrogant and mean. She is cold and distant to all but Doc Reid, Sir Raoul Lazarious and Planktal-Nakton. She is extremely protective and possessive of Lazarious and is constantly at her lover's side; he is her security blanket.

Carlotta finds Planktal-Nakton fascinating and she and her consort both consider him a friend, yet she is always wary of the powerful necromancer. The dragon is also fond of Doc Reid and Vyurr Kly (who she thinks is a mighty warrior and cute), but her only true friend is Sir Lazarious. She finds all the other Rangers (and humanoids in general) to be naive or annoying.
Insanity: None per se, but is terribly suspicious of and competitive toward humanoid women. Can be murderously jealous toward women who flirt with Sir Lazarious.
Experience Level: 7th level Dragon.

Magic Knowledge: Can cast up to 10 spells per 24 hours, P.P.E.: 70 plus 50 P.P.E. in bracelet talisman. Known spells: Circle of flame, magic net, carpet of adhesion, befuddle, cloud of smoke, blinding flash, globe of daylight, heal wounds, eyes of Thoth, concealment, detect concealment, and mystic alarms.

Psionic Powers: I.S.P.: 30. Astral projection, clairvoyance, object read, presence sense, sense evil, sense magic, and telepathy.

Natural Dragon Abilities: Metamorphosis: Can maintain the form of a woman (or any other) for 14 hours per every 48 hour period. Fly 50 mph (80 km), nightvision 90 ft (27.4 m), see the invisible, impervious to fire, senses nearness and general direction of ley lines and nexus points (20 mile range), teleport 36%, and bio-regenerates 1D4 × 10 M.D.C. every five minutes.

Combat Skills: Hand to Hand: Basic. Claws inflict 2D6 M.D., bite 2D4 M.D. (counts as hit point damage against vampires). Ice breath (5D6 M.D., range 60 ft/18 m), kick attack inflicts 3D6 M.D. and a restrained punch 2D6 S.D.C. plus P.S. damage bonus.

Attacks Per Melee: Four (4).

Bonuses: +2 to strike, +3 to parry, +3 to dodge, +16 to S.D.C. damage, +2 to roll with impact, +2 to pull punch, +5% I.Q. skill bonus, +3 to save vs psionics, +4 to save vs magic, +4 to save vs horror factor, +4 to save vs poison, 50% to invoke trust or intimidation, and 83% of invoking charm or to impress.

Weapon Proficiencies: None.

Weapons & Special Equipment: <u>Techno-wizardry & magic</u>: Psionic mind shield that makes one impervious to psionic attack (see **Rifts**, page 96), P.P.E. powered Wilk's 447 laser rifle and 320 Wilk's laser pistol (10 blasts, 2D6 M.D. each, range: 2000 feet rifle, 1000 feet pistol; see **Rifts**, page 95). Two talismans from Planktal-Nakton: a pendant of shadow meld (3), and a bracelet that is a P.P.E. battery (contains 50 P.P.E.).

Triax TX-500 Borg rail gun and ammo-case containing six belts (6D6 M.D. per 30 round burst, 13 bursts per belt, range 4000 ft/1200 m, normal M.D. ammunition, not anti-vampire). Also carries a dozen wooden stakes, a silver crucifix and a silver dagger.

Body Armor: Frequently wears Crusader body armor to help perpetuate the belief that she is human.

Bionics & Cybernetics: None!

Money: Carries a million credits' worth of gems on her at all times (you know how dragons tend to hoard valuables) and has another two million credits' worth of gold, gems and the occasional magic items hidden at a secret place known only to her and Lazarious. She has little trust in credit cards, but does have a universal card with 250,000 credits.

Skills of Note: <u>Magic</u>: Read magic, use scrolls, recognize magic circles and enchantment, can use techno-wizard devices intuitively. <u>Conventional skills</u>: Radio: basic 80%, computer operation 75%, land navigation 65%, track animals 55%, horsemanship 69%, pilot hovercraft 75%, streetwise 49%, basic math 80%, sing 70%, languages: Dragonese and American at 98%, and Spanish at 85% (4th level).

Description: Surprisingly, few people realize that Carlotta is a dragon. Most believe that she is a powerful D-Bee, D-Bee sorceress, borg or bot. Few have made the connection between her and the nameless dragon that is known to frequently join Sir Lazarious on missions. Some have decided that "the dragon" is Carlotta's familiar or pet. To maintain her secret, she and Lazarious disappear for hours or days at a time (Lazarious finds both Carlotta the woman and Carlotta the dragon to be equally wondrous). Carlotta the woman will often wander off or go on reconnaissance *alone*, or with Sir Lazarious, so that she may revert to her dragon form and save her metamorphosis for when she must associate with humanoids. Everybody who travels with her learns that Carlotta can take care of herself and none of Reid's Rangers, except for the newest and foolish, ever worry about her when she wanders off in hostile territory.

Carlotta the White is a strange creature of magic and her relationship with Sir Lazarious is even stranger, for both, dragon and human, are deeply in love with each other. Although she is ultimately more powerful than Lazarious and will live centuries after he is dead, she is very affectionate and submissive toward him. She obeys his every command and satisfies his every desire. She would fight to the death to protect her most beloved or offer her life for his, such is the bond between them. Note that the feeling is mutual and Sir Lazarious would never betray or abandon his lady love, nor ask her to foolishly jeopardize her life. No one knows how the two met nor why a dragon would be so submissive to a fragile human. Their relationship has lasted over a decade.

The ice dragon is capable of anything. She is truly anarchist, with leanings toward evil. In her human guise, Carlotta is a beautiful platinum blonde vixen with hair that flows below her waist, a voluptuous figure and sparkling blue eyes as deep as the ocean. Many men desire her, a fact that she has often used to seduce information from the foolhardy or to distract the enemy. She is as conniving and treacherous as she is beautiful and has lured many men to their doom. She is one hundred percent loyal only to herself and her love, Raoul Lazarious. Regardless of her relationship with Sir Lazarious, Carlotta does not relate well to humans or humanoids. Likewise, she shuns her own kind, preferring the company of her cyber-knight above all others. If not for Lazarious, she might live like a hermit or become the scourge of a countryside. She secretly looks for a fountain of youth or source of immortality so that Lazarious may be at her side forever. (Author's note: No, becoming a vampire is not an acceptable option for immortality.) **Note:** All the original Rangers know that Carlotta is a dragon and keep her secret. However, this knowledge makes Carlotta nervous.

Pequita the Faceless One
One of the more notorious of Reid's Rangers

Real Name: Unknown (P'Kweet Tarl)
Alignment: Anarchist, with strong leanings toward miscreant evil.
Hit Points: 39, **S.D.C.:** 24, **M.D.C.:** 50, Body Armor
Weight: 160 lbs, **Height:** Typically 6 ft, but has varied 4 to 8 ft,
Age: 207, **Species:** Palladium Changeling
P.P.E.: 150, **I.S.P.:** None
Attributes: I.Q.: 11, M.A.: 21, M.E.: 28, P.S.: 15, P.P.:13, P.E.: 8, P.B.: 8, Spd: 15

Note: Being a changeling means the character can assume any humanoid form, changing her size/height from 3 to 10 feet, although her physical mass remains the same (e.g., short and fat or tall and skinny. Attributes remain constant. Although P'Kweet Tarl has elected to use a female gender and name, changelings are asexual and can transform into either gender. A transformation takes about 30 seconds (two melees).

Disposition: Gregarious and playful, but selfish, petty, greedy and envious. Tends to be deceptive and secretive. Loves the freedom and power of being a Ranger. Although considered one of the original Rangers, Pequita was the last to join their ranks and has never been very close to any of them. She associates with all the heroes, but keeps her distance. She really considers none of them her friends, and views them all, not as people, but as a means to an end.

Insanity: A bit paranoid, as changelings tend to be.

Experience Level: 7th level Wizard/Ley Line Walker

Magic Knowledge: P.P.E.: 150. Spell strength 14 (victims need 14 or higher to save). In addition to the usual line walker abilities (see **Rifts**, pages 83-84), Pequita knows the following spells and rituals. <u>Offensive Spells</u>: Blinding flash, turn dead, energy bolt, ignite fire, circle of fire, fire ball, wind rush and superhuman speed. <u>Other Spells</u>: See aura, sense magic, tongues, thunderclap, chameleon, levitation, swim as a fish, fool's gold, purification, reduce self, escape and teleport: lesser.

Psionic Powers: None.

Combat Skills: Hand to Hand: Basic. Kick attack (1D6 S.D.C.), critical strike on natural 19 or 20.

Attacks Per Melee: Three (3)

Bonuses: +1 to strike, +2 to parry, +2 to dodge, +2 to pull punch, +2 to roll with impact, +2 S.D.C. damage, +7 to save vs psionic attack, +3 to save vs horror factor (plus amulet +2), 65% chance of invoking trust or intimidation.

Weapon Proficiencies: W.P. Blunt and W.P. Energy Rifle.

Weapons: Neural mace (**Rifts,** page 205), silver plated war hammer (1D8 S.D.C. or 2D8 to vampires), six wood stakes and a mallet, L-20 pulse rifle (2D6 or 6D6 M.D.; 50 shot clip), six fragmentation grenades (2D6 M.D.), and two plasma grenades (5D6 M.D.). Magic items: Amulet: protection against the supernatural (+2 to save vs horror factor), scrolls: anti-magic cloud (1), mystic portal (1), restoration (1) and fly as the Eagle (1).

Body Armor: Urban Warrior (50 M.D.C.)

Bionics & Cybernetics: None.

Money: Pequita has lived a long time and has gathered and lost a fortune more than once. Currently, she has accumulated about 500,000 credits' worth of artifacts, a million in magic, and 180,000 in universal credit.

Skills of Note: Transformation disguise skill 74% (+4% per each additional level of experience) and imitate voices 56% (+4% per

Reid's Rangers: Carlotta the White, Sir Raoul Lazarious, Planktal-Nakton the Necromancer, Pequita the Faceless One.

each additional level of experience). Climbing 75%/65%, running, land navigation 64%, wilderness survival 65%, horsemanship 66%, pilot hovercraft 85%, basic math 85%, biology 65%, anthropology 60%, demon lore 65%, speaks Gobblely and Dragonese 98%, and Spanish 75%.

Description: During an earlier era, in a different dimension, changelings were the greatest assassins, spies, thieves and masters of deceit. They could infiltrate anywhere by taking the form of any person. Their disguises were perfect, for the change was not cosmetic, but real flesh and blood mystically molded by means of a mysterious supernatural transformation. A single changeling could conquer a kingdom by assassinating the king and assuming his place, or just as easily topple it by taking the king's place and giving a command of deadly consequence or betrayal. Changelings became feared above all others and a massive campaign was launched by all races to terminate the horrible creatures. Virtually every race, from humans to goblins, joined forces to destroy changelings whereever they were encountered. The changelings faced genocide and nearly perished. Even today, eons later, their numbers are pitifully few and people's knee-jerk reaction is to slay them without hesitation or question.

As a changeling, Pequita has no natural gender; the creature can be male or female. In this particular instance, the changeling identifies more closely with the female gender, so she has adopted a female appearance and the name Pequita. Of course, this does not prevent Pequita from assuming the form of a man. A changeling can transform into any humanoid form, humanoid being a large intelligent being with one head, two arms, two hands, two legs and feet (no wings or additional appendages). The body may be covered in hair or be completely hairless. Skin can have any texture and color, the eyes any shape, the apparent age can be old or as young as a child, human or monstrous. The change takes only 30 seconds to a minute. The shape can be general features or those of a specific individual, but imitating people requires practice and knowledge about that person. **Note:** Although a changeling may be an identical twin in physical appearance, the voice, inflections, mannerisms, knowledge, skills, etc., are not. To successfully imitate somebody, the creature must know as much as possible about him or her to complete the disguise, otherwise only those least familiar with that person will be fooled.

To afford protection and to create the illusion of the supernatural, Pequita deliberately changes her appearance every week, sometimes daily. The addition of mystic knowledge provides her with greater protection and helps to create and maintain the illusion that she is a powerful supernatural being.

Vyurr Kly the Hunter

Hero of Eagle Peak

Real Name: Same
Alignment: Anarchist
Hit Points: 71, **S.D.C.:** 58, **M.D.C.:** 70, Bushman Body Armor
Weight: 160 lbs, **Height:** 6 ft, **Age:** 35
Species: Psi-stalker
P.P.E.: 6, **I.S.P.:** 154
Attributes: I.Q.: 9, M.A.: 13, M.E.: 24, P.S.: 21, P.P.: 26, P.E.: 25, P.B.: 7, Spd: 44 (30 mph/48 km)
Disposition: Some what secretive keeping his deepest thoughts and emotions to himself. Wild, carefree, cheerful, but sarcastic, often disrespectful, rowdy and mischievous. Loves to party. Doesn't take anything other than combat, vampire stalking, and partying too seriously. Although a resourceful and experienced warrior, Vyurr is not a leader. He realizes this and actively avoids the mantle of leadership, staying in the background rather than the forefront.

He stays with the Rangers out of a sense of duty, bound by the hype and reputation he has created for himself as a hero of renown. Another enticement is the incredible freedom and respect he enjoys as one of Reid's Rangers. However, he is a free spirit and feels little loyalty or friendship toward anyone except Doc Reid, Mii-Tar, and Grizzly Carter. He thinks of Lazarious as a pompous windbag, Carlotta as a snooty bitch, and Planktal-Nakton as the devil himself; not that he has ever openly expressed such an opinion to Planktal, Vyurr is too savvy for that. Meetal could be a nice kid but takes life way too seriously. Pequita ain't human and is none too friendly, so she's not to be trusted.

Experience Level: 9th level Wild Psi-stalker (wilderness scout).
Magic Knowledge: Lore.
Psionic Powers: I.S.P.: 154, master psionic. In addition to the usual psionic powers possessed by all psi-stalkers, Vyurr Kly has the powers of mind block, object read, see aura, see the invisible, sixth sense, and total recall.
Combat Skills: Hand to Hand Assassin. Entangle, knock-out/stun on a roll of a natural 17-20, kick attack (1D6 S.D.C.).
Attacks Per Melee: Six (6)
Bonuses: +8 to strike, +12 to parry, +12 to dodge, +10 S.D.C. damage, +5 to roll with impact, +3 to pull punch, +5 to save vs poison, +20% to save vs coma, +6 save vs horror factor, +9 save vs magic, +4 save vs psionics, +5 to save vs mind control.
Weapon Proficiencies: W.P. Sword, W.P. Blunt, W.P. Paired Weapons, W.P. Energy Pistol & Rifle.
Weapons: <u>Magic items</u>: Pair of magic flaming swords (4D6 M.D. each), a magic talisman with three globe of daylight spells (last 27 minutes each), and an amulet of turn the undead (vampires, zombies and mummies are held at bay).

<u>Conventional Weapons</u>: Morning star with silver plated spikes (1D8 normal S.D.C. or 2D8 to vampires), matching pair of silver plated daggers, dozen wooden stakes and a mallet, Coalition C-14 Fire Breather assault rifle (**Rifts,** page 203) with a dozen extra grenades and six extra E-clips.
Body Armor: 60 M.D.C. Bushman body armor.
Equipment of Note: Multi-optics helmet, dosimeter, portable motion detector and RMK robot medical kit. TK-engine converted hovercycle is his main ride (210 mph/336 km, requires 10 I.S.P. per 50 miles of travel; see **Rifts,** page 92, #11).
Bionics & Cybernetics: None.
Money: Vyurr lives for the moment and has acquired little money that has not been spent. Equipment, medical treatment, food and shelter are provided by the Doc or by the people, so there is little need for cash, at least from his perspective. Carries 20,000 in gold and 50,000 in credits. Has an additional 60,000 in universal credit at Fort Reid.
Skills of Note: Boxing, body building, general athletics, running, gymnastics, climbing 92%, swimming 90%, prowl 80%, wilderness survival 98%, tracking (humanoids) 98%, detect ambush 75%, escape artist 75%, streetwise 52%, pick pockets 60%, palming 55%, concealment 48%, and languages: American, Spanish, Euro at 98%, Gobblely and Dragonese at 75%.

Description: Vyurr Kly is a tall, lanky ragamuffin who looks like something the wolf dragged in. He is the life of a party, although he will become increasingly wild as he gets drunker and drunker, his actions deteriorating into a brawl, malicious prank, name calling, and/or breaking things; all in a friendly/playful kind of way.

Even when sober, Vyurr Kly is a laid back, carefree fellow. He believes that people take life and themselves far too seriously. He is especially intolerant of unnecessary rules, laws, authority and protocol, which is why he avoids civilization. "A man's a man," Vyurr is often known to quote, "Polite words and fancy clothes don't make 'em a better man than he is." Then with a chuckle he'll add, "Might make 'em prettier, but not better."

Vyurr's demeanor may be casual and sarcastic, but there is nothing undisciplined about his warrior ways. Even during the most relaxed times, Vyurr is alert and ready for action. He may be carefree, but never careless. When it comes to battle, the psi-stalker is one of the absolute best, serious, observant, cunning and quick to action. He is a skillful and thinking combatant, seldom takes foolish chances and works well in a team, as well as alone. His lightning reflexes and speed makes him a whirling dervish on the battlefield, attacking here, then running there to engage another foe or to aid an ally. Unlike Sir Lazarious, Vyurr Kly does not find combat challenging or pleasurable. Fighting is simply what he's good at and he doesn't know what else to do.

Vyurr often says that his idea of the good life is laying back and enjoying good booze, good company, good women, and good fun brawling and breaking windows. But Vyurr is a victim of wanderlust, and, though he denies it, he likes to explore and see the world. Much to his chagrin, he has become close to, "A bunch of goody-two-shoes and their good habits are rubbing off on me." He is referring to Grizzly Carter and Mii-Tar the Destroyer, both of whom are dear friends and now he finds himself thinking and doing noble and kind things; "What a revolting development."

Mii-Tar the Destroyer

Famous Warrior and Lieutenant in Reid's Rangers

Real Name: Same
Alignment: Scrupulous Good
Hit Points: 111, **S.D.C.:** 500, **M.D.C.:** 200, natural body armor (alien), plus specially designed body armor (an additional 200 M.D.C.).
Weight: 940 lbs, **Height:** 12 ft, **Age:** 27
Species: D-Bee (Heroes Unlimited alien).
P.P.E.: 11, **I.S.P.:** None
Attributes: I.Q.: 8, M.A.: 20, M.E.: 10, P.S.: 30, P.P.: 20, P.E.: 30, P.B.: 12, Spd: 23
Note: Mii-Tar the Destroyer is a D-Bee from an alien world.
Disposition: Despite his enormous size and nickname of "The Destroyer" (as in destroyer of evil), Mii-Tar is known for his gentleness, especially with children. He is cheerful, optimistic, always laughing, gentle, kind, generous, merciful, compassionate, trusting (too trusting of his fellow Rangers) and trustworthy. His oath is his bond. A true paladin, he is completely loyal to Doc Reid and all of his companions. Mii-Tar is especially close to Vyurr Kly, Meetal the Butcher and Grizzly Carter. Doesn't really know Doc Reid very well but believes in him implicitly. Trusts the other, original Reid's Rangers, and considers them all his friends, including Pequita, Lazarious and Planktal-Nakton.
Experience Level: 7th level Headhunter.
Magic Knowledge: None.
Psionic Powers: None.
Combat Skills: Hand to Hand: Expert. Kick attack (1D6 S.D.C. plus damage bonuses), critical strike on a natural 18-20, paired weapons.
Attacks Per Melee: Three (3).
Bonuses: +5 to strike, +6 parry, +6 dodge, +2 roll with impact, +2 pull punch, +15 to S.D.C. damage, +8 to save vs magic, +8 to save vs poison, +30% to save vs coma/death, and +80% to invoke trust or intimidation.
Weapon Proficiencies: W.P. Sword, W.P. Chain, W.P. Energy Pistol, W.P. Energy Rifle, W.P. Heavy Energy.
Weapons: Stun gun (**Rifts,** page 245), giant size wood nunchaku (2D8 normal S.D.C damage, 4D8 to vampires), pair of giant size silver plated swords (2D6 normal S.D.C damage, 4D6 to vampires), NG-P7 particle beam rifle.

Mii-Tar often uses an NG-101 rail gun (**Rifts,** page 226). Doc Reid has developed special anti-vampire rounds for rail guns, shards of wood with tiny bits of metal imbedded in the base of the wood projectiles. The blast of wood flechettes inflict only one or two M.D. per burst (30 rounds; roll 1D4: a roll of one or two equals one M.D. of damage, while a roll of 3 or 4 inflicts two M.D.), but is devastating to vampires, inflicting 2D4×10 S.D.C/H.P. damage. A called shot is still needed to strike a vampire in the heart and immobilize him. 40% of the flechettes shoot right through the vampire's body. Range is half (2000 ft/609 m).
Body Armor: Giant size armor specially made for the big D-Bee, 200 M.D.C. (has three additional suits in storage), with an attachable Wilk's jet pack (half speed, 60 mph, because of Mii-Tar's bulk). Also owns and pilots a Titan TR-002 exploration and light combat bot, 300 M.D.C. (**Rifts,** page 215), on long range missions or for heavy combat.
Bionics & Cybernetics: Right leg is bionic and has the following features. Concealed ion rod (4D6 M.D., 2000 ft/609 range), two medium size storage compartments. One contains a pocket laser distancer, PDD audio disc player and his six favorite discs, 100 credits worth of gold coins and a universal credit card with 4D6×1000 in universal credit (in case of emergencies). The other contains two pair of handcuffs, a tube of protein healing salve, a canteen of water, and a magic talisman (three heal wounds).

Additional augmentation includes a multi-optic eye, and clock calendar.
Money: Mii-Tar spends most of his money on the poor, buying them food, clothing, tools, cybernetics and medical care. Has 175,000 in universal credits back at Fort Reid. Usually carries about 40,000 in gold and gems and 40,000 in credit.
Skills of Note: Detect ambush 70%, detect concealment 70%, tracking 65%, land navigation 70%, wilderness survival 70%, weapon systems 10%, read sensory equipment 10%, radio: basic 90%, radio: scrambler 75%, pilot jet pack 78%, pilot tank/APC 70%, pilot robot & power armor 69%, pilot: basic robot combat, demon lore 65%, and languages: American, Spanish, Gobblely, all at 98%.
Description: The initial sight of Mii-Tar is a terrifying one. The gargantuan alien towers 12 feet tall and is as broad as a barn. His obviously non-human features are unnerving, as are his incredible strength and physical endurance. However, it quickly becomes evident that the giant is a gentle and loving creature with a high regard for other life forms. With the possible exception of Robert "Grizzly" Carter, Mii-Tar is the most noble, honorable and dedicated of all the Rangers. He is a true hero, with high ideals and the courage to challenge the impossible. It is these high ideals coupled with a sweet naivete that is both admirable and dangerous.

Mii-Tar sees only the good in people and the beauty in the world. He is a dreamer and an eternal optimist. This means Mii-Tar gives people a great deal of latitude. He trusts his friends and allies implicitly and generally dismisses "lies" about them (rumors of misconduct or evil acts). For example, he will readily admit that Vyurr Kly is lazy, rowdy and drinks too much, but he will excuse this by citing innumerable incidents where Vyurr risked his life without hesitation to save others, and a long list of other acts of kindness and selflessness. In regards to Planktal-Nakton or Sir Lazarious, Mii-Tar can only speak for what he has personally seen and both men, though a bit cold and merciless, have acted as heroes in his eyes.

Now, while Mii-Tar may be naive and easily duped (average I.Q. coupled with his trust in others), he is not stupid. He has his fears about Doc Reid's sanity and has made a point to ignore increasing rumors of dishonorable acts by some of the Rangers, including Sir Lazarious, Carlotta, and Colonel Wilding, for fear of what he may discover if he looked into the accusations. However, if Mii-Tar believed there is some terrible injustice being perpetrated, especially against innocent people, he will fight to protect the innocent and right the wrong, even if it means combating an old friend. It seems inevitable that one day the gentle giant will clash with Planktal-Nakton or Sir Lazarious.

Meetal the Butcher
Famous Hero of Eagle Peak and Lieutenant in the Rangers

Real Name: Meetal M'zz
Alignment: Unprincipled
Hit Points: 58, **S.D.C.:** 36 , **M.D.C.:** Body Armor
Weight: 125 lbs, **Height:** 5 ft, 6 inches **Age:** 29,
Species: Psi-stalker
P.P.E.: 7, **I.S.P.:** 120
Attributes: I.Q.: 15, M.A.: 10, M.E.: 20, P.S.: 18, P.P.: 22, P.E.: 20, P.B.: 13, Spd: 27 (18.5 mph/29.7 km)

Disposition: Tough, independent, self-reliant, bold and brave. Takes herself and her job as a Ranger very seriously. She often finds herself fighting to be professional and to do the right thing rather than act on emotions and selfishness.

Meetal tends to be a quiet lone wolf, keeping her observations to herself until she deems it appropriate to speak. When Meetal does express herself, she can be very outspoken and obstinant. She is especially rude and cold toward Vyurr Kly, whom she thinks of as a cocky, reckless, and undisciplined warrior. Still, she respects his skills and abilities as both a wilderness scout and warrior (which irritates her all the more; what a waste of talent). Meetal fears and doesn't trust Planktal-Nakton. She respects Lazarious and Carlotta, but does not like how they conduct themselves (sees them for the beasts they are). Meetal is only close to Robert "Grizzly" Carter, who she respects above all others (may even have a crush on him). She also likes Mii-Tar the Destroyer. She is completely loyal to Doc Reid and believes in his ideals, but is beginning to recognize the cruelty and madness of his indiscreet experiments.

Experience Level: 7th level Wild Psi-Stalker
Magic Knowledge: None
Psionic Powers: I.S.P.: 120, master psionic. In addition to the usual psionic powers possessed by all psi-stalkers, Meetal has the powers of mind blank, clairvoyance, empathy, telepathy, presence sense, and see the invisible.
Combat Skills: Hand to Hand: Expert. Kick attack (1D6 S.D.C. damage), paired weapons, critical strike on a natural 18-20.
Attacks Per Melee: Three (3).
Bonuses: +6 to strike, +7 to parry, +7 to dodge, +3 to S.D.C. damage, +2 to pull punch, +2 to roll with impact, +10% to save vs coma, +3 to save vs poison, +6 to save vs magic, +6 to save vs horror factor, +5 to save vs mind control.
Weapon Proficiencies: W.P. Archery and Targeting (5th level, +3 to strike, rate of fire is five, range is 740 feet/225.5 m), W.P. Knife, W.P. Chain, W.P. Energy Pistol and Rifle.
Weapons: NG-Super laser pistol, NG-E4 plasma ejector (6D6 M.D., 20 shot clip, 1600 ft/488m range), vibro-knife (1D6 M.D.), two wood knives (2D6 damage to vamps, 1D6 normally), six wooden stakes and a mallet, nunchaku (1D8 normal S.D.C. or 2D8 to vampires; usually hidden in boot), wood crucifix, pocket mirror, two smoke grenades.

Trying to emulate her hero, Grizzly Carter, she tries to use a long bow, of Carter's design, as often as possible. Has two quivers of arrows with the following types of heads:

Special Combat Quiver
4 High-Tech flares, burns for 60 seconds.
4 High-Tech smoke, fills a 20 foot (6 m) area.
4 High-Tech tear gas, affects everyone in a 10 ft (3 m) area.
2 High-Tech neural disrupters, works the same as neural mace.
4 High-Tech light explosive, 1D6×10 S.D.C. damage
8 High-Tech high explosive, 3D6 M.D.
8 Magically endowed for double range, silver tipped.
6 Magically endowed for double range, high explosive (3D6 M.D.).
4 Magically turns into magic fire bolt, 4D6 M.D.
2 Magically turns into magic lightning bolt, 6D6 M.D. plus double normal range.

Standard Quiver
24 hunting arrows, 2D6 S.D.C. damage.
12 silver tipped, 2D6 normal S.D.C. damage or 4D6 to vampires.
12 wood with sharpened tips (same as previous listing).

Note: The high-tech arrowheads are found on page 58 of the *Rifts Sourcebook One*. The magic arrows are NEW!

Body Armor: Explorer body armor (70 M.D.C.) with the Falcon 300 jet pack (120 mile/192 km range, −20% prowl).
Riding Animal: From the pages of the *Palladium RPG*, a rare, trained gryphon! Gryphons are creatures of magic that are half eagle and half lion.

Meetal's gryphon is named Strato. Size: 4 ft tall, 7ft long, 210 lbs. Hit Points/M.D.C.: 71, in the world of **Rifts,** the gryphon becomes an M.D.C. structure. Horror Factor: 13. Combat: Three attacks per melee, claws inflict 2D6+4 M.D., bite 1D6 M.D., +6 to strike, +6 to parry, +6 to dodge in close combat, +9 to dodge in flight, +2 on initiative, +7 save vs magic and poison, +2 on all other saving throws. All bonuses are accounted for. Natural Abilities: High animal I.Q. (about equal to a human I.Q. 5), P.E. 24, P.B. 18, P.S. 20, P.P. 20, super keen vision like a hawk, 180 degree arc for peripheral vision, track by sight 54%, prowl 66%, fly 88 (60 mph/96 km). Note: Strato is very gentle and obedient to Meetal. Friendly toward Grizzly Carter, Vyurr Kly (which irritates Meetal), Mii-Tar the Destroyer (loves to play with the giant), and children. Strato has a good command of American (level of understanding is 50%) and Spanish (level of understanding is 40%), and a few words in Dragonese (25%). Hates vampires.

Bionics & Cybernetics: None.
Money: Meetal has spent most of her money on her equipment, mount, and on the poor. Has 95,000 in universal credits and 200,000 credits worth of gold and artifacts. Always carries 1D6×1000 in gold and gems and 50,000 in universal credits.
Skills of Note: Body building, general athletics, running, gymnastics, climbing 75%/65%, swimming 80%, prowl 65%, land navigation 65%, wilderness survival 90%, tracking (humanoids) 65%, detect ambush 60%, escape artist 65%, streetwise 44%, horsemanship

(gryphonship) 84%, pilot jet pack 71%, and languages: American, Spanish, and Euro at 98%, Gobblely and Dragonese at 70%.

Description: Meetal is an idealistic, female, psi-stalker who dreams of becoming a great warrior and champion of the people like her idol, Robert "Grizzly" Carter. To this end, Meetal practices constantly and studies others in combat. She tries to use her head and to stay cool under fire, which is very difficult for her. She is often discouraged by her fiery nature which prompts her to act out of emotion rather than logic. She feels that she is constantly fighting with herself to stay cool, to think, and to do the right thing (as an unprincipled alignment, Meetal is tempted to be selfish and callous). She is amazingly observant, intuitive and an excellent warrior, though a bit fanatical about discipline.

The young psi-stalker was only 15 during the Battle of Eagle Peak and has been embittered by the massacre. She loathes vampires and necromancy, which is one of the reasons she became one of Reid's Rangers. Her loathing of vampires and other supernatural creatures, especially the undead such as mummies and zombies, is the reason why she chops off the heads of her victims and, circumstance permitting, burns them. This act of perceived brutality has given her the nickname, "The Butcher." Meetal's disgust for the undead also makes her uncomfortable around the necromancer Planktal-Nakton, who she is certain to be untrustworthy and dangerous.

Grizzly Carter has finally accepted the psi-stalker's pleading to take her under his wing to tutor her in archery, the long bow, and combat. Although she doesn't realize it, Meetal is falling in love with her handsome mentor.

Robert "Grizzly" Carter
Hero of Legend and a Lieutenant in Reid's Rangers

Real Name: Rowbyr Kertri
Alignment: Scrupulous
Hit Points: 59, **S.D.C.:** 50, **M.D.C.:** Body Armor or magic.
Weight: 190 lbs, **Height:** 6 ft, 6 inches, **Age:** 380, but looks 30.
Species: Palladium Elf
P.P.E.: 23, **I.S.P.:** 67
Attributes: I.Q.: 14, M.A.: 19, M.E.: 21, P.S.: 19, P.P.: 22, P.E.: 20, P.B.: 26, Spd: 16
Note: Grizzly Carter is an elf from the Palladium RPG who came through a rift and has made his home in the western Americas for over 250 years.
Disposition: Cool, intelligent, careful, thinks before he acts. He is reserved, quiet, keeps to himself, but can be quite outgoing and cheerful. He is generous to a fault, not only sharing his food and possessions with the needy, but donating most of his money to the poor, buying them food, candy, clothing, medical treatment and supplies. He is a team player who is always quick to lend a hand when needed.

Carter likes and respects Meetal and has taken it upon himself to be her mentor. He is also deeply fond of the irascible rogue Vyurr Kly and the gentle giant Mii-Tar the Destroyer. He views Sir Lazarious as a dangerous fanatic and has taken great pains to stay out of his way. Carter knows that Carlotta is a young ice dragon and Pequita is a changeling, both native to his homeworld (Palladium). Planktal-

Reid's Rangers: Robert "Grizzly" Carter, Meetal the Butcher, Vyurr Kly the Hunter, Mii-Tar the Destroyer.

Nakton is known to the elf warrior as a treacherous sociopath (anti-people) and the source of true evil within the Rangers. He keeps a wary eye on the necromancer and is prepared for the day that he must try to destroy him. For now, the mage stands on the side of the good and is spared. Grizzly Carter also realizes that his one-time friend Doc Reid is becoming increasingly deranged. He remains with the Rangers because of their vast potential to do good and to keep an eye on the evil forces that may threaten that good.

Insanity: None

Experience Level: 13th level Wilderness Scout (Palladium Ranger)

Magic Knowledge: Lore.

Psionic Powers: Minor psionic, 67 I.S.P., powers are limited to bio-regeneration and psychic purification.

Natural powers: Nightvision 90 feet (27.4 m), average life span 600 years, youthful appearance.

Combat Skills: Hand to Hand: Expert. Kick attack (1D6 S.D.C. plus P.S. bonus), paired weapons, Judo body throw, critical strike on a natural roll of 18-20 or knockout/stun on a natural roll of 18-20, critical strike (triple S.D.C. damage) or knockout from behind.

Attacks Per Melee: Four (4).

Bonuses: +2 to strike, +5 parry, +5 dodge, +7 damage, +2 to pull punch, +2 to roll with impact, +3 to save vs psionics, +3 to save vs magic, +3 save vs magic, 60% chance of evoking trust or intimidation, 80% chance to impress or charm.

Weapon Proficiencies: Archery and Targeting (bonuses with long bow: rate of fire is eight (8) per melee, +5 to strike, range 900 feet/274 m, +1 to parry). W.P. Knife, W.P. Sword, W.P. Energy Rifle all at 13th level.

Weapons: Pair of silver plated throwing knives, pair of animal skinning knives, pair of magic gryphon claw gloves (can be mentally regulated to inflict 2D6 S.D.C. or 1D6 M.D.C. damage each and does 4D6 H.P. damage to vampires), Wilk's laser scalpel (for skinning animal hides), and a Wilk's 457 laser pulse rifle (3D6+2 M.D. per single shot, or 1D6×10 per triple burst, 40 shot clip). Magic Scroll: Teleport: superior (1) and repel animals (2).

Favorite weapon is a long bow of his own design and two quivers of arrows with the following types of heads:

Special Combat Quiver
2 High-Tech flares, burns for 60 seconds.
2 High-Tech tracer bugs: radio signal, 8 mile (12 km) range.
4 High-Tech smoke, fills a 20 foot (6 m) area.
4 High-Tech tear gas, affects everyone in a 10 ft (3 m) area.
2 High-Tech neural disrupters, works the same as neural mace.
2 High-Tech light explosive, 1D6x10 S.D.C. damage
6 High-Tech high explosive, 3D6 M.D.
6 Magically endowed for double range, silver tipped.
6 Magically endowed for double range, high explosive (3D6 M.D.).
8 Magically turns into magic fire bolt, 4D6 M.D.
6 Magically turns into magic lightning bolt, 6D6 M.D. plus double normal range.

Note: The high-tech arrow heads are found on page 58 of the *Rifts Sourcebook One*. The magic arrows are NEW!

Standard Quiver
24 hunting arrows, 2D6 S.D.C. damage.
12 silver tipped, 2D6 normal S.D.C. damage or 4D6 to vampires.
12 wood with sharpened tips (same as previous listing).

Body Armor: Explorer body armor (70 M.D.C.) with the Falcon 300 jet pack (120 mile/192 km range, −20% prowl).

Equipment of note: Has a hovercycle and two fine riding horses; prefers to ride a horse whenever possible. His black steed is named Midnight; 45 hit points, +4 to dodge, average speed is 33 (22.5 mph/36 km), but can reach a maximum speed of 58 (40 mph/64 km) and maintain that speed for two hours.

His second and favorite horse is a grey mare called Shadow that is fast and has great stamina; 41 hit points, +5 to dodge, average speed is 33, but can reach a maximum speed of 62 (48.5 mph or 77 km) and maintain that speed for four hours!

Special horse armor (barding): Lightweight super plastics affording 45 M.D.C. protection and a magic talisman purchased from a mage that can create the Armor of Ithan around the horse (3 uses, last eight minutes each). **Note:** Horses and over 200 other animals plus monsters can be found in the pages of *Palladium's Monsters & Animals*.

Bionics & Cybernetics: Bio-system prosthetic right hand.

Money: The elf has given a fortune to the poor because he has little need for money in the wilderness. Still, he has amassed a nice nest egg in the way of weapons, artifacts, and magic items; about five million credits worth. He also has 335,000 in universal credit.

Skills of Note: Wilderness survival 98%, land navigation 98%, track animals 98%, fishing 98%, hunting, identify plants 98%, holistic medicine 98%, cooking 98%, prowl 98% (minus armor penalties), skin and prepare animal hides 98%, boat building 95%, carpentry 95%, pilot sailboats and canoes 98%, pilot motorboats 98%, pilot hovercraft 75%, horsemanship 98%, general athletics, running, swimming 98%, climbing 98%/98%, gymnastics, and languages: Dragonese (Elf), American, Spanish, all at 98%.

Description: Rowbyr Kertri is an elf from the world of Palladium. In that world he was a master of the long bow, a ranger and adventurer. He took part in the games at Lopan and wandered the Eastern Territory and Great Northern Wilderness. It was in the northern lands that he and his companions came upon the mysterious wizard's tower known as the *Palladium of Desires* and fell victim to enchantment. One moment he was in his homeworld, the next in a strange, alien world. No way home, Rowbyr became an adventurer in this new land of **Rifts-Earth**.

Having appeared at the Calgary rift, he worked his way southward and made his home in the old American States of Wyoming, Colorado, Arizona, and New Mexico. The longevity and handsome youthfulness of the elven race creates the illusion of immortality, thus the name "Robert 'Grizzly' Carter *the Immortal*". Over two hundred years of heroics and tall tales have made Grizzly Carter a beloved folk hero that many to the east believe is a purely mythical character.

Grizzly Carter is a good and noble champion of the people and has made a career of wandering the savage lands of the western plains to help relieve the suffering of all races. His many exploits include comparatively simple acts of charity and heroics, such as finding a child lost in the wilderness, healing the sick, killing a crazed animal, helping dig a well or rebuilding a barn, and providing food for the hungry. The most flamboyant exploits involve combating monsters and madmen. From time to time, Grizzly Carter has joined groups of other like minded heroes, but has mostly been a lone wolf. His association with Reid's Rangers has been his longest involvement with a group; ten years.

The elf has the accumulated wisdom of nearly three centuries and is incredibly self-reliant and resourceful. He knows and understands people and the evil that too often drives them. He sees this evil swelling in too many of his associates among Reid's Rangers and that worries him. He believes it is his duty to stay among the Rangers and make certain that the organization continues its dream to create a better, kinder world safe from monsters and tyrants of all kinds. However, he clearly recognizes the madness in his old friend Doc Reid, and the ambition of the likes of Sir Lazarious, Carlotta, Pequita, and Colonel Wilding. As for Planktal-Nakton, the elf prepares himself for the day that he must try to destroy this man of evil who thrives on the pain of others and the carcasses of the dead and dying.

Colonel William Wilding

Real Name: William Bedford Wilding
Alignment: Miscreant
Hit Points: 35, **S.D.C.:** 42, **M.D.C.:** Body Armor
Weight: 175 lbs, **Height:** 6 ft, 2 inches, **Age:** 31
P.P.E.: 8, **I.S.P.:** 73
Attributes: I.Q.: 12, M.A.: 9, M.E.: 17, P.S.: 20, P.P.: 18, P.E.: 14, P.B.: 11, Spd: 132 (bionic; 90 mph/148 km)
Note: Lost legs in the heroic service of the CS, his reward was a pair of bionic replacements. He quit the CS four years later, but still has fond memories about the Coalition.
Disposition: Cool, confident, capable, but mean, greedy, selfish, petty and vengeful. Loves his job because it gives him the degree of power he desires and the opportunity to use and abuse others. He is totally loyal to the necromancer Planktal-Nakton who has given him his position as head of internal security. Wilding is fairly loyal to Doc Reid, but thinks him a lunatic; sees Planktal as the true leader and power behind the Rangers. Likes and respects Sir Lazarious and is infatuated with Carlotta, and will do shady favors for them. Dislikes the goody-goody Rangers, especially Grizzly Carter.
Experience Level: 7th level Military Specialist; ex-Coalition.
Magic Knowledge: None.
Psionic Powers: Major psionic: 73 I.S.P., see aura, sense magic, sixth sense, alter aura (great for disguise), levitation, and telekinesis.
Combat Skills: Assassin, entangle, knockout/stun on natural 17-20.
Attacks Per Melee: Four (4)
Bonuses: +4 to strike, +5 to parry, +5 to dodge, +3 to pull punch, +3 to roll with impact, +9 S.D.C. damage, +1 to save vs psionics.
Weapon Proficiencies: W.P. Energy Pistol and Rifle, W.P. Heavy Energy, W.P. Sub-machinegun, and W.P. Targeting (2nd level).
Weapons: Favorite conventional weapons include C-27 plasma cannon, CR-1 rocket launcher, TX-5 pump pistol, and neural mace. Vampire killing gear includes the usual stakes and crossbow, plus TW water shotgun, TW water pistol, 20 TW storm flares, 20 daylight flares, conventional water pistol, and 9 mm sub-machinegun with a 40 shot clip and silver bullets. Has access to all power armor, bots, vehicles, surveillance, and equipment, and manpower in the Ranger's possession at Fort Reid.
Body Armor: SAMAS or heavy Coalition Dead Boy armor is worn in combat, also owns a suit of Bushman, Crusader and Hopper armor.
Bionics & Cybernetics: Two bionic legs, concealed laser rod in the right leg, left leg modified with a concealed TW water pistol, and two vials of holy water and a small silver cross are kept in a secret leg compartment. Other items include a built-in radio receiver and transmitter headjack and speech translator, and toxic filter.
Money: Has 180,000 in universal credits, plus a secret stash of 90,000 credits' worth of gold and gems.
Skills of Note: Intelligence 66%, disguise 65%, forgery 60%, escape 70%, pick locks 70%, tracking 65%, wilderness survival 70%, land navigation 70%, lore: demon & monster 65%, pilot hovercraft 90%, robot combat elite: SAMAS & Enforcer, computer operation 75%, literacy: American 70%.
Description: Colonel Wilding is a conniving weasel who craves power and wealth. He is not a power crazed maniac, but has sought and acquired a position of internal security within the Rangers, a job he loves. His position as the fort's peace keeper and internal security gives him authority over most of the troops and citizens at Fort Reid. It also gives him the power to do what he pleases when he pleases. The authorities he is answerable to are Doc Reid and the original Reid's Rangers. His evil alignment, greed and selfishness has created a very strong camaraderie between Col. Wilding and Planktal-Nakton, Raoul Lazarius and Carlotta the White, but especially with Planktal-Nakton, to the point that one might consider the Colonel his chief henchman. In many respects, Wilding conducts himself like an elite mobster. He is known to gamble, take bribes, seize property without cause, use unnecessary force, take women against their will, brutality, and is petty and vengeful. With a word from the necromancer, he and his goon squad will set up secret surveillance, fabricate evidence, and make troublemakers disappear (sometimes permanently).
Wilding's Elite Peace Officers: Wilding has a group of tough ex-mercenaries who see themselves as the "new," elite Reid's Rangers. They include: **Rem Fields**, a sullen, sadistic bully and 7th level Operator O.C.C. who serves as Wilding's surveillance and gimmick expert. I.Q. 14, M.E. 10, M.A. 7, P.S. 18, P.P. 17, all others average; human, age 25, 6 feet tall, 31 H.P., 20 S.D.C., anarchist alignment. Minor psionic: 30 I.S.P., object read, total recall, resist fatigue and sixth sense. Skills of note: Computer operation 10%, computer programming 10%, computer hacking 10%, computer repair 70%, electrical engineer 80%, mechanical engineer 75%, weapons engineer 70%, locksmith 70%, radio: basic 90%, radio: scramblers 80%, surveillance systems 75%, TV/video 70%, literacy in American 70%, and hand to hand: basic.

Mad Martin, a wild, rambunctious, and super-hyper/jumpy reactionary who is Wilding's right-hand man. 6th level Juicer O.C.C.; I.Q. 10, M.E. 12, M.A. 9, P.S. 27, P.P. 23, P.E. 28, P.B. 11, Spd 77; human, age 22, 6 feet, 5 inches tall, miscreant alignment, 54 H.P., 345 S.D.C., plus the usual juicer bonuses. Has been a juicer for three years. Skills of note: Intelligence, detect ambush, escape artist, wilderness survival, W.P. Energy Pistol and Rifle, W.P. Heavy Energy, W.P. Targeting, W.P. Sword, Hand to Hand: Martial Arts, speaks American, Spanish and Gobblely.

The rest of his elite security force includes: **Consuela**, a third level ley line walker (knows a total of 14 spells; magic is mostly 1-4 level spells suitable for espionage and vampire slaying, plus heal wounds). **Zenaida**, a fifth level burster, **Vic** and **Cassie**, a mated pair of 4th level mutant dogs, four third level city rats skilled in surveillance, four 5th level headhunters, and four 4th level headhunters with NG Samson power armor. All are of evil alignments.

Freak Shows, Circuses, and Travelling Shows

Entertainment in the *big* cities is as varied in the world of **Rifts** as it is in our own modern world of today. The typical big city like *Lone Star, Chi-Town*, and *Free Quebec* offers a hundred or more television and radio channels, movie theaters, live theaters, comedy clubs, taverns, bars, bowling alleys, gambling casinos, parks, etc., but even in these cities, a travelling show, especially a circus, will bring out the crowds. Among the wilderness towns, villages, small kingdoms, and even the burbs of the bigger cities, entertainment is minimal and travelling shows are an exciting diversion from a gloomy or laborious routine.

Freak shows are generally smaller and less scrupulous than a circus, and delivers on shock value rather than real performing arts. Their stock in trade is the frightening and the bizarre. They present shrunken heads, wild men, monsters, mutants, and the exotic. In many cases the living attractions are prisoners, D-Bees and animals locked in cages. The exhibition of oddities is likely to present strange weapons, the bones of monsters, man-eating plants, fossils, magic items and alien and/or pre-Rifts artifacts, all with wondrous yarns spun around them (none of which are likely to be true). Many such items are fake, created by the show's staff or commissioned from artists. Freak shows may also sell souvenirs such as animal teeth (passed off as vampires' fangs or other monsters'), pets (including birds, snakes, lizards and the occasional exotic animal), elixirs of all kinds (usually with a narcotic or alcohol zing to it), booze (beer or moonshine), candy and/or exotic food.

Some freak shows will also sell uncommon, unique or decadent goods and services. Typically these include pre-rifts artifacts (mostly junk), weapons, E-clips, batteries, body armor, healing potions, and the services of psychic or magic healers, prostitutes and fortune telling.

The circus is generally much larger than most other travelling shows and the most professional. Although a travelling circus will have its museum of oddities, freak show, and hawkers, the main distinction is its emphasis on performance. Something is going on all the time at a circus with a dozen different attractions and shows going on throughout the day. The typical circus will offer two dozen or more shows a day (depending on the town), plus the *main event*, a two to four hour blockbuster show in the big tent, every evening. Entertainment includes clowns, comedians, jugglers, acrobats, magicians (often the real McCoy), animal acts, animal rides, mechanical rides (often powered by magic energy), fortunetellers, mind readers, minstrels, singers and sing-alongs, dancers and dancing, games of skill like knife throwing, archery and shooting, and some even show movies (pre-rifts movies attract the largest crowds).

Travelling Shows and Medicine Men are usually one to six wagon shows run by three to thirty individuals. Like the freak show, the scam is usually selling something shocking, frightening, tasty or illegal. The smallest shows will have one main attraction and one or two other points of interest, from spectacle to material goods. Most sell moonshine and a vast variety of potions to fix what ails you (many are heavy on alcohol, narcotics, or hallucinogens). The larger shows will have six to eight wagons and will have two or three main attractions, as well as sell many more potions, tonics, charms, booze, candy, and exotic services. Services often include fortune-telling, psychic or magic healing, doctoring or veterinary doctoring, and the selling of herbs, books, tools, weapons, E-clips, artifacts, and news.

The success of a travelling show, from circus to medicine man, varies from town to town and time to time. Thus, the price of admission, at least for the smaller shows, can range from a credit to ten credits (sometimes each individual attraction has a price of admittance), to free if the show is a con-game designed to trick people into buying goods, especially worthless goods like fake potions and booze. Most shows will accept items in trade rather than credits (many wilderness communities don't deal in credits). Items accepted as trade include silver, gold, precious and semiprecious gems, artifacts, quality magic or high-tech weapons and equipment, furs, alcohol, food and other supplies. During the worst of times, even the best and most reputable shows may offer a spectacular performance or services (including manual labor) in exchange for a hot meal, feed for the animals and/or gasoline for the vehicles and a warm bed to spend the night.

A Source of Evil

Travelling shows have the opportunity to use their unique situation to earn profit above and beyond mere showmanship. The shows are wonderful sources for gathering information and making contacts with a large variety of people. As they travel from town to town, with their shows, the performers can make road maps and map a town accurately, noting places and people of importance. They can inconspicuously study the people, their philosophies, laws, defenses, army, leaders and defenders. They can make note of the community's wealth or poverty, its racial mixture, the people's loyalties, and their leanings toward magic and other activities.

This information has many, many applications. It can be sold to the highest bidder, criminals or other interested parties (like the Coalition), used for blackmail, and wrongdoing. The least scrupulous not only deliberately spy on unsuspecting towns, but may act as agents, performing reconnaissance for bandits or mercenaries (or the Coalition), or may be bandits themselves and work as assassins, thieves, smugglers, extortionists, terrorists, and scoundrels of all sort. This is less true of the circuses, especially the larger and older circuses, but all too commonplace among freak shows and other small travelling shows. In many cases, the owner and his performers are con-men, criminals or hardened mercenaries to begin with, and the travelling show is just a front for the brigands. The opportunity for easy money can't be resisted. Such evil and illicit deeds has given medicine men, in particular, a bad reputation, with freak shows not far behind them.

Game Master's Note
About Travelling Shows

Travelling shows operated by unscrupulous opportunists and brigands can lead to many fun and strange encounters, as well as clashes with unique enemies. The freak show, circus or medicine carnival can be much more than a bunch of no-name bandits and can go a long way to adding color, suspense and action to a story. On the down side, to really make a side show work, a fair amount of thought and character development is required on the part of the GM, but it can pay off big if done right and if used as continuing characters/villains (remember, these scoundrels travel all over the country).

Of course, not all are operated by evil villains, but even the most honest and friendliest travelling show can be a great source of information, news, and rumors. Many can also provide medical treatment and/or sell food and supplies, including weapons (it depends on the specific show). If nothing else, the show will provide some amusing entertainment.

Designing Travelling Shows

Creating a Travelling Show

Step One:
The Size and Orientation

Travelling shows come in all sizes and variety. There are **six** basic types of shows presented here along with the total available points one can spend on show features. The smaller the show the less features available. GMs with specific needs, ideas and requirements may bend these rules, because the design rules for the travelling show are meant to serve as a guideline not constant data for all shows. Also, while the emphasis is in the design of unscrupulous or even criminal organizations, the same features can be used to create honest and good travelling shows; just skip the criminal sponsors, criminal activity and select an anarchist or good alignment.

Each basic type of show will list the initial number of points one can spend on the "features" of the show. The sponsoring force behind the show will also add points that can be spent on features, though some of these may have to be spent on a specific feature. Obviously, the smaller shows will have fewer all around features and resources, which is as it should be. Specific, individual characters in the show may add to the overall power and dangerousness of the performers.

Side Show
Freak Show
Travelling Medicine Show
Travelling Troubadours
Small Circus or Carnival
Large Circus

1. **Side Show.** This is a very small show, usually consisting of about six to twelve people, including the show's owner, performers, and operatives. The typical side show offers a combination of entertainment (minstrels, tumblers, acrobats, jugglers, magic), fortune-telling (a must whether the fortuneteller is really psychic or a charlatan), and an array of oddities. The oddities are mostly inanimate objects, including supposedly alien devices, pre-rifts artifacts, stuffed animals, strange or monstrous skulls or skeletons, and usually one "live" freak (the main attraction and often fake). The side show usually runs on a shoestring and will have very few resources and even less political power (virtually none; considered to be second-rate and charlatans by most). Often return to the same towns and places where they have done well in the past.

   110 POINTS, plus an additional 10 Points for vehicles and 30 Points for acts.

2. **Freak Show.** Most freak shows are about twice the size of a side show and often have 12 to 32 personnel, but are frequently just as poorly budgeted. The show's owner, performers, workers and the freaks, are usually willing members of the show. The emphasis of a freak show is the bizarre, horrific and the frightening. Other than the show's barker (announcer/host) and the possible inclusion of a juggler, tumbler, fortuneteller, minstrel or magician, there are no performers; the freaks are the show.

   There will be at least six to ten living freaks, many of whom are fakes, but at least two will be genuine and truly impressive; one, if not both, will be a show stopper. But even with the real freaks (often D-Bees, mutants, or shape changers) are not as disgusting or dangerous as they appear to be. A great deal of hype and theatrics are involved in the best of the travelling shows.

   In addition to the living freaks, the show always has a display of the strange and exotic. Much like the side show, these include alleged pre-rifts and alien artifacts, demon and monster skulls and skeletons, stuffed animals, the occasional strange or cute D-Bee animal (alive), supposed magic items, castings of footprints, mummies, and other oddities, many of which are fake. Freak shows are seen as a bit off-color, potentially dangerous (part of the attraction) and eccentric. They are usually run on a shoestring and have few resources and even less political power (virtually none; considered to be rogues and charlatans by most). Often return to the same towns and places where they have done well in the past.

   150 POINTS, plus add an additional 20 Points for Freaks (acts) and 10 Points for equipment features.

3. **Medicine Show.** The infamous medicine show can be as small as three or four people to a traveling show of some size (10 to 30 people) with entertainers and side show freaks, but the emphasis is always SELLING product. Medicine shows are almost always a vehicle for flimflam men and charlatans. The typical show will offer a number of potions, tonics, salves, herbs, alcohol and charms to cure whatever ails you. Often the selection of brews is staggering and can number over a hundred!

   The sad thing is that most of the potions and tonics are useless fakes, sugared or spiced water or fruit juices spiked with alcohol or narcotics. Only the herbs are mostly authentic and even then it's best if one knows exactly what he's buying rather than trusting the salesperson. Generally, S.D.C. poisons, herbs for holistic medicine, garlic, wolf bay, mushrooms, spices, candy, salt, fruit juices, beer, wine and moonshine are available in abundance. Magic potions, amulets, talismans, scrolls and similar items (usually kept behind the closed doors of a special wagon for that special customer) should be viewed with the greatest suspicion!

   Entertainment is likely to include stage magic focusing on sleight of hand (palming, escaping from handcuffs, etc.) and a minstrel/singer or tumbler (great distractions while another member or two of the show slips through the crowd picking the richest pockets). A fortuneteller (psychic or not) and healer or doctor (may only know first aid) are also typical members of a medicine show. The rest of the show's members are salespeople, workers, pickpockets, guards and assistants. May return to the same towns and places where they have done well, but will avoid places where they ran into trouble with the law or were accused of trickery, fraud or other illicit activity.

   140 POINTS, plus 10 Points for internal security and 20 Points for criminal activity.

4. **Travelling Troubadours.** Unlike the previous three travelling shows, troubadours or minstrel shows are all entertainment. Generally, the troupe will put on a half dozen to a dozen short performances (each about a half hour long) throughout the day, ending in a big nighttime show (about two hours long). The big show can be a drama or comedy play, stand-up comedy, a pre-rifts movie (always fascinating), or music, or music and dance. The pre-rifts movie and music and dance (especially if the townfolk can dance along) are the two most popular attractions and will pack them in every time. The shorter daytime shows can include musicians, singing, sing-alongs, short comedy plays, story-telling, puppeteers, juggling, tumblers, acrobats, magicians, and sleight of hand. Often return to the same towns and places where they have done well in the past.

   160 POINTS are available, plus 10 Points for equipment and 20 Points for outfits.

5. **Small Circus or Carnival.** The small circus will have the usual elements already discussed about circuses. Typically, entertainment will include a main nightly show that lasts two or three hours, preceded by several smaller shows during the day. Most circuses will have acrobats, tumblers, jugglers, clowns, magicians, fortunetellers, animal tamers, games of chance and souvenir and concession stands. They may or may not have a freak show or may or may not show pre-rifts movies. The typical small circus will employ 200 to 500 people.

Carnivals are similar to circuses except that there is less emphasis on performances (no long show) and more emphasis on rides, side shows, games, and experiences. The typical travelling carnival will support 100 to 400 workers and performers and offer at least a dozen different rides, a house of illusion, two or three showgirl performances, one magic show, two or more side shows, and a couple dozen games of chance, as well as concession stands, fortunetellers, etc. Some of the larger and/or more wild carnivals offer gambling and arena style gladiatorial matches to win a cash prize. The fights often allow challengers from the audience to fight one of several champions, for a price, of course. Rides and experiences can include traditional carnival rides like the ferris wheel and less traditional rides like zooming along on a skycycle or tree trimmer, riding giant robots, riding tame monsters and exotic animals (like a pegasus), the house of illusions (using real illusionary magic as well as mirrors and holograms), and so on. Entertainment is limited to freak shows, side shows, museums, fortunetellers, psychics, healers, magicians, showgirls, wandering clowns, jugglers, minstrels, and games of skill and chance (frequently rigged against the player). Carnivals also sell a larger array of trinkets and junk items.

240 POINTS are available, plus 50 on acts and 10 on reputation.

6. **Large Circus.** The circus is still the favorite of all the travelling shows, consequently, there are a number of large travelling circuses throughout the world. Circuses are especially popular among frontier and rural communities that don't have common access to technology or television. A large circus can employ 800 to 1600 people and will offer a huge venue of diverse acts and entertainment.

300 POINTS are available, plus 90 on acts and 20 on reputation.

Note: The points listed are the total available points for all the different show features. Even with 350 points, selecting features can be difficult. Remember that if no points are spent on a particular feature, say Security, then the travelling show automatically has the worst level, #1 — NONE, in that feature.

Step Two:
Travelling Show Features

A. **Sponsorship.** Exactly who is controlling the travelling show, providing them with their leadership, goals, and their real source of funds? Select one. There is no cost for this necessary feature.

1. **NONE. Independent Operative.** The show is owned and operated by an entrepreneur or group of owners who like the business and run the show. Sometimes funded by a larger private business. His goals are to make money as he and his employees see fit. The owner(s) is responsible for the upkeep of the show, the selection of its attractions, payment to the employees and performers, food, supplies and virtually everything else. He (they) answer to no one and go where they please. Add 20 Points to acts and 20 Points wherever desired.

Show Cost: None

2. **Secret.** The performers and staff have no idea who is really behind the organization or what hidden motives there might be in their assignments to stay alert and gather information. For the moment, they are their own bosses, given a free hand at what they want to do, provided they stay within the frame work of the organization. The features and equipment of the show are paid for by this mysterious benefactor.

Add 10 Points for the purchase of additional acts, 10 Points to defense, and 30 Points wherever desired, but remember, they don't know who they are working for or toward what purpose. The characters may find themselves s for on assignments they do not want, or told to do things that may compromise their morals (if the sponsoring agency is corrupt). GMs should take advantage of this as a continuing story subplot.

Show Cost: None

3. **Criminal: Small-Time Bandits.** The travelling show is run by a gang of brigands who use the show as a means to steal, smuggle, gather damaging or reconnaissance information for resale and extortion, spy, assassination, sell illegal or fake merchandise, etc. Add 30 Points for the selection of criminal activity and 10 Points wherever desired.

Show Cost: None

4. **Criminal: Organized Crime.** The show is a big-time crime outfit engaged in everything listed in number three but on a larger and more covert scale. Add 10 Points to internal security, 10 Points to defense, 50 Points to criminal activity.

Show Cost: None

5. **Government.** This kind of show is secretly sponsored by an official government, usually one of the smaller kingdoms, and is covered by the government's legal framework. The group's emphasis can range from crime-busting to smuggling, from scientific research to espionage. This could include internal security, ferreting out moles/spies from other governments, criminals, monsters, and terrorists, covertly investigating and eliminating supernatural dangers without frightening the public, as well as smuggling, reconnaissance and field investigations. **Note:** Not necessarily an evil force, may be good or anarchist in nature. Add 10 points to internal security and 50 Points wherever desired.

Show Cost: None

6. **Coalition Front.** Sponsored, controlled and secretly owned by the Coalition! 75% of the management personnel are Coalition soldiers (military specialists and technical officers), 20% of the employees and performers are Coalition soldiers and the military defense force is entirely CS personnel. The show is a front for the travelling espionage network used to spy on non-Coalition towns, suspected anti-CS supporters/rebels, magic users, free thinkers, and to gather other intelligence. It is also used for terrorism, blackmail, and assassination. The travelling organization is free to set its own policies and to wage war against enemies of the Coalition States as it sees fit; this can include burning a town to the ground and slaughtering hundreds if it can be done without implicating the travelling show/espionage network. Either way, the characters represent a special team of operatives who utilize robots, borgs, high technology, magic and psychic powers. The organization should be predominately evil. Add 10 Points to internal security, 20 Points to defenses, 10 Points to equipment and another 40 Points to wherever desired.

Show Cost: None

B. **Outfits.** The quality and flamboyance of the clothing worn by performers and workers. Replacement of any show outfit is automatic.

1. **None.** The characters are responsible for their own clothing. Costumes tend to be plain and simple. No replacements of any kind are available.

Show Cost: None

2. Utility Outfits. The show has standard uniforms for all its employees and colorful costumes for its performers. Quality is good and designs are nice, but nothing spectacular.

Show Cost: 5 Points

3. Open Wardrobe. A complete range of clothes, uniforms, and costumes of superior quality. Bright colors, spectacular designs, rhinestones, sequins, feathers, capes, hats, and masks are available to all employees and performers. Quality is excellent; replacements and new designs are regularly available.

Show Cost: 10 Points

4. Specialty Clothing. The absolute BEST in uniforms and costumes. A similar array as described in number three are available, only more dynamic, imaginative and colorful. Includes stage armor, fluorescent colors, glow in the dark fabric, wigs, masks, hats, and props, as well as standard uniforms, clothing and special gear. Even civilian clothing is fairly classy, equivalent to what's available in expensive clothing stores.

Show Cost: 20 Points

5. Gimmick Clothing. A full range of quality clothes and costumes equal to number three (add 10 points to be equal to number four), but also includes an array of colorful wigs, fright wigs, masks, complete make-up kits, disguises, and grease paint. Plus "gimmick" costumes like clothes with hidden pockets, body armor, concealed items (flowers, coins, tools, weapons, etc.), wings that are functioning gliders, jet packs, concealed optical systems built into helmets/hats/goggles, etc. The quality is high, very fashionable and believable.

Show Cost: 30 Points

6. Unlimited Clothing. All the quality costumes, uniforms, specialty outfits, and gimmick clothing one could ever want. All quality levels are available and the worlds top designers are on call to specially make appropriate outfits for any need. Replacements and new designs are frequently available.

Show Cost: 50 Points

C. Equipment. This describes the general equipment and supplies provided free of charge by the management of the travelling show. Replacement of any lost or damaged equipment is usually automatic and at the expense of the management.

Special Note: Unlike other categories, it is possible to pay points to purchase more than one of the following equipment features. For example, by spending 15 Points, a show would provide both electronic (#3) and medical (#4) equipment as described below.

1. None. The characters are responsible for buying and replacing their own equipment.

Show Cost: FREE

2. Cheap Gear. Each performer has the basic equipment, props, and materials for his craft and up to 5000 credits of additional equipment available to him. Damage or lost items may not be easily replaced, especially expensive things like cybernetic implants, weapons and vehicles.

Show Cost: 2 Points

3. Electronic Supplies and Good Gear. Good quality gear is provided, along with up to 25,000 credits' worth of common sensory, recording, video, camera, communication, computer, surveillance, and miscellaneous equipment (like language translators, electro-adhesive pads, etc.) are available for each major performer and 10,000 credits' worth for secondary performers. This selection is limited to electronic items only.

Show Cost: 5 Points

4. Medical Equipment. First-aid and paramedic type equipment and pharmaceuticals are available. Includes antibiotics, painkillers, anesthetic, protein healing salve, sodium pentothal (truth serum), dosimeter, E.K.G. and E.E.G. machines, portable lab, bio-scan, oxygen, all commonly available robot medical kits (RMK, IRMSS, Compu-drug dispenser, etc.) and two basic life support units. Plus a budget of 750,000 for emergencies requiring hospitalization and cybernetic organs or prosthetics.

Show Cost: 10 Points

5. Medical Clinic. The traveling show is equipped with full medical facilities equal to a small medical clinic. A full-time doctor (M.D. or Holistic) and one psychic healer are on staff and assisted by four nurses and two paramedics. In addition, the show has an emergency medical budget of 1D4+2 million credits for cybernetics and hospitalization. There is also a small veterinary facility for any circus animals. Replacement of lost or damaged equipment is automatic, but the total amount of medical equipment can never exceed 10 million credits.

Show Cost: 20 Points

6. Unlimited Equipment. The travelling show is a high-tech operation equipped with high quality equipment, electronics, computers, communication systems, props, and all materials and equipment needed for the acts and to operate the show. In addition, there is a superb mobile mini-hospital that can accommodate as many as 40 patients, has six life support systems, three surgery rooms and one cybernetic surgery unit (cybernetics can be repaired and replaced safely). Two medical doctors, one psychic healer, one cyber-doc, six paramedics and twelve nurses comprise the medical staff. Plus one million credits worth of common cybernetic items in stock and an emergency medical fund of 20 million credits. There is also a comparable veterinary clinic for any circus animals.

Show Cost: 50 Points

D. Vehicles. Transportation provided by the management of the show to the characters. Also includes information on the show's fleet of vehicles.

1. None. Can you run? Fly? Swim? We sure hope so, because you're not going to get any kind of ride from the travelling show. The owner has two horse drawn wagons: his personal wagon and living quarters and the supply wagon. Both are so filled with equipment that there is no space for others. Characters must provide their own transportation and tents.

Show Cost: None

2. Basic Transportation. The travelling show has just enough vehicles to accommodate their needs. A third are horse drawn wagons, a third are trucks and motor-home trailers, and the remaining third are old hovertrucks and trailers. Living quarters are cramped and must be maintained by the people living in them. Performers may purchase their own vehicles but maintenance is their cost and responsibility.

Show Cost: 3 Points

3. Company Fleet of Vehicles. The management of the show maintains a fleet of trucks, trailers, motor-homes, and wagons; all are fairly new and well maintained hover vehicles. 1D4+2 construction vehicles such as cranes and bulldozers, and two giant NG-V10 robot labor vehicles complete the standard fleet. In addition, the performers may be assigned their own personal hovercar, hovercycle, or mini-van. Living accommodations are pleasant, spacious, personal trailers for top performers and their families and reasonably spacious accommodations shared by two to six laborers or minor performers. Special travelling arrangements and expenses for commercial airline flights are available upon authorization, with about 500,000 credits in the expense account.   Show Cost: 10 Points

WORLD'S GREATEST SHOW
THE MOST UNIQUE ATTRACTIONS FROM THE FAR REACHES OF THE UNIVERSE!!
COTTON CANDY
COKE
GUSTOVICH

4. Deluxe Fleet of Vehicles. The fleet of vehicles includes new and constantly maintained hover trucks, trailers, motor-homes, wagons, construction vehicles (8), four NG-V10 robot labor vehicles, six mountaineer ATVs, and a small fleet of personal luxury vehicles for the show's star performers (their choice). An expense account for vehicle maintenance, fuel, and rentals, including chartered aircraft and boats, is also maintained at a level of four million credits. All vehicles are high quality, with special vehicles being the top in luxury and performance. Living accommodations for the stars are spacious and luxurious, equipped with video and music disc stereo systems, rich furnishings and attractive in design. Personal trailers for minor performers and workers are also spacious and attractive though shared by families or two to six individuals.

Show Cost: 20 Points

5. Specialty Vehicles. This fleet contains a number of specially designed vehicles, especially large trucks, trailers, animal trailers, vans, motor-homes and construction vehicles (12). Includes six NG-10V robot labor vehicles, a dozen NG-W10 heavy labor bots, six NG-W9 light labor bots, and two dozen T-21 Hopper power armor suits (see **Rifts Sourcebook** for labor bots and hopper power armor)! 20% of the vehicles are outfitted with additional armor (+20% the normal armor), special sensory (radar), electrical (computer), surveillance (camera and bugs), and security systems (locks and alarms) worth about 100,000 credits. 70% are outfitted with short-range radios (6 mile range/9.6 km). Also, a variety of conventional vehicles and luxury vehicles (for star performers) and helicopters are available on a limited basis. All vehicles are top quality, heavy-duty construction, and constantly maintained (ten million credits budget). A team of mechanics is employed full time and includes one techno-wizard, four operators (with robotics and weapon system skills), 12 mechanics, and 12 assistant mechanics. Living accommodations are luxurious (identical to #4).

Show Cost: 30 Points

6. Unlimited Vehicles. Any existing vehicle is available, including rare and expensive pre-rifts models (used in the show), jet packs, aircraft, and all the specialty vehicles and robots listed in number five. 50% of the vehicles are outfitted with additional armor (+40% more than normal armor), special sensory, electrical, surveillance, security, and weapon systems (if allowed by the military/defense feature), or may be modified to techno-wizard systems; up to 500,000 credits may be spent on a vehicle of importance. All are outfitted with short-range radios (6 mile range/9.6 km). Living quarter are the most luxurious. The full-time staff of mechanics is double that of number five.

Show Cost: 50 Points

E. Communications. This is a measure of how good the communications network and devices are in the agency.

1. None. Characters must buy their own and/or relate messages by word of mouth.

Show Cost: None

2. Basic Service. The travelling show has one long-range, wide band radio (500 mile/804 km range), one portable language translator and a walkie-talkie (3 mile/4.8 km range) in each vehicle. No scramblers or bug detectors available.

Show Cost: 2 Points

3. Secured Service. Two long-range radios, all personnel have a walkie-talkie or other short-range type radio, all with scramblers, six language translators, two mini-radar systems, one PC-3000 pocket computer, and a portable video camera and player.

Show Cost: 5 Points

4. Full Range System. Every tent and major vehicle is equipped with a short-range (6 mile/9.6 km range) radio and language translator, plus there are four long-range radios on line, and all personnel have a short-range walkie-talkie available to them. All radios have scrambler capabilities and one of the long range radios has a laser booster system that doubles its range (1000 miles/1600 km). All key administrators have a full computer as well as the PC-3000 and a language translator, lesser administrative personnel have only the PC-3000. Employees have reasonable access to a variety of commercial audio and video disc recorders and players.

A public announcement system is wired throughout the show and a full sound and video recording studio trailer monitors and controls the music and announcements piped through the PA system. It is also used to mix and prepare music, sound effects and videos for the show. Two full-time communication specialists, two electrical engineers and five assistants are on staff. All equipment is good quality and well maintained.

Show Cost: 15 Points

5. Deluxe Communication Network. Identical to number four except that all the equipment is of the highest quality, the communications staff is twice as big, equipment is more plentiful and readily available, there are two recording studios, and a small video theater tent or vehicle.

Show Cost: 25 Points

6. Theater and Superior Communications. Not only does this show have everything provided in number five, but it also has two large screen video theaters, and a massive full screen theater with a complete pre-rifts *film* projection system with the best surround-sound system. This package also provides computerized lighting, emergency generators, and a laser light show system. The two audio, video and film studios have state of the art editing, production and duplicating facilities. Plus a communications command center monitors, regulates and controls the PA system, lighting, surveillance/security cameras, sensor systems, and communications. All administrators have full size and pocket size computers and language translators. Two dozen or more sets of video cameras, lenses, filters, and other portable recording equipment are available to personnel for business and personal use.

Show Cost: 50 Points

F. Internal Security. This is the level of internal infiltration that the show is vulnerable to. Note that this is the only thing that prevents spies and intruders from already having been placed in the organization. Enemy agents, moles, "turned" employees and supernatural interlopers can only be prevented with high levels of internal security.

1. None. No security, anyone can walk in or out, and employees are not screened or given background checks. No supernatural safeguards other than the character's own awareness and powers.

Show Cost: None

2. Lax. A pair of security guards or muscular thugs stand at the main entrance and another pair keep an eye out for thieves and trouble makers (1D4 level experience headhunter, wilderness scout or strong vagabond). No special identification cards or codes are necessary, everybody knows who is an employee and who is not. Only the owner's property and the most important vehicles and attractions have locks and alarms. 25% chance of that one out of every ten employees has a criminal or Coalition background, or is an infiltrator secretly working for himself (skimming off the top) or for another organization. No mystic safeguards other than the player character's own awareness and powers.

Show Cost: 2 Point

3. Tight. Alert security guards and circus personnel keep one eye on the grounds and the other eye open for intruders and troublemakers. Everybody works as a team. One out of every 20 employees is a warrior type whose job is security, plus two security guards protect the main trailer (office/money) or attraction, another two watch the entrance, and two psi-stalkers wander the grounds, especially alert for supernatural and psychic troublemakers (1D4+2 level headhunter, scout, ex-soldier, and two psi-stalkers). All show vehicles and living quarters have good, solid locks, and electronic alarms.

Larger shows have the performer and living areas guarded by another 2D6 security force (same as above) and may require employees to wear electronic picture I.D. cards and have surveillance cameras to monitor the most important areas. A rigid check of prospective employees reduces the chance of Coalition and active criminal infiltrators to 15% (a criminal past is okay). The travelling show family is fairly close knit and protective of each other and the show.

Supernatural safeguards include a security staff familiar with common supernatural and magic occurrences and how to handle them (items such as silver crosses, garlic, and holy water are available). In addition to the psi-stalkers, psychic sensitive and magic trained members of the show will assist in the event that there is trouble (at least one magician, 1D4 psychics/fortunetellers, and 1D4 with minor or major psi-powers). These individuals can sense for evil and magic and observe a person's aura, etc.

Show Cost: 10 Points

4. Iron-Clad. Every entrance, exit, attraction and area of importance is under constant video monitoring and guarded by one or two members of the security force. The security force represents a quarter of the overall staff (they also assist in tearing the show down, putting it up, and other chores). 10% of the force are at least partial reconstruction borgs, 10% juicers or crazies, 25% psi-stalkers or dog boys, 20% headhunters or ex-military, and the rest have some level of combat or street experience (city rats, scouts, tough vagabonds), plus one or two psychic and magic O.C.C. security personnel. All are 1D4+2 level, the head of security will be 1D4+4 level. Common M.D. and S.D.C. weapons, body armor, optical enhancements, and sensors are provided by the management with good availability. 30% will have power armor or robot vehicles available (no Coalition or Triax Ulti-Max).

Other security measures include high quality locks and alarms on all show vehicles and attractions, hidden compartments/safes, floodlights, emergency generators, motion detectors, heat sensors, mini-radar, and camera surveillance of areas of importance, including the personnel's living area. Magic wards of alarm or incapacitating magic are strategically placed in areas off limits to the public. Patrons attending the show are asked to check weapons at the door and a metal detector is used to scan those entering (15% chance of slipping by or around the scanner). Robots are not permitted on the show grounds.

Supernatural safeguards include the previously mentioned mage and psychic characters on the force, as well as psychic and magic performers, and the occasional protection circle, amulet, talisman. The security staff is familiar with common supernatural and magic occurrences and how to handle them (items such as silver crosses, garlic, and holy water are available). The members of the show are a tight-knit family that watches out for each other and the show. A rigid check of prospective employees reduces the chance of Coalition and active criminal infiltrators to 10% (a criminal past is okay).

Show Cost: 20 Points

5. Paranoid. Top security and then some; all the measures taken in number four plus. Suspicious characters may be strip-searched or denied entrance, and no one can so much as enter a bathroom without surveillance. Multiple check-points and constant personnel checking prevent intruders from entering the restricted areas of the show. Several psychic sensitives and mages are employed as part of the security force. The average level of the security force is 1D4+3. In addition to the human security force, eight NG-W9 light labor bots with illegal military/defense programs and two Triax dyna-bots patrol the area, plus one Triax Ulti-Max or Glitter Boy is deployed at all times (see **Rifts Sourcebook** for new bots).

Supernatural safeguards include a dozen protection circles, amulets and scrolls (including negate magic, dispel magic barrier, turn dead, exorcism, constrain being, remove curse, globe of silence, globe of daylight, locate, negate poison, purification, and apparition; 1D4 of each). The owner and chief of security's rooms are protected by a sanctum spell and several mystic alarms. Superior protection circles, wards, and similar safe guards are scattered throughout the compound. The members of the show are an extremely tight-knit family that watches out for each other and the show. The chance of Coalition and active criminal infiltrators is a mere 5% (a criminal past is okay).

Show Cost: 40 Points

6. Impregnable! An vast amount of time and resources have gone into this security system; similar to number five, only with the absolute best locks, alarms, equipment and experienced personnel (add one experience level to each member of the security force and double the number of psychics and mages). The security force has developed a system of secret verbal signals and hand signs and counter-signs to warn each other of danger and trouble. Reaction to trouble is swift and discreet. Surveillance cameras, motion detectors, heat sensors, and other measures protect the attractions and property of the show. The personnel's living area is protected by a microwave fence (in addition to the other safeguards) and a full radar and ground sensor system is also used. The members of the show are fanatically protective of their people and property. There is only a 2% chance of an infiltrator being found anywhere in the organization.

Show Cost: 60 Points

G. Defenses/Military Power. The amount of military force that the show can command directly. This is the number of defenders and special defensive weapons, bots and equipment available to security and personnel in the event of attack.

1. None. The characters must provide their own weapons and equipment and fend for themselves or rely on the internal security force, if any.

Show Cost: None

2. Basic Defenses. A small number of basic arms have been distributed to the members of the show. These will include basic, inexpensive body armor like the urban warrior and plastic man, and weapons like the NG-57 ion blaster, NG-33 laser pistol, NG-L5 laser rifle, and L-20 pulse rifle. Anti-vampire weaponry includes wooden crucifixes, garlic, wooden stakes and mallets, spears, and the occasional (about one in eight) crossbow with wood bolts.

The management also provides six highway-man motorcycles with machinegun mounts, four ATV hovercycles with laser mounts, two suits of power armor (no Glitter Boy or Ulti-Max) and two giant robot combat vehicles of the more common and basic variety (like Titan or NG-V7 Hunter).

Show Cost: 5 Points

3. Weapons & Armor. A more deadly selection of arms and armor has been distributed to the members of the show. Any type of body armor is available, with the majority being the heavier armors such as Gladiator, Crusader, Bushman, Explorer, or armor of choice. 10% of the personnel have NG-Samson, Titan, or TX-Hopper power armor. 40% of the vehicles have been fitted with weaponry, including rail guns, and additional vehicle armor. In addition, the organization has a special rescue team of ex-military and combat personnel who comprise a 12 man force. All are 3rd to 6th level (1D4+2) and at least two will have psychic powers and two will know magic. All have the best weapons and equipment, four wear power armor of choice (excluding Glitter Boy and Ulti-Max), two pilot giant robot combat vehicles (any).

Show Cost: 10 Points

4. Militia. The travelling show has a 32 man force of warriors; all are 2nd to 5th level (1D4+1) and have the best weapons, body armor and equipment. Six wear power armor (any excluding Glitter Boy and Ulti-Max), six are borgs, six pilot giant robots (any, excluding GB or UM), eight are psychics and/or mages (at least one is a mind melter or burster, two are ley line walkers). The remaining are experienced fighters, including headhunters, juicers, crazies, scouts, ex-Coalition soldiers, psi-stalkers, mutant animals, and D-Bees; all have their own vehicle (hovercycle, jet pack, car, etc).

All show personnel have the same type of equipment listed in number three, as well as performers who may know magic or possess psychic or other powers. 50% of the vehicles are fitted with weapons and sensory systems like radar. Weapons and equipment are of good quality and damaged or lost items are immediately repaired or replaced (20 million credit budget).

Show Cost: 20 Points

5. Private Army. A small unit of 40 combat veterans comprise this elite force; all are 5th to 8th level (1D4+4). One is a Glitter Boy or Ulti-Max (or giant bot of choice), six pilot giant robots, 12 pilot power armor of choice (excluding Glitter Boy or Ulti-Max), six are psychics and/or mages (at least one is a mind melter or burster, two are ley line walkers). The remaining are experienced fighters, all are equipped with the best armor and most powerful weapons, including rail guns, particle beams, plasma, mini-missiles, etc. In addition to the human troops, there are 12 NG-W10s with black market military programs, armed with pulse rifles (4 with light rail guns), as part of the defense force. Anti-vampire weapons, explosives, jet packs, and body armor of all variety are also available. Half are constantly on duty and all are ready to mobilize in a moment's notice!

As usual, weapons and armor have been issued to all personnel and 60% of the vehicles have an extra 1D4×100 M.D.C. armor and weapons added to them. Weapons and equipment are of the best quality and damaged or lost items are immediately repaired or replaced (35 million credit budget).

Show Cost: 40 Points

6. Strike Force. Identical to number five plus the following additions to personnel and equipment. Seven Triax dyna-bots, four more psychics or psi-stalkers or mutant animals, two full conversion borgs or two men of magic, two healers, another Glitter Boy or Ulti-Max (or bot of choice), and twelve additional fighters; 60 troops in all (plus the show's personnel). Add one experience level to all characters in the strike force.

A usual, weapons and armor have been issued to all personnel and 60% of the vehicles have an extra 1D4×100 M.D.C. armor and weapons added to them. Ammunition is plentiful. Weapons and equipment are of the best quality and damaged or lost items are immediately repaired or replaced (50 million credit budget).

Show Cost: 60 Points

H. Types of acts. There are no limits to the number of acts or combinations of acts that one can purchase from this feature. The same act can be selected as often as three times (although the same basic routine, each is different from the other). The more spectacular shows are the most costly but also the biggest money-makers.

1. Average Clowns. Six clowns, all are first and second level vagabonds who have a knack for comedy. All paint their faces and wear funny, colorful costumes. A typical clown can make funny voices and faces, tell jokes, and perform short, silly stories with a lot of sight gags and slapstick. Show Cost: 1 Point

2. Expert Clowns. Six clowns, all are excellent comedians and experienced clowns (1D4+2 levels, any O.C.C., retired, turned to clowning). These men and women can usually sing, dance, play a musical instrument, do back flips, cartwheels, tumble, and balance (gymnastic skill), as well as the usual funny clown antics.

Show Cost: 2 Points

3. Jugglers. Four jugglers, all first or second level vagabonds with high physical prowess and a knack for juggling and comedy. Can usually dance and tell funny stories; nothing more.

Show Cost: 1 Point

4. Expert Jugglers. Four jugglers, all are experienced performers (1D4+1 levels, any O.C.C. turned to performer). These fellows can dance, juggle and throw knives (W.P. Targeting), and perform sleight of hand (concealment, palming, and pick pockets) and may be tumblers as well (gymnastics).

Show Cost: 5 Points

5. Expert Tumblers. Four people skilled in tumbling, falling, rolling, pulling punches, back flips, cartwheels, balance and other feats of physical prowess on the ground (all gymnastic and general athletics abilities).

Show Cost: 5 Points

6. Average Minstrels. Four handsome characters (P.B. 12+) that can sing, dance and play at least two different musical instruments each. Speak at least two languages. Typically second or third level vagabonds. Reasonably good quality.

Show Cost: 2 Points

7. Expert Minstrels. Four handsome performers (P.B. 14+) who sing, dance, can play at least four different musical instruments, tell stories (both lore skills and possibly anthropology and/or archaeology), and speak at least four different languages (50% are literate in one).

Show Cost: 5 Points

8. Expert Side Show Barker (1). This is the charismatic individual who stands outside the tent or wagon and shouts out descriptions about the wonders of the show or exhibit that awaits within, and also serves as the announcer during the show(s). They are consummate salespeople and often con-artists. Barkers speak loudly, quickly, clearly, and have a knack for exciting people by their words.

Typical attributes required: I.Q.: 9+1D6, M.A.: 18+2D6, M.E.: 10+2D6, high P.B. is a nice asset but not a requirement. Typical skills: Radio: basic, T.V./video, first aid (is always there for the public), prowl, anthropology, archaeology, all lore, basic math, and speaks at least three languages and literate in two. Frequently a 1D4+1 level rogue scholar or scientist O.C.C. turned carny-man (may still practice O.C.C. skills/profession, but it's as a barker that the person makes his money).

Show Cost: 5 Points per each Barker.

9. Fortuneteller (non-psychic): This your classic reader of tarot cards, tea leaves, crystals, palms, lumps on the head, and crystal balls. They tend to create a lot of atmosphere and suspense but all of their predictions and intuition is showmanship; none is real. Usually a low level vagabond or city rat turned carny. An M.A. or P.B. of 18 or higher is typical. A typical reading costs 10 to 60 credits depending on the skill of the reader and the complexity of the reading.

Show Cost: 2 Points per each fortuneteller.

10. Psychic or Mystic Fortuneteller. These are the real McCoy. True psychics or sorcerers with the ability to see into the future and/or sense emotions and thoughts. These guys can pull in the big bucks, 2D4×100 credits per individual reading, always amazingly accurate. Psychic sensitive or mystics with the psi-abilities of clairvoyance, object read, empathy, telepathy, total recall and see aura are the very best!! They can see the future and use empathy and telepathy to read the patron himself interpreting emotions and thoughts to tell the person what they want to know. Object read is great for locating people or telling whether a lost person is alive or dead. Many magic spells can produce similar results.

Show Cost: 6 Points

11. Expert Stage Magician. The stage magician knows no real magic but is a master of sleight of hand. They are frequently city rats, vagabonds and thieves who have turned their unconventional skills toward entertainment. However, they may be encouraged to continue their thieving by the managements of the less scrupulous travelling shows, picking pockets and fleecing the public. Skills include concealment, palming, pick pockets, pick locks, prowl, streetwise, and escape artist (special, no skill bonus). Other skills common to the trade are hand to hand basic, expert or assassin, climbing, running, general athletics, computer operation, computer hacking, basic math and additional languages. Generally, the magician will have an M.A. or P.B. of 20 or higher. 1D4+4 levels of experience.

Show Cost: 6 Points.

12. Pickpocket and Shill. This is an unofficial member of the travelling show who pretends to be a spectator. The petty crook will pick pockets, break into vehicles, and perform other acts of theft. As shill, the person helps work the crowd by being amazed by performances and claims or statements of fact (loud oohing, ahhing, excited exclamations, fear, fainting, applause, etc.), to provide supposedly independent verification of facts ("I've been a trapper in these hills for years an' I kin say thet thing is real. An' I ain't never seen nothing like it."), volunteering to drink potions and tonics with immediate and wonderful effect, and so on. Generally, the shill will have an M.A. and M.E. of 18 or higher. Skills include concealment, palming, pick pockets, pick locks, streetwise, and hand to hand: basic. Typically, a low level city rat or vagabond turned carny.

Show Cost: 6 Points

13. Expert Acrobats. A group or family (80% likelihood of being a family) of eight individuals of varying ages, two are attractive females. These performers have learned the art of acrobatics from an early age on as a profession. The two oldest members will be 30+3D6 years old and have 6+1D6 levels of experience, the youngest will be 6+2D6 years old and have 1D4 levels of experience, and the other four will be 18+1D6 years old and have 2+1D6 levels of experience as acrobats. Skills include dance, acrobatics, gymnastics, general athletics, body building, climbing, running, and hand to hand: expert.

Show Cost: 15 Points

14. Expert Animal Tamer. One star animal tamer (1D6+5 levels of experience), two secondary tamers (1D6+2 levels of experience) and six assistants, two of which are psi-stalkers or simvan monster riders (1D4 levels).

Show Cost for Performers: 15 Points.

Show Cost per Animal Act: Each specific animal act must be purchased separately. Select as many acts as desired.

12 trained dogs of all kinds; dance and do tricks. One Point.
24 snakes for snake act. One Point.
Four bears; dance and do tricks. Three Points.
Six horses; dance, leap, do tricks. Four Points.
Six elephants; dance and do tricks. Five Points.
Four African lions; leap through flaming hoops, do tricks. Five Points.
Two tigers; same tricks as lions. Five Points.
Two leopards; same tricks as lions. Five Points.
Small dinosaur; tame, does tricks, can be ridden. Five Points.
Larger herbivore dinosaurs; same tricks as small. 10 Points.
Common monster; tame, does tricks, can be ridden. Five Points.
Exotic monster (like gryphon, pegasus, rhino-buffalo, etc); 20 Points not tamed — 30 Points tamed.

15. Real Magic Act! An experienced wizard (1D4+3 level ley line walker or mystic) and his assistant (1) perform an exciting, but safe, magic show using real magic. Illusionary magic is ideal along the lines of spells like concealment, levitate, fool's gold, trance, escape, fly, superhuman strength, invisibility: lesser, ignite flames, fuel flames, circle of flame, extinguish fire, and impervious to fire. Healing and curative magic is always a plus.

Show Cost: 12 Points

16. Healer (psychic or magic). This is a service oriented performer (level 1D4+3) who will provide conventional doctoring along with magic or psychic healing. The more complex the ailment the more costly the service. This can be a very lucrative feature, especially in areas where medical treatment is costly, poor or not available at all.

Show Cost: 12 Points

17. Showgirls! Eight voluptuous women, P.P. and P.B. attributes 12+2D6, usually 1D4+1 level city rats or vagabonds, but can be any scholar and adventurer or psychic O.C.C.s. Skills of note: dance, sing, cook, pick pockets, streetwise, body building, speaks at least two languages.

Show Cost: 10 Points

18. Live Freaks. Two strange, alien, D-Bee, frightening looking mutant, or disfigured intelligent life forms (not necessarily humanoid). Or 6 fake freaks (make-up and an act; look very convincing).

Show Cost: 12 Points

19. Side Show attractions. 12 inanimate oddities. Can include alleged magic items, pre-rifts artifacts, the skulls or skeletons of aliens or monsters, inanimate mummies, strange plants, and similar.

Show Cost: 10 Points

20. Pre-Rifts Movie! The showing of pre-rifts movies is always an incredible draw. People are fascinated about life before the time of the rifts. They will pay 10 to 40 credits to watch the absolute worst love stories, dramas, comedies, and horror movies and sit glued to their seats, just to see what the world was like. Color movies about city life are among the most popular. High quality, blockbuster action/adventure movies, historical, and science fiction movies are the most popular and can command 50 to 100 credits a person! Some movies can get even more. One of the most famous movies is called "The Day of Destruction," which claims to show the cataclysm caused by the arrival of the rifts. What this clever entrepreneur did was acquire a cache of super-rare disaster movies, made copies, spliced, edited and redubbed them together to show the destruction of the earth. The three hour movie spectacle includes scenes from Earthquake, Towering Inferno, Crack in the World, The Day the Earth Caught Fire, Airport, Poseidon Adventure, and Die Hard. Other shows have shown unedited copies of Wizard of Oz, 2001: A Space Odyssey, the Star Wars trilogy, Terminator and Taxi Driver to standing room only crowds for years. The films are under exclusive ownership and NOT reproduced or sold to others; too lucrative to flood the market. Monster movies (too close to reality) and comedies (often not humorous in this future world) are the least popular.

Show Cost: 15 for projector/theater system (FREE if Communications #6 has been selected). Plus the cost of the film.
Lousy film of any kind. 5 Points (3 if black and white).
Good film drama, gangster, adventure. 10 Points
Great film drama, gangster, adventure, or fair sf. 15 Points
Great Science Fiction! 30 Points

21. Rides.
Pony ride, six animals: 1 Point.
Horse ride, six animals: 2 Points.
Elephant ride, four animals: 4 Points.
Other unusual animals, like camels, lamas, buffalo, ostrich, etc. (four animals): 5 Points.
Exotic Animals (two animals): 10 points.

Carnival rides like those typically found in modern traveling carnivals (ferris wheel, spinning rides of all kinds, etc.). Note that big rides like roller coasters require too much construction, materials, time and labor for a travelling show. 3 Points each.

22. Games of Chance. These are all types of simple games of skill and chance, like throwing knives or darts, tossing a hoop over a target, target shooting, and similar arcade games.
Show Cost: 1 Point per each game.

23. Gladiatorial Arena. Patrons may challenge the shows' champions. Credits or prizes may or may not be offered as a reward to the participants. Taking bets is usually allowed. The typical arena is a large tent with a roped off area indicating the combat zone. Fights are usually limited to fisticuffs and ancient style weapons (swords, maces, etc.). Fights are rarely to the death.

Set-up comes with one 9th level warrior, typically a crazy, juicer, or simvan, trained in hand to hand expert, martial arts or assassin. P.S., P.P., and P.E. attributes are a minimum of 22, one or two are often much higher. Three secondary gladiators level 1D4+2, possessing one extraordinary physical attribute P.E., P.P., P.S. or speed are the other fighter's arena management. The animal tamer may allow one of his bears or other animals to fight as well.
Show Cost: 15 Points

I. General alignment of the personnel. The majority of the workers and performers fall into this category; 80%.
1. **Evil: Miscreant and Diabolic.** Show Cost: None
2. **Evil: Miscreant and Aberrant.** Show Cost: None
3. **Anarchist.** Show Cost: 2 Points
4. **Anarchist and Unprincipled.** Show Cost: 4 Points
5. **Unprincipled and Scrupulous.** Show Cost: 6 Points
6. **Scrupulous and Principled.** Show Cost: 8 Points

J. Criminal Activity. In addition to petty crime, con jobs, theft and brutality, the travelling show has some very developed areas of criminal expertise. The following are special personnel skilled in the criminal arts, offering illegal services like assassination, blackmail, and coercion (beat people up, break legs). Like the "acts" and some other features, several of the criminal activities can be purchased, and the same activity can be purchased as often as four (4) times.

1. Medicine Man (1). Same as "Barker" (see Acts #8, except is a con-man who pitches/sells fake, stolen, dangerous, illegal or worthless medicines and goods. Skills same as barker, plus palming.
Show Cost: 5 Points

2. Prostitutes (3). Ladies of the night who sell sexual favors. Also used in blackmail schemes, gathering information and spying. P.B. attribute is 10+2D8 but M.A. is only 6+1D6.
Show Cost: 5 Points

3. Expert Forger (1). Typically a 1D4+4 level scholar, scientist or military specialist turned to crime. Skills of note: Forgery, literacy in at least three languages, basic math, art, photography, and computer operation.
Show Cost: 10 Points

4. Expert Worms (3). Two warriors trained in espionage (military specialist, crazy or wilderness scout) and a city rat; all are 1D6+2 levels. Skills of note include: Disguise, intelligence, tracking, radio: basic, surveillance systems, basic electronics, computer operation, streetwise, and literacy in American and/or Spanish. Ideal for map making, targeting wealthy or poorly secured houses, reconnaissance, and blackmail.
Show Cost: 10 Points

5. Cyber-Doc (1). A cyber-doc and one assistant nurse illegally practice the science of cybernetic and bionic augmentation.
Show Cost: 10 Points

6. Pickpocket team. A pair of 1D4+4 level pickpockets. Typically city rat, vagabond or thief. Special bonuses in addition to all others: +15% to pick pockets, +10% palming and +5% prowl.
Show Cost: 8 Points

7. Gang of Robbers. While the show is going on, a gang of 2D4+2 thieves and thugs rob the empty houses and mug people in the alleys and dark shadows. Usually 1D4 level city rats, vagabonds, headhunters, or thieves/smugglers. They try not to seriously injure or kill anybody, but beatings of victims are commonplace. No member of the gang is officially affiliated with the show, but the observant individual will notice these shady characters hanging around the circus and they do have a secret hideout in the show's living area.
Show Cost: 10 Points

8. Smugglers and Sellers of Contraband. 1D6+2 specialists in smuggling, 1D4+3 levels of experience. Skills of note include concealment, palming, prowl, basic math, literacy, forgery, detect ambush, detect concealment, escape artist. Buy, sell and transport scarce, illegal, or dangerous goods, most notably poisons, drugs, pre-rifts artifacts, magic, weapons, cybernetics and bionics. Will also carry and deliver secret packages, contraband and information for outside clients; individuals, other crooks, the black market, and the Coalition.
Show Cost: 15 Points

9. Expert Assassin (1). An evil, 1D4+4 level, warrior who specializes in murder; can be any Men of Arms O.C.C., but borgs, crazies, juicers, psi-stalkers, or wilderness scouts are the best. Skills of note: Tracking, sniper, hunter, land navigation, prowl, hand to hand assassin or martial arts, and physical and W.P. skills.
Show Cost: 15 Points

10. Psychic Enforcer (1). A psychically powered individual whose job is to enforce the wishes of his boss and the organization. Assignments include torture, frightening and hurting people, elite bodyguard, protection and murder. Typically a 1D4+2 level mind melter or burster.

Show Cost: 15 Points

11. Special Forces: A pair of super warriors used for special missions such as jail breaks, assaults/raids, and murder. Typically a pair of 1D4+3 level crazies, juicers, borgs, or a dragon (or other supernatural powerhouse) and a psychic or mage.

Show Cost: 20 Points

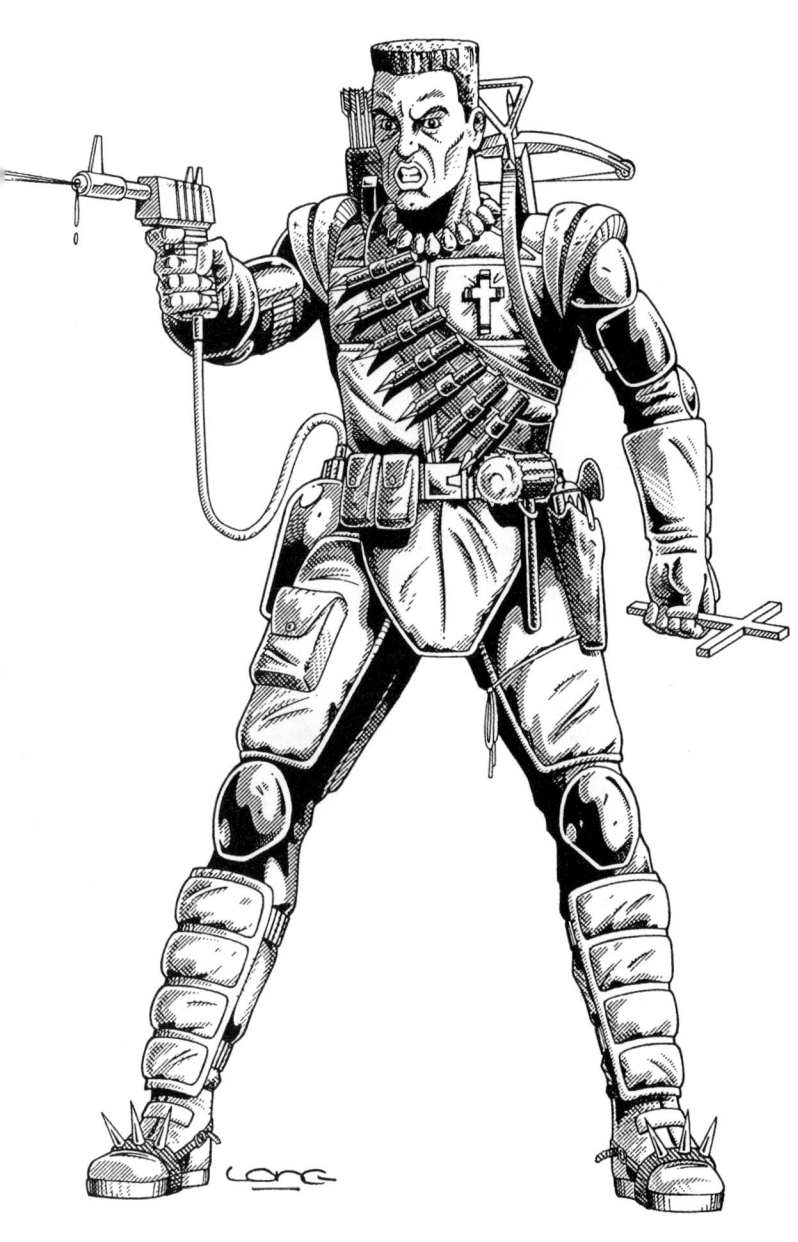

K. Travelling Show's Reputation/Credentials. Just what is the reputation of the show? The credentials determine just how much respect characters can command.

1. Hunted. The group is rumored to be criminal, con-artists, or troublemakers, and viewed with great suspicion by everybody who encounters them. The authorities of several towns are hunting them because they owe fines or for damage caused to their towns and/or they are wanted for questioning about crimes, or they are wanted criminals for known criminal activity, or they are wanted out of vengeance for criminal or cruel acts. There is a 1-40% chance that one of these hunting parties will find them whenever the show stays in or near a community more than three days (roll for each day after three). Cooperation from authorities, particularly police and militia, will be slow and reluctant. Still, the show will draw a crowd.

Show Cost: None

2. Scoundrels. The show and its personnel are viewed with suspicion. The public assumes them to be a group of criminals, outlaws, flimflam men, quacks, freaks or fanatics. Feared and not trusted. But still draws a crowd. Cooperation from authorities, particularly police and militia, will be slow and reluctant.

Show Cost: 1 Point

3. Unknown. No one has even heard of the show. They get no special cooperation and receive no overt attention from the town or the authorities. Draws good crowds. Communities will try to be fair and give the visitors reasonable doubt, but will tend to side with fellow citizens and other authorities; will believe the worst about the show if from a reputable source.

Note: Increase the typical level of pay by 10%.

Show Cost: 5 Points

4. Known. The show is known to have been around for years as a source of good entertainment or product. There are no rumors about the show having ever been involved in criminal or negative activities (regardless of whether the show is operated by scoundrels or not). Tends to draw bigger and more excited crowds. Police and local authorities will help in matters that are in their jurisdiction.

Note: Increase the typical level of pay by 25%.

Show Cost: 10 Points

5. Excellent Reputation. The travelling show has a reputation for providing high quality entertainment and goods. Even if there are rumors of trouble or crimes, nobody holds it against the show (after all, hooligans follow such popular shows to prey on the attendees and the innocent show gets blamed), or the show is so spectacular that people are willing to take the risk. The management is known as "good guys" who deserve all the help they can get. Draws excellent, large crowds.

Police will overlook minor infractions such as brawls and drunkenness, and will gladly dismiss minor criminal charges like petty larceny if the show's management makes restitution to the victim, pays a big fine (double the usual) and promises to keep out of further trouble. Authorities will help and cooperate to their fullest in any investigations and operations; tend to give the show the benefit of the doubt.

Note: Increase the typical level of pay by 50%.

Show Cost: 25 Points

6. Famous! Either a Sparkling or Villainous Reputation. The show is known to be sensational!! The performers are bigger-than-life stars displaying incomparable skill, death defying courage and the best entertainment around! Any authority and citizen would jump at the chance to have the show visit their community, even if it means risking trouble that may come with the show. The show always receives favorable press, gets lots of free advertising, is swamped with adoring fan letters and requests, and draws huge crowds. Shows with truly sterling reputations (are not evil or criminal) receive the same cooperation and adulation as visiting dignitaries; perhaps more. The show is always given benefit of the doubt and the authorities will always side with the show unless there is concrete evidence to the contrary.

Those with notorious reputations (may even be known or suspected crime rings) are still accepted with open arms because they are known as spectacular entertainment. These performers have the same star status and are adored by thousands. The only difference is that a cloud of controversy and trouble seems to follow this show wherever it goes. Authorities will do their utmost to prevent trouble and may increase police patrols or call in the militia just in case there is trouble. Authorities may suspect otherwise, but will always give the show the benefit of the doubt unless there is concrete evidence to the contrary. Brawls, drunkenness, larceny, and petty theft are completely ignored. Even major crimes may be ignored (especially if the show is leaving soon) out of fear of retribution by the show's dark forces.

Note: Double the typical level of pay.

Show Cost: 50 Points

L. Salary. The amount of money received weekly by the employees will vary depending on the size of the show and the show's reputation.

1. None. The performers pass the hat and hope for the generosity of the spectators. Criminal groups make their real money fleecing the crowds. The take is generally small and varies dramatically from crowd to crowd. A place to live, food and costumes may be provided on loan from the management or may be the responsibility of the performer. **Typical Week's Pay:** $3D6 \times 10$ for workers and $5D6 \times 10$ credits for performers.

Show Cost: None

2. Freelance. The performers and workers are paid a small commission based on the profit of each show. No profit means no additional pay but they receive living quarters, food and the use of the show's other resources (costumes, vehicles, etc.). Performers and workers have no binding contract and can be fired or can quit with a moment's notice. **Typical Week's Pay:** $4D6 \times 10$ credits for laborers, thugs, and lesser performers. $1D6 \times 100$ credits for expert performers and criminal specialists (always get paid more than the average Joe).

Show Cost: 2 Points

3. Pittance Salary. The show employs the characters on a full-time basis, but is strapped for money. The show provides living quarters, food, supplies, costumes, and access to other facilities and benefits at no charge. Performers are likely to be signed to one to four year contracts. **Typical Week's Pay:** 180 credits for laborers, thugs and lesser performers. 275 credits for minor performers and 400 credits per week to star performers and expert criminal specialists.

Show Cost: 5 Points

4. Good Salary. In addition to room and board and access to the show's facilities, the employees receive a good salary. All performers and important laborers sign a two to four year contract. **Typical Week's Pay:** 250 credits for laborers and minor performers, 350 credits for the average performer and 650 credits for star performers and expert criminal specialists. Bonuses of $1D6 \times 1000$ are paid to star performers every quarter and $1D4 \times 100$ to others.

Show Cost: 10 Points

5. Excellent Salary. In addition to room and board and access to the show's facilities, the employees receive an excellent salary. All performers and important laborers sign a three to six year contract. Performers and key people may get additional perks in the way of special accommodations, a private vehicle, special billing, etc. **Typical Week's Pay:** 350 credits for laborers and minor performers, 600 credits for the average performer and 2000 credits for star performers and expert criminal specialists. Bonuses of $2D6 \times 1000$ are paid to star performers every quarter and $2D4 \times 100$ to others.

Show Cost: 20 Points

6. Outrageous Salary. All the usual accommodations and perks plus spectacular pay!! **Typical Week's Pay:** 600 credits for laborers and minor performers, 1200 credits for the average performer and 5000 credits for star performers and expert criminal specialists. Bonuses of $1D6 \times 10,000$ are paid to star performers and expert criminals every quarter and $1D4 \times 1000$ to others.

Show Cost: 40 Points

Other Information

Each travelling show should have a name, logo/insignia, and banners. It's a good idea to come up with an owner/manager, an executive officer, a couple star performers, and a few other key characters. Remember that interesting guards, performers and scoundrels can make a travelling show much more interesting. The more colorful the details the greater the atmosphere.

Example of a Circus
Mr. Drak's Travelling Circus

Here's how designing a travelling show might work. A total of 450 Points are available to the large circus for the different features. A minimum of 20 must be spent on reputation and 110 on acts.

A. Sponsorship: Independent Operator	0 Points
B. Outfits: #6 Unlimited Costumes	50 Points
C. Equipment: #6 Unlimited	50 Points
D. Vehicles: #5 Specialty Vehicles	30 Points
E. Communications: #5 Deluxe Network	25 Points
F. Internal Security: #4 Iron Clad	20 Points
G. Defenses: #4 Militia	20 Points
H. Acts: Many	177 Points
I. Alignment: #6 Scrupulous & Principled	8 Points
J. Criminal: NONE	0 Points
K. Reputation: #6 Famous	50 Points
L. Salary: #5 Excellent	20 Points

Total Points Spent: 450 Points

Note: Available Points not spent are forever lost; they can not be saved and used at a later date.

The following pages offer two of the more infamous shows that frequent the territories west of the Mississippi River and into Mexico. Rules for creating the foundations of villainous travelling shows is also provided. Specific details and characters will need to be added.

Mr. Drak's Travelling Circus

By Steve Sheiring and Kevin Siembieda

Mr. Drak has assembled one of the most renowned entourages of travelling entertainers in the Rifts world. Quite often, the mere rumor of the Drak's Circus being nearby is enough to attract people from miles away. Special performances for royalty and powerful political figures are a common occurrence.

The members of the circus are more than mere performers. They frequently use their unique talents and abilities to heal, foretell the future, and offer other special services; all for the proper price. As a travelling circus, Drak and his performers have unique access to many towns and the important figures of those towns. Like many travelling shows, they use their unique situation for obtaining profit beyond that gained from performance by gathering and selling information to interested parties. However, Mr. Drak and his circus family has never deliberately sold information that could hurt innocent people. Nor do they align themselves with evil or militaristic parties. Although **Mr. Drak's Travelling Circus** is welcome in the Coalition States (but NEVER inside the cities), and Mr. Drak has sold the CS information and small services in exchange for political or monetary reward, he is always extremely careful not to betray good people of any race, belief or origin. His trade with the Coalition is a carefully prepared political game.

Mr.Drak's Travelling Circus tends to attract nomadic traders and merchants as well. The larger merchant organizations may even travel with the circus for a short period of time in order to take advantage of their drawing power. In exchange, Mr.Drak receives goods, services or a percentage from the merchant. Merchants who refuse to cooperate or try to cheat the cliental suffer a string of bad luck until they leave or comply. This synergistic relationship is welcomed by Mr. Drak because of the circus' own constant need for fresh food, water, and goods and services. In addition, there exists a certain kinship among nomads of all kinds.

Mr. Drak and his circus performers have earned a special place in the hearts of the people and it is one of the most renowned circuses to travel the countryside (west or south in the spring and winter, Midwest in the summer and fall). Laughter and fanciful entertainment are rare commodities in the turbulent and uncertain world of Rifts. Providing even a few hours of these rare commodities is enough to warrant great admiration and fondness. **Mr. Drak's Travelling Circus** is, of course, unparalleled in its ability to create and sustain the laughter, fantasies and dreams of the audience. As a result, the members of the circus are treated well and regarded as celebrities. No one would dare attack a member the Drak Circus and woe to anyone who would even think of such evil. Consequently, the circus performers are often allowed to violate minor local customs and laws without reprisal.

The members of the circus have been gathered from all over the Rifts world, and even beyond. Mr. Drak is constantly seeking fresh, interesting, and unique talent for his shows. Unfortunately, there are no auditions for this circus. Either you are invited to join or don't bother asking. The only exceptions are those who were born into the circus and raised by the existing circus members.

Acrobats, animal tamers, escape artists, clowns, jugglers, fortunetellers, fire-eaters, court magicians, and side show freaks are just a few of the types of characters employed by the circus. Humans, giants, dwarves, cyborgs, crazies, mutant animals, floopers and D-Bees of all kinds are all part of the circus. Sadly, many have entered the circus life to escape their pasts or persecution from humans or the Coalition. It is not uncommon for the entertainers to assume false names and disguises. As a result of this common fate, the entertainers have developed an unusually close bond among themselves and function as dedicated members of a surrogate family. Racial and physical prejudices rarely exist within the circus family. Additionally, the circus has no specific political or religious allegiances or prejudices.

The major acts and performances take place in the evening or in a dark environment. This serves to focus the audience's attention on the entertainers themselves and create a more mystical environment. Some entertainers prefer to perform indoors, others outdoors. The many mobile arenas, bleachers, and tents of Mr. Drak's circus can accommodate either preference. The daytime performances are usually the less popular and less spectacular performances, especially in wilderness towns where the population spends their day hard at work. The daytime shows tend to be oriented towards little children, with an emphasis on wandering clowns, jugglers, dancers, puppet shows and animal rides, all at greatly reduced prices (often free). The daytime shows are also used to try out new acts.

Some acts require or request audience participation. This participation can take many different forms and is seldom life threatening. Sometimes the audience is asked for suggestions, other times they may be asked to clap, chant, or sing along, or members from the audience are taken on stage and included as part of the performance (usually a comic element) and given simple roles or assignments with props. Audience participation is greatest during the day performances.

The big performances are given only once per day, but the entertainers may be involved in many different acts throughout the day and evening. The exceptions to this rule are those attractions designed to accommodate only a handful of people at a time or small groups of spectators. These include jugglers, puppeteers, clowns, fortunetellers, side show freaks (constantly on display), barkers, healers, workers at concession stands, etc.

Mr. Drak serves as the master of ceremonies for most of the night performances, and has several assistants to manage the daytime activities or to relieve him of his nighttime responsibilities.

Customers are encouraged to dress in their favorite clothes or costumes and to get their faces painted by circus artists. Discounts and prizes are given for unusual or appealing costumes. Occasionally, "MDTC entertainer" look-alike contests are held. Each circus entertainer has his/her own particular costume, look and style. Some are scary, some are unique, and some are silly. Personally, Mr. Drak likes to dress like Count Dracula (not many people in the Rifts world know about Count Dracula).

The common ground area includes, but is not limited to, the games of chance, games of skill (knife and dart throwing, toy laser gun target shooting, etc.), face painters, balloon sellers, fortunetellers, healers, tattoo parlors, massage pallors, side show freaks, exotic displays, animal rides, animal training arenas, concession stands, merchandise booths, entertainer autograph and interview areas, and the museum of **Mr. Drak's Travelling Circus** that tells the history of the 35 year old circus, complete with strange artifacts, fun facts, posters, photographs and information about famous circus performers of the past (this is a free exhibit). Each of these have their own additional costs, which are established by the entertainer operating the specific tent or area. The entertainers are generally excellent salespersons and well schooled in "bait and switch" techniques.

The common ground area is also populated by many wandering entertainers and troubadours. Their purpose is to appease those waiting in long lines, as well as giving the crowd a small sample of what can be expected at the more expensive performances. The wandering entertainers often give out free promotional items like silly trinkets, balloons, and discount coupons for the less popular or more expensive acts. Time schedules for specific events are posted throughout the common ground area. In addition, announcements regarding upcoming events are made periodically throughout the day. The term "day" is used loosely since the MDTC never really closes once it has set up.

The fees for the MDTC performances are as follows:

1) Entrance into the common ground area — 6 credits. Entertainment and access is limited to the simpler wandering troubadours, jugglers, and other free acts, the side show and common area tents which charge individual admission fees.
2) Daytime performances ticket — 20 credits. Allows access to the common ground and the special attractions like the lion tamer and freak show, as well as the main day show, about two hours of entertainment in the big tent (acrobats, clowns, animal acts, etc).
3) Nighttime performances ticket — 75 credits. Allows unlimited access to the circus grounds all night, including the big, four hour evening performance and the many other nighttime performances in the smaller tents.
4) All day ticket — 135 credits. Unlimited access to all events, shows, rides and customer areas day and night.
5) Special group tickets — special price. For many wilderness towns and villages, the arrival of any circus is a big event, but the arrival of Mr. Drak's Travelling Circus is a special event. In many cases

the entire town will want to come out to see the sights. In these cases, Mr. Drak and his administrators strike a bargain with the town official or village elders, agree on a price in credits, precious metals or trade (often supplies or services). The cost per all day ticket will then drop to about 70 credits and a village-wide festival is declared (lasts two or three days). Mr. Drak and his circus performers also enjoy additional perks in the way of celebrity status, special discounts on purchases and star treatment.

Tickets are valid for one particular day only. Each day the circus changes the tickets so that they cannot be reused. While the circus does make an attempt to prevent unauthorized entry, they are not overly concerned if one or two people defeat their security, especially children. Normally, they will let such individuals stay and enjoy themselves. Unauthorized access to Mr. Drak or the entertainers' dressing rooms and living quarters is never tolerated and will result in immediate expulsion from the grounds. Mr. Drak and his fellow administrators have an office where people can come and visit, talk business or lodge complaints.

Access to Performers

Access to the circus performers is limited to sporadic interview and autograph sessions. Special tents have been set aside just for this purpose. A daily schedule, including the times and names of entertainers appearing, is posted outside of each tent. These sessions are held throughout the day, rarely in the evening. Normally, an autograph session opens with the entertainer(s) making a brief speech or giving a quick demonstration of his/her/their skills, answering up to 10 audience questions, and then signing autographs for 15 or 20 minutes. Once the performer has left the session, the public is prohibited from any further interaction. The only other means of contact is watching their act or through the MDTC public relations tent (common ground area).

The public relations people screen all requests for special performances or offers. If worthwhile, they will pass the information to Mr. Drak and the individual entertainer and an appointment will be scheduled. Meetings also take place at the public relations tent or at Mr. Drak's office. Conference tables, chairs and drinks are provided free of charge. Each entertainer may charge a fee for his time; after all, time is money, and charging a fee tends to discourage those with less than serious business proposals. Private shows at homes and businesses can be arranged, but only with Mr. Drak's approval and guarantees of the performer's safety. Fees for such performances, unless a charity performance, are incredibly high (ranging from 500 to 5000 credits an hour), split 50/50 between Mr. Drak and the performer(s).

The entertainers' living quarters are set apart from the public access areas and guarded. Unauthorized people causing mischief in this area will be treated in the following manner (depending upon the circumstances and the individual): 1) A stern scolding and warning, 2) immediate and permanent expulsion from MDTC grounds, 3) arrested and fined, 4) severe beating(s) or other just punishment for the crime (including death). Note that circus people have little faith in the laws and justice systems of most communities and tend to secretly deliver their own punishment to offenders who hurt or steal from their people. **Mr. Drak's Travelling Circus** is no different and uses its own form of justice in dealing with violators of common law. In other words, you are at their mercy. Guards and warnings are posted so that no one can "accidentally" stumble into an unauthorized area. The circus' attitude is, "If you got there, you meant to be there." So be forewarned!

The size and lavishness of an entertainer's quarters are directly proportional to his/her/their popularity and profitability. Needs and special circumstances (a giant would not be put into a small trailer) are also taken into consideration. But it is the roar and approval of the audience, and the feeling of safety and camaraderie for which the entertainers live, not lush quarters and vast wealth. These are society's misfits, they realize this and are happy to have found some semblance of peace, prosperity and fame.

The circus tours the world nine months of the year (the world generally being limited to the Americas). You never know exactly where or when they may appear nor why they have chosen to perform at a specific location — such decisions are made by Mr. Drak himself. The only certainty is the excellence of their performances.

The remainder of the year, the circus spends its time developing and refining acts. The location of their headquarters is a closely guarded secret and changed every few years. The reason for this should be quite apparent, with all of their many fans and groupies, the members of the circus would never have any time for rest, relaxation, or enhancing their shows.

The performers in this circus are free agents. None are slaves or prisoners and all are welcome to stay as long as their work is of good quality. A performer can leave whenever he pleases, providing he has fulfilled his current contract or has reached an understanding with Mr. Drak. As one might expect, the entertainers are extremely loyal to Mr. Drak and their circus family and friends. The majority have been with the circus for years and have no intention of leaving. For many, the circus is a refuge from the terrible anti-human/anti-mutant world around them. Most members are content with their circus lives and few would betray the circus or reveal any of its tricks or secrets, at least not intentionally. Mr. Drak tries to avoid violence and usually acts only in the defense of his circus and his performers. This doesn't mean that He doesn't bend or even break the law sometimes, but never with foul intent.

Non-Player Characters from Mr. Drak's Travelling Circus —— Unusual Performers of Note ——

Mr. Drak
Owner and Manager of the Circus
Real Name: Thomas Draklinski
Alignment: Scrupulous
Species: Human
Hit Points: 61, **S.D.C.:** 20, **M.D.C.:** 50 M.D.C. magic or body armor
Weight: 190 lbs, **Height:** 6 ft, 3 inches **Age:** 47
P.P.E.: 8, **I.S.P.:** 67
Attributes: I.Q.: 18, M.A.: 24, M.E.: 22, P.S.: 15, P.P.: 14, P.E.: 19, P.B.: 14, Spd: 11
Disposition: Usually reserved, gentle and soft-spoken, but quite the opposite when angry or challenged; confident, tough, forceful. Compassionate, friendly and inquisitive, he finds life an endless adventure and sees ALL people as fellow adventurers. He likes to share what he has learned and loves to make people happy. Although Mr. Drak publicly treats children in a gruff, exasperated and detached manner, he enjoys their company and curious minds. It is his unofficial policy to allow inquisitive and poor kids to sneak into the circus without incident or to give them free tickets.

Experience Level: 10th level Rogue Scholar
Magic Knowledge: Lore.
Psionic Powers: Minor psionic, I.S.P. 67; mind block and ectoplasm.
Combat Skills: Hand to Hand: Basic. Kick attack (1D6 S.D.C.), critical strike on a natural roll of 19 or 20, and judo throw.
Attacks Per Melee: Four (4)
Bonuses: +1 to strike, +2 to parry and dodge, +2 S.D.C. damage, +4 to roll with impact, +4 to pull punch, +2 to save vs poison, +2 to save vs magic, +4 to save vs horror factor, +4 to save vs psionic attack, 80% to invoke trust or intimidation, and +4% on all skills (I.Q. bonus has been added to all skill percentiles).
Weapon Proficiencies: W.P. Blunt, W.P. Automatic Pistol, W.P. Energy Rifle.
Weapons: An ornate walking cane specially designed for combat. The cane is made from mega-damage material and has exceptional balance. The head of the walking stick is shaped in the form of a roaring lion, made of silver (great against vampires). The cane also conceals a silver-plated rapier style sword (also an M.D.C. structure). Cane & Sword Bonuses: Superior craftsmanship, +1 to strike, +1 to throw, +2 to parry, +2 to S.D.C. damage, effectively indestructible by S.D.C. damage. Weapon damage: 2D6 S.D.C. plus bonuses as a cane/club, and 1D6 plus bonuses as sword.

Other weapons include a Wilk's 320 laser pistol, Wilk's 457 laser pulse rifle (3D6+2 or 1D6×10 M.D.), a Wilk's laser wand, a Browning GP 35 9mm pistol (2D6 S.D.C., 13 shot clip, has case of silver bullets), silver cross, and pocket mirror. Also has a concealed arsenal in his living quarters that includes three additional 9mm pistols and Wilk's 320 pistols, a TX-5 pump pistol (4D6 M.D.), a 9mm sub-machinegun (2D6 S.D.C.), a shotgun, two Wilk's 457 laser pulse rifles, a TX-30 ion pulse rifle (2D6 or 6D6 M.D.), two NG-Supers, two NG-P7 particle beam rifles, a silver and normal mace, morning star, quarterstaff and the usual vampire equipment. He also has two of each of the following magic scrolls: Armor of Ithan, turn dead, befuddle, fear, sleep, carpet of adhesion, repel animals, superhuman speed, fly as the eagle, dispel magic barrier and heal wounds; has six magic nets. All are at sixth level.
Note: Always has the cane, laser wand, laser pistol, 9mm pistol, cross and mirror on his person.

Body Armor: Mr. Drak's Ringmaster suit is magic and affords him 50 M.D.C. protection. He only wears body armor when he expects to be in a hostile environment. On such occasions that armor will be the Explorer (70 M.D.C.) or T-21 Terrain Hopper power armor (see **Rifts Sourcebook #1**, page 38, 170 M.D.C.).
Bionics & Cybernetics: Headjack, fingerjack (left hand), molecular analyzer, and toxic filter. The fingerjack allows easy, direct access to computers and his robot watchdog, Jack.
Money: Drak carries three credit cards with 500,000 available credits each and 100,000 credits' worth of gold and gems on his person at all times. He also has one of the best collections of pre-rifts music discs (over 2000) and video/movie discs (394), as well as several hundred books, a 1999 Jaguar sports car (restored to mint condition), select articles of jewelry, a half dozen paintings, and other artifacts with an estimated value of 29 million credits. **Note:** The artifacts, other than the car, are hidden when in CS territory and protected by magic and electronic means.

Drak also has several large accounts reserved exclusively for the circus (payroll, equipment, maintenance, expenses, etc.): six million universal credits are in a bank account at **Lazlo**, one million at **Whykin**, one million at **Kingsdale**, two million at **Lone Star** and **Chi-Town**, and eight million at **Northern Gun/Ishpeming**. The payroll wagon will typically carry 1D6×100,000 in gold, gems and other valuables and 1D6×100,000 in credit receipts. The cost of running and maintaining a circus of this size is quite costly.
Skills of Note: Literate in American, Spanish and Techno-can 98%, languages include American, Spanish, Techno-can, and Gobblely at 98%, Euro and Dragonese 79%, basic math 98%, computer operation 98%, computer programming 98%, computer hacking 64%, lore: demons 94%, lore: faerie 94%, anthropology 79%, archaeology 79%, astronomy 84%, chemistry 89%, paramedic 98%, streetwise 60%, palming 69%, basic electronics 69%, automobile mechanics 74%, pilot automobile 98%, horsemanship 77%.
Description: Mr. Drak is a kind and caring individual with a desire to travel and see the world. He loves people and history and learning.

His mind is sharp, analytical, and inquisitive. Like the proverbial cat, his curiosity has gotten him into his fair share of trouble, especially in his youth. Today, experience and maturity have tempered Drak's curious nature with diplomacy and caution, which has made the circus owner a master of smooth talk, gentle persuasion and cool reserve.

Jack —— Mr. Drak's Robot Watchdog

Jack functions as a robot familiar that helps Mr. Drak keep an eye on what's happening at the circus. The bot dog roams around the circus, looking for signs of trouble, and either takes care of the problem itself or reports back to its master. By means of his fingerjack, Mr. Drak can plug right into the bot and view/hear everything the robot has seen or heard as it really happened. The bot looks just like a real life golden retriever, complete with fur, sculpted features, and realistic looking eyes. Jack is clever, loyal and resourceful.

Size: Medium. **Speed:** 88 (60 mph/96 kmph). **Robot Armor:** 200 M.D.C., 300 lbs (−10 to prowl). **Intelligence:** Increased simple intelligence, equal to an I.Q. of 10. **Alignment:** Scrupulous good, completely loyal to Mr. Drak and the circus. Kind and gentle with children. **Skill Program:** Military: Espionage Rogue. Skills include intelligence, pick pockets, palming, concealment, prowl (−10%), and streetwise, all at 60%. Military Technical Program includes photography (built into the robot's eye), computer operation, literacy in American, Spanish, Euro, Techno-can, Gobblely, and Dragonese, all at 94%. **Power Source:** Nuclear, five year. **Optics:** Advanced robot system, telescopic, and external video and audio surveillance system. Realistic looking eyes. **Sensors:** Sensory antenna (motion, heat, touch) and Bio-Scan medical survey unit. **Weapons:** Bite or claw or by small hand weapon/pistol. **Special features:** Prehensile tail and a pair of small, retractable hands and arms are concealed in the lower sides of the bot, used for operating computers and equipment, opening doors, using handguns, etc. **Combat:** Three attacks per melee, bite 2D4 M.D., small claws one M.D., leap kick 2D4 M.D. and a 50% chance of knocking opponent down (loses one attack), counts as two attacks. Or by handgun or knife (retractable arms). **Bonuses:** +1 to strike, +2 parry, +4 to dodge, +2 on initiative. Robots are found in the **Rifts Sourcebook One. Note:** Jack can speak and read the different languages listed in the skill program at 94%.

Floopers —— Silly D-Bee performers

Alignment: Any, but usually unprincipled or anarchist.
Horror Factor: None
Species: D-Bee, creature of magic.
Hit Points: Not applicable. **M.D.C.:** 2D6×10 plus 1D6 per level of experience.
Weight: 1D4×100 pounds, **Height:** 4 to 5 feet tall, very round and flabby. **Age:** Typical life span 200 years. Mr.Drak's Floopers range from 20 to 90 years old.
P.P.E.: 1D6×10, **Average I.S.P.:** 25 to 50 points
Typical Attributes: I.Q.: 9, M.E.: 10, M.A.: 22, P.S.: 9, P.P.: 20, P.E.: 10, P.B. 14, Spd. 14.
Player Character Attributes: I.Q.: 2D6+2, M.E.: 3D6+1, M.A.: 4D6+6, P.S.: 3D6, P.P.: 3D6+7, P.E.: 3D6+2, P.B. 3D6, Spd. 4D6
Disposition: Friendly, goofy, always smiling and talkative, and always looking for a deal or a good trade. Lazy in the extreme when it comes to physical labors.
Experience Level: Equal to the Psi-stalker R.C.C.; Those in Mr. Drak's Travelling Circus are 1D4+2 levels.
Magic Knowledge: None.
Psionic Powers: Minor psionics. I.S.P. 4D6+M.E. and 1D6 per level of experience. Powers are limited to empathy, mind block and sixth sense.

Natural Powers: 1. <u>Double-jointed, ambidextrous and possess high physical prowess.</u> These abilities make the Floopers natural gymnasts, acrobats, escape artists, and thieves. They can roll, tumble, do cartwheels, back flips, juggle, and endure falls from great heights. Being ambidextrous means they can use either hand with equal dexterity and skill. Automatic paired weapons skill and one additional melee attack or action (accounted for in combat description). Also see R.C.C. skills.

2. <u>Flooping!</u> The power of flooping is the strange ability to completely disappear! Not become invisible, but to momentarily vanish without a trace by teleporting into a limbo like dimension. The dimensional teleport can be performed instantly and is as natural as a thought to a Flooper. One moment the D-Bee is there, the next, "floop," and he's gone (a "floop" sound is made when the little fellow blinks out and in). The maximum period of time the Flooper remains gone is one melee (15 seconds) per each level of experience, but he can return at any time prior to that. During that time, the Flooper is in limbo and can take no action in that dimension or any other. When he reappears he can pop (well, "floop,") back at the exact location from which he disappeared or three feet away (in any direction) per level of experience. **Note:** Flooping costs three (3) I.S.P. points per each round trip; disappearance and reappearance.

Combat Skills: Typically none (two attacks/actions per melee) or hand to hand: basic (plus one attack per melee). Too lazy to learn anything more intense than that.

Attacks per Melee: Two to Five.

Bonuses: In addition to attributes and skills combined, the Flooper is a creature of magic and enjoys the additional bonuses of +2 to save vs magic and +2 vs horror factor.

Weapon Proficiencies: See skills; typically, W.P. Targeting (thrown weapons, not archery), W.P. Blunt, and W.P. Knife (for throwing).

Weapons: Typical weapons include throwing knives, darts, batons, clubs, rocks or other items, vibro-weapons and energy handguns, but any weapons can be used.

Cybernetics: Prefer none.

Skills of Note: The Floopers in Mr. Drak's Travelling Circus know the following skills: Dance, cook, radio: basic and scrambler, first aid, wilderness survival, land navigation, identify plants, climbing, running, prowl, and the spoken languages of American and Spanish, as well as the R.C.C. skills. **Skills of Player Characters:** <u>R.C.C. skills:</u> Acrobatics, gymnastics, prowl (+5%), climbing (+10%), escape artist (+20%), two languages of choice (+10%) and W.P. Targeting. <u>Other skills:</u> Select two other W.P.s, and eight additional skills at level one, two at level four, two at level eight and two at level twelve. <u>Available skills:</u> Communication (any), Domestic (any), Electrical (none), Espionage (any), Mechanical (none), Medical (first aid or paramedic only), Military (none), Physical (any, except hand to hand combat: expert, martial arts or assassin, boxing, and wrestling), Pilot and Pilot Related (any), Rogue Skills (any, except hacking, +15%), Science (basic math only), Technical (any, +5%), W.P. (any), Wilderness (any, +5%).

Description: <u>Floopers</u> are short, potbellied, silly looking, floppy eared D-Bees who serve as clowns, tumblers, and jugglers and operate many of the information booths, games and exhibits at Mr. Drak's Travelling Circus. Less reputable travelling shows often employ Floopers as expert thieves and spies. Despite their weight, Floopers are incredibly nimble and fast. They are ambidextrous (can use both hands with equal proficiency), double-jointed and possess high physical prowess and natural acrobatic and gymnastic abilities. They can roll, tumble, do cartwheels, back flips, juggle, and endure falls from great heights without suffering damage. This is in part because they are mega-damage creatures and partly due to their natural prowess and Flooping ability. *Flooping* is the ability to momentarily shift into a limbo like dimension. Flooping can be mentally engaged in an instant to avoid the impact from a fall or to hide from an enemy.

Floopers will do anything for a laugh and are masters of slapstick. They make great circus performers and goofy assistants, because they look silly, are terrible show-offs, love to make others laugh, and love to be with other people regardless of race, origin, or philosophy. Unfortunately, the typical Flooper is also a lazy thief. Combine their laziness with their natural easy-going, playful disposition and natural abilities and you may have the strangest expert thief known to man. It has taken Mr. Drak years of discipline and the patience of a saint to break most of his circus Floopers from stealing and there is still the occasional theft.

In their natural habitat, Floopers live off the land, gathering food, freeloading off others (offering a laugh rather than muscle), or stealing from more ambitious and prosperous creatures. Floopers don't mean to be bad, they just hate work and like to play a lot. Ironically, the silly little D-Bees can exhibit untiring stamina and boundless energy when excited or doing something they enjoy, like playing, making people laugh, talking, or making a trade for something (trades are seldom for anything that has much value to a human).

The richest Flooper will live in a hovel that's ready to tumble on its head, rather than spend energy to fix it himself. Nor will they trade a beloved possession on anything as frivolous as repairing their hovel. They are so lazy that the creatures will let garbage and debris accumulate to the point of being buried before they will — no, not clean it up, but *move* to a new, less cluttered location! Floopers would rather lounge in the sun, munch on sweets and goodies, sleep, play, talk, and talk, and talk, and spend hours and hours discussing trades and trade possibilities. Only the silly creatures' curiosity and need to socialize with other life forms rival their incredible laziness.

A Flooper will always mention that he is willing to trade news about the world or other useful information/rumors (non-circus related) for equally exciting news or unique items and oddities. If the flooper is especially pleased with a transaction, he will utter a "floop floop" sound and perform a back flip instead of shaking hands. A delighted Flooper will perform several cartwheels, followed by hand stands and a back flip, while shouting, "floop floop, yippee, floop floop, zowie!"

Note: 16 Floopers are employed by Mr. Drak's Travelling Circus.

Shapers —— An Intelligent D-Bee Animal

Alignment: Can be any, but typically scrupulous, unprincipled, or anarchist.

Horror Factor: None if known to be a Shaper, but 2D6+3 when disguised as a ferocious beast.

Species: Intelligent D-Bee animal with innate magic abilities.

Size: About four feet tall (1.2 m), but can shape change to three times that size (approximately 12 feet/3.6 m).

Weight: 110 lbs **Hit Points:** see M.D.C., **M.D.C.:** 1D6×10 (average is 30 M.D.C.)

P.P.E.: 2D4×10, **I.S.P.:** None

Age: Average life span in the wild is 50 years, in captivity 80+ years.

Typical Attributes: I.Q.: 5, M.E.: 3, M.A.: 18, P.S.: 9, P.P.: 9, P.E.: 18, P.B. 10, Spd. 30.

Player Character Attributes: I.Q.: 1D6+2, M.E.: 1D6+1, M.A.: 4D6, P.S.: 2D6+3, P.P.: 3D6, P.E.: 4D6, P.B. 3D6, Spd. 1D6×10.

Disposition: Laid back until someone or something stirs them up. Then it's total chaos and silliness until they began to tire. Love sweets and are easily amused by silly and stupid acts. Love to watch crowds and have fun imitating the actions of the people (when in ape form) or putting on a show of silliness for spectators.

Experience Level: May be considered an R.C.C., with skill limitations as listed here. Those in Mr. Drak's circus are 4th to 6th level.

Magic Knowledge: None

Psionic Powers: None

Shaper in its natural form.

Shapers having fun.

Natural Powers: 1. Selective metamorphosis. This is the ability to shape change a specific body area or appendage without altering the other portions of its body. As few as one to as many as a dozen different changes can be made in a single instant. This means that the Shaper's normal half canine, half monkey appearance can be completely disguised. The creatures can look like a chimera or bizarre creatures of its own design; the tail of an alligator, the head of a rhinoceros, the feet of a lion, the ears of a donkey, the body of a lobster, etc. It can even add four additional appendages such as wings, horns, extra arms or legs, etc. ALL changes must be animal features, NEVER human. Oddly enough, they cannot assume the shape of any *one* animal. Thus, they cannot turn into a wolf or cat, etc., but can turn into a dog with the head of a cat! Unlike dragons, the number of times a metamorphosis can be performed is once every melee/15 seconds, with no limit as to how long the Shaper can maintain the shape. However, the silly D-Bees quickly tire of any one particular shape and like to change often.

Fortunately, regardless of how the Shaper may look, the creature retains only its normal number and methods of attack and abilities. Consequently, the armored body of a crab does NOT give the Shaper extra M.D.C. nor do wings provide flight. Furthermore, the alien creatures are friendly, playful and easily frightened. *Also see Description.*

2. Keen animal vision, with color. The Shaper's vision is sharper than the average human's and it can see clearly, in the same color spectrum as humans, for twice the distance.

3. Nightvision. A natural light amplification system provides them with passive night sight; 120 foot range (36.5 m).

4. Enhanced sense of smell. Recognizes and accurately identifies specific smells/scents from up to 100 feet (20.5 m) plus 20 feet (6 m) per level of experience. Base skill at scent recognition: 50% +2% per level of experience; +10% if the smell is very common or very well known to the creature.

5. Scavengers. Shapers are not hunters but scavengers that will eat just about anything. This has given them great resistance to poisons/toxins. Not aggressive, quite social and timid.

Combat Skills: Natural, animal instincts, mostly self defense. Bite causes 3D6 S.D.C. damage, claws 1D6 damage, or may use a blunt weapon or small weapon like a knife, sword, vibro-blade, neuro-mace and even a handgun (S.D.C or M.D.). **Note:** Despite the appearance of the Shaper, which may include stingers, or spikes, or huge claws, extra limbs, etc., the creature is always limited to its natural number of attacks and types of attacks.

Attacks per Melee: Three (3)

Bonuses: Natural. In addition to attribute bonuses, Shapers are +2 on initiative, +1 to parry and dodge, +2 to save vs poison, +2 to save vs magic, and +2 to save vs psionic attack.

Weapon Proficiencies: See skills; typically, W.P. Blunt.

Weapons: Blunt, thrown rocks or other items, natural claws and bite, or handguns (not common among wild shapers).

Cybernetics: Prefer none. Can not shape change that portion of its body, but can still transform other parts of its body.

Skills of Note: The Shapers in Mr. Drak's Travelling Circus know the following skills: Dance, cook, radio basic, first aid, wilderness survival, land navigation, identify plants, climbing, running, prowl, and the spoken languages of American and Spanish. **Skills of Player Characters:** R.C.C. Skills: Prowl (+5%), climbing (+10%), wilderness survival (+15%), land navigation (+10%), and identify plants and fruits (+20%). Other Skills: Select six additional skills at level one, two at level three, two at level six and two at level nine and twelve. Available skills (no bonuses apply except for wilderness skills): Communication (radio basic only), Domestic (any), Electrical (none), Espionage (escape artist only), Mechanical (none), Medical (first aid only), Military (none), Physical (any, except hand to hand combat, boxing, acrobatics and SCUBA), Pilot and Pilot Related (none), Rogue Skills (only palming, pick pockets, pick locks), Science (none), Technical (art but, −20%), W.P. (Blunt, Knife, Sword, and Pistols only) Wilderness (any, +10%).

Description: Shapers are strange alien animals that possess an almost human intelligence and comprehension roughly equivalent to a young 7 or 8 year old child. Like the Floopers, the creatures are generally silly and playful creatures of magic. Unlike the lazy Floopers, Shapers are energetic and helpful, although sometimes too silly to be of much help. Their natural shape seems to be ape-like or a fur covered humanoid with a hyena-like head. Their natural power is to instantly metamorph any portion of their body from one animal form to another, mixing and matching the elements of two to twelve different animals into one.

The transformation happens in the blink of an eye. Shapers use their shape changing ability as a means of defense to scare away attackers, as well as a means of entertainment. They seem to get immense pleasure from creating bizarre appearances and will laugh uproariously at one another. When one of them does something that really strikes the other's fancy, always silly, stupid, or outrageous, all the Shapers may start imitating the instigator. This can lead to unbounded chaos and hours of non-stop stupidity; always a crowd pleaser. The more their kin and/or spectators laugh, the sillier the Shapers get. To a Shaper, laughter and silliness is contagious.

In some instances a Shaper will keep changing its appearance from one form to another so quickly (once per melee/15 seconds) that he'll get dizzy and fall over in a fit of uncontrollable laughter. Such a silliness overload will completely incapacitate the stupid beast for 3D6 minutes. Everything that is said or done is funny (no matter how dangerous), and all the D-Bee can do is roll on the ground, laughing uncontrollably; it can not attack, run, hide, dodge, talk, or anything else. Even seeing somebody get hurt is, for the moment, gut busting funny. Don't even think about trying to get its attention until the critter starts getting tired. Despite their intelligence, a Shaper's silliness limits how well they can be trained. A typical shaper can be taught simple domestic chores, like cooking, clean-up, or lending a hand, and two human languages, in addition to their own animal language that consists of squeaks, chortles, hoots, and howls. Unfortunately, Shapers have a low mental endurance and are easily distracted, enticed to wander or act silly, and are easily frightened. Shapers will only fight when cornered or when a loved one (humanoid friend, mate, or kin) is threatened.

Unscrupulous individuals have trained the animals to operate as spies, guards (turning into a frightening monster), and messengers, although there is always the risk that the Shaper may forget its purpose, act silly, or lose interest in their mission. Mr. Drak simply puts them in a padded cage and lets them act as stupid and silly as they want. The Shapers are so good-humored that it takes very little to get them to act silly and keep them going for hours. When not entertaining, the Shapers help with clean-up and perform minor chores. They are treated with kindness and are loved by Mr. Drak, the circus personnel (well, by most of them, anyway) and by the audience, particularly children.

Note: 20 Shapers are employed by Mr. Drak's Travelling Circus.

The Amazing Doctor Gray Matter
Coalition Experimental Psi-Borg

Alignment: Anarchist
Horror Factor: 10 (acts odd in a frightening, inhuman way).
Hit Points: see M.D.C., **M.D.C.:** 420 M.D.C. HI-B3 cyborg armor.
Weight: 1500 lbs, **Height:** 6 ft, 8 inches, **Age:** 27
P.P.E.: 5, **I.S.P.:** 99 (special)
Species: Human Cyborg
Attributes: I.Q.: 10 (but total recall), M.E.: 12, M.A.: 8, P.S. (bionic): 26, P.P. (bionic): 20, P.E.: not applicable, P.B. 10, Spd 132 (90 mph/144 km).

Disposition: Appears to be lost in thought most of the time. Cold, dispassionate, unfriendly, everything is a matter of fact, shows little emotion except when agitated; a loner. Tends to be short-tempered, cranky and easily antagonized if not left alone. Often bitter and spiteful. Loves to insult others by calling them stupid or making them feel stupid by his arrogant or omnipotent attitude. Flies into a temper tantrum when frustrated or angry. Fears and dislikes the Coalition and bionic/cybernetic scientists. Completely dedicated to Mr. Drak and the circus, and will fight to the death to protect either.
Experience Level: Equal to 15th level Scholar & Scientist.
Magic Knowledge: Lore
Psionic Powers: Special, considered a master psionic. 99 I.S.P. Experimental bionic implants make Doctor Gray Matter impervious to all psionic attacks, including telepathy and empathy, and even a see aura on Dr. G.M. is unreadable. Absolute total recall is automatic, see Description. Conventional Psionic Powers: See the invisible, total recall, levitation, electrokinesis and mind bolt.
Combat Skills: Hand to Hand: Expert at 10th level. Kick attack, judo style body throw, paired weapons, critical strike on a natural roll of 18-20.
Attacks per Melee: Four (4)
Bonuses: +5 to strike, +8 to parry, +8 to dodge, +2 to roll with impact, +14 S.D.C. damage. Impervious to all psionic attacks and communication, mind altering drugs, and +6 to save vs illusionary magic.
Weapon Proficiencies: W.P. Archery & Targeting, W.P. Blunt, W.P. Sword, W.P. Energy Pistol, W.P. Energy Rifle, W.P. Heavy Energy.
Weapons: C-27 heavy plasma cannon, C-18 laser pistol, pair of vibro swords (2D6 M.D.), crossbow, water pistol, pair of silver daggers and the typical vampire weaponry.
Cybernetics/bionics: Full conversion borg with special brain implants that provide the unique psionic abilities. Right hand and arm: Laser finger blaster (1D4 M.D.), laser utility finger (S.D.C.), fingerjack, silver-plated knuckle spikes (3D4 normal S.D.C. damage, double to vampires). Left hand and arm: Retractable vibro-blades (2D6 M.D.), concealed arm laser rod (1D6 M.D.). Legs: One large secret compartment in each leg; one contains credit card with 97,000 universal credits, 50,000 credits' worth of gold and gems, and a canteen of water. The other leg contains one fragmentation grenade, a silver cross, and four wooden spikes. Other bionic features: Cyber-disguise Type AA-1, bionic lung with gas filter and oxygen storage cell, built-in loudspeaker, universal headjack and ear implant (amplified hearing) and sound filtration system.
Skills of Note: All skills are at the 98% level of proficiency. Remember, while a vast range of skills are known, Dr. Gray Matter has no interest in learning new skills (though he remembers everything he sees, hears and reads), and only remembers skills and information on an as needed basis (almost reflex), which means he cannot adequately teach. Skills known: All science and technical (speaks fluently and is literate in all known languages), first aid, computer hacking, computer repair, automotive mechanics, mechanical engineer, weapons engineer, basic electronics, radio: basic, radio: scrambler, optic systems, read sensory equipment, navigation, and weapon systems. Piloting skills include: hovercraft, jet pack, automobile, motorcycle, truck, tanks/APCs, helicopter and horsemanship.
Description: Doctor Gray Matter (real name unknown) is a cybernetic experiment that failed. The Coalition State of Lone Star was experimenting with the idea of augmenting the human brain with advanced storage and retrieval systems, and adding resistance to psionic influence. A sort of combination of bionics and M.O.M. conversion. They desired to push the human brain to its very limits and beyond. Doctor Gray Matter was the result.

The strange borg is a living encyclopedia of knowledge, able to memorize and totally recall everything he reads, sees and hears.

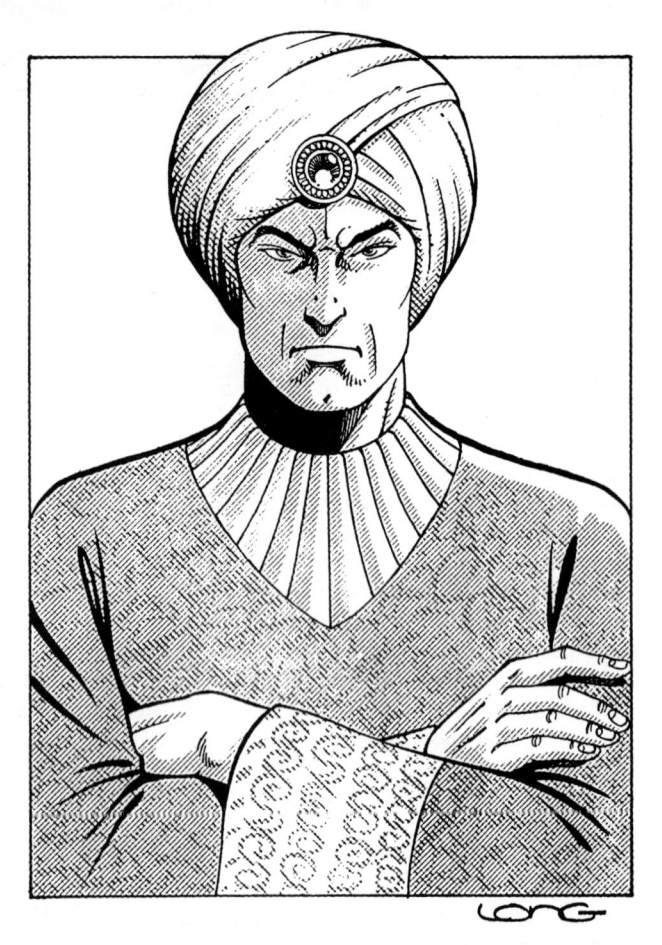

Unfortunately, there were unforeseen side effects. The amazing borg began to lose the ability to learn and think for himself. He truly became a living sourcebook, but lacked emotion, passion and curiosity; a living computer. To complicate matters further, the subject gained complete access to a massive amount of super sensitive military data, including Coalition city access codes, troop strength and dispersement, a 10 year plan for deployment, weapon systems, security, city plans, locations of military manufacturing facilities and laboratories, and other top secret information regarding the Coalition States in general, and specifically, Lone Star, Chi-Town and Missouri. The Coalition scientists decided to terminate the experiment and destroy the test subject in order to cover up their massive mistake. Somehow, Dr. Gray Matter survived, escaped, and joined Mr. Drak's Travelling Circus. Few Coalition authorities know the full details about the failed borg experiment and all parties believe the test subject to have been destroyed years ago. All further research in this area has been suspended.

Only Mr. Drak knows Doctor Gray Matter's Coalition history and is aware of the secret information locked in his head. Dr. Gray Matter, himself, is unaware of the value or the potential danger the information presents. All he knows is that the Coalition is his enemy and that he must hide from them or be destroyed. Mr. Drak, fully realizes that the CS data could, in the wrong hands, destroy the Coalition States. Though he has no love for the Coalition, he will not be party to the Coalition States' destruction, which would mean that tens of thousands, perhaps hundreds of thousands, of innocent people would die. And the end of the Coalition could very well mean the demise of humankind in the Americas. Mr. Drak will never sell or give away dangerous information.

Even five years out of date, the information is extremely damaging to the CS. As it stands, Dr. Gray Matter can make flawless passports, military identity cards, courier cards, citizen cards, contraband cards, weapon permits, and automatically knows the codes to open 69% of the security doors in Lone Star and Missouri and 45% at Chi-Town, as well as the ability to access military and IC Clearance computers, etc. The thing about the Coalition data and all the information in this poor fellow's head is that he doesn't know he knows this information until he needs it, and then, he can just do it, or has the data on the tip of his tongue. **For example:** If somebody asks what kind of CS machine the Abolisher robot is, Dr. Gray Matter would respond something like, "Abolisher Assault Robot, model type IAR-2, one pilot and four man crew, infantry unit." Other specific questions will elicit specific data, right down to projected manufacturing numbers and deployment as intended about five years ago by the Coalition (so not necessarily accurate information today). Likewise, if somebody asks what kind of creature some sort of animal is, he will instantly respond with all available data, including its scientific name, species, and whether it is male or female.

The borg can still learn more data and remember it completely, though he must now concentrate to do so. Like everything the good doctor knows, he instantly forgets the new data until he is called upon to use it. The massive amount of data and dulled emotions gives Dr. Gray Matter a constant zoned out look, with wide, seldom blinking eyes, and emotionless expression (unless agitated). A mental block prevents Doctor Gray Matter from remembering his real name, the Coalition experiments on him, and the events involving his attempted destruction. All he knows is that the Coalition created him, tried to destroy him, fear him, and seek his destruction for reasons unknown to him. Consequently, he fears and dislikes all aspects of the Coalition States. Dr. Gray Matter's personal memory (not skill knowledge and data) begins with waking up to see the smiling face of Mr. Drak and his robot dog, Jack. Life begins with the circus.

Dr. Gray Matter is easily recognized by his stylish capes, clothing, headdresses and turbans. The borg's bionic limbs are cosmetically concealed beneath fake human looking skin and other natural features. It is only when the borg utilizes his superhuman strength or speed, or bionic weapons and body armor, that his cybernetic nature is evident. Mr. Drak had the borg's face rebuilt with a full cybernetic disguise system, which continues to mask his original face.

Note: Drak keeps the Doctor away from Floopers and the circus staff in general (but especially Floopers). To help keep people at a distance, Mr. Drak has perpetuated the rumor that the borg is unstable and should not be pestered or angered. Dr. Gray Matter's cranky disposition and temper tantrums also help in this regard.

Types of routines and performances: 1. "Mr. Knowledge" — ask him about famous people, major news events, history, animals, geography, etc., and he will immediately answer the question correctly! 2. A variation worked into the show is "The Human Calculator." Ask him to solve a mathematical puzzle or amazing computation and the Amazing Doctor Gray Matter will provide the correct answer in less than 2 seconds. 3. "The Riddler" — pose a riddle and see if he can solve it; 98% chance of answering successfully. The prize for stumping him is 100 credits. 4. Game Master — plays chess and a vast variety of card games (counts/remembers the cards); often plays 5 or more opponents simultaneously. Beat him and win an all-week pass to the circus and 50 credits. 89% chance of winning every time. Occasionally engages in games of skill (bionic P.S., P.P. and augmented senses provide a great advantage). **Circus Labor:** The borg assists in maintaining and repairing vehicles, computer systems, communications, and weapons, as well as translating languages and performing other useful skills.

Captain Daring — Escape Artist Supreme

Real Name: James Buccanan
Alignment: Anarchist
Hit Points: 31, **M.D.C.:** 70+ TW modified body armor
Weight: 160 lbs, **Height:** 6 feet, 2 inches, **Age:** 26
P.P.E.: 141, **I.S.P.:** 37
Species: Human
Attributes: I.Q.: 15, M.E.: 14, M.A.: 14, P.S.: 12, P.P. 17, P.E.: 18, P.B. 15, Spd 10
Disposition: Cheerful, cocky, daring, flamboyant, charming, and aristocratic. Loves the cheers from a crowd; a real ham bone.
Experience Level: 5th level techno-wizard.
Magic Knowledge: Remember, all magic is at half duration, range, damage and power when cast as a spell; normal when built into a machine. Spells: Blinding flash, globe of daylight, ignite fire, fuel flame, fire bolt, call lightning, energy bolt, impervious to energy, telekinesis. Specific Spells selected for escape: **escape** (no lock picks necessary), **time slip** (a nifty way to move into the future and out of trouble and the quick escape), **energy disruption** (many purposes, from creating diversions to rendering electronic devices inoperative), **concealment** (a perfect way to palm a lock pick, key, tool, mini-oxygen cell, etc.), **detect concealment** (always a good spell to have, especially against other wizards), **fingers of the wind** (handy for creating diversions), **reduce self** (a terrific way to slip out of any shackles), **eyes of the wolf** (to see the invisible in the dark and other unique features), **superhuman speed** (quickly move or dodge out of harm's way, and great for quick changes of clothing), **breathe without air** (great underwater and when confined in airtight compartments), **swim as a fish** (great for underwater tricks), **teleport: lesser** (teleport tools, lock picks, etc., to hiding places on the set or in clothing or in the trunk/compartment before he is put into it, but after it has been inspected by a spectator from the audience), **mystic portal** (can pass through solid walls or teleport hundreds of feet away, perfect for impossible escapes), **shadow meld** (great for hiding in shadows and moving unseen), **dispel magic barrier** (to escape magic confinement), **negate magic** (handy against other wizards and magic forces).
Psionic Powers: 37 I.S.P., considered a minor psionic. Mind block, speed reading, total recall, and tele-mechanics.
Skills of Note: Radio: basic 75%, computer operation 65%, computer programming 55%, computer repair 55%, basic electronics 65%, read sensory equipment 60%, automotive mechanics 55%, land navigation 57%, basic math 85%, prowl 50%, palming 45%, pick locks 55%, locksmith 45%, pilot hovercraft 75%, pilot jet pack 58%, carpentry 55%, literacy American & Techno-can 60%, languages include American 98%, Spanish and Techno-can 85%.
Combat Skills: Hand to Hand: Basic. Kick attack does 1D6 S.D.C. damage.
Attacks per Melee: Three (3)
Bonuses: +2 to strike, +3 to parry, +3 to dodge, +2 to pull punch, +2 to roll with impact, +2 to save vs magic, +2 save vs poison, +6% to save vs coma.
Weapon Proficiencies: W.P. Energy Pistol and W.P. Rifle (3rd level).
Cybernetics: Gyro-Compass only.
Weapons (conventional): Wilk's 320 laser pistol and 447 laser rifle, both converted to P.P.E. power. 48 smoke grenades (3 different colors of smoke) and 72 micro-smoke grenades, easy to palm and conceal, creates a 20 foot cloud, half the size of the regular grenades; used in the act. Gold crucifix and gold chain (to be worn around the neck), a larger silver cross, 6 wooden stakes and a hammer, a water pistol, and a water cannon.
TW Weapons & Magic Items: Amulet of turn dead worn underneath clothes and talisman, ring, contains an extra 50 P.P.E. (for emergencies). Scrolls include multiple images (1), purification (1), mystic portal (1), superhuman strength (1), and magic net (2). One TK Flyers, one wing board, and one field generator. TK-Machinegun: A converted Wilk's 447 rifle. Damage: 2D6 M.D. per burst. Range: 4000 feet (1200 m). Payload: 80 bursts. Recharge: 20 P.P.E. per 8 bursts. Market Value: 120,000 credits. TW Body Armor: Modified Explorer Body Armor, 70 M.D.C. plus impervious to energy (20 P.P.E. to activate, duration 10 minutes per activation), levitate (5 P.P.E.), superhuman speed (10 P.P.E. to activate, 5 minutes duration), and escape (8 P.P.E.). Market value: 500,000 credits. Has two identical suits.
Special Techno-Wizard (TW) Devices: What follows is a list of specially made techno-wizard items created by Captain Daring for his performances. He has spent years developing and creating his magic gimmicks and will not reveal nor sell his secrets or designs. Of course, similar versions of the less impressive items like his goggles and air filter may be available on the open market in places where magic abounds.

- **RMK knitter TW conversion:** Captain Daring has modified the button size robots from Robot Medical Kits to techno-wizardry and for the purpose of escape rather than surgery. The tiny bots are easy to conceal; in fact, four are disguised as buttons on his sleeves (two per sleeve) and another two are concealed in his belt buckle but are easy to palm or hide anywhere, and automatically engage in escape procedure the moment they are activated. TW modifications are as follows.
    1. P.P.E. powered, providing a longer life and easy recharging.
    2. S.D.C. laser (one S.D.C. point per melee/15 seconds) for cutting rope and other bonds.
    Initial creation cost in P.P.E.: 200. Market Value: 75,000 credits each.

- **Capt. Daring's Fire Wand:** A magic wand with a large ruby at the top and a small one in the bottom. Can be used to cast the following spells. All are equal to the spell of the same name. Initial creation cost in P.P.E.: 75, plus 6000 credits for the two rubies. Market Value: 12,000 credits each.
    1. Globe of Daylight: Costs 2 P.P.E. to activate.
    2. Ignite Fire: Costs 2 P.P.E. to activate.
    3. Fuel Flame: Costs 5 P.P.E. to activate
    4. Fire Bolt: Costs 7 P.P.E. to activate.

- **Capt. Daring's Flash Gun:** Looks like an odd pistol or gun style flashlight. Can create a blinding flash whenever the trigger is pulled. Has a P.P.E. energy source that holds 10 flashes. Costs 15 P.P.E. to recharge. Effective Range: 10 feet (3 m); affects everybody in a 10 ft radius of the flash, except the person using the gun (minus 5 to strike, parry and dodge). Same as spell in **Rifts,** page 168. Initial creation cost in P.P.E.: 10. Market Value: 5000 credits each.

- **Capt. Daring's Breathe Without Air Filter:** Costs 5 P.P.E. to activate. An ordinary air filter has been redesigned to enable its wearer to breathe normally in a toxic or airless environment. Breathe without air spell, duration: 15 minutes. Initial creation cost in P.P.E.: 200 . Market Value: 10,000 credits.

- **Capt. Daring's Diver's Suit:** This is a simple skin diver's wet suit with a crazy looking contraption built into the belt. The TW gizmo instills the magic powers of swim as a fish and breathe without air. Costs 11 P.P.E. to activate. Duration: 15 minutes. Initial creation cost in P.P.E.: 600. Market Value: 50,000 credits.

- **Capt. Daring's Goggles:** The magic goggles contain the following sensory magic and can be activated individually or all simultaneously. Initial creation cost in P.P.E.: 140. Market Value: 50,000 credits.
    1. Detect (magic) Concealment: Costs 6 P.P.E. to activate. Same as spell.
    2. Eyes of the Wolf: Costs 25 P.P.E. to activate. A multi-optic system the enables the wearer to see the invisible — 75%, nightvi-

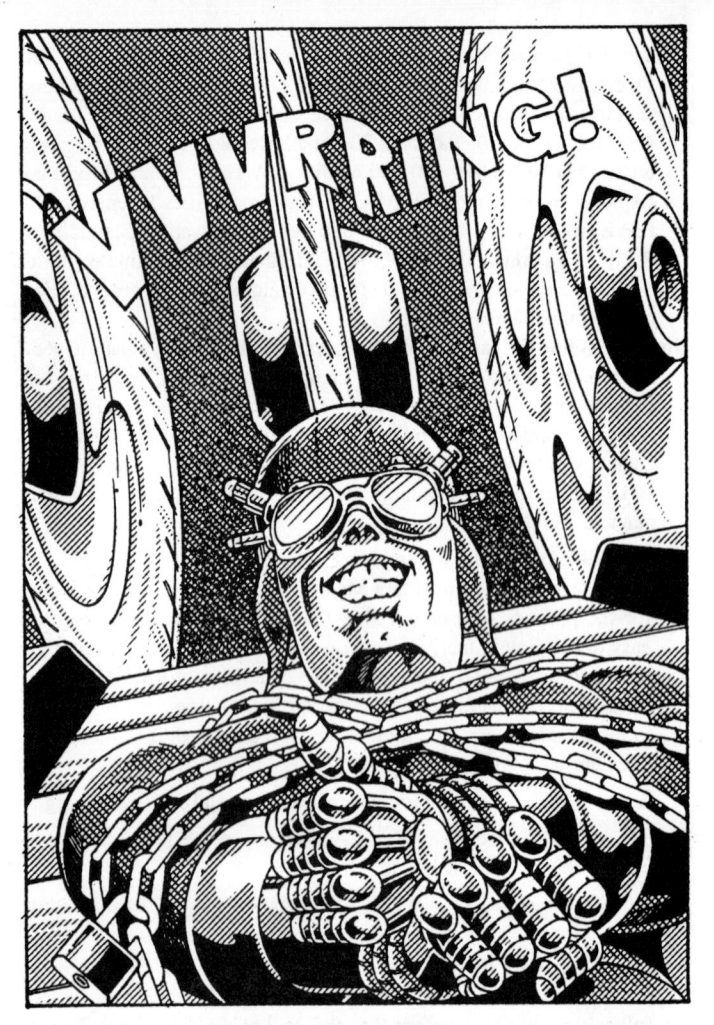

sion — 60 ft/18.3 m, as well as recognize poison — 65%, identify plants & fruit — 70%, identify tracks — 85%, and track — 50%.

3. Globe of Daylight: Costs 2 P.P.E. to activate. Rather than a globe appearing, the daylight illuminates from the goggles as a beam of light, like a flashlight, enabling the wearer to shed light wherever he looks. Range: 48 feet (14.6 m).

- **Capt. Daring's Super Escape Gloves:** The gloves appear to be part of a metallic suit of power armor. Of course, they are powered by tiny P.P.E. generators and six amazing powers. Initial creation cost in P.P.E.: 3200. Market Value: 4.5 million credits.

1. Ion finger: Costs 2 P.P.E. to active. 3D6 M.D. per blast, 10 blasts, costs 20 P.P.E. to recharge. Range: 300 ft (91 m).

2. Concealment: Cost 6 P.P.E. to activate. Enables the wearer to palm and conceal small objects (like lock picks, tools, etc.). Duration: 25 minutes.

3. Fingers of the Wind: Costs 5 P.P.E. to activate. By pointing and wiggling the fingers, the mechano-magic hands create invisible fingers of wind that can be used to knock over an object, put out candles, flick switches, etc.; ideal for creating distractions. Duration: 15 melees (3.7 minutes).

4. Escape: Costs 8 P.P.E. to activate. The gloves/hands can pick any lock, escape any bond in one melee (15 seconds). The gloves/spell must be activated for escape every time a lock or bond is to be removed (spell only removes one restraint every per each activation). Range: Touch.

5. Energy Disruption: Costs 12 P.P.E. to activate. The gloves will temporarily disrupt/knockout electrically powered devices; see spell in **Rifts**, page 174. Range: Touch. Duration: 15 minutes.

6. Teleport lesser (objects): Costs 15 P.P.E. to activate. The gloves can teleport any small object(s) held in its hands. 50 lb (22 kg) limit. See the spell in **Rifts**, page 177. Requires two melees (30 seconds) to teleport. Range: 5 miles (8 km) maximum.

7. Mystic Portal: Costs 60 P.P.E. to activate. Allows its wearer to teleport or pass through solid objects; see spell in **Rifts**, page 184. Range: Must touch the object to pass through it or concentrate to teleport.

- **Capt. Daring's Aviator Wonder Helmet:** Hidden under the lining of the soft sheepskin helmet is a complex system of power crystals and circuitry that provides a multitude of mystic powers. Each magic power can be triggered individually, or as many as four simultaneously as long as sufficient P.P.E. is pumped into the helm. Initial creation cost in P.P.E.: 3500. Market Value: Four million credits. The magic built into the helmet is as follows:

1. Time Slip: Costs 20 P.P.E. to activate. Same as spell in **Rifts**, page 177.

2. Telekinesis: Costs 8 P.P.E to activate. Used to help untie self, pick locks, sneak tools, and cause distractions. Same as spell in **Rifts**, page 171. Range 60 ft (18.3 n). Duration: 5 minutes.

3. Reduce Self (6 inches): Costs 20 P.P.E. to activate. Duration: About 12 minutes (50 melees). Same as spell in **Rifts**, page 177.

4. Shadow Meld: Costs 10 P.P.E. to activate. Used to hide in shadows to create the illusion that he has disappeared or escaped. Duration: 10 minutes (40 melees). Same as spell in **Rifts**, page 173.

5. Dispel Magic Barrier: Costs 20 P.P.E. to activate. Range: 100 ft (30.5m). Same as spell in **Rifts**, page 178.

6. Negate Magic: Costs 30 P.P.E. to activate. Same as spell in **Rifts**, page 181.

- **Capt. Daring's Trick Restraints:** The clever performer has created a variety of trick restraints that are designed to unlock/open/untie (escape spell) when they are activated by 8 P.P.E. Each appears completely normal and do NOT radiate magic until activated. His trick restraints include a straitjacket, leg irons, manacles, handcuffs, rope, blindfold, trunk, boxes, and an M.D.C. safe.

Description: *Captain Daring* is a techno-wizard specializing in escape artistry and death defying stunts. This handsome daredevil has many clever techno-wizard devices of his own design. For instance, some of the very instruments used to entrap him in his acts (chains, straitjackets, boxes, etc.) actually enable him to escape whenever he pumps any P.P.E. into them. He has also created a number of magic devices, enabling him to escape from just about any type of restraint, under the most adverse conditions. Additionally, he is a fairly good stage magician, with good stage presence and sleight of hand skills. The Captain, with his bold, defiant and confident air, always thrills the crowd with his death defying feats. He is quite the showman and will go far as a circus performer.

Types of Performances: Escape artist and daredevil usually with no apparent safeguards or nets.

Hans and Franz
Juicer Strongmen and Acrobat Duo

Real Names: Carl Tominski and Lorenz Von Brunn
Alignment: Scrupulous and Unprincipled
Horror Factor: None
Species: Human
Hit Points: Hans: 60, Franz: 52
S.D.C.: Hans: 341, Franz: 350, **M.D.C.:** Juicer body armor or gladiator armor.
Weight: Approximately 240 lbs of pure muscle (and juice).
Height: Both are 6 ft, 5 inches, **Age:** 19 and 20
P.P.E.: 6 and 7, **I.S.P.:** None
Attributes: Hans: I.Q.: 10, M.A.: 14, M.E.: 12, P.S.: 28, P.P.: 25, P.E.: 28, P.B.: 11, Spd: 87 (58 mph/93 km). Franz: I.Q.: 9, M.A.: 13, M.E.: 12, P.S.: 29, P.P.: 24, P.E.: 29, P.B.: 10, Spd: 88 (60 mph/96 km)
Disposition: Both are always cheerful, energetic, friendly, cocky, and arrogant (in a cheerful way which makes them all the more irritating).

Experience Level: Both are 5th level Juicers.
Magic Knowledge: None.
Psionic Powers: None.
Combat Skills: Martial Arts: Karate kick (1D8 S.D.C. plus damage bonus), jump kick (critical damage), entangle, carry up to 5600 lbs (2.5 tons) and lift up to 11,200 lbs (about 5.5 tons)!

Acrobatic and gymnastic skills/abilities: Sense of balance 95%, walk tightrope 85%, climb rope 98%, back flip 98%, work parallel bars & rings 85%, 40% climb ability.
Attacks per Melee: Five (5)
Bonuses: +7 to strike, +8 to parry, +8 dodge, +13 S.D.C. damage, +4 on initiative, +7 roll with impact, +3 to pull punch, +4 save vs psionics, +6 save vs mind control, +15 save vs poisons/drugs, +7 to save vs magic, +48% to save vs coma/death.
Weapon Proficiencies: W.P. Knife, W.P. Energy Pistol, W.P. Energy Rifle, W.P. Heavy Energy Weapons.
Weapons: Hans: JA-11 assassin's rifle, Wilk's 320 laser pistol, Wilk's 457 laser pulse rifle (3D6+2 or 1D6×10 M.D., 40 shot clip), pair of daggers, and a pair of wood daggers. Franz: JA-9 Variable laser rifle, C-40 Coalition rail gun (1D4×10 M.D., 10 bursts, 4000 ft range), NG-57 ion blaster, vibro-dagger, silver dagger and wooden cross. Vampire weapons include crossbow, wooden stakes, wooden knives, and water cannons. Favorite vehicles are hovercycle or motorcycle.
Cybernetics: None.
Money: 35,000 universal credits each; spend their money like crazy.
Skills of Note: Boxing, acrobatics, gymnastics, body building, swimming (3rd level) 75%, radio basic 75%, wilderness survival 55%, land navigation 61%, pilot hovercraft 80%, pilot motorcycle 80%, pilot jet pack 74%, and languages: Euro, American, gobblely 80%; illiterate.
Description: Hans and Franz are juicers and the resident strongmen. They devote their entire waking hours to various physical activities: gymnastics (with incredible leaps and somersaults), acrobatics, tumbling, jumping, weight-lifting, martial arts, boxing, knife throwing, sharp shooting, and any type of physical challenge imaginable. They never use nets or any means of protection in any of their acts or stunts. In fact, taking any type of damage just makes them feel more macho. Nor would they dream of wearing armor for an act; body armor is used only for "real" combat. Their incredible stamina and need to stay busy has them performing three major day time shows, two evening shows, and an additional dozen small acts on the circus grounds throughout the day. They also assist in security, ever alert for trouble makers and scoundrels.

The stage name of Hans and Franz is based on characters they saw on a pre-rifts video disc. Both speak with a Euro accent and both have nearly identical physical builds. Hans and Franz often ridicule those who rely heavily on high-tech armor and weapons, especially borgs and bots, and make sarcastic comments to such techies as: "Oh, look at the little glitter boy wearing that girlie armor. I don't see how he can pump-up in a suit like that, maybe all his muscle slid down to his seat."

Both young men are new attractions to the circus, but are extremely loyal to Mr. Drak and protective of their fellow performers. Both have served as mercenaries for the Coalition in Minnesota, as well as mercenaries for Kingsdale. Mr. Drak has tried to convince them to get into a detoxification program, but neither will hear of it. Hans will die in four years and eight months. Franz will die in five years.

Types of Performances: 1. Weight-lifting: Can carry two and a half tons and lift an incredible five and a half tons! The act includes lifting a pile of vehicles over their heads, playing catch with a one ton safe, and pulling heavy objects with their teeth. 2. Shoot cannonballs at their stomachs from less than 20 ft away (6.1 m). 3. Breaking chunks of brick and logs with their heads (sometimes with a running start) and karate kicks, as well as feats of acrobatics, gymnastics, and juggling. 4. Wrestling alligators, bears, and monsters without any kind of weapon or armor. 5. Playfully wrestling or fighting challengers from the audience; blood is seldom drawn, played for comedy (lots of jokes and sarcastic jibes). 6. Sharp shooting and knife throwing.

The Night Arcade & Freak Show

The **Night Arcade & Freak Show** is a den of iniquity and evil, engaging in gladiatorial fighting, gambling, prostitution, theft, blackmail and murder. The entertainment and rides are really more of a cover for criminal activity than the acts of a travelling show. Worse, the carnival is a cover for the activities of the undead. Mr. Morricco and many of the performers and carnival workers are vampires.

As you may have guessed, Mr. Morricco is not your run of the mill vampire, but a *Master Vampire* and the vampire carny people are his vampire minions (about 70 secondary vampires and a few wild). Mr. Morricco considers the carnival a perfect mechanism for drawing people (victims) to him. He loves the idea because it is a truly excellent, maniacal deception and artful manipulation of the stupid, lesser human beings. The human crowds are like sheep coming to graze, and Mr. Morricco and his demonic minions are the wolves in sheeps' clothing. Ironically, not only is he using the unsuspecting public as cattle, but the carnival has become a lucrative travelling carnival and is quite famous.

Mr. Morricco takes great pleasure in the intrigue of this never ending con-game. Living for all eternity can be boring, even for a vampire. He has also surrounded himself with non-vampire companions who have suffered such cruelty at the hands of humans and others that their pain and hatred toward their one-time persecutors rivals that of the vampires. They compose a veritable army of embittered and vengeful beings who are loyal to Mr. Morricco and strike down their own kind, the living.

Should one or two people disappear from a crowd of spectators, who will notice? Large crowds and carnival noises are ideal for drowning out the screams of victims. If a body is found, one can only presume he or she fell prey to bandits, a wild animal/monster or one of the wandering vampires that roam the land.

Anything more substantial than mere rumors about his travelling show might soil his reputation and ruin his business. So precautions are taken. From Morricco's viewpoint, it is better to eliminate a problem, like a nosey intruder, than take a chance of being found out. Unlike modern movies where the vampire hovers over his victim and licks his lips for what appears to be hours, Mr. Morricco believes in a swift and precise kill. His henchmen then dispose of the body by feeding it to one of the circus freaks or monsters. Any worthless possessions of the victim, like clothing, are destroyed. All other evidence is completely eliminated; sold, hidden, destroyed. **Note:** Even possessions of great value, including magic, may be eliminated if there is a real possibility that the items could implicate the Arcade in supernatural wrongdoing. After all, Mr. Morricco has centuries to gain wealth — why take chances?. Despite Mr. Morricco's careful plans and caution, the devilish activities of his travelling show do not go completely unnoticed. The show is known for its somewhat dark, dangerous, and bawdy nature, as well as for its frequent accidents between the freaks, monsters and performers with members of the audience. There are hundreds of stories about freaks who escaped and either attacked or tried to attack members of the audience, or ran amok through town. Oddly enough, the elements of danger and the terrifying only add to the goose bumps and lure larger crowds to witness, firsthand, the spectacles of the **Night Arcade**.

Many are the rumors linking the show to theft and other criminal activity. With rare exception, there is the predictable disappearance of at least one or two individuals during the show's visit to every town. Some suspect the show to be cursed and that evil hovers over it like a foreboding storm cloud that inevitably follows the travelling show wherever it goes. Some speak of dark magic, others the supernatural, and still others of the black market or Coalition, but none speak of vampires. Some communities won't allow their citizens to attend the show. Yet despite its dark legacy, most folk greet the infamous carnival with open arms, attributing the crimes and disappearances to bandits who follow all successful travelling shows. Of course, there is also some risk because of the dangerous nature of the Arcade's freaks and monsters, who may also be responsible for some of these incidents, but that's all part of the thrills and chills of the **Night Arcade & Freak Show**.

The vampire lord and his minions have created a marvelous vehicle of subterfuge that has entertained and destroyed life with equal appetite for over a decade. Yet the veil of deception is not always in place. There have been occasions when the vampires returned to a small village, already scouted out during a previous visit by the carnival, and laid it to waste. Such sieges are the scenes of mass murder, torture and frenzied feasting on the unsuspecting inhabitants. All are slain and the homes plundered and/or burnt to the ground. After the carnage, the undead fly back to the carnival a hundred miles away. And nobody is the wiser.

In some cases, especially among small peasant villages with little or no technology, far from civilization, the vampires and their mortal henchmen terrorize the people, but leave most of them alive. These places are pit-stops used by the undead as regular feeding grounds without fear of resistance. But even at these places, the carnival paraphernalia is left several miles away, so that the people do not know that it is members of the **Night Arcade & Freak Show** who are responsible (the peasants presume they are a nomadic tribe of vampires who return once or twice a year).

The carnival henchmen that aren't vampires are freaks, mutants, D-Bee or humans; all are fiends who prey on the weak and unsuspecting. The non-vampires protect their undead leader and his people during the day. At night, the vampires join their human allies to breathe life into the **Night Arcade**. Humans and vampire criminals slip into the *night* crowd (incognito), looking for prey to feed upon or victims to molest. The best victims are transient individuals travelling alone or in a small group; they will not be quickly missed (if at all) by the local townfolk.

The Night Arcade & Freak Show Stats

The infamous carnival of the southwest travels all of Mexico, Central America, and as far north as the old American Empire States of Arizona, New Mexico and Colorado; seldom crosses the Rio Grande River. The Night Arcade is a small travelling carnival with an emphasis on oddities (and crime). A total of 370 Points are available to the carnival for the different features. A minimum of 50 must be spent on acts, 50 on criminal activity, 10 on internal security, 10 on defense, and 10 on reputation.

A. Sponsorship: Organized Criminals	0 Points
B. Outfits: #3 Open Wardrobe	10 Points
C. Equipment: #3 & #4 Electrical & Medical	15 Points
D. Vehicles: #5 Specialty Vehicles (vampire)	30 Points
E. Communications: #4 Full Range	15 Points
F. Internal Security: #5 Paranoid	40 Points
G. Defenses: #5 Private Army	40 Points
H. Acts: Many; see description.	150 Points
I. Alignment: #1 Miscreant & Diabolic	0 Points
J. Criminal: Several	50 Points
K. Reputation: #3 Known	10 Points
L. Salary: #4 Good	10 Points
Total Points Spent:	**370 Points**

Note: Available Points not spent are forever lost; they can not be saved and used at a later date.

Performers, Acts, and Criminals

12 Average Clowns
4 Average Minstrels
2 Side Show Barkers
2 Shills & Pickpockets
4 Non-Psychic Fortunetellers
1 Mind Melter Fortuneteller
1 Mystic Fortuneteller
10 Real Live Freaks
6 Fake Freaks (look real)
1 Side Show with 12 oddities and other filler items
6 Rides
3 Animal acts: 24 snakes, 12 wolves, one monster.
16 Showgirls (6 are vampires)
6 Prostitutes (2 are vampires)
3 Expert Worms
1 Pair of Expert Pickpockets
1 Gang of a dozen Robbers/Thugs

Note: About 70 secondary vampires, 120 non-vampire workers and 80 performers compose the carnival staff of about 270 people.

Mr. Esteban Morricco
Ringmaster/Owner/Villain

Horror Factor: 14, when he reveals his vampire nature.
Alignment: Diabolic
Hit Points: 130, **M.D.C.:** Special Limited Invulnerability: vampires are impervious to most normal and energy weapons. Vulnerable to silver, wood, water and magic. Occasionally wears body armor.
Weight: 155 lbs, **Height:** 5 ft, 9 inches **Age:** Appears to be 30ish.
P.P.E.: 50, **I.S.P.:** 100 **Note:** The I.S.P., P.P.E., & bonuses of the Mystic O.C.C. are not applicable after the transformation into a vampire.
Attributes: I.Q.: 20, M.A.: 24, M.E.: 22, P.S.: 30 (supernatural), P.P.: 23 , P.E.: 21, P.B.: 24, Spd: 28 (18.5 mph/29 km)
Disposition: Malicious, spiteful, and cruel. Loves to torture and torment non-vampires. Incredibly arrogant, sees himself, and vampires in general, as superior to humans and their kin. A calculating and a masterful liar. Can be extremely charming and convincingly pretend to be the nicest, most trustworthy guy in the world and then turn on you like a viper.
Experience Level: 7th level Master Vampire. Was a 4th level mystic!
Magic Knowledge: Previous Mystic O.C.C. (4th level): Globe of daylight, cloud of smoke, chameleon, thunderclap, befuddle, fear, armor

of Ithan, fuel flame, fire bolt, carpet of adhesion, blind, repel animals, float in air, calling, and eyes of Thoth; 50 P.P.E.

Psionic Powers: Vampire, 100 I.S.P., mind control, link with minions, death trance, alter aura, empathy, mind block, presence sense, sense evil, deaden pain, induce sleep, hypnotic suggestion, and super-hypnotic suggestion, as well as psi-powers from life as a mystic: exorcism, clairvoyance, sixth sense, see the invisible, see aura, astral projection, psychic diagnosis, psychic surgery and empathic transmission.

Natural Abilities: Limited metamorphosis, super-regeneration (2D6 H.P. per melee and can regrow new limbs and body parts), limited invulnerability, smell blood a mile away (1.6 km), nightvision 1600 ft (488 m), does not breathe, summon rodents, canines, fog. See the section on **Vampires** and **Abilities Natural to Vampires**. Supernatural strength: can carry 1500 lbs (675 kg) and lift 3000 lbs (1.5 tons)

Combat Skills: Master Vampire (supernatural): Killing bite 3D6 M.D., restrained punch 4D6 S.D.C. plus P.S. bonus (+15 in this case), full strength punch 2D6 M.D., power punch 1D4×10 but counts as two attacks.

Attacks Per Melee: Six (6)

Bonuses: +4 to strike, +4 to parry, +4 to dodge, +15 S.D.C. damage, +3 on initiative, +5 to save vs horror factor, +3 to save vs magic, +4 to save vs psionics, impervious to all forms of mind control, poisons, drugs, magic sleeps, and paralysis. Also impervious to fire until staked through the heart, and impervious to most weapons. 80% likelihood of evoking trust or intimidation, 70% chance of being charming and impressive.

Weapon Proficiencies: W.P. Sword, W.P. Knife, W.P. Energy Pistol, W.P. Energy Rifle.

Weapons: Pair of silver daggers, vibro-sword (2D6 M.D.), C-18 laser pistol, NG-P7 particle beam rifle, four fragmentation grenades (2D6 M.D.), three plasma (5D6 M.D.) and two smoke. Magic scrolls: two animate & control dead (5th level) and one negate magic (6th level).

Body Armor: 40 M.D.C. simple body armor, easy to remove. Worn during most performances and when arriving at an unknown town. The armor also helps to convince people that he is not a vampire.

Bionics & Cybernetics: None

Money: 500,000 credits in gems, one million in gold, 400,000 in pre-rifts artifacts, and two million in universal credits are hidden near the coffin of Mr. Esteban Morricco. The Night Arcade also has 1.5 million credits at Cuidad Juarez.

Skills of Note: Radio: basic 66%, dance 66%, play the guitar and keyboard (synthesizer piano) 71%, horsemanship 68%, pilot motorcycle 78%, pilot hovercraft 71%, wilderness survival 66%, disguise 51%, streetwise 43%, demon & monster lore 51%, basic math 66%, literate in American 56%, and spoken languages include Spanish 98%, American, Euro, and Gobblely 86%. I.Q. bonus included.

Description: Medium height, black hair, spanish features, quite handsome and debonair. Exudes confidence and charisma, but there is also the touch of evil present and his supernatural essence will be instantly recognized by psi-stalkers and mutant dogs.

Mr. Morricco's Living Quarters

Mr. Morricco's living quarters are at the very center of the entertainers' living area, and therefore, the least accessible to intrusion. Around him are most of the tents and trailers of his vampire minions. Security is tight, with surveillance cameras, guards, and dogs monitoring the grounds.

Appointments with Mr. Esteban Morricco are made at the administration trailer (common ground area, behind the public relations tent). The public relations people screen all who inquire to see the carnival owner and they take care of most complaints, fears, or suspicions without ever bothering Mr. Morricco. The common excuses for the master vampire's whereabouts during the day are that he is asleep (having worked all night, till the wee hours of the morning), busy and cannot be disturbed, or away till evening. Even in the evening, meetings will take place at the administration trailer or other locations, never his personal trailer. Mr. Morricco is present at the administration tent only when he has an appointment, otherwise he is found monitoring and directing the affairs of his carnival.

Mr. Morricco's Trailer: A plush, expensively furnished dwelling that seems befitting the successful carnival owner. The trailer has been reinforced with mega-damage material (500 M.D.C.), wired with an alarm system, and the outer door is bolted with a pair of complex electrical locks. The windows have automatic shutters (5 M.D.C. each) that slide into place during the day to keep out sunlight. They also have a pair of normal venetian blinds. The inner doors all lock and are also M.D.C structures (20 each). A large, 100 M.D.C. safe contains many of the circus's valuables.

During the day, two loyal D-Bees stand guard inside Mr. Morricco's trailer (one is a fifth level burster in Bushman armor, the other a 3rd level headhunter in T-21 Terrain Hopper power armor; see **Rifts Sourcebook #1**). Outside, a pack of canines (20 dogs, 10 coyotes) patrol the premises around the trailer; they will alert the carny members of trouble by barking, chase away the curious and tear apart the persistent. One of Mr. Lizzaro's lizards also keeps an eye on the trailer. Anyone caught trying to enter Mr. Morricco's locked and guarded quarters is, generally, tortured for information and put to death that evening (food for the undead). Only the most innocent incidents will be dismissed without repercussion, and even those people will be kept under close watch while the circus is in town.

The vampire's coffin is hidden in a secret compartment and will take at least three people executing an extensive search 15 minutes to locate it. The compartment is wired with a silent alarm that sounds in Mr. Lizarro's and Mad Melody's quarters, as well as the private army's command headquarters. The coffin itself is an airtight mega-damage structure (100 M.D.C.), locked from the inside by two complex electronic locks and two hand-pulled bolts. A small, secret hole in the bottom of the casket can be opened from the inside to allow the vampire to mist out, rather than open the lid. **Note:** Always sleeps with his vibro-sword, C-18 laser pistol, and magic scrolls. A second, identical coffin is hidden in Mad Melody's trailer, on the other side of the carnival grounds, in case the primary coffin is destroyed. A third, simple, pine coffin (filled with soil) is located in a stockroom near the animal pens. Mr. Morricco's native soil is Mexico.

Private Army: The carnival is protected by a small, private army consisting of 40 combat veterans (mostly D-Bees) of 5th and 6th level experience. All have the best body armor, pulse rifles, and heavy weapons. Six are clad in NG-Samson power armor and four in X-10 Predator power armor, one Glitter Boy, and six others patrol the grounds in X-500 Forager Battlebots! **Note:** Most of the carnival employees and vampires also have weapons and body armor to fight off attackers if necessary.

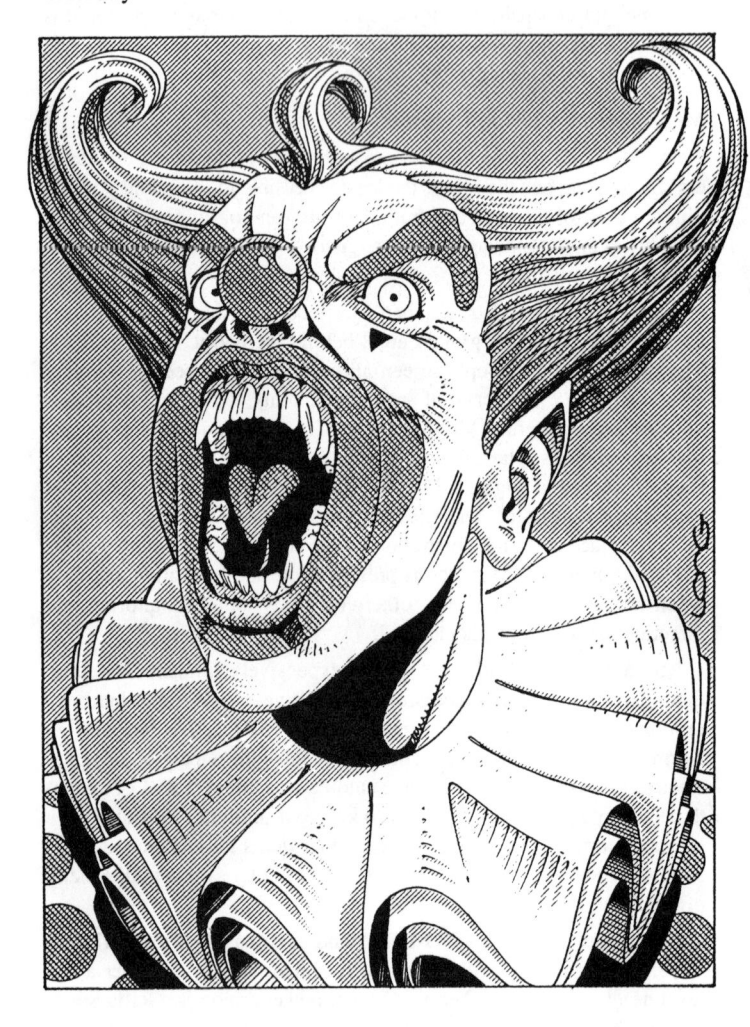

Vampire Clowns — Secondary Vampires

Alignment: Miscreant
Horror Factor: 12
Hit Points: 80 each, **M.D.C.:** Special Limited Invulnerability: vampires are impervious to most normal and energy weapons. Vulnerable to silver, wood, water and magic. Occasionally wear body armor.
Average Weight: 160 lbs, **Average Height:** 6 feet, **Age:** Late 20's
P.P.E.: 20 each, **I.S.P.:** 90 each
Average Attributes: I.Q.: 13, M.A.: 21, M.E.: 18, P.S.: 25 (supernatural), P.P.: 22, P.E.: 19, P.B.: 10, Spd: 22 (15 mph/24 km)
Note: Most are natives of Mexico.
Disposition: Appear cheerful and silly, but are really vicious monsters. Take great delight in fooling humans and other humanoids about their true, undead nature. Arrogant, cruel, malicious.
Experience Level: 4th level Secondary Vampires.
Magic Knowledge: None
Psionic Powers: Vampire, 100 I.S.P., considered major psionic. Mind control, link with minions, death trance, alter aura, empathy, mind block, presence sense, sense evil, deaden pain, induce sleep, hypnotic suggestion, and super-hypnotic suggestion.
Natural Abilities: Limited metamorphosis, super-regeneration (2D6 H.P. per melee and can regrow new limbs and body parts), limited invulnerability, smell blood a mile away (1.6 km), nightvision 1600 ft (488 m), does not breathe, summon rodents, canines, fog. See the section on **Vampires** and **Abilities Natural to Vampires**.
Combat Skills: Secondary Vampire (supernatural): Killing bite 2D6 M.D., restrained punch 3D6 S.D.C. plus P.S. bonus (+10 in this case), full strength punch 2D6 M.D., power punch 4D6 but counts as two attacks.
Attacks Per Melee: Five (5)
Bonuses: +4 to strike, +4 to parry, +4 to dodge, +10 S.D.C. damage, +2 on initiative, +3 to save vs horror factor, +5 to save vs magic, +5 to save vs psionics, +5 to save against all forms of mind control, poisons, drugs, magic sleeps, and paralysis. Also impervious to fire until staked through the heart, and impervious to most weapons. 65% likelihood of evoking trust or intimidation.
Weapon Proficiencies: W.P. Blunt, W.P. Knife, W.P. Energy Rifle.
Weapons: Vibro-claws (2D6 M.D.), dagger (1D6 S.D.C.), L 20 laser pulse rifle.
Body Armor: None
Bionics & Cybernetics: None
Money: Each clown will carry 1D6×100 gold on his person. Another 1D6×1000 gold and an equal amount in credits are hidden in their coffins.
Skills of Note: Gymnastics (4th level), climbing 60%, dance 50%, play one musical instrument 55%, land navigation 45%, pilot automobile 68%, pilot hovercraft 70%, basic math 65%, and speak the following languages: Spanish 98%, American and Gobblely 70%.
Description: The vampire clowns dress and look like your typical clowns except for their fangs. They juggle, tumble, act silly, perform skits and tell jokes. They are particularly useful in luring women and children to their doom. See the description on vampires, their powers and weaknesses. **Note:** The Night Arcade & Freak Show has eight vampire clowns and four non-vamp clowns, all look pretty similar.

Vampire Carnival Thieves — Secondary Vampires

Alignment: Miscreant
Horror Factor: 12
Hit Points: 90 each, **M.D.C.:** Special Limited Invulnerability: vampires are impervious to most normal and energy weapons. Vulnerable to silver, wood, water and magic. Occasionally wear body armor.
Average Weight: 150 lbs, **Average Height:** 5 feet 10 inches,
Age: Late 20's to 40 years old in appearance
P.P.E.: 20 each, **I.S.P.:** 90 each
Average Attributes: I.Q.: 10, M.A.: 19, M.E.: 18, P.S.: 26 (supernatural), P.P.: 22, P.E.: 19, P.B.: 9, Spd: 22 (15 mph/24 km)
Note: Most of the undead are natives of Mexico.
Disposition: Appear cheerful and helpful, but are really vicious monsters. Take great delight in fooling humans and other humanoids about their true, undead nature. Arrogant, cruel, malicious.
Experience Level: 3rd level Secondary Vampires.
Magic Knowledge: None

Psionic Powers: Vampire, 80 I.S.P., considered major psionic. Mind control, link with minions, death trance, alter aura, empathy, mind block, presence sense, sense evil, deaden pain, induce sleep, hypnotic suggestion, and super-hypnotic suggestion.

Natural Abilities: Limited metamorphosis, super-regeneration (2D6 H.P. per melee and can regrow new limbs and body parts), limited invulnerability, smell blood a mile away (1.6 km), nightvision 1600 ft (488 m), prowl 50%, does not breathe, summon rodents and canines. See the section on **Vampires** and **Abilities Natural to Vampires**.

Combat Skills: Secondary Vampire (supernatural): Killing bite 2D6 M.D., restrained punch 3D6 S.D.C. plus P.S. bonus (+11 in this case), full strength punch 2D6 M.D., power punch 4D6 but counts as two attacks.

Attacks Per Melee: Five (5)

Bonuses: +4 to strike, +4 to parry, +4 to dodge, +11 S.D.C. damage, +2 on initiative, +3 to save vs horror factor, +5 to save vs magic, +5 to save vs psionics, +5 to save against all forms of mind control, poisons, drugs, magic sleeps, and paralysis. Also impervious to fire until staked through the heart, and impervious to most weapons. 55% likelihood of evoking trust or intimidation.

Weapon Proficiencies: W.P. Blunt, W.P. Knife, W.P. Energy Rifle.

Weapons: Vibro-claws (2D6 M.D.), dagger (1D6 S.D.C.), L-20 laser pulse rifle, and NG-57 ion blaster.

Body Armor: Light vampire type, 30 M.D.C.

Bionics & Cybernetics: None

Money: Each carries 1D4 × 100 gold on his person. Another 1D6 × 1000 gold and an equal amount in credits are hidden in their coffins.

Skills of Note: Prowl 50%, pick locks 50%, pick pockets 45%, streetwise 36%, land navigation 45%, radio: basic 65%, pilot hovercraft 70%, basic math 65%, and speak the languages Spanish 98%, American and Gobblely 70%.

Description: The vampire thieves dress in either work clothes, overalls, or like the people who attend the show (to blend into the crowd). Some work the various games and booths, while others work the crowd, picking pockets, stealing and mugging. **Note:** The Night Arcade & Freak Show has 20 vampire thieves/city rats that fit this general category; half are native Mexicans, the others are D-Bees; half are women.

Vampire Carnival Henchmen — Secondary Vampires

Alignment: Miscreant

Horror Factor: 12

Hit Points: 70 each, **M.D.C.:** Special Limited Invulnerability: vampires are impervious to most normal and energy weapons. Vulnerable to silver, wood, water and magic. Occasionally wear body armor.

Average Weight: 150 lbs, **Average Height:** 5 feet, 10 inches to 6 ft.

Age: Early 20's to 40 years old in appearance

P.P.E.: 20 each, **I.S.P.:** 90 each

Average Attributes: I.Q.: 8, M.A.: 19, M.E.: 20, P.S.: 24 (supernatural), P.P.: 20, P.E.: 19, P.B.: 9, Spd: 22 (15 mph/24 km)

Note: Most of the undead are natives of Mexico.

Disposition: Appear cheerful and silly, but are really vicious monsters. Take great delight in fooling humans and other humanoids about their true, undead nature. Arrogant, cruel, malicious.

Experience Level: 3rd level Secondary Vampires.

Magic Knowledge: None

Psionic Powers: Vampire, 80 I.S.P., considered major psionic. Mind control, link with minions, death trance, alter aura, empathy, mind block, presence sense, sense evil, deaden pain, induce sleep, hypnotic suggestion, and super-hypnotic suggestion.

Natural Abilities: Limited metamorphosis, super-regeneration (2D6 H.P. per melee and can regrow new limbs and body parts), limited invulnerability, smell blood a mile away (1.6 km), nightvision 1600 ft (488 m), prowl 50%, does not breathe, summon rodents and canines. See the section on **Vampires** and **Abilities Natural to Vampires**.

Combat Skills: Secondary Vampire (supernatural): Killing bite 2D6 M.D., restrained punch 3D6 S.D.C. plus P.S. bonus (+9 in this case), full strength punch 2D6 M.D., power punch 4D6 but counts as two attacks.

Attacks Per Melee: Five (5)

Bonuses: +2 to strike, +2 to parry, +2 to dodge, +9 S.D.C. damage, +2 on initiative, +3 to save vs horror factor, +5 to save vs magic, +6 to save vs psionics, +5 to save against all forms of mind control, poisons, drugs, magic sleeps, and paralysis. Also impervious to fire until staked through the heart, and impervious to most weapons. 55% likelihood of evoking trust or intimidation.

Weapon Proficiencies: W.P. Blunt, W.P. Knife, W.P. Revolver, W.P. Energy Rifle.

Weapons: Pair of daggers (1D6 S.D.C.) and L-20 laser pulse rifle.

Body Armor: None

Bionics & Cybernetics: None

Money: Each carries 2D6 × 10 gold on his person. 1D4 × 1000 gold and an equal amount in credits are hidden in their coffins.

Skills of Note: Prowl 50%, pick locks 50%, pick pockets 45%, streetwise 36%, land navigation 45%, radio: basic 65%, pilot hovercraft 70%, basic math 65%, and speak the languages Spanish 98%, American and Gobblely 70%.

Description: The vampire henchmen dress in either work clothes, overalls, or like the people who attend the show (to blend into the crowd). Some work the various games and booths, while others work the crowd, picking pockets, stealing and mugging. **Note:** The Night Arcade & Freak Show has 30 vampire henchmen that fit this general category; half are native Mexicans, the other half D-Bees.

D-Bee & Human Henchmen —— Non-Vampires

Alignment: 25% are Anarchist, 50% Miscreant and 25% Diabolic.
Horror Factor: None
Hit Points: 45 each, **M.D.C.:** Body Armor
Average Weight: 150 to 220 lbs, **Average Height:** 5 to 7 feet.
Age: Early 20's to 40 years old in appearance
Average P.P.E.: 7, **Average I.S.P.:** None
Average Attributes: I.Q.: 9, M.A.: 9, M.E.: 14, P.S.: 18, P.P.: 14, P.E.: 19, P.B.: 9, Spd: 14
Note: Game Masters can add other unique and interesting characters to these henchmen, as well as the other freaks and performers.
Disposition: Misanthropes who hate humans or other life forms, or who enjoy hurting people. Cruel, merciless, uncaring.
Experience Level: 1D4 level vagabonds, headhunters, scouts, and crazies.
Magic Knowledge: None
Psionic Powers: Generally none or minor.
Combat Skills: Generally Basic and Expert
Attacks Per Melee: Generally three (3)
Typical Bonuses: +2 to strike, +3 to parry, +3 to dodge, +4 S.D.C. damage, +2 to roll with impact, +2 to pull punch, +1 to save vs magic.
Weapon Proficiencies: W.P. Knife, W.P. Revolver, W.P. Energy Pistol, W.P. Energy Rifle.
Weapons: Vary; include energy.
Body Armor: Bushman, Crusader, and Urban Warrior most common.
Bionics & Cybernetics: None or few.
Money: Each carries 1D6×10 gold on his person. 1D6×100 gold and 2D6×1000 in credits are hidden in their trailers.
Skills of Note: Tend to be rogue, wilderness, physical, pilot and weapon/combat related. All know radio: basic, pilot hovercraft, and speak Spanish 98%.
Description: Typical workers and carnival personnel.

Psi-Fi —— Psychic, Mutant Siamese Twins

Alignment: Sylvia is diabolic, Fiona is miscreant.
Hit Points: Sylvia: 48, Fiona: 47, **S.D.C.:** Sylvia: 40, Fiona: 20
Weight: 118 lbs, **Height:** 5 ft, 9 inches, **Age:** 23
P.P.E.: 9 each.
Attributes: Sylvia: I.Q. 15, M.A. 14, M.E. 20, P.S. 16, P.P. 12, P.E. 19, P.B. 8, Spd 8.
Fiona: I.Q. 10, M.A. 19, M.E. 14, P.S. 11, P.P. 15, P.E. 20, P.B. 8, Spd 8.
Disposition: Quiet, shy, meditative except when performing — then they become extroverted and entertaining.
Experience Level: 6th level mind melter and burster.
Magic Knowledge: None.
Psionic Powers: Sylvia (Mind Melter): Master psionic, I.S.P. 220. Powers: Mind block, detect psionics, alter aura, see aura, see the invisible, sixth sense, sense magic, presence sense, telepathy, bio-regenerate (self), psychic diagnosis, psychic purification, psychic surgery, death trance, nightvision, impervious to fire, impervious to poison, ectoplasm, and summon inner strength. **Sylvia's Super Psionics:** Bio-manipulation, bio-regeneration: super, hydrokinesis, mind wipe, mind bond, mentally possess others, psi-shield, psi-sword, telekinetic force field, telekinesis: super, and mind block auto-defense.

Fiona (Burster): Master psionic, I.S.P. 154. In addition to the pyrokinetic powers described on pages 102 and 103 of **Rifts**, she possesses mind block, levitation, and resist fatigue.
Combat Skills: None, rely on psionic powers.
Attacks per Melee: Both women have two physical attacks/melee actions, or two psionic attacks each, for a total of four!
Bonuses: Sylvia: +2 to save vs psionic attack, +2 to save vs magic, +2 to save vs poison. Fiona: +3 to save vs magic, +3 to save vs poison, and is 55% to invoke trust or intimidation.
Weapon Proficiencies: Sylvia: W.P. Targeting, W.P. Sword, W.P. Energy Pistol, W.P. Energy Rifle. Fiona: W.P. Knife, W.P. Energy Pistol, W.P. Revolver.
Weapons: Sylvia: Vibro Sword, NG-97 Partical Beam Rifle, Wilk's 320 Laser Pistol and a Crossbow. Fiona: Small Silver Knife concealed in boot, NG-57 Ion Blaster and a .38 caliber revolver.
Cybernetics: None.
Skills of Note: Sylvia: First aid 10%, literacy: American 10%, computer operation 80%, streetwise 54%, demon & monster lore 65%, swim 75%, pilot automobile 77%, pilot truck 65%, basic math 80%, languages: American, Spanish, Gobblely 98%, and Dragonese and Chinese 70%. Fiona: Cooking 70%, preserve food 60%, sewing 75%, pick pockets 60%, pick locks 65%, streetwise 54%, land navigation, swim 75%, pilot hovercraft 85%, pilot sailboat 95%, boat building 60%, languages: American and Spanish 98%.

Description: Psi-Fi is the stage name of Sylvia and Fiona, twin, mutant sisters physically joined at the head and who possess fabulous psionic powers. In addition to their more traditional abilities, they know what the other is thinking and feeling unless one or the other is using a mind block, and can also willingly supplement each other's psionic abilities with their own I.S.P. Both women trust the other implicitly, but Sylvia, the Mind Melter, is more intelligent, strong-willed, aggressive, and tends to dominate Fiona.

The two mutants hate intelligent life forms in general, and humans in particular, because they have always treated the girls as monsters. Years of persecution, physical and sexual abuse, and ostracism from polite society have made Sylvia and Fiona evil and vengeful. Having grown into powerful psychics, the two use their powers to make those who once tormented them suffer as they were once made to suffer themselves. First at the hands of townspeople, then by a wilderness scout who promised to take the girls to a safe haven, but instead, sold them to a freak show after having his way with them repeatedly. At age seven they were the star attractions of a filthy little freak show. The heartless proprietor and his employees abused the girls, verbally, emotionally, and physically, on a daily basis for over three years, before selling them to a larger, marginally kinder freak show.

It was not until the age of 13 that the girls' full range of psychic powers blossomed. They had always been able to read each other's minds and emotions, but now they experienced an even greater symbiotic relationship. A relationship of power. At age 16, Fiona, with Sylvia's prompting, set the show on fire and burnt it to the ground. The owner and six others died in the blaze. It took four years to find the original freak show that had so proudly displayed them. Along the way four towns were destroyed and a score of other abusers were slain by the sisters. No longer would they suffer degradation at the merciless hands of the smug, prettier humanoids who thought themselves their superiors. Their first tormentors, once found, were each slain, but only after weeks of slow, horrible torture, both physically and mentally.

The sisters continued their rampage of vengeance, causing much pain and suffering to all they encountered on their way southward. About a hundred miles north of Mexico City, they met Esteban Morricco and struck their unholy allegiance with the vampire and his *Night Arcade and Freak Show*.

Sylvia and Fiona are fairly loyal to Esteban and his carnival of evil. It is an excellent means for them to extract their own bloody vengeance against humankind, while enjoying the favor and protection of other powerful freaks and vampires who prey on the innocent. The sisters are just one of the vampires' daytime protectors.

Types of Performances: 1) Psi-Fi perform a mind reading act using telepathy, empathy and psychic sensitive powers. 2) Spectacular healing by Sylvia; takes volunteers from the audience and seemingly cures them of phobias by erasing painful memories or mentally controls them, or may actually perform psychic surgery (also a method of torture). 3) Convince a volunteer that he is actually an animal or to react to unseen stimuli (bio-manipulation, etc.). 4) Feats of telekinesis and other psychic prowess. 5) A spectacular fire act. Occasionally, they will operate one of the fortuneteller or healing tents.

Mr. Lizzaro —— Lord of the Reptiles

Real Name: Hhrrusst
Alignment: Diabolic (can be any, but usually selfish or evil).
Horror Factor: 12
Species: Lyvorrk. D-Bee race of intelligent and psionic reptilian humanoids; a handful (under 100) have come to Rifts-Earth.
Hit Points: 67, **S.D.C.:** 2900, **M.D.C. Equivalent:** Natural toughness from fine, scaly, alien skin provides the equivalent of 29 M.D.C.; roll 6D6×100 to determine S.D.C. points (remember 100 S.D.C.=One M.D.C.).
Weight: 150 lbs, **Height:** 5 ft, 4 inches plus tall (5 feet plus 1D6 inches). **Note:** Is cold-blooded.
Age: 40, average life span 150 years.
P.P.E.: 24 (roll 5D6), **I.S.P.:** 82
Lizzaro's Attributes: I.Q.: 14, M.E.: 21, M.A.: 11, P.S.: 13, P.P.: 11, P.E.: 23, P.B. 7, Spd. 18.
Player Character Attributes: I.Q.: 3D6+2, M.E.: 4D6, M.A.: 3D6, P.S.: 3D6, P.P.: 3D6+2, P.E.: 5D6, P.B. 2D6, Spd. 4D6.
Disposition: Sinister, cruel, vindictive, arrogant, bully. Total fruitcake. Hates humans and dislikes most mammals. Likes to dispense pain and evoke fear. Tends to be sluggish during cold weather. Loves to sun himself.
Insanity: Obsessed with reptiles and loves to be around them (likes to scare people with them too). Phobia about scientists: bad experience; fears them and will avoid scientist like the plague. Lizzaro will fight like a madman if cornered by one, cries and pleads for mercy and/or freedom if captured by scientists. **Note:** All Lyvorrk have some insanities; player characters roll once on obsession and once on the phobia tables.
Experience Level: 6th level vagabond and side show performer. **Note:** Lyvorrkian characters are a Racial Character Class (R.C.C.).
Magic Knowledge: None
Psionic Powers: Special. I.S.P. 82, considered a major psionic. The special psi-powers are not available to mammals. 1. Control Reptiles: Through a combination of empathy, telepathy, and mind control specifically oriented to reptiles, the character can control all cold-blooded reptiles including, lizards, snakes, turtles and reptilian varieties of dinosaurs (not all dinosaurs are cold-blooded or reptilian). The animals will understand and obey the character's every command, verbal or mental. Range: 100 feet. Duration: Indefinite. Number of reptiles that can be controlled: 40 plus 10 for every level of experience, regardless of size. **Mr. Lizzaro** can control up to 100 different reptiles! Bonus: +10% to ride untamed dinosaur reptiles.

Controlling intelligent reptilian life forms is also possible, but the victim gets a saving throw and the other conditions are different. Range: 50 feet. Duration: One minute (4 melees) per level of experience. Number of intelligent reptiles that can be controlled: One per level of experience, regardless of size. Saving Throw: Standard. Victims cannot be forced to do something that is completely abhorrent to them.

2. Psionic Empathy with reptiles: Lyvorrkians automatically have an affinity with reptiles of all kinds, including many varieties of dinosaurs. Reptiles take an immediate liking to the creatures. Reptilian predators will never stalk these D-Bees. Snakes and dinosaurs will not bite nor lizards run in fear. Furthermore, the reptiles are friendly, docile and will do their best to please. Poisonous snakes and dinosaurs make excellent watchdogs and will fight to the death to protect their D-Bee lord.

3. Telepathy with Reptiles: This ability is similar to normal telepathy except that it only works on cold-blooded animals of a reptilian nature.

Conventional Psionic Powers: Death trance, mind block, resist hunger, resist thirst, resist fatigue, and nightvision.
Natural Abilities: Minimal need of water. Can survive on as little as one pint of water a month. Derives moisture from the bodily fluids of its food. Primary diet is rodents and insects, eaten raw, often swallowed whole, but will occasionally eat prepared meats and the flesh of larger prey such as cattle and humans. This also means that the creature has a remarkable stomach and is resistant to poisons, spoiled food/water, and drugs (+2). They are good burrowers and

Mr. Lizzaro with Speedy, Grunt, and Benito.

natural climbers (base skill is 60/50%), also have keen hearing, polarized vision, quick reflexes (+2 on initiative, +1 to strike and parry, +2 to dodge, +2 to roll with impact), love hot climates; not adversely affected by heat. As one might expect, the D-Bees are found in hot climates.

Note: Reduce bonuses and spd attribute by half when exposed to climates colder than 50 degrees Fahrenheit for more than four hours. Bonuses and abilities are restored to full after exposure to warmth (70 degrees or hotter) for two hours. Like all lizards, the Lyvorrkians keep warm during cold desert nights by burrowing under rocks or dirt to retain heat, or, of course, use a climate controlled environment such as a house or vehicle with temperature control or a source of heat. Also see combat data for extra melee attack.

Combat Skills: Hand to Hand Assassin: Entangle.

Attacks per Melee: Four (4) plus one in warm climates. **Note:** Lyvorrkians get one additional attack per melee in warm climes, but are minus one in cold climates (less than 50 degrees Fahrenheit).

Bonuses: (include combat skills, attributes, and natural abilities) +3 to strike, +4 to parry, +5 to dodge, +4 S.D.C. damage, +2 on initiative, +5 to roll with impact, +3 to pull punch, +3 to save vs psionics, +5 to save vs magic, +7 to save vs poisons/drugs, 18% to save vs coma.

Weapon Proficiencies: W.P. Targeting (crossbow, sling and spear are specific areas of interest), W.P. Energy Pistol, W.P. Energy Rifle.

Weapons: Sling with normal and silver sling bullets (1D6 S.D.C., double damage to vampires, 80 ft), also uses grenades with the sling. Crossbow with normal bolts and 12 high explosive (3D6 M.D.), six paralysis (1D6 minutes), and 6 smoke. Spear made of M.D.C. material (retains sharpness, 4 M.D.C.), NG-Super (likes those grenades), and an L-20 laser pulse rifle. **Body Armor** is worn only when he knows he is going into combat; crusader style armor. (55 M.D.C.).

Cybernetics: None, although Lyvorrkians are not opposed to bionics.

Money: 750,000 credits in gold (hidden in his trailer), 50,000 credits worth of pre-rifts artifacts; doesn't believe in credit cards. The treasure-trove is protected by poisonous snakes.

Skills of Note: Mr. Lizzaro: Palming 55%, pick locks 60%, prowl 55%, streetwise 50%, basic math 70%, horsemanship 60%, and in this case includes riding dinosaurs at 70% (+10%), land navigation 61%, and languages include Lyvorrkian 98% and Spanish at 75%.

R.C.C. Skills of Player Characters: Lyvorrkian characters are a Racial Character Class (R.C.C.). Skills available to that R.C.C. (unless a specific O.C.C. is selected) are limited to communication (any), domestic (any), basic electronics, military, physical (any except martial arts, and acrobatics), pilot (any), pilot related (any), rogue (any except hacking, +10% bonus), basic math, technical (any), W.P. (any), wilderness (any), +5%). A total of 10 skills may be selected.

Available O.C.C.s (do not select R.C.C. skills if a specific occupation): Men of arms: Borgs (not a likely prospect), headhunter or military. Scholars & Adventurers: City rat, vagabond, wilderness scout; hate academia. Magic: Any! Love to study magic; magic is a new and interesting phenomenon to Lyvorrkians because magic does not exist in their native world.

Description: *Mr. Lizzaro* is a tamer of wild creatures. He specializes in baby dinosaurs, snakes and lizards. Why? No one really knows what motivates him. Lizzaro is completely unpredictable and a borderline psychotic. Conversely, he is a brilliant performer and will do anything for the sake of entertainment. He considers himself an artist and is always looking for new methods and means to advance and perfect his craft.

Other than his menagerie of reptiles, who he loves more than people, his only "friend" is Mad Melody (see below). Through

Melody's summoning, Lizzaro has been able to obtain bizarre, monstrous reptiles for his acts.

Types of Performances: 1. Dancing lizards: Mr. Lizzaro makes his lizards dance in a human-like manner. The act includes his riding carnivorous dinosaurs and dinosaurs and lizards jumping through hoops and performing tricks.

2. Snake charmer: The D-Bee performer covers himself in poisonous snakes (mostly rattlers) and makes them perform a variety of tricks, including spelling the words, "the end" with their bodies (they're the only two words he can read in American).

3. Dueling dinosaurs: A pair of dinosaurs wrestle each other in what appears to be a deadly battle. However, the entire show is carefully and psionically controlled and orchestrated by Mr. Lizzaro and often includes fake blood. He will sometimes let humans and other mammals fight his dinosaurs for a fee (additional betting is common). About 40% of the time there is a tragic "accident" in which the mammal is seriously injured or killed by the dinosaur(s). However, if one of his reptilian companions is killed, Mr. Lizzaro is likely to seek blood revenge.

Lizzaro does not always keep a tight rein on his creatures and they do get loose and attack the audience from time to time. Lizzaro finds the shrieks and terror of the panicking audience amusing. Ironically, this potential danger serves to attract larger crowds.

Many of his creatures are painted, shaved, or dressed to fit the mood of Lizzaro. "New-wave or punk-looking" dinosaurs are indeed a bizarre sight, but if that's what Lizzaro wants, that's what he gets. Lime-green and turquoise are one of his favorite color combinations. Lizzaro is a fruitcake and liable to come up with any bizarre idea you can imagine.

Note: Mr. Lizzaro and his reptile minions guard the circus and protect their vampire friends during the daytime, when Mr. Lizzaro is at his maximum power. Lizzaro is quite loyal to the vampires because they share his hatred of mammals and feed on them just as he does. Working with them also gives him greater strength and protection from human antagonists, for the vampires and other freaks help to protect him as much as he protects them.

Lizzaro's Menagerie

Benito the Bruutasaur

Benito is a giant reptilian humanoid summoned by Mad Melody. He has become Lizzaro's right-hand enforcer and bodyguard. The dinosaur-like D-Bee towers 11 feet tall (3.3 m) and is a wall of muscle. He is a natural predator and comes from a world where his people are primitive hunters and have little use for technology. Oh, Benito and his kind (no others of which are known to be on Rifts Earth) can use the occasional handgun or even rail gun, but they are more animal than human in intelligence and live as hunters by instinct. In their own habitat, the Bruutasaurs are nomads that travel in small, tribal, hunting packs of 20 to 100 members. They prey on smaller, less intelligent reptiles, dinosaurs and mammals of all sizes. Mammals are their favorite food.

Alignment: Miscreant, but can be any (tend toward selfish & evil).
Horror Factor: 10
Species: Bruutasaur. D-Bee race of semi-intelligent, carnivorous theropods.
Hit Points: See M.D.C., **M.D.C.:** 130 for Benito; natural M.D.C. skin like a dragon's (2D6×10 M.D.C. is rolled to determine M.D.C.) plus 10 M.D.C. per level of experience.
Weight: 950 lbs, **Height:** 11 ft tall; the average bruutasaur is 9 feet plus 1D4 feet. **Note:** Is cold-blooded.
Age: Benito is 21; average life span in natural habitat is 50 years (could be twice as long in a different world, under the circumstances).
P.P.E.: 9 (roll 3D6), **I.S.P.:** None
Benito's R.C.C. Level: 4th (same table as dragons)
Benito's Attributes: I.Q.: 6, M.E.: 18, M.A.: 6, P.S.: 24, P.P.: 17, P.E.: 25, P.B. 7, Spd. 22 (15 mph/24 km), but can run twice as fast in short bursts lasting about 1D4 minutes (used to catch prey).
Player Character Attributes: I.Q.: 2D6, M.E.: 4D6, M.A.: 2D6, P.S.: 4D6+6, P.P.: 4D6, P.E.: 5D6, P.B. 2D6, Spd. 6D6
Benito's Disposition: Aggressive, cruel, bully. Very pushy and intimidating. Hates humanoid mammals, loves to eat 'em. Most Bruutasaurs are extremely dominating, aggressive and mean, particularly the dominant males.
Magic & Psionics: None
Natural Abilities: Natural hunters, very alert, quick reflexes. Heightened sense of smell adds to his alertness: Track by smell 60% +2% per level of experience, recognize specific scent 40% +4% per level of experience, identify edible food 60% +4% per level of experience. Good runner, can run for six hours before beginning to tire. Leap 10 feet plus one foot for every P.S. point. Heal twice as quickly as normal. Special Bonuses: +1 on initiative, +1 to strike, +1 to parry, +6 to save vs magic, +2 to save vs psionics.
Combat: Equal to Hand to Hand: Expert.
Number of Attacks per Melee: Four (4), plus one at level seven and fourteen.

> **Damage:**
> Restrained punch/claw — 6D6 S.D.C.
> Punch/claw — 2D6 M.D.
> Power punch/claw — 4D6 M.D., counts as two attacks.
> Bite — 2D6 M.D.
> Slashing tail — 1D6 M.D.
> Leap attack — 4D6 M.D., counts as two attacks; 60% chance of knocking an opponent under 20 feet tall (6 m) down; victim loses one melee attack. If knocked down, there is a 35% chance that the victim may be pinned and unable to attack or defend. The monster can bite its helpless prey until forcibly removed or lets go. Roll to see if the prey is still pinned at the beginning of every melee round.

Benito's Bonuses: +3 to strike, +5 to parry, +4 to dodge, +9 S.D.C. damage, +1 on initiative, +2 to pull punch, +2 to roll with impact, +6 to save vs magic, +4 to save vs psionics.
Weapons: Vibro-sword (2D6 M.D.) and NG-P7 particle beam rifle specially fitted for his giant hands, but prefers to use claws and teeth. **Note:** Has no money of his own. Mr. Lizzaro provides all.
R.C.C. Skills: Wilderness survival (+20%), land navigation (+20%), track animals (+20%), track humans (+10%), hunting, prowl (+5%), swim (+10%), and W.P. blunt. Can also select two Rifts languages (+10%), two additional W.P.s (any), and three other skills from the categories of domestic, wilderness, pilot (limited to automobiles, trucks, hovercraft, and boats), technical (any), and W.P. (any). Two additional skills can be selected at levels four, eight, and twelve.
Armor: Benito wears black, giant size, gladiator style body armor with 120 M.D.C. points.

Speedy and Grunt
Small predatory dinosaurs

Both understand Spanish and obey both Mr. Lizzaro and Benito. In their natural habitat they feed on small animals and other dinosaurs, however, they have come to prefer human flesh.

Alignment: Effectively miscreant.
Horror Factor: 10
Species: Dinosaurs: carnivorous theropods.
Hit Points: See M.D.C., **M.D.C.:** 20 each.
Weight: 90 lbs, **Height:** 4 ft. **Note:** Is cold-blooded.
Age: 4, average life span is 20 years.
P.P.E.: 6 (roll 2D6), **I.S.P.:** None

Attributes of Note: Animal I.Q., P.S.: 20, P.P.: 16, P.E.: 18, Spd: Speedy Spd 66 (45 mph/ 72 km) and Grunt Spd 50 (35 mph/56 km).
Natural Abilities: Natural hunters, very alert, quick reflexes and incredibly fast (about twice as fast as most small theropods). Heightened sense of smell adds to their alertness: track by smell 60%, recognize specific scent 44%. Good runners, can run for three hours before beginning to tire. Leap 20 feet.
Bonuses: +1 on initiative, +3 to strike, +2 to parry, +4 to dodge, +8 to save vs poison, +4 to save vs magic, +4 to save vs psionics.

Combat & Number of Attacks per Melee: Three (3)
  Damage:
    Restrained punch/claw — 4D6 S.D.C.
    Claw — 1D4 M.D.
    Bite — 1D6 M.D.
    Leap Claw Attack — 3D6 M.D., counts as two attacks. Tears at victim with its powerful hind legs and large clawed feet. 40% chance of knocking an opponent under 10 feet tall (3 m) down; victim loses one melee attack. No chance of pinning prey.

Pokey — A giant turtle-like armored dinosaur

Pokey is a massively built nodosaur encased in heavy body armor covered in large and small, bony spikes along the sides and front of the body. She is a quiet critter who plods along at a calm, slow, pace grazing on grass and other plants. However, when angered, she charges like a rhinoceros and is amazingly fast and maneuverable! She can be quite ferocious in her acts or when genuinely threatened.
Alignment: Effectively anarchist.
Horror Factor: 8
Species: Dinosaur: herbivorous Panoplosaurus; nodosaur family.
Hit Points: See M.D.C., **M.D.C.:** 820
Weight: 4 tons, **Height:** 5 ft (1.5 m) tall, but 15 feet long (4.6 m) from head to toe. **Note:** Is cold-blooded.
Age: 11; average life span is 40 years.
P.P.E.: 6 (roll 2D6), **I.S.P.:** None
Attributes of Note: High animal I.Q., P.S.: 40, P.P.: 16, P.E.: 24, Spd: plods along at a speed of less than 10, but can reach a speed of 50 (35 mph/56 km) and maintain that speed for up to a half-hour!
Natural Abilities: Incredibly nimble and sure-footed, sense of balance 70%, fair climbing 55%, good swimmer 70% and can hold its breath for up to a half-hour, but is a land animal. In its normal habitat the panoplosaurus feeds on the vegetation that grows in and around rivers and other bodies of fresh water (commonly found along the Rio Grande and the rivers of Mexico). Good vision and good sense of smell (no special bonus). Cannot be moved when the beast plants itself (locking hips); a combined strength of 60 is needed and pestering the animal is likely to provoke it into attacking. Generally, Panoplosauruses attack only when provoked or feel trapped or are startled.
Bonuses: +2 to strike, +2 to parry, +6 to dodge, +25 S.D.C. damage, +6 to save vs poison, +4 to save vs magic, +4 to save vs psionics.
Combat & Number of Attacks per Melee: Three (3)
  Damage:
    Restrained head butt — 2D6 S.D.C.
    Normal head butt — 4D6 S.D.C. +25 from P.S. bonus.
    Full force head butt — 1D6 M.D. and a 40% chance of knocking an opponent under 15 feet tall (4.6 m) down; victim loses one melee attack. No chance of pinning prey.
    Stomp — 1D6 M.D.
    Trample — 4D6 M.D., counts as two attacks.
    Bite — 1D6 M.D.
    Short charge ramming/butting attack — 3D6 M.D., counts as one attack and a 50% chance of knocking an opponent under 15 feet tall (4.6 m) down; victim loses one melee attack.
    Full charge/ram — 6D6 M.D., counts as two attacks; 70% chance of knocking down an opponent under 20 feet tall (6 m). Victims lose one melee attack and are likely to be knocked 4D6 feet away. If knocked down, there is a 40% chance of being trampled too, as the dinosaur runs right over you. **Note:** If the dinosaur stands on top of a vehicle or robot or giant and makes itself immobile, it will pin that vehicle in place until it lets go.

Other Reptiles
Note: Most conventional snakes and lizards are found in Palladium's **Monsters & Animals**.
- **24 Rattlesnakes:** +2 to strike, bite does 1D4 S.D.C. and poison: 6D6 S.D.C. per each bite. A successful roll to save vs poison means half damage.
- **12 Cottonmouth:** +3 to strike, bite does 1D4 S.D.C. plus poison: 1D6 S.D.C. for 1D6 melees. A successful roll to save vs toxin means half damage; must roll for each melee affected.
- **4 King Cobras:** +3 to strike, bite does 1D4 S.D.C. and poison: 1D6 S.D.C. per each 4D4 melees; roll to save every melee.
- **6 Yucatan Boa Constrictors.** Not poisonous; crush victims.
- **4 Gila Monsters:** Bite does one S.D.C. and poison: 2D6 S.D.C. per each bite. A successful roll to save vs poison means half damage.(poisonous).
- **30 different kinds of lizards:** All harmless.

Mad Melody
The Carnival's Mistress of Magic

Real Name: Maria Moreles
Horror Factor: None normally, but H.F. 16 when opening a rift or when supernatural forces appear to be at her beck and call.
Alignment: Miscreant
Hit Points: 38, **S.D.C.:** 20+ 30 from supernatural link.
M.D.C.: Body armor or magic.
Weight: 120 lbs, **Height:** 5 ft, 7 inches, **Age:** 28
P.P.E.: 192 (142 natural, plus 50 from link to the supernatural: same vampire intelligence as Esteban Morricco, **I.S.P.:** None
Attributes: I.Q.: 14, M.E.: 20, M.A.: 15, P.S.: 13, P.P.: 11, P.E.: 12, P.B. 14, Spd. 10.
Species: Human
Disposition: Aloof, intense, independent, loner, self-centered. Takes crazy risks, likes to flirt with danger. Always singing or humming. Her link to the vampire intelligence makes her the official super protector of the carnival vampires, especially of Mr. Morricco.
Experience Level: 6th level Shifter.
Magic Knowledge: In addition to the usual abilities of the shifter O.C.C.(sense rifts and dimensional rift home), O.C.C. bonuses and bonuses from her familiar and supernatural links, Mad Melody knows the following magic spells and rituals. **Note:** +1 to spell strength.
  Various Spells (mostly defensive in nature): Sanctum, sense P.P.E., sense magic, tongues, concealment, chameleon, shadow meld, time slip, blinding flash, cloud of smoke, energy bolt, call lightning, breathe without air, swim as a fish, armor of Ithan (60 M.D.C. for six minutes), and invulnerability (+35 M.D.C., 1 and 1/2 minute's duration), impervious to energy, get extra bonuses, and more; see **Rifts,** page 178)
  Summoning & Control Magic: Blind, mute, globe of silence, trance, speed of the snail, apparition, fear, exorcism, animate & control dead, turn dead, constrain being, repel animals, summon and control canines, control & enslave entity, summon entity, summon lesser beings, protection circle: simple & superior, close rift and dimensional portal (open rift).
Psionic Powers: None

Mad Melody in her street clothes, accompanied by Oltec.

Combat Skills: Hand to hand: basic. Kick attack (1D6 S.D.C.), critical strike on natural 19 & 20.

Attacks per Melee: Three (3)

Bonuses: All bonuses from attribute, O.C.C., familiar, and supernatural link are included. +1 to strike, +2 to parry and dodge, +2 to pull punch, +2 to roll with impact, +1 on initiative, +10 to save vs horror factor, +4 to save vs magic, +5 to save vs psionics, +6 to save vs mind control, +1 to save vs poison.

Weapon Proficiencies: W.P. Automatic Pistol, W.P. Energy Rifle.

Weapons: 9 mm Pistol (2D6 S.D.C. per round; has clips of silver bullets from rogue vampires), silver-plated dagger, sacrificial short sword (handle is jewel encrusted, worth 25,000 credits), 4 inch, gold cross that is also a magic amulet (sense the presence of spirits/entities). Plus C-18 laser pistol, C-10 light laser rifle, CS vibro-knife and CS neural mace.

M.D.C. Body Armor: Mad Melody likes Coalition equipment especially their lovely armor. Has two suits of CA-2 light "Dead Boy" body armor (50 M.D.C.) and one CA-1 heavy armor (80 M.D.C.).

Cybernetics: None

Money: Has 290,000 in gold and gems, 80,000 credits worth of pre-rifts artifacts, and 125,000 in universal credits.

Skills of Note: Land navigation 66%, wilderness survival 60%, prowl 52%, palming 47%, streetwise 40%, sing 65%, cook 60%, holistic medicine 50%, horsemanship 60%, pilot hovercraft 75%, astronomy 80%, demon and monster lore 65%, faerie lore 60%, basic math 85%, and languages include Spanish 98%, American, Dragonese, and Gobblely at 90%.

Description: *Mad Melody* is a female shifter specializing in spectacular summoning, which rivals any current day Broadway play or rock concert. Through the effective use of mood creating devices such as music and sound effects systems, lasers, smoke and optical illusions machines, and creative costumes, she can create an incredible spectacle of light, color, and monsters. The audience feels that they are part of the summoning, and indeed they are, for Mad Melody draws on their P.P.E., often requesting their concentration to help her with her summons.

In some cases, the performance is all illusionary, but when performing near a ley line or nexus point, she will actually open a dimensional rift or open herself to new, unknown supernatural forces. Obviously, this can result in unforeseen and dangerous events, but that just makes her show all the more exciting.

"Staged" summoning will involve light shows and illusions, both magical and mechanical. The creature summoned had been previously summoned and prepared for the show or may be Bonecruncher or Benito dressed in a costume. At the proper moment, the monster will seemingly appear out of nowhere. Usually, the audience is so focused on Mad Melody and her light show that they don't realize that the summoning is fake.

Like Lizzaro, Mad Melody is a temperamental artist and borderline lunatic. The two like each other quite a bit and make a formidable team. The friends are seen together often and are quick to come to each other's aid.

Types of Performances: 1. Monster summoning & rift opening! Starts out with small, normal creatures and light show, slowly working her way up to the Grand Finale, usually of a supernatural or dimensional nature. Often Mad Melody summons a creature and Lizzaro tames it for her or uses it as one of the monster/freak attractions.

2. Magic show. A combination of sleight of hand, smoke, light and simple real magic.

3. Light show and stage magic. This will be one of her less impressive summoning acts or fake summoning; no rift opening or major monsters. To assist in creating the right mood, Mad Melody will use the spells blinding flash, fear, and apparition, as well as summon up a couple mischievous entities like poltergeist (see **Beyond the Supernatural** for entities and other supernatural beasties).

Oltec — Mad Melody's D-Bee Familiar

Real Name: Oll-tctlo
Alignment: Miscreant, but can be any selfish or evil alignment.
Hit Points: Not applicable
M.D.C.: Natural 75 M.D.C. (2D4×10+15)
Weight: 50 lbs, **Height:** 2 ft, 6 inches
Age: 57, average life span is about 150 years.
P.P.E.: 70 (roll 2D4×10+10), **I.S.P.:** None
Species: Krpt: D-Bee animal race of magic creatures (the magic is mostly air elemental in nature); reminiscent to a sub-level of flying imps and may, in fact, be cousins.
Oltec's Attributes: High animal intelligence, almost human, but not quite, thus the strange creature can be used as a familiar. I.Q.: 7, M.E.: 18, M.A.: 6, P.S.: 9, P.P.: 7, P.E.: 19, P.B. 7, Spd. 8 running, 50 flying (35 mph/56 km).
Player Character Attributes: I.Q. (human equivalent): 2D4, M.E.: 4D6, M.A.: 2D6, P.S.: 2D6+2, P.P.: 2D6+2, P.E.: 4D6, P.B. 1D6+2, Spd. 2D6 running, 2D4×10 flying.
Disposition: Sneaky, malicious, spiteful and treacherous, but completely loyal to Mad Melody. Regards Mad Melody with love and loyalty, with the same fervor as a loyal watchdog; quick to obey and happy to do it. He is most happy when he can steal something for her, or protect her, or perform some other service that makes his mistress happy. When alone with her, Oltec often acts like a little child with a crush. He can be silly and is easily embarrassed by Melody.

All Krpts tend to be sneaky, mean, greedy and self serving. They are known to hoard treasure and magic items in an attempt to be more human and because they covet things of value, even if they have no use for them. The more an intelligent (powerful) life form values or wants an item, the more the Krpt wants it too. In some cases, the little fiends will secretly keep items that their master needs or wants. Mad Melody wisely allows Oltec to keep a treasure hoard and rewards him often with little trinkets.

Experience Level: Oltec is 5th level; same table as dragon.
Magic Knowledge (innate abilities): 70 P.P.E., Natural magic R.C.C. powers: Sense evil, sense magic, see the invisible, climb, float in air, breathe without air, resist fire, extinguish fire, globe of daylight, blinding flash, thunderclap, heavy breathing, fingers of wind, wind rush, tongues, turn dead, heal wounds, minor curse, and spoil. **Note:** Can not learn additional spells.
Psionic Powers: None
Natural Abilities: Prowl 55%, nightvision 800 ft (244 ft), keen color vision, exceptional hearing (initiative bonus), heals 10 time faster than humans, prehensile tail (like a third hand and adds one additional attack/melee action, barbed tail (poison).
Combat & Number of Attacks per Melee: Three (3) hand/tail to hand or two magic.
  Damage:
    Bite — 1D6 S.D.C.
    Restrained Rear Claws (flying attack) — 3D6 S.D.C.
    Full Strength Claw Attack — 1D4 M.D., because a magic monster.
    Tail Attack — 1D4 S.D.C. from tail spikes plus victim must roll to save vs poison every time blood is drawn. Poison inflicts 2D6 hit point/S.D.C. damage and also makes its victim dizzy; −4 to strike, parry and dodge, spd reduced by 1/3. A successful save means 1D6 damage and no dizziness.
Bonuses: +2 to strike, +2 to parry, +4 to dodge, +2 on initiative, +2 to roll with impact, +7 to save vs horror factor, +3 to save vs magic, +3 to save vs psionics, impervious to poison and drugs.
Weapon Proficiencies: W.P. Knife, W.P. Revolver (or automatic pistol), and W.P. Energy Pistol.
Weapons: .32 caliber revolver (silver bullets are available), TX-5 Pump pistol (4D6 M.D., 800 ft range, 5 rounds), Wilk's laser scalpel, and a dagger.
Body Armor: None
Bionics & Cybernetics: None
Money: Has 45,000 in gold and gems hoarded away, along with a silver cross, wood dagger, squirt gun, a magic amulet (charm: +1 save vs magic & psionics), and a couple scrolls: fire ball and eyes of the wolf (both 5th level).
R.C.C. Skills: These are instinctive abilities that do increase with experience. Like a chimpanzee, the D-Bee animal can learn certain basic routines, skills, and even to understand and speak a few languages. <u>Equivalent Skills</u>: Wilderness survival (+10%), land navigation (+20%), native language is a guttural version of Gobblely 89%, three W.P.s of choice (excluding rifles, heavy weapons, spears, staves and polearms, all are too big). Can also select two Rifts languages (+5%), and three other skills from the categories of domestic, wilderness, Pilot (limited to motorcycle, horsemanship and sailboat), rogue (any +5%, except computer hacking), and W.P. (any but the previously noted exceptions). One additional skill can be selected at levels three, seven, and eleven.
Description: All Krpts are ugly, little critters that stand two and a half to three feet tall. They are slightly hunchbacked, with a prominent bony spine running down the back. The arms are long and rimmed with a leathery membrane that's similar to a bat's wing. Krpts tend to walk and run hunched over, on all fours. The head is long, ending in a hard, beak-like mouth lined with tiny, pointy teeth. The ears are large and floppy.

Krpts are vicious little monsters that love to cause trouble through lies, instigation of evil acts by others, and cruelty. Their numbers are presumably few and are seldom seen in groups larger than three. The creatures seem to prefer the company of larger, supernatural creatures and practitioners of magic, particularly those of evil inclination. Thus, they are often the willing familiars of evil wizards or assistants to intelligent monsters. Even in the wild, a Krpt will rarely associate with his own kind, instead sharing a lair with a bear or lion or other large animal.

Bonecruncher
Freak Strongman & Dragon Slayer

Horror Factor: 12
Alignment: Anarchist
Hit Points: Not applicable, see M.D.C.
M.D.C.: 1D4×100; Bonecruncher has 400 M.D.C.
Weight: 1D6×1000 lbs, Bonecruncher is 3000 lbs.
Height: The average Pogtal giant is 3D6+10 feet, Bonecruncher is 21 feet tall (6.4 m).
Age: Bonecruncher is 61, but the average life span is 300 years.
P.P.E.: 2D6×10, Bonecruncher has 80 P.P.E., **I.S.P.:** None
Bonecruncher's Attributes: I.Q.: 14, M.E.: 15, M.A.: 9, P.S.: 40, P.P.: 21, P.E.: 27, P.B. 6, Spd. 16.
Player Character Attributes: I.Q.: 3D6+1, M.E.: 4D6, M.A.: 3D6, P.S.: 5D6+10, P.P.: 4D6+2, P.E.: 4D6+6, P.B. 1D6+1, Spd. 4D6.
Species: Pogtal, a race of D-Bee giants, also known as the "Dragon Slayers." In this particular case, Mad Melody's opened a rift and summoned him, but other Dragon Slayers are known to exist in the Magic Zone, eastern North America and Atlantis.
Disposition: Merciless and fearless in combat. Tough, aggressive, bully, likes to roughhouse. Hates humans and most of the handsomer races because they fear him. Treats humans and their kin with disdain.
Experience Level: 8th level Dragon Slayer! Same experience point table as Dragons.

Magic Knowledge: Knowledge is limited to lore, but the Pogtal do possess some innate magic powers. Invisibility (equal to superior, but can only turn self invisible), see the invisible, energy bolt (S.D.C. damage; energy bolts can be fired from fingertips), and negate magic (same as spell).

Energy Aura (special): The Pogtal generate an invisible energy field that helps to protect them in combat. The creation of the field automatically engages, instantly, like an adrenaline rush, when the giant is frightened, angry, excited, or exerting himself/combat. The invisible aura of energy adds 100 M.D.C. (subtract damage from this energy aura first) and covers everything the giant is wearing or holding. Depleted M.D.C. from the aura is restored within 24 hours.

The additional effect of the mega-damage aura is that the energy field turns ordinary, hand-held, S.D.C. weapons/items into M.D.C. extensions of the Pogtal! Thus, a strike from an S.D.C. giant sword, club, dagger, or uprooted tree inflicts the 4D6 M.D. of a full strength punch from the giant. Damage from energy weapons and vibro-blades is not increased. The damage from magic weapons is the higher amount of damage; i.e., a magic weapon that inflicts 2D6 M.D. will inflict the 4D6 M.D. of the punch, while a magic weapon that inflicts 6D6 M.D. will inflict 6D6 M.D. because it is higher than the normal full strength punch. **Note:** The extra 100 M.D.C. may be used up and can not be regenerated for 24 hours. However, the field still turns S.D.C. wepons/objects into items that inflict the M.D.C. nature of hand-held weapons. In such a case, mega-damage. The S.D.C. items are not damaged by the M.D. impact of the attack, but only have an equivalent of 4 M.D.C. and can be blasted into bits if 5 or more M.D.C. is inflicted in any one attack. Of course, another item can be grabbed and used as a replacement weapon (or an M.D.C. weapon may be used in the first place). Note that the S.D.C. object only has M.D.C. when held by the Dragon Slayer. As soon as it is dropped or put aside it is instantly an S.D.C. item.

Natural Abilities: Impervious to magic fire (dragon fire)! High resistance to magic, natural M.D.C. skin/body, inflicts M.D.C. damage from punches, bites and other attacks. The giants are also impervious to normal fire, cold, and S.D.C. weapons. Special bio-regeneration can be used to instantly restore 1D6×10 M.D.C. three times per day (24 hours). Bonuses: +3 to save vs magic, +3 to save vs psionic attack, +5 to save vs horror factor; supersensitive hearing is equal to the cybernetic amplified hearing and adds the bonuses of +1 to parry, +2 to dodge, and +3 on initiative. Great strength and agility provides one additional attack or action per melee.

The mouth is lined with two rows of large teeth; if a tooth is lost, a new one will grow to replace it in a matter of two weeks. The muscles and bone structure of the jaw enables the giants to unhinge the jaw (similar to many snakes) so that they can take massive bites and swallow large chunks of food. This also prevents the jaw from being broken. Dragons and dinosaurs are these giants' principal prey; consequently, the teeth are so sharp and hard (2 M.D.C. each), and the jaw so powerful, that the Pogtal warrior can bite through dragon flesh and crack dragon bones (dragon bone marrow is a favorite). Mouth can be opened large enough to inflict about a four feet by about four feet (1.2 m) bite. The giants been known to bite off the entire hand of power armor and bots in a single bite.

Psionic Powers: None
Combat Skills: Martial Arts: Paired weapons, entangle, leap attack (critical), jump kick (critical), kick attack, critical strike on the roll of a natural 18, 19, or 20.
Attacks per Melee: Four (4)
Mega-Damage:
    Bite — 6D6 M.D.
    Restrained Punch — 1D6×10 S.D.C. + P.S. bonus (25)
    Full Strength Punch — 4D6 M.D.
    Karate Style Kick — 5D6 M.D.
    Leap Kick — 1D6×10 M.D., but counts as two attacks.

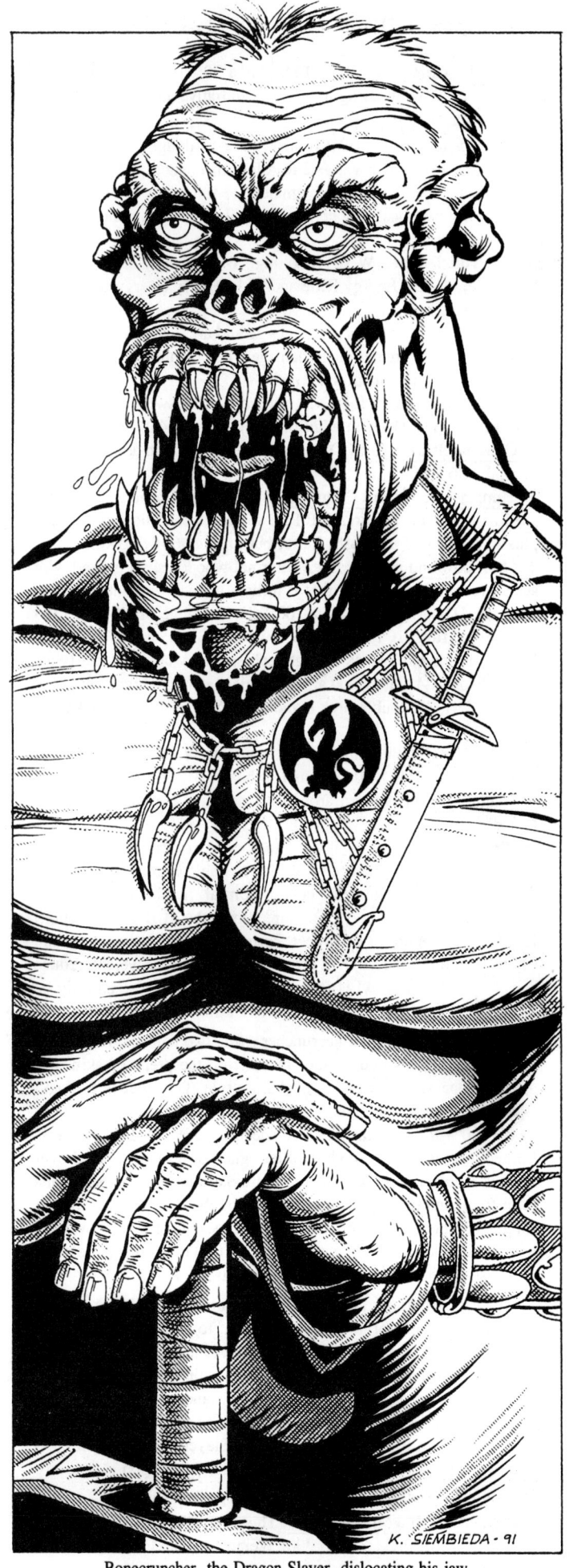

Bonecruncher, the Dragon Slayer, dislocating his jaw.

Body throw — 2D6 M.D. plus victim loses initiative and one attack that melee.

Body Block/Ram — 2D6 M.D. plus a 70% chance of knocking an opponent down causing him to lose initiative and one attack that melee. Counts as two attacks.

Bonuses: +5 to strike, +7 to parry, +7 to dodge, +25 S.D.C. damage, +3 on initiative, +2 to roll with impact, +5 to save vs horror factor (+7 with magic amulet), +9 to save vs magic, +3 to save vs psionics, impervious to poison, drugs, and S.D.C. weapons/damage.

Weapon Proficiencies: W.P. Targeting, W.P. Knife, W.P. Sword, W.P. Blunt, W.P. Energy Rifle and W.P. Heavy Energy are known by Bonecruncher.

Weapons: All hand weapons are giant size and are made out of M.D.C. alloys and inflict greater mega-damage when combined with Bonecruncher's own supernatural strength.

1. His favorite is a 15 foot (4.6 m) two handed sword, 50 M.D.C, that inflicts 2D6 M.D. in addition to his normal 4D6 M.D.

2. Giant battle axe: 30 M.D.C, inflicts 1D6 M.D. in addition to his normal 4D6 M.D.

3. Human size bastard "flaming" sword (hangs around his neck) used as a dagger, requires 7 P.P.E. to activate, inflicts 4D6 M.D. plus 4D6 M.D. if used as a knife, but only 4D6 if thrown.

4. Short bow and arrows. Even a normal wooden shaft is fired with such strength and velocity that it inflicts a small amount of mega-damage: 1D4 M.D. or 1D4×100 S.D.C.; range: 1000 feet (305 m), rate of fire: six (6) and +4 to strike. Giant arrows can allow for double the explosives of high-tech specialty arrows (cost twice as much too). 24 giant wood arrows, 6 giant standard high explosives (3D6 M.D.), 12 double high explosives (6D6 M.D.), 6 smoke (40 ft cloud).

5. NG-202 Rail Gun with a case of ammunition. Range: 4000 feet, mega-damage: 1D4×10 per burst, 8 bursts per 300 round belt.

6. Magic Amulet is worn around his neck; +2 to save vs horror factor.

Body Armor: May vary from none to special construction full plate armor (looks like a giant robot vehicle). The cost for giant size (13 to 16 feet) is three times the cost of normal, human size armor, is three times as heavy, and offers three times the M.D.C. protection. Really giant armor, 17 to 28 feet, costs 8 times the normal cost and offers eight times the M.D.C. protection (10 times the weight; reduce speed by 1/3 and prowl is impossible). Special armor can only be built at facilities that manufacture body armor or giant robots.

Dragon skin armor. Bonecruncher owns two suits of the Dragon Slayers' traditional body armor made from the prepared skin of a dragon. One set of armor is gladiator style, the other is a cloak. Both have 260 M.D.C. (seen some wear). Weight: 1100 lbs. Penalties: −30% to prowl and reduce speed by 20%. Market value is limited; useful only to another 20 foot giant or possibly draped over a giant robot or to be cut down and remade into human size suits (a difficult and time consuming task), thus there is not a big market for giant dragon skin armor, especially in the south or west. However, in the east, one suit might get as much as 300,000 credits (wholesale purchase price, resale is 600,000+ credits).

Dragon skin armor can be made in a variety of styles, including the common gladiator and crusader styles, to robe or long cloak or a set of baggy clothes (pants, shirt/coat/tunic). The dragon skin armor is a surprisingly heavy M.D.C. fabric that looks like a bulky, four inch thick, padded leather with thousands of tiny scales. As one might expect, dragon's view the armor as abhorrent as do many other intelligent life forms. The Dragon Slayers wear the armor as a badge of honor and skill, because traditional dragon skin armor is made by the wearer from a dragon slain by his hands.

Human size dragon skin armor: This is not the ideal body armor for humans. M.D.C.: 250 to 300. Weight: About 110 lbs, more if taller than 6 ft (add 1.3 pounds/.52 kg for every additional inch up to 7 feet). Restrictions: Requires a minimum P.E. of 20 and P.S. 20 to wear and be maneuverable (anything less, reduce number of attacks, speed and combat bonuses by *half* and use fatigue/encumbrance rules: cannot be worn for extended periods of time). Not recommended for characters with less than a P.E. and P.S. of 24 (or higher), but even they suffer the following penalties: −40% to prowl, −1 to strike, parry and dodge, reduce speed by half. Penalties apply unless either the P.S. or P.E. is 30 or higher and the other is not less than 26, then same penalties as the giant's: −30% prowl, reduce speed by 20%. Robot Note: The armor is really not suitable as additional protection for robots. Draping a giant bot in the armor requires special modifications/alterations of the armor's design and may still block and prevent use of robot weapons, jets, and sensors. Covering cooling vents, exhausts, or jets may cause overheating, too. Also adds to clumsy and awkwardness factor; usual penalties apply plus −1 to parry and dodge. The cost is also prohibitive; it's cheaper and more efficient to get conventional armor.

Bionics & Cybernetics: None, although Dragon Slayers are not opposed to mechanical augmentation. The giant size increases the cost proportionately.

Money/valuables: Has 145,000 in gold and gems hoarded away, along with a silver, gem encrusted cross (worth 50,000 credits), a giant wood cross, about a dozen different human size swords and daggers kept as souvenirs, 20 dragon's teeth, a horned dragon skull, a human size flaming sword, two human size TK-gliders, a giant size squirt gun, and 48,000 in credits (prefers gold and precious gems).

R.C.C. Skills: These are learned skills. Note that while, theoretically, the Pogtal are intelligent enough to learn any skill, including the sciences, they are not oriented in that area. The Pogtal are warriors from a savage land and natural, instinctive, big game hunters.

R.C.C. Skills: Hunting, wilderness survival (+25%), land navigation (+20%), track animals (+20%, includes dragons and dinosaurs), skin and prepare animal hides (+20% large animals, +10% small), hand to hand martial arts, swimming (+10%), W.P. Targeting and W.P. Blunt and two ancient skills of choice. Speak Dragonese and Gobblely at 98%.

Other Skills: The Pogtal may select six other skills at first level and two other skills at levels three, six, nine, twelve and fifteen. Available skills are limited to Communications (radio: basic and scrambler only), Domestic (any, +10%), Espionage (tracking, sniper, intelligence only, +10%), Medical (first aid or holistic medicine only), Physical (any except acrobatics, +10% when applicable), Pilot (limited to horsemanship of giant animals, and boats), Science (math and astronomy only), Technical (languages, literacy and lore only), W.P. (any, lean toward ancient types), Wilderness (any, +10%).

Description: The Pogtal Dragon Slayers are a race of warrior giants and are creatures of magic. The Pogtalian's native world is a lush wilderness of tropical and subtropical forests broken only by the occasional desert and sea (no grasslands, many swamps and marshes). The dominant life form are dragons and dragon-like predators (the latter being more like the Great Wooly Dragon or dinosaurs than the more intelligent dragons). The Dragon Slayers have evolved to survive in this hostile land of giants by themselves becoming giants and developing resistance to magic as well as a variety of other features that enable them to combat their natural nemesis, the dragon. The giants' maws are designed for biting through the M.D.C. flesh of their prey, the stomach for digesting raw meat.

Over the eons, the giant humanoids have become the predators of the dragons and dinosaurs (and vice versa). Males and females alike are skilled hunters and wilderness scouts. The typical community is a small tribe of 20 to 100 members. Some are stationary communities while others are nomadic. The level of technology is low, with ancient style weapons and armor. Even when high tech energy weapons are made available the giants prefer the challenge of hand to hand combat. They pride themselves as dragon slayers and as the greatest warriors in the universe. This also means that they are generally arrogant, extremely aggressive, quick to fight, and merciless in combat. They eat the raw flesh, drink the blood, and eat the bones of their prey (most hate cooked meat). In the world of **Rifts,** they prey on dragons, dinosaurs, large mammals, and other giants. Although they are frequently called savage cannibals, they NEVER eat the flesh of their own kind, but have been known to eat other humanoids. With the exception of the occasional rogue, Dragon Slayers seldom terrorize unarmed humans or other tiny people. The giants are proud warriors and there is nothing to be proud about in the slaughter of unarmed opponents. As warriors, they do not look for treasure or a people to rule, but rather seek adventure and combat. They love to fight giant robots and find conflict with monsters and wizards a great challenge.

Bonecruncher is the stage name for the Dragon Slayer that works at the **Night Arcade & Freak Show**. He is a favorite attraction and his dislocating his massive maw to the four or five foot height, accompanied by a blood curdling roar, has been known to make women and children faint or run in terror. Bonecruncher's acts exhibit incredible feats of strength and combat skill. He will accept challenges of hand to hand combat from any member of the audience to fight him one on one, including giant robots and power armor (no long range weapons). Using mind control magic or psionics is forbidden and results in disqualification or worse (some sort of punishment). The prize for beating bonecruncher is 50,000 credits. In order to be eligible for the prize money, the combatant(s) must pay 50 credits. A combatant may wager any amount over 50 credits, as long as Bonecruncher or Mr. Morricco is willing to accept. Multiple combatants against Bonecruncher are permitted at the giant's discretion.

Bonecruncher is also active in the general security and defense of the travelling show.

The Mysterious Yucatan

A doorway to another dimension

Many people say that the Earth no longer belongs to humankind. That it has been completely transformed and now belongs to other, alien creatures. That the dominion of humankind is shrinking and falling into the hands of supernatural monsters. Few places on Earth exemplify this more than the Yucatan. The Yucatan Peninsula, home of the ancient Mayans, is no longer a part of the planet earth, at least not as we once understood the Earth.

Traveling to the Yucatan by air

Flying above, from the air, there is no Yucatan. The warm waters of the Mexican Gulf seem to have swallowed the tropical lowlands a hundred feet beneath the water, just as it has the Texas and Louisiana coastline. All that appears to remain is the southern portion of Mexico and Guatemala, the peninsula is gone. Even flying a foot above the waves shows no sign of land until the new coastline, which starts north at Ciudad del Carmen and runs southeast, touching the old pre-rift cities of Villahermosa, Flores, Poptun, and Puerto Barrios. Consequently, most eastern map makers, including Erin Tarn and the Coalition, do not show the Yucatan to exist! Most northern scholars dismiss the stories of the Yucatan Peninsula existing or co-existing in another dimension as folk tales. Remember, very few northern explorers have ever traveled as far south as the Yucatan and have returned to tell the tale.

Some scholars and ley line walkers have noted that a 250 mile ley line runs parallel to the new coast at what was (is) the base of the Yucatan Peninsula. The ancient Mayan ruins of **Palenque, Yaxchilan** (also near Bonlampak), **Seibal, Machaquila,** and **Pusilha** mark the straight line of the mystic energy stream. 20 miles north of the ley line is the new Yucatan coast. **Pusilha** is a ley line *nexus* that is linked with another major ley line that stretches 100 miles, starting south, at **Copan**, running north to Quirigua and to Pusilha, and another 400 miles northwest to Uxmal. The speculation is that the entire Yucatan Peninsula is a giant triangular ley line nexus with twenty multiple ley lines within its boundaries, making it a ley line nexus times twenty; a super nexus.

It is also interesting to note that the conflict that began the rifting of the ley lines was in Central America, perhaps somewhere near the Yucatan? Coincidence?

Without a doubt, the level of mystic energy permeating the land and the Palenque-Pusilha ley line nexus junctions plays a significant role in the Yucatan mystery. For you see, the Yucatan Peninsula still exists, only it exists in a different dimension. The dimensional anomaly is even stranger, because while the peninsula is not visible nor accessible from the air, it is both visible and easily accessible from the land. Landing on the apparent coast is easy for bots and power armor (the coast is jungle with no beaches or flat land for airplanes). A moment after landing, the ocean is gone, having been replaced by forest stretching three hundred miles to the north.

Taking to the air again, there is a shimmering of the sky and disorientation as the flyer is suddenly engulfed in clouds (a sudden storm?). The instrument panels go crazy and all sense of direction, even up and down, is lost. A lucky flyer will suddenly find himself over the Gulf of Mexico, the Yucatan once again buried underwater. An unlucky flyer may find himself trapped in the cloud covered limbo of a trans-dimensional vortex.

GM Note on surviving the trans-dimensional vortex: The vortex is the same type of phenomenenon reported countless times by aircraft and boaters in the pre-rifts Bermuda Triangle. Getting lost in the vortex can mean oblivion. Time and space are crushed and compressed, and released like a spring, thus what may seem like 15 minutes could be the passage of 15 years or 15 centuries. Every time a character exits the Yucatan Peninsula by air, at any point north beyond the Palenque-Pusilha ley line, he will be temporarily caught in the trans-dimensional vortex. Roll percentile dice four times. One must roll between 1 and 55% two out of the four times to escape the vortex. Two successful rolls means that he or she is suddenly back in the rifts world and at the correct moment in time.

A failed series of rolls means one of the following. Roll percentile.

1-25 Lost in a limbo-like dimension of endless clouds. After a while, the character lapses into a peaceful, trance-like sleep and flies through the limbo for all eternity. Or until some outside force yanks him into a different dimension or time. Rolling up new characters may be applicable.

26-50 Lost in the cloud limbo for what seems like days, but do not fall into the limbo state. After what seems like three or four days (vehicle never loses power nor consumes fuel) the character(s) begins to see blurred shapes and shadows among the clouds (astral travelers). He also hears voices occasionally calling to him, but can never seem to find the source.

Finally one clear voice is heard and leads him to a bright light, passing through the light the character finds himself out of limbo and back to real time. Unfortunately, it is another dimension. A shifter or Palladium summoner should be able to open a dimensional rift and return home (in fact, a shifter can return to his home dimension and correct time from the limbo or anywhere else, it's bringing his companions back with him that may be difficult). Rolling up new characters may be applicable. Or the GM can opt for a brief adventure in a different world (any of the other Palladium RPG settings are appropriate).

51-75 The limbo state lapses into the trance state, remembered as an experience like falling asleep for who knows how long. Suddenly, the characters are back in the real world, only 1D6×100 years in the future! Rolling up new characters may be applicable.

It is possible to go back to the past to the specific point that they disappeared in the vortex (not beyond), but requires the skills of a shifter and his home-sensing abilities, or a creature with similar dimension traveling skills (includes sensing the right period of time). Time travel is extremely difficult and using the vortex means that the characters can only travel the straight line back to when and where they first entered the vortex. Back to the right time, they must then exit the Yucatan vortex either astrally, with the help of the shifter, or roll again on this table. **Note:** Shifters will always sense the right direction out of a dimensional vortex, it is a simple dimensional corridor he has passed through many times. A shifter can also teleport himself and his companions back to the right dimension and time by opening, or using an already opened, dimensional rift to the Yucatan vortex. Of course, the shifter can return home by himself far more easily than dragging along companions.

76-00 The limbo state occurs, but a short time afterward the person(s) wakes in a panic state, frantic to get home. The psychic energy released by the panic propels him home, only it's 4D6 hours later and he is 6D6×10 miles off course (any direction the GM chooses).

Note: Characters lost in the limbo dimension can be rescued or intercepted by a shifter/summoner or supernatural being (while in the vortex they are at the mercy of outside forces that can manipulate dimensions). The trick to being deliberately rescued is finding them in limbo. A shifter or Palladium RPG summoner can sense limbo travelers (not including astral travelers) by opening a dimensional gate/portal and peering/sensing into it. The shifter can sense familiar auras, physical manifestations (an anomaly in this dimension), magic, and other aberrations not natural to that dimension; only astral and psionic emanations are natural. He can then draw the alien object to him, like a magnet attracts iron, until he can see it clearly and even summon it into his own dimension. Searching for specific people in the limbo is incredibly difficult; 3% chance of success per level of experience per every four hours of concentration. There is also the possibility of accidentally latching onto something undesirable/monstrous; GM's option.

Another way to get out of the limbo is to leave one's physical body and enter the astral plane. The limbo dimension functions on the astral plane, thus characters in their astral bodies will suddenly have a better sense of direction and should be able to find their way back to the right dimension the same way they would return from the astral plane (see psionic power of astral projection in **Rifts**, pages 119-121). Likewise, an astral traveler can enter the limbo plane and search for specific people in the dimension/vortex by concentrating on them. The odds of locating people by means of astral projection is far better than the shifter's; same procedure to locate somebody as it is to return to one's astral body. A series of lucky rolls could mean instant success. To bring the people back to their dimension is the same as rolling to return from the astral plane, with the astral traveler guiding the others (conscious or unconscious) home.

Traveling The Yucatan Peninsula By Land

Traveling the Yucatan Peninsula by land is strange only in that there is no apparent entry zone into the dimension that contains the missing Peninsula. One simply walks across an invisible dimensional border. There is no sign, no shimmering wall of light or strange cloud, only rain forest, and lots of it. Exactly when and how one enters the dimension is unknown. Apparently, the entire length of the Palenque-Pusilha ley line is a giant dimensional doorway. Those who know of such things speculate that the physical and ley line connection to the land holds the Peninsula to the dimension of earth, from which it originated. Had it been an island, the Yucatan might have been swallowed by an alien dimension. Travelers can cross back and forth from the Earth Mexico and Guatemala to the Yucatan dimension without the slightest sensation. Except for the supernatural creatures and occasional alien foliage, one would never know that he is not still on Earth.

Air travel is dangerous in that it could fling the traveler out of the Yucatan dimension and into the limbo void and, if lucky, back to Earth, where the Yucatan does not exist (Must fly to the coast and land to get back to the Yucatan. The experience can be extremely disorienting if one does not understand dimensional travel.) Flying at speeds faster than 300 miles (482 km) an hour and/or an altitude of higher than 600 feet (183 m) above the floor of the Yucatan will throw the traveler into the limbo dimension previously described.

Speed and Visibility

Staying on the ground or travelling at tree-top level is the safest way to avoid dimensional sling-shotting. However, travel is not easy or safe. The rain forest is incredibly hot (90 to 120 degrees Fahrenheit), humid (80%+), and the jungle is so thick that travel by foot reduces the character's speed by half (and even that is a quick and potentially reckless pace). Creatures like borgs, bots, juicers and others with unnatural or enhanced speed will find that even traveling at half speed is hazardous. **Any speed above 12** (8 miles per hour) means that the character is traveling too fast to notice everything around him or even in front of him. This means he could run into an ambush, fall into a pit, step into a swamp or quicksand, startle a dangerous creature (in the trees or hidden in the thick underbrush), or step into a hostile village just beyond some trees.

Visibility is limited to about 200 feet (61 m) and even within that limited area there are a score of places where human size and smaller creatures can hide, that's how dense and cluttered with leaf and vine the rain forest is. A hasty pace opens one to potential danger because he can not examine his surroundings properly and is making so much noise rushing thorough the underbrush that it will alert predators and enemies to his presence and to his direction of travel. Such are the perils of the rain forest.

Eighty percent of the Yucatan Peninsula is rain forest. The northern tip of the peninsula is tropical savanna and light forest. The tropical savanna of the Yucatan is composed of tall grass, shrubs, thorny plants and vines, broken by occasional trees or patches of light forest. The humidity is considerably less here too, especially during the winter dry season. The old city of **Merida** was located in this area and the famous Maya ruins of Uxmal lay just south of the grassland, nestled in the northern edge of the forest. Along the northwest coast, between the ruined pre-rifts cities of Campeche and Progreso, is a strip of marshlands surrounded by the tall grass and vines of the savanna. A similar swampland is found on the northeast side of the Peninsula between Felipe Carrillo Puerto and Chetumal, but is surrounded by rain forest.

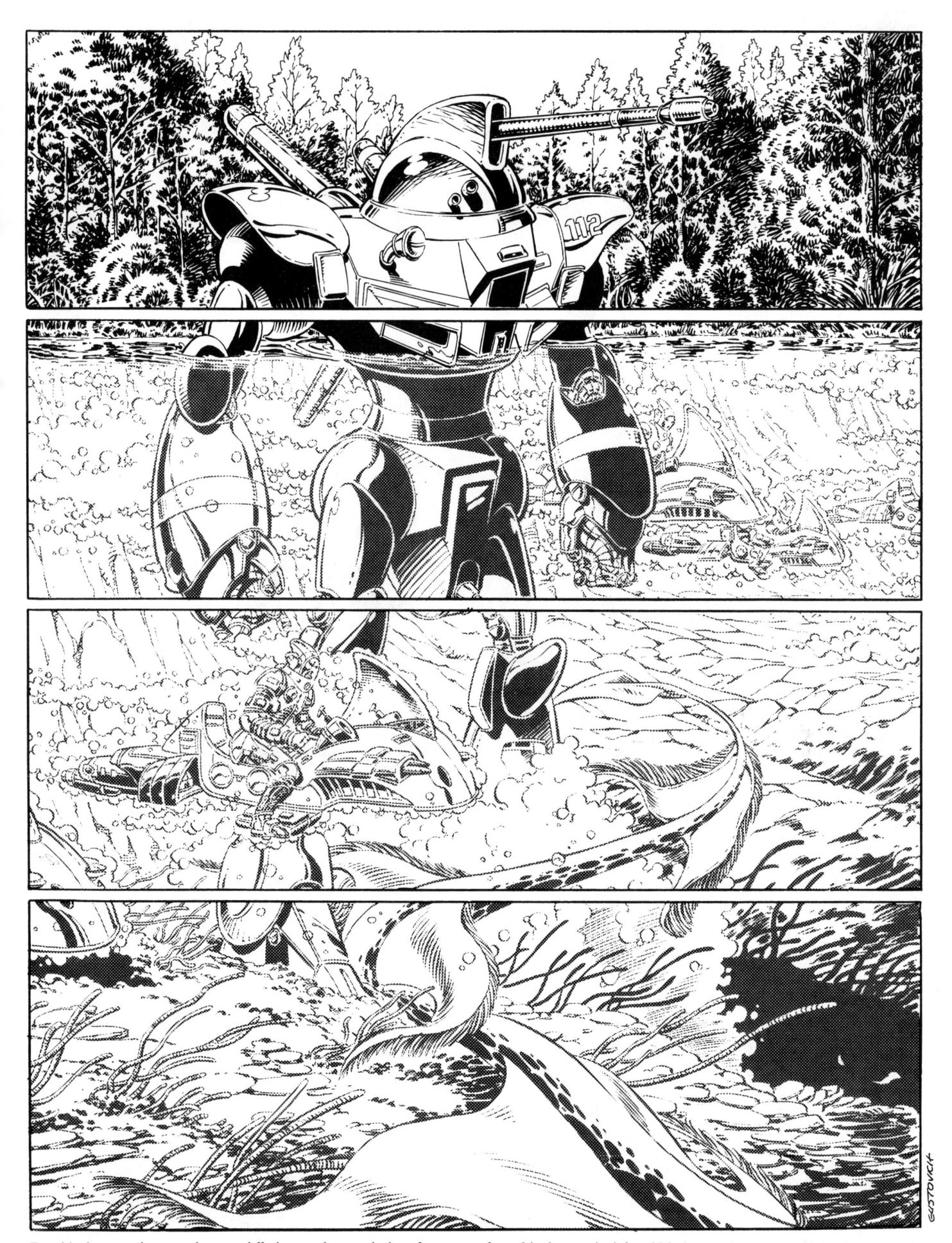

Travel by boats on the water, but especially in or underwater is the safest means of travel in the vampire infested Mexico and Central America.

Of course, there are other menaces like the Agenor River Serpent.

Travel by Water

One of the preferred methods of travel in the Yucatan, Central America and Mexico is on, in, or along the water by following the rivers, lakes and waterways and land, hopping from one body of water to another. Water travel makes one far less vulnerable to vampire attack. However, there are two disadvantages. One, the path of a river is seldom the most direct route from one place to another, although many tiny humanoid communities can be found near the waterways. Second, other predatory monsters and demons not vulnerable to water have learned to stalk these areas, for the prey is plentiful.

Leaving the Yucatan Peninsula by boat is the same as flying out. About two miles (3.2 km) from the coast the watercraft is engulfed in a strange fog that turns into the cloud limbo. Getting out of the limbo is the same as with aircraft. However, sailing along the coast is just like walking through the forest, except once the dimensional border is penetrated (near Ciudad del Carmen) the Yucatan Peninsula is suddenly gone. Sailing back the way you came offers only miles of water (a one-way dimensional door by sea, leading back to Earth or to limbo). Plunging into the limbo dimension only happens when sailing away from the *peninsula*, not sailing from the Earth dimension of Mexico or southern Guatemala toward where the Yucatan should be. One can take a boat through where the Yucatan should be, in from the Gulf sea, without incident. Since flying and sailing, starting from the peninsula and moving away from it, sends people into limbo, experts suspect that the peninsula may it self co-exist in the limbo dimension, or, more likely, exists in a pocket dimension (the pocket contains only the Yucatan Peninsula) accessible from Earth and through the limbo dimension.

Yucatan Notes & Features

1. Land area: 202,000 square miles (approx. 335,000 km), including most of Guatemala, Belize, and portions of Honduras and El Salvador.
2. The rainy season starts in May and lasts through September. The rains are generally quite heavy, occurring 1D4 times a week, almost always in the afternoons (**seldom at night**), and last 2D6 × 10 minutes. Sometimes a light drizzle, lasting 1D4 + 1 hours, will occur rather than a heavy rain. It is also extremely hot during this period.
3. From September through November, storms in the Caribbean are common and bring intermittent rain and drizzle during the day and part of the night (about once a week).
4. Dry winter from December through March; cool weather (low 70's and 80's, cooler in the mornings, no rain).
5. The pre-rifts city of **Merida**, once the capital of the State of Yucatan, is a monster haunted ruin. Highway 180 is cracked and much of it is rubble, but it still leads from Merida to the Mayan & Toltec ruins of **Chichen Itza**, one of the most powerful ley lines in the Yucatan.
6. Highway 180: Chichen Itza is approximately 75 miles (120 km) east-southeast of Merida. Highway 180 also continues to the Caribbean side of the Peninsula and to the pre-rifts locations of such cities as Cancun and Puerto Juarez, Puerto Morelos, Playa del Carmen, and the Maya ruins of Tulum (and near Coba).
7. Edible animals include deer, wild boar, caoti, paca, rabbit, opossum, armadillo, monkey, lizard, snake, turtle, pheasant, wild turkey, wild chickens (from the once domesticated bird), quail, partridge, and varieties of pigeons and parrots.
8. The ratio of humanoid habitation is one per every 50 miles. Of course, a person may travel hundreds of square miles without encountering a soul, and most humans and D-Bees are found in clusters of nomadic tribes or little villages. Most humanoid communities are found in or around water; rivers, lakes, streams, cenotes, the gulf coast. There are no humanoid cities or large towns in the trans-dimensional Yucatan. A typical community will have 4D6 × 10 members.
9. Vampires are found in the Yucatan Peninsula dimension, especially during the winter dry season (December - March) and, to a lesser degree, the mostly rain free summer nights (April - August). At least four vampire intelligences live in the Yucatan. Some scholars believe they too, may be responsible for the trans-dimensional aspect of the Peninsula.
10. Supernatural and alien monsters abound in the Yucatan. Most notably, these include the vampires, death weavers, dybbuk (a vampire-like demon), boschala, malignous, adram, dragon, the worms of Taut, and a variety of serpents, lizard and snake people, and alleged deities. **GM Note:** Monsters not found in this book are found in *Beyond the Supernatural* and *Palladium's Monsters and Animals*, all of which are given specific **Rifts** stats in the **Rifts Conversion Book**.
11. The ancient Toltec ruins of **Tikal** and much of the old province state of Peten (what was once northern Guatemala) is a transformed nightmare realm known as Xibalba, "Region of Phantoms." The dreaded place dominates the center of the Yucatan rain forest.
12. Over 3000 Maya, Toltec or other ancient ruins exist in the entire Yucatan Peninsula, including Guatemala and Belize. 90% mark a ley line or nexus.

A brief pronunciation key to Mayan words.

"a" sounds like the a in far.
"e" sounds like the e in prey.
"i" sounds like the double (long) ee sound, like see or eel.
"o" sounds like the o in obey.
"u" sounds like the double o in zoo or toon.
"Ua" has a "wah" sound, like the a in water.
"c" has a hard "k" sound, like cat.
"x" has a "sh" sound, like shoe or shout.

Example: Tikal (Tee-kal), Uaxactun (Wa-shak-toon) and Xultun (Shul-toon; the "X" is always pronounced with an "sh").

Yucatan Overview

Palenque
Home of the Jaguar People

Palenque is the ruins of a rather expansive, ancient Mayan city and a ley line nexus. It is located not far from the pre-rifts city ruins of Villahermosa, about 70 miles (112 km) northwest of Palenque. The city has a long history of being a place for ghosts and monsters, but in the last hundred years it has become the home for a tribe of jaguar people (werebeast). An estimated hundred Jaguar people inhabit the ruins. As animal-like predators, they have little need for a formal society or fancy dwellings. Consequently, the smaller family groups are scattered throughout the vine and tree covered ruins, living in various parts of the buildings as they would a cave or den. They are surprisingly gentle, tolerant and compassionate with each other. The tribe works well together and are very protective of each other and the humans who worship them. They feed primarily on animals and the occasional humanoids killed in battle (they always devour those they kill). They also love to hunt and destroy vampires, which consumes most of their nighttime leisure activity.

A hunting tribe of about 180 indians lives among the Palenque ruins and worships the supernatural Jaguar People as holy forest spirits (and friends). The tribe calls itself the "Children of the Jaguar," and they paint their faces with white fangs, whiskers, and cat eyes. They think nothing of co-mingling with the werebeasts and the two tribes help

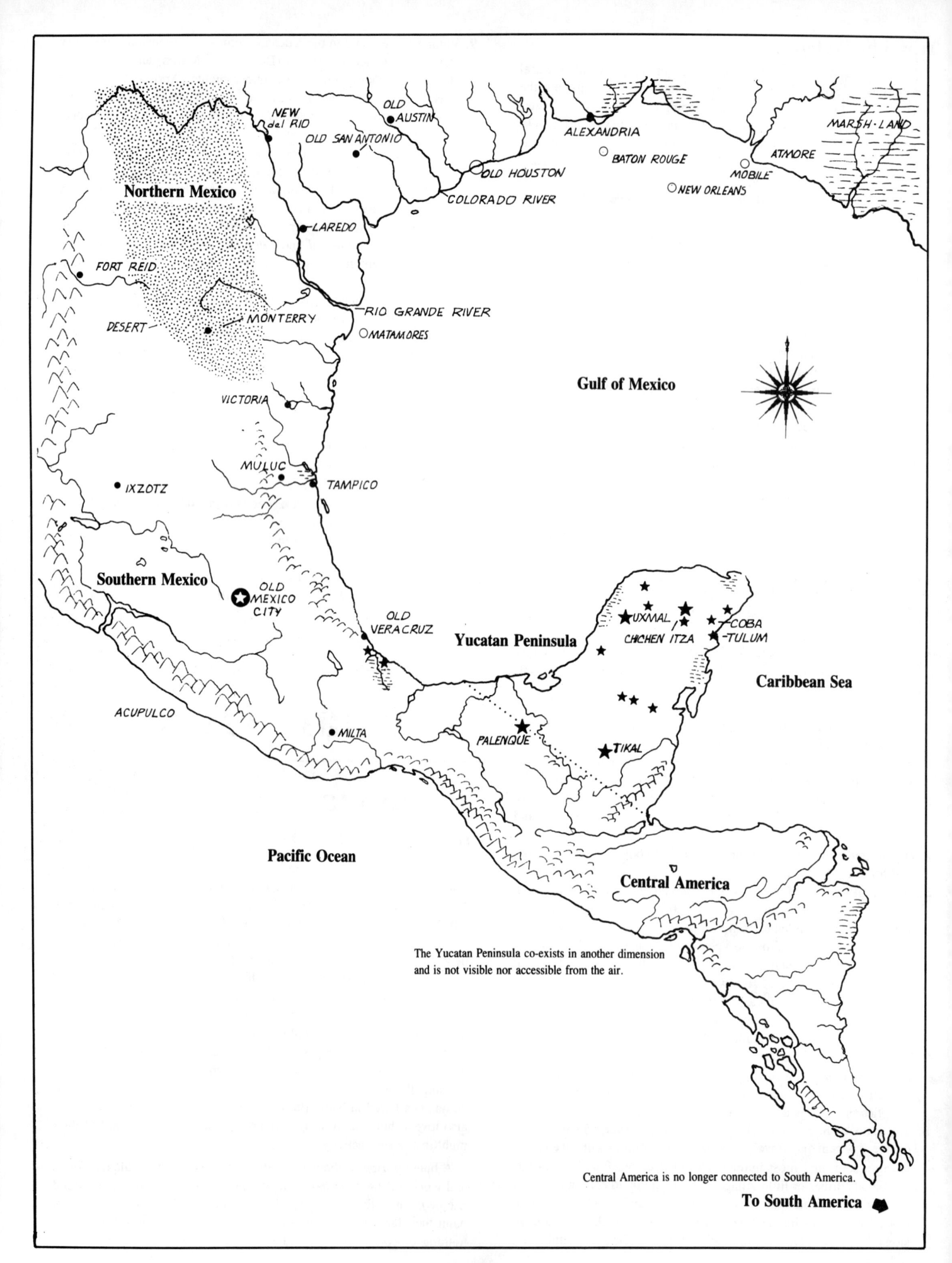

Northern Mexico

- NEW del RIO
- OLD AUSTIN
- OLD SAN ANTONIO
- ALEXANDRIA
- BATON ROUGE
- OLD HOUSTON
- ATMORE
- MOBILE
- NEW ORLEANS
- MARSH·LAND
- COLORADO RIVER
- FORT REID
- LAREDO
- DESERT
- MONTERREY
- RIO GRANDE RIVER
- MATAMORES
- VICTORIA

Gulf of Mexico

- MULUC
- TAMPICO
- IXZOTZ

Southern Mexico

- OLD MEXICO CITY
- OLD VERACRUZ

Yucatan Peninsula

- ★ UXMAL
- ★ CHICHEN ITZA
- ★ COBA
- ★ TULUM

Caribbean Sea

- ACUPULCO
- MILTA
- ★ PALENQUE
- ★ TIKAL

Pacific Ocean

Central America

The Yucatan Peninsula co-exists in another dimension and is not visible nor accessible from the air.

Central America is no longer connected to South America.

To South America ➤

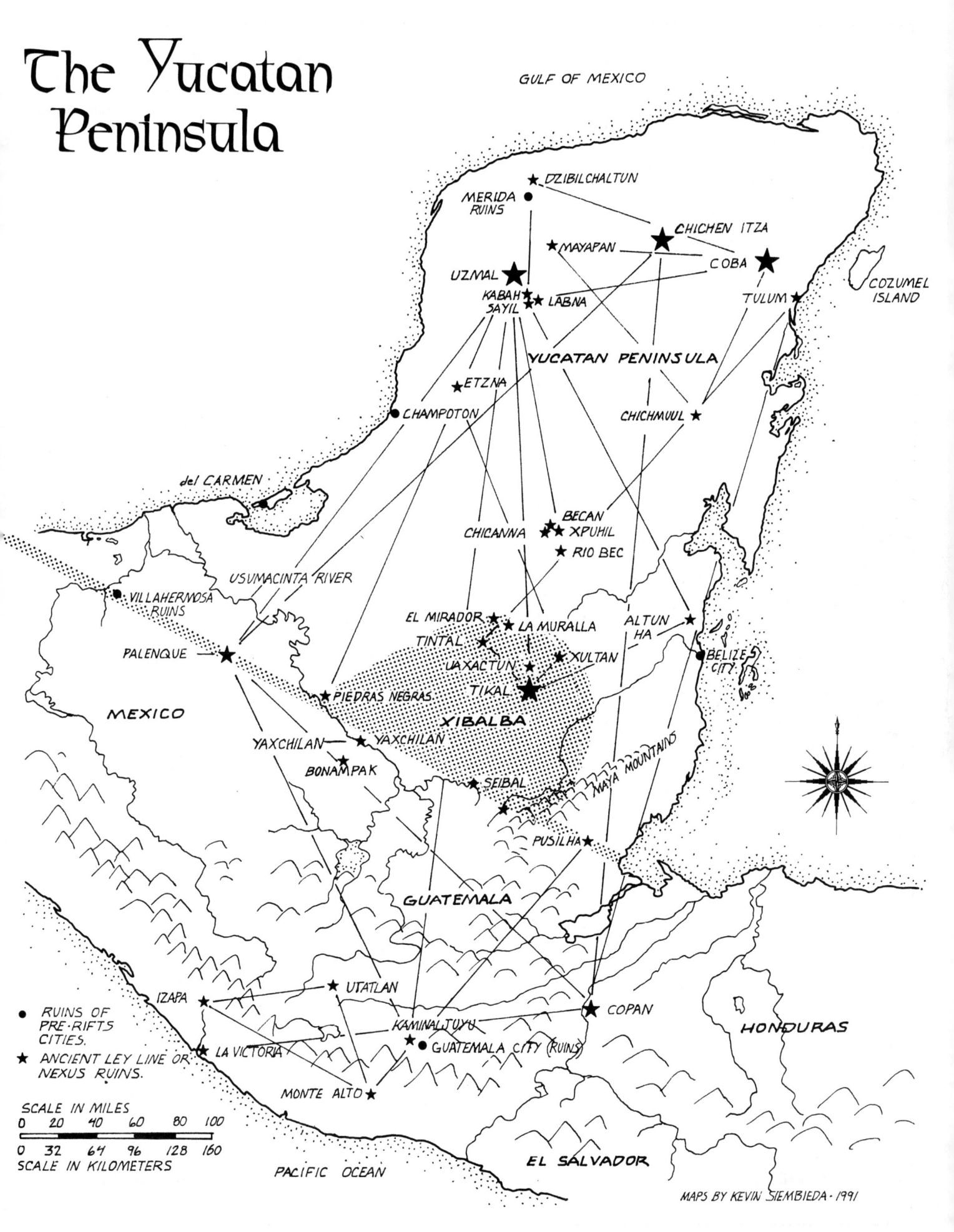

The Yucatan Peninsula

GULF OF MEXICO

★ DZIBILCHALTUN
● MERIDA RUINS
★ MAYAPAN
★ CHICHEN ITZA
★ UZMAL
★ COBA
★ KABAH ★ LABNA
SAYIL
★ TULUM
COZUMEL ISLAND
YUCATAN PENINSULA
★ ETZNA
● CHAMPOTON
★ CHICHMUUL
del CARMEN
★ BECAN
CHICANNA ★ ★ XPUHIL
★ RIO BEC
USUMACINTA RIVER
● VILLAHERMOSA RUINS
★ EL MIRADOR ★ LA MURALLA
★ ALTUN HA
TINTAL
★ PALENQUE
★ UAXACTUN ★ XULTAN
● BELIZE CITY
★ PIEDRAS NEGRAS
★ TIKAL
MEXICO
XIBALBA
YAXCHILAN — ★ YAXCHILAN
★ BONAMPAK
★ SEIBAL
MAYA MOUNTAINS
★ PUSILHA
GUATEMALA
★ IZAPA
★ UTATLAN
★ COPAN
HONDURAS
★ KAMINALJUYU
★ LA VICTORIA
● GUATEMALA CITY (RUINS)
★ MONTE ALTO

● RUINS OF PRE-RIFTS CITIES.
★ ANCIENT LEY LINE OR NEXUS RUINS.

SCALE IN MILES
0 20 40 60 80 100

0 32 64 96 128 160
SCALE IN KILOMETERS

PACIFIC OCEAN

EL SALVADOR

MAPS BY KEVIN SIEMBIEDA · 1991

159

each other in their work, hunting, defending the village, and tending the sick and injured. The humans will fight to the death to protect their village and the Jaguar People. The werejaguars feel the same and both have fought their share of invaders, human, demonic and vampire, who have tried to capture the Palenque ruin and ley line nexus for themselves.

A dozen other small tribes of about 30 to 80 humans and D-Bees exist in a 50 mile radius around Palenque. They worship the Jaguar People as forest gods, but they are terrified of the werebeasts and of the tribe of men that walks among the gods. In times of trouble, these other tribes will flee, unless forced to fight by the Jaguar People.

A handful of lone hunters and small family groups of werejaguars (and the occasional werewolf) prowl the forests of southern Mexico, parts of northern Mexico, the Yucatan, and parts of South America.

Yaxchilan

Nestled on the tall hills along the western shores of a horseshoe bend in the great river *Usumacinta* are the ruins of the Mayan city of Yaxchilan. The ruins are 100 miles (160 km) southeast of Palenque, on the border of what was once southern Guatemala. It is also located near the giant ley line that runs across the base of the Yucatan Peninsula, which places it just outside the border of *Xibalba, the Region of Phantoms.*

For 80 years the ruins were populated by a prosperous rural community of humans and D-Bees. Encircled by the waters of the Usumacinta, they were safe from vampires and many other potential enemies, but a devastating disaster of some sort killed them all. Most suspect the demons of Xibalba, just across the river, others blame a legion of vampires, but nobody knows. Since then, about 40 years ago, Yaxchilan has been deserted. The occasional sorcerer may visit from time to time, when the ley line energies swell, and travelers often stop for a night or two, seeking shelter under its crumbling roofs, but few live there.

The only regular inhabitants are a family of five Jaguar People (all of anarchist alignment), and 8 Ti-Xibalban Mirror People (5 are dopplegangers of 3rd level native hunters and three are peasant women, 3rd level vagabonds; all are miscreant demons of Xibalba sent to lure strangers into their domain), but no others. Mercenaries, demons and monsters from Xibalba (frequently allies of **Hun-Came**, ruler of the demon city of Xultun) often camp at the ruins for 1D6 days on their journeys to and from the Region of Phantoms. They and the Ti-Xibalban Mirror People sometimes set traps for unsuspecting hunters and travelers to capture as slaves, or lure victims into Xibalba for the amusement of their demon lords.

Ten miles southwest of Yaxchilan is **Bonampak**. Both Bonampak and Yaxchilan rest on a 300 mile long ley line that connects with *Chichen Itza* in the northern lowlands of the Yucatan. They are occasionally visited by tribal shaman and supernatural creatures, but are otherwise uninhabited.

Across the Usumacinta River is Xibalba, The Region of Phantoms, once part of northern Guatemala, now a place of horror. The river itself continues to snake southeast into the dense and mostly unpopulated rain forest of northern Guatemala. A tributary branches northeast and will carry travelers to the Maya ruins of **Seibal**, still along the southern border of Xibalba. The city of Seibal boasts of a great temple dedicated to a Mayan king. On top of the temple is what was a symbolic gateway to the underworld, how ironic that it faces toward Xibalba.

The Region of Phantoms

Xibalba (pronounced Shee-bal-ba) means "Region of Phantoms" and it was the Quiche Maya term for the underworld or hell. In ancient, pre-rifts times, the derivative word was *Chi-Xibalba,* which meant the devil/demon, or the dead, or vision/phantom. The word *xibil* meant "to disappear like a phantom." The Maya performed a dance called *Xibalba ocot*, meaning "dance of the demon." The Quiche Maya indians believed that **Xibalba** was an underground region "inhabited by the enemies of man." The religious myth may have been based on some fact. Xibalba was not a netherworld hell, but another dimension, perhaps accessible through an opening in the Mayan Mountains as believed by the Mayans (a natural, periodically opening rift), and demons (xibil) may have been summoned by means of mystic ritual and the "dance of the demon." A temple at the ruins of **Copan** was said to be a portal to Xibalba; perhaps it was.

The Maya priest of old perceived Xibalba as an invisible, pervasive, ambient presence. A parallel world that could be seen during a trance. The coming of the rifts and the multi-dimensional aspect of the transformed Yucatan has apparently made this fabled place of evil more than an ambient presence, it is here. A dimensional melding of the Xibalba dimension that has transported a small portion of that dimension into the Guatemalan jungles of the Yucatan Peninsula, (**Note:** This also makes teleportation into the full dimension of Xibalba very easy from any nexus point within that part of the Yucatan jungles.)

The Xibalbans (Shee-bal-bans) have claimed and rebuilt the Mayan ruins of **Tikal** (Tee-kal), **Uaxactun** (Wa-shak-toon) and **Xultun** (Shultoon). Each is a major, hellish city ruled by a demonic lord. Tikal is the largest and is ruled by **Cuchumaquiq** (Kook-hoo-ma-qook), Lord of Xibalba and Lord of Darkness and Death. **Vukub-Came**, "The Phantom," rules Uaxactun and **Hun-Came** (Hoon-kam-eh), "One Death," rules Xultun. The Lord of Darkness rules all of Xibalba, with his two lieutenants assisting him. The three demonic rulers and their Xibalban subjects are all supernatural creatures that take delight in testing, challenging, teasing, tricking and tormenting humans. Xibalba is also a land that welcomes and protects vampires, entities, and other "enemies of man" (all intelligent humanoid life forms). Fortunately for humans, none of the Xibalbans can travel beyond their boundary of their dimension, thus they can never leave the kingdom of Xibalba. Only the Demon Lord and a handful of his minion can venture beyond their kingdom, often in a diminished, spectral form.

The Kingdom of Xibalba is especially dangerous to humans because it appears to be a safe, impressive, and thriving community of fellow humans. Many travelers, human and D-Bee, have blissfully wandered into the demons' cities to meet a terrible fate at inhuman hands. The inhabitants of the Xibalba region are mostly evil and predominately supernatural. Although not all who live in Xibalba are demons, only creatures of evil are permitted to live among them. A handful of human and D-Bee tribes and wilderness scouts live in the alien domain, but they are suspicious of all strangers and avoid encounters with everybody.

Most Xibalbans and their demon lords, are masters of deceit and treachery, thus they do not necessarily pounce on travelers nor torture and kill everyone they encounter. Instead they try to befriend travelers, weaving convincing yarns about their own travels, village, fears and desires. They may play the helpless jungle peasant whose village or livelihood is threatened by a monster and plead with the wandering heroes to slay the horrible beast. The impending conflict is of great amusement because the heroes are pitting their lives against a monster for no reason other than the fact that the Xibalban has tricked them into it. Or the horrible creatures may pit them against rival supernatural forces and other enemies, including real humans. The lords of the three demon cities also enjoy testing and teasing each other, so the fiends may dupe travelers into attacking, or stealing from, or vandalizing their sister cities just to antagonize their demons buddies (all for a laugh or good sport). As you can see, this is a place of phantoms. Not just ghosts and apparitions, but a place where it is often difficult to distinguish between what is real and what is not. Who is friend and who is foe? Which people are humans and which are demons or people of wood? Who speaks the truth and what are the lies? The deceptions, illusions, and treachery of Xibalba are legendary.

All is not fun and games or deception in Xibalba. The Xibalbans have a craving for humanoid flesh, blood, and death and enjoy inflicting pain and misery whenever possible. Consequently, it not unusual for small groups of 2D6, with murderous intent, to attack travelers. They may fight to the death, employ hit and run tactics, lure people into greater danger (more Xibalbans or monsters), or flee like crying babies, it all depends on the attackers and the composition of their foe. Often interlopers are captured and taken back to one of the cities. Here they will be presented to the ruling demon lord as a plaything or as food, or enslaved (manual labor; beaten and ridiculed frequently, life expectancy is short), or tormented (physically and/or psychologically/psionically tortured), or tortured and eaten, sometimes eaten alive.

Tikal
The Domain of
Lord Cuchumaquiq

The ruins have been masterfully rebuilt from their original design, with a few extra demonic looking temples added. It is the largest and most populated of the three demon cities. The inhabitants of the city include three distinctly different life forms, true Xibalbans, who look like humans, but are really supernatural devils/demons, Ti-Xibalbans, who are identical to Xibalbans/humans but are really *people of wood*, and the Lord of Darkness, Cuchumaquiq.

Tikal was once one of the greatest of the Mayan cities. It is significant again as the capital of the Xibalba region and as the fourth most powerful ley line nexus in the Yucatan. Only Uxmal, Chichen Itza and Coba are more powerful (in that order). Here rests the throne of the Demon Lord himself.

Tikal Population: Approximately 500 Xibalbans, 300 Ti-Xibalbans, 150 slaves of all races, and a few dozen other monsters and demons. At any given time an additional $1D6 \times 100$ Xibalbans roam the vast rain forest of the Region of Phantoms, typically in pairs or fours.

Note: The region that Xibalba dominates is all dense rain forest. There are few human inhabitants.

Xibalbans — Demons

Horror Factor: 8, only when they exhibit their supernatural aspect or when a person knows that he is confronting a Xibalban.

Alignment: Miscreant or Diabolic.

Hit Points & S.D.C.: Not applicable

M.D.C.: $2D6 \times 10$

Weight, Height, and Appearance: Equal to that of a human, except their natural skin color is a reddish bronze, the ears are pointed, the eyes dark, the teeth more canine, and they have a long, bony, hairless tail that ends in a point.

P.P.E.: $2D6 \times 10$

I.S.P.: $4D6 \times 10$

Attributes: The number of six-sided dice to roll is indicated, but the physical attributes are uniform for all Xibalbans. I.Q.: 3D6, M.A.: 4D6, M.E.: 3D6, P.S.: 19, P.P.: 19, P.E.: 20, P.B.: 17, Spd: 22.

Disposition: Mischievous, mean-spirited, deceitful, enjoys causing pain and sorrow, but also clever and tricky.

Experience Level: Equal to 6th level.

Magic Knowledge (limited): Average P.P.E. 60; concealment, death trance, fool's gold, mask of deceit, fly, calling, tongues, and invisibility: superior; also see natural abilities.

Psionic Powers (limited): Master psionics. Average I.S.P.: 140; bio-regeneration of $1D6 \times 10$ M.D.C. three times a day, astral projection, see the invisible, see aura, sense magic, empathy, telepathy, empathic transmission, psi-shield, psi-sword, mind bond and mentally possess others.

Natural Abilities: Can change physical features and skin color to that of any of the human races (indian, asian, negroid, caucasian, etc.). Metamorphosis into a dark colored owl with glowing yellow eyes. Plus turn invisible at will, nightvision 600 feet (183 m), climb 88%/80%, swim 88%. Flesh is a mega-damage structure, thus impervious to S.D.C. weapons and damage, HOWEVER, silver-plated weapons (knives, swords, bullets) inflict 1D6 M.D. to the demons.

Combat Skills: Special

Attacks Per Melee: Four (4)

Bonuses: (Includes attribute bonuses) +3 to strike, +5 to parry and dodge, +5 to pull punch, +5 to roll with punch, +10 to save vs horror factor, +10 to save vs poison & drugs, +4 to save vs psionics, +4 to save vs magic.

Damage:
Normal punch or kick — 2D6+4 S.D.C. damage.
Power punch — 1D6 M.D., but counts at two attacks

Weapon Proficiencies: W.P. Blunt, W.P. Sword.

Weapons: Whatever's handy.

Body Armor: Never wears any.

Bionics & Cybernetics: None.

Money: None.

Skills of Note: Dance, sing, fish, play the flute, horsemanship, basic math, demon & monster lore, radio: basic, first aid, pick pockets, and pick locks, all at 70%.

Description: Human in appearance except as previously noted. Like to trick and torment other intelligent creatures. Feed on the flesh, bones, and blood of other creatures, which accounts for some of the Maya human sacrifices.

Ti-Xibalbans — The People of Wood

(Some become the Mirror People)

Horror Factor: 10, but only when they exhibit their supernatural aspect or when a person knows that he is confronting a Ti-Xibalban.
Alignment: Anarchist as zombies, Diabolic as mirrors of the living.
Hit Points & S.D.C.: Not applicable
M.D.C.: 2D6×10
Weight, Height, and Appearance: Equal to that of a human, except the creatures are made of wood.
P.P.E.: 1D6×10, **I.S.P.:** 1D6×10
Attributes: All Ti-Xibalbans have identical attributes unless they have become the demonic clone of a living person, then they possess the identical attributes of that person. I.Q.: 10, M.A.: 5, M.E.: 10, P.S.: 10, P.P.: 10, P.E.: 20, P.B.: 10, Spd: 10.
Disposition: Rather quiet and zombie-like servants who perform the majority of the labor within Xibalba. In many respects they are like demonic zombies made of wood, or a human size wood Golem. Mischievous, mean-spirited, deceitful, enjoy causing pain and sorrow, but also clever and tricky.
Experience Level: Generally first level.
Magic Knowledge: Generally none. Only those who have become the mirror of the living possess magic and skill knowledge. Average P.P.E. 30.
Psionic Powers (limited): Minor psionics. Average I.S.P.: 30; sense magic and telepathy.
Natural Abilities: As creatures magically created from wood, they do not breathe, are not affected by gases or poison, do not require food, water or rest; never fatigue. This also means that bio-manipulation, neural-maces, stun guns, tear gas, bad air, no air, fumes and magic clouds have no effect. Likewise, many illusionary magics designed to frighten humans will not be as terrifying to Ti-Xibalbans. They do float on water and do burn, possess nightvision 600 feet (183 m), can climb 60%/50%, swim 88%.

Generally impervious to S.D.C. weapons. Mega-damage weapons inflict normal damage; feels minimal pain. **Fire** is the most feared element in the world to these creatures. Fire does double damage, so a 50 S.D.C. fire blast will inflict 100 S.D.C. or the equivalent of one M.D. point of damage, while mega-damage and magic fires inflict M.D. double damage to the vulnerable creatures. **Regeneration**: Unless the wooden person is completely destroyed (-10 M.D.C.), it can regenerate completely within 24 hours. All it needs is some good dirt (not sand or clay) to plant itself in, and it can regrow. It requires 8 hours to restore the first 10 M.D.C., but after that the creature is restored at a rate of 8 M.D.C. an hour. New limbs are regrown, scars and burns disappear. **Damaging to vampires:** As a creature made of wood, their punch, kick and bite inflicts 2D6 damage direct to the vampire's hit points, but the undead will immediately realize that they are fighting a Ti-Xibalban duplicate. (**Stupid note:** No, the wood person can not sharpen his fingers or arm to be a wooden stake or knife. However, he could sharpen his teeth.)

The Ti-Xibalban's most frightening power is the ability to become, in the words of the ancient Maya, "a mirror of the living." Basically, the wood people can transform into a demonic, animated, wood clone of a living, flesh and blood person. This is done by a slow process and strange ritual. The Ti-Xibalbans will only transform themselves when commanded by Lord Cuchumaquiq or one of his demon lords or messengers. Typically the living subject is already a captive of the Xibalban. The creature of wood is brought to the restrained person it is to duplicate. The living victim is made to bleed (not enough to kill him, must be kept alive a while longer), the blood is soaked up by the wood demon, who then sprouts long, climbing roots in a matter of minutes. The roots cover the bleeding victim and attach themselves to the skin (no pain, minimal discomfort). Over the next four days the wood person becomes covered in a weave of roots and fuzz that seems cocoon-like. On the fifth day the cocoon cracks open and an *exact* physical duplicate of the living person stands before him! The slightest feature, scars, moles, eye color, everything is re-created, including the victim's every memory! The wood doppleganger has every memory, every desire, skill, ability, powers, P.P.E., I.S.P., experience level, voice, everything the person was is possessed by the creature of wood.

Fortunately, there are differences. They were called the "mirrored people" by the Maya because they appear as a mirrored duplicate image. If the original being was right-handed, this creature is left-handed. A scar above the left eye is now above the right eye, and so on. Still, one will be amazed at how few acquaintances will notice such a minor change, and if they do, often they assume they must have been mistaken (1-62%). Only wives, lovers and close friends of several years tend to notice the differences immediately (1-95%), thus they usually fall victim to accidents and mysterious deaths. Other differences are that the creature never ages, does NOT increase in experience or skill, and is distinctly evil. The alignment is always miscreant or diabolic and the mirror person is still completely loyal to the demon lords of Xibalba and dedicated to a life of evil. Worse, unlike his zombie-like brothers, the mirror person can leave Xibalba and enter the world of men to create sorrow and pain!

Note: Only one mirrored copy of a single person can be made, not an army. If the wooden duplicate is destroyed, only then can a second duplicate be made. However, the original, living person is usually slain or imprisoned in Xibalba immediately after the first duplicate is made.
Combat Skills: Special
Attacks Per Melee: Two (2) as normal Ti-Xibalban zombies, or equal to the person of whom they are a mirrored duplicate.
Bonuses: (Typical zombie person of wood) +1 to strike, +2 to parry and dodge, +1 to pull punch, +1 to roll with punch, +5 to save vs horror factor, impervious to poison, drugs, and gases, +3 to save vs psionics, +3 to save vs magic, impervious to petrification. If a duplicate, it will possess all the skills and bonuses of the person it has copied. But the skills and abilities never increase.
Damage:
Normal punch or kick — 1D6 S.D.C. damage.
Power punch — 1D4 M.D., but counts at two attacks.
Weapon Proficiencies: W.P. Blunt or duplicate knowledge.
Weapons: Whatever's handy.
Body Armor: Typically never wears any unless a duplicate.
Bionics & Cybernetics: None. Duplicates can only copy the appearance, not the mechanical mechanisms themselves.
Money: None or that gained by theft or murder.
Skills of Note: Dance, horsemanship, basic math, demon & monster lore, radio: basic, four human languages of choice, all at 70%. Or those gained by duplication.
Description: Human in appearance in every way, except seems a bit sluggish (and are made of wood, but not obvious). Duplicates may look human or like a humanoid (alien/D-Bee) and can be a dwarf or giant in size. Obedient, unquestioning slaves unless they become a mirror person, then they possess the personality of the duplicated person, with an evil spirit. Enjoys tricking, hurting, and killing other intelligent creatures.

Cuchumaquiq, Lord of Darkness
Lord of all of Xibalba & Ruler of Tikal

Horror Factor: 17 when in his natural form or when one knows who they confront. H.F. 10 even when in human form; radiates evil.
Alignment: Diabolic
Hit Points & S.D.C.: Not applicable
M.D.C.: 1500
Weight: Ten tons,
Height: Human or 20 ft (6 m) monster
P.P.E.: 1000, **I.S.P.:** 200
Attributes: I.Q.: 21, M.A.: 21, M.E.: 30, P.S.: 40, P.P.: 21, P.E.: 30, P.B.: 21 in human form, Spd: 33 (22.5 mph/36 km). **Note:** Vulnerable to all mega-damage weapons, magic, psionics, and silver (silver-plated weapons inflict 1D6 M.D. to the demon).
Disposition: Cruel, tormentor, torturer. Loves to dispense pain, misery and death. A maniacal manipulator who prefers to cause suffering through deception, subterfuge, temptation and humanoid pawns; playing on people's greed, lust, hatred and desires.
Experience Level: 13th level sorcerer.
Magic Knowledge: P.P.E. 1000, spell strength 15; all level 1-3 spells, all summoning, all metamorphosis, plus heal wounds, restoration, create scrolls, astral projection, teleport: lesser and superior, eyes of Thoth, tongues, calling, locate, oracle, memory bank, transferal, mystic portal, close rift, and dimensional portal. Offensive Spells: fire ball, sleep, blind, mute, domination, agony, life drain, sickness, spoil, minor curse, luck curse, curse: phobia (and remove curse), energy disruption, wisps of confusion, repel animals (10x normal effect), turn dead, animate & control dead, negate magic, dispel magic barrier, anti-magic cloud, and impenetrable wall of force.
Note: The demon lord is especially powerful when in Tikal or the other two demon cities. His close proximity to his minions enables the fiend to draw upon an additional 200 P.P.E. every melee!

Bonuses: (Includes attribute bonuses) +5 to strike, +7 to parry, +7 to dodge, +5 to pull punch, +5 to roll with punch, +12 to save vs horror factor, +10 to save vs poison & drugs, +4 to save psionics, +8 to save vs magic.
Damage:
Restrained punch or kick — 6D6+25 S.D.C. damage.
Full strength punch or kick — 6D6 M.D.
Power punch — 2D6×10 M.D., but counts at two attacks.
Bite — 1D6×10 M.D.
Killing touch — 2D6 direct to hit points (6D6 M.D. to mega-damage creatures such as dragons and many supernatural beings); counts as two attacks. The victim suddenly feels sick, nauseous, burning up with fever, weak; penalties: reduce speed by half and lose one attack that melee per each touch (even affects dragons). Cuchumaquiq must announce that he is going to kill the target of his death touch before it can be effective; something like, "Now you shall feel the caress of death," or "Now you die." Characters protected by M.D.C. body armor or who are partial reconstructed borgs suffer half damage and minimal side-effects (no penalties). Characters in power armor, robots, or who are full conversion borgs suffer no damage or side-effects from the demon lord's killing touch.
Weapon Proficiencies: W.P. Blunt and W.P. Sword.
Weapons: Any that strike his fancy. Usually relies on magic and supernatural powers.
Body Armor: None, other than for disguise.
Bionics & Cybernetics: None.

Money: Has collected a treasure of gold, silver and gems worth 2D6×10 million credits, and a variety of weapons and armor to tempt, corrupt and lure foolish humanoids. Weapons of note include one Triax Ulti-Max, two X-10 Predators, a suit of magic power armor and some magic weapons and scrolls.
Skills of Note: Disguise, forgery, math: basic and advanced, astronomy, all lore, all common languages (plus Mayan, Olmec & Toltec), and writing, all at 92% proficiency.
Description: Can appear to be completely human or other humanoid form and a handsome or beautiful one at that (can assume either gender). However, the demon Lord of Xibalba's natural form is that of a bloodthirsty monster. The body is a lump of flesh with two long, gnarled arms and disproportionately long fingers, supported by a pair of small legs. In the front of the body mound is a huge 15 foot (4.6 m) maw with six foot (1.8 m) long teeth. Three sunken eyes peer from above the upper lip, and horns protrude from the top of the head. Ancient myth has it that the giant maw was to devour the bodies of the dead, freeing their spirits from their bodies. But the Lord of Death is so ravenous that he often lures those not yet ready for death into his deadly embrace. He was also deemed responsible for disease, rot, famine and natural disasters, such as earthquakes, so that he could feed. Much human blood was shed on the sacrificial alters of Tikal and Copan in an attempt to satisfy Cuchumaquiq's hunger to prevent pestilence and disaster.

Again, myth and reality collide, for the horrid monster eats corpses, savoring the flavor, though its main food is P.P.E. from the ley lines and the life around him.

Like his minions, Cuchumaquiq can not venture beyond the border of the Xibalba dimension. However, he can leave his physical body to become a demonic, semi-opaque, spectral shadow of himself. This spectral form looks like a ghostly, dark grey mist in the vague shape of a man, with glowing white eyes. In this form the Demon Lord can fly at a speed of 66 (45 mph/72 km) and prowl at a skill level of 60%. He can use his psionics to attack or communicate (usually preferring to incite trouble rather than attack out right) and can also use the following magic powers: sickness, spoil, repel animals, animate and control the dead, calling, tongues, and teleport: superior, but all magic has a reduced spell strength of 12 (instead of 15). He can also use his killing touch but must physically touch his victim.

The spectral self is a shadow of the true monsters real self, thus it is vulnerable to energy weapons, silver, psionic attack, exorcism, banishment, and is powerless against protection amulets and protection circles. A globe of daylight will hold the demon lord at bay, as will the cross, like a vampire. Daylight is blinding and painful, causing the spectral self to hide in darkness until nightfall. The spectral body only has 150 M.D.C., and depleting the M.D.C. will force it instantly back into its physical body, miles away. The pain and shock of the experience prevents it from traveling in spectral form again for 1D6 weeks, another reason to avoid confrontation as its shadow self.

Uaxactun

Uaxactun is a half day's journey from Tikal, about 12 miles (20 km). Its Maya ruins have also been restored to their former splendor and it is the second largest of the demon cities. A gargantuan pyramid-like structure is the most prominent building and is the lair of Vukub-Came. The pyramid is located directly on a ley line nexus and the arch mounted on the top is a dimensional doorway.

Uaxactun Population: Approximately 300 Xibalbans, 200 Ti-Xibalbans, 100 slaves of all races, and a dozen other monsters and demons.

Vukub-Came, "The Phantom," Lord of Uaxactun

Horror Factor: 14
Alignment: Anarchist
Hit Points & S.D.C.: Not applicable
M.D.C.: 800
Weight: One ton, **Height:** 12 ft tall; pale grey human, ghostly in appearance.
P.P.E.: 500, **I.S.P.:** 100
Attributes: I.Q.: 15, M.A.: 20, M.E.: 25, P.S.: 20, P.P.: 20, P.E.: 27, P.B.: 8, Spd: 88 flying (60 mph/96 km). **Note:** Vulnerable to all mega-damage weapons, magic, psionics, and silver (silver-plated weapons inflict 1D6 M.D. to the demon).

Disposition: Mischievous, cruel, tormentor. Loves to engage in games of wit and cunning (win or lose). Enjoys gambling and taking chances. Loyal to Cuchumaquiq only because the Lord of Xibalba is more powerful than he.

Experience Level: 8th level wizard.

Magic Knowledge (limited): P.P.E. 500, spell strength 14; all level one spells, all illusionary magic, plus fly, fly as an eagle, levitate, float in air, astral projection, escape, multiple image, shadow meld, see the invisible, invisibility: simple and superior, teleport: lesser and superior, eyes of Thoth, tongues, calling, turn dead, life drain, call lightning, summon storm, calm storm, fingers of the wind, wind rush, negate magic, dispel magic barrier, and dimensional portal.

Note: The demon lord is especially powerful when in Uaxactun or the other two demon cities. His close proximity to his minions enables the fiend to draw upon an additional 100 P.P.E. every melee, and Uaxactun is located on a ley line nexus. The throne room of Vukub-Came is located on the top of a Mayan pyramid at the nexus' center. This means that the demon lord can draw on an additional 30 P.P.E. per hour (like he needs it), his own P.P.E. recovers at a rate of 20 P.P.E. every half-hour, and the range, duration, and damage of magic spells is tripled!! **Players,** remember that all practitioners of magic enjoy the increased power of their magic near a ley line nexus; see **Rifts**, page 163.

Psionic Powers (limited): Major psionic, I.S.P. 100; astral projection, mind block, clairvoyance, telepathy, see the invisible, sense evil, sense magic, nightvision, and telekinesis.

Natural Abilities: Fly (see attributes), prowl 60%, nightvision 600 feet (183 m), and sharp normal vision.

Combat Skills: Supernatural

Attacks Per Melee: Four by hand, or two by magic, or two by psionics.

Bonuses: (Includes attribute bonuses) +5 to strike, +6 to parry, +8 to dodge, +5 to pull punch, +5 to roll with punch, +10 to save vs horror factor, +4 to save vs psionics, +6 to save vs magic.

Damage:
Restrained punch or kick — 3D6+5 S.D.C. damage.
Full strength punch or kick — 2D6 M.D.
Power punch — 6D6 M.D., but counts at two attacks.
Mystic javelin — 6D6 M.D., 2000 foot (610 m) range.

Weapon Proficiencies: W.P. Targeting and W.P. Sword.

Weapons: Prefers the bow and arrow, javelin and spear. Magic javelin: can make a shimmering javelin appear out of thin air and hurl it up to 2000 feet (610 m); equal to a lightning bolt that inflicts 6D6 M.D.; usually relies on magic and supernatural powers.

Body Armor: None.

Bionics & Cybernetics: None.

Money: Has collected a treasure of gold, silver and gems worth 40 million credits, and a smattering of various weapons, armor and magic items to tempt, corrupt, and lure foolish humanoids.

Skills of Note: Math: basic and advanced, all lore, all common languages (plus Mayan, Olmec & Toltec), and writing all at 92% proficiency.

Description: Appears as a semi-transparent, pale grey human dressed in a glowing white. The face is pale and thin, with a long mane of full, white hair blowing in the wind (even when there is no wind). Like his minions, the Phantom can not venture beyond the border of the Xibalba dimension except by means of astral projection.

Xultun

This is the smallest of the demon cities, but the most savage and war-like, mainly because its demon lord is a warrior king. Its main structure is a comparatively small sacrificial pyramid, which is also the lair of Hun-Came. The stairs are decorated with carved human skulls and the stairs themselves are littered with real skulls and the skeletal remains of hundreds of victims. Snakes writhe at the foot of the throne and a foul, sweet smelling incense, reminiscent of burning flesh, fills the air. One of Hun-Came's warriors (his current favorite is a secondary vampire who is unmerciful in combat) and one of his monster allies stand at either side of the throne as his personal guards.

Xultun Population: Approximately 200 Xibabans, 50 Ti-Xibalbans, 200 slaves of all races, and nearly a hundred other monsters, demons, and evildoers with a taste for combat and human blood (10% are vampires). Xultun is located about 40 miles northeast of Tikal and 20 miles northeast of Uaxactun.

Hun-Came, "One Death" Ruler of Xultun

Horror Factor: 14
Alignment: Miscreant
Hit Points & S.D.C.: Not applicable
M.D.C.: 1000
Weight: Two tons, **Height:** 5 to 30 ft tall, human in appearance.
P.P.E.: 400, **I.S.P.:** 100
Attributes: I.Q.: 14, M.A.: 15, M.E.: 25, P.S.: 30, P.P.: 22, P.E.: 26, P.B.: 14, Spd: 44 (30 mph/48 km). **Note:** Vulnerable to all mega-damage weapons, magic, psionics, and silver (silver-plated weapons inflict 1D6 M.D. to the demon).

Disposition: Cruel, enjoys torture and maiming, merciless in combat. Aggressive, arrogant, and murderous. Loyal to Cuchumaquiq.

Experience Level: 12th level warrior.

Magic Knowledge (limited): P.P.E. 400, spell strength 14; all level one spells, plus swim as a fish (superior), breathe without air, fly as an eagle, levitate, float in air, escape, chameleon, invisibility: superior, teleport superior, eyes of Thoth, eyes of the wolf, tongues, calling. Offensive spells: Armor of Ithan, invulnerability, energy bolt, fire bolt, fire ball, circle of flame, call lightning, summon storm, calm storm, globe of silence, life drain, speed of the snail, turn dead, banishment, negate magic, dispel magic barrier, and dimensional portal.

Note: The demon lord is especially powerful when in Xultun or the other two demon cities. His close proximity to his minions enables the fiend to draw upon an additional 100 P.P.E. every melee and Xultun is located on a ley line nexus. The throne room of Hun-Came is located on the top of a Mayan pyramid at the nexus' center. This means that the demon lord can draw on an additional 30 P.P.E. per hour (like he needs it), his own P.P.E. recovers at a rate of 20 P.P.E. every half-hour, and the range, duration, and damage of magic spells is tripled!! **Players,** remember that all practitioners of magic enjoy the increased power of their magic near a ley line nexus; see **Rifts,** page 163.

Psionic Powers (limited): Major psionic, I.S.P. 100; mind block, death trance, impervious to fire, impervious to poison, resist fatigue, resist thirst and hunger, and summon inner strength.

Natural Abilities: Can alter his size (clothing and weapons adjust proportionately) from 5 feet (1.5 m) to 30 feet (9 m); attributes and M.D.C. remain unchanged. Has keen natural vision, nightvision 120 feet (37 m). Heals ten times faster than a human, about 100 M.D.C. a day, and can metamorphosis into a giant snake (10 to 30 feet long; four attacks in snake form by bite, or two by magic, but prowls at 66% and swims 96%).

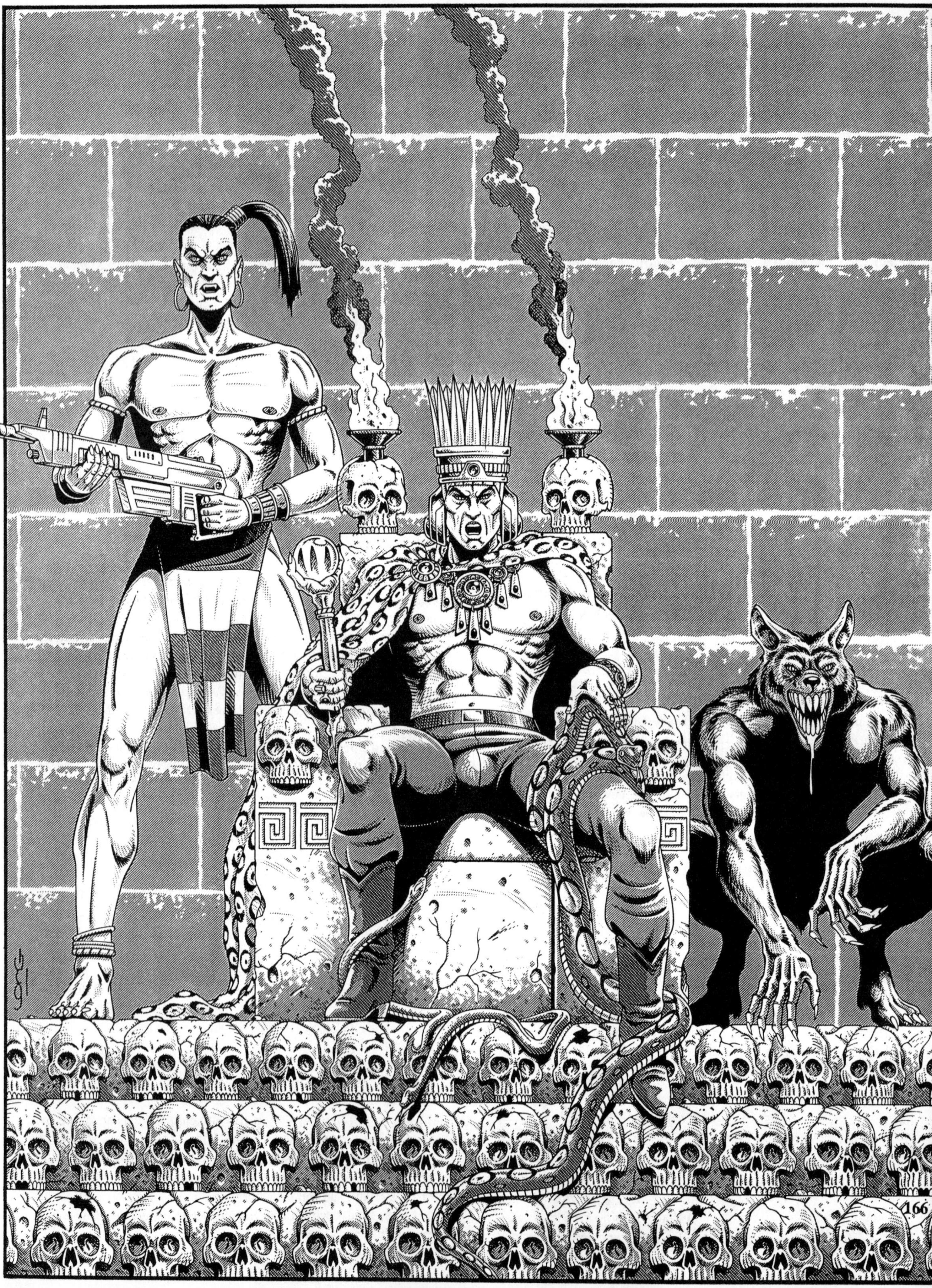

Combat Skills: Supernatural. Loves to engage in hand to hand combat.

Attacks Per Melee: Six hand to hand, or one hand to hand and two by magic, or two psionic actions.

Bonuses: (Includes attribute bonuses) +6 to strike, +9 to parry, +9 to dodge, +5 to pull punch, +5 to roll with punch, +10 to save vs horror factor, +5 to save vs psionics, +6 to save vs magic.

Damage:
  Restrained punch or kick — 4D6+15 S.D.C. damage.
  Full strength punch or kick — 3D6 M.D.
  Power punch — 1D6×10 M.D., but counts at two attacks.
  Body throw — 2D6 M.D.
  Leap kick — double damage (6D6 M.D.), uses all melee attacks.
  Critical strike on a natural, unmodified roll of 18, 19, 20.
  Magic Weapons — see weapon description.
  Snake bite — 3D6 M.D.

Weapon Proficiencies: W.P. Targeting, W.P. Blunt, and W.P. Sword.

Weapons: Magic scepter/war hammer: 4D6 M.D., is indestructible, and can cast the following spells three times daily: heal wounds, purification, and turn water to wine. Serpent net: Works like the magic net spell, with a horror factor of 16, plus the snakes will bite those who try to escape. Those bitten must roll to save vs magic sleep (12 or higher). Flaming two-handed sword: Powerful magic sword inflicts 6D6 M.D. Also uses a bow and arrow that inflicts 2D6 M.D., with range of 3000 feet (915 m). Otherwise relies on magic and supernatural powers.

Body Armor: None.

Bionics & Cybernetics: None.

Money: Has collected a treasure of gold, silver and gems worth 10 million credits, and a smattering of various weapons, armor and magic items to tempt, corrupt, and lure foolish humanoids.

Skills of Note: Math: basic and advanced, all lore, all common languages (plus Mayan, Olmec & Toltec), and writing, all at 92% proficiency.

Description: Appears as a powerfully built Mayan warrior king, dressed in jaguar fur cape, feathered headdress, long black hair, and usually holding a royal scepter which doubles as a war hammer. Hooked to his belt is a magic net of living snakes. He can grow to 30 feet tall (9 m) at will and loves to fight, torture, and maim; permanently disfiguring or crippling somebody is more satisfying to this fiend than actually killing, but killing is fun too. Like his Xibalban minions, the demonic warrior lord can not venture beyond the border of the Xibalba dimension and has no spirit or astral self to explore what lays beyond his kingdom. This can be frustrating to the Hun-Came and sometimes sends him into a fury, particularly when prey escapes him by stepping beyond the border of the Region of Phantoms. It is for this reason that he has gathered about him his mercenary troops of monsters and madmen who have no such mystic restrictions.

El Mirador, La Muralla and Tintal

Three other ruins of Maya cities are clustered within a 20 mile (32 km) area near the northern border of Xibalba. A mile north, beyond El Mirador, and one is free of the Region of Phantoms. None are a formal demon city or village, but 2D6×10 Xibalbans and 1D6×10 Ti-Xibalbans are present at any given time (attracted by the mystic energies).

Travelling in nearly a straight line north of El Mirador, through 180 miles (240 km) of rain forest, is the fabled ruins of Uxmal, 80 miles (129 km) northeast is Chichen Itza and 80 miles southeast of it is Coba, three of the most powerful ley line nexus points in Central America!

Altun Ha

Long ago, the city of Altun Ha was a major Maya community, five miles from the coast of the Caribbean Sea, in the country of Belize. Today it can hardly be recognized when one sees its crumbling temples and the surging energy of the ley line nexus.

About 20 miles (32 km) South, on a little peninsula, is the pre-rifts ruins of **Belize City**. A human fishing village of about 300 live in and around the ruins. In addition, a tiny band of 20 warriors have reclaimed the airfield there and have established a base of operations. The fighters are dedicated to the eradication of the undead. The band has discovered the existence of vampire intelligences and has learned that destroying the intelligence will obliterate its legion of vampires. Having lost 130 men (including five cyber-knights) in a campaign against a vampire intelligence at **Rio Bec** (and failing to destroy the intelligence), they fled to Belize where they have regrouped and are trying to rebuild their forces. The group is lead by a one-time Ried's Ranger, Lupe Madero (7th level wilderness scout), and a cyber-knight, Sir Anthony the Brave (8th level cyber-knight, also known as Sir Anthony the Mad, because he is obsessed with destroying vampires). The average level of the other 18 warriors is 5th level, half of which have Titan or Hopper power armor. While they gather their forces (they have already added a mated pair of werejaguars to their numbers), they have taken to exploring the rain forest and protecting innocent people from vampires and monsters.

Rio Bec

Rio Bec is a Maya ruin occupied by a vampire intelligence, located on a ley line nexus. The vampire intelligence has surrounded itself with flocks of bats (scares people away) and a tribe of human cannibals (200 warriors, average 3rd level, quite bloodthirsty; 20% use captured energy weapons) taught by their god (the intelligence) to drink the blood and eat the flesh of their fellow man. An insane warrior shaman leads his cannibal warriors to glory before his god. The man is young, powerful, knows psionics and magic, and is gifted by the genius that sometimes comes with madness. He is a wildman who takes wild chances, fights like a demon and is a natural at strategy and tactics. Some believe he is the human embodiment of their god. **The Shaman, Atu Caotz:** Diabolic, but fanatically loyal to his god. Age 23; I.Q. 14, M.A. 24, M.E. 9, P.S. 24, P.P. 21, P.E. 18, P.B. 8, Spd. 22. 5th level shaman/ley line walker. Major psionic: 56 I.S.P., astral projection, mind block, clairvoyance, presence sense, telepathy, see the invisible, sixth sense, total recall. Magic powers of note: 127 P.P.E., chameleon, climb, swim as a fish (superior), levitate, escape, fly, eyes of the wolf, impervious to fire, superhuman speed, reduce self, armor of Ithan, globe of daylight, fear, turn dead, energy bolt, fire bolt, call lightning, sleep, carpet of adhesion, trance, cure minor disorders, heal wounds, commune with spirits, and exorcism. Skills of note: Holistic medicine, astronomy and all wilderness.

Note: 2D6×10 secondary vampires are also in the area of Rio Bec to protect their creator. Six dybbuk demons have been accepted into the tribe and also protect the intelligence.

The Becan Cluster

Twenty miles (32 km) northwest of **Rio Bec** is a cluster of ancient ruins that form a small triangle of ley lines. Each ruin is about two miles away from the other and each is a small nexus point, but **Becan**, which is also linked to Mayapan, 200 miles (320 km) to the north, is the most powerful.

Each ruin is inhabited by a Death Weaver spider demon. The one at Becan is the most powerful, an 8th level shifter, while the other two,

An adventurous Simvan Monster Rider on his Ostrosaurus mount.

one at **Xpuhil** and the other at **Chicanna,** are both 6th level. Although Death Weavers seldom associate with others of their kind, these three are sisters and they work together, gathering mystic knowledge and treasure so that they may one day become gods. The three are diabolic evil and attack anybody who appears to be a potential threat or rival. They have successfully defended their triplex against several would-be invaders, including a new, weakened vampire intelligence. The sisters and their minions amuse themselves by experimenting with magic, summoning demons, and opening rifts. This brings all types of monstrosities into the Yucatan Peninsula, many of whom find their way to Mexico and South America.

To help them in their endeavors, they have acquired six slaves/assistants, five warriors (all 5th level wild psi-stalkers), and a young thunder lizard dragon (4th level); all are evil and fairly loyal to the spiders.

The demon spiders have also amassed a treasure-trove. The Becon treasure is the largest (the others are half as big) and contains six million credits worth of gold, silver, jade and gems, two TW flaming swords, a dozen scrolls, several TW water weapons and devices, a dozen energy pulse rifles, a suit of SAMAS power armor, and the mechanical remains of two Coalition full conversion borgs. Plus two crude, clay statues of twin giants. Closer inspection will show that they are really two mud caked, but otherwise pristine, pre-rifts Glitter Boys with boom guns and ammo and bearing the American empire's USA logo and flag emblem; worth more to some collectors as relics than as war machines.

Etzna — Lair of the Muluc Intelligence

The ruins of Etzna lay about 30 miles east of the Gulf coast, and about an equal distance northwest are the ruins of the pre-rifts city of **Champoton**. Fishing villages dot this coast and the village of Champoton has a huge population of 1200 people (70% human, low tech, fishers & farmers).

Etzna is rumored to be a place of evil and avoided by the humanoids in the area. Indeed, it is the secret lair of the vampire intelligence responsible for the **Muluc Vampire Kingdom** off the gulf of southern Mexico. The horrid creature keeps a low profile, seldom ventures outside and is protected by only 24 secondary vampires and its demon familiar.

Uxmal

Maya ruins mark one of the most powerful ley line nexus points in the **Rifts** world. So powerful that no vampire intelligence or supernatural being has been able to claim and control its energies for himself, though many have tried. Like the Calgary and St. Louis Archway rifts, the Uxmal rift tears open, out of control, to spew forth new horrors into the already demon plagued world. Remember, Uxmal and all of the Yucatan Peninsula ley lines are **unknown** to the rest of the world, because the Yucatan Peninsula exists in a different, parallel dimension (many don't know the Peninsula still exists). Only some of the practitioners of magic and supernatural creatures native to the land know and use these formidable places of magic power.

Uxmal is located about 40 miles (64 km) south of the pre-rifts city of Merida and approximately 85 miles (136 km) west of Chichen Itza. About halfway between Uxmal, Merida, and Chichen Itza are the ruins and ley line nexus of **Mayapan**. About six miles north of Merida are the ruins of **Dzibilchaltun**.

Merida

Merida was the major pre-rifts metropolis of northern Yucatan. Several highways ran along the coast and highway 180 weaved around Chichen Itza to Coba. When the cataclysm of the Rifts Time came, virtually all of the Yucatan coastal and lowland cities were obliterated by tidal waves and the seismic eruption of the rifts at nexus points and along ley lines. It was only the mystic energy that had been channeled through the Maya temples and pyramids for thousands of years that preserved the majority of the Maya cities; after all, that is what they had been built for. Shortly after the eruption of the rifts, the entire Yucatan Peninsula was *shifted* into a different dimension, tied to the rest of the continent by its physical connection to the land and its mystical connection of ley lines that ran through and beyond the Peninsula, holding on to at least some part of it, like magic sutures.

The cataclysm was so devastating that most of the Peninsula remains unclaimed by humanoids and demons alike. The old pre-rifts cities mangled and covered by vegetation.

Chichen Itza — The Lair of Camazotz

The pyramids and temples at Chichen Itza were the most famous Maya ruins in pre-rifts times. The city is located approximately 75 miles (120 km) east-southeast of the pre-rifts city of Merida. Today it is the home of a creature who claims to be the return of the Quiche-Maya god, **Camazotz, Lord of the Bats.** Whether it is really the Maya god or not, the creature is more powerful than the average vampire intelligence. It has forced the intelligence that previously inhabited the small ley line nexus into obedient slavery. The intelligence still lives, but obeys Camazotz' every command and its minions answer to the Lord of the Bats, not the vampire intelligence that created them. However, Camazotz' power must have its limits, because it has not seized control of any of the other vampire kingdoms or intelligences.

The bat god is an evil creature of darkness that thrives on chaos and agony. Thus, it sends its 2000 vampire minions into the rain forests of the Yucatan, Central America and Mexico to kill and cause mayhem to humanoids and vampires alike. Part of the mayhem is to cause trouble between the vampire kingdoms of Mexico by creating dissention between the rival factions. This may involve lies and manipulation, to outright attacks on villages, vampires and humanoids owned by the other vampires, while disguised as members of rival kingdoms.

Note: In addition to the vampire intelligence and the intelligence's demon familiar that protect and serve Camazotz, there are usually 3D6×10 secondary vampires (night) and 2D4×10 zombies (day) wandering the ruins of the city, as well as the occasional visiting demon.

The Healing Well of Chichen Itza

A new feature of Chichen Itza is that the old fresh-water cenote for which the city was named, "the Well of the Itza," has mystical healing properties. All wounds, no matter how grievous, are healed with but one sip of the Itza water. **RPG Note:** Always stays fresh tasting and cool to the touch no matter how long the water has been removed from the well. A well person will feel totally refreshed. To an injured person the water restores all hit points and S.D.C., or the M.D.C. of supernatural creatures, instantly! The waters will also instantly negate magic curses and ailments. It is even rumored to bring the recently deceased back to life by completely immersing the corpse in the healing waters. Any person of a good alignment who died at the hands of a true, supernatural demon (undead included) will be brought back to life, as long as the individual has not been dead for more than a week. The healing water does NOT restore missing limbs or organs.

Unfortunately, the well is right in the middle of the city complex and in plain sight of the pyramid lair of Camazotz and the vampire intelligence. Consequently, there are always 3D6 secondary vampires or zombies around the well. Furthermore, there is a 1-55% chance of trespassers being noticed by the vampire intelligence, and a 1-36% chance of being noticed by Camazotz himself. As a result, few have ever heard of the healing well and fewer still have ever stolen its waters. A sip (about an ounce) of Itza water can command as much as 30,000 to 60,000 credits on the open market. Super, super rare!!! Virtually nonexistent.

Camazotz — Lord of Bats & Darkness

Horror Factor: 17 when in his natural form, none in humanoid guise.
Alignment: Diabolic
Hit Points & S.D.C.: Not applicable   **M.D.C.:** 2500
Weight: 200 lbs, **Height:** human, 6 ft 4 inches
P.P.E.: 3000, **I.S.P.:** 1000
Attributes: I.Q.: 18, M.A.: 18, M.E.: 28, P.S.: 28, P.P.: 18, P.E.: 28, P.B.: 18 in human form, Spd: 38 (25 mph/40 km). **Note:** Natural form is a 10 foot globe of blackness, like mini-black hole. Physical form is that of a black (as in pitch-black) human male. Vulnerable to all mega-damage weapons, magic, and psionics. **Disposition:** Always seems relaxed. Speaks in a warm, gentle voice, but is cruel, vindictive, domineering and a sadistic tormentor. Loves to create confusion, chaos, and misery. Demands to be worshipped by lesser creatures, especially those who are of a bat-like nature.

As Lord of the Bats, it believes that the undead and their vampire intelligences that created them, should bow down to him as their master. His goal is to make the vampires of Mexico and Central America acknowledge him as their ultimate lord. Sees humans and D-Bees as interesting, often underestimated creatures that make excellent pawns and allies.

Experience Level: 15th level sorcerer.
Magic Knowledge (limited): P.P.E. 3000, spell strength 16; knows all spells level 1-7, all summoning, all metamorphosis, and all dimensional travel magic (including teleport & time hole), plus oracle, commune with spirits, transferal, negate magic, dispel magic barrier, anti-magic cloud, id barrier, create magic scroll, create zombie, restoration, and transformation.
Psionic Powers (limited): I.S.P. 1000, astral projection, mind block, empathy, telepathy, object read, presence sense, see the invisible, sense evil, sense magic, exorcism, psychic diagnosis, psychic surgery, psi-shield, psi-sword, hydrokinesis, and mind block auto-defense.
Natural Abilities: Nightvision, 600 feet (183 m), keen normal vision, bio-regenerate 1D4×10 M.D.C. every minute (every fifth melee round).
Combat Skills: Supernatural
Attacks Per Melee: Four (4) by hand, or three by magic, or three by psionics.
Bonuses: (Includes attribute bonuses) +5 to strike, +4 to parry, +4 to dodge, +2 to pull punch, +4 to roll with punch, +14 to save vs horror factor, +7 to save vs poison & drugs, +7 to save psionics, +7 to save vs magic.
Damage:
   Restrained punch or kick — 6D6+13 S.D.C. damage.
   Full strength punch or kick — 1D6×10 M.D.
   Power punch — 2D6×10 M.D., but counts at two attacks.
Weapons & Weapon Proficiencies: Relies on magic and psionics.
Body Armor: None, other than for disguise.
Bionics & Cybernetics: None.
Money: Has collected a treasure of gold, silver and gems worth 10 million credits, and a variety of weapons and armor to tempt, corrupt and lure foolish humanoids.
Skills of Note: Disguise, math basic and advanced, astronomy, all wilderness, all lore, all common languages (plus Mayan, Olmec & Toltec), and writing in Maya and Dragonese/elf both at 98% proficiency. **Description:** Appears as sphere of black light or a black skinned human.

Coba

Coba was another of the famous pre-rift archaeological sites of Maya mastery. Over the years, it has been fought over by a number of supernatural powers. Currently, it is held by an adult great horned dragon for purposes unknown.

One of the interesting features of Coba is that one of its temples has an active teleportation/dimensional portal to Xibalba. The portal will instantly transport an individual to **Tikal,** in the Region of Phantoms, or to **Copan,** far away on the northern border of Guatemala and Honduras. **Copan** has a similar portal, hidden in the tall hills, that will teleport a person from Copan to Tikal or Coba. Note that the great horned dragon does not appreciate sudden guests, while the Lord of Xibalba enjoys visitors immensely (the same can't be said of the visitors).

Other Monsters

Monsters common to the Yucatan, Southern Mexico & South America

The Children of Cihuacoatl

One of the Aztec myths speaks of the goddess Cihuacoatl, which means "Serpent woman," and was believed to have born humans from snakes. Now Cihuacoatl has bore herself new children, or so it is believed by the peasants of Southern Mexico. Giant 10 to 20 foot long serpents with four lashing tentacle arms and human eyes and intelligence. The monsters are seen as horrible demons and attacked on sight. There have been dozens of Cihuacoatl attacks during the last year when they first appeared.

Although seen as one of the most horrible of demons, the Cihuacoatl are not demons at all, but aliens from another dimension. There are two factions of Cihuacoatl (they call themselves Vernulians): military invaders who have been dimensionally teleported to Rifts-Earth to see if the planet should be considered for conquest and colonization (the verdict will probably be no, because the environment is too hostile and unstable/constantly changing) and Cihuacoatl refugees who have escaped from their persecuted existence to find and build a new life on a new world. A rebel force started a riot and was able to take over the dimensional teleport facility. Approximately 1200 refugees were transported to Earth, to southern Mexico. Many have since dispersed and live in the forests of southern Mexico, the Yucatan and South America. Only a handful travelled north and few of them survived.

The refugees escape to Earth is of great concern to the Vernulian military, and the soldiers who followed are charged with seeking out and terminating the rebellious refugees as an example, as well as reconnoitering the planet for possible colonization. The military serpents are aggressive, cruel and war-like. They attack at the slightest provocation and are merciless in combat. The reptilian warriors feed on mammals and have been known to eat slain humanoids, supporting the belief that they are demons.

The refugees tend to be far less hostile and have a respect for all intelligent creatures and a high regard for life. The Cihuacoatls/Vernulians can be amazingly kind, gentle and loving, but a life of persecution, and now being attacked as monsters, has made the nicest Vernulian paranoid, secretive, and suspicious of all strangers and acts of kindness. The trouble and pain they have endured has turned some into the cold-hearted and cruel monsters they believed to be. These individuals are as bad as the members of the military and government that they loathe. They will steal, hurt and kill to survive, or to get what they want, and have little regard for life other than their own, or for their own people (about 30% of the refugees are Vernulians of this misanthropic nature).

Cihuacoatls/Vernulians — Optional Player Character

Horror Factor: 14

Alignment: Any; commonly unprincipled, anarchist and miscreant. The soldiers are usually anarchist and miscreant.

Hit Points: 1D6 × 10,

M.D.C.: Main body: 1D6 × 10, natural body armor. Each tentacle has an additional 10 M.D.C. Soldiers and some refugees have a energy field generator collar that creates an invisible force field of 140 M.D.C. and regenerates M.D.C. at a rate of 10 an hour. See body armor description.

Weight: 3D4 × 100 lbs,

Height: Can rear as high as three-quarters of their over-all body length,

Length: 2D6 + 8 feet,

Average Life Span: 90 years; reach full size and maturity at age 10.

P.P.E.: 6D6,

I.S.P.: 1D6 × 10 plus M.E. and 1D6 + 1 per level of experience.

Attributes: The number of six-sided dice are indicated as follows. I.Q.: 3D6, M.A.: 4D6, M.E.: 4D6, P.S.: 4D6, P.P.: 4D6, P.E.: 4D6, P.B.: 1D6, Spd: 4D6

Note: It is impossible for humanoids to tell a male from a female without a thorough physical examination.

Disposition: Varies, like humans. The military and embittered rebels tend to be aggressive and mean, the refugees tend to be quiet and pleasant, but all fear and distrust other life forms, especially humans.

Experience Level: Average military: 1D4 + 1 levels, average refugees are 1D4 level scholars and adventurers, mostly vagabonds, city rats and rogue scholars.

Available O.C.C.s: Any! The Vernulians are intelligent, high-tech creatures. The tech-level is easily equal to the Coalition, with a bit of techno-wizardry mixed in.

Military characters are the equivalent of the CS grunt (40%), military specialist (10%), technical officer (10%), RPA elite (20%, bot vehicles & power armor), and 20% are full conversion borgs!! Same basic weapons and bots, and enhancements as Coalition equivalents, only shaped to conform to the multi-limbed and serpentine body.

Non-fighters/refugees can be any of the scholar and adventurer O.C.C.s, or techno-wizard with a psionic/I.S.P. orientation. P.P.E. and the other forms of magic are foreign to them, but in time, the Vernulians can learn magic too.

Magic Knowledge: None

Psionic Powers: All are considered major psychics and possess telepathy, telekinesis, and mind block, plus select a total of four additional powers from the categories of healing, sensitive and/or physical; no super psionics. Average I.S.P. is about 45 to 75.

Natural Abilities: Instinctive swimmers 80%, excellent climbers 90%/80%, and prowl 38%.

Combat Skills: Military: The usual hand to hand skill selections and abilities; typically hand to hand: expert, martial arts, and assassin, plus two (2; not four) additional attacks per melee. Non-military: Three (3) attacks per melee without any combat training, or two (2) plus hand to hand skill abilities; usually basic or expert. Paired weapons and Special parry attempt on all attacks except from behind.
Bite attack — 3D6 S.D.C. + P.S. bonus.
Tentacle punch/whip — 3D6 S.D.C. + P.S. bonus.
Tail punch/whip — 4D6 S.D.C. + P.S. bonus.
Head butt — 4D6 S.D.C. + P.S. bonus.
Body flip: Counts as one attack, opponent loses one attack and there is a 1-70% chance that the serpent can entangle/pin the off balance individual.
Special Entangle: Can entangle/pin one opponent with two arms and attack him or another, or parry with the other two arms.
Bear hug/pin: Can wrap body or two tentacles around an opponent and pin him so that the person is completely immobile and cannot make any physical attacks/actions (can still use psionics or magic attacks). Can only break free by pulling the tentacles off, but needs a combined P.S. of 10 points higher than the serpent's, or somebody else can try chopping the tentacle off (or can be released by the serpent).

Attacks Per Melee: Two, in addition to hand to hand/combat skills.

Bonuses: In addition to those acquired from attributes and skills: +2 to parry, +2 to save vs poison.

Weapon Proficiencies: Varies with O.C.C. background

Weapons: Vernulian weapons have triggers that are activated by telekinesis rather than physically depressing a trigger. The being's innate psionic abilities allow them to exert just enough telekinetic pull to depress a trigger, button or keyboard without expending I.S.P. They can also operate humanoid weapons the same way.

Body Armor: The Vernulian military has created an energy field generator collar that creates an invisible force field of 140 M.D.C. and regenerates M.D.C. at a rate of 10 an hour. Limited to 12 hours a day use or the system temporarily overloads and shuts down for 24 hours. Consequently, the machine is engaged only when needed. The device also provides warmth to keep the body's metabolism high (peak combat) during cool periods, like desert nights. Engaged telepathically/mental command, expends no I.S.P. Serpent Power Armor: An impressive and frightening sight is one of these four-armed serpents in robot-looking armor. M.D.C. by Location: Head 100, tentacles (4) 100 each, main body 300, hover jets (6 underside) 25 each, main hover jets (2 on back) 75 each. The jets are used for low altitude flying (maximum height is 300 feet/91 m), maximum speed is 400 mph (640 km).

Bionics & Cybernetics — Serpent Borgs: Full conversion borg: Standard bionic attributes: P.S. 30, P.P. 26, Spd (slithering/loping with arms) 50 (35 mph/56 km). Optional: Bionic legs: Spd: 220 (150 mph/241 km running, only 30% add bionic legs), or a detachable jet pack: Spd 365 (250 mph/400 km; 70% prefer the jet pack rather than add legs). Standard Weapons: One retractable vibro-sword (3D6 M.D., giant size) or one set of retractable vibro-claws (3D6 M.D.; four 10 inch, hooked blades pop out of the front of a tentacle), two tentacle blasters (same as human forearm blasters), tail mounted blasters (same as forearm blasters but bigger, doubling the range and adding 2D6 M.D. to the blast). Body armor: Medium Infantry: 350 M.D.C. Other Features: Plus 1D4+2 additional bionic or cybernetic weapons or implants.

Skills of Note: Depends on O.C.C. skills. Telepathic nature allows the Cihuacoatl to learn one new language every level of experience or every year, whichever comes first; +25% bonus.

Jaguar People — Werebeast

Centuries before the coming of the rifts, *legends* abounded with tales of shape-changing men and demon-men who appeared to be normal humans by day, but were transformed by moonlight into beasts. The werewolf is the most famous of these beast-men, but legends from other lands tell of a great variety of werebeasts. Canines seem to have been the most common, but other animals included bears, panthers, jaguars and tigers.

Werebeasts are shape-changing predators of supernatural origin. Their true form is that of half-man and half-beast, e.g. the wolf-man, or similar to the intelligent mutant animals that are becoming so common in North America. However, werebeasts can magically metamorphose completely into animal or human shape. As an animal, the only things that distinguish the creature from the normal animal kingdom is its size (nearly twice as large as the typical animal), and its seemingly human intelligence. Most werebeasts are fairly intelligent, and the werejaguar is one of the most intelligent; thus they can, for brief periods, pass themselves off as being completely human. However, they are creatures born to hunt and kill. That is their life, purpose, and pleasure, and they cannot disguise this aggressive, animal tendency for long. Nor can the werebeast tolerate being cooped up in a confined environment; it needs to run free.

Despite contrary belief, most werebeasts, the jaguar people included, prey mostly on animals and, in the rifts world, other supernatural creatures. In fact, the werejaguars are an instinctive enemy of vampires. The undead also prove an exciting and challenging foe. Werejaguars enjoy deadly games of sport, and delight in the challenging combat offered by vampires, humans, D-Bees and other intelligent life forms. Like most cats, the fun of recreational hunting is in the stalking, chase, and capture of the prey. Unless you are a vampire, there is a good chance of being let free after the "cat and mouse" game is over.

Werejaguars roam the Southern forests of Mexico and parts of the Yucatan and South America. The old Mayan ruin of Palenque (Southern Mexico, near the Yucatan) is the lair for a community of an estimated one hundred werejaguars and is known as the Domain of the Jaguar People. Most locals leave the Jaguar People alone, because they protect the area from vampires and are not too troublesome if not antagonized. The werebeasts living in an established community collect the occasional object of value such as some gold, silver, gems, weapons, and works of art (decorations).

The Werejaguar — Optional Player Character

Horror Factor: 12 in the their natural half-man/half-beast monster shape. The horror factor does not apply to human form.

Alignment: Feline werebeasts, like the jaguar people, are typically anarchist or any evil (occasionally unprincipled) alignments. Canine werebeasts tend to be evil, occasionally anarchist.

Size: 6 to 7 feet tall in human and humanoid monster form, 5 to 6 feet long in animal form.

Weight: 200 to 300 lbs (90 to 136 kg).

Hit Points (Special): 6D6+10. Like the vampire, the werebeast is invulnerable to most weapons, including mega-damage energy weapons, explosives, bullets, fire, wood, steel, poisons and toxins. However, also like vampires, werebeasts are vulnerable to ordinary silver. Weapons that have at least a 50% silver content inflict double damage to the supernatural things. Thus a silver plated dagger, which normally inflicts 1D6 S.D.C. damage, inflicts 2D6 points of damage direct to the monster's hit points. Although werebeasts possess bio-regenerative powers, they are nothing like the vampires', so being bludgeoned or stabbed by silver can kill the creature without requiring decapitation and staking.

I.S.P.: 5D6,
P.P.E.: 2D4×10+10.
The Eight Attributes of the Werejaguar: The number of six-sided dice are indicated as follows: I.Q.: 2D6+2, M.E.: 3D6, M.A.: 4D6, P.S.: 4D6 (never less than 16), P.P.: 4D6 (never less than 16), P.E.: 4D6, P.B.: 4D6, Spd. 6D6
Experience Level: Average 1D4, same as psi-stalker.
Natural Abilities: The abilities listed are specifically for the werejaguar, other werebeasts may differ. Speak while in animal shape, prowl 80%, swim 60%, climb 90%/80%, acrobatics 80%, track by smell 60%, nightvision 300 ft (91.5 m), and bio-regeneration: restores hit points at a rate of 2D6 H.P. an hour.

Limited invulnerability: See hit point description. *The creature is vulnerable* to magic, psionic attack and weapons made of *silver* (double damage). Wolfbay and garlic will hold all werebeasts at bay, like a vampire, but the cross, sunlight and running water have no adverse effect. Powerful mega-damage attacks and explosions that inflict great amounts of damage may knock the creature down or stun it. Same *Knockdown/Impact* table as for vampires.

Shape-changing power: The myth is that a werebeast is human by day and beast by night, but this is not true. The creature can shape-change at will, day or night. The metamorphosis takes about 15 seconds (one melee) and there is no limit to the number of times the creature can perform a metamorphosis or how long he can maintain that particular shape. As stated previously, the creatures are quite intelligent, thus they generally assume the less frightening form of human during the bright sunlight hours when humans are on the prowl, and into monster humanoid form or animal shape during the night. Also, since they are *nocturnal* hunters, they tend to sleep most of the day and are active during the night. The three (3) shapes are human, jaguar, and its natural shape of jaguar humanoid (half man, half jaguar).

Magic: Tongues, chameleon, astral projection, repel animals, heal wounds, metamorphosis: animal, and metamorphosis: human.
Psionic Abilities: Sixth sense, see the invisible, mind block.
Attacks Per Melee: Five (5) in natural monster or animal form; two (2) in human shape.
Damage:
  Claws do 1D6 plus P.S. bonus to damage, bite does 2D6 damage.
  Human shape punch — 2D6 S.D.C./H.P. + P.S. bonus.
  Restrained claw — 4D6 S.D.C./H.P. + P.S. bonus.
  Power claw — 1D6 M.D.C., counts as one attack.
  Power punch claw — 3D6 M.D.C., counts as two attacks.
  Normal Bite — 2D6 S.D.C.
  Power Bite — 1D4 M.D
Note: All S.D.C. damage from claws or bite inflicts full damage to the hit points of vampires and other werebeasts.
Bonuses: In addition to possible attribute bonuses, the werejaguar is +1 on initiative, +2 to strike, +2 to parry and dodge, +6 to save vs horror factor, +2 to save vs psionics, and +2 to save vs magic.
Skills: Werejaguars can speak Spanish 98%, land navigation 90%, and can learn a total of seven additional secondary skills at first level and two additional skills at levels three, six, nine, eleven and fourteen. Use the same experience table as the psi-stalker. Hit points and skill proficiency increase with each level; no special skill bonuses unless indicated. Available skill categories include domestic, espionage, science: basic math only, technical: language, lore, and photography only, W.P. any (lean toward ancient), wilderness (any, +20%), pilot: automobile, motorcycle, hover vehicle, boat, and horsemanship.
Note: Werebeasts are found all over the world. The werewolf or similar canine is the most common and are found in Europe (especially Eastern Europe), Canada, USA, Africa, Australia and Japan. The werebear is known to exist in northern Canada, Alaska and Russia. The weretiger and panther are found in India. Evil sorcerers sometimes summon werebeasts as assassins and protectors.

Spider Demon — The Death Weavers

The Cunto Indians of South America knew of the "Death Weaver," a vile supernatural creature that appears as a giant spider with a hideous, half human head and a death's skull emblazoned on its hindquarters, long before the Time of Rifts. The Indian legend says that the Death Weavers were overlooked by the gods as lowly predators of vermin. The spider demons were much more intelligent than any suspected and stole the gods's secrets of magic, throwing them to the wind, scattering magic across the world where mortal man could learn its secrets. For eons, the spiders have searched the globe, retrieving the magic and mastering its secrets for themselves, so that they might become gods. In Rifts Earth, the spider demons are back and more powerful than ever.

The Death Weavers see humans as three things: food, pawns, and a source of potential psychic energy. Over the centuries, they have often manipulated primitive people to worship them as gods (or demons), or have established secret death cults. The spiders are cunning, ruthless and more than a little insane.

Horror Factor: 16
Alignment: Diabolic or miscreant (occasionally aberrant).
Size: Stand 6 to 8 feet tall (1.8 to 2.4 m) and equally long.
Weight: 600 to 1000 lbs (272 to 453 kg).
M.D.C.: 2D4 × 10; on the magic saturated Earth the demons are M.D.C. creatures.
I.S.P.: 2D4 × 10,
P.P.E.: 1D4 × 100 + 100.
The Eight Attributes: Not applicable; but very devious and cunning; I.Q. equal to 14, Spd. 22
Level of Experience: Typically 1D6 + 1 ley line walker or shifter.
Natural Abilities: Can walk, run, climb on most surfaces with amazing speed (15 mph/24 km), upside down, straight up, and so on, like a real spider. Only smooth, glassy surfaces impede its movement (half speed). Nightvision 200 ft (61 m), prowl 80%, and can spin a web (for climbing and ensnaring) at a rate of 200 ft (61 m) per melee (15 seconds). The web is tough, like light M.D.C. rope, but deteriorates quickly (within 4 minutes/16 melees) unless a bonding resin is secreted from the spider's mouth over the web. The Death Weavers can also use the web as a rope to entangle and tie creatures up; very strong, one M.D.C. point per stand.
Magic (typical knowledge): Knows all protection circles and protection magic (like sanctum), summoning magic (rituals), armor of Ithan, invulnerability, invisibility simple and superior, breathe without air, float in air, mystic portal, close rift, and dimensional portal, as well as 15 spells selected from levels 1-8 and 6 selected from levels 9-15. Older more experienced death weavers may know more (GM's discretion).
Psionic Abilities: Presence sense, total recall and hypnotic suggestion. Equal to a second level psychic.
Combat: Supernatural.
Attacks Per Melee: Four (4) physical or two by magic.
Damage:
  Strike by leg — 4D6 S.D.C.
  Mandible bite — 3D6 M.D.C.
  Entangle in web — No damage, 69% chance of being incapacitated, pinned, cannot move or attack, until the character can untangle himself (takes one melee). Vulnerable to cocooning and other attacks while entangled. Roll first to strike an opponent with the web, then roll percentile to see if entangled (69%). An entangle attack can be attempted only once per melee; counts as one attack.

  Web cocoon — No damage, but completely encases the victim in a web cocoon/straight-jacket. The trapped individual is completely immobile, unable to perform any physical actions. The only way to get free is to be cut or torn out, but the average cocoon has an M.D.C. of 1D6 × 10. Or an untreated cocoon (no resin) will deteriorate within 2D4 minutes. A cocoon treated with the spider's bonding resin does not deteriorate and adds an extra 10 M.D.C. to the silky encasement. Note that the cocoon is porous and allows air to pass through its walls, so even a person encased from head to toe can breathe.
Bonuses: +2 to strike, +4 to parry, +4 to dodge, +4 to save vs magic, +3 to save vs psychic attack, +10 to save vs horror factor. Vulnerable only to mega-damage weapons in the Rifts dimension.
Weapons: Prefers to use magic.
Bionics and implants: Possible, but not likely.
Skills: All lore 89%, literacy in Dragonese 98%, basic and advanced math 98%, astronomy 89%, radio: basic 89%, land navigation 89%, tracking (humanoids) 50%, identify plants & fruits 60%, holistic medicine 50%, and can learn to speak 1D6 different languages, and literacy in 1D4 written languages (+20%).

Dybbuk — The Demon Ghoul

The dybbuk is a horrifying demon that has stalked mankind since the time of the Egyptians. In the ancient, pre-rifts Earth the Dybbuk, the "Eater of Flesh," was said to have been summoned by a power mad necromancer who opened a doorway to the dybbuk world in an attempt to summon an army of the savage creatures. Unfortunately, he greatly underestimated their power and became their first human victim. During those pre-rifts days the dybbuk was an S.D.C. creature, but even then he was a formidable supernatural foe. In the world of **Rifts**, where mystic energy abounds, the dreaded monster of old can enter the Earth dimension at will, and is more powerful than ever.

The dybbuk loathe humankind and delight in its torture. It looks at all humanoids as humans, so even elves, goblins, ogres and other D-Bees are in danger. These demonic beings are intelligent, cunning and deadly; capable of learning human skills to destroy humankind. Despite their wiles, they are extremely intolerant of their own kind and will bicker incessantly whenever two or more are forced together. For this reason, they shun the company of their own race. A dybbuk will frequently work with an evil sorcerer, demon or other maleficent forces to cause mayhem and inflict agony.

The natural form of the demon-ghoul is a massive, barrel-chested humanoid with no neck, vaguely human head, bald, and large maw rimmed with a double row of pointed teeth. In place of the arms are a pair of oversize limbs, like those of an ape, thickly muscled, with massive, clawed hands, like shovels, that drag across the ground. These arms are used to dig up the graves of the dead and to rend flesh from large prey. Tucked under them is a second pair of arms: spindly and delicate, a little shorter than a human's, and half as thick. The hands are small, with long fingers tipped with four inch long, razor sharp claws used to dismember its food and feed itself.

The dybbuk can not tolerate the light of day, which completely blinds them and physically hurts; 1D4 M.D. damage per minute of exposure. A globe of daylight will have the same effect on a dybbuk as it does on a vampire. As a result, the sinister creatures venture out only at night or during rainy, overcast days. Their favorite habitats are city ruins, graveyards, caves and slums (including Ciudad Juarez and the Chi-Town Burbs). The dybbuk's favorite food is dead, rancid meat (animal or human), but they have grown to enjoy fresh human and elf flesh almost as much.

Horror Factor: 14
Alignment: Diabolic or miscreant.
Size: 6 to 8 feet (1.8 to 2.4 m) tall.
Weight: 400 to 700 lbs (181-317 kg).
Hit Points: 2D4×10, **M.D.C.:** 6D6+30
The Eight Attributes: The number of six-sided dice are indicated. I.Q.: 3D6, M.E.: 4D6, M.A.: 2D6, P.S.: 5D6, P.P.: 4D6, P.E.: 4D6, P.B.: 1D6, Spd. 3D6.
I.S.P.: None. **P.P.E.:** 4D6
Disposition: Mean, vindictive, blood thirsty. Likes to kill and inflict suffering.
Magic Powers: None.
Psionic Powers: None.
Natural Abilities: Superior nightvision - 600 ft (183 m) but blinded by sunlight (-8 to strike, parry and dodge). Artificial light is hard on the eyes — 30 ft range of vision without sunglasses. Can dig through packed dirt or clay at a rate of six feet (1.8 m) per minute, and almost always constructs a network of tunnels in its lair to escape intruders. Enhanced healing (6× times faster than a human), impervious to cold, resistant to fire (half damage), track by smell 85%, prowl 50%, swim 50% and can learn 2D4 human secondary skills equal to third level proficiency.

There is one more aspect about the dybbuk that makes it ever more so dangerous. The damnable thing can physically inhabit the recently deceased. If the body is not badly damaged and it is one hour or less since the time of death, the dybbuk can discorporate itself and enter the dead body. Immediately, the body will come to life, possessed by the demon-ghoul. The memories, skills, personality and essence of the person are all gone. It is an empty, lifeless husk that the dybbuk now inhabits. A perfect disguise to walk among humans. It can maintain the body, without it deteriorating, indefinitely, as long as it feeds daily on human blood.

Combat: Supernatural.
Attacks Per Melee: Six (6) in dybbuk form, but four (4) in human form.
Damage:
  Human form punch — 3D6 S.D.C. + P.S. bonus, if any.
  Restrained slash by big claws — 4D6 S.D.C. + P.S. bonus.
  Full strength slash by big claws — 1D6 M.D.C.
  Small razor arms — 2D6 M.D.
  Normal Bite — 6D6 S.D.C.
  Power Bite — 1D6 M.D.
Bonuses: In addition to probable attribute bonuses, the dybbuk is +1 to parry and dodge, +4 to save vs horror factor and +4 to save vs magic. In Rifts Earth the creature is invulnerable to conventional weapons and can only be hurt by mega-damage weapons, psionics, magic, and poison/drugs.

Incubus & Succubus

In their natural, "true" form, the incubus and succubus, also known as the Dar'ota, are large, slimy, scaly, hunchbacked humanoids that resemble a monstrous lizard. The head is a huge, misshapen bag of flesh with a gaping mouth loaded with fangs three to six inches long (76 to 154 mm). The creatures are vampires. Not undead, but creatures with the ability to shape-change into an attractive human, seduce its victim, and kill him or her, tearing out the throat and drinking the blood. The fiends must feed on blood, preferably human blood, every two days.

Many cultures have myths about the succubus (female) and incubus (male); shape-changing demons who would charm and seduce unsuspecting humans for the purpose of manipulation, torment, or murder. They are cruel, maniacal beings who enjoy abusing humans in every possible way. The dar'ota will often ally themselves with a wicked wizards or other dark force to promote pain and suffering.

In human form, the creature will have the beauty and appeal of a movie star. Only the monster's inhuman strength and malignant aura (for those who can see such things) will hint that the beauty is not what she or seems to be. The dar'ota can remain in human shape for days, but must revert to its monstrous shape to feed (ideally, every 2 days). The demon will also revert to its true identity when engaged in prolonged combat (more than two minutes/8 melees). They are lethal combatants in either form, but devastating as a lizard-thing. It is important to point out that all dar'ota are psychotic killers who love to hurt and murder.

Horror Factor: 18 when the transformation from human to monster is witnessed, 15 as the lizard-like Dar'ota, and none in human guise.
Alignment: Always diabolic or miscreant.
Size: Five to six feet tall (1.5 to 1.8 m). **Weight:** 300 to 600 lbs (136 to 272 kg).
Hit Points: Not applicable, see M.D.C. **M.D.C.:** 2D4×10+40; tough, scaly skin.
I.S.P.: None. **P.P.E.:** 1D6×10+10 in Rifts-Earth
The Eight Attributes: The number of six-sided dice are indicated. I.Q.: 3D6, M.E.: 3D6, M.A.: 5D6, P.S.: 5D6 (minimum strength is 18), P.P.: 4D6, P.E.: 4, P.B.: 1D6 natural Dar'ota form, 5D6 in human form (minimum of 20), Spd. 5D6.
Disposition: Cool, confident, masters of lies and deception. Arrogant, treacherous; sees themselves as superior beings. Enjoy killing and anarchy.
Natural Abilities: The Succubus can shape-change into a beautiful adult female human (or human-like D-Bee) and the incubus into a handsome human male. Nightvision 60 ft (18.3 m), keen normal day vision, resistant to fire and cold (does half damage), smell blood up to a half mile away (0.8 km), track by scent 50%, climb 60%/50%.
Magic Abilities: Average 40 P.P.E., spell magic only, equal to a 4th level sorcerer, which means a 13 or higher is needed to save vs magic. Spells include: Death trance, sense evil, concealment, befuddle, calling, and charismatic aura and three additional (GM's choice) from level one and/or two.
Combat: Supernatural
Attacks Per Melee: Three (3) hand to hand or one magic.
Damage:
  Restrained punch/claws — 3D6 S.D.C. + P.S. bonus.
  Full strength punch/claws — 2D4 M.D.C.
  Normal Bite — 6D6 S.D.C.
  Bite — 1D6 M.D.
Bonuses: In addition to probable attribute bonuses, the succubus and incubus is +1 to parry and dodge, +10 to save vs horror factor and +1 to save vs magic. In Rifts Earth the creature is invulnerable to conventional weapons and can only be hurt by mega-damage weapons, psionics, magic, and poison/drugs.

MINDOLAR —— The Mind Slug

The mindolar are giant slug-like beings that can be summoned from another dimension by men of magic. The mindolar seldom come to Earth intentionally, although the incredible amount of magic energy and chaos makes Rifts-Earth a far more appealing place to visit. A mindolar can not be controlled by humans, because of its superior psychic mind, but it can control a human like a puppet on a string. This makes them very attractive to evil practitioners of magic and power hungry rulers. The summoner must be careful not to fall under the creature's control or he will become its pawn rather than vice versa. But the mindolar is not a mindless savage and will psionically see or feel an evildoer and will listen to any proposition the summoning mage may have to offer. If the creature likes what he hears (chaos and carnage) it will agree to work with the one who solicited its aid. And the pitch better be a submissive and respectful one. The mindolar does not appreciate arrogance and will attack or betray anyone who belittles it. If an agreement can't be reached, the creature will ask to be sent home, but only after a warning about how a puny human should not play with forces he can not possibly control. If angered the monster will attack, take over the mage or kill him and find his own way home (or see the sights for a while).

A mindolar is observant, a quick learner, and quick to react. If betrayed or tormented, it is likely to make a quick snack of its tormentor (the only thing humans are really good for, eating). The Mindolar has a formidable array of psychic abilities, but its most dangerous power is its *mind controlling bite*.

Horror Factor: 16
Alignment: Anarchist, Miscreant or any evil.
Size: 7 ft (2.1 m) long. **Weight:** 600 lbs (272 kg).
Hit Points: 3D6×1000 and M.D.C. equivalent of 30 to 180; average is about 100 M.D.C. **Note:** The body of the mindolar automatically returns to its own dimension when killed.
The Eight Attributes: I.Q., M.E., and M.A. are all superior to a human's, ranging around 24 to 30. The following indicate the number of six-sided dice for the remaining attributes. P.S.: 2D6, P.P.: 3D6, P.E.: 4D6, P.B.: 1D6, Spd. 2D6.
I.S.P.: 2D6×100,
P.P.E.: 1D4×10
Disposition: Ruthless and cruel, vents its frustration on the puny human race and their sub-human cousins (D-Bees). Love anarchy, often considered a demon of chaos and darkness.
Level of Experience: Equal to a 10th level mind melter.
Magic: None.
Psionic Abilities: Master psionic, Average I.S.P. 900. All psychic sensitive powers, plus exorcism, healing touch, increased healing, deaden pain, induce sleep, resist fatigue, bio-manipulation, empathic transmission, hypnotic suggestion, mind block auto-defense, and group mind block. **Mind Controlling Bite:** The victim of a Mindolar's bite must roll to save vs magic (a 15 or higher). A successful save means the character is still himself. Three successive saves against the magic bite means the character is immune to ALL of its mind altering powers and will be perceived to be a serious threat to its existence. **A failed roll** places the person under the slug's complete control. The effect is exactly like the magic spell "domination," except there is no limit to the range or duration. The bite also enables the mindolar to place the victim in a trance, identical to the spell "trance." The person is enslaved, with no chance of fighting free of its control, as long as the creature is alive or in our world. When slain or sent to another dimension, the slug's mind control is broken and the victim(s) returns to normal. **Note:** A single mindolar can control as many as 200 human beings simultaneously.
Natural Abilities: Understands all languages, but must use a human pawn to speak. Bio-regenerates at a rate of 4D6×100 Hit Points per hour. Resistant to cold and drugs/poisons (1/2 damage) and high saving throw. Climb 20%, prowl 30%, and swim 30%. Impervious to mind control of any kind. In Rifts-Earth the demonic thing's hit points are so great that it is effectively a mega-damage creature but is vulnerable to S.D.C. weapons, as well as mega-damage weapons, magic, psionics, and supernatural enemies.
Combat: Supernatural & Psionic.
Attacks Per Melee: Three psionic or three physical attacks.
Damage:
    Bite — 2D6 S.D.C. plus the victim must roll to save vs magic mind control (15 or higher).
    Tiny hands punch — 1D6 S.D.C. +2 damage.
Bonuses: +4 to parry, +10 to save vs psionic attack (this includes M.E. bonus), +10 to save vs horror factor, +3 to save vs magic,. It can not be possessed or mind controlled.
Skills: Can learn eight new skills in six months from the skill categories of technical and science all with a skill bonus of +20%.

Agenor River Serpent

The rivers, lakes and oceans of the Rifts-Earth are filled with what can only be considered sea serpents and sea monsters. Some are dinosaurs, while others are supernatural monsters. Some are intelligent, others animal predators. The Agenor river serpent is one of the animal-like sea serpents that are fairly common in the many rivers of South America, the Yucatan, Mexico, and the Rio Grande into New Mexico and Colorado. They are found only in rivers (deep and shallow), typically feeding on dinosaurs and mammals that come to the water's edge.

As humans in Mexico and Central America become more and more aquatic oriented, travelling and living near, on and in the water to avoid vampires, they become more and more of a target to these 40 to 60 foot leviathans. Although they will gobble up the occasional lone swimmer, they are typically attracted to schools (groups) of swimmers, large robot vehicles and large watercraft (fishing boats, barges, etc.), as well as large animal prey.

Horror Factor: 14
Alignment: Animal predator, generally considered anarchist or miscreant.
Size: 1D4×10+20 feet long. **Weight:** Four tons.
Hit Points: Not applicable.
M.D.C: 4D6×10
The Attribute Equivalents of Note: I.Q.: animal, P.S.: 40, P.P: 24, P.E.: 30., P.B.: 12, Spd. (swimming): 1D6×10+10, Land spd. is half.
I.S.P.: None, **P.P.E.:** 4D6
Disposition: Hunter, gets involved in a feeding frenzy and will fight to the death after it has lost half its M.D.C., otherwise may give up on a particularly resistant foe.
Level of Experience: Equal to a 10th level mind melter.
Magic: None. +3 to saves against repel animal spell.
Psionic Abilities: None.
Natural Abilities: Swim 98%, nightvision 200 feet (61 m), polarized and keen vision underwater and above water, sense water up to two miles (3.2 km) away. Can and does occasionally come on to dry land and can breathe/survive on land for 1D4 hours without adverse effect, after which the creature will experience some difficulties (reduce speed and bonuses by half), but can survive another 1D4 hours before it begins to severely dehydrate and die.
Combat: Animal.
Attacks Per Melee: Three (3) physical attacks.
Damage:
    Bite — 4D6 M.D.
    Body slam/ram — 4D6 M.D.
    High speed ram — 6D6 M.D., counts as two attacks.
    Crush/Squeeze — 5D6 M.D. per melee; crush by coiling around it's victim and constricting. 60% chance of pinning/incapacitating its prey and can still bite.
    Suffocation — Can slay some prey by coiling or biting and holding on, then drags the prey underwater until it drowns.
Bonuses: +6 to strike, +8 to dodge underwater (automatic, like a parry), +3 on initiative, +8 to save vs poison/drugs, +8 to save vs magic, +3 to save vs psionics, +8 to save vs horror factor. It is difficult to mind control.